D1076762

WITHOUT WARNING: AFTER AMERICA

Also available from John Birmingham and Titan Books

Without Warning
Angels of Vengeance

WITHOUT WARNING
AFTER AMERICA

JOHN BIRMINGHAM

TITAN BOOKS

Without Warning: After America
Print edition ISBN: 9781781166154
E-book edition ISBN: 9781781166161

Published by Titan Books
A division of Titan Publishing Group Ltd
144 Southwark Street, London SE1 0UP

First edition: February 2013
1 3 5 7 9 10 8 6 4 2

This is a work of fiction. Names, characters, places, and incidents either are the product of the author's imagination or are used fictitiously, and any resemblance to actual persons, living or dead, business establishments, events, or locales is entirely coincidental. The publisher does not have any control over and does not assume any responsibility for author or third-party websites or their content.

John Birmingham asserts the moral right to be identified as the author of this work. Copyright © 2010, 2013 by John Birmingham. All rights reserved.

No part of this publication may be reproduced, stored in a retrieval system, or transmitted, in any form or by any means without the prior written permission of the publisher, nor be otherwise circulated in any form of binding or cover other than that in which it is published and without a similar condition being imposed on the subsequent purchaser.

A CIP catalogue record for this title is available from the British Library.

Printed and bound in Great Britain by CPI Group Ltd.

Did you enjoy this book? We love to hear from our readers.
Please email us at readerfeedback@titanemail.com or write to us at
Reader Feedback at the above address.

To receive advance information, news, competitions, and exclusive offers online,
please sign up for the Titan newsletter on our website:
www.titanbooks.com

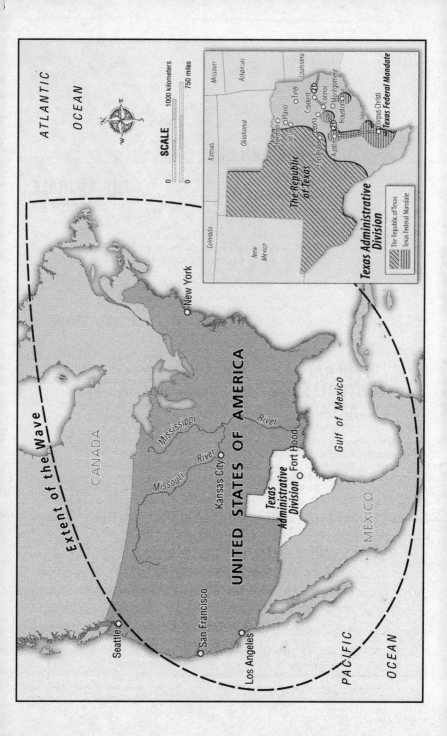

ATLANTIC OCEAN

PACIFIC OCEAN

Extent of the Wave

SCALE
1000 kilometers
750 miles
0
0

CANADA

New York

Mississippi River

Missouri River

Kansas City

UNITED STATES OF AMERICA

San Francisco

Seattle

Los Angeles

Texas Administrative Division

Fort Hood

Gulf of Mexico

MEXICO

Texas Administrative Division

New Mexico

Colorado

Kansas

Oklahoma

Missouri

Arkansas

Louisiana

The Republic of Texas

Texas Federal Mandate

Sherman
Plano
Dallas
Fort Hood
Leona
Austin
Crockett
Tyler
Connor
Montgomery
Houston
Corpus Christi

The Republic of Texas
Texas Federal Mandate

PROLOGUE

SEATTLE, WASHINGTON

"Man, being president sucks."

"Try being married to the bozo who's always complaining about how much being president sucks."

Kipper flinched as Barb pinched a small fold of skin just below his Adam's apple while trying to fasten the top of his dress shirt.

"Oh my God, Kip. You are such a baby. It's lucky none of your marines can see you right now."

"They're not *my* marines," he protested, finally stepping away from his wife to peer around her shoulder at the full-length mirror in the bedroom of their private quarters.

Hmmph. He was a wearing a fucking penguin suit. With tails and everything. It was all he could do not to make little barking penguin noises.

"Do I really have to do—"

"Yes, Kip. You really have to. It's part of the job."

"But *poetry*…"

Kip turned from the mirror as Barbara fiddled with her earrings at the antique dresser in their bedroom.

"Come on, Kip," she teased. "Rhyming couplets aren't the worst things you've had thrown at you the last couple of years. It might even be fun."

Maybe. If he was allowed to get a few beers in, and who knew, the poems might even rhyme. He could hear the musicians, some sort of small local chamber orchestra, playing downstairs. Violin music and the growing murmur of a small crowd pushed up through the dark wooden floorboards of their bedroom. Kipper mentally ticked off the hour, at least, he would have to wait before ripping the top off his first brew.

"Mister President, if you're ready, sir."

Barbara smiled at their protocol chief. "Oh, Allan, he'll never be ready, but I've done the best I can. Let's go downstairs."

Kipper hadn't seen anyone appear at their door, but he wasn't surprised to find him there. Privately he referred to Allan Horbach, the White House protocol chief, as Casper because he was always spooking around somewhere, although admittedly Kipper needed more protocol wrangling than your average president. Barb and Allan fell into a hushed but animated conversation as the three of them made their way down the hallway toward the main staircase. As the background noise swelled to a reasonable roar, Kip estimated that there had to be nearly two hundred people crammed into the reception area on the ground floor of Dearborn House. He'd long ago done away with a good deal of the formality that made these events so punishing, meaning he did not now have to endure that nearly unbearable moment when Allan announced their arrival as though he were stepping onto the bridge of an aircraft carrier or something. Even so, as they came down the stairs smiling and waving, it seemed as though everybody there turned as one toward them.

And then, just like stepping off the bank into a deep, fast-flowing river, he was pulled into the crowd.

Half of Seattle had somehow crammed itself into the music

room and formal parlor of Dearborn House. He winced to see the Greens' leader, Sandra Harvey, bending the ear of his appointments secretary, Miss Hughes, and made a note to remind Annie that when Sandra came calling, he was always out. He had just enough time to register Jed Culver, his chief of staff, deep in conversation with Henry Cesky, the construction magnate. He wondered what dark schemes those two could be cooking up, and then Allan was suddenly at his side, gently directing him by the elbow toward the British and French ambassadors who appeared to be arguing over something to do with Guadeloupe.

He was pretty sure that was a country, not a tapas dish, but not sure enough that he wanted any part of the argument.

"Mister President," said Horbach, "we must greet the ambassadors, then the speaker of the House, the governor, the…"

Kipper zoned out. They were no more than a minute into this reception, and already he was screaming inside. He had no idea how Barb smiled and chatted through it all as though she were actually enjoying herself. Christ, maybe she was. The next thirty minutes passed in a painful series of meet 'n' greets with a procession of dignitaries, foreign guests, senators and Congressbots, and Seattle City Council officials, all of whom had been elected well after he'd left the City Engineers Department. It was with a truly pathetic sense of gratitude that he spotted Barney Tench, his old college bud and now reconstruction czar, working the buffet over by the windows.

"Barn! Man, how you doin'?" he called out over the heads of the crowd, instantly drawing the attention of about fifty or sixty people to Tench, who was caught stuffing a giant piece of crabmeat into his mouth. Allan Horbach actually face-palmed himself, and Barb gave him a small kick in the back of his leg.

"But I need to talk to Barney," he protested. "It's about work."

"Not now, Mister President," the protocol Nazi insisted. "Mister Ford is about to perform."

"The poet?" said Kip. "Oh. Great."

Back through the press of the crowd they went, every step blocked by somebody who wanted a small piece of his time, all the way up to the front of the room, where Kip was introduced to a thin, nervous-looking man in a slightly ill-fitting suit. He instantly felt for him. Ford looked no more comfortable than he did.

"Mister President," said Allan Horbach, "might I present our first poet laureate of the new age."

That's what we're calling it now, he thought. *When did we start calling the end of the fucking world a new age?*

He shook Ford's hand and leaned in close to be heard over the crowd.

"Don't worry, buddy; by tomorrow this'll all just be a terrible nightmare."

"What?" Ford looked shaken. "Oh. A joke. I see. Okay, then. Shall I read now?"

"I think the president wants to say a few words first," said Horbach.

"Well, I don't really *want* to," Kip said, earning a glare from his wife, "but what the hell. We're not getting any younger. Let's do it to it."

A bell rang somewhere as he ascended the small dais that had been erected and then tapped the mike.

"Hey, everyone, how you doing?" Kip said as the soft roar of two hundred voices finally trailed away. He winked at Ford. "As you all know, I'm not a big fan of these formal shindigs, but I do believe it's important to pull on a monkey suit every now and then. As my grandmother used to say, if something is worth doing, it's probably worth wearing a clean pair of pants."

Polite chuckles washed up at him from the crowd, but no more than that, except for Barney, who was stuffing more crabmeat into his face at the back of the room and laughing such a big genuine laugh that Kip worried his old friend was in danger of choking. *God,* he thought, *these are so not my people.*

"Anyway," he continued. "Tonight is definitely worth pants."

He gave Adam Ford a big thumbs-up and was rewarded with what looked like a real smile from the poet, whose eyes were twinkling a little more brightly the longer Kipper had the floor.

"Barbara and I invited you all here tonight to… well, hell, you know why you're here. We've got us a new poet laureate!"

He boomed out that last, as though announcing that the local college football team had brought home the national championship. The applause and some of the whoops of approval that rolled back up at him from the floor were actually heartfelt this time.

"I'm glad to see you're as stoked as I am about this," said the president, settling into his delivery, "because this *is* totally stokeworthy. You know, a lot of what we've been about the last few years, it's been little more than brute survival. Feeding ourselves, defending our homes, just keeping our kids alive, has been…"

He paused, searching for the right words. To the endless frustration of his staff, Kipper rarely delivered prepared speeches or even spoke from notes.

"…it's been, well, calling it a challenge would be… inadequate. It's been hell."

The room was quiet now.

"Our world went to hell on March 14, 2003. That's the only way I can describe it, because we still don't know what happened, and frankly, I don't think we ever will. I have hundreds of scientists still working away at this every day, throwing all sorts of theories and tests and experiments at it, trying to tell me where that Wave came from and where it took all our friends and families. They've been studying it for years now, and they are no closer to knowing. So perhaps it's time to come at it from a different angle, a different kind of knowing. That's why Adam Ford is here tonight. He's not a scientist, he's a poet, and from where I stand looking back at everything that's happened since the Disappearance, I reckon his way of trying to come at the meaning of it all is every bit as valid as all those scientists writing all those reports for me. Probably more so." He gestured to the poet to make his way to the microphone. "Adam?"

Loud applause carried the poet laureate up onto the stage and the president down from it. Ford pulled a single sheet of paper out of the breast pocket of his jacket and coughed before thanking Kipper and waiting for the minor roar to die down. When the room was quiet again, he read.

"This is a poem called 'Aftermath,'" he said.

> *"They weren't lost at sea. They are not missing in action.*
> *We weren't at their side as they breathed their last.*
> *There are no bodies to identify.*
> *They were here. Then they weren't.*
> *We're left behind with nothing to point to,*
> *No evidence that says, 'This happened here,'*
> *No shadows burned into the sides of buildings,*
> *No mountain of glasses, suitcases, and shoes,*
> *No pile of skulls, no handheld footage*
> *Of papers and shattered glass raining down.*
> *Just the near-infinite density of collected grief*
> *That distorts our universe like a black hole—*
> *Grief that we, who remain,*
> *All bear as one as we search for our place*
> *In this strange, new, far-too-different world."*

01

NEW YORK

"No siree, Mister President, you do *not* get these from pettin' kitty cats."

James Kipper nodded, smiling doubtfully as the slab-shouldered workman flexed his biceps and kissed each one in turn. His Secret Service guys didn't seem much bothered, and he'd long ago learned to pick up on their unspoken signals and body language. They paid much less attention to the salvage crew in front of him than to the ruined façades of the office blocks looking down on the massive, rusting pileup in Lower Manhattan. The hard work and unseasonal humidity of Lower Manhattan had left the workman drenched in sweat, and Kipper could feel the shirt sticking to his own back.

Having paid homage to his bowling-ball-sized muscles, the workman reached out one enormous, calloused paw to shake hands with the forty-forth president of the United States. Kipper's grip was not as strong as it once had been and had certainly never been anywhere near as powerful as this gorilla's, but a long career in engineering hadn't left him with soft fingers or a limp handshake.

He returned the man's iron-fisted clench with a fairly creditable squeeze of his own.

"Whoa there, Mister President," the salvage and clearance worker cried out jokingly. "I need these dainty pinkies for my second job. As a concert pianist, don'tcha know."

The small crush of men and women gathered around Kipper grinned and chuckled. This guy was obviously the clown of the bunch.

"A concert penis, you say?" Kipper shot back. "What's that, some sorta novelty act? With one of those really tiny pianos?"

The groan of his media handler, Karen Milliner, was lost in the sudden uproar of coarse, braying laughter as the S&C workers erupted at the exchange. That did put his security detail a little on edge, but the man-mountain with the kissable biceps was laughing the loudest of them all, pointing at the chief executive and crying out, "This fuggin' guy. He cracks me up. Best fuggin' president ever."

Kipper half expected to be grabbed in a headlock for an affectionate noogie.

That *would* have set his detail right off.

But after a few moments the uproar receded.

Kipper's gaze fell on a woman, who'd remained unusually reserved throughout. Doubtless one or two of his detail were watching her closely from behind their darkened sunglasses. He caught her eye and favored her with an indulgent grin by which he meant to convey a sense of amused pity. She obviously did not fit in with this gang of roughnecks. Her features were fine-boned, and she didn't look like somebody used to long days of heavy manual labor. As he so often found when he traveled around to "meet the peeps"—his daughter's term, not his—the peeps intrigued him. This nation of castaways and lost souls all had their stories. And you had to wonder what paths had brought biceps guy and this quiet woman to New York three years after the Wave had dissipated as mysteriously as it had arrived.

"Mister President," Karen Milliner said, "we really need to get a move on—the schedule, you know."

Jostled out of his momentary ponderings by the director of communications, his flak catcher in chief, he nodded and smiled apologetically to the workers.

"I'm sorry, guys. Just like you, I am a mere civil servant, and my boss here"—he jerked a thumb at Milliner—"says I gotta get back to work."

The small crowd booed her but cheered him as he waved and began to walk away with his personal security detail shadowing every step. Cries of "Thank you, Mister President" and "Way to go, Kip" followed him down into the graveyard of corporate America.

The stillness of the ruins soon returned. Grit and debris crunched underfoot as the party picked its way through the wreckage of Wall Street. Only the sound of the pigeons, which had returned to the city in plague numbers, broke the silence. The ecosystem within the Wave-affected area seemed to be outstripping all scientific predictions in terms of recovery. Wood chips and piles of tree branches lined the streets. The buzzing roar of chain saws joined in with the heavy metal crash of machinery. Much of the cleanup work in places like Manhattan pertained just as much to brush clearance as to vehicle pileups or burned-out buildings. It wasn't like the great charred wastelands left by the firestorms that had covered so much of North America. There was life here, of a sort. He could smell it in the fresh-cut timber of an island fast reverting to its original, heavily wooded state.

Away from the raucous cheers of the salvage crew, Kipper fell deep into the well of his own thoughts. He took in the sight of a Mister Softee ice cream van that had speared into the front of the Citibank at the corner of Wall and Front streets. A couple of bicycles lay crushed under its wheels, and jagged shards of glass had ripped through the scorched, filthy rags that once had clothed the riders. He had to remind himself that they hadn't died in the auto accident.

They had simply Disappeared like every other soul in this empty city, like everyone across America four years ago.

"Traffic's not too bad here," he ventured to Jed Culver for want of something better to say. "Not like back on... what was that last cross street, where those guys were cleaning up?"

"Water Street, sir," one of his Secret Service detail offered. He was a new guy. Kip didn't know his name yet, but his accent was local. You had to wonder what that was doing to his head.

"Most of these cars were parked when the Wave hit," Culver added. "Mostly pedestrians and bike riders through here, health nazis, that sort of thing. Water Street was busier."

Culver's soft Southern drawl, a Louisiana lilt with a touch of transatlantic polish, trailed off. The silence of the necropolis, a vast crypt for millions of the Disappeared, seemed to press the air out of him. Kip turned back to gaze down the shadowed canyon of the old financial district. The intersection of Water and Wall was a wrecking yard of yellow cabs, private cars, and one armored van that had been broadsided by a dump truck and knocked completely over. The impact had smashed open both rear doors, and a few buff-colored sacks of old money still lay unwanted on the ground. None of the salvagers bothered with the dead currency, which long since had been replaced by the less valuable New American Dollar. They had returned to attacking the tangle of metal with earthmoving equipment, sledgehammers, chains, and pure grunt.

It was the loudest noise in the city.

Kip shook his head and turned back.

"Come on," he said. "Let's keep going."

At the corner of the JP Morgan Building they encountered the weather-worn façade of the New York Stock Exchange. A large soiled and tattered American flag hung loosely from the Roman columns of the neoclassical structure, held in place by creeping vines as much as by nylon ropes. Kipper had never been to Wall Street, or New York City for that matter, and photographs of the Street always made it appear larger than life. Now, here, in the presence of what had been the most powerful engine of capitalism on the planet, it felt small and almost claustrophobic.

Down at the end of the street he could see a church of some sort, dwarfed by the skyscrapers of Lower Manhattan. Kipper wasn't a religious man, but the sight of the steeple deepened his melancholy, driving it toward the deeper blue depths. More than a few nut jobs had proclaimed their own end of days interpretations of the Wave. For his part, he still believed that there had to be a rational explanation.

But what that explanation was, nobody knew.

He indulged himself in a melancholy sigh.

The party was small for a presidential caravan: just Kipper, Jed Culver—Karen Milliner, and half a dozen security men in dark coveralls and heavy combat rigs. There was no getting rid of them. An army of looters was currently denuding the eastern seaboard of everything from sports cars and heavy equipment to computer game systems and jewelry. Kip often found himself contemplating the lot of Native Americans when whitey turned up. An entire continent was ripe for the taking, and nobody seemed to care that a small number of locals already had a claim on the place.

The irony, or tragedy he supposed, was that most of the Native American population had been wiped out by the Wave. He wasn't sure how many remained. Next year's census would, he hoped, shed some light on that. There simply hadn't been time to organize a full survey of the population since the Wave. There was too much to do just keeping their heads above water. For one thing, the East Coast was overrun with raiders and pirates. Many were part of big criminal syndicates out of Europe and South America, some of them operating with tacit state backing—where states still existed to give that backing—and the balance was a swarm of smaller private operators mostly based in the Caribbean but sometimes hailing from as far away as Africa and Eastern Europe. From the briefings he'd had back home in Seattle, he knew you really didn't want to tangle with *those* guys. Half of them were whacked off their heads on weird-ass cocktails of jungle drugs. They came for the luxury cars and high-end goods. They came for the salvage potential of so much copper, iron, and steel. They came for the jewels, gold, and art, leaving MOMA and a dozen other museums stripped bare, their treasures scattered to the four winds.

And some came specifically to kill any American they could get in their sights.

According to Jed, on any given day there could be up to eight or nine thousand freebooters in New York, and unlike the army or the militia, they were not hemmed in by rules and law. "You ever work here, Jed?" Kip asked.

"On the Street, you mean, Mister President? No. I did a stint in New York about eight years back. Worked in-house with Arthur Andersen. But never on the Street, no."

The president craned his head upward, looking for the Marine Corps sniper teams that had slotted themselves into the buildings above his intended route. He couldn't see them and had to suppress a shiver. There was just something wrong about this place. Vegetation had come back much more quickly than anyone had imagined, probably helped by the flooding and storms of the last few years, and the entire city reminded him of a weed-choked cemetery—a cemetery that was also a battleground.

It had taken one of the U.S. Army's remaining brigade combat teams, augmented by militia units, to clear just the southern end of the island for his visit. And even that clearance was less than perfect, leaving porous gaps through which everyone and anyone could slip. It took an additional force of marines, special forces, and private contractors to secure a solid wedge from the World Trade Center down to Battery Park and across to the ferry terminal for his visit—and once secured, a battalion of Governor Schimmel's

Manhattan Militia irregulars threw up a cordon none could pass without lethal consequences.

Karen Milliner stepped up to his elbow and spoke quietly.

"The media are on site, Mister President. We'd best a get a move on."

He wasn't sure why she felt the need to keep her voice down. He had specifically said he wanted to make this part of his inspection alone, just himself and his chief of staff. Karen came along simply because of the media events that bracketed his stroll through the dead city.

Kip turned away from the NYSE only to pause and stare at the grand Doric columns of Federal Hall. Washington's statue still stood on a plinth in front of the building, which had gotten through the last few years in much better shape than some of the larger, more modern buildings around it. A cleanup crew had swept away any debris and vegetation from the stone staircase, and the first president's statue gleamed as though freshly scrubbed.

"Just gimme a minute," he said.

Kipper crossed the street, prompting his security cordon to follow him, with Culver huffing and puffing to keep up. At the steps of the building he gazed into the upturned eyes of George Washington before reading the inscription at the base of the statue.

> ON THIS SITE IN FEDERAL HALL
> APRIL 30, 1789
> GEORGE WASHINGTON
> TOOK THE OATH AS THE FIRST PRESIDENT
> OF THE UNITED STATES
> OF AMERICA

"Mister President?" Culver tugged at his arm.

Kipper frowned at his chief of staff. He'd labored manfully to get Culver to call him Kip or even Jimmy—ordered him to more than once, in fact—but the former attorney insisted on the formalities. Kip suspected he enjoyed them. Jed's considerable bulk was constrained in a dark blue three-piece suit, which must have been a terrible inconvenience; the president wore jeans, tan Carhartt work boots, and a ballistic vest over an old L.L. Bean shirt. Even that modest outfit was uncomfortable in the heat and humidity. The damn weather, it was still all over the goddamn place.

"Just one more minute, Jed."

Looking at the statue, Kipper wondered what truly had gone through Washington's mind on that day. He was the leader of a newborn nation on the brink of a vast wilderness surrounded by both real and potential enemies. He had given up command of the army against the advice of many officers who'd argued against the move. Faith in the system he was helping to establish—that was the lesson Kipper took from Washington.

Reading presidential biographies was a self-imposed requirement for a job he felt poorly qualified to do, yet they never truly got to the heart of the men who were his predecessors. Of them all, Kipper really identified only with Truman, who felt as if the barn had fallen in on him when Roosevelt died.

At least he knew it was coming, Kipper thought ruefully. He marveled at the path he had traveled: from being an anonymous city engineer in Seattle to provisional president and ultimately elected to a full four-year term as president of the much reduced United States in January 2004, not long before the Wave finally lifted. A hell of a trip.

"Okay, I've probably seen enough," he conceded. "Just thought it was important, you know, to have a look for myself."

"That's why people like you, sir." Culver smiled. "You *like* to get your hands dirty. Come on, shall we get back to the convoy? This place gives me the creeps."

They retraced their steps along Wall Street, carefully picking their way around the occasional pile of rags that had not been blown or washed away. There weren't many left after so long. Jed and Kip both swerved to avoid a rusted three-wheeled baby stroller that had tipped on its side. They studiously avoided looking too closely at its contents. At one point a shaft of light between two burned-out buildings illuminated a small galaxy of twinkling stars on the footpath. Some of the smaller, more desperate freebooters did nothing but sweep the streets clear of rings, watches, bracelets, and other smaller bejeweled trinkets left behind when their owners died. There was a mountain of such stuff still lying around. As Kip sidestepped an pricey-looking silver watch, the thud of faraway gunfire reached them. His detail chief spoke briefly into a radio, but even Kip knew the small battle was too far off to concern them.

The convoy was waiting back at the intersection with William Street, four black Secret Service Humvees and three Strykers bristling with machine guns and grenade launchers. More security men hurried toward his walking party as they approached.

"Trouble?" Jed asked.

"Nothing we can't handle, sir," replied the agent in charge. "Just a little flare-up over on Canal. It won't bother us, but we should get moving anyway."

Kipper distinctly heard the crump of multiple explosions somewhere far off in the city. The muffled thrum of helicopters grew louder but faded away before he could see them. *At least they're ours,* he thought. You couldn't always be sure these days. The detail hurried him over to his vehicle and almost pushed him inside. Jed climbed right in after him, followed by Karen Milliner. The young woman's expensive-looking black silk slacks were covered in dust and grime. She pulled herself into the cabin and seated herself directly in front of Kipper.

"Sorry, sir, but I've just been talking to the Service, and I'm afraid I probably have to advise against going on with this. There's been three big-ass firefights across the island this morning and more over in Brooklyn. A real humdinger near JFK with air force security forces."

Kip enjoyed Karen's totally ingenuous use of words like "humdinger."

"Karen, there are gunfights all over this city every day and night," he said. "Mostly freebooters and pirates fighting among themselves. There's never going to be a time when you get the nice quiet background vision you want. Just roll with it."

Doors slammed up and down the convoy, and the engine turned over in their vehicle, a heavily armored SUV.

"And while we're on the topic, sir, respectfully and all, you really should have let me assign a camera crew to at least shoot some pool vision of your little walk around back there. I mean, what is the point of all that meetin' and greetin' if we don't get any good coverage out of it?"

Kip smiled and shrugged as the vehicle lurched forward. "The point? To meet and greet folks?"

Karen opened her mouth to protest, but Jed cut her off.

"Give it, up, darlin'. You'll never win. I've been trying to get him to dress like a grown-up ever since I took this job, and he still looks like he's about to go and boss a crew of ditchdiggers somewhere."

Kipper waved his hands back in the general direction of the salvage workers they had just met.

"Well, mostly that's what I do, Jed. This job is not what it used to be. Matter of fact, it's not far removed from my old job for the city, and I'm just fine with that. The country doesn't need a commander in chief nearly as much as it needs a chief engineer, if you ask me. Just look at the work that needs doing in this city if it's gonna be our main eastern settlement again."

Jed gazed morosely out the windows as the convoy slowly rumbled down Broad Street. The fire-blackened shell of Goldman Sachs loomed just ahead.

"But Mister President, we cannot do that work without securing the ground first. Those people we just met back there—they could not be doing what they're doing unless that part of the city had been cleared of raiders and pirates. And now that we have cleared them, that is, killed them all and cordoned off that part of Manhattan, we'll need to hold the area, which will mean sustaining militia forces and at least a brigade of regulars, and securing JFK, the bridges and roads between here and—"

Kipper held up his hands to cut Jed off.

"I know all that, Jed. You don't have to remind me. Some days I feel like I'm living in some weird-ass History Channel show and we're trying to settle, or resettle, the Wild East. I got hostile powers to three points of the compass, a weakened military, massive debt, feuding state and federal governments, and an economy that pretty much ceased to exist four years ago. None of this is news to me, buddy. But when I agreed to do this job, I agreed on one condition: that it was to be about rebuilding. And yes, I know that retaking ground and fighting off all comers is part of that. But it's not the main game. Not for me. Restoration, reconstruction, and renewal are my three R's. Otherwise I just walk away."

He shook his head and folded his arms to emphasize the point. Nobody would ever doubt that James Kipper meant what he said. He wasn't even sure he wanted to run in the next election, and he had been entirely open about that, a level of honesty that drove his handlers to distraction most days.

Culver threw up his hands in mock surrender. "You're the boss."

"Yes, I am," said Kip. "It says so on all my underwear."

02

TEXAS, THE FEDERAL MANDATE

An icy morning crust crunched and melted beneath Miguel Pieraro's boots as he knelt down to grab a fistful of cold, damp soil. He sniffed the richness of the East Texas earth, worked the black gritty loam between his fingers, and marveled at the sea of emerald that spread before him under a heavy gray sky. His horse, Flossie, tied to a fence post, dipped her head and pulled at the grass, tearing great clods and mouthfuls of feed from the ground with a hard, ripping sound while his oldest daughter patted and stroked the chestnut mare's twitching flanks. A warning rose in his throat, but he stifled it. Sofia was still a teen, a young teen, but she had an easy confidence around horses born of a lifetime's experience.

Miguel turned back to surveying his domain. One thousand acres of land. Government land for the moment, but it would be his in a few years. As would the livestock and all the capital, the homestead, the barns and equipment, everything. And something else, too, something even more precious. Citizenship. *Belonging*. For now, however, he and his family worked for Presidente Kipper, and he was a happy man for the chance to do so. As he watched, a dozen Bedak Whitetails wandered over the next ridgeline, big four-legged beef factories imported from Australia. Heads down, tails swishing, they methodically mowed through the dense carpet of feed at their hooves. Here and there the grass cover was thicker and appreciably more lush. Miguel had learned early on that such dense clumps of verdant growth often signaled the final resting place of a previous occupant of the ranch, usually a longhorn, but not always. Although many animals had survived the initial appearance of the Wave, many more had perished during the ecological collapse afterward.

"Sofia," he called out. "It is time to saddle up and check the back ninety."

He spoke in English to his daughter, as he insisted on speaking to all of his clan these days. English was the language of their new home, and they would settle in here with much greater ease if they all spoke it well. He did not ban Spanish or Portuguese, the two crib languages of the Pieraro household, but he did not encourage them, either. In Miguel's mind, his family members, all of his extended family, were not simply farmers. They were settlers, making a new history for this country, and he wanted his children especially to be able to play as full a part in that new story as possible. They, too, would probably work this ranch, but *their* children might one day go to one of the universities in the Northwest or even, God willing, in the East, once the bandits and criminals were driven away and the cities were reclaimed for respectable people.

His daughter led both horses over: his own and her smaller gray pony.

"Dad, is it lunchtime yet?" she asked with just a slight trace of an Australian accent, a legacy of eighteen months in the refugee camp outside Sydney that had given all his children a flat, nasal way of speaking that sounded harsh and alien to his ears. He did not bother to correct them, however, certain that within a few short years they would have adapted to the local Texan drawl. Of course that was just as foreign to Miguel, but at least it was familiar.

Not that he had anything against Australia. Life had not been so bad there, he had to admit. Certainly not as hazardous as it had been on Miss Julianne's boat. His family had shelter and food, and the children were schooled properly while the adults worked six days a week on government projects. Agricultural work mostly but also some rail construction for the army in the last couple of months. But as the world had slowly, painfully returned to… well, not to normal… as the world had *settled,* say, after the madness of the Disappearance, Miguel and his wife had finally begun to look beyond the end of each day, to think about the future as something more than a food handout and a cot in a refugee camp.

"Papa? Lunch?"

"Lunchtime will come and go without us noticing on this trip, biggest sister," he quipped, but the classical reference was lost on her. Sofia probably had no idea who John Wayne was. For Miguel, he was still the vaquero's vaquero.

She pulled a face at him and produced an apple from her saddlebag, crunching into it, then dramatically rolling her eyes as the pony implored her to share the good times. Miguel unhitched his mount and swung up into the saddle, taking a moment to enjoy the view across his land. Or what would be his land. There was a powerful difference, he had to admit, between laboring for a bossman and pouring your sweat into soil that you could call your own. Acres of greensward swayed in a gentle breeze, rippling downslope to fields of genetically modified spinach and silverbeet and durum wheat in the back ninety, the new strains growing at a greatly accelerated rate and for longer each year, increasing the yield of his holdings at least threefold. They could handle the harsh cold and heat of Texas far better than the pre-Wave crops could. And if there were any problems with them, Miguel had not noticed yet.

He was not much fussed about the GM crops himself. Whatever

worked for his family was an unqualified good in his estimation, although he knew that the Greens in both the national Congress and the Washington statehouse were forever conniving to ban the wonder plants. He shook his head as he nudged the horse away from the old wooden fence. Why would they do that? It was madness when the country had so much trouble feeding itself now. Not through a lack of good land or seed stock but from want of experienced farmers and the—what was the word?—the infrastructures to harvest and deliver crops to market. Finding parts for the farm equipment was a hit-or-miss affair. And once the crops were harvested, moving them from the farm gate to the grain silos was often a matter of long horse-drawn convoys, which in this part of the country were liable to be set upon by bandits.

Sofia ambled up beside him, and he felt his heart swell with pride at her ease on the horse and the straightness of her back. She was a good child and would be a fine woman in a few years. He would be needing his shotgun, especially as the district filled up with more settlers, as surely it must. For now they shared the valley with just a handful of families, at least half of them, like him, hailing from abroad. He liked the Poles the best. They were quiet, hardy folk from good farming stock. The Yankees who had moved here from Seattle, in contrast, though pleasant people, were softhearted, soft-handed fools when it came to the ways of the land. They had a lot of funny ideas about the land, which they called Mother Earth or some equally silly-sounding name. Gay something or other.

They were forever at odds with the resettlement authorities over Seattle's insistence that a certain percentage of their crops be the new genetically modified strains. Instead they harangued the inspectors and overseers who came through every few months to be allowed to experiment with their crazy ideas about organic this and biodynamic that. And they were absolutely horrified by the deer hunt that had taken place on Miguel's ranch last fall, riding over to personally protest his murderous ways. When Sofia ran up, covered in blood and gore, and held up the ten-point white-tail she had bagged and dressed that day, one of the folks from Seattle actually fainted. One of the men.

Miguel did not expect them to last.

"What are you smiling about, Papa?" she asked as she finished the apple.

"Nothing," he said contentedly. He was truly at home. The ranch was coming into its own. His herds were expanding, fattened on the lush grazing lands. Even the old apple orchards back at the hacienda seemed to be doing well enough, producing a palatable cider that made Mariela's roadside watering hole very popular with the other settler families. The corn whiskey from his other crops didn't hurt matters, either.

Prosperity beckoned, he thought, patting his horse. Her ears flicked up, eyes darting skyward. She jerked at the bit, pulling at the reins in his hand.

"Easy," Miguel whispered in his native tongue. "Easy."

And then he could hear it, too, the rapid pop and crack of gunfire. A gallon of ice-cold water seemed to sluice into his stomach. The noise reminded him of hail on the tin roof of his toolshed, but he was all too familiar with the sound of weapons fire. Could the uncles be leading a practice shoot for the younger boys? They all practiced frequently with their weapons, but that was usually after dinner and the shots were controlled, designed to improve marksmanship. This was rapid, indiscriminate fire.

Trouble, he thought.

He quickly rode up the small hill blocking his view of the homestead and dismounted before the crest. Sofia followed, unable to conceal the worry on her face. She held the horses while her father inched up to the ridgeline. There were more pops, and he thought he heard screams. With a sick fear twisting in his guts, Miguel pulled the binoculars from around his neck up to his eyes. He could already see a collection of vehicles in various states of repair parked outside the hacienda. Some of them were four-wheel drives mounted on what the gringos called lift kits, giving them extra ground clearance. They were dirty, battered, and heavily burdened with a motley collection of goods. *Plunder,* he thought instantly. Twenty or more men had fanned out through Miguel's property, bearing military-style weapons.

There were bodies.

Miguel felt his innards clench tight as he focused the binoculars on one of the lifeless forms. Little Maya, no more than seven years old, lay on her back, staring up at the gray late-winter sky. Crimson horror flowed out of the ragged mess where her belly had been. Memories arose unbidden of him blowing tiny tummy farts for her while she squealed and laughed and complained how much his bristles were scratching her. Grandma Ana was next to the child, facedown and unmoving in the frost, a knife clutched in her hand. One of the men kicked the old woman's corpse as he nursed what looked like an injured arm.

Sofia, shaky and fearful, reached him from behind.

"What is going on, Papa?"

"Stay where you are, Sofia," he said harshly. His throat had clamped tight and did not want to work.

Screams drifted up from the hacienda: a woman's howl, his own woman. Mariela Pieraro. She screamed in her native tongue, lashing at her tormentors, who all appeared to be gringos, although most of them were so filthy that it was hard to be certain.

Road agents, he thought, the very words like a rattlesnake in his mind. A collection of vaquero pretenders, costumed in a motley collection of army camouflage, urban gangbanger, and cowboy fetish outfits. They ran like vermin all over the outer wastes of the Texas Republic, but Miguel had never known them to venture so far into the Federal Mandate. That was why he had brought his family to settle here, so they would be safe. His head swam and squirmed with horrified rage as he realized how wrong he had been about that. He had led them all here, and now they were dying for it. His hands were shaking so badly, he could hardly make out the scene below. A hard mercy in a sense, because at that moment three men were attacking his wife.

Just a few seconds' exposure to the atrocity was more than enough for Miguel. He could no more stand to watch the unfolding horror than he could have perpetrated it himself. He let the binoculars fall and tried to push himself up from his prone position hidden in the lush greensward on top of the ridge overlooking his family home. His stomach heaved as he did so, and he dry retched, stumbling badly as he turned to hurry down the hill to his daughter.

Perhaps his only surviving child now.

Teetering and almost falling down the slope on legs as stiff and unyielding as a tin soldier's, the cowboy almost knocked over his oldest girl, so blinded was he by the shock.

"Father? Papa?"

He took the reins from Sofia with violently trembling hands and somehow pulled himself up into the saddle. Maybe someone had managed to get away, or perhaps some of the gunshots were from the survivors, trying to fight the agents off. He could ride down there, perhaps help out. Maybe give the survivors a chance to fight back, even the odds.

Maybe, just maybe…

"What is it? Father, Papa, tell me," she pleaded in a small voice cracking with panic. She, too, could hear the gunfire and screams coming over the ridgeline.

Miguel unholstered his Winchester, feeling its deadly promise in his shaking hands. It was too late, far far too late to save his loved ones, but high time indeed for a reckoning with those who had taken their lives.

Maybe…

He checked the load and slid the rifle back into the saddle holster. With a tap of his heels, his mare began to crest the hill. Sofia mounted her animal and followed suit. "I'm coming with you," she cried out to him in strangled English

Miguel shook his head fiercely. "No, you are too headstrong for your own good. Stay here. I will—"

The boom of a large-bore weapon rolled over the crest like a single note of distant thunder. He turned quickly in the saddle, pulling the binoculars up to his eyes so quickly that he smacked himself in the face. His wife's body was slumping to the floor of the wide veranda that ran around the hacienda, leaving a dark smear on the whitewashed wall. One of the rapists spit at her, as she lay on the ground.

A small sound escaped from Miguel's lips, something between a groan and a strangled squeak. His vision grayed out to the edge, and dark blossoms of poison night flowers bloomed in front of him. He swayed and very nearly passed out.

The guns fell quiet and silence filled the atmosphere, broken only by the cackles and shouts of the road agents. He scanned the landscape for some forlorn hope that one of his sons or Mariela's brothers had made it to cover, waiting with their own weapons to back him.

Sofia was suddenly by his side. She took the binoculars from him and surveyed the scene herself.

"No," she whispered. "No, please."

"It changes nothing," Miguel hissed, his head clearing. "Wait here."

Sofia reached over and took the reins of her father's horse in her hand. He turned on her with a look that caused her to flinch away. She drew back a bit but did not drop the reins, however, keeping them firmly in her hands.

"Sofia." His tone was low and even. "Give me the reins."

"No, Papa, please. Don't leave me up here alone. Don't go down there. They will kill you, and I will have no one."

His daughter's face, a contorted mess of terror and pain, began blurring and running in front of him as tears filled his eyes. Miguel had trouble speaking. "Sofia, you may think you are too old for a whipping," he choked out, "but I will give you one if you do not hand me the reins."

"I will gladly suffer that if it keeps you alive," she said. *"Pleeease."*

Miguel felt as though he might die. Whole continents of loss, huge tectonic slabs of grief and rage, were breaking up and grinding around inside his body. It was entirely possible, that his heart might explode. Through it all only one thing grounded him and kept him tethered to reality: Sofia's small pale hand gripping his arm, stopping him from rushing headlong into violence and annihilation.

As tremors racked his upper body, she stood in the saddle and examined the property with his binoculars. Engines turned over amid shouts of pleasure and curses of aggravation. A few random shots pierced the air, but none in their direction.

"They are leaving," Sofia said. "They have not seen us."

Miguel reached for the binoculars, causing Sofia to pull back farther, taking Miguel's horse with her.

"Please," Miguel said. "The binoculars." He did not wish her to see any more.

She handed them over.

The road agents pulled away from the hacienda, taking a few potshots at the windows. One of the vehicles stopped by the chicken coop. It was a faded sky-blue Ford F-150, an older model, rusty in places and in need of a muffler. A driver remained at the wheel while the other men went for the chickens. The birds, already spooked by the gunfire and screaming, took fright and scattered in all directions as the main body of the agents' convoy rounded a bend in the road and disappeared from sight. The stragglers made no move to join them. Instead, the driver of the truck climbed out of the cabin to join his comrades in chasing the chickens. He was carrying a small cooler, from which he took a can of beer.

Miguel's eyes narrowed.

Three to one was much better odds than twenty to one, he thought silently. This would be a start.

"Here." He tossed the binoculars at his daughter's face. "Catch."

He heard her yelp as he swiped the reins from her hands and rode off.

"Stay here," he ordered, from the crest of the hill. "I mean it, Sofia. I will call you down when it is safe."

He didn't look to see if she obeyed. The lack of hoofbeats behind him told him she was staying in place. Miguel drew his Winchester again and levered a round into the breach. The reins he laid lightly in his lap, controlling the horse with his knees and occasional shifts of body weight. This was not Hollywood. He did not charge down the slope or scream his vengeance to the skies. He rode slowly at first, increasing his pace to a canter as he drew within range. The three road agents were entirely distracted attempting to round up his chickens, presumably for their lunch or dinner. They were even laughing at their own haplessness and incompetence. The moronic sound of it drifted uphill toward him.

The awful scenes of murder and violation that assailed him on all sides, he ignored. Or rather, he simply shut down any human reaction to them, letting a crust of dried blood as hard as an iron carapace form around his heart. An easterly breeze blew the smell of spilled blood and corruption into his face, carrying with it the harsh laughter of three of the men who had destroyed his family. He could tell now they were drunk, staggeringly so. As his horse pulled up in a clatter of iron-shod hooves on hard-packed dirt, one of them, the driver, finally noticed him. A look of dumb incomprehension clouded his bovine features as Miguel dismounted. He half smiled, half waved before finally raising his beer can to take a sip.

The driver was at least a hundred yards away, and two bodies lay between him and Miguel, one of them the cowboy's son. The other looked like old Armando, Mariela's uncle. A swollen river of black hatred poured through Miguel's head.

"Hola," the road agent slurred. *"¿Cómo estás?"*

Miguel lifted the rifle mechanically and shot the road agent in the forehead. The beer can from which he was drinking exploded fractionally before his head flew apart and his body tumbled over backward.

"Hey!"

"What the fuck?"

The other two had noticed his presence at last. The man farthest away, a fat stringy-haired gringo in blue jeans, circus cowboy chaps, and a long leather jacket, had actually managed to grab one chicken. He at least had the presence of mind to drop the bird and try to retrieve the assault rifle hanging from his shoulder, but Miguel gutshot him before he was able to lay a hand on the weapon. He screamed and fell to the ground, his body shuddering under the impact of two more bullets.

The last intruder turned tail and ran for the truck. Whether he was going for his guns or attempting to escape, Miguel did not know. He tracked the running target for two seconds before shooting him in the hip. The man went down like a galloping horse that had snapped a leg in a gopher hole. His screams were pitiable, animalistic. Miguel chambered another round and advanced on him without mercy. He was a scrawny specimen, although possessed of a potbelly he had tended well over the years. Like his friends, he was dressed in an eccentric combination of Wild West castoffs and modern hoodlum chic. As he scrabbled through the dirt, still trying to reach the sanctuary of the pickup truck, he kept one clawlike hand clamped on his ruined hip, from which geysered thick dark gouts of arterial blood keeping time with his failing heartbeat.

Miguel ground his teeth together so painfully that he thought they might shatter as he stalked past the body of his son. Every good and decent instinct in his body was drawing him toward the little boy, urging him to scoop up his body gently as though he were just sleeping and might be revived by a father's kiss upon his eyelids.

But Miguel knew from a brief horrified glimpse at his wounds that his only son was gone. He squeezed off any good or decent feelings that might have remained in his heart as though he were crushing a small bird within his fist.

He was just dimly aware of one small surviving voice of rationality, a mere whisper in the chorus of rage and loathing that filled his mind. It was his own voice, speaking from a better time, telling him he had no choice but to preserve the life of this man in front of him no matter how wretched a creature he might be, because he needed to know who had done this and why. But a hot gust of intemperate hatred blew that small, reasonable voice away. With his face distorted in a rictus of pain and malice, he very carefully and slowly walked up to the whimpering, moaning creature attempting to escape from him. When he was in range, one swift boot into the rib cage flipped the man over, causing him to cry out anew. Miguel raised his knee and stamped down viciously with the heel of his boot on the man's face, muffling his scream of protest and agony. Again he stomped down, shattering a mouthful of teeth and shredding lips and cheeks.

Stomp.

Stomp.

Stomp.

By the time he was finished, by the time the demon that had arisen inside his head and apparently taken over his body was finished, Miguel's leg ached. His boots and jeans were soaked with blood and smeared with gobs of brain and bone chips. The road agent's head was no more than a gruesome pancake. A cold wind seemed to pass through him, and he collapsed to the earth, shivering.

03

WILTSHIRE, ENGLAND

Caitlin awoke to the crying of her baby. The child would be hungry and in need of changing, and today was Bret's morning off, which sounded a lot more indulgent than it really was. He might get to hide under the covers for a few minutes more while she tended to little Monique and brought the coal-fired stove back to life for coffee. It was a good idea to keep the fuel banked up overnight and never to let the stove go out completely. Not unless you felt like flapping around before dawn with a cold draft blowing up your nightdress as you got down on all fours to jam rolled-up paper and fresh coal into a dead hearth. Caitlin tried to rub another night of broken sleep from her eyes and squinted at the glowing dial of her watch. Looked like about oh-four-hundred-twenty hours. "Omigod-thirty," as Bret referred to anytime before the sun rose. She swung her long, finely muscled legs over the side of the lumpy mattress and dropped in bare feet to the flagstone floor. A fair drop, too. The antique wrought-iron bed was huge.

"Want me to get her?" Bret mumbled without much enthusiasm

from under the duck feather duvet. Summer was not far off, but the weather had been chilly since the Disappearance, and although it did seem to be returning to normal, they still often slept under a couple of layers of woolen blankets and one oversized quilt.

"Not unless you can grow a pair of working udders in the next three minutes," Caitlin croaked, aware of just how swollen and heavy with milk her breasts were again. Monique was a good sleeper mostly, for which they were profoundly grateful, but that meant that Caitlin woke up most mornings needing to get her on for a long feed. Bret's half snort, half snore told her just how sincere the offer had been.

She wearily worked her feet into a pair of slippers and padded through into the baby's room, ducking under the low wooden lintel. At least he'd offered, and if she had genuinely been too tired to deal this morning, he would have dragged himself into the nursery to change the diaper before sliding Monique into bed beside Caitlin for a feed and a cuddle. They had all fallen asleep like that more than once.

The baby's cries, which had been short, disjointed, and scratchy when she first awoke, were growing longer and more insistent as she realized she was both hungry and trapped inside a large, wet, and very unpleasant square of not-so-white toweling cloth. Disposable diapers were almost impossible to get now, and as Caitlin gently wrestled with her daughter in the semidark, she tried to tell herself she was doing the right thing for Mother Earth. She quickly scraped Monique's poop into a chamber pot, wrinkling her nose in distaste. They routinely saved the malodorous contents for recycling in the farm's composting pits, but doing so was a hell of a hard sell at omigod-thirty with a thrashing baby kicking her heels in a puddle of what looked like undercooked chicken curry.

"Goddamn, sometimes I think I'd rather be back in Noisy-le-Sec," Caitlin muttered without conviction as she wiped the baby's bottom the way the midwife up at Swindon had shown her.

"Midwitches, more like it," she whispered to Monique as the offending mess went into a bucket by the change table and a fresh new terrycloth diaper and liner went under the infant's now clean butt. The liners, too, were very scarce. They were impossible to find on the open market, and the National Heath allotted them only seven per week. She really didn't want to wash and reuse them, but what choice did she have? This kid needed six or seven changes a day, not a week.

She marveled at how the quick, spare movements to secure the diaper in place had become second nature, even in the dark. She could do it blindfolded, although, of course, she could also field strip and reassemble the small armory of weapons on the manor under the same conditions. It wasn't so much the ease with which she had adapted to the thousand little tricks of parenthood that gave Caitlin pause for thought. It was the very fact that she'd become a parent in the first place. Settling into the enormous cracked leather armchair overlooking the southern fields, she eased little Monique onto her right breast while she watched the first stirrings of movement in the workers' camp beyond the security wall. The foremen were already awake, moving quietly up and down the long lines of ex-British Army tents, seeing to the campfires and the cooking wagons. For just a few moments of lingering darkness, it looked as though a regiment had bivouacked on her farm, so familiar was the strict and orderly fashion in which the men went about the job of rousing the sleepers from the long straight lines of tents. But as the baby sucked at her nipple and squirmed into a comfier position, the first hint of dawn softened the faraway line of the horizon over the Savernake Forest, and the true nature of the camp revealed itself.

Her workforce was composed almost entirely of refugees, mostly American but with a leavening of Continentals, with a cadre of former military types from the Home Guard to keep them all in line and on the job. They were the foremen she could see moving around before everyone else. After a few minutes Caitlin carefully hoisted the baby up onto her shoulder and patted her on the back waiting for the hearty burp she knew was coming, without any milk vomit, she hoped, to further stain and stink up her dressing gown. She didn't indulge herself in any limp, liberal bullshit about feeling sorry for the refugees or guilty for living in relative luxury here in the old stone manor while they slept and toiled in the fields. She did her fair share of toiling, and the bottom line was that they had all chosen to stay in the United Kingdom even after it became possible to return home to America. They were earning their room and board, to use a local phrase. Two years' labor for the Ministry of Resources and they would be free to settle wherever they wanted in the British Isles or the wider Commonwealth. Despite what some people said, England wasn't a gulag. All the men or women working her fields or those of her neighbors were at liberty to take themselves down to Portsmouth, where a free berth to the United States was available. Of course, once they stepped off the boat at the other end, they'd find themselves obliged to work for Uncle Sam for *five* years as payment for their passage.

Caitlin shifted Monique to her left breast and stroked the baby's head as she struggled to stay awake. She heard Bret grunt and throw back the covers in the next room. He soon appeared in the doorway, dressed in brown U.S. Army boxers and a white T-shirt.

He yawned. "You want some coffee?"

"When she's finished," she answered, stroking Monique's head again. "I had one while I was feeding her the other day, and man, it was like she'd snorted a line of speed or something. Didn't sleep all day. Warm milk and honey would be nice, though."

"Got it," he said in a voice still hoarse with sleep. Her husband disappeared into the depths of the farmhouse to stoke the wood-fired stove and dole himself out a small serving of black market coffee, another perk of her job. The rattle and tink of metal cooking pots drifted across the small stream from the camp, which was quickly coming awake as people spilled out of the big twelve-man tents.

She could see quite a few children already, picking up the games they'd been forced to abandon by nightfall the previous evening, running through the dew-soaked grass, chasing and being chased by four or five dogs. Strictly speaking, the young'uns were supposed to be boarded elsewhere; there were schools for foreign children, again mostly Americans, in both Swindon and Basingstoke, but Caitlin had heard nothing good about them, and she quietly used her connections in London to allow as many families as possible to stay together at Melton Farm. One of the tents was given over to an all-ages school run by three teachers who'd been traveling through Italy when the Wave hit. It was one of the things that made placements on their farm so popular.

Bret returned just as Monique fell off the breast, fast asleep and sticky with milk. "Look at her, would you." He smiled as he passed Caitlin her warm honeyed milk, making sure to keep it away from the child. "It's a good thing she got your looks and brains, sweetheart, because she is a lazy-ass sleepin' fool just like her old man, and she's gonna need something to fall back on in life."

Caitlin nodded, honestly wondering how her nearly-narcoleptic husband had ever made it through ranger school.

"Well, we don't know that she'll be a rocket scientist," she said. "But she is pretty."

"Like you," Bret said as he leaned forward to kiss her on the forehead.

"Guess I could have had my coffee, after all," she said.

"Take mine," he offered. "I don't mind milk and honey."

"I can't do that. You're down to half a bag of beans."

He shrugged. "You'll get more. You are still going to the city, aren't you?"

She nodded, a little distracted. She was already planning her morning run. Maintaining her fitness was not negotiable. Bret did not bother as much now that he was a self-proclaimed househusband, although farmwork kept him fit and strong enough.

Caitlin, however, had no choice. She still answered to her old paymasters even though she was no longer on field duty.

She had run five miles just a couple of days after Monique had been delivered by elective cesarean. (And hadn't there been some tut-tutting from the midwitches over *that*.) A week further on and she was back in the gym she and Bret had set up in a sunroom overlooking the swimming pool. And yes, she *had* been more than a little surprised to find a working English farmhouse with a heated in-ground swimming pool, but that had been one of the things that had attracted them to the property. That and the peppercorn rent paid to the government, an indulgence in return for her services as a "consultant" to Echelon.

Bret stood by the window, silhouetted by the rising sun, causing Caitlin a momentary rush of blood. There had been a time in both their lives when they would have instinctively avoided exposing themselves in such a manner. Her husband had been able to get over it.

She hadn't.

Arguably, Caitlin did not need to maintain her combat readiness and field craft the way she did. Her consultancy consisted almost entirely of analytic and training work, and having hunkered down here in the heart of the English Home Counties, they could hardly be more secure. Bret had tried to get her to ease up, but her Echelon training had taken hold down at a cellular level. She could not stop being who and what she was. Looking at her husband, she often envied his ability to simply walk away from his army past.

Monique stirred and grumbled in her mother's arms, perhaps disturbed by her dark shift in mood. Bret turned away from the window where he was watching the workers' camp come to life and offered to take the baby. His limbs were all heavily muscled, and the small swaddled infant disappeared into the crook of one arm without waking. He started to pat her lightly on the back, rocking her gently and humming an old Willie Nelson standard.

"My Heroes Have Always Been Cowboys." The song never failed to have a magical, soothing effect on the baby, and Caitlin could tell that Monique was falling more deeply asleep in her father's arms.

She stepped back into their bedroom and quickly changed into her running gear: black Lycra leggings, an old T-shirt of Bret's, and a Berreta M9 pistol in a specially fitted holster at the small of her back. Her husband didn't give it a second glance. He had spent his adult life around weapons and knew his wife well enough to understand why she would never stop carrying one.

"Are you riding up to Swindon today to that GM crop briefing?" she asked. "I'll just tell the stable guys is all, if you're gonna need one of the horses."

Bret eased the baby back into her crib and stood up, stretching his back with an audible cracking of bones. Like her, he carried a good deal of scar tissue and old injuries.

"Thought I might take the mountain bike up if you don't mind," he said quietly. "I could do with the cardio workout."

"You could," she teased him, grabbing for a fold of skin at his belly. He wasn't carrying any fat, but he batted her hand away defensively anyway.

"Hey, you squeeze it, you buy it, lady."

"Really?" she said, closing on him.

When she grabbed at him this time, he didn't resist.

An hour or so later, jogging on the spot to keep her heart rate elevated, Caitlin enjoyed taking in a deep draft of chilly morning air and shooting one last glance at her home before plunging back into a long cross-country run. Thick tendrils of coal smoke were creeping out of the kitchen chimney, where Bret would be preparing hot drinks for the foremen before briefing them on the day's work. They'd be plowing the new GM soy into the eastern paddock today, half a mile up the road toward Stitchcombe, and without a gasoline ration, as usual these days, it would all be done by hand. Most of the camp would turn out for that, although a smaller number would be at work in the southern fields, scattering a new weed-n-feed mix as part of a trial for the Resources Ministry. They were being paid in fuel coupons for letting the government's eggheads conduct field tests on their property.

She shook her head at that again.

Their property.

The previous owner, a minor Saudi prince, had lost the farm during the "resettlement" period in the year after the Disappearance. Caitlin's mouth quirked downward at the bloodless euphemism. "Pogrom" would be more accurate: ethnic cleansing on a scale to put into the shade the earlier atrocities in the Balkans. The prince had not complained, however. He'd been at a wedding in Damascus when the Israelis nuked the city.

She shook off the grim memories and took off again, shortening her stride as she dropped down a hillside where long summer grass covered the tangled roots of chestnut and elm and holly oak trees. She didn't need a sprained ankle or worse to teach her not to run blindly over treacherous ground. Small families of birds took flight at her approach, starlings and robins as best she could tell. They'd experienced something of a population boom earlier this spring, rebounding from the collapse of their populations after the pollution storms. Turning onto Thicketts Road, which wound down through the hills toward the village of Mildenhall, Caitlin settled into a long, loping stride. She felt good this morning and decided to add another couple of miles to her course by circling the village a few times. That way she might even catch Bret and Monique on the way home if he was cycling up to Swindon as planned. She played her thumb over her wedding ring. It was still so new, she hadn't built up a callus on her palm beneath it. Just as her mother and father had. She remembered the feeling of their hands as though she had just let go of them, a tactile memory so sharp that she had to wonder whether it had anything to do with the tumor that had been cut out of her brain. The doctors had said there would be side effects from the treatment.

She pushed away the troubling idea that her mind was not quite right and never would be again, preferring to concentrate on her breathing and balance as she powered along the country road.

She and Bret would build up their own calluses, their own family history, here or back home in America, with Monique and any more children who came after her. She knew they would. There would be a long time ahead of them for all that.

04

NEW YORK

Culver took a spot at the back of the press conference in Castle Clinton, the old sandstone fort at the northern end of Battery Park. It was possible, standing on the freshly raked gravel and staring over the heads of the reporters, to look at the skyline of Lower Manhattan and imagine that not much was wrong in the world. You merely had to ignore a few scorch marks and broken windows, maybe squint your eyes a little to fuzz up the details, and you could have been standing in the New York of old, with life teeming around you, ten million people, seemingly twenty million cars, the subway rattling and roaring underfoot as you walked downtown, the smoky, earthy fragrance of frying meat from a hundred street carts, the clip-clop of horse-drawn carriages around the park. It was almost as though he could close his eyes and be back there, strolling up to Redeye, his favorite bar and grill, for a perfectly cooked fillet of Chilean swordfish with San Moriglio sauce.

Instead, the thump of two Blackhawk helicopters circling the southern tip of the island drowned out what little ambient noise there was, mostly distant gunfire or the crash, rumble, and grind of salvage work.

The White House chief of staff folded his arms and pushed the pleasant daydreams away. It would be a long time before anyone in this country could indulge in daydreams again. While Karen Milliner warmed up the audience by taking questions on the issues of the moment—Jackson Blackstone's antics down in Fort Hood, the Indo-Pakistani wars, and the congressional hearings on the Lands and Homesteading Act—Culver contented himself with scoping out the scene. The colonnaded cloisters of the roughly circular fort were deep in shade with the sun climbing high overhead, and he could make out Secret Service details stalking through the shadows, ever watchful. The reporters were arrayed on plastic chairs in front of Karen Milliner, who spoke from a plain black podium.

Jed turned his attention to the reporters who were going back and forth with Karen as prelude to the main game, Kipper's appearance in a few minutes. The national networks, for want of a more accurate term, had sent their heavy hitters; the bloggers were a bit of a rabble, as always, and the news sites and daily papers had assigned their national security guys rather than their Seattle correspondents. That told him right away how they were going to play the resettlement story: as a battle for the Wild East.

Kip wasn't going to like that.

He really did prefer to concentrate on the constructive side of nation building, or rebuilding. The uglier, more violent aspects of reclaiming the frontier were something he considered a grim necessity, best left to the experts.

Jackson Blackstone—Culver refused to refer to the man as "General," since he had been forcibly retired—was undeniably one of those experts. However, you could hardly count the elected territorial governor of Texas as one of the president's men.

The White House chief of staff suppressed a rueful grin as

someone questioned Milliner about Fort Hood again.

"Ms. Milliner, my sources indicate there are significant efforts to evict and deport families vetted under the Federal Homestead Program. Does the president intend to do anything about the racists and rebels at Fort Hood?"

That had come from a blogger, of course, Krist Novoselic from the *Seattle Weekly*. Culver still didn't know why Kip had insisted on accrediting any of those assholes. They had zero respect for the conventions of the old press corps. You couldn't even leak to them without the fact of it appearing in the opening paragraph of any resulting story, as he had discovered to his undying chagrin very early in the administration.

"We are monitoring the situation in the Texas Territory, Krist. The president isn't pretending to be happy about it. But he's not about to go hauling out the big stick to beat on Mister Blackstone just to prove that he's a tough guy. Frankly, President Kipper is a busy man, Krist, and Fort Hood is a tenth-order issue at best. I probably shouldn't have to remind you, either, that Mr. Blackstone is not a rebel. He was actually elected. So no, we won't be sending the cavalry. And if that's what you were hoping for to boost your traffic stats, I'd suggest you prepare for disappointment."

A ripple of amusement ran through the arena. Milliner was famous for her refusal to coddle the press. It was why Kip had chosen her for the job and kept her on in the face of some frenzied back-channel protests from the surviving old school media.

Culver winked at her as she gave the blogger a taste of her own big stick, but she was professional enough to ignore him, of course. A small flock of starlings zipped overhead, and he watched them disappear out over the water. The birds were one of the first things he'd noticed on getting back. There seemed to be a lot more of them than he remembered. More birds. Fewer rats. He was going to have to ask somebody about that one day.

"Is the president planning on talking to the Commonwealth

prime ministers about speeding up the repatriation process, do you know, Ms. Milliner?"

That question came from Ted Koppel at National Public Radio, and Culver winced as soon as he heard it. Two million of the estimated fifteen million surviving Americans had made the choice to stay in the foreign refuges, mostly in the other English-speaking democracies. They were a real point of friction with the country's surviving allies. Hell, Koppel himself didn't even live in the United States, preferring to stay at the NPR field office in London, which made him a bit of a hypocrite in Culver's book for even asking the question. But Jed couldn't really blame Koppel or those two million others. Those people were desperately needed back home, but home wasn't nearly as friendly a place as it had been once upon a time. The hungry time after the Wave was still fresh on everyone's mind, and many were convinced they had not yet turned the corner on food production and distribution. Food shortages were still a very real problem.

"Freedom of movement is still one of our fundamental rights, Ted," Karen said, quickly throwing up her hands. "And before anyone gets on my case about the Declared Areas, can I just say, grow up. They're declared for good reason, and you know it. As to our expatriate community, what can I say? Every American is free to come and go as they please. This stuff I've been reading about foreign governments impeding their return, it's just hogwash. Obviously, we would prefer to have everyone back home again. We need all hands on deck to rebuild this country, but we are not in the business of forcing people to do anything."

Koppel was on his feet again, waving a pen at Milliner to beg her indulgence for a supplementary question.

"How can you say that, Ms. Milliner, when the administration indentures returnees for five years?"

Karen smiled.

"That's overstating the case, don't you think, Ted? People are free to return of their own volition, and if they do it at their own expense, they are free to live and work wherever and however they choose. But I don't think it's wrong to ask people to give something back if they rely on the taxpayer to get them here and support them when they arrive. There are no freebies anymore, Ted. Everyone works. Everyone pays. Everyone does their bit. The Congress and the president have made that clear, as have the American people, given their repeated endorsement of the mutual obligation policy at the ballot box. Was it not Captain John Smith at Jamestown who said, 'He who does not work, shall not eat'? We are not asking anything less than Smith did."

Culver almost rolled his eyes at Milliner's chutzpah, but he remained outwardly blank-faced. Very few people had the resources to get themselves home from overseas, which left most returning expatriates with only one option: to hitch a ride with Uncle Sam. And it most definitely was not a free ride. Koppel looked like he was gearing up for a head-butting session with Milliner, but she cut him off with a wave and a disingenuous smile as Kipper suddenly appeared from within the shadows behind her, where he'd been waiting, skimming the notes Culver had prepared for him, they hoped. The boss was notorious for refusing to stick to his talking points and for going off topic at the merest provocation. He did like talking to people, and even reporters were people, as he'd told Jed more than once. Kipper squinted briefly as he passed from shadow into the bright, warm light of high spring. He seemed to sniff the air and took the time to look around as he made his way to the podium.

Karen Milliner formally introduced him, and everyone stood for a moment, which was where the formalities pretty much ended. James Kipper did not enjoy the formal trappings of office and shook them off at every opportunity. He took his place behind a single microphone that was used to record audio for all the assembled media, his hands in the pockets of his jeans. He'd ditched the flak jacket before appearing in front of the press, some of whom were still in their own.

"Thanks for coming, everyone," he said chattily. "I know it's a hell of a trip getting out here, and I appreciate the effort involved. It's important."

Koppel waved his pen at the president, probably hoping to take up where he'd left off with Milliner, but all he got was a cheeky grin.

"I'm sorry, Ted. I'll be happy to talk your ears off about the Homesteading Act and the whole mutual obligation thing on the plane going back, but we're here to talk about one thing this morning, and I have promised Karen and Jed that's all I'm gonna talk about." Koppel did a good job of looking chagrined, but he settled back to listen.

"As you know from the precautions we had to take getting you all here today, this city is not the safest place. My security guys had what my granny would've called a fit of the vapors when I told them we were coming here."

Jed watched the audience closely. Only a few of them smiled.

"Right now," Kip continued, "while we're sitting here in this old fort, there are probably a minimum of eight thousand looters, scavengers, whatever you want to call them—a horde stripping this city of anything they can carry off. There are tens of thousands more up and down the East Coast and all the way around into Texas. Most of them are just small-time racketeers, crooks, and so on. But there are a couple of big organized criminal groups out of Europe and Africa, too. The navy and coast guard have been doing what they can to interdict them, but we just don't punch at the same weight we used to. A lot of them get through, and they are stripping the cities bare. Some of them are even pushing into the interior."

Jed resisted the urge to let his head drop into his hands. There was just no telling Kipper. As much as he tried to teach his boss the dark arts of spin and issue management, the guy was determined to speak his mind, no matter how damaging. Culver could see the headlines already. "President Admits the East Is Lost." "Raiders Pushing into the Heartland." Most of the reporters were already madly scribbling away on their notepads. He shared a quick, furtive, and despairing glance with Karen Milliner as the president pushed on.

"Now, while I agree that capturing and killing as many of these thugs as we can is important," Kip said, "it's not the only answer. I could order the army to kill every single pirate in New York today, and a month from now the city would be crawling with them again." More furious scribbling. "President Throws in the Towel." "President Admits Piracy Problem Is Beyond Him."

"There is only one way to reclaim the eastern seaboard, and for that matter the interior of our continent. And that is to actually reclaim it."

Kipper paused to let the moment sink in. *Here it comes,* Jed thought. *The money shot.*

"This morning I signed an executive order requiring the armed forces to seize and secure eighteen strategically important sites on the East Coast, including here in New York. We will spread out from those sites, which will become colonies, if you will, where any returnee who is willing to take on the risk can settle freely anytime six months after their repatriation. Those six months will be spent in full-time preparation for resettlement. Additionally, any immigrant willing to take the fast track to U.S. citizenship can settle freely after two years, including eighteen months of mandated service and six months of settlement training. Long story short, that's it. Any questions?"

It took all of half a second for the press corps to react, but when they did, it reminded Jed of the ringing of the bells at the old stock exchange. In one master stroke the president had outbid the foreign powers for U.S. human capital and most likely performed an end run around Blackstone down in Texas at the same time. The reporters all seemed to explode suddenly out of their seats, flinging questions at Kipper, who smiled and waited for the uproar to die down a little before pointing at Joel Connelly from the *Seattle Post-Intelligencer.*

"So, Mister President, you're rescinding the requirement for returnees to work in the National Reconstruction Corps for five years?"

Kip smiled and shook his head. "Only if they take on the risk of settling in one of the new colony sites."

"What about exemptions for veterans?" Novoselic asked. "Will they be obligated—"

"They've already given their pound of flesh," Kipper replied. "We won't be asking anything more of them."

More furious questions flew up at the podium, but Connelly won out again.

"Well, just how risky will it be?"

"Very," said Kip. "It's a frontier, Joel. And frontiers, as we know from our old history books, are dangerous places. Some of our efforts will fail. Some people will die—"

Kipper never finished the sentence. Two Secret Service men suddenly slammed into him, driving him backward off the stage a second before Jed heard a high keening whistle that quickly became a screech before disappearing inside an abrupt, roaring concatenation of thunder. Time stretched out as though the whole world existed on the skin of a balloon that was quickly inflating around and away from him, slowing everything as it receded. He saw the reporters start from their seats, some sprinting in slo-mo replays of Olympic runners flung from the blocks by a starter's gun, others half standing, then sitting, bobbing up and down like puppets jerked around by a small child. Everything moved so slowly even as he knew everything had accelerated, and then— *oof!*—an agent clad in black coveralls shoulder charged him, lifting his considerable bulk right off the ground, two clear inches of air between the soles of his oxfords and the white, crunchy gravel as he was driven back into the shelter of the colonnade like a water boy T-boned by a linebacker.

The world clock caught up with his fear-quickened senses, and a rush of visions flowed over him. Dirty orange blooms of fire consuming the heavy earthmoving equipment on the muddy, torn-up grass outside the fort. An explosion above him, off to the right, as something detonated on the old roofline, sending dark, wicked fangs of black roofing slate scything away through the air. A deep rumbling in the earth as the volcanic eruption of fire and thunder built to a crescendo. A woman, a reporter, running full tilt, right into a blossoming explosion that roughly quartered her body, flinging the remains to all points of the compass.

Then more men, all clad in black body armor, all over him, slamming his shoulder into something hard and unyielding. A wall? A door frame? It was dark, and he couldn't see anything beyond the spots of light blooming in front of his eyes. Jed felt himself thrown to the floor, a polished wooden floor he noted just before his cheekbone cracked into the boards. The thunder rolled on outside but became distant, muffled. Black spots spread over his vision, and he fell into them.

05

NEW YORK

Yusuf Mohammed was unimpressed by his fellow fighters. Although many of them were older than he, some by many years, they behaved like foolish children. He did not imagine that most would survive an encounter with the Americans when they came. Looking out across the river, craning to catch a glimpse of the great broken spires of Manhattan, Yusuf knew the Americans could not be far away now. He crouched in his fighting pit, chosen for him by one of the emir's very own lieutenants, and wondered where the other men of his *saif* might be.

To judge from the yipping cries and gales of laughter that reached him between the volleys of rocket fire, they were still dancing and capering around the launchers. Yusuf shook his head in dismay. He was no more than fifteen, maybe sixteen years old. Nobody knew for sure. But he had been a soldier for nearly ten of those years, and he had seen unknowable numbers of men and women and of course children, such as he had once been, who had died because they did not take the business of war seriously.

Another string of missiles shrieked away into the sky, describing a great soaring arc over the river, traced by dirty gray trails of smoke. From his makeshift bunker, where he clutched an AK-47 to his chest and leaned against a canvas bag full of loaded magazines, he could not see the launch of the rockets or where they fell on the far side of the water. But he could hear them as they crashed down on the heads of the infidel, the thunder rolling back across the river like the sound of God's judgment.

Laughter and the words of an obscene Somali drinking song also reached him.

Drinking!

He sighed heavily. Allah's judgment would fall heavily on both sides of the river today.

Yusuf risked a peek over the barricade of broken concrete blocks and bricks and loose black soil behind which he was hidden. Amid the roaring rush of the missile barrage he thought he heard the distant buzzing of attack helicopters, a terrible sound he knew only too well. From his vantage point overlooking a large rectangular field covered in thick, tall swards of grass and a small forest of gray stunted trees, he could not see the southern end of Manhattan, but he had a clear view of another large island directly across from the mouth of the large dock that all but cut Ellis Island in half. A small swarm of black metal insects appeared to be rising from somewhere within the middle of that island. They had been told by the emir's officers that it was a base for one of the American militias and that they could expect the response to their attack to come from there.

Yusuf tightened his grip on his weapon and marveled just a little at how nervous he was. He had fought in many battles in his short life, but most of them of course had been in Africa against other primitive forces. As the vague dark shapes resolved themselves into the outlines of the helicopters he knew as Apaches, the young fighter allowed himself a small measure of pride in how far he had come. There was a time when he thought of his first allies, the small band of Ugandan child fighters by whom he had been abducted and with whom he fought for five years, as the finest, the toughest, the most ferocious warriors in the world. Now, hunkered down thousands of miles from home, or at least from the continent he called home, he thought of his first band of comrades and their fabulously cruel commander Captain Kono as nothing more than stupid savages. They fought for the same reason he had fought. Because Captain Kono and his men had taken them from their homes, murdered their families, and threatened to kill them if they did not fight for him. Yusuf checked his weapon one last time, looked around in vain for the other mujahideen who were supposed to be manning a strongpoint with him, and mouthed a quiet prayer of thanks for the opportunity the emir had given him not just to escape Kono and the ridiculous Lord's Resistance Army but to lift himself up into the light and the forgiveness of the one true God.

"Allahu akbar," he said quietly to himself. Not fiercely, not boastfully, but quietly and piously and most of all with great love in his heart for the infinite forgiveness that Allah had bestowed upon a former infidel such as he.

He crouched down below the lip of his fighting pit. The emir's men had trained him well. He knew all about the wondrous technology with which the Americans still fought in spite of the great blow God had smashed down upon them. He knew that merely popping his head up for just a second or two might be the last thing he ever did. It made the stupid, animalistic laughter and shouting of the other fighters, who were *still* apparently dancing around the rocket trucks somewhere behind him, all the more galling. Had they learned nothing?

The answer came in the form of a sudden high-pitched screeching sound as the Americans finally reached out with their own rockets and missiles. Yusuf burrowed as deeply into his little pit as he could and breathed out to protect himself from the waves of overpressure that surely would follow the impact of the aptly named Hellfire missiles. Huddled into a tight ball, pressing himself into the earth, he had only the vaguest impression of the sky above the island suddenly turning lethal. Whereas their rockets, launched from the back of trucks driven in darkness over the long causeway from the mainland to this former migrant-processing center, had lanced through the air like the spears of Zulu warriors, the American attack seemed to fill the entire space a few feet above his head with roaring death. There was no *whoosh-whoosh-whoosh* of volleying rocket fire. There was only a huge and instantly terrifying eruption of noise and fire and smoke as the very earth seemed to shake beneath his cowering form. Shock and horror rolled over the boy soldier as he thought it possible the Americans might just demolish the entire island, pouring fire onto the rubble until it subsided beneath the waters of the river.

He did not know how long he lay there, quaking in fear. His abject terror was so great, so overwhelming, that a few times he felt himself subject to a whole-body hallucination, the feeling that he was being squeezed out of his mortal remains in the bottom of his bunker. His mind seemed to float free of the hell in which his body was trapped, but it did not escape, falling instead down a long dark tunnel at the end of which a smaller, younger version of himself lay quivering in fear many, many years ago. As in a dream, he had no grasp of the hard edges of this vision. It was more a sensation and a few half-remembered images he had long ago tried to forget. His mother screaming in pain after Captain Kono's men had cut the lips from her face. His tiny, spindly little boy arms shaking and useless, all but paralyzed with mortal dread as he held a makeshift club and stood over his uncle Bongani while Kono screamed in his face to kill the old man if Yusuf wanted to live.

Of course in those days his name was not Yusuf Mohammed. He did not remember what his name had been when he lived in the village with his mother and uncle and brothers and sisters and all his cousins. He did not remember being happy, but at times even now he assumed he must have been, even if that happiness was born of ignorance.

Yusuf Mohammed forced himself out of the waking nightmare before it could get any worse. And it could get much worse than the memory of his murdering a kindly and much loved uncle just to save his own life. He forced himself to open his senses to the real world even though it was a hell of fire and death. He was surprised to find himself lying on open ground a few feet from his dugout, which was smoking and ruined as though from a bomb blast. His heart, already trip-hammering, lurched sickeningly in his chest as he caught sight of a disembodied arm and a leg trailing the gruesome tendrils of torn flesh and muscle and meat he knew so well from the battlefield. But as he pushed himself up off the ground, he knew they were not his limbs. He was still all in one piece.

His weapon was still secured to him by its strap, but the canvas bag full of magazines was missing, and his chest throbbed with a great dull pain as though he had been struck heavily.

A terrible sound like the clanging of a large metal press brought him further back to his senses as one of the Americans' Apache helicopters flew overhead, hosing long lines of machine gun fire into an unseen target. A scalding hot rain of empty brass shell cases began to tinkle around him, burning his skin whenever one touched him. Yusuf scrambled to his feet but stayed crouched as low as he could, running for cover into the nearest building. He nearly tripped on the remains of one of his fellow fighters who was lying a few yards away. A head and maybe a third of the upper torso, the rest just viscera and bloody ruin. He thought he recognized Abayneh the Ethiopian. An unbeliever gone to his punishment. He had probably been one of the drunken fools cavorting around the rocket launchers. Why did the emir's lieutenants allow the consumption of liquor among the janissaries? Among the fedayeen it was strictly forbidden. At the end Abayneh remained a pirate and an ally of convenience, nothing more. Most of the men on the island were like him. Only a handful of the righteous had been salted through their number to stiffen their resolve and attend to the technical aspects of managing the rocket barrage so that it fell as close to the target as possible.

As one of the righteous, Yusuf knew his duty. He rushed toward the nearest building clutching his weapon, his lungs burning as much from the smoke as from the exertion. For the first time since the American counterattack had begun he heard voices, speaking in Arabic. His spirits soared. Some of the fedayeen must have survived and rallied together in this building. He rushed onward, his feet seeming to fly across the ground as a burst of machine gun fire from above scythed down the chest-high grass in front of him. He ran on regardless of the danger. If it was Allah's will that he should die, then he would die.

But he did not. Diving through a shattered doorway, he found himself inside a large room, empty except for what looked like some desks and chairs that had long ago been pushed into one corner and covered with a heavy dust cloth. He came up out of his roll, clutching his weapon as he had been taught, and found two comrades shouting orders out of a window. It was hard to hear them clearly over the uproar and the clatter of American fire, but merely hearing the familiar sound of their voices was enough to give him heart for the fight.

"Allahu akbar," he cried out.

One of the men spun around, pointing his gun at Yusuf but smiling a little wildly, perhaps even crazily, when he saw it was the Ugandan convert. The young warrior recognized Mustafa Ali, one of the officers responsible for coordinating the rocket barrage. A Pakistani, a good man with a large family over in one of the outlying camps. "Come, come quickly," he cried out to Yusuf. "They are here. Quickly now, follow us."

Ali and his comrade, an Arab that Yusuf recognized but did not know, grabbed a pair of RPG-7s leaning against the windowsill and ran for a doorway at the end of the room, motioning for Yusuf to follow them. He did so, catching a glimpse through the window of the truck-mounted rocket launchers on the roadway outside. They had been destroyed, utterly destroyed, as if a giant had smashed his fist down on top of them. The wreckage was aflame, and occasionally small explosions tossed twisted metal refuse into the air as ammunition or fuel cooked off. Of the janissaries, or the foolish drunken pirates as he thought of them, there was little to be seen beyond a few chunks of burning meat and random limbs scattered here and there.

It meant nothing to Yusuf. The carnage of battle was familiar to him, even if the terrible intensity of the American attack was something new. Feeling dizzy, with his legs wobbling and his ears ringing, he hurried to catch up with Ali and the other fedayeen. The rolling thunder of rocket and bomb blasts had abated somewhat in the last few minutes, giving way to an increasingly furious crescendo of gunfire and the clattering roar of helicopters. The three men ran toward an internal staircase, passing a couple of pirate mercenaries on their way. The pirates were no longer laughing and singing. They looked shocked and furious. Indeed, so murderously angry did they first appear that Yusuf thought it possible they might turn their weapons on the fedayeen. He almost raised his own gun, but Mustafa Ali was in the way. Probably a good thing. The pirates would almost certainly have turned on them if he had reacted that way. Instead they simply ran past one another, shouting incomprehensibly in some language he did not recognize. Yusuf followed Ali up the staircase, covering two flights of steps in what seemed like no time.

The Arab and the Pakistani exchanged a few brief words on the second floor and came quickly to an agreement. Beckoning Yusuf to follow them, they ran down along the corridor with ruined offices on one side and a long line of mostly shattered windows looking out over the burning wreckage of the rocket launchers on the other. Every inch of flesh on Yusuf's body crawled sickeningly as an American helicopter swept by. It was one of the fat troop transports they called Blackhawks. A door gunner seemed to look right into his eyes as he worked frantically to clear a jam on his weapon. Yusuf jumped in surprise as Ali fired an RPG out of the window without any sort of warning. Thick acrid smoke filled the corridor and burned his eyes, but he was still able to watch the long looping flight path as the rocket-propelled grenade sped out of the building and flicked across a short distance to the second lumbering metal bird, striking it squarely in the cockpit.

All three of the fedayeen warriors yelled in surprise and delight as a greasy orange ball of flame engulfed the front of the Blackhawk, wrenching it out of its flight path. Yusuf saw the door gunner flung backward into the cabin just before a secondary explosion tore the main body of the helicopter in two. It dropped from the sky with sickening speed, spilling four—no, five—of its occupants out into clear air. Two of them were engulfed in flames, but the others looked like rag dolls as they fell. Exaltation and horror swirled in Yusuf's mind. He made to run over and congratulate Ali on the fluke shot, but even as he took the first step, his comrades flew apart in front of his eyes, their bodies disintegrating as the corridor around them suddenly was chewed up by a savage storm of return fire.

The boy soldier dropped to the ground without conscious thought. He could hear the pounding *thrum* of the helicopter that had swept in immediately after the first one had gone down. It must have been very close, because the sound of its miniguns spewing thousands of rounds into the space where his comrades had stood, living and breathing just half a second ago, seemed to fill the world right out to its very edges. Though he couldn't see it, he thought it must have been one of the small egg-shaped helicopters from the gunfire, which sounded like the ripping of a great sail. They had warned him about those metal devils. Giving no conscious thought to his actions, Yusuf moved with animal quickness, crawling through the nearest open door and getting a couple of inches of solid brickwork between himself and the lethal rain of fire. Not that he had any illusions about the safety of hiding behind a wall should the Americans turn one of their satanic cannons on him, but by hiding at least he might escape their attention.

His skin felt as though he were on fire. He realized he had soiled his pants, but it did not matter. At least he was alive. The frightening hammering sound of the helicopter's machine guns trailed off, and with it the dull thumping beat of its rotor blades. He gave himself a minute to recover from the shock before crawling out of the room and into the corridor, where all that remained of Ali and the other man whose name he did not know were a few bloody rags and scraps of smoking meat. Yusuf kept his head down and his weapon in front of him as he belly crawled away from the horrible scene as quickly as he could. He was certain he could hear harsh flat voices shouting in English somewhere nearby, and he imagined the whole building filling up with cruel American soldiers. There was nothing for it but to get himself away from here so that he might fight another day.

Reaching the stairwell up which they had just climbed, he dragged himself back to his feet and hurried down unsteadily. He knew that to run out of the building was to invite almost immediate death from the circling helicopters, and so as soon as he reached the ground floor, he turned down another hallway and ran as fast as he could on rubbery, shaking legs and with his lungs burning as though he were drowning in blazing gasoline. He did not see any other fighters, which was probably a good thing. If they were as traumatized and unbalanced as he, they were likely to kill one another. Hurrying away from the part of the island where the rocket launchers had been parked, he found himself in unfamiliar surroundings. The noise of battle dropped away just a little, but his confusion increased. He soon found himself at the end of the hallway where a door, apparently shattered by gunfire, opened onto an area of concrete tarmac and beyond that the water. Driven by fear now, and humiliation, Yusuf threw his assault rifle away and sprinted out the door and into daylight, covering the short distance to the edge of the water in just a few seconds. A single loop played in his mind. He could not let himself be captured. None of the fedayeen were to allow themselves to be captured. Gunfire cracked somewhere behind him, and it felt as though every muscle in his back was clenched tight in anticipation of the bullet that must surely be coming for him, but he ignored it and ran on, launching himself into the air and out over the dirty green water. He did not expect to survive.

06

NEW YORK

"Incoming fire!" the Blackhawk pilot shouted.

Milosz winced as his headphones amplified the man's cry to painful levels.

Between the crackle and chatter of the headset and the hammering blades of the helicopter, Sergeant Fryderyk Milosz could not hear the distinctive and all too familiar sound of the BM-21 rockets that were pounding Castle Clinton. But he didn't need to. He could easily follow the bright arc of their flight paths as they zipped in over the river, and the results were laid out beneath him like a grotesque work of art painted in blood and fire. It greatly distressed the former Polish Army GROM operator to see his new countrymen scurrying about, trying to avoid the pepper-black bursts of high-explosive warheads. It distressed him even more to see some of them fail. Scattered around the grounds of Castle Clinton were a number of mangled bodies, some still crawling, some limping heavily, others writhing on the ground in agony. Here and there a few crimson lumps did not move at all. Fortunately, the bastards behind this atrocity were very poor artillerymen. Many of the rockets fell short into the river, throwing up plumes of dirty brown water or not exploding at all. A handful of warheads flew wide, crashing into the surrounding skyscrapers, detonating with extravagant blasts of color that rained deadly shards of glass into the concrete canyons of the city below. A largely empty city, he thought, thank the Virgin Mary.

"I have them. The island at two o'clock," Milosz called out over the intercom, pointing at a collection of massive, aged brick structures on the island to the north of the big Liberty Lady statue. "In the car park behind the buildings. There! See?"

He pointed out the launch plumes to the ranger fire team in the cabin. Great eruptions of smoke and flares that would not have been visible from ground level on Lower Manhattan, hidden as they were behind the buildings.

"Copy that," the pilot said. "Viper one-three, this is Saber six-one, approaching Ellis Island from the northwest for a visual."

"Viper one-three copies," Milosz's headset told him. He glanced out over the water to see if he could catch a glimpse of Viper one-three, an Apache tank killer assigned to the security detail. He found the helicopter and turned his attention back to the island. "Approaching low from the east. ETA thirty seconds."

"They are BM-21s!" Milosz shouted, scoping the truck-mounted launchers with his rifle. They were still too far off for a decent shot. Plumes of smoke obscured one or more multiple rocket launch systems, Katyushas. As the Blackhawk, flying high and out of reach, orbited Ellis Island, a voice in his headset crackled, "I count six, seven... no, make that a dozen combatants and two launchers."

"Viper, this is Saber. Did you copy last?"

"Viper copies. Stay clear of the island. It'll be rotten with RPGs," Viper one-three said.

"No! Get us closer," Milosz insisted, taking aim at one of the combatants, African by the look of him, clad in ragged olive drab fatigue pants and a ludicrously loud yellow and red patterned shirt. "I can take them. Get us in there."

"Not no, but *hell no,*" the pilot called back.

"But if you get us closer, I can take them out," Milosz argued.

"Negative, Sergeant," the pilot replied. "They'll be waiting in there for us with RPGs."

"Saber six-one, this is Viper one-three. I count fourteen combatants around four truck-mounted BM-21 launchers parked in the parking lot of Ellis Island on the west side. Possible combatants in the museum complex. I am not authorized to fire on a historic landmark," Viper said.

Milosz felt as though his head was going to turn inside out.

These Americans will lose their country yet, he thought, amazed and not a little angry at their reluctance to fire on the enemy. He gauged the range at well over a thousand meters away, too far to make a decent shot with his M14 rifle. It was a good weapon, especially with the Leupold scope, but not quite what he needed for the nig nogs on the island. Now, if he had a fifty-caliber, the story would be very different. Milosz had to content himself with scoping the launchers as a furious exchange went back and forth between the pilot and somebody higher up his chain of command. Even at this distance, with the vibration of the Blackhawk shaking his view in the sight, he could tell the pirates were whooping it up down there, loving every minute of this. They danced and twirled, and a few even performed somersaults as the rockets flew away. Milosz shook his head.

Fools. He tuned out an argument between the Blackhawk's crew chief and the pilot over whether to engage with the M240 door gun. The crew chief lost the argument, fueling Milosz's frustration that much more. He lowered the scope and shook his head at the other three rangers in the bird: Wilson, Sievers, and Raab. Hollywood pussies, he had once called their sort, and his time among them had not changed his opinion entirely, even if it had made him more circumspect about expressing it. They were good men, dedicated, but not as dedicated as his former comrades in the Polish Army. When Germans and Russians have had their boots on your throat for generations, you learn to explore new whole levels of dedication to the task of defending yourself from their ilk.

"Eager to die for your new home, Fred?" Master Sergeant Wilson asked, a thin black man who served as Milosz's squad leader.

The Pole shook his head. "No, I am eager to kill the enemies of my new home."

"The chance will come soon enough," Wilson said, holding a pair of binoculars up to his face. "Looks like Africans or Arabs, do you think? Maybe Jamaicans."

"What does it matter?" Raab asked. "One dead fucker's the same as any other, right?"

"Angolans or Yemenis most likely," Milosz replied, ignoring Raab's contribution.

"Why do you say that?" Wilson asked.

"Those states operate that particular model of BM-21," he said. "They have many to spare and run big looter gangs here, no? It is nothing to loan one to these so-called pirates. That is why I say this."

"Could be anyone," Wilson said, examining the scene below as they banked around to the west.

"We shall see," Milosz said. He watched a U.S. Army AH-64D Apache Longbow come to a hover over the water, outside the reach of the few on the ground who noticed it.

"Stand by," Viper one-three said over the headset. "Engaging. Missile away."

"Put a hurtin' on them fuckers," the Blackhawk pilot said.

Smoke and the flame of more steel javelins climbing away from the launchers in the parking lot obscured the enemy, but as Milosz watched, a barrage of 2.75-inch folding-fin Hydra 70 rockets sliced through and struck the vehicles, tearing them apart in a maelstrom of explosive fire. The cabin of one truck went spiraling high into the air, lazily describing a tumbling flight path back toward a big patch of cleared ground on the Jersey side of the bay but falling well short, dropping onto the causeway that ran out to Ellis Island.

Milosz heard the words "chain gun" through a rush of static just before dark charcoal-gray bursts of smoke began chewing over the parking lot, which quickly disintegrated into a storm of torn steel and fleeing men. Meat and metal swirled in the air, caught in a tornado, as the 30-millimeter cannon fire set off secondary explosions in the wreckage of the Katyusha launchers.

"Yeah!" the Blackhawk pilot whooped. "No one's coming back from that party."

Weapons fire winked at them from one of the larger buildings, a rather beautiful and ornate structure to Milosz's mind, somehow reminiscent of a wedding cake, with four green domed turrets, at least two of them occupied by hostiles. He instinctively reached for a grab bar as the chopper dipped and turned to avoid a line of tracer. The brutal ripping noise of the chain guns sounded again, and when the helicopter had leveled out and he had regained his balance, Sergeant Fryderyck Milosz could see that those turrets were no more.

So much for not shooting up historical monuments, he thought wryly.

"It is good, yes," he said to nobody in particular. "Better that monuments get shot up than Milosz."

An RPG spun forth from a window on an unerring heading, straight toward the Blackhawk.

"Incoming!" Milosz shouted.

The chopper banked and surged, and his stomach felt as though the patron saint of alcoholics had reached inside him and tried to rip it out through his ass. G-forces pressed him down into the deck, and he had trouble holding his head up to watch the action below.

His efforts were rewarded by the sight of another Blackhawk taking an RPG round in the cockpit.

* * *

The fast rope insertion went without incident. The four-man team dropped onto the flat roof of what looked like the second largest building, under the shadow of a towering water tank and northwest of what Milosz continued to refer to as the wedding cake building. He thanked the Lord that no shooters had thought to position themselves up there, although he had to admit, that if they had, the Apaches would have reduced them to pink gruel by now.

"On me," cried Master Sergeant Wilson, and the operators rushed to follow him across the roof toward the small cabin that would give them access to a stairwell dropping down into the structure. It was maybe a hundred yards, but it felt like a mile to Milosz, who could not help glancing over at the smoking wreckage of the nearest turrets on the wedding cake. What chance that some new hobgoblin would suddenly pop up there and start spitting fire at them? The hammering thud of an orbiting gunship providing them with cover allowed him to wrestle his thoughts back to the here and now. He fingered the safety on the matte black Mossberg 590 shotgun he had substituted for his M14 back on the chopper. The first shot in the chamber was a breaching round, a shell filled with wax-bound metal powder that would be no good in a fight unless you jammed the muzzle right into the face of your man. It was, however, purpose-built to destroy deadlocks, hinges, and door handles. The team made the entry point as a stray bullet caromed off the sheet metal roof structure. Milosz heard the sudden roar of the Apache's chain gun but did not turn around to see the results. Wilson and Raab took up positions on either side of the door.

Milosz wasted no time, calling out "Clear!" as he ran up, took aim, and blasted a melon-size hole where the door handle had been. Racking another round into the chamber, a man killer this time, he kicked in the door and fired into the interior.

"Frag out!" Raab called as Miloz sidestepped and the corporal tossed a grenade into the breached doorway. They all took cover from the explosion, which seemed to shake the entire roof structure beneath their boots. Sievers entered with his M249 squad automatic weapon up and ready to hose off any resistance, but no answering shots came from below.

"Man in left," he called out, and Milosz entered, his finger with a half pull on the trigger, the muzzle pointed down the dark musty stairwell. The rangers switched on their tac lights, illuminating a small world of mold, peeling paint, and pigeon shit. The stairs were slick with four years of inattention to care and cleaning.

Wilson and Sievers followed him, the team moving down the steps like a death adder with its teeth out. The crash and uproar of the battle outside fell away only marginally, and Milosz could tell from the heavy drilling sounds below them that at least one heavy weapon was still firing from this building. Every so often, he could hear the *whoosh* of an RPG climbing away.

Wilson held a closed fist up to halt the squad in place in the stairwell while he queried the enemy's position via his headset. Milosz moved up with Sievers to cover the door leading to the top floor.

"This is Romeo one-one to any element," Wilson said. "We've effected entry. Request location of hostile elements, over."

Milosz could not hear the reply on Wilson's headset. He watched the black soldier nod his head once, twice, then a third time.

"This is Romeo one-one, verifying. North side, one floor down from the top floor, one heavy machine gun and an unknown number of RPGs. Is that correct?" Wilson asked the unseen, unheard voice.

After a fourth nod, Wilson signed off. Milosz often wondered why, in the American Army, he could get a headset in the Blackhawk but they did not have individual headsets for soldiers. Delta Force had them, those few he had encountered, GROM had them, and even the British doled them out to their troops, but not the Americans. And so in this way the Americans wasted vital time yet again.

"Okay," Wilson said in a low voice. "Like I said, one floor down, at least halfway along the northern face of the building, we got a crew-served machine gun, something heavy and nasty, and a couple of RPG launchers, which are pinging our birds. Some prisoners would be good but not essential. Let's go. Sievers, you've got the SAW, so you got the lead."

"And lovin' it," Sievers said without any real enthusiasm.

The team moved out behind him, sweeping the hallway in front of them as they went. Milosz brought up the rear, pausing and turning to cover their asses every ten yards or so. There was no indication of any hostile activity on this floor, no sounds of gunfire or voices. Outside the building, though, all was murder and bedlam. They turned the corner at the end of the corridor and flowed around into the next hallway. Rocket fire had struck heavily on this side of the building and opened it up to the outside, collapsing part of the floor between this level and the one below. Small fires burned here and there, and Sievers brought the team to a halt well short of the worst of the devastation. Milosz could see the sky through an enormous hole that looked as though some hungry giant had taken a bite out of the top floors of the structure.

A rocket-propelled grenade whooshed away into the air from somewhere below. Milosz heard a babble of excited Arabic that he lost in the roar of a heavy machine gun from the same location. The team perched silently, their weapons trained on the enormous breach. Wilson signaled to Milosz to ready a couple of frags, and they all inched toward the opening. The thunder of battle rolled on outside, with the crump of rockets and the pounding of guns drowned out by the percussive roar of close-quarter Blackhawk and Apache flybys. The ranger fire team took up position just back from the ragged edge of the collapsed floor and wide-open façade, every man tossing his grenade at a signal from Wilson. The detonation hammered at the floor underfoot like a short, spastic tom-tom beat, and when Milosz's ear stopped ringing, he could hear nothing of the men below.

"Clear," called Raab, who had moved up to take a quick, furtive look over the edge.

"Right, let's keep moving," said Wilson.

Milosz was exhausted. He had not been this tired at any time in Iraq. But then, he had not been involved in such dangerous, close-quarter battles there.

An hour after the last shot sounded in anger, Miguel lifted a cigarette to his lips with a badly shaking hand.

Why didn't I stay in Poland?

He knew the answer to that. There was no future in Poland. But having just nearly been killed in a room-to-room firefight with three dozen doped-up pirates who weren't worth... what was Wilson's phrase? Ah yes, hen shit on a pump handle. A good phrase. He would note it down in his little book of useful American words. Yes, having nearly been killed by these fools, he did have cause to question his decision to move out here with his brother's family. They were safely tucked away in some big homestead down in Texas where the cowboys lived while he was being shot at by pirate fools who did not even have the decency to allow him to get close enough to stick his fighting knife in their gullets to settle the score.

When Raab and Sievers had attempted to capture one of the wounded pirates, the crazy man had blown himself up, killing Raab and crippling Sievers and very nearly doing the same to one Fryderyk Milosz, too.

Perhaps he would be better off behind a mule, like his brother. Perhaps it was preferable to holidays in the woods of Washington State trying to harden soft volunteers into rangers who were less soft. Perhaps behind a mule would be better than filling out requests for the Special Forces qualification course, the next step on his journey toward Delta Force. A maddeningly slow journey since the U.S. Army made him go through the hoops regardless of his GROM service.

But farming was not an option, of course.

He was here because his service had bought the ticket that allowed his brother Stepan and his family to join the federal settler program down in Texas two years ahead of time. He hoped his brother appreciated it, Milosz thought as he manhandled a naked and wounded Somali out of the building and toward the Manhattan militia patrol boat.

The Somali was naked because neither Milosz nor Wilson would take his surrender without proof that he had not booby-trapped himself like his crazy-ass Arab friend. Two civilians in khakis and dark polos took the man without comment, probably superspooks from the National Intelligence Agency. He was not the first naked pirate they had carted off, apparently. Milosz gladly washed his hands of the African fighter and made his way over to the ruins of a barge, stepping over the guts and brains of a recently departed combatant without batting an eye. A pair of Navy SEALs were in the debris, sifting through it all.

"Anything?" Milosz asked.

"Who the fuck are you?" one of the SEALs asked.

"Fryderyk Milosz, staff sergeant, army rangers," he growled back. "That's who the fuck I am, you dolphin-fucking dickwad. So. Did you find anything?"

"No, Sergeant," the SEAL said, not much chastened. "Aside from some old Soviet-era manifests, we haven't found shit. Some of these crazy fuckers preferred blowing themselves up to giving it up for us. Ended up shooting most of them. Anything else, *Sergeant*?"

Milosz grunted and walked away. He sometimes grew tired of the xenophobia of some Americans, especially ones who should know better. Did he not just prove himself to this man? Had he not been proving himself since he set foot here and took up a rifle for his new country? Seemingly not.

He left the SEALs to do their work and returned to the Blackhawk, where a subdued Wilson was sitting with his legs dangling from the cabin, pouring the contents of a Tabasco sauce bottle into an MRE meal pack.

"Want some, Fred?" Wilson asked. He set the bottle on the floor of the Blackhawk with a badly shaking hand and started to turn the food over with a shit-brown spoon. "Got chili mac for once. They are getting harder to find."

"No thank you," Milosz said, squatting down beside Wilson. He removed his kevlar helmet and proceeded to rub his scalp until the blood flowed again.

"Don't let that asshole bother you," Wilson said. "I'm glad you've got my back."

"Yes." Milosz nodded wearily. He jerked his thumb back toward the barge. "I am not to be upset by asshole who eats the pussies of rotting beached whales, no. I am tired and upset by Raab and Sievers. They were good guys, yes?"

Wilson exhaled raggedly, "Yes, they were. I only knew them since getting out here from the West, but they were a good team. We all were, Fred. You were a big part of that. Still are."

"Thank you," the Pole said as he leaned against the chopper and felt waves of lassitude roll over him. "Is it normal, these pirate bitches blowing up themselves and good guys like Raab and Sievers? It reminds me of crazy men in Iraq, yes? Before Jews turn them all into melted glass."

The senior NCO gave two empathetic shakes of his head.

"No way," he said. "I was here for the sweep and clear of Lower Manhattan. Didn't see nothing like that. Didn't see much resistance at all, really. Pirates just sort of melted away."

"Have you heard anything yet about who these brazen nig nogs were to be shooting rockets at President Kipper?" asked the Pole.

Wilson pursed his lips and shook his head.

"Fred, you're gonna have to learn to watch your words, my

brother. You're an American now. You cannot say things like that."

Milosz tilted his head, genuinely perplexed. *Does Wilson think I am referring to him as well?*

"Like what?"

Wilson looked as though he'd been struck by a bout of the squirting assholes and was straining to stay puckered.

"You know, the N-word."

"Nig nog?"

Wilson winced yet again. "Yes, please. Don't say it anymore."

Milosz shrugged. Never mind that he heard many black soldiers saying far worse to each other. He had seen more than one confrontation erupt when someone who was not black also said it. The rationalizations and counter arguments made his head spin. What was the saying?

Oh, yes: not the hill you want to die on.

"If you say so."

They were strange, these Americans, he thought as he dug a half-melted chocolate-covered cookie, a track pad as they called them, from one of his pockets.

They would think nothing of killing a thousand nig nogs in a morning's work but became entirely discomfited if you referred to the nig nogs in any but the most delicate of terms.

He had come to a very peculiar place.

07

TEXAS, FEDERAL MANDATE

They used bedsheets and coverlets as shrouds for the dead. Few words passed between them. Sofia seemed too stunned to say anything. Miguel had expected her to cry or lose control of herself, but that had not happened. Sofia moved mechanically to collect her rifle from the house along with a first-aid kit. She took the keys to the gun cabinet from him without a word. Even though he implored her not to, she passed from body to body, checking vitals to see if anyone was left among the living. He managed to stop her before she reached little Maya; that was a task from which he wanted to spare her. She flatly refused his offer to remove herself from the scene of the massacre and stand watch for the road agents.

The agents had turned right at the main gate to the ranch less than an hour ago, probably headed for the village of Connor, a few minutes up the road toward the junction with Route 21. Perhaps they had looting to be getting on with up there, or perhaps they had carried on to one of the other settler ranches. For now Miguel's main concern was to be gone before they returned in search of their dead comrades. But before he could get Sofia safely away, he had his own dead to attend to.

He carried all the bodies inside the homestead himself. One of the few times he did speak to Sofia was to tell her not to pick up her little brother.

"No, no," he said softly as she bent over Manny like a poorly strung puppet, all stiff limbs and awkward swaying. "I shall do that. Go inside and get me some more blankets." He spoke as gently as he could, adding "please" as an afterthought.

Miguel did not need any more sheets or shrouds; he had plenty, but nothing was served by having the girl there.

He was determined that she would not carry through life a memory of the terrible dead weight of her brother in her arms. One day, with God's blessing perhaps, she might remember Manny smiling and squealing as they wrestled on the floor of the homestead.

What God? he thought bitterly. No loving God could visit such horror on the world.

He turned again to Sofia. "Could you see to the dogs, I can hear them barking; they are still tied up in the barn out by the pond."

She nodded stiffly, as though she had hurt her neck, before moving slowly away. Miguel spit into the mud and tried to ignore the acid burning in his guts. Much of his body felt numb, his limbs in particular, as though he had lain awkwardly for hours and cut off his circulation. His fingers sometimes tingled painfully, however, a feeling not unlike having grabbed an exposed electrical wire. Having felt like it might explode out through his chest earlier in the day, his heart now beat slow and hard like a pile driver.

He covered Grandma Ana in the bright patchwork quilt she had begun knitting in the evenings in the refugee camp in Australia. Darkness stole in at the edge of his vision and a thick crust of salt hardened around his heart as he draped an army blanket over his son, little Manny. It had been given to them by the federales in Corpus Christi when they arrived to take up their place in the resettlement program. The children had driven Mariela to the edge of madness turning it into a tent in the lounge room on rainy days all through the winter just passed.

Corpus Christi, he remembered, was where he had first heard about the road agents, in a lecture from an FBI man about the dangers of the frontier. He had said nothing about them being Fort Hood's men, but Miguel had made it his business to find out as much as he could about them. He had thought he was being careful, but it had not helped.

As he moved from one member of his family to the next, covering them for the last time, he tried to murmur a prayer for each one, but found that the words would not come. He had no prayers to offer. Just once in the terrible business of collecting his dead did he falter, when he picked up Maya. Still so small and looking as vulnerable in death as she had in life. A high-pitched keening sound caught in his throat, and he had to bite his cheek hard enough to draw blood to regain some control over his feelings. He would mourn for her later. He would mourn for them all later, but for now Sofia still lived and it was to her safety and welfare he would have to attend first, after seeing to the remains of his family.

Only Mariela, his wife, his lifelong love, did he pick up and carry into the homestead without first wrapping her body in some kind of shawl. Her eyes were closed, mercifully. He would not have wanted to look into those lifeless orbs. It was bad enough having to hold her and feel her dead flesh against his. A primitive, irrational part of his mind tried to will his life into her where their bodies touched, skin on skin, hers still warm but slick with blood and so terribly still. He kissed her lightly on the forehead as he maneuvered through the screen door into the parlor, for all the world looking like a newly married man carrying his wife across the threshold of their future together. Miguel laid her gently on the couch and shook off the admonishing voice in his head that scolded him for getting her blood on the fabric. Mariela's voice, of course.

Once inside, he could hear Sofia upstairs in her room, crying like a small child. Obviously, she had not made it down to the barn to untie the dogs. He could still faintly hear their frenzied barking off in the distance. Sofia's crying reassured Miguel, oddly enough. It was at least a change from the cold, nearly unresponsive puppet of a few minutes ago. Part of him knew he should fly to her and fold her in his arms. But that was not possible. There were hard necessities of the situation that could not be avoided or denied.

The screen door clanged as he pushed through it out into the yard to continue gathering up his dead. The sun had climbed a little higher in the sky, but the morning was still cool. Trees on the horizon slumped heavily under a sheen of ice and a few clumps of snow, dragging their branches low to the ground. Overhead a pair of black crows cawed at him, the noise sounding like the laughter of cruel and stupid men. Dizziness came over him in waves, and he feared he might pass out, falling to the ground and possibly never getting up again.

But there was still Sofia. He had to get her away from here and the agents as soon as he could. The need for haste helped, hurrying him through the awful business of collecting the bodies of his family and carrying them inside so that he might escape with all that remained for him in the world. With Sofia.

The silent farmhouse sat nestled at the edge of a thick glade of myrtle and basswood trees on the southern foot of a small rise overlooking his fields of lima and pole beans. A whitewashed two-story wood-framed house with deep verandas around three sides, it had been crowded with all his relatives crammed inside, but Mariela had insisted on keeping everyone together. He chose not to dwell on the bitter irony of that as he carried the last of his extended family into the parlor.

He could not bear to stand and look at them, even shrouded as they were, for more than a few moments. It was not just that he could feel his heart seizing up painfully; there seemed a good chance that he might go mad if he gave in to the urge to lie down among them and give up. Instead he forced himself to make the sign of the cross before backing out of the room and closing the door. He would never set foot in there again. Instead, he trudged upstairs, where he could hear his daughter still crying.

The door to her bedroom was closed, the room she had shared with her little sister Maya. He hesitated outside for a moment before pressing on to the master bedroom. Everywhere he saw evidence of violation: drawers pulled out and the contents emptied, clothes on the floor, toys scattered around, a chair knocked over and left lying halfway out the door. On a normal day Mariela would never have allowed such chaos in her domain.

He clenched his jaw, tasting his own blood, and hurried into the bedroom, quickly stuffing spare Levi's and shirts and two pairs of boots into a sports bag. He dug an army surplus arctic-rated sleeping bag out of the bottom of the closet and a thick lamb's wool coat. There would be nights when they would not be able to find shelter, and the chill of the deserts and badlands after dark was enough to finish off the unwary. Although he would doubtless be able to scavenge much of what they needed on the trail, there was no point leaving things to chance at this early stage. The main thing right now was to get the hell away from Blackstone's territory with Sofia, to seek out help wherever he could.

He knew he was alone among his neighbors in believing the road agents to be tools of Jackson Blackstone, but Miguel had invested a good deal of time, before arriving here, consulting much more widely than the "experts" on offers to prospective settlers. He had sought out a number of Mexican sources, vaqueros like himself, some of them settlers, some bandits working the border regions. To them there was no question. The agents did the bidding of Fort Hood.

Miguel was about to leave when his eye fell upon a small silver-framed photograph of Mariela and the children resting on an old mahogany chest in which all the drawers stood open. Hesitating momentarily, he finally picked it up and carefully removed the picture from the frame. His hands were shaking but he allowed himself a few seconds of indulgence, gazing at his family as they had been just a few short hours ago. He struggled with the enormity of it all. That happy time was now as distant and impossible to touch as the surface of a cold star twinkling in the night sky. How could there be so much life in his gnarled brown fingers as they stroked the image of his beautiful wife and children when they were all gone now.

Miguel stuffed the picture into his wallet before his emotions could boil up again and unman him.

He padded softly out of the room with his bag, painfully aware he would never set foot in there again. The vaquero paused outside his daughter's room, listening to her wretched, strangled sobs. He knocked lightly and entered, not waiting for a reply. Sofia lay on her side with her knees drawn up under her chin, shivering violently, crying, and hugging a small stuffed bear she had carried with her from the day she had found it on the *Aussie Rules*. Aware that every moment's delay put her in danger, he nonetheless approached quietly and cautiously, easing himself down on the mattress beside her. She jerked away from him, her tear-reddened eyes wide with fear. Miguel tried to brush her long hair away from her face, but she flinched.

"Easy, Sofia. Easy. I know it is hard," he said softly, "but we must go. Now. The men who did this will be back, and if they catch us here, I cannot protect you."

She drew in a shallow hitching breath and tried to speak but was unable to form any words at first. Miguel was worried by the violence of the tremors racking her slim body. He glanced briefly out her window, which overlooked the area in front of the house, including the driveway winding up toward the main road. How long would it be before the road agents returned?

"I am sorry, but we must go; we have to get you away from here, Sofia. We have to go now if you are to live."

"I... I d-don't want to l-live," she cried pitiably.

Another glance out the window.

Nothing yet.

He took a moment to lay down beside her and fold her into a hug. She did not resist, although she was shaking so hard, he wondered whether she would have been able to anyway. Miguel tried to speak, but his throat was tight with grief, forcing him to push his feelings down tight. When he knew he could talk without falling apart, he spoke quietly into her ear.

"Crying is good; you must cry for all of them. But we must go, too, Sofia. Your mother, your brother and sister, all of your uncles and aunts, they will haunt me if I do not get you safely away before those men come back. And they will come back, Sofia. Very soon. So we must go."

He kissed her head, which felt hot with fever, and rubbed his callused hands gently on her upper arms as he spoke. Slowly the tremors that shook her body trailed off and the awful, gut-wrenching tenor of her cries became less like the sounds of an animal and more like the bawling of a little girl to whom something bad had happened, something very very bad. When Miguel judged her sufficiently in control of herself again, he eased up, pulling her with him.

"Come on, then, come with Papa," he said softly. "You can bring your bear and a few personal things, small things like photographs, but you must gather them quickly and keep them all in one bag. Pack some clothes for traveling, for trail riding, warm clothes. And be quick, Sofia. Those men will be back for their friends soon, and we will give them nothing. Nothing, do you understand?"

She sniffed and nodded uncertainly.

"Do we have time to bury them? To say prayers?"

He shook his head firmly.

"No. We must be gone, but we will not leave this house to the agents, and we will leave no one to the dogs or the wolves. "

She nodded shakily and tottered over to her dresser drawer on stiff unsteady legs. When he judged her sufficiently composed, he left the room and hurried downstairs, where he tossed the bags and heavy jacket onto the kitchen table. He fetched a couple of saddlebags from the utility room at the rear of the house in order to pack them with trail food. Rice, beans, dried meat, sugar, coffee, and a bottle of vitamins. Mariela had baked biscuits that morning, and the rich, malty smell of them was still thick in the kitchen. He found a jar of cookies in the pantry and wrapped a few in an old tea towel. They would do for a quick meal this morning, and he felt it important not to leave them behind.

Finally he unlocked the cupboard under the main staircase and flicked on the bare lightbulb inside. Using a key on a separate ring hanging from his belt, Miguel opened a small gun cabinet he had fixed to the rear wall. He took out his favorite rifle, a Winchester Model 1894 Lever Action 30.30, and his saddle gun, a double-barreled Sicilian-style Lupara. He then grabbed six boxes of ammunition for the long arm and two boxes of shells for the sawed-off shotgun. He threaded a heavy clublike Maglite torch through one of the big steel key rings on his belt. Sofia had already collected her hunting rifle and the ammunition for it. He was not keen on her carrying the Remington on a regular basis, although if she had had it with her this morning…

Stop it, he told himself as he tried to figure out what other weapon to get for his child. Neither of them was a soldier and he didn't want to be loaded down with a lot of useless ironmongery. As it was, they simply couldn't carry enough weapons to fight off more than a very small band of road agents.

He grunted and decided that the Remington would have to do.

Shuttling all the supplies out to the horses required four trips, with Sofia joining him on the last run. He was glad to see she had changed her clothes and carried her personal belongings in a small backpack with the head of her teddy bear sticking out of the top. She remained subdued, and he could tell from the furtive way in which her eyes sometimes darted here and there that she was wondering where he had laid out the bodies. Miguel did not want her dwelling on such things. He gave her a bag of beans to carry out to the horses and told her to transfer the rifle he had ridden out with this morning to her own mount.

"For the next few weeks we must always be armed," he said. "Both of us. Until we get somewhere safe."

"Are we going to Corpus Christi?" she asked in a small voice. "Wouldn't they expect us to go that way?"

The sky had grown dark with gathering storm clouds. Lightning strikes crackled over the hills to the southwest, and a few drops of icy rain splashed Miguel's face as he looked up.

"Yes," he said. "I do not think we can go south. They probably would expect that. We would have to pass through Blackstone territory, and his men would make it difficult for us. We shall ride north, to Kansas City. The federales are strong there. We need to tell them what has happened. They will do something."

Sofia said nothing. He wondered how much she knew of the political situation in Fort Hood, of the standoff between the Federal Mandate and Governor Blackstone's regime. It was not something the adults had discussed in front of the children. The horses twitched their ears and shivered while he loaded them with supplies and allowed them to drink from the trough lying in the shade on the eastern side of the house. Miguel did not let himself dwell on the moment that was coming, the abandonment of the ranch that had been the best hope for his family.

He remembered the day they arrived in a salvaged school bus loaded down with supplies from Corpus Christi. A civilian from the Federal Mandate had helped them get settled in, logging their location on a laptop and taking a few pictures of the family. It had been difficult, getting the children to settle down long enough to gather for a photograph. The men had inventoried the salvageable equipment and the structures for the government man while Mariela and the women put out the best spread they could manage. Everyone sat around a cobbled-together table, sampling freshly butchered and roasted beef while enjoying bottles of a New Zealand red wine they had brought with them.

After dinner Mariela was waiting for him in their bedroom, her skin glowing under the candlelight. She held out her hand...

Miguel shook the past away. He took a deep breath and held it for a second lest his self-control finally fail.

He could not afford to think about this, to let go of hope entirely. He had to look to the future, to Sofia.

The dogs were still barking, and he again asked Sofia to ride over to the barn to release them. "They will be upset," he said.

She nodded, her face a dull mask as she placed one boot in the stirrup and swung up into the saddle.

"Good. If the men come back, you must ride out immediately. Head into the forest. They won't be able to follow you in there, not in vehicles. You know the clearing? In the middle of the forest? You wait for me there at the northeast corner."

He considered telling her to make for the militia post at College Station if he didn't turn up, but she was fragile enough as it was. He did not think his daughter would cope with the prospect of something happening to him while she rode away. Miguel checked that she had transferred the rifle to her mount then waved her off.

He flicked his eyes down to the main road, past the bodies of the road agents, which he had not bothered to move. A pair of black crows, their oily feathers glistening with raindrops, pecked at the wounds of one of the dead men, pausing momentarily as Sofia's horse approached. Miguel watched her stiffen in the saddle as she rode past them with her head turned away. He ducked back inside for just a moment, bending down to open the bottom drawer in the kitchen, from which he removed a small sheaf of papers in a plastic Ziploc bag. His settlement documents, proof that the government in Seattle had chosen his family to run this farm as part of the reconstruction program. He tucked them away inside his jacket, then pushed a light straw Stetson down on his head and donned a pair of wraparound sunglasses. From the cupboard under the sink he fetched a one-gallon drum of lamp oil, unscrewed the cap, and splashed the contents all over the kitchen.

For a few seconds he hovered on the edge of indecision, unable to do what he had to. But the barking of the dogs reached him, telling him Sofia was releasing them from the barn. With his face contorted into a rictus of loathing, he struck a match and tossed it on to the nearest patch of oil, which ignited with a *whoomp*. He stalked out of the house without a backward glance.

08

WILTSHIRE, ENGLAND

The ambush was a simple affair, two cars in a herringbone formation blocking Stock Lane, just before the T-intersection with Hilldrop Lane about three klicks outside Aldbourne. Bret spotted it as he crested a rise about five hundred yards short of the trap. Somebody without his experience, a local farmer, say, probably would have ridden right into it, assuming a breakdown or even a small crash had blocked the road. But Bret Melton had been through enough military checkpoints to recognize the unmistakable arrangement of vehicles. In fact, the very presence of two cars was enough to give him pause. Very few people had the resources for private automobile travel anymore. He squeezed the hand brake on the mountain bike as he reached the summit of the hill, very much aware of the baby's presence in a carrier on his back.

"What the fuck?" he muttered before admonishing himself quietly. He was trying not to swear in front of Monique. She wouldn't understand yet, but it was a bad habit he had to give up. He felt her shift in the backpack as he squinted at the cars. There appeared to be four, no, five men down there. Two white and three dark-skinned, probably of West Indian origin. There weren't many from the subcontinent free to wander the British Isles anymore. They appeared to be inspecting the engine of one car. The hood was up and three of the men were bent over it, but that made him even more suspicious. The car was a late-model BMW by the look of it, and on the rare occasions that they broke down, there was very little you could do if you didn't have access to a full suite of computerized diagnostic tools in a licensed repair facility. The baby cried out loudly, and a pulse began to beat in Bret's temple. This just felt wrong.

The men were looking at him now, pointing. One of them waved, gesturing for him to pedal down to them, as though some passing cyclist might be able to help fix their high-tech sedan. Melton checked his watch. He was due in Swindon in about ninety minutes for the meeting with the Resources Ministry guys. He wouldn't be missed back at the farm for hours yet. He shook his head. Something felt *very* wrong about this.

He stood up and pressed down on the pedals as if to trundle down the hill to them but instead turned the bike around and pushed off in the direction of home. A few seconds later the sound of slamming doors and engines firing up drifted over the rise. *Damn.* There was no way he could outrun these guys. They'd be on him in moments. He skidded the bike to a halt, dismounted quickly, and carried it over to the drystone wall that ran alongside the country road. He flung the bike over without any concern about damaging it, then scrambled over, taking considerably more care not to jostle the baby. He ducked down behind the wall as the first car, the BMW with supposed engine trouble, came roaring over the crest.

He dared not risk raising his head for a look as the cars rushed by. Monique was fully awake now and crying loudly. They wouldn't hear her over the noise of their engines, but if the men stopped the cars and climbed out, as surely they must in the next few minutes, the baby would give away their position. He looked around desperately. A two-hundred-yard dash would carry him to the far side of the field and another drystone wall. A few trees stood in the northwest corner of this field, and another clump had been allowed to grow up a few hundred yards farther on in the next field beyond, a roughly rectangular paddock waving with what looked like a barley crop.

Bret didn't debate his next move. He checked that the papoose was securely fixed, then took off at a sprint, bent low, making for the far side of the field. The ground was uneven, recently plowed, and he had to watch his footing lest he turn or even break an ankle. When he was halfway across, he heard the cars returning.

They screeched to a halt just as he made the barrier of the ancient rock wall. Taking it in one leap, he flinched and ducked instinctively as a single shot rang out behind him. He heard voices calling out for him to stop, but they simply spurred him on. If he could just make the next field, he might be able to disappear into the gently swaying sea of grain. Beyond that lay a remnant strip of forest, and from there it was a short, hard dash to the village of Aldbourne and the Home Guard office at the corner of Castle and Malborough. His cardio fitness was not great, not compared with what it had been when he was a ranger or even a correspondent. But he was pretty certain he could outrun the city boys behind him.

For the briefest moment he wondered what the hell they wanted with him and his daughter, but the question answered itself. It probably had nothing to do with either of them. This would be about Caitlin. As soon as he thought of his wife, more guns opened up. He dared not risk even a glance behind as he sprinted toward the wall, attempting to maintain an even, loping stride so as not to shake the baby too much. She was screaming now, a full-throated caterwauling wail.

From the sound of the gunfire he judged his pursuers to be toting light automatic weapons, some sort of machine pistol. A stuttering burst threw up small puffs of dirt about twenty yards to his right. The sorts of light arms they were using weren't very accurate. If he was unlucky, there was a very good chance they'd hit him or Monique by accident.

Monique.

He cursed himself for strapping her onto his back, where she was exposed to the gunfire. He could have slung her on his chest but had chosen not to because it made riding the mountain bike a little more difficult. He reached and vaulted the next boundary fence in one fluid sweep as a burst of fire chipped sharp pieces of stone from the wall. His lungs were already burning, and he fought to control his breathing, drawing in long, deep breaths rather than giving in to the urge to start panting and gulping for air. This field looked to be about three hundred yards across, and beyond it lay the relative safety and cover of the barley crop. A flight of birds took to the sky from a copse of yew trees at the far side of the meadow. Behind him a machine gun coughed and stuttered, and one of the birds exploded in midflight, dropping to the ground ahead of them.

Bret's vision began to blur, and he could feel a stitch gripping his gut just above his old appendix scar, but still he pressed on. *If I can just get to the next field.*

A single shot caught him in the right leg, just above the knee, and he screamed as he went over, throwing his arms out to accept the full weight of the fall so that he would not roll over and crush the baby. He felt a bone snap behind his left wrist, and his jaw smashed into a jagged rock thrown up by the blades of the last plow that had passed through there. He coughed and choked on a mouthful of dirt and attempted to haul himself up again, but the injured leg wouldn't take his weight and it collapsed underneath him. He began to crawl, anyway, ignoring the raucous, braying laughter he heard from behind. They were close now.

A gun roared, much louder, and chewed up the thick brown earth a few feet away.

"That'll be far enough, brother."

The voice was accented slightly. London with an underlay of Jamaica, perhaps.

Bret used his good arm to lever himself up. He'd made it to within ten yards of the wall and lay within the dappled shade of the largest yew tree.

Monique was screaming and trying to crawl out of the backpack.

"Fuck, would somebody shut that little shit up."

That voice was pure East End, and Bret glared at the speaker, a redheaded tough in his early twenties. He wore a short-sleeved T-shirt, and his arms were covered in the fuzzy, amateurish tattoos of a convict.

"Quite a chase you led us, mon," said the darkest of his hunters, the one with the slight Caribbean lilt.

Bret was too short of breath to reply. He merely moved his body to put himself between the baby and their captors. Not that it would do any good. They had him at their mercy, and their mercy looked thin indeed.

"What do you want?" he asked at last as they stood over him. His leg was in agony, and the broken wrist felt as though it were on fire.

"It's not what we want, mon. It's who. Where is your wife at, eh? The lovely Caitlin? She wasn't where we were told she would be. She is supposed to run along here, mon. But here you are, and where is she?"

He felt nauseous with the pain and with something deeper and uglier, a creeping sense of his failure.

"If you'd found her," he said, nearly gagging on the effort, "you'd be dead by now."

The redhead with the tatts laughed, and Bret recognized his donkey bray from a few moments earlier.

"You reckon, do you, pal?" He grinned just before his teeth disappeared in an explosion of gore.

A thunderclap from a powerful handgun, a Beretta, rolled into a series of short, flat explosions, almost impossibly close together. Another three of the men went down as huge gouts of blood and tissue erupted from the center mass of their bodies. The West Indian, his eyes suddenly as wide and white as Ping-Pong balls, loosed off a wild unaimed burst from his sidearm, an old Heckler & Koch MP5. It clicked empty after a brief stutter of fire, and he turned to run just as Bret caught a flash of color in his peripheral vision, a blurred figure leaping the drystone wall.

Caitlin.

She seemed to materialize instantly at his side in a combat shooter's crouch and snapped off two more rounds. The fleeing man cried out as the bullets' impact and his own momentum lifted him off his feet and slammed his body hard into the ground.

Caitlin's voice was harsh and clipped, almost alien in its tone. "You all right? The baby's all right?"

Monique was still screaming, but she sounded distressed rather than in pain.

"We're fine for now, I think." Bret coughed, spitting more dirt from his mouth and ignoring his agonizing injuries.

Caitlin walked quickly over to where the four men she'd first targeted had fallen. Without preamble she executed two of them with a double tap to the head. Another she kicked, but Bret could tell he was already dead, shot through the heart.

The redhead was attempting to crawl away. The lower half of his face hung in tatters and a terrible, animalistic keening sound came from his throat. Caitlin approached him with the muzzle of her pistol trained on the back of his head. She quickly glanced up to where the last of the five, the Jamaican, was also trying to escape, dragging himself back toward the cars. His legs trailed behind him uselessly.

Bret watched as his wife made some grim calculation before firing two rounds into the head of the man closest to her. His skull came apart, spattering her with blowback.

Monique screamed louder with every shot. Bret did his best with what felt like a broken wrist to unhitch the papoose and drag her around as Caitlin stalked over to the sole remaining survivor. Bret was pulsing blood from a bad wound to one of his fingers. White fire burned through shards of glass rubbing against each other in his leg and wrist, but he managed to cradle Monique in his good arm. He kissed the top of her head, humming softly, and rocking her back and forth. He waited for the last shots, but they never came.

Caitlin approached the Jamaican from behind, waiting until he had levered himself up on his arms as he crawled desperately for the imagined safety of his car. She launched a short, vicious kick into one elbow, snapping the joint with a sickening crack. The man screamed and rolled over onto his side, which allowed her to piston another kick into his solar plexus. The howls cut off abruptly as the blow drove all the air from his body. As Bret watched, horrified, his wife placed her running shoe on the man's throat and pressed down, all the while training the pistol on his face. After thrashing around for a short period, his body went limp. She delivered a kick to his groin just to check, but he was lights out.

Holding the muzzle of the M9 against the back of his neck, she searched his pockets, pulling out a cell phone.

Bret's last memory before he passed out was the beeping of the keypad as she called for help.

The hospital, a modern facility, sat next to Junction 15 of the M4 motorway, a relatively short ambulance ride from the scene of the killings. The paramedics assured Caitlin that Bret and Monique would be fine and that she had nothing to worry about, but sitting in an interview room of the Gablecross police station in Swindon, she couldn't help but worry and fret on their behalf. Bret had lost a lot of blood before she was able to tie off his wounds, and Monique was still screaming when they took her away. The police had refused to allow Caitlin to keep Monique with her, and she supposed she could understand their point. She had just shot and killed four men and critically wounded another. Her running outfit was tacky with their blood, and she kept finding small bone chips and worse in her hair.

"We really can't help you if you won't help us," Detective Sergeant Congreve said for the third or fourth time.

The female constable sitting beside him across the table gave Caitlin a sympathetic look, which had no more effect on her than a small bird flying into a brick wall.

"You need to call the number I gave you and tell them what's happened," she said. "I can't help you. There is nothing else I can say."

Congreve, a chubby, dark-haired man with a large drooping mustache, frowned unhappily.

"Somebody will be doing just that, Ms. Monroe, but until then, why don't you tell us what happened. You appear to have been defending your partner and child from armed men. There can be no harm in explaining what happened, can there? Was it just happenstance that you came across the villains while you were running?"

It was total happen-fucking-stance, all right, but she remained silent.

Congreve exhaled slowly.

"Look, Ms. Monroe. You and your 'usband have a good reputation down in Mildenhall. We never hear anything but good things about how you run your farm, and I know from talking to the Resources Ministry that you're in tight with the government somehow. I just don't understand why you can't help me help you. This isn't going to go away, you know. Self-defense or not, 'appenstance or whatever, you can't go gunning down 'alf a dozen people without explanation. Now, if you want to see your family anytime soon, and I'm sure you do, you'll be needing to give me somethin' to go on with. Who were those men? What were they doing in Wiltshire? Do you know them? Do you know why they'd be lookin' to do you or yours any harm?"

He favored her with what her old man would have called a hangdog expression, shaking his head at the bother of it all and imploring her with big wet eyes to just do 'erself a favor.

Caitlin smiled without warmth.

"Call the number."

Congreve rubbed one meaty hand across his face and reached for the off switch on the video recorder.

"Interview suspended at thirteen hundred and twenty-three hours. Go call the fuckin' number, Constable." He sighed. "See what happens."

The uniformed officer excused herself and closed the door behind her. Congreve shook his head.

"What sort of fuckin' teddy bears' picnic have you dragged me into, young lady, eh?" he asked. "Those blaggers we took out of that field, they had the look of nasty men about them, they did. What you left of them, at any rate. And that one you choked off after you shot him, we'll 'ave him identified soon enough, and I'll wager he's no fuckin' altar boy, eh? Not a bad morning's effort for a little lady, was it?"

She shrugged, trying to keep her impatience and frustration under control. She needed to get to her family. Before somebody else did.

"Would you like a cup of tea, perhaps?" The detective went on. "Something to wet the whistle. Might put you in a chattier mood. After all, you've had a bad scare. Might be a bit shocky. Does wonders for the shocky types, a cup of tea does."

"I'm not the shocky type, Detective Sergeant," she said calmly. "A cup of coffee would be great, though."

The door opened behind him, revealing the female constable, who had returned with another cop, a middle-aged man in a dark blue suit.

"Sorry, guv," said Congreve. "Not making much headway with this one."

"No," the suit said in a tired voice. "I can't imagine that you are. And you're not about to, either. We have to let her go."

For the first time, Caitlin saw Congreve struggle to control his temper. The avuncular bumpkin routine slipped for a second, and his face flushed with anger. She had to hand it to him, though; he didn't lash out. A bunching of the muscles along his jawline and the clenching of one hand were the only signs of annoyance he allowed himself.

"Do you mind if I ask why, guv?" he asked.

The suit, whom Caitlin assumed to be the station commander, shook his head.

"Orders, Detective Sergeant. From the Home Office. No questions. No charges. Just let her go. Somebody from London will be down to take over the investigation this afternoon."

Congreve's mouth dropped open before he had a chance to compose himself. "You're fucking kidding me."

"I don't kid, Detective Sergeant. And neither does the Home Office. Ms. Monroe, you are free to go."

"Thank you," she said as humbly as possible. "I'll need my weapon."

"You can collect your personal effects at the front desk."

09

NEW YORK

"Did you hear? They tried to kill the president."

Jules swung the sledgehammer into the tangle of crumpled metal and fiberglass with a bone-jarring *clang!* She was trying to dislodge a Lexus from the rear end of a UPS truck.

"Really, Manny? Who's they?" she asked.

"You know, the pirates, out there?" The small, wiry Puerto Rican waved in the direction of uptown Manhattan. "Fuckin' pirates, man. Africans. Wetbacks. Crazy fuckers, all of them."

The clash and boom of heavy tools on twisted metal and the grumble and roar of the heavy equipment, the dozers and scrapers and skid steer loaders, made it all but impossible to hear him. The clearance crew had been working on the pileup in Water Street all day and had made some obvious progress. An assembly-line process started with knots of vehicles such as the one Julianne's crew was working on, breaking apart the impacted vehicles. Salvaged NYPD tow trucks pulled the smaller vehicles over to the forklifts that would in turn load them onto army HEMTTs. The Heavy

Expanded Mobility Tactical Trucks were eight-wheel vehicles with large flatbeds. Once their beds were full, the HEMTTs would bounce down the recently cleared streets to the river, where barges awaited the busted-up vehicles. Heavier vehicles were moved by army five-ton tow trucks or M88 armored recovery vehicles. All of them where headed to the same location, down by the river.

Another team of free enterprise types, some of them veterans who had served their time and were not subject to the resettlement program, would work over the vehicles. Luxury vehicles such as the Lexus commanded their attention for the leather seats, sound system, and other parts. After being stripped, they were tossed into garbage barges along with the rest of the car wrecks of Manhattan.

So far, the clearance crew had only reached the Flatiron Building. Some streets were still jammed, made worse by the recent fighting that had torn through the financial district during the early days after the Wave lifted. That said, at least there was still a city to be salvaged and cleared. Many urban areas had been reduced to blackened scars of rubble and ruin that stretched for miles in every direction.

Julianne couldn't help feeling the hopelessness of the job when she thought about the whole city still waiting to be cleared and the country beyond that. Not that she would be around to help out. But it did rather get one down if one let one's thoughts stray that way.

"What's that, Manny? What'd you say?"

The Rhino's bellowing voice was powerful enough to be heard no matter how loud or harsh the background noise. Manny leaned on his sledgehammer for a moment and wiped his face with a dirty red cloth, which he then stuffed back into his jeans.

"Fuckin' pirates, Rhino. They took a shot at President Kipper this morning. About an hour after we saw him," Manny explained. "That was all that banging and booming we heard downtown. They fuckin' shot rockets at him, dude."

"I heard it was mortars," said Ryan, a big, raw-boned kid from Kentucky who'd been traveling through Germany when the Wave hit. "Heard they put mortars on top of some building, you know, for the extra range, and they tried to get him while he was doing something down at Battery Park."

"So much for the Green Zone," Manny said.

The Rhino frowned deeply as he swung a massive sledgehammer into the crumpled snarl of the Lexus. Jules took a moment to catch her breath as Manny and Ryan argued about who had the dopest of the inside dope. The Rhino kept swinging and swearing around the stub of a well-chewed stogie. Jules knew that he liked James Kipper, and he seemed more than a little pissed off at the news.

"Who'd you hear this from?" he asked.

"Bossman," said the Puerto Rican.

"Lewis, the security guy," Ryan said.

"But he's okay, right?" Rhino asked. "He didn't get hurt or nothing."

Both men shrugged and shook their heads.

"Don't think so," Ryan said.

"Boss said it was cool," Manny agreed.

The Rhino muttered a few curses under his breath and swung the sledgehammer with an almighty effort. The impact broke apart the grille of the Lexus, freeing up the vehicle. Teenagers with chains and nimble fingers slipped under the UPS truck, hooking the chain to the axle. A waiting tow truck dragged the vehicle away, making room for the next tow truck to remove the Lexus.

"Dial it down, Rhino," Jules said as she moved up beside him. "Don't wear yourself out. We have a long way to go yet."

He nodded and took a breather, moving out of the way of an army five-ton that was inching forward.

"It's just, you know, fuckin' *pirates*. I hate those guys, Jules. Nothin' but worthless fuckin' bottom feeders the lot of them. Never heard of one worth a pinch of shit when I was in the Coast Guard, and these assholes we got running around now are no better. Just scavengers is all. Fuckin' parasites and worms, the lot of them."

"Yes, Rhino, I'm sure, but let's not get carried away, shall we."

She gave him a warning look, one eyebrow raised and her head dipped like a disapproving schoolmistress.

"Okay, Miss Jules. Whatever you say."

Rumors of the attack swirled through the salvage and clearance crew all afternoon. Some said it was a car bomb; others insisted on a lone sniper. At one point Manny became convinced that ninjas were involved.

"As if," Ryan Dubois snorted. "Ninjas and pirates *never* work together."

The gang boss called time at four in the afternoon after a day that had started at four in the morning. The grubby rainbow coalition of people that made up the salvage crews dragged themselves onto a long line of salvaged double-decker New York City tour buses driven by Pakistani survivors of the Indo-Pakistani War of '05. The buses would take them back to their quarters, a hotel in the center of the island's pacified area. Julianne purposefully tuned out of the horrible Pashtun music and local conversation buzzing around her, knowing that nobody on the crew could really have any idea of what had happened earlier in the day. It wasn't that she was not interested, far from it. But until she could access a news source back at the Duane Street Hotel, she saw no point in drinking from the bottomless well of ignorance on the bus.

Instead she closed her eyes and tried to rest. Two weeks they'd been working clearance in New York, and her body was only just getting used to the abuse. Blisters had covered her hands, broken, and been replaced by new and even more painful blisters. Her back ached constantly, and her arms were so tired that she had trouble raising them to wash her hair at night. But, she kept telling herself, a job was a job.

Not the salvage work, of course. Manual labor had never been her thing. That was just a convenient and marginally safer way of getting into Manhattan. But the real job, the Rubin commission that had brought them to the East Coast, promised a payoff that would put her back on the water with a decent boat and a reliable crew. There was no way on God's green earth that Julianne Balwyn was going to play frontierswoman for the rest of her life.

The small convoy of buses and their Humvee escorts, after making sure to hit every bump, pothole, and obstruction in the road, finally pulled up in front of the somewhat stark modernist façade of the Tribeca Hotel. It had been a boutique establishment back before the Disappearance, not at all the sort of place a rough-headed bunch like this would have stayed. But it sat well within the Green Zone secured by the army and the private contractors— mercenaries, for want of a gentler euphemism—and it had its own diesel generators for power and light. Two such contractors with beards and massive arms cradled their M4s, their eyes hidden behind high-end sunglasses liberated from the Big Apple. The zone they protected was an oasis compared with the brute creation that had taken over the rest of the city.

"Drink later?" Rhino asked as they dragged themselves into the foyer.

"Bath first, then dinner, then a drink," said Jules. "I'm knackered."

They parted at the elevators, where Jules punched the button for the fourth floor, a women-only level. They were all grown-ups, of course, and there were no rules against socializing, but Lewis Graham, the head security contractor, had insisted on that measure, and for her part Julianne was more than happy with it. The salvage and clearance crews were not your cookies and cucumber sandwich types, and she didn't fancy having to secure her room at night against any possible incursion by some drunken ape with a whole lot of loving to give.

As she walked slowly toward her room, a couple of the other women from the crew emerged from the second elevator, laughing and talking about the dates they had lined up for later. Jules was in no mood to socialize and was glad to get into her room without having to fob off an invitation to join them. She kicked the door closed behind her and turned left into the bathroom, where she immediately stripped and ran a hot, deep tub. Some bubbles in the bath and a flask of brandy from her bedside table and she was ready to soak her aching muscles for a few hours.

Her palms stung as the hot water hit them, and the muscles in her legs felt as though they were moments from cramping, but gradually the steam heat and the alcohol loosened her knots and helped push the discomfort to the back of her mind, which she was then able to turn to the task at hand. Not the wretched construction work of the clearance crew but her real reason for being in New York.

"Why, Miss Jules, I thought you might have stood me up."

The Rhino had grabbed a table for them in a secluded corner of the hotel's dining room and was washing down the remains of a cheeseburger and fries with a bottle of beer. She didn't recognize the label and wondered if it had come from the hotel's pre-Disappearance stocks.

"What are you drinking?" she asked.

"Well, that is a sad story, Miss Jules. This here is one of the last ever bottlings from the lost and much lamented Dogfish brewery. Four times the grain, twenty times the hops, and about a hundred times better than cat's piss like Bud."

"Rhino, I would never have taken you for a boutique beer man. It's all rather flowery and gay, isn't it?" Jules said as she pulled up a chair.

The Rhino made a show of scowling at her before he finished off the dregs of the beer in his hand.

"This here brew has such a high alcohol content that you could run your old boat off it, if they hadn't taken it from you in Sydney."

"Don't remind me," she said wearily. A waiter arrived, a young woman in the sharply starched blue BDUs of Schimmel's Manhattan constabulary, one of the local Manhattan militia units. The hotel, indeed the whole Green Zone, was officially the concern of New York Territorial Governor Elliott Schimmel. She took Jules's order for a T-bone and baked potato with a side of green beans after first fixing them up with drinks. Another, increasingly rare bottle of India pale ale for the Rhino and a gin and tonic for her. When the waitress had retreated, Jules leaned forward.

"We need to make our move pretty soon," she said in a low voice. "That attack on Kipper this afternoon, I don't like the look of that at all. It has all the hallmarks of some jumped-up gang boss staking out his turf. I fear this city is going to be a very unfriendly place to visit in the near future."

"It's not exactly fuckin' Wally World now," the Rhino said. "But you're right. I checked on the Net earlier. Everyone's talking about it as a warning to Seattle to stay out of the East. Geraldo even had an interview with some Haitian toe rag running a crew out of East Quogue, who said all the pirate outfits would get together to make sure Uncle Sam kept his nose off their turf. Their fucking turf! Can you believe it?"

"Easy there, big boy," she cautioned him, but for once he would not be talked down.

"It's easy for you, Jules. This isn't your country. It's just a place you're working. But I served twenty years to protect and defend America from exactly the sort of bottom-feeding scum suckers who've swarmed all over us since the Wave. It makes a rhino angry is all I'm saying. And an angry rhino is a dangerous thing."

"I'm sure," Jules said, pausing while the waitress returned with their drinks. She signed the chit that would charge the bill back to her account but didn't leave a tip. By federal law you couldn't offer a member of the militia any sort of monetary inducement. It was the woman's duty to ply Jules with gin and tonic. The lavish

catering was also part of the incentive to come to New York or one
of the other Declared Zones. To many it was a damned sight better
than standing in line at one of the many government kitchens in
Seattle waiting for a cup of thin venison chili.

"The fact remains," she continued when they were alone again,
"that we have to get a move on. If Kipper is serious about retaking
New York and settling it, there is going to be an almighty brouhaha
in this place before too long. I wouldn't be at all surprised to see
the freebooters band together, at least temporarily, and it is almost
certain that they'll call in help from their motherships and home
ports. In fact," she said, leaning forward, "I would lay very good
odds that our little holiday resort here will be targeted for a jolly
good rogering by the Jolly Roger crowd in the very near future."

The Rhino sipped his beer and nodded.

"You might well be right about that, Miss Jules. It would sort of
make sense for them to hit hard before Seattle can get a grip on the
city. So where's that leave us?"

Jules smiled and went quiet again as the waitress appeared with
her meal. The food was all flown in from Kansas City or the West
Coast and must have been hideously expensive. There weren't
many working men and women in America who could afford
T-bones and designer beer for dinner anymore, but everything in
Manhattan's Green Zone was subsidized by the federal government,
so although Jules would have to pay for the meal and the drinks, it
was a nominal cost.

"We need to be ready," she said. "When the opportunity arises,
we have to go without hesitation. But if nothing does arise in the
next few days, I think we have to make our own chances."

Jules casually took in the dining room. It was fast filling up with
workers from their crew and the other two that had been clearing
the main arterial roads at the lower end of the island. The room
was noisier, rowdier for sure than it would have been back in the
day. Most of these men and women were veterans of working the

Declared Zones, and they had the hard-bitten, chewed-off look of frontier types. They were coining it, to be sure, but there was no old money style and grace about them, none of the reserve with which she was so familiar from her childhood.

A booth full of roughnecks started a drinking game as they waited for their meals to arrive. Ryan and Manny and some of the younger hands from their crew had colonized another three tables nearby and pushed them together and were raucously playing some sort of networked game on half a dozen PSPs, another rare luxury item. One of the televisions above the bar played archived episodes of *One Life to Live,* which drew the attention of men and women alike, oddly enough. Out in the foyer of the hotel four fully armed members of Schimmel's militia prowled the carpet, occasionally disappearing out onto the street for a few minutes to consult with the private contractors.

Across from her, the Rhino had diced up his steak and potatoes like a master samurai and was inhaling the results. It was his second meal of the night. Julianne was famished after a day of extreme physical labor, but she restrained herself. For all that her father had been a fraud and a scoundrel, Lord Balwyn had instilled in her the importance of at least "looking one's part," and that meant not falling on one's food like a starving wolverine.

"Have you had a chance to talk to that goon Lewis yet?" she asked after thoroughly chewing and swallowing a small forkful of beef. A glass of red wine would have been nice with it, she thought idly, but she had work to do later and instead sipped at her chilled spring water, another expensive luxury.

The Rhino nodded as a fist-sized lump of food disappeared inside his maw.

Jules waited a discreet moment.

"And?"

"I asked him about the attack on Kipper. You know, everyone's asking, and Lewis does love to be the guy with the inside knowledge. Anyway, we got to talking about the plans to reclaim the city and all, and I just casual like asked him how things were going, especially up in the border zones around Central Park and the Upper East Side."

Jules nodded at him to continue.

"He said the park itself isn't too bad. The bandits stay clear of it because they can be interdicted by missile drones so easily."

"As could we," she added quietly.

"Yeah… but anyway, the park is pretty much clear. A lot of midtown's not so sporty as it used to be. Mostly been picked clean the last few years. Main issue where we're headed is that a couple of the gangs did set themselves up on the park, you know, living out of the Plaza and some of the better apartments."

"As one would," Jules conceded.

"Verily indeed," the Rhino quipped in a mock posh accent. "Anyway, that area's a free fire zone now. A true no-man's-land. So it's not permanently inhabited, but it's dangerous as hell to pass through."

Jules pushed back from her plate.

"Why didn't the air force just bomb those places if they knew there were a lot of pirate Johnnies hanging around?"

The Rhino looked momentarily discomfited.

"Coupla reasons. The president, he doesn't like to bomb his own cities and… well, there's a lot of talk that some of those places, like the Plaza, get used as rec facilities."

"As what?"

"Brothels."

"Good lord. Where do they find the talent?"

"Slaves," the Rhino said. "American slaves. So no boom boom while there's boom boom."

Jules found herself blushing, somewhat to her surprise. "Oh, dear. I am sorry, Rhino. I didn't know. I hadn't heard."

He shrugged, pretending he didn't care.

"You're not enslaving them. Anyway, it's all rumor, you know. Chain-gang scuttlebutt. Buncha fuckin' idiots swinging a hammer, daydreaming about what they'd do if they had a hotel full of whores to themselves."

"Well, we knew this wasn't going to be a milk run," Jules said. "Are you still up for it?"

"Hey, lady, the Rhino is permanently *up*."

Julianne shook her head and returned to her meal. "Okay, then. Let me think this through tonight and we'll talk again tomorrow."

Back in her room, changed into track pants and a Teletubby sweatshirt, Julianne poured herself a nightcap of whiskey and soda and secured the locks on her room. With curtains pulled she sat at the small desk and unfurled the papers she had taken from a hidden compartment in one of her backpacks. They showed the floor plans of an apartment overlooking upper Central Park from Fifth Avenue. Others were detailed aerial shots of the neighborhood, some of them pre-Disappearance and others taken within the last few months. She had to wonder at the amount of leverage her client must have used to gain access to what were obviously military intelligence sources. She didn't need more than a glance to know which images had been taken before the Wave and which afterward. The latest photographs all showed a city torn by the riots of nature gone wild and the infinitely more hurtful disturbances of men run amok, up to and including arc light firebombing runs by the remains of the B-52 bomber force. Firestorms could be seen raging in the areas local commanders had written off as unsalvageable, but Manhattan had been spared the worst of it.

Jules looked over the intelligence packet provided by her client. It was a collage of cached Internet files, pilfered recon reports from the Third Infantry Division, news media feeds, and pre-Wave satellite imagery. Rubin had also provided a Macintosh iBook with a series of embedded video files taken from recent drone flights over Lower Manhattan. A copy of an army map for Operation Sinatra showed a series of phase lines, graphic control measures meant to signify objectives for ground forces, slicing the island into a series of small, manageable components. Some of the material was six to eight weeks old, which was regrettable, but it did show the lead elements of the army and the Manhattan militia units penetrating up to 26th Street. It also showed a battery of Marine Corps artillery in a baseball diamond off FDR Drive. The operatic boom and crash of those howitzers could be heard through the night, and if one looked out over the ruins of Manhattan, it was possible to see the shells passing through the clouds, lighting them briefly before screaming on to their destination.

She thought briefly about using the sewers to move forward to their target. A couple of beers in those bars where the soldiers and militia hung out quickly convinced her otherwise. The Army Corps of Engineers had restored some pumps on the island and used the sewers to facilitate the movement of U.S. forces on the island. When the sewers and subways were not in use for troop transport, they were allowed to flood again. Rhino had suggested that Navy SEALs might be able to use the sewers, but with their rudimentary scuba skills, it was a death wish to try it.

Examining the drone feed on a disk, she could see that the life of Central Park had spilled over the iron fences and across the footpaths and tangled wreckage of the avenue, and everywhere greenery had blossomed and surged, burying much of the wrecked and frozen traffic in a lush tangle of vines and bushes and newly sprouted saplings. People had fought back, though, and huge areas of ancient regrowth had been burned out, either deliberately or as a side effect of conflict between the warring gangs.

Jules sipped at her drink and studied the most recent surveillance shots, wishing they were more current than six weeks old. There was nothing to be done about it, though. You just had to go with what you had.

And what she had was the plans to a building in this contested, lethal no-man's-land in which lay hidden a treasure she had been contracted to remove and return to its owner on the West Coast.

10

NEW YORK

Yusuf swam for his life. A great many things floated in the river, dragged along by the tide, sometimes gathering in great rafts of wrack and flotsam that turned slowly in the cold green water as the vast, unstable islands of refuse made their way toward the sea. The thin African boy clutched a half-inflated basketball that he'd found around not far from where he had jumped into the Hudson from the crumbling concrete deck at the northern tip of Ellis Island. At first, he had not kicked or tried to swim away, partly fearing that the Americans would shoot him from the sky if they saw him thrashing about in the water and partly because he was worn out. It was all he could do to limply hang on to the basketball and let the current take him away. Eventually, however, he had to kick against the pull of the water lest he be sucked into the dangerous logjam of refuse.

For a while he worried that he might wash up on the southern end of Manhattan where they had just struck at the infidel or, even worse, on the other island about a mile south, where the American military and militia forces had their main base. As soon as he was in the channel, however, he felt the tug of a much stronger current carrying him north. Being careful not to move in any way that might draw attention to him, he was able to see the effect of the rocket attack for the first time. It was a glorious sight in spite of his own ignominious circumstances. The ancient circular fortress nestled in a park where the vegetation had run wild was partly ablaze. Many vehicles outside the old castle also seemed to have been struck by fedayeen rocket fire, although it was obvious from the spread of destruction across many blocks in that part of the island that a good deal of the bombardment had gone astray. Still, Yusuf thought, with real satisfaction, they had struck a great blow for freedom and righteousness today.

He did not know who in particular they had attacked. It was not for a lowly soldier of a mere *saif* to be privy to such details. But looking at all the flashing lights and thinking back on the savagery of the Americans' counterstrike, there had to have been somebody very important inside that fortress. Perhaps even the governor of New York! What a blow to the Americans' prestige it would be were the emir to reach out and lay the judgment of God on somebody like that. Yusuf allowed himself a small tired smile as he floated past the chaotic scene. He was too far away to make out much individual detail, but he could see that the Americans had been badly hurt. Hundreds of them were running about outside the fort, seemingly without purpose. Wailing sirens carried their panicked notes all the way out to him in the middle of the channel. It was gratifying to see them laid low in God's eye.

At one point, however, a small eddy in the river turned him around, affording the exhausted boy soldier a view of the smaller island from which he had escaped. The scale of destruction there seemed infinitely greater. Over a dozen helicopters looped and circled in the air above fiercely burning buildings, and higher up jet fighters described elongated figure eights over the whole area. No gunfire came from this island, telling him that whatever battle had been fought there was over and the Americans had most certainly won. As he watched, two of the fat, dark green troop-carrying helicopters flew low and straight across the water to land unopposed on the same dock from which he had made his escape. The current turned him around again then and carried him farther away before he was able to observe anything else.

Conveyed upriver at something considerably quicker than a walking pace, Yusuf was soon so far from the scene of the battle that he could no longer make out any details at all. He contented himself with watching the ruins of the city go by. He had been in Manhattan for only three weeks after arriving from the training camp in Morocco, his ship unharmed by the threat of British submarines or warships. They were known to fire on vessels within the so-called exclusion zone that extended many hundreds of miles out from the U.S. coastline. He still marveled at the scale of the metropolis. What a seat of power it must have been when the city still lived. And to think it was just one of many cities across this continent. Perhaps the greatest of them, to be certain, but still only one of hundreds according to their teachers in camp. He wondered how God could have allowed wickedness to be raised so high before finally striking it down. But then, maybe that was the point, he thought, a lesson to the righteous and the evildoer alike, as he floated past what looked like the ruins of some sort of little harbor on the mainland side of the river. For a wonder, a number of sailboats still lay at anchor there. Some others had been thrown up out of the water, presumably by a storm, and lay broken-backed on the docks, which were strewn with debris and rubbish. Other boats were half submerged, their masts broken like matchsticks. These observations were interrupted by a painful bump on the side of his head.

Yusuf found himself at the edge of what appeared to be a huge floating mass of trash. Some of it had originated in the natural world. Large tree branches and even one or two whole trees that looked like they had been knocked over at their very roots were entangled with rotting bulrushes and great accumulated clumps of smaller twig and leaf matter. Caught up with them were car and truck tires, all manner of ruined furniture, and a seemingly infinite number of plastic bags, some of them empty and some of them bulging with unknown contents. His nose wrinkled and he gagged in disgust as he realized that some of the floating island was composed of dead bodies, many but not all of them human. A large, clear plastic bag full of small white balls floated by within easy reach. Yusuf tested it and found it not only more buoyant than his sadly deflated basketball but much easier and more comfortable to rest on. He abandoned the ball and moved across to the bag, on which faded red lettering spelled out beanbag stuffing.

He did not wish to get caught up in the island of floating wreckage and thought it prudent to get as far away from the rotting bodies as possible. He shuddered with loathing when he recognized the bloated corpse of a wild pig not more than a few yards away. The drifting atoll was large enough that it took him a long time to swim around it and, with some added effort, to break free of the slow but significant whirlpool in which it seemed to be spinning.

It seemed that he frog kicked upriver for a long time after that. He was very worried, and his anxiety grew with the distance from Ellis Island. He knew parts of Manhattan quite well from having studied tactical maps on the ship, but his instructors had bidden him to concentrate on learning the street grid in those areas where it was most likely he would have to fight. Down here, on the river, disoriented by the battle, he had trouble placing himself. Other than knowing he was floating up one of the rivers that ran on either side of Manhattan, Yusuf had no idea where he was or how he might get back to the emir's camp. He needed to find a landmark he could recognize and use to orient himself. The boy lay his head on the bag of beans and examined the blank wall of high-rise buildings past which he was sailing. Many of them

looked like ruined shells, fire-scorched and even teetering on the
edge of collapse in some cases. At one point, floating past a series
of jetties, he saw the amazing sight of an enormous skyscraper
that had toppled to one side and now leaned precariously against
another, forming a giant inverted V. You would certainly not walk
under it if you had half a mind. But Yusuf would not be walking
through that part of the city, anyway. His incomplete but workable
understanding of the island led him to believe that he was passing
the territory claimed by a number of competing criminal gangs
from Eastern Europe, mostly Russians and Serbs. He had heard
many stories of both peoples and their wars against the faithful.
It said a lot, he thought, that the emir had chosen to drive the
Americans from their own city before turning on the intruders
who had come to ransack it. Their time would surely come, but he
had to wonder why they had not been dealt with first. Surely they
were not that formidable and fierce an opponent. Well, it was not
his role to question the strategies of his superiors.

He could not help thinking about it, however, and, in doing
so, dwelling on the fighting in which he had really played no part,
Yusuf allowed a gnawing sense of shame to come over him, just as
the chill of the river seeped into his bones the longer he remained
immersed. When he examined his actions devoid of the rush of
adrenaline and emotion that had carried him through the fighting,
he saw that he had bolted like a terrified horse attacked by fearsome
dragons. He had gone into the fight so proud and tall and—looking
back on it—with such unbridled arrogance, but now he had to face
the unpleasant fact that his manhood had vanished altogether at the
very first sight of the Americans. They had robbed him of courage
like Satan's imps, and he had run from them as if they were pitiless
machines, not mortal men with their own fears and weaknesses.

Yusuf shuddered with the shame of it, as though the emir himself
was somehow looking directly at him, knowing of his failure. It felt
as though he were wallowing in the water directly in front of the

maw of a giant shark. A small groan escaped from his throat, and he closed his eyes, horrified, as though waiting to be eaten.

What had he done?

Nothing. He had done nothing but disgrace himself from the very first moment of the battle. A terrible understanding came to him. There was no great shark, of course, nor was it the emir whose gaze he had felt upon him with such weight and significance. It was God's eye. Allah himself had looked down from heaven and judged Yusuf Mohammed as unworthy.

"Oh, no, please…"

He experienced the same debilitating feeling he recalled from the opening moments of combat a few hours before, the feeling that he had somehow become detached from his body and was free-falling through time and space. He felt dizzy, and his head wobbled before dropping onto the bag of beans in despair. Darkness bloomed in his vision as evil memories arose from the past, unwanted and unbidden.

He remembered a dusty road outside of Moroto in Uganda, not long after Captain Kono had come to his village and changed the course of his life. It was so long ago, long enough that he thought of those days as detached from the world in which he now lived, as belonging to a different world altogether. In that world he was not Yusuf Mohammed. He was not a sinner. He was just a child who had come to know that the greatest cruelties in the world could be the work of other children, or at least other children who had been raised by the likes of Captain Kono. The children of the Lord's Resistance Army who had taken him from his village and killed everyone there often competed with one another in games of great brutality and violence. In one awful memory they were walking along the dusty road, and there came an old man on a bicycle. All of Kono's children began shrieking and yelping as soon as they saw him. Captain Kono hated cyclists and had declared that the punishment for riding a bike in his presence was amputation of at least one leg. Two of the grown men who fought with Kono pulled the old man on the bike over to the side of the road. He was shaking with fear but grinning and laughing nervously as if to encourage the idea that this was all some sort of practical joke. Kono appeared, towering over Yusuf. He, too, was grinning, but unlike the old man, his amusement was genuine. He explained to the boy that if he wished to prove himself to his comrades, he would have to chew through the man's leg, right down to the bone. Like a tiger. Kono smiled. *Imitate the actions of a tiger, boy.*

It all came back in diabolical recall. The hot, sweet, coppery taste of arterial blood. The stringy, almost gristly muscle and meat caught between his teeth. The way his throat locked up as though a chain mail fist were choking it off. As a sort of perverse mercy Kono had allowed him to finish the task with the machete, but it took many blows, and when it was done, the little boy Yusuf had once been was screaming louder than the old man whose leg he had taken off.

Moaning pitiably, he kicked for the shoreline, not caring if anybody looking down upon the water saw him thrashing and splashing away. All he knew was that he had to get out of this river, get to shore and somehow to make his way to the camp of the emir to seek forgiveness or at the very least the just punishment of God. The current was very strong, however, and it bore him upstream for at least another mile or two before he had swung close enough to the riverbank to be able to contemplate climbing out. By that point an unexpected sight had presented itself, one that made his heart lurch in momentary fright. One of the great warships of the Americans, one of those from which their planes and bombers used to fly to enforce their will around the world, lay ahead of him. For a few seconds he feared he had swum right into their midst and would soon be captured. The surprise of it, and the renewed feeling of burning shame, all but eclipsed him before he attended to what he was actually seeing rather than what he thought he had seen.

The aircraft-carrying ship was rusting and listed over to one side, so much so that he doubted anyone could have walked safely on its giant flat deck. Some of the planes had apparently broken whatever chains once had held them down and slid to the edge of the deck, where they had tumbled onto a barge far below. A small mountain of twisted metal wreckage had built up there: jet fighters and helicopters and possibly even a spaceship of some sort to judge by its weird twisted form, like a giant white plate... a flying saucer, he believed they were called. This one was bent out of shape like a cheap plastic or even a paper plate.

He thought he remembered this ship from his map lessons. It had been a museum of jihad for the Americans, and although it was a long way from the camp of the emir, he was pretty sure that if he cut across the island from this point, he might have a good chance of finding his way back to friendly ground. Kicking harder to maneuver himself around the many items of floating rubbish that clogged up much of the water, Yusuf set a course for a slightly newer-looking concrete jetty south of the warship. He was not surprised to find that his legs were so weak that they could barely carry his weight when he dragged himself hand over hand out of the water. He was lucky, because either the pier had sunk down into the bed of the river or the waters had risen over the last few years to lap over its edge. Hauling himself out was much less trouble than actually standing and beginning the long, hazardous journey across the city.

11

SEATTLE

She loved Pike Place Market because it was so busy, so full of life,
that you could lose yourself in it and forget for just a moment that
the world had gone to hell. A strong aroma of spices and coffee
mingled with the unmistakable briny odor of fresh fish and crabs
from the sea. Some of the reopened fishing areas off the coast of
California were starting to produce again. Each time Barbara
Kipper came to the market, a little more produce appeared from the
formerly deserted parts of the United States, starting with a bounty
of potatoes from Idaho. Stopping before a stall to inspect a batch of
Vidalia onions from Missouri, Barb thought it was almost possible
to convince yourself that the Wave was a bad dream and that the
hungry times had never really happened. It was all a straight-to-
video stinker with horrible computer graphics and bad acting. She
popped four of the best-looking onions into her string bag before
handing over a two-dollar note that looked even fresher than the
vegetables. The stall owner handed her a few coins in change, and
she passed on to Abe Frellman's Sausage Hut, where she wanted to

pick up a string of the deliciously fat pork and porcini chipolatas Kip liked so much.

"Came out of the smokehouse this morning, Mrs. Kipper," Frellman said, when he saw her eyeing them. "Three newbies a pound."

Barbara smiled. "You can do better than that, Abe. How about two-fifty?"

As they haggled back and forth over the inflated prices, Barbara realized that it was truly impossible to lose herself in the market or the past. The four Secret Service men trailing her as she tried to shop for fruit and vegetables would never allow that to happen. And even though the stallholders and many of the regular customers had grown accustomed to the First Lady buying and carrying her own groceries, Barbara Kipper was still the center of a buzzing circle of gawkers, admirers, and occasional crazy people wherever she went.

"Missus Kipper! Missus Kipper. Over here. Freshest Dungeness crabs on all the West Coast over heeeyah!"

Barb smiled and waved at Sammy Portuni as he held aloft two giant orange-backed specimens, their pincers snapping angrily in the air as a rival seller cried across the heads of the crowd.

"Hell, no, Ms. Kipper. Over here is where you want to be for the finest damn crabs and lobsters and fresh Canadian salmon anywhere."

She turned and waved at Jon Daniels from the Old City Fish Shop, who waved back at her with an enormous shining silver fish that looked bigger than her daughter.

Suzie jerked her mother's hand. "Can we get the big fish, Mommy? The big fish for Daddy?"

"Suzie, I can't carry a big fish like that all the way home, darling," she protested. "And I came here for fresh fruit and vegetables. We have plenty of meat and fish at home in the freezers."

"Oh veg-e-tables," Suzie moaned. "They're no fun at all. And we've got heaps of them in the garden at home. And you're getting sausages, and sausages are meat."

Thankfully, before Suzie could really get going on her antivegetable stump speech, a three-piece band started up: a fiddler, a double bass, and a guitarist banging out some jaunty little Cajun number from the sound of it. Barb forged on through the crowd toward her favorite produce store, reminding herself to stop at the cheese shop for some of the stinky blue stuff Kipper liked on his toast in the morning. She had just noticed a new stall selling handblown glass jewelry when one of the Secret Service men appeared at her side. Momentarily distracted—she hadn't seen a craft store in the markets for years; they were all about fresh food nowadays—she missed whatever he muttered in her ear. She really did want to see that jewelry. It had been so long since anyone had the time or freedom to indulge in such things.

"Missus Kipper, ma'am. You really need to come with us now."

It was the hard edge he put on the last word that finally broke through and caught Barb's attention.

"What's up?" she asked, turning to him. "Is there something wrong?"

She looked around quickly but saw nothing untoward in the markets. They were crowded with midweek shoppers, most of them with their arms full of groceries. Like her, they were probably supplementing the produce nearly everyone grew these days in their home gardens or on the community plots that had taken over so much public parkland. Barb kept her face neutral and her voice low, not wanting to cause a minor panic, even though she was suddenly feeling very anxious.

"Is it Kip?" she asked as quietly as she could. "Has something happened to my husband?"

"If you'll come with us, ma'am," the agent insisted, taking her string bags of onions and celery and carrots and handing them off to another man, who disappeared into the throngs. Three more agents moved in around Barb and Suzie and began to maneuver them toward the exit where Pike Place swung around to climb up a slight incline back to First Avenue. Three black Chevy Suburbans were waiting under the market's famous orange neon sign. The day had clouded over while she'd been shopping, and the lettering stood out sharply against the lowering gray sky.

Barb bit down on her irritation. She had grown used to the ways of the Service and knew they would explain all that they could once she and Suzie were safely out of harm's way. A few people in the crowd noticed that the First Lady was cutting short her regular shopping trip, and there was a momentary surge in the background buzz, but when nobody pulled any guns or started bellowing instructions to her protection detail, the small surge in the crowd's excitement level quickly abated. Just as the city had grown used to the First Family walking and living among them, they had become accustomed to Kipper and Barb occasionally disappearing without notice at the behest of their bodyguards. Three years after the Wave had simply vanished, the world remained a dangerous and unpredictable place. It was always a wonder to Barb that people seemed to have adapted so quickly to the arbitrary and hazardous nature of life in the new world.

"Does this mean we don't have to have vegetables for dinner?" Suzie asked with the eternal hopefulness of childhood as she hauled herself up into the rear seat of the Suburban in the center of the little convoy.

Barb smiled nervously at her daughter. It was a little sad how quickly Suzie had also adapted to an unsettled and uncertain existence. She had been whisked away into hiding so many times in Kip's first year as president that she took it as a natural state of being.

"Seat belt on, darling," Barbara said, as she strained to lock in on some vital piece of intelligence from the chatter of the agents, surrounding the vehicle, fingers to their earpieces, listening to whatever information there was to be had. At times like this, Barb wished she had one of those earpieces.

"I have my belt on, Mom, but you didn't answer my question. Are we having vegetables? Potatoes are okay, especially the crispy ones that Chef Mikey does. Is the chef cooking dinner tonight, or are you, Mommy? If we have visitors, don't you think Chef Mikey should do the crispy potatoes?"

"Suzie, just quiet down for a moment and let Mommy get strapped in, would you?"

The agents were moving with some haste but not scrambling madly the way they had on the day Kip had ordered those Chinese planes shot down over Alaska. That day remained her yardstick for judging when the brown stuff had really hit the fan. The Suburban's engine roared into life, and they accelerated away sharply enough to press her back into the seat. She pushed herself forward with some effort, leaning over to speak to the Secret Service man riding shotgun in the front seat.

"So what's happening, Peter?" she asked. "Is it Kip? Is he okay?"

"Yes, ma'am," the agent replied tersely as they sped up the hill and across First Avenue.

"Yes what?" Barb asked with a flash of irritation.

"Yes, ma'am. It's your husband," he said, but without elaborating.

"Mommy," a small voice asked from beside her. "Is Daddy okay?"

"I'm afraid he's dead," the agent informed him.

"Damn," Jed muttered.

"But I was standing just a few feet away," Kip protested. "I didn't get a scratch. How did he get hit?"

"Mister Koppel was struck by shrapnel, sir," the detail chief, Agent Shinoda, replied. "It was bad luck. He died on the scene while two of my people attempted to stabilize him. One of them was wounded in doing so. Critically."

"I'm sorry," Kipper said. "What was his name?"

"She, sir. Agent Rachael Lonergan. She lost the lower half of her left arm. She's supposed to be on case-vac to Kennedy, but I, uh, need to discuss that with you, Mister President. We don't control that evac point at the moment."

Kipper shook his head in confusion. The three men were huddled in a small subterranean room in Castle Clinton. The rocket attack had been suppressed nearly a quarter of an hour ago, and Kipper could hear only sporadic and muffled gunfire from above them. The end of the battle on Ellis Island, they told him. With no power to provide lighting, they spoke underlit by the white glow of a battery camp light that gave their faces a shadowed, haunted look.

"What do you mean you don't control Kennedy?" the president asked.

His detail chief shook his head.

"I'm sorry, sir. Poor choice of words. We control the secured area of the airport that we came in through this morning, but it is being attacked by irregular forces."

"Pirates?"

"Pirates, mercenary forces, irregulars," said Shinoda. "They're uncoordinated, but there's a lot of them, in four, maybe five elements, an alliance of convenience most likely, cobbled together for the duration of your time in New York. We've seen them ally against each other at times. It would make sense for them to combine against us. Mister President, we cannot take you out of the city via Kennedy."

"Do you think you'll lose control of the secured area?" Kip asked.

"No, sir. A battalion from the First Cavalry Division is there along with an additional battalion of Governor Schimmel's militia and a hundred special operators from Sandline who were on their way out after completing clearance operations in Lower Manhattan. Combined with our firebases, we have more than enough firepower to hold the position, sir. The problem is that it's simply not safe to take you out through that facility, Mister President."

Kip folded his arms and dropped his chin down onto his chest, the universally recognized symbol of an unhappy President Kipper. His ears were still ringing, and he had a monster headache that was refusing to disappear even after a couple of painkillers.

"Well, Agent Shinoda, I'm sure you have any number of fallback plans and alternate routes out."

Shinoda nodded. "Yes, Mister President. We can evac you by *Marine One* to—"

"However," Kip interrupted, "we have, what, fifteen serious casualties from the rocket attack and about twice that again in walking wounded?"

Jed Culver closed his eyes and started shaking his head.

Shinoda nodded. "Mister President—"

Culver tried to interrupt, but Kipper cut him off.

"Not a word, Jed. Agent Shinoda, what arrangements do you have for getting the really badly wounded people out? I assume they would have gone out on some sort of medical flights from Kennedy."

Shinoda looked grim-faced as he nodded. "We'd evac them to the federal health center in North Kansas City. They'll have to wait until we can secure the landing strip, sir."

"That fight could go on for days," said Kip. "Your own briefings said there were a minimum of eight or nine thousand freebooters in New York alone. And plenty more up and down the coast. They picked this fight on purpose. What makes you think they won't just keep pouring men in to keep it going?"

"Mister President, that's not really my area of concern. You'd need to talk to your military—"

Kip waved his hand to cut Shinoda off. "Well, at this very minute it is your concern, Agent Shinoda, because I'm making it so. Are you certain we're not going to lose all of those wounded people while we wait for the fight at the airport to die down?"

Shinoda looked deeply uncomfortable but did his best to answer, raising his voice to be heard over the growing clatter of a helicopter that sounded as though it was setting down inside the castle's walls.

"The irregular forces are very loosely coordinated, Mister President. In fact, calling them coordinated at all is probably an exaggeration. Maintaining a siege of the airport against superior firepower, especially with the air-to-ground assets currently servicing them, well, it's just not feasible sir, not in the long run."

"But our people don't have long, do they? Our wounded, I mean. They need to get out now."

Another Secret Service agent, this one dressed in black coveralls, appeared at the doors. "Excuse me, sirs, but *Marine One* just set down topside."

"Mister President," Jed said. "Perhaps if we could continue this on the chopper."

Kipper shook his head. "Nope. I'm not getting on the chopper until the Secret Service can assure me that all of the seriously wounded have been evacuated to a secure federal facility. You can start moving them out on my helicopter. It's equipped for this sort of thing, and I'm perfectly healthy, so I don't need it."

Agent Shinoda attempted to demur. "But Mister President…"

"Forget it. This isn't a debate. I'm going to have it my way. Now Jed, you go find me whoever is in charge on the military side around here and make sure he knows what I want done. Agent Shinoda, I will stay down here if it makes your job easier, or I can relocate somewhere more secure. I'll leave that choice to you. But I don't leave Manhattan until the wounded are out, do you understand?"

"Yes, sir," Shinoda said with visible reluctance.

"Where do you have the wounded now?"

"We established triage upstairs, Mister President, inside the old gift shop."

"Fine." Kipper nodded to himself. "That sounds safe, so take me there. Right now."

Shinoda looked as though he was going to argue, but a raised eyebrow from Kipper was enough to subdue any resistance.

* * *

"Did you see any pirates, Daddy? They were on the news, but Mom wouldn't let me see it even though you were on with the pirates, too."

Kipper smiled as he held the handpiece to his ear and imagined his daughter back home, fed and bathed and ready for bed—safe and warm and thousands of miles away from this dead city full of murderous crazy fuckers and blood and horror and madness. Her room was next to Barb's and his on the second floor of Dearborn House, and Kipper knew she would be sitting on the thick shag pile rug at the foot of her bed, surrounded by her closest advisers: Tigger, Barbie, and a white teddy bear dressed as a cheerleader that sang, "Oh Mickey you're so fine you're so fine you blow my mind…" at the merest bump or provocation. It was a hell of a lot nicer to think of than his current surroundings, in the back of an armored car somewhere in Lower Manhattan listening to Suzie's voice through a connection of static and beeps.

"No, darling, I didn't see any pirates," Kipper said. "They were on another island. Now, have you brushed your teeth and said your prayers?"

The military radio beeped, indicating that Suzie was going to speak again. It really annoyed Kipper no end.

"Yes," she said suspiciously.

"Well, then it's bedtime, sweetheart. So climb under the covers and let Daddy speak to Mommy."

The radio beeped again.

"Okay, night night, Daddy."

Oh Mickey you're so fine you're so fine you blow my mind. Hey Mickey!

"Good night, Suzie," he called out, but she was already gone. The next beep of the radio heralded the less pleasant segment of this call home.

"Kip, is that you? Are you okay? They said you were fine, but my God, some of the pictures on the news. All those people. I told you not to go out there. I told you. The Secret Service told you. Jed told—"

Barb had gone from relief at hearing his voice, to anxiety, to building rage all in the space of a few seconds. He had to cut her off before she lost it. Hunching over the blinking lights of the control panels in the back of the armored vehicle, cupping his hands over the mouthpiece, he tried to keep his voice down. The two army technicians in there with him did their best to pretend they couldn't hear a word of his developing domestic argument. A bit of static washed over the transmission, cutting Barbara off and giving Kip his chance.

"Whoa, honey," Kip said. "Just settle down. I'm fine. I am perfectly fine. Hardly a scratch. And I'm surrounded by a whole army of… army guys."

The two army techs surreptitiously rolled their eyes at each other. Another beep of the radio signaled Barb's biting retort.

"What do you mean, you're surrounded by army guys? You're supposed to be on a flight back home by now. Where are you?"

Kipper flinched at her tone of voice. This wasn't going to be much fun.

"Well, thing is, I'm in New York…"

"What the hell are you still doing in New York City, James Everett Kipper? I swear to fucking God that you are dumb as a sack of hammers."

The techs shrank at their posts and removed their headsets. The president reined in his temper before it got the better of him. "Two things," he said quickly. "One, the airport we came in through wasn't safe anymore." He didn't explain why. "And two, those people you saw on the news, the ones who were hurt, I put them on my chopper to get them out of here and back to KC for treatment. They'd have died, all of them, if we'd waited."

There was a momentary pause while Barb digested that. Kipper peered out the slits in the heavy steel doors on the back of the…

the... damn, he didn't even know what kind of tank or armored car he was in. This military stuff just was not his thing. Outside on the street he could just make out figures in uniform flitting about and other vehicles moving around, some like his and some Humvees— at least he knew what a Humvee looked like.

"Well, when are you getting out of there, Kip?" his wife asked. "It's not safe."

He resisted the urge to tell her that was exactly why he had to come out to the East Coast, as a first step to making it safe again, but he knew Barb wouldn't be impressed by that sort of BS.

"You know I can't give you exact details of my movements, honey," he said. "Just know I am safe and I will be home soon."

Her reply was lost in static, but it didn't sound very encouraging. Kipper thought he saw one of the techs fiddling with some of the cables on the radio.

"I'm sorry, Barb, what was that?"

"...back... sorry..."

The connection dropped out, and one of the soldiers began stabbing at buttons and muttering an apology.

Kipper reached over and patted him on the shoulder.

"Don't worry, son. I think you just saved your commander in chief from some world-class ass whuppage."

12

SWINDON, ENGLAND

A man from the Home Office was waiting for her at Swindon's Great Western Hospital, a cream-colored modernist structure on the southwestern edge of the town. The man was an unremarkable type, medium build with light brown hair cut short and a well-made but not too expensive gray suit. Caitlin picked him out as her handler, or minder as they said here, as soon as she hurried in through the automatic doors to the reception area. He favored her with a half-raised eyebrow and came gliding over, juggling a document wallet from one side to the other, allowing him to extend a hand in greeting. He smelled of aftershave and pipe tobacco. She noted that although he looked every inch the gray bureaucrat, his grip was strong and his hand was hardened by the same sort of calluses that scarred her own.

"Ms. Monroe, my name is Dalby," he said. "The office sent me from London to help out with your spot of bother."

Still jittery with the adrenaline backwash, Caitlin could not help herself.

"Spot of bother? They tried to kill my fucking family," she snapped back.

"Indeed. I am sorry," Dalby said. "Sometimes understatement gets the better of me."

His speaking manner was an odd mix, a rough-working class accent bundled up in a very polished and, she thought, practiced form of expression. Caitlin made a conscious effort to calm herself and brushed off his apology, "I'm sorry. Please excuse me, Mister Dalby. It's been a hell of a morning. I just want to see my family, if that's okay."

"Of course," he said. "If you'll follow me."

The hospital seemed quiet even for a midweek morning, with only a few people in the waiting area for accident and emergency and no sense of the barely controlled mayhem that characterized most public health facilities in her experience. Caitlin had half expected some sort of delay at the front desk, but Dalby handed her a clip-on badge and indicated that she should follow him by pointing toward a pair of heavy plastic swinging doors that led into the building's interior. None of the staff questioned them or tried to interfere, and she could only surmise that the Home Office man had already established his credentials as somebody not to be fucked with. Not that anyone fucked with the Home Office these days.

"So, you had any luck putting names to the bodies?" she asked as they hurried down a wide corridor past assessment and treatment rooms, most of them empty.

"I have some briefing notes for you," Dalby said. "All of your villains returned positive IDs from the national database, and we had further hits off the Yard and the Home Office's own restricted lists."

"They were professionals?" Caitlin asked.

"That would be overly generous." Dalby snorted. "Three very low-rent criminals and two from a little further up the evolutionary ladder, probably to run the operation, such as it was."

Again, Caitlin found herself intrigued by his voice. He had a definite strain of East London in his flat, nasal tone but spoke as though he'd been coached in elocution at an expensive boarding school. "They were well resourced, though," she cautioned, thinking of the cars and guns, neither of which were easy to come by in the United Kingdom now. Both tended to be assets of the government, not the private citizen.

"Indeed," Dalby said, as they turned a corner into a corridor off which a number of semiprivate wardrooms were accessible. Caitlin noted four beds in each room, about half of them occupied, although mostly by young people. A few years ago she'd have expected to see a good many wrinklies and fatties and chronically unhealthy specimens in a place like this, living off the public tit. No longer. From a few cursory glances she confirmed her suspicion that most of the bedridden were trauma cases, broken limbs and crushed bodies, almost certainly from the many farms in the district just like hers, where strong backs and straining muscles were the order of the day. Her mind wandered briefly, dwelling on the growing demand for horses in the district. She was on a waiting list herself. Caitlin shook the errant thought from her mind.

"Do we know who sent them?" she asked.

"Not yet," Dalby admitted. "Although the chap you left alive is helping us with our inquiries."

"When you say 'us,' you mean…"

"Our office," he answered. "Yours."

"Okay," Caitlin admitted. Dalby was here on Echelon business.

"Here we are, then," he announced as they made one final turn and fetched up outside a private room. Another man in a suit with a bulge under his jacket, much larger and more imposing than Dalby, nodded to them and opened the door.

"I'll give you a minute," Dalby said quietly. "I understand your daughter is asleep and Mister Melton has been lightly sedated."

Caitlin thanked him and pushed past the guard with her heart beating noticeably harder. The room was large and well lit, with a couple of windows looking out over plowed fields to a small lake a mile or two to the west. Monique was asleep, as she'd been told, but Bret blinked groggily and tried to smile at her. She shushed him quickly with a finger to her lips, indicating the sleeping child. A cursory examination showed that the baby was largely unharmed save for a few scratches on her face. Her husband, in contrast, looked terrible. The scars from Iraq, the stitches where they sewed up his shoulder, and his missing finger had new companions. Remnants of his ranger regiment tattoo provided a stark contrast to his pale, pasty complexion. He had lost a lot of blood back in the field and looked drained. Caitlin's stomach was clenched, and she felt a coppery taste at the back of her throat.

"I'm sorry…" he croaked. "Couldn't…"

The room blurred in front of her as the tears came, and she shushed him again, this time with one finger on his lips. They were swollen and cracked, and half of his face was mottled with bruising. One leg was fully bandaged and held aloft with a complicated series of wires and pulleys. He would be limping again, perhaps forever. She'd often teased him about the jagged scar where the combat support hospital in Kuwait had dug an old piece of wood from his ass. Bret usually responded by farting on cue, chasing her out of the bed briefly while she waved away the stench. Laughing at the crude absurdity, she would come back to the bed and find something else to tease him about.

It didn't seem so funny now.

"Don't," she whispered. "You did great, sweetie. Five guys with guns. You were unarmed, yet you protected Monique and you both got out. That's all that counts."

Bret pressed his lips together and squeezed his eyes shut, shaking his head once, emphatically.

"I should have had a—"

"Hush now." She softly stroked his thick brown hair, blinking away her tears. "This is no time for beating yourself up. If I'd married any other man, I'd be a widow now and my daughter would be gone along with my husband. You did an amazing job to get her away from them."

"But we didn't get away," he croaked. "And if you hadn't come along…"

Caitlin shook her head.

"You know better than that, Bret. We don't do what-ifs in our line of work. Or mine, anyway. You're a farmer and a daddy now, and that's the most important thing. To me and the baby. You need to rest and get better and look after our little girl. And you need to let me worry about these bastards. Can you do that, Bret? Can you leave them to me?"

"Hooah," he whispered. "Leave them to you."

The effort of talking seemed to have exhausted him, and he nodded weakly as a long ragged breath leaked out between his lips with a wheezing sound. He groped for her hand and squeezed it.

Caitlin leaned forward and kissed his forehead.

"I love you," she said quietly. "And I promise you this will never happen again."

Still in her bloodied running gear, Caitlin followed Dalby to his vehicle, an unmarked gray Mercedes W203 sedan. A small window tag displayed the logo of the British Home Office, promising to build a "safe, just, and tolerant society." Clouds obscured the sun, snuffing out what little warmth had been left in the day, and she was grateful when Dalby turned up the heat as he started the car.

"Perks of the job," he said. "It often seems this car is the only place where I can escape the chill these days. Bloody weather, being all over the shop."

Caitlin nodded without a word. Even with the resources of her own farm and the indulgences of the government, her family still felt the privations of the rationing system.

"We'll move your family to one of our secure estates," Dalby said as they drove away from the hospital, heading south toward the highway. The effort was slow going as he worked his way around a pod of cyclists and a horse-drawn cart. None of the bike riders were wrapped in Lycra. They weren't pedaling for their health. Dalby's was the only car on the road.

Caitlin watched the sides of the road, scanning for anything unusual.

"You won't have to worry about them," Dalby assured her. "We have secured the area."

Caitlin shook her head. "I can't help worrying, Mister Dalby. They're everything I have now."

"I'm sorry," he said. He seemed to open almost every sentence with an apology. "I meant that we will take care of them. And the farm. We'll keep Mister Melton and your little one under our wing while this situation gets sorted, and a manager has been sent to your estate at Mildenhall. One of our men. A good chap with the right background. His family has farmed this area for many years. But no, of course I didn't mean that you would feel no worry. That would be most insensitive."

"So Echelon sent you? Not the Home Office," Caitlin said, forcibly dragging her thoughts away from the hospital room as they entered the M4, heading west. That surprised her. She had been expecting to go to London.

"It's an interdepartmental issue. The lines of authority are somewhat blurred. Intentionally so," Dalby said as he maneuvered them onto the all but deserted highway. A few army trucks—lorries they called them—and two green-painted buses with British Army markings and steel mesh on the windows were the only vehicular traffic she could see. Dalby was finally able to tap into the power of the car, accelerating away from Swindon.

remaining overseas territories and barred from returning to the newly promulgated "metropolitan area"—Greater Britain and Northern Ireland, in not so many words.

Most of the territorial administrators, such as the military commander of the British base on Cyprus, a major relocation hub, had simply moved them on again, at gunpoint if necessary.

"So what's the current thinking?" she asked. "Richardson was a sleeper, a stay-behind? Or his jailhouse conversion was just a convenience while he was inside?"

Dalby eased back on the gas as the downpour grew heavier, exhibiting the first hint of emotion since she'd met him. If she didn't know better, she could have sworn that he was disappointed. He flicked the wipers to a faster setting and turned on his headlights, although the road remained largely empty.

"We have no preconceived ideas," he said, hunching slightly over the wheel. "But we very much like this Hizb connection as an explanation for why he'd be looking for you—and how he came to get his hands on a couple of prestige motors, a book of petrol coupons, and the small arsenal they were carrying. There is no common or garden-variety criminal angle to this as far as we can tell. But Richardson and his crew taking on a contract job for Hizb ut-Tahrir? That all clicks together very nicely."

"Well, not really," she protested. "I can't imagine the Hizb have much of a network left here since the deportations. Who would have handled Richardson for them?"

"A cutout?" Dalby suggested. "They don't need a full beard to issue the orders. Just someone reliable to pass them along and run the logistics. There's still plenty of villains about, and pickings have been very thin for them the last few years what with all the extra security and rationing and so on. One of the advantages for Hizb in having been so active in the prison system is the number of contacts it gave them with handy infidels, like Richardson's crew."

"None of them flagged as converts?" she asked.

"No. But they'd all done time in prisons with a Hizb presence. Richardson would not have had to sell them a line about doing God's work. All he had to do was tell them he had a paying job. And this job did pay well. Once we had confirmed IDs, the Met raided the last known addresses of the four men you killed, well, three of the four. For one we had no known address. They found envelopes with two and half thousand in euros at two of the flats. At the third, they found a party in progress. Seems young Ed McConaughy's girlfriend couldn't wait for him to get home."

"McConaughy?"

"The nasty little carrot top. I believe you shot him in the face."

"Oh, him. So, two and a half up front. And two and a half at the back end? Plus a bonus for Richardson, an executive fee for running the show?"

"Certainly. Plus the equipment, the cars and guns and so on. And travel passes. They were valid, so that involved a payoff somewhere along the line. We'll know more about that when Special Branch gets back to us. All in all, though, Ms. Monroe, somebody spent a pretty penny to send these villains after you."

Caitlin stared out her window. The rain was heavy enough now to have obscured visibility beyond about fifty yards. The world outside the car had been reduced to formless gray and green shadows.

"So why, if you're going to all that trouble…"

"Do you send a bunch of bloody amateurs like these?" Dalby finished for her.

Caitlin nodded. It made no sense. There had to be better crews around than Richardson's. Professional hitters who could have taken her out from a hilltop with a long barrel. Snatch teams that could have disappeared her from the face of the earth without a trace. Yet somebody had sent a bunch of half-wits and morons who'd been incapable of catching her husband on his bicycle.

And, with the exception of Richardson, their putative leader, they were all dead. Almost as if that was the point of the exercise.

13

TEXAS, FEDERAL MANDATE

Crows and magpies, carrion birds, screeched nearby as the little caravan emerged from the northern edge of the forest through wispy drifts of cold rain. A thin, straggling line of poplars wound away to the north like a green river through the fields of beans and spinach irrigated from a couple of human-made lakes. The sun cracked through the clouds as Miguel rode past the nearest garden beds, and an automatic sprinkler system engaged with a click and a whoosh, creating a small field of rainbows in the arcs of jetting water. Blue Dog, an Australian blue heeler, barked in surprise but settled with a warning glance and whistle from his master. His littermate, a red heeler inventively named Red Dog, appeared to throw a contemptuous glance at her brother. She stuck close to Sofia's horse, a station from which she had not strayed since the girl had released both dogs from the barn back at the farm.

Miguel watched Sofia closely from a few yards behind, where he was leading a string of three more horses. Great storms of emotion swirled and clashed within him, but he ignored them as best he could, focusing his concern on his surviving daughter. She rode tall in the saddle; that was normal enough. The problem was that everything and anything seemed to spook her. Her eyes were constantly darting over every possible place where danger might lurk. He was worried that she would focus so much on what frightened her that she might tumble from her mount like a rag doll. Sofia's agitated mood was easily read by her horse, which in turn grew increasingly twitchy and nervous. Red Dog trotted alongside her, looking up and whimpering occasionally.

They stuck to the tree line even though it doubled the distance they had to cross, winding back east for a few hundred yards, then switching north again before the ground began to rise and the cultivated fields gave way to larger patches of old-growth forest, thick with chalk maple, hackberry, and white ash. The road agents had not appeared again, but Miguel had no doubt the towering pillar of black smoke rising from his homestead would be enough to draw them back to investigate what had happened to their missing comrades. He wanted to put some hard ground between them and his daughter as quickly as possible. The patch of uncleared forest they were headed for would be impenetrable to motor vehicles of the sort the road agents were driving. Indeed, within minutes both he and Sofia were forced to dismount and lead the horses on foot. Blue Dog trotted ahead, sniffing at tree roots and occasionally snapping up a bug. Red Dog stayed close to Sofia, nudging at her leg every now and then.

They bore away from Bald Prairie and the homesteads Miguel knew were a few miles to the north. He did not think it likely the agents would attack those farms. They were home to white families from Seattle, and Miguel believed with all his heart that the road agents were Blackstone's men, and so would do the governor's bidding. That meant driving off beaners like his family even if they were within the Federal Mandate but leaving the right sort of settlers in place. He was confident the forest would keep him and Sofia hidden for most of the next twenty or thirty miles, until the patches of woodland grew thinner and eventually petered out short of Leona. There was nobody up there. It was a pissant little burg that had mostly burned out after the Wave and never been reclaimed. If they could make it by nightfall, it was certain they'd find shelter there, but no sign of the agents or the TDF, he hoped. The Texas Defense Force was supposed to protect settlers from the likes of the road agents, but in Miguel's experience people like him needed protecting from them.

The path widened as the forest thinned out again, and within a few minutes they were able to remount. Following the heavily wooded line of Larrison Creek, they rode in silence for nearly two hours, the only sounds the snuffling of the dogs and the muted footfalls of their mounts on the soft leaf litter of the forest floor. At one point, just after three o'clock, he called a halt for ten minutes after hearing the thudding beat of a helicopter somewhere to the south, but it never moved any closer while he sat quietly, chewing a couple of Mariela's cookies and sipping at a water bottle. Sofia refused the offer of something to eat, but he was relieved to see she took a drink from her canteen. Red Dog growled at the distant noise, but Miguel shushed her immediately.

The first real challenge to their getaway came a short time later when they had to cross the wide-open lanes of Route 21. Emerging from the tree line near the rusting hulk of a pickup that had veered into the ditch and rolled, presumably when its driver had Disappeared, Miguel gave himself a minute.

"Sit and stay," he ordered, and the two cattle dogs dropped onto their haunches as he listened to the world around them.

Sofia unslung her Remington and laid it across her lap, and that unsettled him. She was just a little too quick to reach for her rifle, and he considered taking it from her more than once. However, he couldn't leave her defenseless, and it was better that she be alert than lethargic.

"Is something wrong?" Sofia asked, looking around. "Do you see those men?"

He shook his head but gestured with a hand for her to be quiet while he listened. But there was nothing.

No helicopters.

No aircraft.

No traffic.

Just the rustle of a chilling breeze through the wet leaves of the forest patch from which they had come.

"It's nothing," he said quietly. "I am just being careful. Come on."

They all crossed the roadway at a trot. It was cracked and sprouting with weeds in places, and the clip-clop of the horses' metal shoes sounded very loud after the quiet confines of the forest. But within moments they were over and safely concealed under the forest canopy again. The rest of the day passed without event, giving Miguel to understand just how empty was the land in this part of the country. They skirted two ranches late in the day on the approach to Leona, but the sun was already low in the sky and he could tell from a few minutes' observation with his binoculars that the homesteads were deserted. Not because agents or the TDF had run off new settlers but because they had been empty for years. Grass and weeds grew to chest height right up to the front porches. The roof of one house had been badly damaged in a storm at some point and never repaired, and the other home was blackened with the telltale scorch marks of a small fire. He wondered why the whole structure had not burned but shrugged off the question. A sprinkler system, perhaps. It didn't really matter. Only ghosts dwelled there now.

He cantered up beside Sofia with a flick of the reins and a few clicks of his tongue. Fresh tear tracks ran like dry riverbeds through the dust and accumulated grime on her face. She was not crying at that very moment, however. At best she seemed cold and remote.

"We shall make camp up ahead soon," he promised. "There is a small town not far off. We should be safe there."

Her only reply was a vague shrug.

As the sun dropped into the west, it seemed to grow larger and glow with an almost malevolent orange glare, as though he were staring into a furnace in the Devil's basement. Shadows pooled in the recesses of the last patch of forest, a small wedge of uncleared brushland between Route 75 and the Farm to Market Road. Leaving the shelter of the trees, they diverted a few hundred yards to the north, where a small farm dam glistened in the sunset. As the animals drank their fill from the cool, clear lake, a dog or possibly a wolf howled from not too far off, causing the horses to step skittishly and flick their ears around, searching for the predator. The cattle dogs were instantly alert, with lips peeled back from their teeth as they growled in warning and the short wiry hair on their backs stood up.

"Blue Dog, Red, be quiet," Miguel warned. He leaned forward and patted Flossie on the side of her neck. "Hush now, young lady. Some flea-bitten mutt calling for its dinner is no reason for you to be fearful, no."

Sofia craned anxiously in the saddle, peering into the gloomy distance. Her posture tensed up more than Miguel would have thought possible as she unslung her rifle again and brought the scope to her eye. Again, Miguel fought the urge to take her weapon away from her, though it was good that she thought to scope the town for any trouble.

"See anything?" he asked.

Sofia shook her head. "No, Papa. It looks clear from here."

"Very good," he said.

The cowboy unholstered his saddle gun, stroked the polished wooden stock, and resisted the urge to check the loads. There could be no letting his own nerves get the better of him. Any beast or man bold enough to try his luck with Miguel Pieraro would very quickly find that luck turning sour, especially today. He stood alert, listening as the horses dipped their heads back to the dam. They heard no more of the predator. After a few minutes even Sofia relaxed. With the horses watered, he hauled himself back up into the saddle for the short ride into Leona.

"We'll camp here, Sofia," he said, mostly for the sake of saying something.

They had ridden in silence for most of the day, exchanging only a few words here and there as was necessary.

"Fine," she replied.

Sunset was not far off as the last of the storm clouds broke open to reveal a deep red-orange orb peering through a haze of magenta and purple as it fell toward the western horizon. A few birds trilled and tweeted in the trees as the small caravan slowly approached the edge of the settlement. Sofia remained quiet. What little heat had been generated by the reappearance of the sun rapidly leached out of the day as Miguel scanned the ruins of the town for somewhere suitable to make camp. It looked as though more than half the place had burned after the Wave hit, and many of the surviving buildings were badly storm-damaged. Wrack and refuse littered the two main roads, and a flagpole outside the general store was bent over at nearly forty degrees; a twisted sheet of corrugated iron had wrapped itself around the pole where the flag must have flown in days past. The metal awning over the sidewalk by the ruined flagpole had collapsed and the windows flanking the store's main entrance were broken, but structurally the building seemed fine.

"Perhaps over here," he suggested as he dismounted and led the horses over to a line of wooden fencing that had survived intact.

"Uh-huh." His daughter shrugged, following suit and dismounting. Miguel frowned as he tethered Flossie and the string of remounts before removing his saddle gun and cautiously approaching what looked like a general store. After a few steps he paused and motioned to Sofia to be ready with her Remington. She brought the rifle up to her shoulder and waited for further instructions. Her eyes remained blank, cold. Miguel was worried for her, but he had to press on. He whistled softly to the dogs and waved them ahead of him. The dogs trotted off, sniffing and twitching their ears, but gave no sign of any trouble. Miguel took his time examining the building. A small annex, once given over to a diner, remained in stasis. No windows had broken to let in the elements, and the cowboy could see in the fading light that three of the four Formica tables had been occupied on the morning of the Disappearance. Piles of clothing, stained black and stiff with organic residue, lay draped over half a dozen chairs. In front of them sat plates of food or what had been food. Red and yellow plastic bottles stood on each table accompanied by dried-out bottles of McIlhenny Tabasco sauce.

Miguel couldn't help shaking his head at what the gringos called hot sauce. To his taste it was as bland and sugary as catsup.

Except for a few bones scattered about, it seemed that rats and insects had cleaned up the leftovers. He supposed they had probably cleaned up whatever was left of the customers, too. His nostrils flared in anticipation of the smell, but three summers had probably petrified the remains. Pushing through the door of the main store, he sniffed and confirmed his suspicion. Dust and neglect and the faint iron tang imparted to human leavings by the mysterious action of the Wave were all that lingered.

"Sit," he ordered the dogs. "Outside," he added. They would not now enter the building without specifically being ordered to. He did not want them pawing through any of the human remains in there. It would be disrespectful. Like almost everyone in the post-Wave world Miguel had grown used to the sight of the Disappeared, but unlike some he had never allowed himself to forget that they had all been God's children, had possessed souls, and had left this world without the benefit of those blessings and rites with which all men should embark on their journey into the next life.

"I am just going to check it out," he called back to Sofia. "You keep a watch and come quickly to me if you see anyone approaching."

She nodded more emphatically than he had expected and moved to give herself a better view of the path they had taken from the edge of the forest into town.

Miguel stepped up off the road and onto the front porch, which creaked loudly under his boot. The sun was very low now and it was dark inside, forcing him to haul out his Maglite, which he held in one hand while sweeping the space with his saddle gun. A pair of black workman's boots, Levi's, a checked shirt, and a hat lay on the floor just in front of his feet. The clothes looked stiff and blackened. Moving into the shop, he found two more piles of clothing in the next aisle over. No, make that three. He missed the baby shawl on first glance. There would probably be another set of remains behind the counter, he imagined, but for now all that mattered was that the store was empty and safe.

He found a couple of kerosene lamps and after a few minutes had them going, giving him ample light. He quickly walked the aisles, noting what supplies they might take in the morning and what might be useful for the night. A sealed glass jar of beef jerky on the counter he scooped up immediately. It would do for the dogs. Peering behind the counter, he was surprised to find there were no human remains, but he did note a sealed trapdoor, which was good news. The canned food on the shelves of the store would probably be safe to eat even after three years. But it would have been exposed to high temperatures even with the climatic cooling they had experienced of late, and he had no wish to expose Sofia to the danger of food poisoning. If there was a good cellar, however, any stores down there would be fine.

This looked like a good point to lay up for the first night. He returned to the horses and was pleased to see Sofia keeping a watchful eye on their surroundings. She brought up the scope of her Remington every so often, sighting on something of interest before lowering the rifle. Her movements were rigid, somewhat machinelike. Miguel thought she was in shock, as he himself must certainly be. But there could be no question of coddling themselves until they had covered a safe distance. He began unloading the saddlebags.

"Sofia, you are doing very well, sweetheart. I need you to take the horses into the garden across the road. It is fenced off, and there is a small pond for them to drink. Can you do that while I unpack and set up?"

"Yes, Papa," she answered. She had always worked hard, and he trusted her to look after the horses properly, even as damaged as she was by the trauma of the day. He, too, had been forced to push through his own pain and distress, and he wondered when they might have a chance to simply settle down for a day or two and grieve for their loss. Sofia led all the animals through the deepening twilight into the garden he had indicated. The house there had burned down, but the fence line remained intact. Flossie tossed her head and insisted on leading her mates through the gate and into the knee-length grass.

"Blue Dog, Red, you, too," he ordered. Sofia whistled to the dogs, and they followed her happily. "Guard!" Miguel called out when they were inside the fence before throwing a handful of jerky strips over the gate. The dogs fell on the treat with great hunger. As Sofia tended to the horses, he gathered the saddlebags and returned to the general store.

Full darkness was upon them now, and the light from the kerosene lamps seemed much stronger than before. Miguel's stomach was rumbling with real hunger, and he set up a small gas-powered camp stove on one of the tables in the diner. He took his Maglite and returned to the main area of the shop, where he soon hauled up the trapdoor to the cellar behind the counter. It was pitch-black down there, requiring him to take both the torch and a lamp down the steep wooden steps. He had to stop halfway down and consciously push away the image of his family sitting down to dinner just the previous night. The shock of remembering was like a punch to the heart from an armored fist. He gritted his teeth and forced himself back into the present. There would be time for all that later. Right now he had his daughter to look after.

The cellar revealed itself to be well stocked, with enough canned and bottled goods to feed his family for a year.

He shook his head in disgust at his own weakness. How could he possibly control events over the next few weeks if he could not even control his own thoughts and feelings? He returned to the diner with a can of Dinty Moore beef stew and a can of Del Monte peaches. A few minutes on his camp stove and dinner was ready as Sophia arrived carrying her own saddlebags, her backpack, and her gun.

"Are you hungry?" Miguel asked.

"Sure," she said, showing very little emotion. "Thank you, Papa."

She joined him at the counter, where he had set up the small gas stove. She seemed less aware or possibly just less bothered by the remains of the Disappeared. The younger ones, he noticed, were like that. They seemed to accept what had happened with much greater ease than their elders were able to.

"I am sorry," she said, looking at Miguel. "I should be feeling something, but I can't. Is that wrong, Papa?"

Miguel felt as though his heart might burst from the pressure gathering around it. He took Sofia into his arms and held her close. To his surprise, she stiffened. His own tears came, but they were quiet, unlike Sofia's from earlier in the day. They blossomed in his eyes like small exquisite pearls of acid and burned as he burned.

He would grieve, but he would also have vengeance.

14

NEW YORK

A thorough skin care treatment and a small loss of dignity saved Julianne's life. Her hands had suffered terribly from the gang work, even with the heavy lined gloves she wore, and so, acting on advice from Jenny Janssen, one of the other women on the crew, she'd secured a bottle of Vaseline and a pair of vinyl gloves. Before laying herself down to sleep, Jules slathered the petroleum jelly all over her fingers and palms, which were so dry and cracked that they burned painfully at the first touch. She persevered, however, and soon had both hands so greased up that it was impossible to put on the gloves without smearing Vaseline all over the sheets. With a squish here and a squeegee there, both gloves went on and she was ready for bed.

As soon as she lay down, her nose began to run.

"Oh, bugger," she said irritably.

She plucked a tissue from the box by the bedside, blew her nose, and lay a fresh tissue on the pillow next to her as a precautionary measure. She hated the idea of lying on a snotty pillow and waking up looking like a glazed doughnut in the morning.

Off went the bedside light, and with her hot, greasy begloved hands at her side, Julianne finally laid her head down to sleep. But after a few minutes of lying on her back she turned over. Instantly, a searing pain shot through her right eye, and she sat up in bed, blinking wildly.

The tissue was caught inside the lid of her eye.

"Godshitfuckdamnshit!" she cried out, blinking rapidly to clear the obstruction but only dragging the corner of the Kleenex in deeper under her eyelid.

She tried to grab the tissue, but her hands were so clumsy with the greased-up gloves, she managed only to poke herself in the other eye, smearing Vaseline in there. Shrieking with frustration and pain, Jules tried again. She could only imagine what she looked like, sitting up in bed in a tattered pink Teletubby T-shirt, her tiny ponytail standing straight up on her head and greasy rubber-gloved hands yanking wildly at a Kleenex that was stuck inside one eyelid, flapping up and down on her face while she cursed up a storm.

"God shit fuck goddamn motherfucker!"

Not quite the queen of the seven seas image she'd cut as master and commander of the *Aussie Rules*. She smashed the bedside lamp while reaching blindly for it in the dark, tried to lever herself out of bed, and crashed to the floor when her slimy hands slipped on the dresser. Mercifully, the fall yanked out the tissue, and she stumbled to the bathroom, cursing again as she flicked on the light and got a look at her raw, red eyeballs in the mirror.

It took a long time to settle down after that, perhaps an hour. For a while, she sat gazing out of a dirt-smeared window at the Lower Manhattan skyline, which was dark for the most part with the silver wash of a full moon haunting the empty and occasionally burned-out skyscrapers. A flicker of tracer fire could be seen in the distance, but she could not place the exact location. After calming down, she returned to bed, where the fearful crash of artillery from the firebases on Governors Island sounded like a distant thunderstorm.

Her eyes, heavy-lidded and grainy sore, closed of their own accord as she recalled a party on the roof of a nearby building. The Rhino, Manny, and a bunch of private operators sitting around a barbecue grill smoking cigars and drinking high-end bourbon while the glowing artillery shells passed through the clouds with a brief lightning flash before traveling on to their targets. Helicopters of a dozen varieties hammered the night sky above, but soon Jules fell into sleep and the memory was lost to dreams.

She slept through her alarm, only waking to the sound of Rhino hammering on her door.

"Come, Miss Jules, your carriage awaits! And verily the driver is pissed!"

For the briefest moment she dreamed herself in a Cinderella world where a handsome horse-drawn buggy and a charming young prince did indeed await, but the Rhino's bellowing and hammering quickly ended that.

"Come on, they'll dock us a week's pay if we make them late," he yelled through the door somewhat more prosaically.

Julianne wondered groggily why he cared, given that salvage work was strictly a cover for them and the payday they'd get when they delivered the Rubin package back to Seattle would dwarf the money they were earning here.

A sharp, stunning discontinuity cut off her thoughts with a giant boom.

The dirt-smeared windows shattered and exploded into the room. Shrapnel whistled through the air, burying itself in the plaster walls, and pepper-black smoke rolled into the room as the building shuddered all the way to its foundations. The explosion shook the building so violently that she was seized with a fearful certainty that it would collapse around them. Jules tumbled from the edge of the bed onto the floor with the pillow over her head, falling painfully on a few broken shards of the lamp she had knocked over in the night.

The eruption began to subside, only to be followed by a barrage of smaller, sharper explosions she recognized as rocket fall. Burps of Gatling gun fire spit upward at the rockets from some improvised navy missile defense weapon on the roof. If they had any effect, Jules couldn't tell.

Memories of battles at sea came crowding in: a chromatic rush of images, remembered sounds, and foul smells and then a sudden tug of sorrow for the friends she had lost. All that passed in a twinkling as another explosion blew in the one remaining window. The heavy drapes protected her from flying glass but not from the remains of the broken lamp base, which fell heavily on her bare foot.

"Jules, you okay?" the Rhino yelled.

"I'm fine; stay out there. Dangerous," she called back as she frantically hauled herself into yesterday's filthy jeans, a difficult thing to do with slimy Vaseline hands. The Rhino kicked in the door anyway, and she looked up to find him staring at her, as confused by the bright pink latex gloves as by the attack on the Green Zone.

"Don't ask," she said tersely, stripping off the gloves and wiping her hands on the bedsheets. "What's going on outside? Pirates? A raid or something?"

The Rhino shrugged and then ducked instinctively as a rocket screamed in and detonated a few floors above them.

"This isn't some pissant little raid. They're blowing the shit out of us."

Jules nodded. It wasn't unusual for the occasional rocket or mortar round to come dropping into the Green Zone. That was why they had the navy guns on the roof: to catch some of that stuff. The freebooters did like to let Seattle know it wasn't getting the city back without a fight. But those attacks were small-scale and uncoordinated. This felt like they were being softened up for an invasion.

"I think our work here is done, Rhino," she said, hurriedly pulling on a pair of Carhartt work boots and a thick leather jacket. "Time to toddle off."

The floor bounced against the crump and blast of another

round striking the side of the building. Glass and debris fell past the shattered windows of Jules's room as the building creaked and groaned in a high-explosive maelstrom.

The Rhino didn't seem convinced. "You think so, in this weather?"

Jules picked out the first crackling pops of small arms fire under the din. If whoever was attacking was that close, then yes, it was time to go.

"I don't think we'll be going to work today," she called out over the racket. "Or anytime soon. This is it, Rhino. Time to be about our own business. Let's go. We'll need our bugout bags."

"Fine," he said. "Down on my floor."

Jules took a few seconds to retrieve the small package of documents she'd stashed in her room after studying it the previous night, but she grabbed nothing else. There was virtually no chance she would return to the hotel and that meant leaving a few personal items, but there was no choice. They had to move quickly.

Hastening down the narrow corridor, she was at least a little safer for a moment. Unless the pirates let off some massive bomb directly under the hotel that brought down the entire structure, they were afforded some protection by the internal walls. She ran right past the elevators and wrenched open the door to the fire escape. The Rhino's room was two floors down, and she took the steps three at a time, holding on to the handrail and swinging around at each landing. The sounds of battle outside reached them as hollow booms and thunder, occasionally transmitted right through the fabric of the building as a rocket or mortar bomb made a direct hit.

"This one," the Rhino called as they made his floor.

There was nobody there, either. She checked her watch. Everyone would have been waiting in the bus when the attack commenced, and that caused Jules a momentary pang of survivor guilt. Many of their fellow workers undoubtedly had died in the last few minutes. In fact, their buses may well have been the targets. Eight or nine of them were lined up each morning on Duane Street to ferry the crews out to whichever clearance site they'd be working that day. They made a nice, tightly bunched target.

"Here we go," said the Rhino, stopping not outside his room but in front of the little cupboard where the hotel guests had been able to obtain ice cubes in happier times. The space wasn't used for anything now, not officially, anyway. The Rhino reached in and stood on his toes to retrieve something from high up over the door lintel. With a jump and a grunt he dislodged two small black backpacks. Jules caught the one he tossed to her. It was heavy. She drew back the zipper and removed a strange-looking firearm.

"What the hell is this?" she asked, holding it up to inspect it. The rear half of the gun was effectively a solid block, and the grip at the front was formed from a series of dark metal curlicues, giving it an overall appearance of something alien and wrong. It was obviously a weapon but unlike any she had ever fired.

A look of irritation crossed her face. "I asked you to get us some guns, not a bag of bloody Dr. Who props."

The Rhino allowed himself a guilty smile, removing a clone of the weapon from his own backpack.

"These are mil-spec P90s, Miss Julianne. I picked 'em up cheap, swapped 'em for those food vouchers we scored back in KC. Look here." He tucked the buttstock in against his left shoulder and swept the empty hallway with the muzzle. Jules bit down on her frustration as the barely muffled sounds of battle raged on outside.

"It was designed for support troops by the Belgians, you know, the rear echelon fucks. It's got fully ambidextrous operation," the Rhino said. "Bullpup configuration. Fifty-round mag. Specialized ammo, of which I have an elegant sufficiency, believe me, with much better lethal range, a flatter trajectory, and greater penetration against body armor than—"

"Okay, okay, I can feel the fucking love." She shook her bag up and down, pulling out an equipment vest filled with magazines and a set of black body armor. She set the weapon down and shrugged into the vest, nodding toward Rhino's weapon. "Where's the selector switch?"

He held up his own weapon and pointed out a dial under the trigger.

"You're safe in the S position. One is semi. A is full auto," he explained. "On full rock 'n' roll you have a two-stage pull. Semiauto on the half pull. Then you blow your whole wad with a full squeeze."

"Got it," she said, Velcroing the equipment vest into place. She hefted the unusual weapon a few times to get the feel of it. Despite its bizarre appearance, it did sit very comfortably in her grip.

"Take this and snap it on," said the Rhino, handing her a length of black piping.

Jules scrutinized the pipe. "Flash suppressor?"

"Nope. Well, sorta. But mostly for sound suppression," he corrected her. "P90's already a good deal quieter than, say, an M4. This makes it even stealthier. I'm guessing we'll be sneaking out of here today."

"Yes." She sighed as a heavy automatic weapon started grinding through hundreds of rounds somewhere below them. "Anything you need from your room?"

"Got everything I need right here," he said, nodding at his backpack as he snapped on his silencer. Soon his body armor and oversized equipment vest were in place, leaving his massive biceps exposed for a quick kiss.

"Did I ever tell that you that you don't get these pettin' kitty cats?" He grinned, before sticking an unlit cigar between his teeth.

Jules rolled her eyes as she slipped her arms through the backpack straps and they trotted back to the fire escape. The angry sounds of combat seemed to have settled into something like a rhythm beyond the walls of the hotel, a steady pounding of heavier weapons overlaying short, spasmodic gusts of small arms fire, single-shot three-round bursts, and the regular snarls of somebody letting off whole clips. That would most likely be the attackers, she thought.

The militia and private operators protecting the Green Zone had better fire discipline than that. A pity their professionalism didn't extend to properly securing the perimeter.

The lights in the stairwell flickered briefly as they entered, but only once. Nonetheless, the two smugglers picked up their pace as they made the long climb down past the ground floor and into the service levels, where they hoped they could make their exit. Jules expected to run into drug-fucked pirates at any moment, and once or twice they did hear doors opening and slamming closed above them, but they enjoyed a clear run all the way down. It was only when she carefully pushed open the door on the lower ground floor that they ran into trouble. Two rounds slammed into the wall next to her, sending hot chips of cement into her face.

"Damn it," she cried out. "It's Jules and the Rhino. Who the fuck's out there?"

A pause followed before a shaky voice called back, "It's me, Ryan Dubois. Julesy, is that you?"

She shook her head angrily and yelled at the door.

"Of course it's me, you wanker. I just told you that. Who the hell did you think you were shooting at?"

The door opened a crack as Dubois nervously peered through.

"I thought you were pirates, sorry. I heard they got inside the hotel. Lewis told me to stay down here and keep an eye on the service levels. Gave me this."

He almost waved the chrome .38 special in her face, but the Rhino reached over with one giant paw and pushed the muzzle down firmly but gently.

"Guns don't kill people, Ryan," he said in soft tones, taking the unlit cigar from his mouth to make his point. "Stupidity does. And Rhinos of course. Rhinos are always killing people. Especially stupid ones."

"You said Lewis sent you down here," Jules cut in. "So he's still alive?"

Ryan looked worried, and his shrug was more of a nervous tic than an answer.

"I hope so. He told me to stay here until he came and got me. But I really don't want to stay here. D' you think I could come with you? This place is giving me the creeps."

Jules pushed past him, careful not to get in the way of his pistol, which did not have a safety. The hallway outside the fire escape was poorly lit, with only every third fluorescent tube powered up, and one of them was flickering erratically. Shadows appeared to twitch and shiver organically in the crawl space between stacks of cardboard boxes and laundry carts. The thunder of guns and rockets was muffled to a dull rumble by the concrete foundation. Ryan fell in behind them as the two smugglers cautiously advanced down the subterranean corridor, sweeping the space in front of them, ready to lay fire on any sort of danger.

"So, umm, can I tag along?" he chirped.

"No," they answered in unison.

Jules could sense him walking behind them, anyway. She was annoyed, but Ryan was the least of her concerns at the moment. They had no idea what they were walking into, how many pirates might be out there, in what numbers, or even what their intentions might be. A punitive raid? An attempt to overrun the Green Zone? And what was the militia doing? Or, more important, the private ops, the mercenaries. Most of them had left the zone after securing it, but she knew at least two dozen or more still remained, and she feared them more than any freebooter. The mercs had a reputation for using way more firepower than was ever really warranted, which was why Lewis Graham had insisted on keeping some of them around well after this part of Manhattan had been cleared.

"So it stays cleared," he always said.

Or he used to. Jules wondered if he was still running around somewhere upstairs.

"Ryan," she said, coming to a halt outside a storeroom.

"Uh, yeah?"

"Tell me exactly what happened this morning."

He made a show of searching his memories. "Well, I got up early to make sure I scored some flapjacks because those bastards from the third-floor crew are always scarfing the lot down and—"

"Christ," Rhino said under his breath.

Julianne rubbed at her sore and tired eyes, pulling her hand away when she felt the sting of Vaseline again.

"No. Not what happened at the breakfast buffet. Tell us about the attack. What you remember of that."

The Rhino watched the corridor while Julianne encouraged Ryan to focus.

"Were you out at the bus queue when the raiders hit?"

"No," he said, shaking his head with apparent regret. "No. 'Fraid I was on the crapper. Somebody left a copy of the Seattle papers in the dining room, and I was reading the sports pages from the *P-I*. I had a bet on the Royals-Mariners game, and the radio reception was pretty bad."

The Rhino piped in. "Tell me you did not bet on the Royals."

"I did," Ryan said, almost indignant. "Someone told me they won the World Series once."

"They did," the Rhino said. "Back in '85."

"Oh," Ryan said.

"Fuck me," Jules said heatedly. "Would anyone like to chat about the fucking cricket, perhaps? Good! Stay with me here, Ryan. The attack. It started while you were in the bathroom?"

"Oh, yeah," he said, looking abashed. "Lucky thing. I'd a been toast otherwise. I saw those buses, man, when I came out. They got opened like fucking tin cans, eh?"

"And the militia. And the private operators, what about them?"

Ryan shrugged. "Well you know the routine, Jules. There was probably some of them out at the bus line, just keeping things running. But I guess they got blown up, too."

"Did you go out there, to check?"

"No," Ryan continued. "When I knew what was happening, I started running for my room. But Mister Graham, he caught me and gave me this gun, told me to get down here and stand guard."

The Rhino, who was stealing energy bars from a nearby stack of cardboard cartons, stopped for a second.

"Was Lewis hurt, Ryan?"

The boy shrugged. "Well, duh. He was out with the buses when the rockets hit. Dude was covered in blood. One arm kind of limp and all."

Julianne exchanged a look with the Rhino.

"Sounds like we got caught bent over and pants down."

The Rhino grunted in disgust.

"You would have thought after yesterday they'd have had extra security on. Worked the perimeter harder. Always said that Graham asshole was as worthless as tits on a bull."

Jules began moving again, headed toward a heavy steel door shrouded in darkness at the end of the hallway.

"Well, to be fair, Rhino, they could have dropped mortars on us from well outside the zone."

He conceded the point with a barely perceptible lift of the shoulders.

"Suppose so. They did control this part of town for a long time. Could have prefigured the mortars before they had to give it up. Doesn't sound like any fucking pirates I ever met, though. Their idea of forward planning generally doesn't even extend to checking they got enough paper to wipe their asses before takin' a shit."

Jules nodded as they reached the door. Pressing her ear to the cool steel, she could hear the fighting only distantly.

"Ryan." She put her hand on his chest. "Do not follow us. It will end badly for you."

The Rhino took up a firing position to cover her as she heaved on the horizontal steel bar that opened the door.

15

NEW YORK

"Jesus wept, this just gets better and better, doesn't it?"

Kipper peered through the cracked and heavily grimed window on the second floor of the U.S. Custom House. He could feel his Secret Service detail fidgeting with barely suppressed anxiety behind him. He supposed he shouldn't rile them by exposing himself to danger or even the chance of danger, but from what he could tell, all the action was uptown from their current hiding place. And that's what it was, a hiding place. Agent Shinoda had tucked him away in the massive stone pile of the old customs building that overlooked Battery Park and Bowling Green at the very bottom of Broadway. It was a beautiful building to Kip's eye. Even though it had stood empty and neglected for nearly four years, the lines of the hundred-year-old architecture spoke to that rare and perfect balance of form and function that engineers thought of as elegant. To Kipper, there was no higher praise one could afford a human-made structure.

His appreciation of the old girl was soured, however, by the evidence he could see of the conflagration unfolding up near the

Tribeca area, where many of the clearance crews he'd visited just yesterday were housed. The sun had risen a few hours ago, and with the day came the roar of an explosion that signaled what looked like the start of a small war. And it was a war, he supposed, even if they weren't fighting another country. At least not openly. He'd seen plenty of classified intelligence that clearly incriminated a host of foreign states in supporting the pirates, whether to profit from their raids or simply to kick back against an old enemy. What was that old Arab saying? A falling horse attracts many knives. Or was it a camel?

Black oily clouds climbed high into the air above the city, and although the fighting was some distance way, he could hear and even feel it occasionally.

"Mister President. Time to go, sir. Chopper's on final approach."

"Thank you, Agent Shinoda," he said, turning away from the depressing vista.

Jed was standing mournfully behind him, a sheaf of papers clutched loosely in one hand. An army officer with a black embroidered bird on one collar stood by him. The name tape above his breast pocket read kinninmore. A cavalryman's patch on one shoulder took the form of a shield with a black stripe topped in one corner by the head of a horse.

Kip was still on a steep learning curve with all things military, and even with a radically smaller defense force, he still found himself lost more often than not in a forest of acronyms, units, and ranks. The cavalry patch he recognized immediately, however. The cav had made a big comeback as the army's glamour outfit the last few years, if by glamour one meant they got to fight and die more often than anyone else.

The officer ripped out a parade ground salute even though he looked like he'd just crawled through a few miles of dust, blood, and thornbush. Kipper acknowledged his salute, and Jed Culver made the introduction.

"This is Colonel Alois Kinninmore, Mister President. From the

Seventh Cavalry Regimental Combat Team. They flew in here last night to crack a few heads together over at the airport, but he's... ah... well, I guess I'll let him explain. Colonel."

"Thank you, sir," said Kinninmore. Kipper had expected a ferocious bark to go with the salute, but Kinninmore was soft spoken with a very polished Bostonian accent. "Mister President?"

"Go ahead, Colonel, but walk with us if you would. I suspect Agent Shinoda will have kittens if I don't get my ass down to the helicopter in time."

"Of course, sir."

The small party of men—Kipper, Jed, Colonel Kinninmore, and half a dozen Secret Service agents in black coveralls and body armor—formed up in a loose group and moved out into the corridor, a long, dimly lit but strikingly beautiful hallway finished in white marble.

"Major tactical ops at the airport are mostly done with, Mister President," said Kinninmore. "We're just counting coup on the stragglers now."

"That went pretty quick, Colonel. Did you lose many of your men?"

"Our casualties were twelve killed and fifteen wounded, sir."

Kipper knew, because he had been told time and again, that fighting in urban environments chewed through men at a terrible rate. But a dozen dead and even more wounded still sounded like a heavy butcher's bill. He would have many letters to write when he got back to Seattle. He made it a point to contact the families of any serviceman or -woman who died following his orders. Culver argued that he could delegate that to others, but Kipper insisted in spite of the increasing amount of time he spent writing such letters and the emotional cost it laid on him. It was the very least he could do.

"I'm sorry to hear that, Colonel. I really am. I'd like to come visit your wounded if I could, as soon as possible."

"Thank you, sir. They will appreciate that."

The party passed by a pair of heavy wooden doors standing open to reveal what looked like a courtroom inside. Kinninmore, who was striding alongside Kipper with a helmet tucked under one arm, seemed oblivious to their surroundings as they turned again and hurried down a wide, sweeping marble staircase and past a sign that informed them they were entering the museum level of the building.

"I'm pulling three troops from the Seventh along with two marine companies and redeploying them here, Mister President. Immediately. We should have them here within the hour."

"Three troops?" Kipper asked.

"My apologies, Mister President," Kinninmore said. "Company elements; we call them troops in the cavalry... er, about three hundred men. With the Marines, we should have close to a battalion-size force here."

More terminology. Kipper let it go and nodded for him to continue. He made a point of not interfering with the military's decisions in the field.

"The thing is, sir, I believe there could be something more going on than the looters and pirates simply pushing back at you for trying to retake the city. The elements we fought at the airport were well coordinated, and when we arrived in force, they pretty much melted away. Conducted quite a decent withdrawal under fire and would have got a lot more of their guys out if we hadn't had air support to smack them flat."

Kip had a momentary vision of what that last euphemism would mean in reality: hundreds of bodies torn asunder by high explosives and white-hot metal. He pushed the images away as they marched along a curving corridor flanked by wood-paneled displays of Native American artifacts, feathered headdresses, buffalo-hide shields, tomahawks, and jewelry, all of them still intact. Thick blue carpet muffled their footfalls, and Kip could not help but notice that it was discolored here and there with the dark, telltale stains of the Disappeared. He almost wondered for half a second when their remains had been cleared away but forced himself to stay focused on Colonel Kinninmore.

"My S-2 got out and policed up the battlespace, sir…"

S-2? Was that an intelligence officer? The army has all of these confusing codes for everything. And whatever happened to plain old battlefields? Kipper was pretty sure the colonel meant this his intelligence officer had quickly inspected the remains of the dead and whatever entrenchments they may have occupied.

"…and I have to say we had a few disturbing finds," Kinninmore went on. "Especially in light of the rocket attack on yourself yesterday, sir. Those Katyushas weren't the usual dime-store crap—if you'll excuse me, sir—that you normally find the pirates using. Intel says they were fresh out of the shrink-wrap from Yemen. And the enemy combatants we cleared out of JFK, they were using good new Russian radios and Chinese assault rifles. Type 56 carbines. We also discovered well-concealed command and control bunkers with medical facilities and housing for a larger force."

Kip thought he saw where Kinninmore was going.

"You're surely not thinking conspiracy, Colonel? China's barely a functioning state after the civil war. And Putin's got his hands full with the stans."

The cavalry officer shook his head.

"No, Mister President. Or at least I'm not positing a conspiracy between those states. The Type 56 carbines could have come from what's left of Pakistan or a number of other countries. My point is that the matériel was top-shelf stuff. And it has to be significant that it should suddenly appear, all at the same time, in our eastern theater of operations while the raiders, who spend as much time fighting each other as they do us, suddenly smarten up and start kicking it with battalion-level operations, all coordinated with the best comms gear you can buy on the open market."

Kipper agreed with the officer that it did sound significant. But in what way?

"You've got my attention, Colonel. But do you have anything more in the way of detail? Something other than the equipment and… well, behavorial change? People do learn, after all."

"They do, Mister President. They do. Places like New York, they learn or they die. What I want to know is who's been teaching them. We took a handful of prisoners at Kennedy. Most of them pretty messed up, but we're doing our best to debrief them as soon as possible."

Kipper could imagine that debriefing would not be a pleasant experience for the captives. He'd long ago authorized the army to treat any pirates captured on U.S. soil as illegal combatants. The best they could hope for was immediate deportation, but summary execution was just as likely. Kinninmore, for all his Boston Brahmin airs, did not look like a man who would lose a lot of sleep if he had to execute a bunch of glorified looters, which in the end was all the pirates were.

"The thing is, Mister President," the army officer continued, "I don't think everyone we're fighting right now are simple pirates."

Kipper almost did an exaggerated double take at having had his private thoughts contradicted immediately.

"Go on," he said.

"We're also getting some intelligence back from Ellis Island, where the rocket attack was launched from…"

Kinninmore flicked the briefest glare of disapproval at Kip's Secret Service detail before carrying on.

"…and what we're hearing is that there's some new guys working the city. Professionals. I mean real pros, not just the organized gangs from Russia and so on. These new guys are rallying the pirate gangs and paying them off with tribute and turf."

"Any idea who?" asked Kipper.

"Early days, sir. But it doesn't sound good. Some of the prisoners referred to them as fedayeen. Some called them jihadi."

Kipper's nuts did a slow crawl up into his body.

He was unfamiliar with the first word, but he well remembered the term "jihad" both from the days before the Wave and of course from the French civil war that had followed it.

"What are those fucking wing nuts doing here?" he asked.

Kinninmore shook his head as they reached the foyer of the building. The sound of helicopters was growing louder.

"Mister President, at the moment all I have are the first scraps of information from a very confused battlefield. I can't tell you any more than that. What I can say is that this does not look like a flare-up or an ad hoc resistance movement suddenly self-organizing. It looks to me like somebody who knows what they are doing is pissing in our patch."

Kipper found the colonel's vernacular a strange fit with his cultured accent, but he supposed that Kinninmore must have spent his adult life in the army and so it would be silly to expect him to speak like a merchant banker or art dealer. He stopped just inside the building's entrance, and gave the officer his full attention.

"Colonel, I remind myself every day to listen to people who know what they're talking about. If you feel strongly enough about this to have dragged yourself through the briar patch getting the information to me, I am willing to listen. Right now, though, at this very minute, we have people fighting and dying a few miles from us. First person I'm going to talk to when I get on my chopper is General Franks. I'm going to tell him to devote whatever resources he needs to clearing this city out, once and for all. This is an American city, and it is going to stay that way," Kipper said.

"Hooah," Kinninmore replied in soft but firm agreement.

Kipper continued, "I need you to write me up a report on what you've just told us and forward it directly to Franks as well as your local higher-ups on my authority. I'll have the national security director schedule it as one of our first agenda items for our next meeting, which is…"

He looked across at Jed.

"Three days from now, Mister President."

"Okay, three days. Is that good enough, Colonel?"

Kinninmore straightened his back and nodded. "Very well, Mister President. My S-2 has already prepped a report, with attachments. I will have him e-mail it to you via secure link ASAP."

"Good enough, then," Kipper said, extending his hand. "Colonel. Good luck. Kicking these losers out of New York is a higher priority for me right now than knowing exactly who they are. But I do want to know that, too. And make sure Jed gets details of where your wounded are being treated. I will be visiting them."

"Thank you, Mister President."

Kinninmore saluted again, looking marginally happier than when Kip had first seen him but still very grim as he replaced the helmet on his head. If they were going to be fighting in the city to the end, he was going to lose many more troopers. A thumping roar announced the arrival of *Marine One,* Kip's personal chopper, now finished with evacuating casualties from the rocket attack. The Secret Service agents formed up around them, and Kipper was hustled out into the morning air, where oil smoke, dark and thick, obscured the sun and left a burning sensation in his nose.

Sergeant Ryan Peckham of the Marine Presidential Security Detail ripped off a perfect salute. "Good day, Mister President. If you'll step aboard, please."

Kipper returned the salute, still a sloppy one, he supposed, but Sergeant Peckham took no notice. The president of the United States passed by Peckham's younger brother, Lance Corporal Justin Peckham, who was standing at the ready behind a multibarreled door gun on *Marine One.* It intrigued Kip why two brothers had ended up on his chopper, but he had never had time to ask them about it.

Many things had changed since the Wave, and *Marine One* was a perfect example. No longer a brightly polished dark green and white VH-3D Sea King helicopter emblazoned with the presidential seal, Kipper's rotary wing transport was now a gray, camouflaged, and heavily armed AugustaWestland medium-lift chopper, a joint British-Italian design. The Royal Air Force had fitted out six for his use as part of a complicated facilities and equipment exchange deal negotiated under the new Vancouver Alliance agreement. Climbing aboard, he found the cabin was still configured for medical evacuation, with only four seats available up near the cockpit. It was difficult to hear himself talk over the thunderous noise not just of his aircraft but from the three gunships hovering protectively overhead. As he strapped in, Jed Culver dropped into the seat opposite and raised an eyebrow but said nothing, either. Between the Super Cobras of the *Marine One* escort force and the howling engine over their heads, it was simply too noisy to speak until they were under way.

That took less than a minute, and when they lifted off, Kip felt himself pressed into the seat much more firmly than usual. The floor tilted radically, and the Rolls Royce turboshafts spooled up with a scream. The marines flying him out of New York were not inclined to take chances. They were another sign of the radically changed times. Three marine Super Cobras flew escort for *Marine One* no matter where the president went. The marines themselves were no longer attired in the smart dress uniforms and white gloves of their counterparts back in Seattle. All of the flight crew's members wore desert tan flight suits and came with a heavy load of personal weapons. Members of the Presidential Marine Security Detail wore body armor, standing at the ready by doors and window apertures that bristled with heavy machine guns. When they were safely away and the noise had throttled back some, Kip leaned over to speak to his chief of staff.

"Jed, can you make sure Tommy Franks gets that stuff from Kinninmore? Especially this fedayeenie-whatsit business. Today."

"Fedayeen. And it's already done," Culver said, smiling tightly and waving his mil-grade PDA. "I've scheduled it as an item for discussion at NSC. Second on the list."

"What's first?" Kip asked, wondering what could squeeze out a report of possible foreign interference in the pirate war.

"Well, I'm afraid you're not going to like it, sir, but we do need to get to grips with this Blackstone situation."

Always back to Blackstone. Kip could feel his facial muscles tighten with anger as Jed held up one hand and begged his indulgence.

"I know, Mister President, that you think it's near the bottom of the priority list, and having him down there running wild means fewer federal resources going into border security along the El Paso," Jed said.

"Look, I don't like Mad Jack any more than you do, Jed. But he *was* elected. And you may have noticed that we are a bit short of resources," Kip said.

Even Tommy Franks had pestered him about the importance of controlling the center of the continent, which was part of why there was a heavy federal outpost in Kansas City. But in Kip's eyes Texas just didn't seem worth the aggravation, regardless of what the history books and his own advisers said. If Blackstone wanted to play out some frontier fantasy down there, let him have it. For now. He was still an American. He'd been voted into the governorship fair and square. As big an asshole as he was proving to be, he was a duly elected asshole and that was that. It wasn't like a foreign state had set up shop down there.

"Sir," said Culver, undaunted as usual. "We have to start looking at Blackstone as a major impediment to reconstruction a few years down the path. If we don't get this little dictator slapped into line, we are going to lose control of the South forever. He's not making any bones about that."

"The whole Republic of Texas thing is a joke," Kipper said. "I've been reading up on your briefings. They weren't able to make it work in the 1830s, and I do not see how they'll make it work now. Blackstone can bluster on about holding as many referendums as he wants. Nobody outside of Fort Hood is going to vote to break up the union."

Jed leaned forward in his seat. "It's 'referenda,' and it is no joke, Mister President. Jackson Blackstone *was* legitimately elected territorial governor in 2005, which makes it very difficult for us to challenge his position. It's not like that last little coup by stealth he tried after the Wave. What's more, he has plenty of allies in Seattle who would like to see Texas fast-tracked to independence. The reality on the ground, as the military likes to say, is that neither Blackstone nor his territorial legislature respects the authority of Congress or you, or the courts, or anything other than the threat of the 101st jumping in there to smack him upside the head. And sir, we are getting to a point where I doubt the army will be able to do it. For every officer we have like Kinninmore, Blackstone has three, and for every solid soldier we have, Blackstone has anywhere from three to seven, most of them disgruntled veterans."

"I don't understand why they're so disgruntled," Kipper said morosely. He didn't understand at all, on any level, why so many former members of the U.S. Armed Forces had gone down to Blackstone's self-styled Republic of Texas. Kip was taking care of their health needs and providing them with preferential hiring privileges and free education in a society that did not have much time for such things these days. They got fast-track placements into both the urban and regional resettlement programs. They were exempt from the various compulsory labor laws, yet they *still* went to Texas. Meanwhile, those who stayed under the federal banner often took advantage of the benefits while supporting the rump Republicans, which was a real kick in the head. Not all of them, by any means, but a sufficient number to inflame his acid reflux on a daily basis.

"Different dreams," said his chief of staff in answer to Kip's question. "We haven't offered them a better one. Blackstone has. He is growing and hardening his forces, Mister President, and if you'll excuse me pushing the metaphor perhaps a tad too far, we are gonna get fucked because of it."

Kipper couldn't help but smile in spite of the sense of frustration that welled up as a bilious taste at the back of his throat whenever he was forced to give due consideration to the antics of Jackson Blackstone. Jed would not let this dog lie, and Kipper supposed he would one day have to thank him for that, but right at the moment, the renegade former general turned politician and his Southern political machine were hardly a more pressing issue than the small war that apparently had broken out in the city below them.

He stole a quick glance out of the small window to his left and shook his head at the dismal scene of a large part of Manhattan shrouded in smoke and flames, with the flash of bomb bursts and rockets clearly visible in the dark gray canyons below midtown as long sparkling chains of yellow and green tracer fire lashed up from street level.

The door guns opened up, spewing a stream of red light down on the city, spattering their rounds against the streets. Lucifer tearing the curtains of Hell came to Kipper's mind as the brass tinkled away from *Marine One*. Riflemen took their positions at the rear of the cabin, opening the windows to get a clear shot at whatever might try to kill them. Kipper saw Corporal Peckham swivel his door gun as his brother directed the rest of the detail over his headset.

"RPG! Evasive!" one of the riflemen roared.

Kipper gripped his armrest as the chopper dipped and dropped to the right so suddenly that his stomach felt as though he'd left it a few hundred feet higher up. The door gunner opened up again on an unknown target beneath them, and he caught a black flash out of the corner of his eye as one of the Super Cobras screamed away to lay fire on whatever had caused them to maneuver so violently. The machine gun fire cut off abruptly, and he felt the chopper settle into a new heading that took them directly away from the island. Both Kip and Jed were used to the extremes of flying out of contested airspace, and neither man bothered to check with the air crew. For their part, the crew did not interrupt the presidential party, in line with orders Kipper had issued long ago to just get on with their jobs and not waste time briefing him on every little scare and mishap during flight.

Marine One powered higher above the Manhattan skyline until they were well out of reach of everything short of a decent surface-to-air missile. The marine detail eased back from the windows and returned to their seats, allowing Kipper to refocus on Jed. He sighed heavily, trying to gather his thoughts. It was more a protracted grunt of annoyance, really, and he rubbed his eyes, which were hot and gritty with a lack of sleep.

"Why, Jed? Why now?" he asked over the ringing in his ears from the gunfire. "Don't you think I have enough on my plate out here without starting another fight down South? Mad Jack *loves* it when I get on his case. He fucking lives for it."

Culver reached into a briefcase on the floor between his legs. It was a battered old brown leather satchel that he carried with him everywhere, and Kip was certain it must be a relic of his former life as an attorney. It was out of character, because Jed Culver was a man who even now dressed in only the finest clothes and still wore expensive aftershave, but in Kip's experience most people liked to keep something of the old days close to them, and he assumed that the briefcase was a talisman of sorts for his chief of staff.

Jed passed across an unmarked manila folder that Kip opened to find three sheets of paper and a couple of poorly focused low-res color photos. The printout was a long list of place names and dates followed by notations that made little sense to Kipper. The first read:

- Baker Lake/Madison/14-March-07/Pieraro/TDF- Bravo 2/14.../13CC

"I'm sorry, Jed. What does all this mean?"

Jed tapped the top of the sheet Kipper was holding.

"What it means, Mister President, in the first case there, for instance, is that soldiers from Bravo Company, Second Infantry Battalion of the Texas Defense Force, entered the property of one of our homesteaders, a Miguel Pieraro, three months ago. There they found fourteen members of the Pieraro clan dead. Killed by bandits, according to the TDF report. The state authorities then seized the property and reallocated it to their own settler program under the agreement we signed with them to ensure the Federal Mandates did not lie fallow."

Kipper found himself grinding his teeth together. He felt a sick sort of anger curling tightly in his stomach.

"Bandits, they reckon? And three months ago?" Kipper asked. "Why so long to let us know?"

Culver shrugged. "Travel time required to get the dispatches back to Corpus Christi, according to Fort Hood."

"Bullshit."

"Of course."

Kipper fought to get his temper under control. He looked at the name on the file again. Pieraro. It didn't ring a bell, but he did recall a clear blue day more than two years ago on the deck of an aircraft carrier filled with homesteaders down at Corpus Christi. The photo op included pressing the flesh and handing out warrants for homesteads throughout Texas. A delegation from Fort Hood had been there, watching the ceremony and promising that they would protect the new homesteaders. Governor Blackstone had been notably absent.

"Want in one hand, shit in the other," Kipper muttered.

"What's that, Mister President?" Jed asked.

"Never mind. The fourteen dead homesteaders. Was that all of them?"

"No, sir. Pieraro himself and one of his children, a girl called Sofia, were not found. That doesn't tell us anything, though."

Kipper examined the sheet of paper again. There were dozens of entries, some with subtle differences that he picked up after a moment. He held the report up to Jed, pointing at a word he didn't understand.

"What does 'ivet' mean?"

"Involuntary transfer," Jed replied. "Deportation. The Pieraro homestead was attacked and emptied out by bandits, according to Fort Hood. But some of those other cases detail settlers in the Federal Mandate who've been evicted by Texas Defense Force personnel on Blackstone's orders. Usually citing disagreements over the extent of the Mandate."

Kipper felt a world-class headache sharpening itself up for an assault on his skull. He rubbed his forehead irritably, continuing to read the report. "And K.I.T.O.P.?"

"Killed in transfer operation," Jed said flatly.

That sick bilious taste was rising in his gorge again. "I see. And when did we get this information?" the president asked.

Culver essayed an apologetic dip of the head.

"I've been on at the FBI to collate the figures for about five months now, sir. They have a field office in Corpus Christi, but as you can imagine, it is understaffed, overwhelmed, and mainly dedicated to fraudulent salvage contracts. They finally put someone on this full-time when we got confirmation of the first kitops."

Kipper frowned at the ugly acronym.

"Murder," he said. "The first murders, you mean."

Culver nodded at the photographs behind the printout. "A bureau agent managed to get coverage of a transfer in progress just outside a town called Groveton in Trinity County."

Kip examined the photographs properly for the first time, and his face twisted into a contorted mask of disgust. The images were poor, probably shot from a great distance, but there was no mistaking the story they told. A small group of men, women, and children were being beaten by a larger number of uniformed men. One of the photos appeared to show one of the victims being shot.

"Jesus H. Christ," he breathed. "How extensive is... this..."

Words failed him, and he simply waved the folder at Culver.

"We're still compiling data, sir. And you have to remember that we don't control the south any more than we control Manhattan. Less so in some ways because we're not challenging Blackstone down there like we are challenging these bastards up here."

Kipper ignored the tone of rebuke that Jed had allowed to creep into his delivery.

"But as best we can tell," Culver continued, "over six hundred of our homesteaders have been driven off their land. Only a hundred and twelve have made it back to a federal facility. Now," Culver added hurriedly, "that doesn't mean the TDF killed them. Texas in particular is crawling with genuine bandits and freebooters. There's also the road agents, outlaw gangs, but the FBI believes they are operating with the tacit assistance of Fort Hood. Chances are that most of our people fell afoul of these agents. But it is undeniable that there have been instances where lethal force has been used by the TDF when transfer was resisted. And as terrified as the refugees were of the TDF, they were even more frightened of any encounters with the road agents."

Kipper pressed his lips together and took a moment to calm himself. He gazed around the cabin, taking in the crouched, watchful posture of Corporal Peckham at his door gun and nodding to Agent Shinoda, who was drinking from a water bottle while hanging on to a grab bar near the marines at the back of *Marine One*.

"Lets not dress it up any fancier than need be," he said, turning his attention back to Jed Culver. "Lethal force, involuntary transfer. It's all bullshit, Jed. We're talking about murder and ethnic cleansing. And you're right. I'm sorry. We do need to do something about it."

16

SALISBURY PLAIN, ENGLAND

The large faded yellow and red poster read: warning to the public. danger from unexploded shell and mortar bombs. The words in the middle of the sign were faded beyond legibility, but the last sentence, it may explode, didn't leave much room for doubt that a world of hurt lay around them. The effect was lessened by the pole to which the poster was affixed leaning over at thirty degrees, creating a definite air of neglect, but Caitlin could hear the distant thud of munitions and, occasionally, when Dalby's little car crested a ridgeline, she could make out the dark, heavy shapes of armored vehicles maneuvering through the mist and rain in the distance. Some of them were still painted desert tan, most likely former U.S. Army Abrams and Bradley tanks given to Britain as collateral for her matériel support since the Wave. A mountain of U.S. military equipment and more than a few personnel to maintain and operate it had been "permanently loaned" to a handful of allies in a variation of the lend-lease arrangements from World War II. Although the signage appeared to be neglected, Salisbury Plain itself was alive with thousands of troops training in the wet, filthy conditions.

Dalby didn't spare the warning sign a glance as he sped along the winding country road. They had seen dozens of such posters since entering the restricted military area but Dalby appeared to know his way around, skirting temporary roadblocks and turning down laneways and roads in defiance of the direst warnings.

"Do you come through here a lot, then, Mr. Dalby?" Caitlin asked.

"The last few years, yes, Ms. Monroe. And I spent a lot of time here as a young squaddie many, many years ago. It's a miserable place, truth be known. But convenient."

She nodded in an abstract way, staring at the fresh brown scars of tank tracks that crisscrossed a gently sloping hill to their left. She'd seen paratroopers drop onto a similar rise from a flight of C-17s shortly after they'd entered the Plain an hour earlier and had immediately thought of her husband, who had once run around jumping out of perfectly good aircraft for a living, perhaps even around this very part of the countryside. Her anger flared again. Bret had done a great job protecting Monique, but he had been very badly injured in doing so, losing half of one finger to a bullet and sustaining a fracture from the impact of another bullet on his right leg, along with a badly chipped elbow and a broken wrist from where he'd fallen and rolled. It was a mercy that Monique had come through unscathed, but a cold fury still washed over Caitlin when she thought about how it so easily could have turned out differently. Thinking of Monique, she suddenly realized how heavy and painful her breasts felt, the awareness arriving along with an unexpected moment of grief. She knew she would not be seeing either of them very soon, possibly not for weeks.

She would never breast-feed her daughter again.

She pressed her lips together tightly and stared out the window, trying to disconnect herself from any feelings that might dull her edge or distract her. Grief and mourning were not what her family needed.

"Dear me, here comes some 'appy campers, then," Dalby muttered as they rounded a blind corner and found themselves driving toward the rear of a double file of soldiers, heads down, tramping along the roadway in the cold rain. Dalby slowed and eased over to the side of the road, keeping a few feet of clearance between them. The troops were on Caitlin's side of the car, and she tried not to stare openly at them as they inched past. There looked to be about two platoons' worth of riflemen carrying a mix of SA-80s and M16s, most of them very young, very wet, and very, very disenchanted with the world.

"Conscripts, I'll wager," Dalby said. "Probably first few weeks in by the look of them."

She nodded without comprehension. They did look young, but apart from that, why they'd be draftees rather than volunteers was beyond her. She assumed Dalby had an eye for such things, however, having been there himself.

"And this'll be the slave driver in chief." He grinned, as another young man, tall and seeming to revel in the unpleasant conditions, peeled away from the head of the column and stepped into the roadway in front of them, holding up his hand. The other men kept trudging forward.

"Pass me the clipboard, would you, Ms. Monroe?" Dolby asked as they pulled up alongside the officer. "In my experience, there's no situation a fellow cannot handle with a clipboard and a sense of entitlement."

The lieutenant in dripping wet battle dress twirled one finger to signal to Dalby that he should roll down his window. A pair of Warrior infantry fighting vehicles passed by, drowning out the officer briefly.

"Good morning, Lieutenant. Not a bad day for it, eh?" Dalby chirped as he passed over the clipboard without being asked.

The lieutenant wiped a stream of rainwater from the brim of his helmet, only to see it reappear moments later. He leaned forward, dangerously close to dripping into Dalby's vehicle. "An excellent day for it, sir, and what would you be doing driving around my firing range?"

"Well, if you'll read the top sheet, you'll see it's not all yours, Lieutenant... Hunter. We do have to share, you know."

The officer, who spoke with the polished accent of the English upper class, turned down the corners of his mouth as he inspected the travel pass and Home Office authorization.

"I see," he said somewhat despondently, almost as if he'd been looking forward to roaring through somebody other than his own men. "So it's the village you're off to, Mister Dalby and... Miss..."

"Monroe," said Caitlin, sitting forward slightly. "Caitlin Monroe."

"A consultant to the Home Office," Dalby offered.

The lieutenant frowned. If he cared about her American accent, he gave no indication. "She's not listed on the authorization. You'll have to wait here while I check with my superiors."

"She wouldn't be," Dalby said, letting some of the pleasant tone drop out of his voice. "If you took the trouble to read the note, you'd see that I'm authorized to transport whomever I damn well please wherever it takes my fucking fancy, Lieutenant. If I feel like driving this vehicle right up your ass and parallel parking it in the voluminous spaces there within, then that's exactly what I shall do. And I believe your superiors would concur with that assessment. Luckily for you, however, I'm not so inclined. I just want to carry on to Imber."

Lieutenant Hunter, who looked like he was chewing on a particularly sour dog turd by that point, sniffed in distaste. A drop of rain hung on the tip of his patrician nose. He wiped the brim of his helmet again, spattering a bit of misery onto Dalby's coat.

"Imber. I see. Well, no need for attitude, sir. This is a dangerous part of the country, you know."

"Everywhere is a dangerous part of the country nowadays, laddie. So if you don't mind, I'll have those papers back and be on my way."

The rain was thickening, and the soldier contrived to get quite a bit of water into the warm, dry interior of the little Mercedes as he tossed the clipboard back into Dalby's lap.

"Drive carefully, sir." The lieutenant smiled. "Accidents do happen."

Dalby snorted and shook his head as he raised the automatic window and placed the travel papers on the floor behind Caitlin's seat.

"There's a big puddle up ahead," she said. "If you time it right, you could give him a hell of a dunking."

Dalby smiled.

"Childish but as satisfying as that would be, Ms. Monroe, I shall resist. I do have to pass through here quite a lot, and although Imber is our patch of the manor, it doesn't do to get the tin hats offside. A simple life, Caitlin. I crave a simple life. Do you mind me calling you Caitlin, by the way? That was rather presumptuous, wasn't it?"

"No, you're fine," she said, trying to inject some warmth into her voice. It was difficult with the chill she felt settling around her soul. A killer's cold detachment. "And thank you for looking after Bret and Monique, by the way. I was a bit out of it back at the hospital. I didn't really think to say thank you for all you've done. I'm sure it must have been a hassle organizing everything on such short notice. And I know that resources are always an issue these days."

"Think nothing of it," he said as he drove carefully past the army officer. "Things are always tight; you're correct. Those poor bloody squaddies of his, the conscripts at least, they wouldn't be earning enough for a decent punt on ciggies and pints at the mess. No wonder they look so bloody sorry for themselves. Bloody Russians pay their troopers better than that. But there's money for some things, and our little operation remains flush."

Caitlin wondered why he never mentioned Echelon by name. It wasn't as if the network of agencies, all of them based exclusively within the English-speaking world, was a state secret. Even

Monique, the French girl after whom her daughter was named, had known something of it, gleaned from the pages of the French press before the Disappearance and the intifada. Perhaps Dalby was just an Old World kind of guy.

"Not too far now," he announced a few minutes later as they drove past a plain white two-story building. It had no windows or doors, just empty spaces letting in the weather. She assumed it must be the first of Imber's ghost buildings. The village had been taken by the army way back in 1943 to be used as a training facility for the invasion of mainland Europe, and although the inhabitants of that time had been promised they could return to their homes, the army had kept the place for itself.

"So this place has been off limits for what, sixty-three years now?" she asked.

Dalby made a gentle left-hand turn toward a thin stand of elm trees sheltering two more boxy-looking buildings like the one they'd just passed. Without windows or any of the usual signs of habitation, the empty shells looked entirely forlorn, although Caitlin assumed the army must have spent some time maintaining them. Structurally they appeared very sound, which should not have been the case after more than half a century of exposure to the elements.

"Back in the old days," Dalby said, "before the Wave, the army opened the village up to sightseers quite a bit. After things changed, though, the Imber Range went dark again. Army still uses the village hulks for specialist training, but we have our own reception facility here, in the old pub, and first dibs on the rest of the place. It's well away from prying eyes and secure naturally, being stuck in the middle of sixteen thousand hectares of live firing range space."

The rain had eased to a light drizzle as they swept into the main street of the village. Leaf litter and food wrappers blown by the morning's wind plastered the lower floors of the first structure past which they drove, a long rectangular building with a steeply pitched green roof. It was a featureless, rather ugly structure, not at all what Caitlin would have expected of a well-preserved English village. She caught a glimpse of a church steeple off to the southwest, tucked in behind a thick screen of oak and chestnut trees. The tall gray spire appeared to be leaning slightly off center, and she wondered if the army had maintained it to the same standard as the rest of the village.

"That's Saint Giles through there," said Dalby, who seemed to enjoy taking the role of tour guide. "A rather lovely old place it is, with some very fine wall paintings. From Shakespeare's day, you know. About four or five hundred years old that makes it. Heritage listed."

"Does it get used?" she asked.

"Used to, once a year. But lightning struck the steeple. In the year of the Wave, in fact. It's been closed up ever since. Here we go, then."

He swung the car hard left past a row of five stark and somber-looking whitewashed buildings, all of them exposed to the weather. The narrow gravel driveway opened up into a generous parking lot in which sat two civilian cars and an army Land Rover. A couple of soldiers, much older and more grizzled than the draftees they had passed earlier, walked from one building shell to another, cupping their hands around lit cigarettes as they went. Neither gave Dalby's car more than a glance, and he made nothing of their presence.

"We're over here in the old inn," he said as the car crunched to a halt in front of a long, low-rise building that obviously predated the council flats they had seen.

"Looks old enough that Shakespeare might have stayed a night himself," she said.

"Mmm. Would have had a thatched roof and all once upon a time. The walls are genuine wattle and daub. You can even see the handprints of the original builders here and there, and there's some quite charming touches inside, old reed lamps and suchlike, but

I'm afraid the accommodations are quite basic otherwise. It's hardly boutique these days."

She followed Dalby out of the car and in through the old wooden doors. A fat, cold drop of rainwater plopped right on the end of her nose. Inside, the outline of the old public bar was visible on the dark wooden floor as a lighter area. Very little else remained of the building's history. Most of the long rectangular space was taken up with cheap government desks, plastic chairs, and a few filing cabinets. Dalby nodded to a middle-aged black woman typing at a computer. She smiled back but didn't break rhythm at the keyboard.

"They downstairs, then, Jude?"

"Yes, Mister Dalby. In the old keg room."

"Thanks, luv. Don't forget to take your lunch break today. Can't have you going all light-headed on us, can we?"

It must have been an old in-joke. Jude snickered and rolled her eyes but carried on.

"If you'll follow me, Caitlin, our Mister Richardson is down here."

She expected to follow him into the rear of the inn, but Dalby picked his way between a couple of desks, bent over, and hauled up a trapdoor. From its position relative to the outline of the old bar, she assumed it must have been where the cellarmen passed up supplies.

"The keg room?" she asked.

"Aye," Dalby confirmed as he swung around and went backward down a very steep wooden ladder. "Watch how you go, Caitlin. It's not an easy climb for an old duffer like me or a woman in your condition."

"My condition is fine," she said as she swung over the hole in the floor and slid down the ten-foot drop with her boots on the outer rails of the ladder and her hands only lightly gripping the side. Her breasts did ache a bit as she landed, but she would never admit that to anyone.

"Indeed, my mistake, then," Dalby said with one raised eyebrow. "Through this way."

Huge oaken barrels still lined two walls of the cellar, and dusty bottles, some hidden away behind spiderwebs, filled two wooden shelves along a third. A couple of men in casual clothes playing cards at a fold-up table greeted Dalby and waved him through to the end of the cellar space, where a wedge of yellow light spilled over the flagstones from a room obscured from view by an especially large wooden cask.

One of the two guards winked and blew a kiss at Caitlin as she walked past.

She stopped and smiled warmly, picked up his cards, and cocked an eye at his mate.

"He's holding both red queens, a nine of hearts, and fuck all," she said.

The other man roared with laughter as she walked on.

Dalby stood waiting for her at the entrance to a small, damp room that ran off the end of the cellar. Illuminated by a naked lightbulb, it contained two silent hovering guards and one chair, on which sat Richardson, the man who'd tried to kill or take her family a few hours earlier. Richardson was shaking and attempting to blink away runnels of fear sweat before they stung his eyes. His dreadlocks were matted with mud and leaves, and the right leg of his jeans had been cut away. A dirty, bloodstained bandage encircled his upper thigh, and his left arm had been roughly splinted after she'd broken it at the elbow.

His eyes went wide when he recognized her, but it was Dalby he should have been watching. The quiet gray-suited man moved up beside the prisoner and swung a hard, vicious sword-hand strike into his nose. Richardson screamed as he went over backward, a few drops of crimson blood spraying the slimy whitewashed brickwork.

"Righty oh, then," Dalby said softly, turning to one of the guards, who hadn't reacted in the slightest to the assault.

"I could just murder a cup of tea. I don't suppose you could fetch us a brew, do you, lad? I fear we may be some time down here. What about you, miss?" he asked Caitlin.

She regarded Richardson without obvious emotion in spite of the bloodlust roaring through her head. His eyes were huge with terror.

"Got any coffee?" she asked.

17

TEXAS ADMINISTRATIVE DIVISION

Miguel slept through the night until just before dawn. He awoke wishing he hadn't. Nightmares had haunted him almost from the moment he'd closed his eyes, visions of his family dying while he stood in the middle of the slaughter unable to move, unable to lift as much as a finger to stop it while the road agents laughed and pointed at him, mocking his impotence. When he finally stirred in the dim gray light, he felt as though he had been awake for days. There was no gift of forgetting. He did not wake up thinking himself home in his own bed, even for the briefest of moments, lying next to Mariela, waiting for the first of the children's footfalls to thunder through the house. He simply woke from dreams of loss and horror into the reality.

Sofia twitched and mumbled in her sleep on the bedroll next to his where they lay behind the counter. He resisted the urge to stroke her head, to calm her thoughts. She cried while she slept or during the day when she didn't think he would notice. He suspected she was trying to keep up a brave front for his benefit. As troubled as her dreams would be, however, he preferred her to sleep. They would have another long day in the saddle.

He lay still for a minute, then stretched carefully before inching away from his daughter and standing. He had taken off his jacket and his boots but remained dressed in the clothes he had worn yesterday. They both did. He leaned over and picked up Sofia's bear, which was lying on the floor a short distance from her. After tucking it in next to her, he moved away quietly. The pop of his knees and a cracking back told him that his body would not thank him for the night on a hard floor. His sore ribs, combined with the cold air, made breathing a chore. Whatever aches and pains he may have felt in his body, they were nothing compared with the agonies of his soul, a torment that he had no choice but to ignore.

To add to the discomfort of an aching back and stiff legs, Miguel's bladder was full, but he took the time to pull on his boots and gather his weapons before pushing quietly through the front door of Leona's general store. The sun was peeking over the eastern horizon, washing everything in a soft yellow light that only emphasized the sense of abandonment as he walked down to the intersection at the top of the main road.

As he looked back over the ghost town, burned-out husks of buildings glinted where the dawn's rays struck broken glass or exposed metal and dewdrops glistened like a billion diamonds on grass that had grown wild and high in untended fields and gardens. Certain he was not being observed, he finally relieved himself at the side of the road by the fence where they had secured the horses overnight. Red Dog joined him at the fence, wagging her tail and panting in anticipation of breakfast.

Wiping his hands on the dewy grass and then his jeans, Miguel took a minute to breathe in the chilled air as his gut cramps and chest pains abated. The cry of a night heron drew his attention back toward the main road through town, and he saw the hunched, almost stocky-looking gray and white bird lift off from the wreck of a house a hundred yards down. A flash of red and white zipping from the cover of the ruins gave away the fox that had been stalking it. A rumbling growl began at the back of the dog's throat, but Miguel silenced her with a simple command.

"Quiet, dog. Even the fox must eat, yes?" he said. "And better a useless heron or prairie chicken than some farmer's egg layer."

He heard the screen door bang open as Sofia emerged from the store. She, too, had pulled on her boots, and she was carrying her Remington. Her face looked puffy and pale, and she rubbed eyes that seemed to be rimmed by dark shadows.

"I didn't know where you were," she said almost resentfully. "I don't like it in there on my own."

"That's okay," he said. "If you look after the horses, I will see to breakfast."

She seemed grateful for something to do. If her night had been anything like his, she would be looking for a distraction. The horses would provide one. By the time they had been brushed and had their hooves picked and cleaned and their legs massaged and rubbed down, she would have done at least an hour's work.

"Keep the dogs with you and your rifle close to hand," he said. "I shall not be far."

She gave him a brief, fierce hug as they passed, which made Miguel feel a little better. He had to admit that he didn't care for the ice-cold blankness of yesterday.

He returned to the store, intending to search the cellar properly before he prepared any food. There seemed to be quite a treasure trove down there, but they would have to choose what they took carefully. They did not have the capacity to load up a wagon train, and even if they had, it would have slowed them down too much. He could not shake the conviction that they had to cross a lot of ground very quickly to get Sofia away from the agents.

The cowboy shivered as he reentered the shop. The remains had not bothered him the night before, but now, in the light of day, something like a cold eel slithered up his spine, raising gooseflesh on his arms and causing him to shudder with an unspecified sense of dread. He regarded those taken by the Wave with some trepidation, as though the empty clothes, stiffened and black with the leavings of those who had worn them, might suddenly inflate with their specters and rise from the floor to admonish him—or worse—for living when they had died.

"Madre de Dios," Miguel muttered to himself, momentarily forgetting his own frequent commands to his family to always speak in English. "Get a grip, you ignorant fool," he said more forcefully.

Still, he could not help glancing back over his shoulder to where the dogs sat patiently guarding Sofia as she brushed down his horse in the warming light of morning. The animals seemed not at all perturbed, and he consoled himself that although he was not a stupid and superstitious peon, he had heard it said by such types that dogs were especially attuned to the spirit world and to those who passed, by accident or design, from the place of shadows in the world of real things. If spirits there were in this empty store, Blue Dog and Red Dog were unaware of them. They sat, grinning stupidly, awaiting a feast of canned franks or loose meat.

Tamping down on the very strong urge to step back out into the bright, clean light, Miguel stroked his saddle gun in the oversized holster at his hip and stepped farther into the crypt.

He stopped.

Why had he called it that?

The same shiver seized his whole body this time, and he could feel goose bumps spreading all over both arms and legs. Even his ass tingled with a strengthening sense of free-floating dread.

Miguel Pieraro remained fixed where he stood, and darkness gradually seemed to swirl up like mist from the shadowed recesses of the aisles at the rear of the store. He was certain that were he to turn around, the Disappeared would be standing there, yellow teeth grinning at him through rotted lips, bony claws reaching out to seize him and carry him off to wherever the Devil had taken their souls on the morning of March 14, 2003.

When the dogs began barking, he nearly filled his pants.

The two men were on horses, which wasn't unusual. The fact that they wore white business shirts with clip-on name tags and black ties under their navy blue Columbia windbreakers definitely was. They had been advancing down Leona Road on two chestnut-colored horses until they'd encountered his daughter leveling the business end of her Remington 700 at them. Now they weren't going anywhere. They sat very still in their saddles with their hands in the air. The dogs had taken up guard positions on either side of Sofia and hunkered down on their front legs as their wiry fur bristled and their lips skinned back from cruel-looking fangs.

Miguel lowered his weapon as he emerged from the store and recognized them as Mormons. Another two just like them had come by the ranch almost a year earlier, and at the time he had been struck by the incongruity of their dress. It was a sort of uniform, he knew, and he could think of nobody else who would be dressed in such a fashion this morning in East Texas.

"Sofia," he called out. "It is all right. You can put the gun down."

He was gratified to see that his daughter did not take her eyes off the men even as she lowered the muzzle of the rifle.

"Good day to you, gentlemen," he said, projecting his voice down the empty street. He still held his Winchester, but casually, one-handed, pointing it down into the dust. The saddle gun lay heavy and reassuring at his hip. The riders, he noted, made no effort to place their weapons within easier reach. They each appeared to have modern military-style rifles slung across their backs, and he could see no evidence of a quick-draw saddle gun such as his own Lupara.

"Good morning to you, sir," one of them called back, waving

with what looked like forced cheer. "Do you homestead around here, or are you passing through?"

"Around here," he answered with some care. There was no reason to explain to these men what he and his daughter were doing on the trail. "But I am traveling north. Yourselves?"

"We head north as well. To Kansas City, with a herd of beef cattle."

"Advance riders?" he asked, walking out to meet them in the center of the road.

Sofia turned slightly at the hip to watch him as he walked toward them, her gun pointed down but her finger still firm on the trigger. Miguel could see no sign of a big herd anywhere near town. His horses had trotted up to the fence line of the property where he had secured them for the night. They snorted and whinnied at the new arrivals while the dogs remained on guard on either side of his daughter. Should trouble develop, they would fly at the men's horses with fangs bared. The chance meeting did not feel dangerous, though, despite an air of strain about the men.

"Our main group is some miles back. Near Elwood," said the second rider, who had not spoken before. "We've ridden up to see whether there is pasture and shelter for them here at Leona, or whether it might be best to push on for Centerville. My name is Willem D'Age, and this is Cooper Aronson. Besides driving cattle we are witnesses for the Lord and…"

Miguel waved him off before he could get into his sales pitch.

"I am Catholic," he said. "For what it's worth. That will do me fine for now."

"And on Judgment Day?" Aronson asked.

Miguel gestured to the ruins of Leona behind him. "Some might think that Judgment Day has come and gone and left us all in its wake, my friend."

The Mormons nodded somberly.

"Indeed," said D'Age, letting a moment pass before continuing.

"So you would know this area well, then, Mister…"

"Pieraro. Miguel Pieraro," he answered before walking nearer, extending a hand, which Aronson bent down to shake. "I am a rancher under the Federal Mandate. This is my daughter, Sofia."

The two men bowed their heads and removed their hats, each of them greeting her politely in turn. She nodded brusquely but said nothing.

The two riders exchanged a glance as they replaced their hats.

"You run longhorns?" D'Age asked.

Miguel shook his head. "Bedak Whitetails. My family made it to Australia after the Wave. I have always worked with cattle and was sent to a property tending Whitetails after we were released from camp. They are a good breed. Well suited to this land."

"But you are some distance from your land today, Mister Pieraro," D'Age said, leaving the obvious question unspoken.

Miguel nodded and answered by spitting in the dust.

"Road agents," he said without further explanation. Both men were sweating and high-colored in spite of the morning being cool. The color seemed to drain from the face of the one calling himself D'Age.

Aronson, the taller, leaner of the pair, cleared his throat awkwardly. "And your family?"

Miguel shook his head as he felt great weights and precarious burdens shift around somewhere inside him.

"I'm his family," Sofia said, and left it at that.

"I am sorry," Aronson said. "Some evil has befallen you?" His companion muttered condolences, too, shaking his head.

"Some," said Miguel.

Before dismounting, the riders appeared to consider something between themselves without actually exchanging any words. D'Age shook hands with Miguel while the other man led their horses over to the nearest fence line, where he tied them up. Miguel was surprised to see tears welling in D'Age's eyes.

"I am very sorry," he said again quietly. "Very sorry," he added while half bowing in a strangely formal gesture toward Sofia.

The girl smiled, but the warmth didn't reach her eyes. She didn't come and stand by her father, however, as much as Miguel could tell she wanted to. She knew not to present a small target by grouping together like that. Aronson knocked the dust from his hat by slapping it on his thigh as he walked back from the fence line.

"I'm afraid we have had our own problem with road agents," he said. Miguel noticed that D'Age seemed to stiffen and bunch his jaw muscles tightly as Aronson continued.

"Raiders hit us outside of Trinity," he said. "Near Lake Livingston. Took our supplies, a good number of cattle…"

Miguel waited for them to finish. There was obviously more.

"And some of our people," Aronson confessed at last, forcing out the words like squeezing pus from a wound.

"Your women," Miguel said flatly.

Both men nodded. He noticed something like fear tinged with rage in his daughter's eyes. The vaquero ran one hardened hand through his thick black hair. It came away damp with sweat. The sun was fully up in the eastern sky now, warming the day and causing all three men to perspire. Sofia seemed less bothered by the heat.

"We had six young women with us," Aronson explained. "One of them was betrothed to Willem. The others were riding north to our community in KC. They are a great loss."

"Your raiders came out of Montgomery, most certainly," Miguel said, his voice tired and cracked. "Many banditos infest the ruins of Houston. Not like the big Eastern cities, no, but still many. I believe that Blackstone leaves them alone in there because they threaten the refugee trails coming up from the south. They—"

"You never said anything about that," Sofia interrupted, looking annoyed.

He motioned her silent and continued. "They threaten the federale settlement paths out of Corpus Christi, too, another reason for Blackstone to leave them be. In my opinion."

Both men looked hollow-eyed and raw. Aronson worked the brim of his hat like a length of rosary beads.

"I do not take your point about Governor Blackstone, Mister Pieraro, but do you think it is possible the men who attacked us also attacked you?" he asked.

"Papa?" Sofia asked in a small voice, her eyes looking very large in her face.

Miguel sighed and shook his head. "I don't think agents from out of Houston would come this far. I saw no sign that the men who attacked our farm were traveling with prisoners."

D'Age looked ill. "But that could just mean—"

Miguel cut him off with a chopping gesture.

"No, the men who killed our family were not taking prisoners or hostages. They took nothing. A few who stayed behind were scavenging food, but that was all." He tried to give D'Age a reassuring look. "The men who attacked you were seeking plunder. They will still have your women and cattle."

Sofia surprised him by speaking up and doing so with real force.

"Then we must help them, Papa," she insisted, sounding very much like her mother for just a second. His first instinct was to argue with her, but the fierceness of her gaze gave him pause. He could tell she had made up her mind. Miguel spent a few moments sizing Sofia up. For the first time since yesterday he saw a strong emotion other than sadness in her features.

He saw ungovernable rage, a killing rage suddenly boiled up from within her heart, and it disturbed him greatly.

He sighed.

"You are looking for them, are you not?" he asked. It was more of a statement than a question.

Aronson nodded. "We followed them north as best we could, but we are not country people, really. I am a sociologist by training. I was witnessing in Scotland when the Wave hit, studying at Edinburgh.

All of us came home when it lifted. We have tried to do the best we can, Mister Pieraro, but…"

Miguel could see the that man was losing his composure fast. It was not surprising. Being wrenched from city life onto the frontier and told to make do as best one could, would be enough to break most people, but these poor bastards did not just have surly beasts and stony ground with which to contend. They had fallen afoul of human treachery as well.

The vaquero came to a decision.

"There is a store here in Leona," he said. "It has a well-stocked cellar, protected from the heat and rain. You can take supplies from there. I will show you. As for your raiders, if they are not here and they did head north, they will have set down in Crockett for a few days. It has not been reclaimed, and much of the town still stands. I believe the power failed there after the Wave. If you wish, I will help you take back what is yours."

The men gaped at him as though he had just materialized in the morning air. He was aware that compared with them he must look every bit as rough and untrustworthy as the bandits who had attacked their party. Their questions spilled out one on top of the next.

"You would do that?"

"You would help us?"

"You're sure that's where they would be?"

"Why?"

He shrugged. "We are also traveling north. It will be safer for my daughter if we travel with a large group, even though we may attract more attention. If you will have us as companions, I will help you. Sofia, however, I must insist be protected. If there is fighting to be done, I will do it."

He gave her a stern look, as if to cut short any dissent, but she bristled anyway.

"I want these men as much as you do, Papa," she protested through thin lips.

Miguel folded his arms and shook his head. "They are not the same men, Sofia. And even if they were, it would not be your role to settle our affairs with them. That is my duty and mine alone. Your mother, God rest her soul, would not have it any other way. As you well know, young lady."

The Mormons tactfully found something interesting to look at off on the horizon while the surviving members of the Pieraro clan played out their small confrontation. Miguel did not glare at his daughter. Indeed, he was proud of her for wanting to exact vengeance with her own hands. But although a life of hardscrabble farming had given her great strength and fitness for one of her age and sex, she remained at heart a young girl, and he would do all he could to protect her innocence as much as her life. While she fumed and pouted, he merely stared back at her, waiting her out. After a few moments she expressed her exasperation in the time-honored manner of all teenage girls, rolling her eyes and muttering loudly about the unfairness and indignity of life.

Miguel shrugged.

"We are all heading north." he said to the two men. "It is a dangerous path we take, especially for Sofia. If you help us through Blackstone's land, I will help you through this. Is that a fair trade?"

The dogs sniffed at the feet of both men and wagged their tails, pronouncing them acceptable. D'Age looked the more pained of the two, and Miguel remembered he had lost someone to the raiders.

"Why do you think they will stay in Crockett?" he asked.

Sofia spoke before Miguel could. "To rape the women and enjoy the spoils," she said. "That is what they did to Mama."

Miguel felt sick. He'd hoped to have protected Sofia from that knowledge.

"Come," he said. "We have much to do."

18

NEW YORK

Some people were just lucky, but Ryan Dubois wasn't one of them. The mortar round that exploded and blew him into three large, messy pieces of burned meat merely tossed Julianne through a store window that had already been shattered. She tumbled through the air, eerily detached, recalling a childhood misadventure involving a trampoline and a dislocated shoulder. Her sense of time passing stretched like a rubber band, and then—*snap!* The world sped up again in a violent, jaggy swirl of color and pain and the loudest noise she had ever heard in her life.

Jules screamed in agony as she hit something hard and immovable and the same shoulder was wrenched out of place with a grinding pop. She rolled across a wooden floor, every turn a flaring supernova of pain in her back and side, dark purple blossoms opening in front of her eyes as she fought to hold on to consciousness. Impact knocked the wind out of her, and she had trouble taking a breath, as though she'd just been gut punched by Lennox Lewis. Attempting to push herself up off the floor, she collapsed, screaming again as white-hot flames seemed to shoot down one side of her body. The rolling thunder of rocket fall and mortar fire lashed at the street outside, and she was oddly certain the Rhino was dead, disassembled at high speed just like poor Ryan, but then he unexpectedly landed feet first on the floor next to her. His filthy bloodstained boots crushed a small glass figurine a few inches from her face as he knelt down to help her up.

She tried to cry out, to warn him that she was injured, but he had his arms around her and was dragging her away from the open window before she could protest. The pain was grotesque, unbearable, nauseating, and she did pass out for a few minutes. Another white dwarf of agony exploding somewhere inside her woke her up again to a world filled with death and horror and the screaming of a small child.

After a few seconds she realized the small child was herself and the Rhino had done something to her shoulder. She felt a sting in her neck and then the most delicious warmth as a soothing bath of soft analgesic pleasure flowed out from that point to gently wash away all of her many hurts and outrages. Her eyelids felt heavy and her chin dropped down onto her chest as the Rhino heaved her up off the floor and away into a long, dark tunnel.

Jules came to consciousness slowly, in fits and starts. She was dreaming. A nightmare, actually. Some penny dreadful horror, probably from eating too much Brie and watching that awful *28 Days Later* with Fifi. They'd put the bloody thing in the DVD player only because Mr. Lee had brought a copy back from a trip ashore in Kupang and they simply couldn't sit through another fucking session of *The English Patient*. Now she was fighting to drag herself out of the dreadful nightmare of a world emptied of people—no, haunted by them. The world was haunted by millions of souls who had disappeared, and now they were back, returned from some hell dimension with every trace of humanity sucked from their souls. They had eyes like the milky orbs of dead fish and lips rotted away from yellow teeth, and they were coming for her. Of course, she couldn't run from them. She tried, but she never moved, not an inch, no matter how fast she pumped her legs.

Jules forced herself out of the half-waking state with great effort, pushing back against the vision of hell as if bench-pressing a huge weight away from herself. She finally woke up in her hotel room in New York on fresh white Egyptian cotton sheets, with the prospect of a day's shopping in front of her and a night at the theater with Paul, and dinner at Gabriel's. She would wear her new Kate Spade slingbacks and perhaps the Karen Millen Black Silk Bird Dress, but definitely the Kate Spades, because they were gorgeous and she'd just bought them and the shop was wonderful; it was as if she were floating through it again, turning over and over in the air, with a thousand jagged shards of glass and the disembodied head and upper torso of Ryan Dubois, and she was falling, slamming into the floor, and hurting the same shoulder she had dislocated on a trampoline, and again playing hockey at school, and screaming...

Screaming.

She came fully awake at last with a gasp. Still groggy and disoriented and feeling as though she were at the end of a tumbling free-fall through her personal history.

Paul?

Dear Paul. God, how long had it been since they had dated?

And Fifi was dead.

And she had not shopped in New York for many years.

And those shoes were lost somewhere back in England.

And then she knew where she was. She'd been blown through the front window of a Kate Spade store on the corner of Broome and Mercer streets. She had never shopped there. For an infuriating, irrational moment she could not recall where she'd bought the gorgeous slingbacks her sister had stolen so many years ago. And then she remembered. It was in San Francisco, way back in 2000, at the opening of the store. She levered herself up against a display case, groaning a little at the sudden throbbing ache in her shoulder. This was the third time she'd popped the thing, and every time recovery took longer and was less complete.

"Rhino," she said, coughing as she choked on the dust in her mouth and throat. "Rhino? Are you there?"

"Quiet," he said softly. "Pirates."

That one word brought her rushing back to full consciousness, or close enough that it made no difference. It was dark in the store and outside on the street. She calculated quickly that she must have been out of action for most of the day. She remembered the sudden fall of the rockets, the way a tsunami of explosive fire had rushed toward them up the narrow street, and the weirdly familiar sensation of being blown clear through the air. It was like standing on a ship's deck in a fierce storm and being catapulted through space by the impact of a rogue wave. She remembered with shuddering horror how Ryan, who had been standing a good ten yards away from her, closer to the blast, had simply come apart and spewed his inner life all over the whitewashed façade of the store on the corner.

She understood then that they had not been attacked by pirates or caught in one of their mortar barrages. They'd been mistaken for pirates and targeted by the army. Or maybe not. Perhaps they were just firing blindly into this part of Manhattan because it was crawling with freebooters. She pawed at her chest, seeking the reassurance of the weapon she'd set out with a dozen or so blocks back on Duane Street.

"I've got it," the Rhino said in a low voice. "You're in no state to fight anyone. I put your shoulder back in and doped you up. Now just lie still and try not to get us both kilt."

Kilts, she thought, somewhat baffled. Why would she be looking for kilts?

Her eyelids drooped again, and she dozed off.

It was very dark when she next awoke, but her head was much clearer. The morphine must have leached out of her bloodstream. She blinked her eyes open and shut a few times and carefully rolled her injured shoulder. It was stiff and sore, but she could move the arm even though the Rhino had fashioned a basic sling out of what had once been a very expensive silk scarf.

"You awake?" he asked. "For good now?"

"Water," she croaked, and the former coast guard man passed her a canteen. It was smeared with blood, and she could taste the coppery scum of it as she put her lips to the plastic bottle. The water was warm and tasted brackish, but she gulped it down gratefully.

"S'okay," said the Rhino. "The pirates have moved on. They didn't come in here. Guess this season's fashions are just so 2003, eh?"

He held up a pair of gold leather sandals and grinned.

Jules stared at him.

"I've been unconscious for most of the day, and that's the best line you could come up with?" she asked.

His grin grew wider as he saw she was going to be okay.

"Can you move? Or carry your weapon? Because believe me, I can handle two of these puppies on the leash, don't you worry," he said as he hoisted up both P90s. Julianne sucked in a deep breath, rocked back, and then rolled up onto one knee before standing, exhaling, and taking another deep breath to control her dizziness. The Rhino was quickly at her side with a strong arm for support.

"The fighting's moved downtown and west a ways," he told her. "Lucky thing for us, too. Thought we were gonna get ourselves squashed between both sides for a few hours there."

Jules allowed him to lead her though the wreckage of the store, which was so badly trashed that she couldn't tell what damage was new and what had been done by neglect and the elements over the years since the Disappearance. Here and there she was able to pick out a pile of clothes and accessories that were rigid and black with the congealed leftovers of whoever had been wearing them when the Wave struck. But mostly the store was just a shambles of collapsed shelving, broken glass, ruined stock, and...

"Oh..."

She closed her eyes and swallowed when she saw a disembodied arm poking out from under a blackened display cabinet.

"Damn, sorry, Jules. I thought I'd policed up all the remains."

He moved to pick it up, but Jules squeezed his elbow and shook her head.

"Doesn't matter. Come on. We should get moving. I want to get to Union Square before sunup."

The Rhino helped her out onto the street, which looked like a scene from wartime France, illuminated by the shells of burning buildings. Explosions had picked up car bodies and tossed them willy-nilly, smashing them into shop fronts, tearing the chassis into jagged knots of metal. Tires burned. Shop fittings burned. The long, ruined canyon of Mercer Street, once one of her favorite parts of this city, was illuminated by the oily orange glow of a hundred separate fires. Light rain, more of a sooty drizzle, drifted down, coating the rubble in a thick patina of ash and toxic chemicals.

They picked their way along the cobblestoned street, threading through entanglements of fallen scaffolding and brickwork. A huge steel garbage can blocked the path down near a boutique she vaguely recalled visiting during the three weeks she'd spent here in 2000, shortly after the millennium celebration. The can had been blown high into the air and come crashing down to lie with one end propped up against the first floor of the boutique. It had buckled in the center and now effectively closed off access to upper Mercer.

"Let's cut through," said the Rhino, gesturing at the boutique with one of the P90s. "We should get out of the main thoroughfares, anyway. There'll be a lane or something out the back of these buildings. We can get up the block using that."

Jules muttered her agreement, preferring to concentrate on not tripping and further injuring her arm. They climbed over the windowsill of the nearest shop front, a gutted homewares store, and navigated their way to the rear of the building, first by the light of the fires and then by means of a torch the Rhino clipped onto one of the machine guns. A jet screamed overhead while they searched for a rear exit, chased by the thump-thump-thump of a big antiaircraft cannon. She'd heard of the pirates mounting such things onto pickups but had wondered at the truth of such rumors. Surely the city's road network was too locked up with the rusted remains of all the vehicles that had crashed after losing their drivers.

"Here we go," said her companion as the thin beam of torchlight picked out a heavy metal security door. "Stand back, Miss Jules."

She did as she was told while he pressed down the locking bar and tentatively pushed open the door. No gunfire greeted the movement, and the Rhino slid through.

"Clear," he announced a few seconds later, and she followed him through, emerging into the cold, gritty rain that pattered down into the space between those buildings fronting Mercer and the ass-end of their counterparts on the next block over. She tried to remember which street ran parallel on that side but came up blank. The back alley, as always, was much less disordered than the main streets. There were a few vehicles parked here and there, but they had been parked back in '03 while their drivers ran deliveries to the businesses on either side. The smugglers had learned very quickly, right back at Duane Street, in fact, that such hidden, disused passages were safest when one was trying to traverse the contested island.

She recalled this as they sloshed through three inches of rancid, stagnant groundwater collected in the artificial valley between the two terraced rows of buildings on Mercer and whatever streets. Rats the size of small dogs swam away from the thin shaft of torchlight, trailing V-shaped wakes.

Didn't there used to be alligators in the New York sewers?

"Rhino," she said lightly. "Do you recall whether the Wave disappeared crocodiles and suchlike?"

He halted in front of her and turned around, keeping the torch pointed down to avoid dazzling her.

"Crocodiles? You mean gators?"

"Yes," she said, trying to sound casual.

"No idea, Miss Julianne. What is it they reckon now? It took humans and most of the higher primates. Chimps and apes and so on. And killed about half of anything that had a spinal cord. But not so as you could predict what was gonna get zapped beyond people and apes."

"Don't worry about it," she said, feeling rather foolish.

The Rhino sketched a devilish grin.

"Do gators have spinal cords? Or do they just like to eat them? Hmm. Do you know, Miss Jules?"

"Shut the fuck up and keep moving," she scolded, waving him forward.

The Rhino sniggered and turned back to resume sloshing through the filthy watercourse. The grumble of bomb bursts and far-off cannon fire rolled around the empty chasms of the city, but hidden away in their own deep concrete valley and with a cold rain pressing down, the fighting sounded muted and far away. Jules kicked away a rat that ran across her boots, sending it into a rack of old dresses still waiting to be delivered. They were covered in plastic bags; she wondered idly if any might still be wearable but scoffed at the thought. They'd be moldy and chewed to rags by moths and grubs after so long. After squeezing through a narrow space where the corners of two buildings almost met, they followed the passageway up to the rear of a two-story shop dwarfed by a much larger buildings on either side. The door was jammed open by a large cardboard box that was halfway to total disintegration. The Rhino tried to pull it out of the way, but it came apart in his hands and spilled its contents with a harsh clatter of metal and crashing glass.

"Shit," the Rhino said. He kicked a path through the refuse. As

Jules stepped forward, she realized she'd stood on the remains of whoever had been carrying the box and felt an absurd reflex need to apologize. Hurrying to keep up with the bobbing torchlight, she tried to make out what sort of store it might have been, but the best she could come up with was "eclectic." Clothes. Knickknacks. Hideously expensive objets d'art. There were examples of all those in the small, neat space.

Spring Street, onto which the shop fronted, apparently had reverted to its original form as a stream. At least a foot of brown swiftly running water gushed past outside, lapping at the bottom of the shop's front door, pouring in underneath. The Rhino was less concerned by that than by the chance they might be spotted as they left the cover they had so far enjoyed.

"Why don't we just kick our way into the place over the road?" Jules suggested. "See if we can cut through the block like we just did?"

"That's my plan, too," he replied. "But I'd just like to check the water before I go dipping my toes."

He turned around and smiled wickedly.

"Gators, you know."

19

Richardson broke just after four in the afternoon. He lasted much longer than Caitlin had expected, but she had watched better men than that try to resist torture before. She had even broken some of them herself with nothing more than a sanitary napkin smeared with pig's blood. Everyone had a weakness, some deep fear that could be exploited if one was given time. If time was an issue, there was always the proper amount of pressure, applied in controlled doses. Everyone broke sooner or later. The wonder with Richardson was that he held on for so long, but as Dalby pointed out, it wasn't for the sake of honor or duty.

"I believe he was quite terrified," said the man from the Home Office. "And not of us."

"Not at first," Caitlin corrected.

Dalby seemed to give her comment more consideration than it was really due, sipping contemplatively at his cup of tea before dunking a cookie—or, rather, a biscuit—into it. He stood aside to let the guards drag Richardson's unconscious body past him. The criminal's dark skin was spotted with burn marks and torn by small, bleeding lacerations, hundreds of them, some crusted with salt. He reeked of sour sweat and the stink of his own urine and feces. As Caitlin kept her nose close to the coffee mug, attempting to block out the worst of the smell, she was reminded of a figure from history who used to carry a hollowed-out orange filled with perfume. He would sniff the orange to keep the miasma of the unwanted masses away.

What was that guy's name? She had heard it in some history class eons ago. She couldn't even remember the last time she had seen an edible orange.

Stop it, she told herself. Jesus Christ but her mind was not as sharp at it had been before the tumor. It seemed to wander so much now.

The smell didn't seem to bother Dalby in the least, but he was sensitive enough to her discomfort to move out of the room when the path was clear.

"Lads, why don't we pack our guest off to London?" Dalby said. "For a spell in the Cage."

"Yes, sir," one of the guards said. "Very good, Mister Dalby. We'll see to it."

The funk inside the small cell must have been especially thick, because the air in the musty, enclosed space of the main keg room tasted as sweet as an alpine forest when she was able to breathe freely once more. Caitlin did not tell the Englishman that Richardson's interrogation had brought back some deeply traumatic memories of her own treatment at the hands of al Banna, but Dalby would have been familiar with her file, and he had offered a number of times to take on the responsibility for the hostile debriefing alone.

She'd refused. Richardson and his crew had come after her through Bret and Monique. She wouldn't leave the room until he broke and told them why. Indeed, she believed her presence had probably contributed to undermining his will. He'd seen her execute his comrades, some of them in cold blood, and she gave him no reason to believe that she wouldn't be just as ruthless with him.

"Still and all, he did give a good accounting of himself in there, didn't he?" said Dalby as they reached the foot of the ladder leading up to the old barroom. "That was quite a job of work getting him to talk. Your Mister Baumer really knows how to put the frighteners on a chap."

Caitlin shook her head in disgust.

Bilal Baumer. Al Banna.

She thought she'd seen off that worthless blood clot years ago. But here he was, back in her face, even if it was only through the agency of cutouts and dupes like Richardson. She finished the dregs of her coffee before pulling herself up the old wooden ladder hand over hand. She was amused and a little touched to see that Dalby made a conspicuous effort not to stare at her butt as it swayed past his eyes.

He was good guy, old Dalby, she had decided, even if he was a little too ready with the shaving razor and the Zippo during interrogation. He followed her up the ladder and directed her through the small pod of desks, where the typist she had met earlier was having a late-afternoon tea, nibbling a jam-covered scone and reading an old gossip magazine. Not that there were any new gossip mags being published. Not in paper form, anyway. After all, a big swag of the world's celebrity supply had disappeared back in '03, but more important, the all-powerful Ministry of Resources had deemed august journals such as *Hello!* and *OK!* "surplus to the national emergency requirements," making them prohibitively expensive to publish. Like most of the print media, they had downsized and gone online, where they scrabbled over some very meager pickings from advertising and subscriptions.

"This way," Dalby said, using a key to open a door at the far end of the room. The day had grown even gloomier while they'd been downstairs, and outside it was so dark with the lowering clouds and rain that she could barely see beyond the windows. Springtime in

England, she thought gloomily. A log fire burned in the center of the old barroom, providing welcome light and warmth, but fluorescent tubes hanging from the ceiling shone with a much harsher effect, laying a flat white light over everything. Caitlin tailed Dalby into the room, which looked like it might have been the pub manager's office at one time. It was furnished in the same spare utilitarian style as the main area, but he had softened the space with a few amateurish oil paintings and a potted fern, which he sprayed with water from a plastic bottle before sitting down. There were three framed pictures sitting on his desk, which was otherwise free of clutter. She assumed they were of his family but could not see from her side of the room.

"Sit down, sit down. That's the comfier perch," he said, indicating a very tired-looking leather armchair in a corner behind her. It sat next to a gray metal bookcase that was mostly filled with government documents and a few nonfiction books: *The Legacy of Jihad, Bravo Two Zero, The Disappeared.* There were two novels there, however, lying face up on the top shelf: a well-thumbed copy of *The Cruel Sea* and what looked like an unread science fiction title, *Tearing Down Tuesday.* She assumed it was sci-fi because of the green robot on the cover. She was probably sitting in Dalby's reading chair, she realized. It was, as he had said, a rather comfortable perch.

"I must apologize for the unpleasantness downstairs, Caitlin. It did get rather fraught once or twice."

"Big boys' rules," she said casually.

"Indeed. Which brings us to the question of which rules we're now playing by as regards Mister Baumer."

Caitlin shifted her position slightly in the chair. The mention of Baumer's name upset her more than she would care to admit. She could not avoid the image of her husband and child, her precious family, lying dead in a field had she not been there. And where was she now? Not by their side, that was for...

She forced her mind to stop rambling.

"I thought he was supposed to be chained up at the bottom of some hole in Guadeloupe, helping the gendarmes with their inquiries."

"Indeed," Dalby said with a quirk of the lips that might have been rueful or wryly amused.

"Our last information had him so situated. But that was a year ago, and I'm afraid that communications between metropolitan France and the *territoires d'outre-mer* are not what they might be. Frankly, Mr. Baumer was no longer an active concern of ours once it became obvious that we were never going to be given unfettered access to him. Or any access at all, beyond furnishing the DST with a list of questions they might just pass on to the Directorate of Military Intelligence, which took control of him back in 2003."

"So, what, all of our work on him was for nothing? Or was it because *we* were asking. Rather than MI6 or the Yard?"

"Could be," Dalby conceded with a wave of one hand. "We're not flavor of the month in the Elysée Palace. Never have been, which is only reasonable, I suppose, given our brief. Frankly, I would rather that Echelon had remained a private affair and hence deniable rather than declaring our hand as we did after the Vancouver Conference. I really don't think your Mister Kipper did us any favors there."

Caitlin leaned forward and placed her hands on her knees, locking her elbows straight, imitating her father without realizing she was doing so. She agreed with the Englishman but could not get worked up over it in the same way. Echelon had worked very well in the old world as a secret arrangement among the Anglophone powers to divide up responsibility for spying on the rest of the world. And it wasn't as if the rest of the world didn't know about them. Compromised elements of the DGSE in France had been able to roll up most of Echelon's network there in the first days of the intifada.

"That's all politics, Dalby. And history now. Fact is, we are in the open, we are declared players, and the French are going to have to give up whatever they know about Baumer. This guy is out, and he's running assets again, on our turf, against me."

"You really think it's personal?" Dalby asked. He sounded skeptical.

Caitlin threw her hands into the air. "Richardson was paid by a man called Tariq Skaafe, also known as Terry Skaafe, one of Baumer's old aliases. He was contracted to drive up here and put a hit on my family. He got a bonus payment if he managed to drive back to London with me in a bag. It sounds personal, dontcha think? The guy's been sitting in a fucking hole in Guadeloupe for two or three years, eating his craw, stewing on the infidel bitch who put him there. Fuck knows how he got out, but if Sarko doesn't really control the external territories anymore—and who does have a handle on the fucking Carribean these days?—then it's entirely fucking possible that Baumer got sprung from his spider hole for a packet of fucking cigarettes and a handjob!"

Caitlin, who had leaned far forward in making her case, fell back into the chair, annoyed with herself for losing control in front of Dalby, for losing control at all. If Baumer really was on the loose and coming after her, she was going to need to stay frosty until she could reach into his fucking chest and rip his heart out herself just to make sure the fucker was really dead.

Dalby nodded sympathetically and opened a drawer behind his desk. "Do you mind?" he asked, taking out a pipe. "Helps me to think things through. And I received a new bag of tobacco the other day. From Missouri."

"Knock yourself out, Sherlock," she said, smiling an apology. "I'm sorry to rant, but it's not just about me, you know. Those assholes this morning came after my husband and my kid. It doesn't get any more personal than that."

Dalby tamped down the small bowl full of brown leaf and lit up with the same lighter he'd used to extract the information about

"Terry Skaafe" from Richardson. "You know this al Banna chap better than anyone," he said as he drew in the first puffs. "Do you think there's a chance he's still in the country?"

Caitlin shook her head. "None at all. He'd have moved in and out very quickly. The Skaafe cover was a good one. He didn't use it when I was trailing him. We only found out about it afterward. A solid jacket as a Kurdish-Austrian businessman working in medical supplies. That would have got him all the travel stamps from the Resources Ministry. He was on a clean EU passport, Austrian nationality. Gave him a free pass at border control. Richardson took the job from him six months ago. Paid by small multiple Web transfers into his betting account. He came, he went, he's gone."

Dalby took a long draw on the pipe and closed his eyes, obviously enjoying the indulgence. The smoke had a whiff of port and old leather about it. Rain pattered at the single pane of glass between the office and the training area beyond. A chopper passed by, the hammering blades audible some distance away. *It could lull you to sleep if you didn't mind yourself,* Caitlin thought.

Dalby was quiet for so long, with his eyes shut and his head bobbing slightly, that she was beginning to wonder whether he might have fallen asleep when he spoke again.

"And so where to for Mister Baumer, assuming you're correct?"

She relaxed slightly, relieved that they were moving forward again. She wanted this dealt with so that she could get home.

"Well, not metro France, that's for damn sure. Paris isn't Guadeloupe, and old Sarko runs a pretty hard-hitting crew nowadays, at least in the parts of the country he controls. He's got the migrant ghettos sewed up pretty tight, too. If I had to make a guess, I'd say we'd need to start looking for Baumer in Neukölln, where his mom lived. Still might, if she's alive. Germans didn't go in for the whole ethnic cleansing thing. And they took in a shitload of refugees from France after the war. From here, too, after the Tories took over. A third world shariatown like Neukölln would be a good place for Billy to hole up. He knows the place inside out, and it's crawling with his sort of people. Lots of new faces, too. Makes it hard for the Germans to keep track of the talent. Not that they have time anyway with the Poles and the Russians keeping them busy."

She sighed and shook her head. "What a world, Dalby."

He had the pipe running hot now. Caitlin didn't smoke, but she appreciated the strong, earthy odor after the stink of the interrogation room.

"So you would propose to go back into the field?" he said. "Into Germany as a first measure?"

She nodded. "I had a watching brief on him there for a year. He has a network. Or had one, anyway. The old Doctor Noor outfit…" She paused. "I suppose you can tell me that Doctor No is actually dead, right? The French didn't fuck that up, too."

Dalby smiled.

"No. That half clip of nine-millimeter hollow-point you emptied into his chest back in Paris well and truly sent him off into the afterlife to enjoy his seventy-six raisins with the blessed Prophet. He, at least, is no longer a bother."

"Well, that's something," she conceded. "And to answer your question, yes, I think Germany is the place to begin. I'd like to start as soon as possible."

"I can drive you down to London when we're cleaned up here if you wish," Dalby offered.

"No," Caitlin said. "I'd like to see my family before I leave."

"You know, kickass superspies aren't supposed to have leaky breasts. I checked in the manual. It's like an actual rule or something."

Caitlin swaddled Monique in a fresh blanket and placed her on her back in the cot by Bret's hospital bed.

"Yeah, that might have been a rule once upon a time, but it was superseded by enlightened affirmative action policy ages ago," she said. "Any jihadi whack job or hired killer who tries to take unfair advantage of my leaky breasts is so going to get a severe dressing down from the Advisory Conciliation and Arbitration Service. Plus new moms are perfect assassins. They're supergood at being very quiet, being up late at night, and sneaking around in the dark not stepping on LEGO or shell casings."

Bret smiled, but the effort involved was painfully obvious. Her husband was trying to make light of her departure but failing. He had refused any pain relief so as to be clearheaded when she called, and Caitlin knew him well enough to see that he was trying to hide a serious hurting from her. More important, she knew, he had not forgiven himself for the morning, no matter how many times she told him he had nothing for which to seek forgiveness. He was too much of a soldier to let it go, a ranger no less, no matter how much he tried to distance himself from that past.

He'll never forgive himself, she realized. *Not today, not tomorrow, not ever.*

A low-watt lamp on the shelf by his bed lit the hospital room. Full night had fallen a few hours ago, and the curtains were drawn. Monique gurgled a few times and fell asleep, snoring ever so quietly and all but breaking Caitlin's heart. She had fed her one last time. She gently eased herself down on the edge of the bed next to Bret and took his hand, linking her fingers through his, being careful not to dislodge the IV line or hurt any of his injured digits. She was dressed for travel in jeans, a thick woolen shirt, and her favorite black leather coat, whereas he lay in bandages and a thin cotton nightgown with no ass. It felt wrong, just wrong, to be leaving them, but she had to tell herself that she was not abandoning her family, she was protecting them. And that meant going out into the dark to hunt for monsters.

"That guy Dalby, he's not bad, is he?" Bret said in a quiet, almost croaky voice. "He told me about the arrangements for the farm and the safe house. We're gonna be good to go, Caity, so I don't want you to be worrying about us while you're working. Don't be thinking about having to call and check to see if Monique and I are squared away. Just get on with…"

His soft, battered beautiful face blurred as her tears came. Caitlin leaned forward over him, her tears falling freely onto his cheeks.

"How do you shut an idiot up?" she whispered. She kissed him hard, and for a brief instant everything faded from concern. Bret and Caitlin were the only two people in the whole world. When she pulled away, she could already feel her heart hardening to the task ahead.

"I love you both so much."

"I love you, too," he said.

"And I will be back as soon as I can," she promised. "I'll be fine. And we'll be fine. Everything is gonna be cool."

He squeezed her hand and smiled, but she could tell he did not believe her.

20

"Contact," the pilot said over the cabin speakers of *Air Force One*.
Through his window Kipper watched the smaller plane, a fighter
jet, take on fuel from their escort tanker. He never got tired of
watching the in-flight refueling process. It was a marvel of the
man-machine interface and testimony to the fact that almost any
problem was amenable to rational thought and considered action.

Almost any problem.

"Refueling complete," the pilot of the smaller plane said over the
radio. The fighter pulled away from the refueling probe, and a mist
of fuel vaporized harmlessly over the fuselage as the pilot rejoined
his place in formation against a clear blue sky. Kipper understood,
however, that their plane, *Air Force One,* had no such capability. He
had asked about it and argued with Jed for a different aircraft, one
of the air force C-17s, but Culver and his staff had fallen on that
suggestion like a sack of hammers.

"The aircraft that is *Air Force One* needs to be one that upholds the significance and prestige of the president of the United States," they said.

What prestige? Kipper often wondered as he boarded "his" plane at some lifeless airfield in the middle of nowhere. On this trip, for instance, they'd transferred from the *Marine One* chopper to *Air Force One* at an airbase in upstate New York a couple of hours after escaping the city. A grim, windswept outpost it was, too, manned by a heavily armed company of marines. He shook his head. This really wasn't how he'd expected to be coming home. Again he thought, *What prestige?*

After the brief interlude of the refueling operation, Kip dropped back into the padded leather chair across from his chief of staff and resigned himself to wrestling with a long list of problems for which no elegant solutions presented themselves. As he sat down, he knocked a book off his armrest: David McCullough's biography of Truman. He'd read over the section on the firing of General Douglas MacArthur for the fourth time that morning once they had cleared the dangerous airspace around Manhattan.

"I didn't fire him because it was the easy thing to do," Truman had said. "I fired him because it was the right thing to do."

"So, Blackstone," Kip sighed.

"Well, at least we don't have polling data," Culver said lightly, but he was tired and stressed, and his eyes failed to light up.

He was right, though. No one bothered to conduct polls these days. There were too many other things to do: food to grow, equipment to scavenge, salvage and clearance work, a nation to rebuild. Those with the number-crunching skills to run polls were put to better uses, such as trying to ration the food supply to keep the population fed or balance a federal budget floating atop an economy that had shrunk to a minuscule fraction of its former size and devolved in part to subsistence and barter. Running polls came in a very poor second. If the president of the United States needed to know what the people were thinking, he had only to go for a walk around Seattle or call up a talk radio station in Alaska, although he rarely did that because of the very real danger of being ambushed on air by Governor Palin.

Anyway, he didn't need a stack of polls to know that Blackstone was dividing the nation, literally and figuratively. How many times had General Franks warned him that if Blackstone secured control of the Mississippi River Valley and the Gulf Coast, their efforts on the eastern seaboard would be pointless? The true border of the United States would end right about where Kansas City rested in the heart of a dead nation. How many times had Kipper put off confronting this inconvenient truth?

The problem, as he understood it, was that a good many folks felt Blackstone was doing the right thing down in Texas. Even in Seattle, where he was regarded with equal measures of fear, scorn, and distrust, there had been some grudging support for his move to seize the Panama Canal back from the gang lords who had taken control of it after the Disappearance.

"Defend as far forward as possible," Mad Jack had argued. It was the sort of stuff that made headlines, or "generated political capital," as Culver said.

More unsettling than that, however, had been the foreign support he'd garnered. Eight countries, including Israel, had opened consulates in Fort Hood after Blackstone had secured the canal, and although their consuls were officially accredited to the federal government, it was no secret that the diplomats worked directly with Blackstone's people, cutting the State Department out of the process. Worse still, they were providing Blackstone with operating capital, technical expertise, and political support in exchange for the right to extract oil, technology, and salvage without the fees imposed by the federal government on the western seaboard.

Kip stared unhappily out the window at the plains of Ohio. All this and now a pirate war that may or may not be the start of a holy war the like of which had all but torn France asunder a few short years ago. The president had no doubt that Colonel Kinninmore would be turning the city upside down as he attempted to find any evidence that the fighting there was not just an opportunistic attack by a pack of scavengers who'd decided to band together for as long as it took to convince him the city wasn't worth retaking. But what if he did find evidence of a new threat on the eastern seaboard? Kipper almost wished the plane would never land, because then he wouldn't have to face the consequences of whatever was coming for him in the next few days.

Instead he sighed and took in the view, such as it was.

Patches of black ruin from a city with no name stretched across the horizon below *Air Force One*. Some of the firestorms had expanded out of the cities and into the surrounding burbs and rural areas, chewing up hundreds of square miles of land in spite of the presence of snow back in March 2003. He could see the steel and concrete stumps of what might have been skyscrapers and highways below. Back in Seattle, in Barney Tench's office, there was a map of the United States covered with graphics representing such areas. Dead zones, they were called. Yet Kipper could see plants and trees struggling to take dominion where humanity once had reigned supreme.

He knew that in the unaffected areas of Ohio's flat, glaciated landscape, nature was coming on with a vengeance. The well-defined borders of thousands of farms gone fallow, the extensive road network, it was all disappearing as Mother Nature wiped away the more fragile traces of human settlement. The ruins and the intact smaller farm towns still loomed large on the vast checkerboard of the land below, but they were utterly lifeless, and he wondered sometimes whether they could be reclaimed before brute creation took over again.

"D' you think I made a mistake, letting those diplomats into Texas?" he asked Culver as he stared out the window at the thin sliver of golden light on the western edge of the world.

Jed seemed a little nonplussed at the unexpected tangent, but he waved off Kipper's obvious self-doubts.

"It was a close call, Mister President. Fort Hood is our second biggest population center and Texas is our largest territory in the Wave-affected zone in terms of population. We have a lot of homesteaders down in Texas. And those foreign missions aren't full embassies, just small offices, Chargé d' affaires and a couple of honorary consuls—"

Kip cut him off gently.

"You're covering for me, Jed. You didn't want to accredit any of them as I recall. Said it'd be a big mistake. What's different now?"

Culver sized him up, a look Kip had come to recognize. He was about to get a straight shot to the head.

"The difference is, sir, that they are there now. And if we withdrew recognition of those offices, chances are, their governments would just ignore us and keep them open. It would serve as a demonstration of our weakness. It's better that we just leave them there for now, conniving with Mad Jack, and deal with them once we're done with him."

A steward, an air force staff sergeant, appeared at Kip's elbow with a tray of sandwiches and two cups of cocoa.

"Thank you, son," Culver said, scooping up two thick wedges of corned beef on rye. Somehow the food scarcity that had trimmed Kipper's waistline seemed to have missed Jed's. The man still sported the double chin of someone used to expensive dinners and long lunches. Kipper took one sandwich and his drink, talking around mouthfuls of food.

"I don't think Blackstone is really crazy," he said. "Not like everybody says. I think that whole Mad Jack routine of his is just a smoke screen. Distracts people from his real intent."

"And what would his real intent be, Mister President?"

Kipper drank some of his cocoa before answering.

"I think he's just a very old-fashioned guy, Jed. He sees a chance to take the country back to what he thinks of as its roots. And some of that stuff is good, you know. Respect for institutions and authority. Civic duty. The frontier spirit. All that Kennedy stuff about asking what you can do for your country rather than the other way around. It's no different from what we've been talking about since the election."

"But?" Culver prodded.

"But he gets things confused. This business of running off our homesteaders. He's not. He's only running off some of them."

"The ones with the wrong skin color."

"Yes," said Kipper. "Jack Blackstone looks back on an older, simpler America and likes what he sees. He's trying to remake it down there, but he's making a big mistake. He's confusing people with ideas. He looks at a Mexican, someone like… who was that guy… the first one on the list you showed me…"

Culver had to juggle his sandwich, coffee, and laptop computer, along with a manila folder, but he eventually dug out the piece of paper he wanted.

"Uh, Pieraro," he said. "Miguel Pieraro."

"Yeah. He looks at Pieraro, and he sees an alien. A fucking peasant. Someone not of his world because he looks different. He talks different. Hell, yes, he probably thinks differently about some things because of the world he grew up in. But this Pieraro guy, God rest his soul, I didn't know him, but I do know that he went through our homesteading selection process, which means he is not just some wetback peon with an eye to an easy score. We don't let just anybody into that scheme, Jed. You know they have to prove themselves worthy. They have to *want* it and work for it. Really fucking hard. This guy—" He waved his corned beef on rye at the piece of paper Jed was still holding. "—he had to jump through hoops of fucking fire, backward, singing 'The Star Spangled Banner' just to earn the right to sit the tests that weeded him out from all the losers and pretenders looking to work the program for a free ride. This guy, all of those people we choose for homesteading, they're committed. Their allegiance isn't in question, nor their skills or suitability. But Blackstone won't see that. He confuses the idea of America with an old and seriously out of date image of America. They're two different things. Miguel Pieraro, he died for the idea of America."

Culver began a slow hand clap. "And if you would just stop being so fucking reasonable and get off your ass and out on the stump and give that same fucking speech ten times a day, perhaps people might start seriously questioning what is going on down south, if you'll excuse me, Mister President."

Kipper took Culver's rebuke in good humor. He needed someone like this shifty, misanthropic bastard watching his back.

"I long ago accepted the fact that you are inexcusable, Jed," he said. "But useful because of it. That's why I'm going to leave Mad Jack to you for the moment. I can see this oozing fucking mess in New York is going to be with me night and day. I wasn't looking for a stand-up fight there. You of all people know that's not my way. But we've had one forced on us, and I do not intend to lose. You have Tommy Franks break out his plans for retaking the city—I know he's got them in a bottom drawer somewhere—and have him meet me in KC. No, scratch that. There's no reason to waste his time in transit. Just schedule a vid link to Fort Lewis. I want to go through the options. I also want the latest from that Colonel Kinnymore—"

"Kinninmore," Jed corrected him.

"Yeah, him, on whether this is a coordinated attack by offshore interests, government or private, whether it is some sort of crazy holy war spin-off from France or the Israeli strike, or whether those fucking pirates have just finally gotten their shit together. Whatever the case, I want options for taking that city."

"Well, the options are simple, Mister President," Culver explained in a somber tone. "You can use men or you can use ordnance. The more men you use, the more of them die. But it does less damage to the infrastructure. The more ordnance we drop, bombs and missiles and so on, the more of our own we save, but much less of the city is left standing. You take that logic to its end point, we just pull out and nuke the place from orbit."

"From orbit?" Kip asked, genuinely confused.

Jed smiled, a real smile this time, if tired. "Sorry, classical reference."

Kipper nodded slowly and took a few moments to himself. He wondered idly just how much of New York City he really did need intact. Manhattan, for sure, and the ports. But did he need the entire metropolis? Even with the uptick in immigration and naturalization of refugees from the Indo-Pakistani War and with thousands of Europeans leaving the Old World every month, it would still be years, if not decades, before they could occupy all the infrastructure in just that one city. By then, the ravages of time would require a total rebuild, anyway.

These thoughts he pondered as the C-40 Clipper continued to hum along, attended by her escorts. F-16s, he remembered; the pilots liked to call them Vipers. Far to the north the moon glinted on a large body of water dusted with low wisps of cloud cover, and he wondered whether that might be the southern extremity of the Great Lakes.

"Remind me, Jed," he asked quietly. "Did the military ever actually develop one of those neutron bombs? You know, kills the people but leaves the city standing."

He watched Culver's face turned a slightly pasty shade.

"I don't know, sir. I suppose I could ask."

"You do that," said the president.

The escorts topped up their fuel tanks one more time somewhere over Illinois before making the run into Kansas City. The last dim light of day had fallen well below the horizon when Corporal Peckham, the younger of the two brothers on his detail, appeared at

Kipper's side and bent forward to whisper that the city was visible on the horizon.

"Thanks, son," he said, unbuckling his seat belt and sliding carefully past Jed Culver, who had fallen asleep beneath a drift of briefing papers. Everyone was worn out and ragged, drained by the adrenaline backwash from their experiences in New York. However, Kipper had specifically asked to be informed when KC came within view. After traversing an empty, burned-out wasteland, he wanted to see a living metropolis, all lit up, as they came in on their final approach.

KC, of course, was not just one city but a cluster of them. Most people, even in the post-Wave world, still confused the city with the state of Kansas. However, the largest part of the city was on the eastern side of the Missouri-Kansas border, straddling the two rivers so named. The resurgence of barge traffic on the rivers was key to the agricultural revitalization of the American Midwest. Together with the network of rail lines that snaked through yards in the West Bottoms and in North Kansas City, the region below was easily the best place to engage as far east as possible.

Kip made his way into the cabin, telling the air crew to carry on with their jobs as they came to attention.

"Good evening, Mister President. You here for the view?" Colonel Terri Lowry, the pilot, pointed out of the cockpit toward the lights on the horizon. "You can see the skyline at my one o'clock. We are presently following U.S. Highway 169 on approach to Charles B. Wheeler Downtown Airport. If you look, you can see that the streetlights are all working and we have some vehicle traffic down there."

"Thank you," Kip said. Indeed, he did see a convoy of vehicles crawling along the highway toward the skyscrapers of the city, most of which were still dark. The semi trucks were hauling something in covered flatbeds, most likely grain from the last harvest. From this altitude, he could see the lights of the federal court house and the city hall, where the Midwestern Restoration Authority was headquartered.

"Can you take me for a spin?" he asked.

"We can certainly take an orbit of the city, as instructed, Mister President," Lowry said. "Wheeler Tower, this is *Air Force One*. We'll be orbiting the city for a visual inspection. Copy?"

"*Air Force One,* this is Wheeler. Traffic pattern is clear. Orbit at your discretion."

"Copy that, Wheeler. *Air Force One* out." She banked to the west, crossing over the mansions of Briarcliff West and across the upper reaches of the Missouri River. Below, salvage crews were working through the night to restore the ruins of the Fairfax Assembly Plant. A random lighting strike back in the Wave year had ignited a fuel storage farm near the factory, creating a firestorm that had severely damaged the facility in spite of the heavy rain. Kipper recalled that all the plant's useful items were to be transferred to the Claycomo Ford plant in the Northland, where vehicles and equipment were systematically stripped for usable parts, inventoried, and stockpiled in limestone caverns through the area. If time were not a concern, he would have loved a tour of the facility, but he had other pressing issues.

To Colonel Lowry's left, the skyscrapers of Kansas City rotated below *Air Force One*. The tallest, One Kansas City Place, featured a large gash in the side where a private jet had speared into its flank on the day of the Disappearance. Trains rumbled through the West Bottoms, where large animal pens held herds of feral cattle rounded up from the area. The feral livestock was a godsend to the slowly starving Pacific Northwest, breaking what had been known in the press as the hungry time. Three trains a week made the run between Seattle and Kansas City, connecting a number of small outposts where homesteaders were attempting to bring the land back to life.

The pilot turned southeast out over the state line for a brief moment before heading due east over the cleared but still relatively vacant I-35. The collapsed column of the Liberty Memorial spilled down the north hillside into Pershing Road. Kipper could see trains and lights passing through Union Station as well as lights within the Crown Center shopping and hotel complex, which served as a barracks for homesteaders settling in the Midwestern restoration areas as well as the local militia forces. This was all good, he thought. It never failed to lift his spirits.

"*Air Force One* copies, Wheeler Tower," Colonel Lowry said, turning the aircraft back to the north. "Mister President, if you could return to your seat, we will be landing shortly."

Kipper nodded. "Thank you for the tour, Colonel. It does me good to see what's going on out here,"

"Thank you, Mister President."

Returning to his seat, he found Jed awake and sorting through his papers again, filing some away and carefully placing others on his tray table, which was weighed down with a glass of bourbon he had procured from somewhere. If he stuck to his usual routine, he would sip his drink and work on the papers until *Air Force One* touched down and the seat belt signs were turned off.

"I don't suppose you need me to tell you," Culver said, not lifting his gaze from the papers, "that forcing Blackstone into retirement was a mistake."

Jed had a habit of picking up conversations hours after they had finished. It was disconcerting until one got used to it. Kip had no trouble dealing with it because his wife did exactly the same thing. Like Culver, she also had a spookily forensic capacity for recall and could throw back in his face incriminating statements he had made weeks, sometimes months, after he had foolishly uttered them.

Kip shrugged. "Couldn't leave him in command. Not after Seattle."

Jed looked up. "We could have promoted him off to oblivion. That's what the Romans used to do. If he were a four-star general down in Panama right now, he'd be relatively harmless to everyone but Roberto. A win-win situation there."

It was an old argument between them by now, one that Kipper responded to without much thought. "Some of those Romans didn't stay gone, Jed. Guy called Julius Caesar comes to mind."

Jed shook his head. "Well, Blackstone is no Caesar any more than MacArthur was. But neither is he the idiot that folks in Seattle think he is. He wasn't much of a politician, either, like you," he added, indicating the Truman biography lying open on Kipper's seat. Kipper brought his seat upright and looked out the cabin window.

Air Force One passed over the Missouri River again, this time on the east side of the urban core. The bridges of the city were strung with lights, reminding him of dew-dappled spiderwebs in the moonlit nights of childhood summers. Traffic pressed across the bridges while a salvage barge full of farm equipment made its way to the reconstructed docks on the north side of the river. They would be loaded onto trains and transported to Claycomo for processing. Street lamps flooded the roads with a sickly yellow light on the north side of the Missouri River, where most of the permanent population lived in an area known as Northtown. Futuristic spires and gleaming office buildings filled the dark sky with the brightest light.

Culver caught a glimpse through Kipper's window. "That's the Cerner Campus, home of the Heartland Territorial Government. We've just moved in there. If things go according to plan, we should have Heartland admitted as a state before the next election. That could help us."

"Cerner? Don't they do medical technology?" Kipper asked, ignoring the politics.

Culver nodded. "Yeah, they had a lot of people overseas in 2003. Most of them are back here now in their R&D division, but not with enough numbers to fill the campus. Territorial government took fully serviced office space there in return for tax concessions."

Kipper wondered how Jed kept all this stuff in his head.

"Good morning, Mister President and passengers on board *Air Force One*," Colonel Lowry said over the speakers. "We are due to land at Charles B. Wheeler Downtown Airport shortly. Please secure all belongings and prepare for landing. Security detail and crew to arrival stations."

"Caesar or not, what's done—" Kipper turned away from the window and looked squarely at his chief of staff. "—is done. Question now is what's to be done next. That's up to you, my friend. Turn your devious mind to it and get back to me with a cunning plan."

Jed took a pull on his bourbon.

"For now," he said, "I'd suggest doing nothing. But only for now, while we're distracted in New York. I'll admit, Mister President, I don't like the way things have gone bad so quickly there. It smells. I do have some plans for Texas, but you're right about needing to focus on the piracy issue first. Especially if it turns out we've got something worse than pirates in New York."

"But if we do nothing about these forced evictions in the Mandate, now that we know what's happening, it'll be taken as consent and I'll be held accountable," Kipper said.

Culver shook his head. "I don't think so, Mister President. Not with the fighting in New York. People will believe you're biding your time, waiting for an opportunity to settle up," he said, sipping his bourbon.

"He hasn't given me one," Kipper said.

Jed pointed at a stack of briefing documents on the unoccupied chair next to the president. "In all of those files, do you have any on your officers? Any officer evaluation reports?"

Kipper's face went blank. "No, why? I could get them, I suppose. General Franks would probably ship over whatever I wanted, but what good would they do?"

"Well, for one thing, they'd tell you what other officers thought of Blackstone. His file is interesting. I've studied it deeply. He's aggressive, almost to the point of folly. He has a mouth he can't quite control, which is one reason he was at Fort Lewis in command of I Corps in '03, far away from the main game in the Middle East. He overreaches, especially when in command of a military operation. Sometimes skill and a combination of luck and mistakes by his opponents reward that aggressiveness. And..." Jed finished his drink and smiled wolfishly.

Kipper smiled. "And sometimes his mistakes catch up with him. Like in Seattle?"

Jed nodded. "See, you're learning. We'll make a president out of you yet."

The small windows were full of dawn's breaking light now as they descended toward the tarmac at Charles B. Wheeler Downtown Airport. Culver leaned forward and raised his glass to Kip.

"When Blackstone makes a mistake," he said, "I promise you it'll be a large one. In my judgment, Jack Blackstone is a man who can be led all too easily to foolish and intemperate action, which, by the way, just happens to be one of the many services I provide."

21

NEW YORK

"Man, this is the way to fight pirates," said Wilson.

"This is the way to fight everyone," Milosz said, as he watched sheets of rain drift down past the ninth-floor window of the apartment building on Astor Place. A contrary gust of wind would sometimes blow a few drops in on his face, but compared with the poor bastards doing their fighting down on the streets below, he was warm and dry and relatively safe. This was much more pleasant than flying into a nest of vipers such as the ones they had encountered on Ellis Island.

He sat on a very comfortable leather armchair that was perched on top of a huge oak desk some distance back from the window, providing him with an elevated view of the street without exposing him too much. Wilson, sitting next to Milosz in another chair they'd hauled up on top of a dining-room table, scanned their field of fire for any more hostiles while the Polish commando resisted the urge for another Winston from his growing stash of New York City plunder. He sucked down a little more of the stale Folgers coffee instead and continued his own scan. The weapon, a fifty-caliber M107 sniper rifle, was heavier than he was used to, but he'd traded up because the M107 was a big serious weapon for big serious work, and he wanted to be able to neutralize any threat short of a T-90. With Wilson's help he had stabilized it by screwing the base into a wooden file cabinet that they'd also lifted up onto the makeshift firing platform. The whole arrangement gave the impression of two overgrown boys who'd decided to build a fort in their rich uncle's apartment.

For the moment, there was no movement at all. Using a thermal sight on his rifle, Milosz was able to watch the body heat leaking out of the eight men he had already killed around the Brinks armored truck they had been using to get around the city. He had put two rounds of armor-piercing incendiary into the engine block to stop the truck before sending another round through the skull of the driver. He and Wilson had picked off the rest, before any of them made it to cover. One of them, he noted with interest, was wearing a scarf of the type sported by the pirate... how would you describe them? Commanders? Captains? That seemed too formal. Whatever his role, the dead man's body, like the others, had glowed a fierce cherry red when Milosz had shot him, but now they all registered as dim, wistful ghost images in the AN/PAS-13 scope. Soon, with the cold rain draining all the heat from their corpses, the last trace of their lives would vanish, at least to him. The bodies would stay where they'd fallen until it was safe to dispose of them.

If there was danger in all this, it was that he was so comfortable in the expensive lounger that he might fall asleep. As his eyelids began to droop, he decided on another square of chocolate and a fresh coffee.

"I am getting drowsy, Wilson. I shall make some more shitty Folgers if you would like."

"What I'd like," said the wiry black man, "is three days in bed with some smoking, cocksuckin' hottie. The first two days, just to sleep."

"Ah, that way lies madness, Wilson, believe me. I had a wife once. Am much better now in city of the dead being shot at by pirate bitches and fools."

"Who said anything about a wife?" Wilson asked with real umbrage. It was almost as though Milosz had let slip another nig nog or two. "I'm talking *poo-saay,* my friend."

"Is all the same in end," said Milosz. "All the women, they hold out promise of this mythical *poo-say,* but what you get is nagging and frustration and not so much of the penis gobbling. Being shot at is much more exciting, believe me."

Wilson eased back from the spotter scope for a moment, looking wistful. "I hear Texas is the place for a man to live these days. Frontier country again. Your money can buy anything there. New toys, booze, *real* hotties," he added significantly.

Milosz squirmed, uncomfortable with the direction of this conversation. "Are you thinking about going there? My brother and his family, they farm in Texas on the federal program. They do not so much like this Blackstone."

Wilson pulled back from the scope and shook his head. "Nah, I hear Mad Jack down there, he's cool with the black man, as long as you served, but he has a god-awful number of redneck cracker assholes gathering to his flag who aren't. I'm looking further ahead, no matter how shitty the short run may be."

Milosz patted Wilson on the back. "Good man. Like your famous Gatsby, no? I, too, believe in the green light, the orgastic future that year by year recedes before us. I read your famous books to understand this country, yes? But orgastic? This word I do not know. Explain, please."

"I think it's a sex thing, maybe," Wilson said, uncertainly.

He was not much of a reader as far as Milosz had observed.

"Oh, well, then. I am going to get some of that stale and unacceptable coffee now," Milosz said.

Wilson nodded, taking up the long fifty from Milosz's grip after he had set his own carbine aside. "Take ten. Get a smoke in while you're at it. No one will smell your nasty Winstons up here."

Milosz eased himself out of the lounger and stretched, cracking the bones in his back into place. He peered down into the streets leading back toward the East Village, but without the long fifty's thermal scope, there was not much to be seen. Low clouds blocked any natural light, and the rain had doused many of the fires set burning by the day's combat. A few buildings were still aflame here and there, but no fighters moved anywhere near them. They stood out too starkly on the darkened stage of an empty city. Gunships and A-10 Warthogs circled continuously, waiting for just such targets of opportunity.

The Polish commando, so far from his birth home, walked carefully through the apartment, navigating partly by memory, partly by dint of the fact that he and Wilson had pushed most of the furniture up against the walls while they still had daylight. It gave him a clear path back into the kitchen, where he'd set up a little Coleman stove in the sink. He could use it safely back here without fear of the tiny blue flame giving away their position. Milosz brewed two cups of strong coffee and contemplated adding a slug of brandy—the apartment had been furnished with an excellent bar—but it was an idle thought. He had also salvaged a bottle of vodka, which he would enjoy when they came off the line, but for now, he was so sleep-deprived and physically exhausted that a mouthful of alcohol might be the end of him.

The fighting had not ceased completely with the fall of darkness. Both sides enjoyed the advantage of night vision equipment, and a small battle appeared to be raging in the foul weather some ten or fifteen blocks to the north. But the rain had flooded huge tracts of Lower Manhattan, making tactical movement difficult, if not impossible, and the huge brigade-level encounters of the morning had died down as conditions had deteriorated. At first the Americans had been choppering in, right on top of the pirates—or looters, as Milosz insisted on calling them. To him the word "pirates" sounded a bit too glamorous for the lowest forms of criminal scum, scavengers raking over the junk heap of a dead city. But so many men and helicopters were lost to shoulder-fired rockets that all movement was now either on foot or by armored fighting vehicle, and even they could fall prey to giant bombs hidden at the roadside or in piles of refuse and wreckage. All in all, Milosz was more than happy to sit up here in his well-furnished eyrie, picking off random targets as they presented themselves. A troop of cavalry had his back, securing the lower levels of the building against infiltrators, and the Apaches circling beneath the cloud cover would swoop down on any large group attempting to rush their position. Forward observers even coordinated concentrated bursts of accurate cannon fire from the army and the naval vessels on the East River now. It was such an agreeable setup, all things considered, that it could not possibly last.

He returned with the coffees and a Mars Bar chopped in two with his Gerber knife, a prize from a game of poker with Wilson two weeks back.

Happier times.

The master sergeant leaned forward in his own luxury armchair, pressing his fingers up against the single earpiece of their radio. Milosz, without a headset on, could not hear the exchange.

"This is Gopher one-three," Wilson said, using the latest in an ever-changing series of call signs. "Go with your traffic."

Milosz waited for Wilson to finish his conversation.

"Gopher copies," Wilson said. "Out."

He took the hot coffee from Milosz and inhaled the chocolate bar all in one go.

"Sorry, spring break is over. Militia company pushed a little too far forward up on Madison Square, got 'emselves surrounded. The disco lights just started up from that direction. We're moving up with the cav to dig 'em out."

Milosz took a few moments to savor his half of the Mars Bar and sip the rest of the coffee. His gear was ready to move at moment's notice, and he did not know when they might eat again.

* * *

The nig nogs were flooding in from…

Milosz forced himself to back up and rephrase that. He had promised Wilson there would be no more nig nog talk. And anyway, not all the looters were nig nogs. Many were ragheads. Some were beaners. There were even a few outfits from his part of the world, Slavic crews out of Serbia and Russia. The latest intelligence even had a few dozen players from the Chechen mafia working the north end of the island. For some reason, though, the loose coalition of bandits who were actually spoiling for a fight were mostly African or refugees from the Second Holocaust, a grab bag of different Arab nationalities and Iranians. They were flooding into the blocks around Madison Square Park, where Alpha Company of Governor Schimmel's First New York Militia Regiment was cut off and in danger of being overrun.

"The better part of Alpha has holed up here," said the colonel as he pointed at a strange map surrounded by cups of stale coffee, pencils, rulers, and message printouts on a dusty conference room table. It showed not only the street grid for that part of the city but 3D-like drawings of the buildings. They reminded Milosz of a tourist guide to Rome he had once owned. He had never been there, of course. Sergeants in the Polish Army did not earn that sort of money. But as a staunch Catholic he often dreamed of visiting the Pope in his hometown, even when the blessed John Paul II had passed on to his reward and been replaced by that creepy German, Ratzinger. So he had bought a copy of that guide to Rome, which featured maps just like this one.

The colonel, whose name tag read kinninmore, stabbed his finger down again, pointing to a richly illustrated wedge of parkland.

"Unfortunately," he continued, raising his voice over a wash of radio chatter that spilled out of a makeshift communications area. The sound of panic filled the room until someone turned the speakers down, reducing the gunfire and shouts to a tolerable level. The colonel resumed his speech. "Unfortunately," he said, "there's a platoon and spare change pinned down out here, in the open. They have good tree cover and have dug themselves in as best they can, but the pirates are pouring it on. They want to wipe out a whole company. We're shielding them with protective fire out of our ships on the river, but they're running low and resupply is dicey at best."

Again with the pirates, Milosz thought. They really needed a better name for these asswits. There. Asswits. That would do perfectly well. Master Sergeant Wilson could not complain about that that because asswits, in Fryderyck Milosz's long and all too common experience, came in a variety of colors and ethnicities. Whereas the pirates who had first raided New York in the weeks after the Wave rolled back came from one place only, Nigeria, specifically the port of Lagos. They were real, modern-day pirates, too, who until then had made a living seizing and ransoming container ships in the Gulf of Guinea when they didn't simply kill the crew and take the cargo for themselves. The news of the first of their number to strike out across the Atlantic and come home with a hold full of treasures saw most of the port's pirate cohort immediately slip anchor for the New World. Then most of the port's other inhabitants followed them. Then, increasingly, competitors from neighboring countries, from the Caribbean and South America and of course from the benighted wastelands of all those lands destroyed by the Israelis' nuclear strikes.

As far as Milosz could tell, the original Nigerian pirates weren't even operating here anymore, having been driven off by larger, better-armed and -organized competitors. So it just wasn't correct to call them pirates anymore. Whereas "asswits"—a term he had picked up from a British officer in Iraq—well, asswits very much appealed to him.

Colonel Kinninmore, however, was sticking with "pirates."

"The pirates we're looking at here are probably sourced from over a dozen different crews, until recently none of them coordinating very well but all of them pretty well established in the AOR, and with good equipment. Suspiciously good equipment. They have solid Russian AKMs, PKMs, a lot of Chinese Type 56s, and some crew-served stuff, which they've taken off the trucks since we started interdicting them by air. They have some night vision capabilities, a mix of Chinese and Russian gear, which seems to be unevenly distributed. Same with body armor; even got some scavenged NYPD vests thrown in. Their comms gear is very good. Although their radio security is not."

Milosz stole a glance out the window of the conference room. It was on the fourth floor of a nondescript office building near Union Square, looking out across a little park. All the big boys had been brought to the conference, special operators from all four branches of the U.S. military along with private contract operators from Sandline. One of the Navy SEALs from Ellis Island recognized Milosz and nodded to him.

Dolphin fucker, Milosz thought, nodding back and taking notice of one of the females in the room, a blond woman who could have been army or air force, it was hard to tell. She stood, popping her bubble gum, next to a very large... African American.

"Our first priority with this mission is getting those militia boys out of the shit," said Kinninmore. "But there is a secondary consideration, too."

The assembled men and women appeared to perk up at that.

"I said before that the pirates weren't very well coordinated until recently. But you'll all be aware that's changed in this latest round of fighting. Those of you who fought on Ellis will have encountered the guys there with the scarfs. They seemed to be providing tactical-level command. We've seen the same thing here on the big island. You'll also know we haven't yet been able to capture one."

Milosz remembered the mess one of those crazy fucks had made of Raab and Sievers.

"As a secondary, and for now I mean *secondary,* consideration, the National Command Authority would very much like it if we could obtain one of those gentlemen for a full and frank exchange of views on what the fuck they're doing in New York."

The room filled with grunts and a few curses. Everyone knew of somebody who'd been taken out by one of the exploding bad guys. Milosz peered out into the darkness. From here you could see flashes and snaking flights of tracer fire farther uptown. The open area below was well lit up as Strykers and Humvees poured into the staging post. Two converted M1 Abrams tanks fitted with massive plows and Mk19 grenade launchers were grunting and chugging thick clouds of hot exhaust that caused the paint to peel on the abandoned cars. They cleared the intersections of wrecks, piling them up into a makeshift berm in case everything went wrong and the Americans had to retreat to a strongpoint.

"Anyway, that's where you come in," said Kinninmore, and instantly Milosz switched his full attention back to the briefing. The ads were over, and it was time for the main feature, as Sergeant Wilson would say.

"I need you to work in behind the enemy, determine their lines of approach, and mark them for interdiction. If, *and only if,* you can grab one of our mystery men without getting yourself blown to pieces, then you're tasked to do that, too."

"We getting full air this time, Colonel?" Master Sergeant Wilson asked in a familiar tone, teetering between hope and resignation. "Sounds like we can't count on arty."

"We are," said Kinninmore, surprising everyone. "We've got aircraft stacked up in holding patterns up to thirty thousand feet, all loaded for bear. We also have air force operators who will be assigned to each of your teams. The gloves are off, gentlemen. We have fast movers in play right now, in-flight tankers to keep them there. And they are ready to bring death and sadness down on the city. So you will be calling in the real deal. Whole blocks are gonna get leveled if the payoff demands it."

"Most excellent!" Milosz blurted out before he could stop himself.

Kinninmore did not seem put out by the interruption; instead, he grinned appreciatively.

"Indeed, it is most excellent Sergeant... Milosz."

He pronounced it wrong, but his sentiments were in the right place.

"No more dicking around, people. We have new orders direct from the president himself. Kill them all."

"Ah, I knew I liked this president," said Milosz. "He is reminding me of Clevinger, Yossarian's foil in Mister Heller's *Catch-22*. Has anyone read it? An excellent novel for military men, no?"

He knew they were serious this time, because he was back in a helicopter, and they would be flying through rocket swarms before his feet touched the ground again. If they ever did. Outside of the Blackhawk, other helicopters orbited the rooftop, waiting for Milosz and Wilson to get clear in order to pick up the other teams waiting for insertion at their objectives. The woman from the briefing was sitting across from Milosz. She leaned forward and offered her hand.

"I don't believe we've done the formalities. Tech Sergeant Bonnie Gardener," she said. She nodded toward her partner, a large man with an M240 machine gun. "And this is my spotter, Staff Sergeant Veal."

The machine gunner merely nodded in response.

"Tactical air controller, air force special ops," explained Wilson as the engines spooled up and made normal conversation difficult. "We mark the targets. She calls 'em in."

"And what if asswit pirate boy is sitting in the Metropolitan Museum of Art?" asked Milosz. "Can be we bomb statutes and paintings now?"

Gardener grinned; an evil-looking grin it was, too.

"I'm from Alabama, Sergeant. We never did care much for art down there. 'Cept for that very special form of performance art created by five-hundred-pound bombs. Or dynamite and iron anvils. Y'all ever seen that done?"

Wilson laughed. "I like you already, Gardener. You're my kinda cracker."

And there was much to like about this Gardener, thought Milosz. She was a very attractive woman, although he knew better than to make anything of her sex. This Veal was a very ugly-looking guard dog indeed. Oh, well, the U.S. military took its warm bodies wherever it could find them these days. He was proof of that. And Gardener did not seem at all bothered to be heading into a roiling snake pit, even though women captured by the asswits had a much tougher time of it than men—and male prisoners were routinely tortured, humiliated, and killed in the most gruesome fashion, often on video, for propaganda. Gardener, however, seemed unconcerned.

He felt liftoff press them all into their seats before they banked away from the rooftop helipad. For just a moment he was afforded a clear view of the battle raging a dozen blocks north. The solid, rectilinear landscape of dead Manhattan, miles of right angles and straight lines soaring skyward in the bleak, inky blackness under a lowering sky, was broken and lit up in one small tile of open space where flaring light and fire raged. He could see small, single pinpoints of light moving through the rain from the north and west, like fireflies drawn to a spitting campfire. Across from him, Gardener checked her equipment as Wilson did the same thing. It was busywork. They had all checked and cross-checked their loadouts before climbing on board.

Milosz had switched up again, opting for an M4 fitted with an M203 grenade launcher from the traveling weapons locker that accompanied the ranger teams everywhere they went. He looked it over for any problems, performing a function check on the carbine while in flight. Sighting through the ACOG scope, the M4 felt impossibly light, even with the forty-millimeter launcher mounted under the carbine. He would have preferred a solid AKM with the same grenade launcher but was shot down every time he asked. No weapons that looked like those of the opposing forces, which was just as well since the SAPI plate in his body armor and the weight of three days' food, rations, and ammunition more than made up for the lightness of the carbine. For good measure, Milosz also packed a pair of claymores, eight rounds of HEMP for the 203, a quartet of frags, and a block of C-4.

Be prepared, he always said.

Wilson and Gardener looked over their M4 carbines. He noticed that Gardener also carried two pistols in combat rigs holstered on her thighs, plus a couple of thermite grenades, probably to destroy the radio and her laser designator.

She smiled when she saw Milosz looking at the pistols. "Nice, aren't they? Nothing better than an M1911 forty-five for knockdown power. I'm not going easy into that good night, Sergeant."

Milosz nodded.

Veal growled, "We ain't going at all."

"Ah." Milosz grinned. "That is orgastic Gatsby spirit, yes?"

The air force grunt just stared back, saying nothing. Another illiterate, then.

"Y'all think we'll be laying hands on any of those scarf-wearing motherfuckers?" Gardener asked.

Wilson was emphatic.

"No. I lost of couple a good guys to one of those whack jobs on Ellis. You see one, Technical Sergeant, you bring the fucking sky down on top of him. We won't be getting close. Agreed, Fred?"

"Orgastically." Milosz grinned.

The Blackhawk swooped around far to the west, well away from the main concentration of enemy forces. But even so, ground fire reached up for them as they hammered low over the unlit warren of Greenwich Avenue and the West Village. Metallic pings and pops signaled a couple of lucky hits, but the pilot forged on, describing a snaking path up the island that never exposed them to a line of fire for more than a few seconds. As they crossed West 23rd Street, Gardener toe-tapped Milosz on the side of his boot and jerked her thumb, pointing east. Milosz had a clear view of seven or eight rocket-propelled grenades as they described tightly swirling arcs through the air to detonate in a spectacular constellation of starbursts against the façade of a high-rise. Falling glass and metal twinkled in the light of other fires. And then they had swept past and the destruction was reduced to unseen flashes and sheet lightning.

Master Sergeant Wilson, he noted, had his eyes closed and might even have been sleeping. Veal yawned expansively. Milosz knew it was common among combat veterans, especially airborne forces, to doze fitfully while flying into a landing zone. It was not bravado. This was simply one of the few times over the next few days they would get to sit quietly without having to remain constantly alert to enemy movements. Unfortunately, Milosz had never learned the art of blocking out the infernal racket of a helicopter in flight and so contented himself by furtively sneaking glances at the air force woman.

She was a fine and fierce-looking warrior encased in her body armor and festooned with weapons, and it had been many months since Milosz had enjoyed any quality time with any woman. He sighed and shook off such thoughts as best he could. This was going nowhere. She was very heavily armed.

"Help you, Sergeant?"

Damn, she had caught him sneaking a peek.

"No," he replied, bluffing. "You catch me daydreaming of better world, yes, except it is not day, and there is nowhere better in the world to be."

"Oh, yeah. It's nice work if you can get it," Gardener happily agreed, although she looked as though she knew exactly what he had been up to. She didn't seem to care, though.

Milosz reached through his body armor to his sweat-soaked T-shirt and pulled out the small cross he wore on a chain around his neck. He kissed it and asked God for the strength to keep his mind on the job and out of Technical Sergeant Gardener's pants, where it seemed inclined to stray.

"Two minutes!" barked the Blackhawk's crew chief. He had stuck a Velcro patch on his uniform that read number one infidel.

Milosz saw Gardener smiling at it and was annoyed to find himself feeling a brief pang of jealousy.

Veal blinked groggily like a man awakened far too early from a much-needed nap. Wilson came awake like a cat, all at once.

"Lock and load," he ordered. Magazines came out of ammo pouches. Wilson and Gardener both tapped mags against their helmets before slapping them into the magazine well. Milosz skipped the meaningless helmet tap and locked a round into place. For good measure, he pulled a fat forty-millimeter high-explosive grenade from his webbing. As he slid the 203 into the breech, he tried to crush the image of his very own weapon slipping into the air force lady.

Oh, Milosz, he scolded himself. Pope John Paul would be very disappointed.

He leaned sideways as the chopper began to angle around for a fast insertion. They were setting down on a clear, flat rooftop, and Milosz fired up his night vision goggles, set for low light amplification, and slapped them down over his eyes, turning the world a cool, fuzzy green.

"Ten seconds," said the Number One Infidel.

The Blackhawk slowed to a hover as the crew chief threw the ropes out. Milosz was up and on the rope first, grabbing it with his hands.

The chief sought clearance from the cockpit and received it.

"Go-go-go!"

Milosz stepped out of the aircraft, his feet gripping the cord between his ankles in one fluid motion. He slid down into the maelstrom below.

22

TEXAS ADMINISTRATIVE DIVISION

"You have more of these?"

Miguel held up the heavy black goggles to admire them. They did not look very comfortable, but if they did what Aronson claimed and allowed the wearer to see in the dark, they would be more than worth a little discomfort. The Mormon leader—Miguel had come to recognize him as the head of their party—shook his head.

"I am afraid not," he said. "We only have two pair. We originally picked them up to keep an eye on the herd at night. It never occurred to us that we'd need them for any other reason."

Miguel placed them back on the faded Formica top of the table in the diner attached to Leona's general store. He made no comment on Aronson's lack of foresight. The night vision goggles had been designed for soldiers to use in night fighting. Surely it must have occurred to someone in their party that they might have a purpose beyond babysitting cattle through a long Texas evening. It was not his place to question other people's judgment, however. After all, he was the man who could not save his own family. At that thought he could not help taking a quick, flitting glance at his daughter to reassure himself that she was nearby.

Sofia was no more than a few feet away at another table in the diner, helping sort through stores brought up from the basement. She was still very subdued, but he could tell she was making an effort to be pleasant with the new people. For their part they were solicitous of her feelings, and Aronson's wife Maive in particular seemed to be trying very hard to look after her. Miguel was grateful for that. He moved the night vision goggles off the road map they had spread out on the table, where it covered a dark black stain left by whoever had been having a meal here when they Disappeared. All the remains were gone now, respectfully removed and buried in soft ground at the back of the store. Not that there were many "remains" as such, just a lot of clothing, stiffened and stained by the noxious organic waste that the energy wave had left behind when it hit people. Not knowing the faith of those they had buried, the Mormons had enacted a small brief ceremony of their own that seemed specifically tailored to mourning those who were not of their church. Miguel had kept a respectful distance, but Sofia had seemed interested in the unusual prayers and display of faith, and he had no objection to her watching more closely if the Mormons did not mind. They did not.

"It is a pity about the goggles, then," he said. "We will need to hit them at night if they are as numerous as you say."

"There were at least two dozen of them, I'm sure," Aronson said.

The cowboy nodded. "I have never heard of Blackstone's men traveling in small bands."

Aronson looked up from where he had been studying the map and frowned. "You keep referring to them as Governor Blackstone's men, Miguel," he said. "But they are just bandits. Blackstone has outlawed them."

Miguel waved away the distinction.

"They serve his ends," he said, "even if he denounces them. I have spoken to other settlers about this. Many agree with me. As do the banditos from south of the Rio Grande. Did you know they will not cross the agents' territory? They consider it Blackstone land already."

Aronson looked like a professor challenged by a particularly obdurate student, but even if he felt like arguing, Willem D'Age was in no mood to be distracted.

"We need to catch up with them, to cover this ground as quickly as possible," he said as he swept a hand over the map. "And we will need to travel at night. Is that right, Miguel?"

He nodded. "Not at first, when we set out from here. But yes, we must assume they have scouts out the closer we get to them. We will need the darkness then. It is the only way. There are many more of them, and… they will be seasoned killers. Your party, Aronson. It is…" He trailed off.

Aronson conceded the point with a lift of his shoulders. "No, you're right; we are not like them. There's no point pretending otherwise."

"We will need to take them by surprise," Miguel said. "It will be difficult and unpleasant. Very unpleasant. I have been thinking about how we might do it and have written down a few ideas and a list of supplies we will need."

He reached into his jacket pocket to fetch an old folded envelope on which he had sketched out his plan, such as it was. Instead, he accidentally brought out the photograph he had taken from the homestead just before they left. Seeing his wife smiling and surrounded by their children, he felt as though he had been struck a blow just below the heart.

"Excuse me," he said quietly as he returned the photograph carefully to his pocket.

The day was heating up outside, turning into one of the warmer days Miguel could remember in quite some time. It had been a hard winter in East Texas, but the air in the diner grew thick and close

as morning closed in on noon. The Mormon women, with the help
of Sofia and the two boys, Adam and Orin, were progressing well
with the job of restocking the group's supplies. He was glad that
Sofia had work to distract her. It was undoubtedly better that she
not spend today in the saddle dwelling on what had happened back
at the homestead. Helping these people would help her; he was
sure of it. Unfortunately, there could be no doubt that helping the
Mormons would also serve to put his daughter in the way of grave
harm, because that was where Miguel himself was heading.

"It will be a difficult business scouting this town," he said as they
surveyed the map of Crockett. "Although if I was driving a herd
of stolen cattle and looking for an easy time of it, I would probably
graze them here on the southeastern edge of the city. Near this
school or college." He pointed at a cluster of buildings and playing
fields on the map.

"Well, none of us are real cattlemen, Miguel," said Aronson.
"We're willing to take your counsel on that. So then, do you think
that's the direction we should approach from?"

"Not directly," he said. "And we do not even know they are
there in town, let alone camped in this particular field. If they are,
it would be best if we came in through cover. You cannot tell from
this map, but we must hope there is forest or brushland along any
line of approach we might take. But unless there is someone among
you who knows this town well, we shall just have to be careful and
scout it out properly."

The screen door behind him creaked open, admitting to the diner
a giant by the name of Ben Randall. He carried sledgehammers and
clothing wrapped in a giant bundle.

"Got what you wanted," he said to Miguel.

"Good. Just put them over there on the table next to the women."

Randall unburdened himself of the load, which landed on the
table with a dull crash. He was one of the biggest men Miguel
had ever seen, some sort of engineer in his former life who'd

been working on an oil rig somewhere off Indonesia when the Wave struck. He had grown up on a farm, however, and of all the Mormons, except Peter Atchison, their senior horse wrangler, he seemed the most comfortable in the wild. Joining them at the map, he wiped a thin film of sweat from his brow as he appeared to take in all the squiggles and lines converging on the town.

"Guess we'd better pray for some cover."

"Pray if you must, Mister Randall," Miguel said. "But I believe the good Lord will look after those who are best prepared and who have investigated their enemies."

Aronson looked troubled, and it was not long before he spoke up. "On that matter, Miguel. How are we to approach this? I am not comfortable splitting up our group. We would have to leave one or two men behind with the women, including Sofia, and even that is no guarantee of their safety. And what happens if our scouts do find these agents in Crockett? They will then have to backtrack for the other men if we are to have enough guns to have any chance of pulling this off."

Randall and D'Age looked to the cowboy for an answer. That was only natural. Unlike Miguel, they had no experience of leading men in a situation like this and, until they were attacked by the road agents, probably had precious little experience of fighting them, either. Miguel had been bossing vaqueros for twenty years, during which time he had regularly had to enforce his will with boot and fist. And of course he had had his fill of deadly violence escaping from Mexico with his family on Miss Julia's boat. His brow creased, and he grunted as he pushed away the memory of the massacre yet again. It flashed before his eyes many times every day, distressing him greatly. Until Sofia was safe, surrounded by the armies of Presidente Kipper, he could not indulge in the weakness of memory and regrets. First came her safety, then came vengeance, and only then, if he still lived, would there be time for mourning.

He chewed his lower lip as he thought over the difficulty Aronson had raised. A couple of errant whiskers got caught between his teeth.

"You are right," he said. "I must admit I have been worrying about this very matter all morning. The bandit gangs are pushing much deeper into the Federal Mandate than they have before. And there seem to be more of them. I do not think it would be wise to split up into smaller groups that could be easily picked off. Altogether we have, what, six men, two boys, your two women, and Sofia. If they can all pull a trigger to protect themselves and if we are careful, that is enough to give the agents pause. A smaller group, however, they will simply overrun, especially if they know there are women to be had."

Aronson nodded, seemingly satisfied with that line of reasoning. "So we all travel together."

"Yes," said Miguel. "But if we are successful in tracking them, only the men will fight. There will be work for the women tending the animals and, when we are done and if we are lucky, looking after the wounded. This fight will be no place for them."

The chatter of voices from the other side of the diner had gone quiet while Miguel spoke. He turned around to find Sofia and the two Mormon women looking at him. He thought that his daughter might say something in protest. He recognized the flame of indignation in her eyes, but before Sofia could speak, Maive Aronson leaned across a bag full of beans and squeezed her arm.

"Do you think you could go find Mr. Atchison for me? I have need of inquiring with him about how much we can load in these saddlebags. I believe he is tending to the horses. Here, Adam can help you go find him."

The youngest of the Mormon men, a pink-faced boy of maybe sixteen or seventeen, pulled up short as he tried to wrestle a big cardboard box into the room. His companion—Orin was his name if Miguel recalled correctly—bumped into him from behind, almost knocking him over. It was enough to break the tension. Sofia did give her father a cool glare as she left the diner, but Miguel was man enough not to be troubled by the poor opinion of a teenage girl. He even smiled slightly as she swept out of the room with as much dignity as she could muster, pulling Adam along in her wake. His grin lingered for a moment when he saw that the other boy, Orin, was genuinely put out not to have been chosen for escort duties. And then the black fog of sorrow descended upon him again.

"We should travel fast and light," he said, almost sighing. "Perhaps we should leave everything here that we will not need in the fight. Your herd can be secured here."

Cooper Aronson looked as if he was about to say something, but Miguel cut him off. "There *will* be a fight, Mister Aronson. "

The Mormon leader nodded reluctantly.

Miguel continued, "You are all carrying the same weapons, yes?"

Ben Randall answered, "Yep. Government-issue M16s. They hand them out when you get off the boat in Corpus Christi. I'm surprised you and your daughter don't have them," he said before suddenly blushing bright red and stumbling over an apology. "Oh, I'm sorry. I didn't mean…"

Miguel waved it away with one hand. "We were issued three army rifles when we arrived, but I do not like them as guns. We are not soldiers, and they are unreliable in any case. I took some time when we arrived at the homestead to seek out more appropriate firearms. Some for killing snakes," he said, patting the cut-down shotgun in the oversized holster at his hip, "and some for farmwork, like my Winchester. I prefer a weapon with which I am familiar. And I have used a Winchester all my life."

"And your daughter's rifle?"

"She hunts," Miguel said. "It is no matter. She will not be involved in this. She can protect herself and the women with that Remington."

"Is she a good shot?" Aronson asked.

Miguel nodded. "She brought down a ten-point whitetail buck at three hundred yards." He paused for a second. "I do not believe she will hesitate before pulling the trigger on a man."

Aronson took a moment to digest all that before looking to his wife. "How are the supplies?"

"We will have what we need to see us through the next week," she answered.

"That will be more than enough," said Miguel. "We will resolve this one way or another in two days."

23

"Maybe Union Square's not such a good idea," said Jules.

The rooftop garden, which had gone wild in the last three years, afforded them with an excellent view of the soldiers pouring into Union Square, where Jules had been hoping to lay up for the night. She and the Rhino leaned over the guardrail in the constant drizzle and passed a pair of binoculars between them, scanning east on 14th Street to where the army apparently was gathering… well… a small army of some sort as far as Jules could tell. Jules's injured shoulder forced her to use the binoculars one-handed when she took them, and the image was correspondingly shaky. Her shivering from hunger, cold, and fatigue did not help matters. Only a day had passed since her shower before bed back on Duane Street, yet she was already sweaty, itchy, and greasy from the rain.

"Looks like they're getting together some sort of armored task force to punch a few blocks north," said the Rhino, shaking a shower of raindrops from his army surplus Gore-Tex jacket.

All manner of armored vehicles and even a few tanks were

rumbling into the streets around the little park. They couldn't see much to the northeast, but from the martial thunder and lightning in that direction there was something untoward going on.

"Well, that's just marvelous," Jules replied sunnily, relatively dry in her own Gore-Tex jacket. "We're going north; perhaps we could thumb a ride… That's sarcasm, by the way," she added. "Just in case you got all excited at the idea of a ride on a big bloody tank."

He continued to peer through his binoculars, not bothering to answer.

"Perhaps if we headed down to the river," she suggested more seriously, stepping back from the sheer drop to West 14th and pushing through the wet, overgrown foliage to a small open vantage point a little farther down. The rooftop garden thinned out there, possibly because it would be in the shade of a looming elevator shaft for more than half the day. The road far below them was badly congested with crashed cars and, for some inexplicable reason, dozens of Dumpsters. It looked as though a small river was running along the street, and at the corner of Seventh Avenue she could see an extraordinary sight: a veritable geyser gushing up from underground through the entrance to the subway there. It made her wonder whether the entire city might collapse in on itself and sink into the rivers that surrounded it.

"Nope, can't go west," the Rhino said, as he moved a piece of chewing tobacco from one cheek to the other. Julianne prepared herself for the inevitable stream of spit, and…

There it was.

She felt like shuddering every time he did that, but if he wasn't smoking cigars—and he wasn't right now because of the chance they'd be spotted in the dark—the Rhino insisted on getting his tobacco hit via plugs of the foul "chaw," as he called it.

"Can't do that, Miss Jules," he continued. "I endured a good long time picking Lewis's tiny brains about who controlled which parts of the city, and he said everything north of Eighteenth and west of

Eighth was being fought over by Serbs, Russians, Chechens, and Rastas. You don't want to be tangling with any of them."

An enormous blast a mile or two to the north sent a bright white ball of fire and sparks high into the sky.

"Do I have to make the obvious point that I don't want to be tangling with any of these fucking munters?" she asked.

"Sarcasm again, Miss Julianne?"

"Yes. Sarcasm. I'm afraid that at the moment I have only the lowest form of wit to offer. And to think I took a first in rhetoric at Cambridge."

"Didn't you cheat your way through college?"

"Cheated and bonked, but I did have a base level of competence, you know. It's in my nature. Daddy virtually lived off his wits until he blew his brains out."

The Rhino lowered his binoculars and joined her in the small clearing. Jules could recognize a few of the plants that had gone wild up there—some Japanese maples that had burst out of their pots and colonized a large square of native grasses, a thicket of tomato vines, and what looked like zucchini—but most of it was just anonymous shrubbery and scrappy urban jungle. The Rhino spit out the rest of his chaw, plucked a small tomato off the vine, and bit into it, but then he screwed up his face and spit out the pulp.

"Nasty."

The tom-tom beat of a heavy weapon started up, and within seconds Julianne flinched as a jet fighter slipped down out of the clouds and released a couple of bombs that detonated with enough force to shake the city. Pulling out of the dive, the jet fighter climbed back into the clouds, its engines howling at the skyscrapers. The drumbeat did not resume.

"Bloody hell," she said as the rumble subsided. It never ceased to amaze her. The sounds on the battlefield were not like the movies at all. You never heard the jet until it was too late to do anything about it, especially if you were the target. She hoped that did not happen to her.

"Yeah." Rhino showed his tobacco-stained teeth. "Fuck, yeah. They're not dicking around anymore, are they?"

"Perhaps they're avenging all our deaths," Jules suggested with no real sincerity.

"I sorely doubt it," the Rhino said. "But it looks like the president has decided he's had enough of caring and sharing."

The way he said "the president" gave Jules to understand that the Rhino most definitely approved.

"So what are we going to do?" she asked. "We need to get to that apartment and get out of the city with Rubin's papers if we're to be paid."

The huge, slab-shouldered sea dog appeared to think about plucking a zucchini and trying his luck but decided against it. The rain came down heavier for a moment, then eased off, as though the downpour had given its all before petering out.

"I'm gonna suggest we keep pressing on, Miss Jules. If we thread ourselves up between the ragheads who started this fight—" He jerked one thumb over his shoulder back toward Union Square. "—and the crazy fucking Ivans down by the river—" He nodded toward the Hudson. "—we might just show 'em all a clean pair of heels."

Jules frowned, unconvinced, but there didn't seem to be many alternatives. If the Rhino was right and this was the first day of a battle to retake the city, the army would roll up the island block by block, probably destroying everything in its path. They had to get to Rubin's apartment and retrieve his documents before that happened, even if it meant dialing up the risk for a day or two. This gig was a big score. If it paid off, she could probably retire from assing about in the smuggling game and set up a legitimate business out on the West Coast, running salvage charters down to LA or something. Or, rather, not running them in person, just raking off the cream while some other poor bastards did the hard work as her contractors and remitted all the profits back to her.

She shivered as the wind knifed in off the river. Her shoulder ached terribly, and she longed to be out of the cold. Across the water New Jersey was a dark continent with just a few mystery points of light to give some sense of the vastness of the graveyard it had become. She wondered idly who or what those lights might be. Freebooters? Scavengers? Some sort of special forces camp with a lot of unwashed Lord Jim types sitting around eating roasted rats off coat hangers?

Possibly not.

There were still mountains of canned and vacuum sealed food in the big cities to make a resort to hobo's chicken—one of her father's favorite jokes—a rarity. Another jet plane—no, two of them—came shrieking down out of the night sky, flying just under the low ceiling of cloud, which lit up with their exhausts and running lights. They appeared to drop a stick of bombs somewhere near Gramercy Park.

The Rhino grunted in approval but frowned.

"Miss Jules, I'm going to do something that a good Rhino never does," he said. "I'm going to lower my horn and back the fuck up. This looks to me like a fight that is only just getting warmed up, and I wonder if we should be heading out into it just yet."

"We could end up like poor Ryan," she said.

"Yeah. I vote we hunker down here for a few hours, get some rest, review our plans, and see whether there's a lull anytime before sunup when we could move a few more blocks."

Julianne shivered inside her Gore-Tex. The thought of getting somewhere warm and dry appealed in a way that no trip to the Virgin Islands ever had.

"Sounds good to me. Let's see if this building had a penthouse, shall we?"

* * *

"May God strike me down if the worst thing about the end of the world isn't the impossibility of securing a decent cup of tea when I fucking need it. I could murder a pot of Twinings right now."

Jules stood at the black granite island bench in the massive, luxuriously fitted out kitchen with hands on hips and frustration acid etched into her face.

The building did not boast a single penthouse, but the top-floor apartments were considerably larger than those below, there being only four of them in all. The Rhino had tried to kick in the door of the first apartment they came to, but it seemed to have been secured by something as extravagant as thick metal locking bolts driven deep into the walls. His size-twelve boots boomed off the hardwood surface without any appreciable return on the effort. The next apartment door, however, yielded to his second kick with a terrible splintering and cracking of the door frame. The noise was awfully loud inside the empty building but insignificant when one considered the uproar of the street fighting a mile or two away. The two smugglers swept the darkened entry hall and a large open-plan living room beyond, but it was obvious that no living soul had set foot in there for years. After securing the wreckage of the front door by pushing a heavy couch up against it, they went about settling in for a few hours: drawing curtains so they could turn on a battery-powered camp light, firing up a small gas stove, and searching the kitchen cupboards for any usable supplies, whereupon Jules was yet again confronted by the barbaric habits of Americans high and low.

"There simply is no fucking tea in this place," she complained.

The Rhino snorted his amusement.

"Got plenty of stale coffee if you want. Or drinking chocolate. Does that stuff keep?"

"Let me see," she said, taking the small white canister from him. A twelve-ounce tin of Dagoba organic. Jules rolled her eyes. "Well, it's hardly Vosges La Parisienne Couture cocoa, but I suppose we'll see. At least it's never been opened."

As the Rhino set to brewing a small pot of water poured from his canteen, Julianne retrieved their commission papers from her small backpack. In addition to the satellite maps and out-of-date intel on the surrounding area, she carried a private *lettre de course* from Samuel Rubin's attorney in Seattle, authorizing them to search Rubin's New York apartment and seize any and all documentation relating to his disputed claim to part ownership of the new Sonoma "Sunset" gas and oil field, along with detailed floor plans of the apartment and instructions for accessing a hidden safe in the library. She also found their original letters of acceptance into the Manhattan clearance and salvage program. She was about to toss them away as being no longer necessary, when caution stayed her hand. The only safe and sure way into New York, a Declared Zone, had been via the salvage program, and given how everything had gone so spectacularly wrong in the last twenty-four hours, it might turn out that those crumpled form letters were their only way out of the city as well. They wouldn't stop an F-16 from dropping smart bombs on them should they be mistaken for villains, but if they ran into any U.S. ground forces, it probably would pay to have a piece of paper explaining how they came to be in the city.

Of course, what they were actually doing was illegal in a Declared Zone, even with Rubin's letter to wave in the face of any overzealous state-sponsored busybodies who might care to interfere.

The Rhino used their single fluorescent camp light to search the kitchen for coffee mugs. The white glow threw long, swinging shadows over the living area as he moved from cupboard to cupboard.

"Damn, but these folks lived well," he said. "They gotta have eight different types of noodles in here."

Jules looked up from the sat maps of the Upper East Side she had been studying to find the Rhino waving a packet of linguini around.

"That's pasta. Not noodles," she said.

"Here we go. Cups and saucers. Got a special cupboard just for themselves. How pretentious is that?"

"Depends on the make of china," she said, standing up straight and stretching her back muscles. "Tell you what, Rhino. How about you come over here and update these maps. Draw in what you know of who controls which parts of the city now. It might help us find a way through to Rubin's place. I'll make supper."

"Huh, good luck with that," he scoffed. "These snobs didn't have anything worth scavenging from the larder. You know, we'd be a lot better off looting from dead rednecks. Score ourselves a whole chicken in a can or some Vienna franks. Have to be better than these... what the fuck are these? Imported dog turds?"

He held up a small plastic packet and scowled at it in the lamplight.

"Give me those," said Jules, suddenly excited. "Oh, my God, you fucking Philistine, they're dried porcini. We may well dine in style yet. Let me see if I can find any decent oil. I'm willing to bet a place like this will have top-shelf extra virgin. It keeps for years."

"Just don't burn my hot chocolate while you're getting carried away there, Martha Stewart."

He had a point. The pot of water on their little primus stove was but a moment away from bubbling merrily, so Jules put off her grocery search to make the drinks. Her injured arm was still half numb and next to useless, which meant doing everything one-handed, a slow, frustrating process. The Dagoba drinking chocolate came in a powder that had all but solidified in its cardboard canister. With some difficulty and discomfort she managed to hack off a couple of chunks, which she stirred into the hot water. She checked the walk-in larder, hopeful of finding a tin of condensed milk, but that was too much to expect, and she resigned herself to the necessity of a thin, stale brew. The scent of it was still heady enough to make her mouth water and her stomach grumble in protest.

"Do you have those energy bars you pinched from the hotel?" she asked the Rhino, who was searching for something, presumably a pencil or pen with which he could shade the sat maps as she'd asked.

"In my smaller pack, over by the ugly coffee table," he answered as he methodically opened and closed a line of drawers in a blond wood sideboard on top of which sat an enormous flat panel television. "Hot damn! Check this out."

Jules expected to find him holding up a new gun or perhaps even chicken in a can but was genuinely surprised to find him standing there patting what looked like a Viking helmet on his head.

"Pretty sweet, huh? There's nothing a Rhino likes more than extra horns."

She refused to bite. "Just try the kitchen drawers if you're looking for something to write with," she suggested. "Even the rich write notes to themselves." As she fetched the energy bars, Jules marveled that he called his ruck a small pack. It was large enough to serve her as a full-size backpack.

The Rhino left the ridiculous helmet on his enormous head, where, unfortunately, it fit perfectly. He picked up his mug of chocolate as he walked past.

"I've never asked you," said Jules. "Are you going to take an up-front fee from Rubin when we get back—"

"If we get back," he corrected, finding a marker in the first drawer he tried.

"Of course. How very Pollyanna of me. So *if* we get back. An up-front fee or the equity deal?"

The Rhino stopped by the end of the island bench to sip his drink and consider her question. He actually scratched one of the giant protuberant cow's horns on his newfound head gear as he did so.

"Well, I have done some thinking on that, Miss Jules, I must admit. The prospect of a straight-up payday does appeal. I could set myself up in fine style with a quarter million new bucks. Finding a boat's no problem at all, of course. There's plenty of them lying around with no owners to lay claim. But manning them, provisioning, fuel oil, it all adds up. A payday would be mighty useful."

Julianne took a few experimental sips of her own drink. It

wasn't too bad, and she was desperately hungry. "You couldn't be thinking of going back into the charter business, surely? There's no market for it."

"No," he agreed as the rumble of an especially large explosion rolled over the building. "I was thinking more in terms of a small trader, you know, zipping around the islands, maybe even down south to some of the secured ports. Old Roberto is a murderous thug, but he does run a tight ship down there in the federation now, and he's looking to do business. Coffee. Cocoa…" He held up the steaming cup. "Even sugar from the Caribbean. They're all paying well now."

"That's all?" she asked skeptically. "You wouldn't be tempted to run a little marching powder up the coast?"

He looked truly offended at the suggestion.

"Miss Jules, I was a career coast guard man! My whole life was about chasing bad guys, not being one."

"Rhino. You're a smuggler now. A people smuggler for a year after the Wave. Contraband and zone runner ever since."

He blew her off with a flip of one hand.

"Bullshit. I might be bending the odd law here and there, but I'm doing what's right. Those rich assholes we got out of Acapulco, yeah, they were rich and kind of assholey, but that didn't mean they had to die there, and that's what would have happened. And Miguel and his family, they were good folks who just needed a break. We gave them one. As for Rubin, the man says he owns a chunk of that oil field off Sonoma. Says he has the papers to prove it. Half a dozen fucking foreign oil companies say he doesn't. You know what I think? I think he does and they're just trying to frighten him off the claim, keep it for themselves. So sure, I'm breaking the law going into a zone without the exact right papers and passes signed and stamped in triplicate, but goddamn, this is still the United States, and I will go where I please, and I will be ass fucked by rabid monkeys before I stand by and let a little guy get bullied out of what's his by a bunch of giant foreign oil firms."

Jules was smirking by the time he'd finished his small speech, unsure whether he was kidding or if indeed he might have convinced himself of his own rectitude and heroic status. She moved around from behind the granite-topped island bench and into the living area to retrieve one of the energy bars.

"So, seriously," she said. "Will you be taking the quarter million up front? Or a share of the Sonoma field? And before you answer, you should know I cannot take seriously anything you say while you are wearing that ridiculous helmet."

24

NEW YORK

In another era, perhaps he would have held his council in a grand war tent, sitting on fine pillows and handwoven rugs. Instead, the emir made war from a third-floor office in an anonymous building in the midtown region of Manhattan. He was of course more familiar with this sort of environment than he was with grand war tents or the stony deserts in which the Prophet had pitched them when he first brought the word of God to the heathen tribesmen of Arabia, but he found it hard to romanticize the image of a holy war generaled from the entirely unromantic command post of some dead heathen's windowless office. Perhaps it would help if it were not all going so badly.

The emir, surrounded by his most trusted lieutenants, leaned over the huge map of Manhattan that had been spread out on the dead man's cheap chipboard desk. From where he stood, with his knuckles resting on the New Jersey Turnpike and the upper reaches of Central Park, he could see a broken photo frame lying on the floor in the corner of the office. A pretty blond woman and two children dressed in cowboy outfits smiled out from behind the shattered glass, presumably the family of the man who had worked in this office.

The photograph reminded the emir that this was not a simple blood feud with an old foe. It was certainly that, but even more it was now a struggle to claim a new homeland for those who had survived the Second Holocaust. Many of his warriors had brought their families with them not because they wanted to but because there was nowhere left for them in the old world. This was especially true of those who had been forced from Great Britain.

Fortunately, their families seemed to be safe for the moment. He had worried privately that the Americans might bomb the makeshift villages they had established for the women and children, but for the moment they seemed to have gone undetected. It was, after all, a very large and empty land these days.

As he examined the map again, he wasn't sure if they'd be safe much longer.

"It may have been best had we waited and stuck to our original schedule," he thought out loud.

"No," insisted Abu Dujana, the Indonesian, one of the few who had come without his kin. "It was a rare opportunity to cut off the head of the taipan, and you were right to strike when you did. We all agreed then, as we all agree now."

Dujana looked at each man in turn, searching their eyes with his own for any sign of disagreement. But there was none. The emir had consulted with each of them and sought their counsel sincerely before making the decision to bring forward their attack when they learned that President Kipper would be in New York.

"Are we not told by the Prophet himself to fight and kill the disbelievers wherever we find them?" Dujana asked. "To lie in wait and ambush them using every stratagem of war?" The four men around the table were all intimately familiar with the holy Koran. They nodded in agreement.

The emir stood up straight, stretching his back and trying to get some distance from the immediate crisis so that he might have time to think, to see a way through. He was young for one to whom such a momentous undertaking had been fated and as fit as any man under his command, but he felt tired and worried. The problem was that unlike the Prophet he was not a military commander and had no pretensions to being one. That was why he surrounded himself with men like Dujana, famed for taking the battle against the Indonesian military dictatorship right up to the gates of the presidential palace. The emir was not burdened with false modesty. He knew that inspiring men, and even women when necessary, was a special talent gifted to him by God. However, to lead men in battle, particularly in an environment such as New York, required a very different set of skills, which he did not possess.

Amin Bashir, like him a German but unlike him a man experienced in the extremes of urban warfare, pointed to an area of the map at the southern end of Manhattan. Bashir had brought all of his family with him. Three of his five sons were fighting alongside him, and the emir knew he was willing to sacrifice them all if need be.

"Such a somber mood does not well suit what we have achieved in this battle," Bashir said. "We do not serve God if we underestimate his enemies. Just like Mohammed and the first converts from Medina, we face a people given to war with a mighty prowess. But they are not invincible. Even before God laid them low they were not invincible. Right here, at this crucial juncture, their arrogance caused them to overreach, and many hundreds of their men were led into slaughter at the hands of mere janissaries. It might seem an evil thing that this Kipper still lives. But how can it be anything but the will of God?"

The emir and his advisers mumbled assent. What Bashir had said was true, or at least not to be argued with. The emir could not help doubting himself, though. The casualties among the janissaries were very high, and although his own men had suffered commensurately, they were far fewer in number. It could not be long before the leaders of the bandit gangs with whom he had struck an alliance began to question the arrangement. After all, what did it profit a man to have a whole city at his feet if he had no means by which to plunder it? The submarines and warships of many countries already cut into profit margins by boarding or sinking a percentage of treasure ships as they crossed the Atlantic Ocean. Some of them were little better than pirates themselves in his opinion.

"Amin is correct," he conceded. "It saddens me that Kipper survived our attack, but it is the will of Allah, and to wish it any other way is not just weakness, it is a sin."

He stood back from the makeshift map table and smiled at his comrades, his friends. The office in which they were gathered was small and looked out on a much larger area in which stood nearly two dozen desks, at least half of them occupied by his officers as they worried away at the details of their particular responsibilities within the widening firestorm engulfing Manhattan. So hastily had they had to move after the Americans targeted the last command post that there had not even been time to properly clear away the remains of those who had died there when Allah's sword swept all life from this continent. The noxious remains had been piled up in a mountain of stiff, blackened clothing over in the far corner. A couple of janissaries had been employed for that work, a fatwa from the grand mufti having declared the remains of the so-called Disappeared to be unclean.

"I am afraid I have sinned," the emir confessed, quickly raising his hands to forestall any disagreement. "I am sorry, but in trying to strike down Kipper I could not help but see myself holding the spear that pierced the heart of Gordon at Khartoum. A failure of humility on my part and a grave insult to Allah, blessed be his name. It may even be why this pig still lives and why the fight goes so hard."

The other men looked on somberly, none of them rushing to disagree but all of them looking very uncomfortable.

"Still, although we have not cut the head off the snake, we have stamped it beneath our boots and, I believe, injured it gravely. Kipper is much weaker now than he was this time last week. He is not a warrior. He does not rush to the fight as we do or even as his soldiers do. And yet he is drawn into this battle unwillingly, halfheartedly. We all know where that path leads."

Abu Dujana folded his arms and took on a defiant air. "Our onslaught will not be a weak faltering affair," he said, quoting from the Prophet. "We shall fight as long as we live. We will fight until they turn to Islam. We will fight not caring whom we meet. We will fight whether we destroy ancient holdings or achieve hard-won gains. We will mutilate every opponent. We will drive them violently before us at the command of Allah and Islam. We will fight until our religion is established. And we will plunder them, for they must suffer disgrace."

The emir nodded approvingly, although he did not necessarily see the need to quote chapter and verse at the great length to which Dujana was often given. A simple "Let's kick their fucking asses" would have sufficed. Dujana was a traditionalist, however.

"And that is how it shall be," he said, smiling at the warrior from Indonesia. "Kipper's survival does not make the Americans stronger; it makes them weaker. He is a weak man without the stomach for war or the strong-arm with which to make it."

As he spoke, the emir became more confident that what he said was actually true and not merely an empty platitude mouthed for the benefit of his followers. It was true that one could not ask for a better opponent than this president. Such reluctance to fight in a so-called commander in chief was a rare gift to his opponent. It must surely be the will of Allah.

"The more we draw him in here, the more blood we let, the weaker he will become." He waved away the map of Manhattan lying before them as though it were of no concern at all. "Perhaps if he is weakened enough, this crazy man Blackstone will finally take his Texas Republic away from Seattle and tear this country asunder. That may well be our purpose here, my friends. If we are penitent, if we humble ourselves before God, he may well show us that his design did not end with us leading our armies to the gates of Seattle like Dujana led his men to the palace in Jakarta."

His Indonesian comrade bowed humbly in acknowledgment of the compliment as the emir continued.

"Such arrogance is hardly befitting servants of God. But if the Americans turn on each other as the desert Arabs turned on each other in the day of our Prophet, then our work will be done and we will yet bring peace to this land that once dared threaten the House of Peace."

Dujana and Bashir nodded enthusiastically as though they were students who had suddenly come to understand a difficult mathematical theorem. The fourth man in the room, a great barrel-chested Turk by the name of Ahmet Ozal, folded his massive arms and nodded slowly but had a deep scowl on his face. It looked as though he were examining a deal in which he was almost certain to come off poorly. He had not spoken at all in the meeting, and the emir waited on his reply with some trepidation. Ozal commanded the largest contingent of fedayeen in the city, and his men were by far the best trained, equipped, and led. He was also the man the emir relied on to manage their relationship with the pirate gangs. Although he had pledged his allegiance to the cause and his obedience to the emir, his agreement was not a given. Ahmet Ozal was very much his own man, and he would choose to serve Allah in his own way. After an excruciating half minute, he nodded gravely and finally spoke.

"You are very wise for one so young, Emir."

A sly smile stole across his broad, brown face. "It must be the Turkish blood winning out over your German heritage," he said before clapping his hands loudly. "I agree. We must draw the Americans in here and defeat them on their own land, fighting for their own home. If we do that, we will break them here. We will break them everywhere. Then this will become our new home, and it will be a House of Peace."

The emir smiled, unafraid to show that he was relieved he still had everyone with him. He might not be an expert on urban warfare, but he was an expert on dealing with people, and he knew it was as much a mistake to demand loyalty as it was to expect it unconditionally. He needed these men. Allah needed these men.

"How goes it with the janissaries?" he asked the Turk. "They have suffered fearful losses and few gains, and unlike us they have no higher cause."

Ahmet Ozal waved his hand dismissively.

"For now they fight because the gains are enough. The leaders have been well rewarded with plunder from the other cities, and the fighters themselves are well supplied with strong drink and kif and of course the promise of loot, land, and slaves."

The emir looked to Dujana, expecting him to protest the use of drink among the janissaries. It was a sticking point with the Indonesian, but for once he remained silent. Perhaps with the balance of the battle so delicately poised he was willing to contemplate a loosening of his rigid doctrinal standards for even a small tactical advantage. The bandits did fight with much greater ferocity and abandon when their minds were inflamed with drugs. The emir was not sure it made them a more effective tool of war, but if it kept them running at the American lines, wearing down their numbers with the sheer relentlessness of their attacks, it could not be a bad thing. Especially not if it meant that when the time came to reconsider their truce with the bandit leaders, the janissaries were much weakened.

He was about to bend himself to the task of disentangling the mess of differently colored squiggle lines and *saif* designations on the big map in front of him when a commotion in the outer office drew his attention. Two of the janissary guards were manhandling a small African boy toward the door. The emir did not recognize him, but he had the look of a street fighter about him, and from the filthy scarf around his neck he was obviously fedayeen, even if only a lowly spear carrier in one of the *saif*. The boy was struggling fiercely and seemed very distressed. Bashir and Dujana looked unconcerned, but Ahmet Ozal glowered furiously at the scene before turning his back on the map table and stalking out into the main room.

"What the hell is going on here?" he roared. "This boy fights with one of my *saif*. Let him go now."

The janissaries seemed unsure what to do. They obviously had a reason for detaining the boy, and they looked to the emir to resolve the dilemma. They were charged with securing this office, and the boy had no good reason that the emir could see for being in there. But Ozal was fiercely protective of his men, and they were fiercely loyal to him. The emir smiled as warmly as he could at the two guards while waving them away and indicating to the young one that he should come forward.

"What is your name, boy? And whose *saif* do you fight with?"

Ozal frowned and answered for him. "I do not know his name, Emir. But from his keffiyeh I'd say he fought with Mustafa Ali on Ellis Island."

A hush fell across the room as the boy came forward. He looked frightened but also angry. When he spoke, it was in slow halting English rather than Arabic, which told the emir that he was probably a recent convert who was still learning the language of the fedayeen. The fact that he was fighting in Manhattan, however, marked him out as someone with some skill and experience of at least township war and possibly full-blown urban conflict. Possibly more so than the emir himself could boast.

"Yusuf Mohammed, my sheikh," answered the boy. "And yes, I was on Ellis Island."

He seemed ashamed to admit as much, but to the emir there was no mystery about that. Every man he had sent to Ellis Island was either dead or captured. If they were fedayeen, the former only. The holy warriors had all taken a vow to die, by their own hands if necessary, before allowing the infidel to capture them. Again, the grand mufti had issued a fatwa absolving any man who took his own life in such circumstances. Greater glory in heaven awaited those who took a number of the enemy with them, of course. The emir was curious as to how and why this young man had escaped such a fate, especially since he must have traversed the city to make it to this command bunker.

"Bring us some tea and some fruit," he commanded nobody in particular. One of the junior officers hurried out to the little kitchen down the corridor where they kept a small stash of field rations. "You must be hungry and thirsty, is that right, Yusuf?"

The boy's eyes went wide, and he nodded with nervous vigor.

"Yes, my sheikh. But I… I did not…"

The emir smiled and walked over to pat him on the shoulder, steering him toward a chair. He gestured for the boy to sit. Seeing this Yusuf Mohammed treated with such deference and respect changed the atmosphere in the room from surprise and a vague sense of threat to something more akin to curiosity. A small bowl of dried apricots and dates appeared, followed shortly by a steaming mug of black tea.

"I'm afraid we have no milk or sugar," the emir explained. "It's just a guess, but I imagine that you learned your English on a mission station somewhere, perhaps in Uganda or Kenya."

The boy regarded him with frank disbelief. He nodded slowly. "I was taught by nuns… sorry, infidels… in a village not far from Moroto. But I do not remember much of that time," he hurried to add.

Ahmet Ozal lowered his massive frame to sit on the desk next to the boy, towering over him. He encouraged Yusuf to eat from the small bowl of fruit and to take a drink of tea.

"You will need your strength, boy, if you have somehow escaped from the Americans and made it here through the Serbs and the Russians. Is that the way you came? Through their territory on the western shore?"

Yusuf nodded anxiously. It appeared as if he was about to pour forth some long explanation of his trip before Ozal silenced him by gesturing at the dried fruit again.

"Eat up, boy," he said before turning back to the others to explain. "Yusuf would be one of a number of converts we found among the barbarians of the Lord's Resistance Army in the borderlands between what used to be Uganda and Somalia. Child fighters, mostly. They have attended to the message of the Prophet and allowed him into their hearts with great sincerity and eagerness, for the most part."

The emir regarded the boy with some respect.

"That is hard country, Yusuf, especially since the abomination of the Jews' atomic strike. You have done well to make it to such a ripe old age. What are you, fifteen or sixteen years old?"

The boy soldier shook his head.

"I do not know, my sheikh. I was with the LRA for a long time, and I was very young when they came and took me from the village."

The emir let his compassion show openly on his face.

"I can understand that after being forced to fight for most of your life you might have wanted something other than a warrior's fate when the fedayeen liberated you. I must thank you, Yusuf, for having the faith and the courage not to walk away from your calling. It is a good thing you have done coming here to the city, a good thing you did in the battle at Ellis Island, and an even better thing you have done finding your way back to us to add your strength to ours for the battle yet to come."

Nobody spoke or even seemed to so much as breathe while the emir thanked the thin African boy for his service. The rumble of battle was distant but forever with them as the Americans expended enormous stockpiles of heavy ordnance in trying to pulverize the faithful and their allies at the southern end of the island. The whining scream of jets, the thud of helicopters, and the occasional *tock-tock-tock* of heavy weapons fire did not relent. But in the stuffy third-floor office where the emir had established his temporary command post, a blessed silence held. Yusuf Mohammed seemed overwhelmed. His eyes welled with tears, and all his limbs shook. Hitching sobs began to rack his upper body.

"But I'm not worthy… I didn't…"

The emir squeezed his shoulder and hushed him.

"Only God can judge our worthiness at the end of days, Yusuf. It is not for me to sit in judgment on you who have had so much harder a time of it in this battle."

The boy blinked away tears and pressed trembling lips together in an effort to maintain the last of his dignity.

"Are you still willing to fight, Yusuf? Will you take God's message to the heathen who would bar it from this land?" the emir asked.

"Yes," he answered in a small, quavering voice. "Always."

"Then God will judge you worthy of his mercy and indulgence in this life and the next," said the emir. "Go now. Get some rest. Spend this night in my own harem and be sure to tell Sheikh Ozal's men everything of what you learned on Ellis and in the territory of the Slavs. It will be useful. It may even be important."

The boy looked as though he wanted to say more, but in the end he simply put aside the small bowl of dates and apricots he held and reached out to kiss the emir's hand.

Bilal Baumer, sometimes known as al Banna and now the putative emir of the promised lands, rubbed Yusuf's filthy, matted hair with obvious affection and shooed the lad away.

Within an hour the story of the emir's generosity and kindness would spread all the way to the front line. Especially the bit about the harem, a small caravan of captured women he saved for just this sort of thing. Although he would never actually partake of them himself—God only knew what sort of filth a ragamuffin like Yusuf was carrying—the idea that he might share his bedroom slaves with the lowest ranks of the fedayeen would add powerfully to his myth.

25

LONDON

The London Cage occupied one part of a former paper-recycling plant on the river at Creekmouth, an industrial suburb east of the city. Caitlin and Dalby set out along the A13 after overnighting at the Ibis Hotel on Commercial Street in Aldgate. More than half the hotels in London had closed over the previous three years, but the Ibis chain had survived by virtue of a contract with the government to provide discounted accommodations to civil servants traveling for work. Caitlin had stayed there before. She'd been too young to work behind the Iron Curtain, but she imagined that the old Soviet-era tourist hotels had probably been something like this. Clean but drab, with at least one "experience" to be savored in every room. A threadbare towel. A half-empty bar fridge. Flickering lightbulbs. Reused soap. And surly, off-putting security staff, a disconcerting number of whom were forbidding bull dykes seemingly recruited from some underground lesbian wrestling league. They prowled the floors constantly. Her first stay at the Aldgate Ibis, one had knocked on her door three times during the night, to "check that everything was in order," leaving her alone only after Caitlin had jammed the muzzle of a Glock 17 in her face and shouted that apart from her not being a morning person, everything was "just fucking fine."

This trip they checked in well after midnight and left just after dawn, with Dalby brushing aside all the usual demands for travel warrants, internal passports, and itineraries with a brusque refusal to cooperate and an imperious flick of his ID badge into the bleary, sleep-deprived face of the night manager, who was still on duty at six in the morning.

"You know, sometimes I think we should be done with it and just get ourselves Gestapo outfits," Caitlin said. "You know, some really spanking long black leather coats and dark fedoras. Then we wouldn't even have to worry about badging people or waving Glocks in their fucking faces. Everybody would just know to *fear* us."

Dalby gave her a quizzical look as they rode the elevator down to the car park.

"Sometimes with you Americans it is impossible to know whether you are being funny or simply far too enthusiastic."

"Jeez, Dalby, and they reckon *we* don't get irony."

"Nobody gets irony anymore, Caitlin. We live in a post-ironic world."

She slung her backpack, a small overnight bag really, into the back of Dalby's precious little car and folded herself into the passenger seat. He turned on the radio after doing up his belt, locking the doors, and keying the ignition—the exact same sequence of actions he performed every time they climbed into the compact Mercedes. Caitlin wondered why he didn't just leave the radio on, but she was coming to understand that Mister Dalby was a man of very particular habits. The only music he ever played in the car was a CD compilation of popular classics. And when he wasn't playing that, he would listen to BBC Radio 4, which was what she would have called a news radio channel.

He flicked that on now as Caitlin ran her fingers through still-damp hair, tying it back with an elastic band. She'd had time for a quick shower this morning but not for much else in the way of personal grooming. At least the water had been reasonably hot this time. On her last extended trip to the Cage the hot water in the hotel had been out for two days, and when it did come back on, it smelled strongly of sulfur. Dalby drove out of the car park as Charlotte Green finished a report on trials of GM wheat and soy in Wiltshire.

"We were part of that," said Caitlin. "Bret was supposed to go to a briefing up in Swindon before Richardson's crew tried to hit him."

Dalby turned onto Whitechapel Road before negotiating the turn onto the A13. Traffic was very light as always, just a few commercial vehicles and a bus coming in from the suburbs. It was three minutes before they saw another private car like their own. Most of the shops along the retail strip were still closed, many of them boarded up for good. Here and there, though, she did see a new café, and in one case a knitwear store had opened. So perhaps the chancellor of the Exchequer was not talking entirely through his ass when he spoke about a few "promising green shoots" poking through the ashen wasteland of Britain's post-Wave economy. After all, they had been getting increasing orders for Bret's farmhouse goat cheese these past three months, which was very much a luxury item, something he had begun pottering about with, in the English style, after reading an article on Britnet about artisan cheese making.

"Do you enjoy the farm, Caitlin? It's not in your family history, is it? Farming, I mean. You were an air force child as I recall."

She had never told him that, but she wasn't surprised that he knew. As soon as Dalby had been given her case, he would have called for her personnel file and had probably even spoken to her old controller, Wales Larrison, who worked liaison in Vancouver these days. Thinking of Wales gave her an unexpected pang of homesickness.

"My grandparents on Mom's side scratched at the Dust Bowl for a while in Oklahoma," she said. "But not for long. So no, I wouldn't say we were farming folk. But I do enjoy it, Dalby. It's... peaceful, you know. Even getting out of bed at four in the morning to go fist some poor cow in a freezing barn... it's better than being stuck in the cells at fucking Noisy-le-Sec, let me tell you."

"You don't have to tell me," he said without elaborating.

The six o'clock bulletin came on, read by Alan Smith.

"Fighting continues in New York," he announced, "after a failed attempt on the life of President James Kipper yesterday. U.S. forces press on with their counteroffensive to retake the strategic port against heavy resistance. Prime Minister Howard will call the Cabinet Security Committee together this morning to discuss what help might be offered the U.S. administration."

"Do you really think that business was an assassination attempt on Kipper?" Dalby asked as they passed a small convoy of Ministry of Resources vans heading into town. "I mean, it seems a rather ham-fisted way to have at a chap, I would have thought. It's not as though your Mister Kipper doesn't present himself as a tempting target most days of the week, anyway, with this living among the people rubbish of his."

"Why, Dalby," Caitlin said in a delighted voice, "I do believe that's the most disapproving tone I have ever heard from you. Not a Kipper man, then, eh?"

The Home Office man nearly blushed at his indiscretion.

"Oh, I'm sure I don't have any opinion at all of U.S. politics, Caitlin. I find the plethora of new green parties and millennarian crazy men to be quite beyond fathoming. As I'm sure many of your country folk must long for the certainties of the old two-party system."

"Like here?" She smirked.

"Point taken," he muttered as they drove slowly past a minibus that had been pulled over by heavily armed special constables. The occupants were filing out, hands on heads, and lining up by the side of the road in front of a cash and carry and a money transfer bureau, apparently both owned by the same Indian family. A hand-painted sign hanging in the window of the money transfer announced "Fresh Basmati this Tuesday!" The minibus passengers looked like they were probably Pakistanis, or 'deshis from the Enclosures in South London, being bused into the city for a work detail. They had a sullen, beaten-down air of resignation about them and paid no heed to the three Indian children who came laughing and spilling out of the shop to watch. One of the specials crouched down on one knee while keeping his MP5 trained on the detainees to exchange a joke with the smiling, chattering children. Caitlin wondered whether the detainees envied those on the watch list who'd been deported. The Enclosures was a very grim and isolated place.

And then they were past the scene. Alan Smith continued in his calm, almost sublime way, recounting tales of horror from the night. The firebombing of a Hindu corner store in Newham that had killed the family of eight sleeping in the rooms above. The famine in western China. And an Amnesty International report on death squads in President Morales's South American Federation led into a final bookend report on Brazil's resurgent nuclear weapons program.

Caitlin listened despondently, wondering whether there might be a lighter story at the end of the bulletin simply to lift the spirits. But before handing off to the sports desk, the newsreader finished with a reminder that government inspectors would be double-checking ration cards this week after a significant increase in the incidence of forgeries.

"Enough gloom for one morning, I think," Dalby said, and he switched the audio to his classical compilation CD. The track that came on was Albinoni's *Adagio in G Minor,* which to Caitlin's way of thinking wasn't exactly "Disco Inferno." It was more "music to eat your pistol by," and she did her best to block it out.

"Have you sent anything to Wales about Baumer yet?" she asked. "He'd want to know."

"Mister Larrison, you mean? Yes. Vancouver liaison gets a routine weekly brief from the Cage on all of our doings and a-goings-on.

And given your involvement, I sent an extraordinary update as soon as I had enough detail."

Caitlin sat up in the passenger seat.

"So did Wales have a reading on it?"

Dalby frowned. "I'm afraid that with this business in New York all of your government's intelligence resources have been retasked onto the pirate issue. Indeed, most of ours, too. A good deal of Echelon's continental and African assets are now actively attempting to interdict the pirate traffic at the source. So although Mister Larrison was concerned and sent his best wishes, he was happy to leave the running on Mister Baumer to me and thee. Like you, he saw this as a personal vendetta and best dealt with… personally."

Caitlin was a little pissed off that Dalby hadn't told her about the contact with Wales, but he had been so good about everything else that she let it slide. After all, her old controller had effectively shined them on, and he would have been hell busy with New York.

Instead, she concentrated on the view outside. As bleak as that was, there were a few pleasant interludes. They stopped behind two buses outside a small park just after Wharf Lane. She could see a few families over the brick wall, laboring away at their vegetable plots while smaller children played in the trees. They had probably come down from the council flats behind the converted garden and seemed to be enjoying themselves tending the rows of carrots, peas, and potatoes. An older man, half stooped and white-haired, a geezer in the local parlance, shared a thermos of something hot with a large black man, a West Indian, she guessed, who wore the bright red patch of a London council auxiliary sewn on his sweater. He leaned on an ax handle while enjoying his "cuppa." He would be there to discourage any raids on the site by gangs of chavs or munters who, in Caitlin's opinion, could do with a bit of fucking Enclosures themselves.

By the time they had driven down as far as the All Saints station on the East India Dock Road, the residents of the flats that lined both sides of the street were beginning to shuffle out into the gray, wet morning to join lengthening queues for buses and trains. Dalby's zippy German car attracted many envious looks as he subtly increased his speed through the area, and more than a few of the waiting commuters resentfully gave him the finger.

They drove for another twenty minutes, passing thousands of people trudging to line up for public transport into the city, if they were lucky. Many would have to make multiple transfers, and as much as everybody had once bitched about being caught in peak-hour traffic, it seemed much worse when there was no traffic at all save for the fleets of buses. It had never been an issue for Caitlin, of course, but she had read that it wasn't unusual for people to spend up to four or five hours a day in transit, and she often wondered why they didn't just move closer to wherever they needed to be.

They passed another park given over to agriculture, except this one was much larger than the little plot closer to the city. It looked big enough to have hosted a whole complex of sports fields at one time, and she could tell at a glance that the two tractors plowing the rich black soil were preparing it for a single seed planting. It must have been a ministry operation, as modest little council plots did not run to the sort of gas allowance one needed for tractor farming, although the small crowd she saw huddled at the rear of the field undoubtedly meant the actual planting would be done by hand.

"Must make you a bit homesick for your own place, then, eh?" said Dalby.

She sighed and shook her head, imagining how cold and miserable those people were going to be. They were probably on a work-for-the-dole scheme.

"I forget sometimes how good we have it down there, Dalby," she said. "I mean, we have refugees and everything, and so you're always reminded of how fucked things are for some folks. But even for them, it's gotta be better than trying to scratch together a living up here."

"Well, I imagine that's why there is such a long waiting list to get onto farm stay programs like yours and Mister Melton's. I cannot think I would remain long in London were it not for work."

He swung off the A13 at River Road, just before the Lyon Business Park, where there wasn't a lot of business being done. Indeed, half the premises seemed to be shuttered up, but Creekmouth wasn't completely derelict. Trucks rumbled to and from the nearby gravel pits, and the sewage plant across Barking Creek was churning away as always. The Thames Café and Daddies Snack Bar were open, serving chip butties and sweet tea to a few hundred workers who had precious jobs in nearby metalworks and manufacturing plants. There was a surprisingly healthy marine engineering trade, an industrial cleaning plant, a wire factory, a joinery, and a food wholesaler. One of the largest, most modern facilities belonged to DHL, the courier company, a German engineering firm had just taken over six large factory buildings on Long Reach Road, and there was talk of them opening an engine plant for the new BMW compact under an EU redevelopment program. As far as Caitlin could tell, however, nothing had changed at the abandoned site beyond the erection of a high razor-wire fence.

Dalby drove past all this activity, carefully avoiding the jouncing trucks that rumbled along the crumbling, potholed road, spewing black diesel fumes and not much caring whether they sideswiped him. They carried on past the Crooked Billet pub, an honest drinking hole that smelled of stale food, refried grease, and cigarette smoke. Caitlin had lunched in there once and been taken by the stained-glass windows and an unusually large collection of Pat Benatar tracks on the jukebox but not so much by the grim Dickensian atmosphere and the openly lecherous stares of some of the factory workers nursing their pints and roll-yer-owns.

A minute on from the pub Dalby took a sharp turn just before the old power station and motored down a long driveway past a row of very obviously empty sheds and a large, quiet fenced-off area in which shipping containers were stacked three and four on top of each other. The Thames, gray and wind-flecked, flowed past a hundred meters away, where two men were unloading heavy boxes from a small boat tied up at the end of an old pier. They waved to Dalby as he pulled up and climbed out of the Merc, then went back to their work. The assassin and her handler took their luggage from the backseat and walked through a muddy parking lot in which sat more rusting shipping containers, piles of car tires, at least a dozen rotting wooden boats, and a few mounds of gravel covered in once-green tarpaulins that had been bleached nearly white by exposure to the elements. After a short passage through this junkyard, turning left and right as they threaded through the piles of rubbish, they came to an eight-foot-high electrified fence topped by more razor wire. A blockhouse where a young, well-built man in civilian clothes sat drinking from a paper cup guarded the entrance.

He greeted Dalby by name but insisted on seeing their papers anyway.

The hair on Caitlin's neck stood up as she sensed herself in someone's sights, but she didn't react to the uncomfortable feeling. She knew that snipers covered everyone who came to the Cage through the front door. As long as you had business there, you were fine. It was only those who came through the delivery entrance who had reason to be worried.

The guard thanked them for their time and apologized for the inconvenience of the painstaking accreditation check. The gate slid open smoothly, and they stepped through into Echelon's London op center.

26

TEXAS ADMINISTRATIVE DIVISION

"These are definitely no banditos," Miguel said quietly. "They are road agents."

He passed the night vision goggles to Aronson. They were an excellent tool, he thought, well worth stopping in the next large town they might pass to salvage a pair for himself from a hunting supply store or army surplus outlet. He could easily make out a wealth of detail around the Hy Top Club, a slumping structure of old wooden slats with a broken-back roofline and a half-collapsed awning dropping down over a front veranda.

Aronson also spoke quietly, although without whispering. "Is there a difference?"

Miguel took back the goggles and resumed his surveillance of the old nightclub, or dive bar, or whatever it had been. The small town may have been a mausoleum haunted by the seven thousand souls of those who had Disappeared there, but one would not have known that if all one could see of Crockett, Texas, was the Hy Top Club of South Cottonwood Street. The agents who had attacked the Mormon party, stolen the better part of their longhorn herd, and ridden off with half a dozen of the women were doing their best to push back the darkness. The club roared with life—rude, vicious, drunken, and barbarous, but life nonetheless. The uproar had made it all too easy for Miguel and the Mormons to locate their quarry after cautiously approaching the ghost town from the southwest. Two days it had taken. Two days of nerve-racking stealth and caution, rewarded now by the road agents' total ignorance of the danger that had come upon them.

Miguel estimated the agents' fighting company at twenty strong, give or take, and in addition to the six Mormon women they had taken, there appeared to be another seven or eight camp followers with them. All of them were female, but some of them were not really old enough to be called women. About the age of his own daughter, Sofia, he thought with a glare that was hidden by the absolute darkness of the night.

His blood burned with the need to reach out and hurt someone, even though these men were not the ones who had attacked his farm and family.

Well, they would do for now.

"The banditos are all from the south," he explained to Aronson. "They raid into Texas, but they do not base here. Some say they are sent by my old friend Roberto Morales. I once knew him, you know. Before he became so famous."

The frank disbelief on Aronson's face was discernible even by starlight. Morales, the president for life of the South American Federation, was quite a name for a homeless Mexican cattleman to be dropping. But Miguel did know him, even if only in passing. They had worked together

"I joke, of course," Miguel continued. "He was not my friend at all. But I did know him for a short while, long before he knifed Chávez in the back. Whatever the case, the banditos they come and they go, taking what they can and doing their best to avoid

Blackstone's troopers. If caught, they are hung... what is the word... summary?"

"Summarily," Aronson corrected him. The man's face writhed with warring emotions—anxiety, fear, impacted fury—all of them barely contained by the need to remain hidden from the men who had taken everything from him. Screams intermittently reached them in their hiding spot, a thicket of loblolly pine and pecan trees a block west of the club. The women's cries unsettled Miguel, too, reminding him of his family's last moments. It was all he could to restrain himself from storming in there right now. He wondered if Aronson was able to recognize any of the ragged, terrorized voices and prayed that he could not. It would be too much for any man to bear. Certainly if his own daughter were being held and abused by such human filth, Miguel doubted he would be able to remain detached.

He calmed himself with the thought that Sofia, at least, was safe for the moment. Hidden well outside town with the rest of the Mormons, she would not be exposed to the ugliness of what was going to happen there this night.

"For banditos, Blackstone's Texas is a hard country," he explained patiently. "Deadly if they are caught. For these men, however, not so much."

He jerked his chin in the direction of the Hy Top, which was illuminated by fires burning in oil drums. Rock music thumped and howled from inside. White man's music. Crunching guitars and pounding drums to drown out all but the loudest wailing of the female prisoners. He stilled his sense of outrage, which was considerable, and regarded the scene with a heart crusted in salt and black ice. The camp followers were easy to distinguish from the Mormon women. Although just as likely to be struck or kicked or even dragged into the darkness by the agents, they did enjoy a noticeable freedom of movement not granted to the newest captives. They also enjoyed the privilege of kicking down on the other women.

As he watched through the NVGs, two of the camp whores delighted a small number of agents by tripping one of the captives after she had delivered a tray of beers outside. They fell on her, pinning her struggling form to the ground, and then one sat on her face and shook her ass, laughing and yelling something that Miguel couldn't make out but that he was certain could only be a cruel taunt. It reduced the audience of road agents to helpless laughter.

Hot waves of fury washed through his head, making him dizzy.

Lying on the thick carpet of pine needles, he felt Aronson go tense and start to move. Miguel reached over and grabbed the man's upper arm, digging into the flesh with fingers as hard as rail spikes.

"No," he said firmly but quietly. "Now is not the time."

"But… they're… that's Jenny over there, Willem's betrothed."

Miguel drilled the tip of his thumb into a nerve bundle beneath Aronson's bicep. The Mormon was not a soft man, but the pain was excruciating and overwhelmed any other considerations. When Miguel was certain he was subdued again, he let go.

"I am sorry, Aronson, but if you move against them now, you will die and she will die. Possibly all of your women will be killed. And not quickly. The agents will make sport of it. We must wait. The others will not move until we report back, and we need all of them."

Aronson was silent for a moment, allowing more screams and reports of debauchery to reach them from South Cottonwood Street.

"This is intolerable," he said at last in a weak, broken voice.

Miguel nodded in the dark.

"Yes. We should withdraw for now, back to the meeting place. I can return and watch the agents' camp by myself. It might be better, anyway. I need to move around them, and I want to scout out the field where they have left the cattle. We must find out how many of them are on guard there, and I can do that without being caught. Probably. You, probably not. Let us go, then."

Without allowing the poor man another second to think about it, Miguel was up, drawing the Mormon to his feet and exiting the overgrown lot where they had been conducting their surveillance. The agents had set themselves up in a poor area of town, southwest of the main business center. Miguel could see that even before the Wave it would have been home to the poorer folk of Crockett. Many of the houses that still stood looked small and mean, especially on the western side of Cottonwood Street, where remnant forest still covered the hills and fields. A good deal of refuse and rusted machinery lay where it had been abandoned in gardens and driveways long before the inhabitants had Disappeared, but unlike the town center and some of the more affluent neighborhoods, the area had not been ravaged so completely by fire and looters. To judge from the scenes he had just witnessed, the Hy Top Club had not been relieved of its liquor supply in the years since the Wave had swept away its clientele.

He pondered that.

Perhaps one of the road agents was a fortunate local, someone who had been out of the country in 2003. Perhaps with the army in Iraq. If so, he could have led his comrades here after they had attacked Aronson's people. In the post-Wave world a little local knowledge could be a very precious resource.

The two men retreated carefully through the darkness. This far from the club, with so much scrubland in the way, not much light made it through from the burning oil drums, but the stars burned with cold brilliance high above and a half moon laid an opalescent glow over the ruins of the town, allowing them to pick their way through. They took it slowly, retracing their steps of an hour before, finally emerging into a small open area where the surrounding forest of hickory, elm, and sweetgum gave way to knee-high grass and a few thin saplings. In twenty years, thought Miguel, it would all be forest again.

Aronson whistled, a trilling call like a night bird, and five silhouettes arose from the grass in front of them. Miguel was impressed. Had he not known the Mormons were secreted in the little glade, he would not have spotted them unless he was especially alert. They had even taken care not to tamp down the grass, leaving a telltale path as they walked over it. He recognized the outline of Willem D'Age as the man spoke in a low, anxious voice.

"What have you seen, Brother Aronson? Are our women alive? Are they well?"

"They are alive, for now," Miguel said, before the other man could set off a panic among his fellows or tell D'Age anything that might tip him over the edge into a righteous fury. "And they will stay that way if we keep our heads about us. Gather around."

The group clustered around the returned scouts. Miguel deferred to Aronson, who delivered a competent report of what they had seen on the edge of town. He managed to contain his obvious distress about their women and shaded the details to spare his comrades. Nonetheless, they could not help themselves.

"So these animals, they have taken the women as chattels?" D'Age asked.

"They treat them very roughly, brother," said Aronson.

"Then we should go now and release them from this veil," another voice piped up. "We shall lay the Lord's vengeance on them for their trespasses."

The speaker was young, and Miguel recognized him as one of the boys, Orin. He was waving around a military assault weapon, and Miguel could tell even in the starlight that every line in his body was tensed and quivering like a bow drawn too far and held too long. He reached over and placed his hand over the boy's where it gripped the front end of the rifle.

"Boy," he said quietly but with great firmness, "this is no game. We shall kill these men tonight. Or they shall kill us. It is not play. Put your weapon away until it is needed. Until blood is the only outcome…"

Miguel hoisted his own rifle, his much-loved Winchester, and held it in front of the boy.

"I have leveled this gun at five men. They are all dead now. Do you understand? Do not wave your weapon around. It is not a toy."

Not only the overexcited lad fell still, but all the men around him.

"Good," said Miguel. "Then we can prepare."

Miguel heard the lowing of the cattle, well before the stench of the animals reached him, and then the wind changed and the familiar bovine reek was in his nostrils, at the back of his throat, everywhere, thick as fresh shit on the heel of a new boot. He smiled thinly. He did not imagine for a moment that the road agents guarding the stolen livestock would be savvy enough to detect his particular smell on the night breeze. To get stuck with a job like this when there was a party to be had, they would be the bottom feeders of the crew, the new recruits with nothing to leverage. Still, he would pay them the heed due to men who would kill without a qualm, given the chance.

That was why they would never get the chance.

Two hours he had been watching them as they made their rounds of the football field that butted up against the big loop road that swung around the southwestern reaches of the town. The sporting field was fenced, and the fence line had not deteriorated too badly in three years without maintenance, providing the agents with a convenient area to pen their newly stolen herd within a reasonable distance of the Hy Top Club. It was, he estimated, no more than a ten-minute walk through the darkness, depending on whether you risked turning an ankle or even breaking a leg by cutting across the overgrown gardens that lay in between.

The sounds of revelry had died away in the last twenty minutes. No more music or laughter drifted through the newly grown forest that was quickly reclaiming the outskirts of Crockett. The occasional scream did so, however, and Miguel could only hope that the Mormons would be able to contain themselves until the moment was right. Before they could move on the main body of the agents, he had to dispose of these two quietly. Even two men, well armed, arriving at the wrong moment could be enough to turn the tide against them.

Miguel settled himself against the rough, sticky trunk of a pine tree and brought the night vision goggles up to his eyes again. There were two of them, both young, as he had thought. One was taller, however, and, unusually for these times, quite fat. A prodigious belly spilled over his belt buckle, and as Miguel watched, he appeared to be shoving some sort of long bread roll into his face. They were both dressed in a ridiculous mishmash of Hollywood outfits he would have thought of as cowboy biker: jeans with chaps, buckskin shirts, studded black leather vests, and wide-brimmed hats. The shorter and thinner of the two was also wrapped in what looked like a full-length black leather coat. They each carried pistols in hip holsters, but Miguel assumed they were modern semiautomatics, not revolvers. They were for show at any rate, because each was also armed with an assault rifle. Some sort of M16 variants if he was not wrong.

The smaller one was smoking and occasionally drinking from a flask he would take from inside his full-length coat. That was good, the vaquero thought. *Drink up, my little friend. Drink up.* They shivered and stomped around a small campfire they'd lit near the northern end of the running track that ran around the football field.

Or did they call it a gridiron field here? he wondered. True football was a game played with a round ball between civilized people.

Miguel waited another five minutes, until total silence had fallen over the empty wastes of suburban Crockett. When he was certain the main body of partygoers had exhausted themselves with debauchery, he made his move.

First he removed his shoes and dropped his pants—took them right off—before putting his boots back on.

Then he donned a leather motorcycle jacket salvaged by Ben Randall from an auto shop in Leona two days earlier, thankfully, not from the remains of its former owner. After his scare in the general store, that would have been too much. Miguel was certain he would have felt the dead man creeping all over him within a few minutes of pulling it on. But the jacket had been hung cleanly on a hook in the workshop of the town's garage. It matched the clothing of one or two of the road agents he had spied back at the club. They had also sought out other equipment, but without luck. Thus, he had no silenced pistol or hunting bow with which he might quietly send these two worthless *chochas* into the next world to account for themselves.

But he did have a plan.

And so, without pants but leather jacketed, with a bright yellow Caterpillar baseball cap pulled down over his face, he emerged from his hiding spot and began a long, staggering walk across open ground, waving a half-empty bottle of bourbon around.

He was praying that with the night being so dark and the agents partly blinded by the small campfire, his bizarre approach would disarm their suspicions. If it did not, he was dead and the Mormon women almost certainly, too.

Miguel kept his head down as best he could, allowing himself only brief glimpses of his quarry as he staggered theatrically every few yards or so. The guards noticed him when he was about fifty yards out, the shorter of the two pointing and laughing.

"Hey. Is that James? Jimmy James Jefferson? Y'all brought us some bourbon but none o' that tight Mormon pussy, you dumbass?"

A few of the nearest cattle bellowed and snorted, but they moved away and resumed dozing, chewing their cud, or swatting flies with their tails.

Well before Miguel entered the full glow of the campfire where he would have been identified as an impostor, he deliberately stumbled facedown into the dirt, where he stayed, groaning, with his ass pointed squarely at the road agents.

He hoped they would not be so familiar with the ass of this

Jimmy James Jefferson that they would be alerted to his ruse.

From their braying laughter, they did not seem much perturbed.

Typical, thought Miguel, that men of this ilk would do nothing to help a fallen comrade with neither pants nor dignity to his name. They seemed content to chat to each other while he lay in the dirt.

He groaned loudly again and pushed himself up on one his elbows before throwing one arm out and crashing down again, this time with the bottle of bourbon where they might see it draining away.

"Hey!" cried one of them, the smaller man, he was certain. "Don't spill it all."

Miguel dragged the bottle back toward himself and waited.

He forced himself to go completely limp as he heard both sets of feet approaching. He had his right hand tucked away inside the leather jacket, his fingers wrapped around the handle of the footlong Bowie knife. A cattleman, he had worked with knives all his life and knew what speed, strength, and a finely honed blade could do to living flesh when driven with enough force and skill and merciless intent.

When he felt the men's hands grab for him roughly, he rolled over and struck out in one, two, three flashing movements. He whipped the knife through a short vicious arc that took the killing edge of the blade deep into the throat of the smaller man, who could not even scream, so quickly was his trachea sliced in two. As he continued to sweep around, launching himself like a coiled rattler, he switched to a backhanded stabbing grip and drove the evil-looking steel shaft deep into the temple of the second man, whose eyes seemed almost to pop out of their sockets at the very moment the last spark of life died in them. He reversed the flow of his attack, ripping the blade out, bringing huge gobbets of flesh and slivers of bone chip with it. With a final lunge he drove the Bowie up under the floating rib of the first man he had cut, making sure of his end by ramming four inches of hardened steel into his heart.

A few cattle bellowed in protest but stayed where they were.

Grimacing with disgust, Miguel stood and stripped off the leather jacket. He was bathed in hot, dark blood, but there was no time to clean up.

He hurried back to where he'd left his pants and his guns.

There would be more such work before he was done for the night.

27

KANSAS CITY, MISSOURI

Compared to most big urban centers, Kansas City was relatively intact. As he took in the view from his temporary office on the Cerner Campus in North Kansas City, Kip played connect the dots in his head. He could hear the trains rumbling down the tracks on the other side of Highway 210. He would use those trains in conjunction with the Missouri River to resettle St. Louis at the eastern end of the state, where advance salvage crews were already busy stripping the Boeing plant, among other things. Once St. Louis was resettled, they could begin to reassert control over the Mississippi River. With control of the river, he would hold the beating heartland in his hands and could turn his attention south or east.

This was the part of his job that thrilled and fascinated Kipper. The politics he left to Jed. The necessity, the inevitably of conflict, of war, he was coming to accept as a part of binding up the fabric of a continent that had been torn apart. He was already at war in all but name on the island of Manhattan, and that rat bastard down in Fort Hood seemed intent on pushing him to the edge of a sectarian conflict at some point in the future. But the challenge of rebuilding and renewal, marshaling all the resources at the nation's call, as diminished as they might be, and applying them in the best way at the right place and time—that was engineering on a scale that went well beyond the merely epic. This was world building. He indulged himself in a few moments of happy satisfaction as he watched school buses full of men and women in overalls and brightly colored safety vests chug out of the parking lot across the street from another Cerner building that had been converted into a dorm. More buses would be collecting workers from Crown Center, the hotels at Harrah's and Ameristar Casinos farther to the east, and a nine-story loft apartment complex in Northtown. The workers, a mix of people from all over the planet, would fan out across the city to perform their duties and earn their places by dedicating themselves for seven years to the renewal of the republic.

Some would head out to the Hawthorne Power Plant to assist in restoring the facility to its full 435-megawatt capacity. Maybe they'd be clearing the roads of tangled auto wrecks, although KC's road net wasn't too badly jammed up by the insane megasnarls Kipper had seen in New York. Anyone with railroad experience, mostly refugees from India, was tasked with restoring the myriad rail yards scattered through the Kansas City area.

Their work might be altogether grimmer, of course. If they had been chosen for their jobs because they had an employment background in the medical sector or had worked with hazardous materials or environments before, there was a chance they were heading out to clean up the remains of the Disappeared. There were still tens of thousands of them to be put to rest, and the God botherers in Congress had kicked up an almighty stink when they'd discovered that the first clearance teams in KC had simply scooped up the leftovers of former residents and burned them in Hawthorne Unit 5's coal-fired furnace. The Greens hadn't been too happy, either, although of course those wing nuts had complained about the loss of precious biomass and the carbon footprint of the reclamation efforts, especially pertaining to the reactivation of the coal-fired power plants. Man, he really didn't relish their likely reaction when they learned that the Wolf Creek nuclear generating station in Coffey County was next on the list of plants to be reactivated.

Kipper rolled his eyes. You would have thought they'd have been content with the collapse of the global economy. That had wound back carbon emissions to early-twentieth-century levels once you corrected for the one-off addition of the toxic firestorms back in '03. But no, the Greens had the swing votes in Congress, and they had proved themselves to be entirely ruthless in using their numbers to play off the old Republicans and Democrats. They were even worse in many ways. Their party discipline was kind of frightening. Probably it had something to do with that weird messianic fervor they all seemed to share. In private, he and Jed often referred to them as the Borg, and he was very much looking forward to leaving them behind when his term was over. The next president of the United States could argue with them about who should actually be running Reconstruction. In his darker moments he really hoped Sarah Palin would run. They deserved each other.

"Mister President?"

Kip turned away from the window and found a young woman waiting at the door with a clipboard.

"The chief of staff is here, sir. And your secure link to Pearl Harbor will be up in the conference room in five minutes. Oh, and Mister Tench is here early. I've given him a doughnut and a coffee downstairs."

The president laughed out loud.

"If Barney is early, you're going to need some more doughnuts. Tell him I'll be down as soon as I can."

He thanked the young lady and said good morning to Jed as he bustled into the room, also carrying a doughnut. Kipper wondered where they came from. Surely they weren't being flown in from Seattle.

Jed was hauling around a couple of ring binders under one arm, which he dropped onto the bare, rather cheap-looking desk. The office was remarkably spartan for the nation's chief executive, but Kip liked it because of the great view it afforded him of the reclamation work. From the southwest corner of the building, it was possible to see the rail yards of North Kansas City, the planes coming into Charles B. Wheeler Downtown Airport, and the skyline of Kansas City, Missouri, proper. Trucks and buses rumbled down Highway 210 laden with workers, salvage, and supplies. A good many horses and bicycles could be seen plying the roads as well. If he looked due west, it was possible to see the restored and fully operational North Kansas City federal medical facility. Kipper felt a pang of guilt, knowing that some of his soldiers were in there struggling for their lives. He needed to get over and see them before he returned to Seattle. Turning away to the east, he could see the stream of smoke rising from Hawthorne Unit 5's power plant, which provided power for the entire metro area. He hoped he would be able to get out there before the end of the day and personally see how things were going. Or to micromanage the chicken shit and put everyone's teeth on edge, as Culver put it.

"Good morning Mister President," said his chief of staff, who was dressed in a perfectly pressed charcoal-gray three-piece suit. Kipper wore chinos and a blue denim shirt, a casual ensemble that was justified in his mind, by all the site visits he'd be making later in the day and possible because his wife was not there to hassle him into a monkey suit.

"Any good news out of New York overnight?" Jed asked. "I've been caught up with Treasury."

"Nothing I'd call good," said Kip. "Forty-eight confirmed dead on our side, mostly from the clearance teams we saw yesterday. About as many again badly wounded and enormous destruction of the city between Union and Madison squares. The casualties will be flown out to Northtown Medical later today."

"I see," Culver said. "Any news of enemy casualties?"

Kipper rubbed his eyes, which were grainy and red. He never slept well the first night in a new bed at the best of times, which these weren't.

"Six hundred plus, according to the cav. But there's plenty more where they came from. Including our mystery men. We've apparently got an updater coming from Colonel Kinninmore later in the day about that. And what about you, Jed? What complications do you have for me this morning?"

He meant it to be a joke, but it came out a little surly and undignified.

"Sorry," Kip added. "I'm tired and pissed off. And I have forty-eight very sad letters to write later today."

Culver joined him at the panoramic windows to look out over the city.

"Well, you know my views on that," he said.

"And you know mine," Kipper shot back with a slightly warning tone. "It is not a waste of time, Jed. It is something I have to do. They're just short notes, but I know they mean a lot to the families."

Thankfully, Culver chose to ignore yet another of their old arguments.

"The press isn't too bad this morning," he said, choosing to plow on in his usual pragmatic style. "They're getting right behind us in Manhattan. Calling it the Battle of New York."

"Has anyone started speculating on this business of the—" Kipper checked his notes. "—the fedayeen involvement?"

"Not yet," said Culver. "But it's early days, and there are half a dozen or so reporters and war bloggers embedded with our guys and Schimmel's militia over there. If it's a live issue, they will get onto it before long."

Kipper gazed down at the hospital where casualties would be

arriving from New York throughout the day.

"Good," he said. "Maybe they can get us better info than official channels. You know, if they're writing and filing their stories from the front."

Culver looked skeptical.

"Unlikely, sir. If they're embedded, all of their reports are going through our links and getting censored by our intel guys. They're not going to let raw data like that get out to the public till they've had time to work out their own spin."

"That's actually kind of a pity, Jed," Kipper said, and meant it. "Sometimes it's good to get an alternative reading of a situation. What chance you reckon any of these embeds might be able to file independently, via satellite phone or something?"

"I suppose they could," said his chief of staff. "But it's unlikely they'd ass fuck the army like that. The embed system works for them. Increases traffic to their sites. Mostly, they won't jeopardize that relationship. They're on board. Look at what happened after the attack. I was wrong to think the casualties from Castle Clinton would turn them against us. Even Arianna is baying for pirate blood now. I think staying behind while we evacuated the casualties on your chopper really helped."

Kipper frowned.

"Jed, it wasn't about spinning the story. Those people would have died."

"I know, I know," he apologized. "But someone has to think the ugly thoughts in this administration, Mister President, which brings us to Blackstone. I've had a few ideas…"

"Just hold that thought, Jed. We can work through your Texas problems later today."

"My Texas problems?" Jed replied archly.

"Yes." Kipper smiled. "Yours. Didn't you get the memo? I'm sure there was a memo. Anyway, that's for later. Right now I want to talk to a man about a bomb."

"You'll have to wait, Mister President," said Jed Culver with a touch of satisfaction. "It's only three a.m. in Honolulu, leaving plenty of time to work through my Texas problem."

The man charged with guarding and maintaining the strategic deterrent of the United States of America found himself staring out at a light blue Pacific sky not long after sunrise. A glass of juice sat untouched on a paper napkin on his desk while he waited for the video link to tie him in to his commander in chief. While he waited, Admiral James Ritchie looked over the latest updates from the Pacific Fleet's deterrent force of Ohio-class submarines, six boomers in all, down from a pre-Wave total of eighteen, deployed in a pattern to allow maximum coverage of all potential targets on the face of the globe. After sixty years during which the awful specter of nuclear war sometimes seemed to be the only thing preventing it, some people had grown awfully blasé about tossing atomic weapons at each other. The death toll from Israel's first strike in 2003 was now conservatively estimated at six hundred million as the secondary die-off continued. They had decimated humanity.

But who was he to think ill of them, having played his own part in firing a nuclear warning shot across the bows of Hugo Chávez a few days later?

The Russians had nuked three of their own former republics six months after that, and of course the Indo-Pakistani War had killed another two hundred million before the surviving nuclear powers intervened with a threat of general annihilation for both countries. Meanwhile Brazil had restarted its nuclear weapons program for the South American Federation, something Ritchie knew long before the news media did. And nary a week went by without the Australian ambassador calling on him to inquire about transferring two of those decommissioned boomers into her country's rapidly growing arsenal. Some days Ritchie thought it was a blessed wonder that anyone was still alive on this poor little planet.

"Links secure," an army communications officer said on the twenty-six-inch widescreen, breaking the admiral's train of thought.

President James Kipper appeared on the big Sony display, his image slightly pixelated and jerky. Chief of Staff Culver sat in the background, pen in hand. There seemed to be nobody else in the room, which looked like some sort of hotel conference space. Ritchie had worked with Kipper's administration long enough to know the president's informal ways, but there were times he wondered whether the president understood he wasn't just running a city council department anymore.

"Mister President," Ritchie said. "Mister Culver."

Kipper waved, and Culver nodded.

"Admiral," said the chief of staff. "Good to see you again. Did you get that package I sent you?"

Ritchie held up his untouched glass of juice. "Yes, I did, sir. I appreciate the gesture."

"And did you have a chance to look over my query concerning the use of special weapons in tactical situations?" Culver asked.

"Neutron bombs, Admiral," the president interrupted. "Let's not be coy. He means neutron bombs. I want the option for New York if necessary. To cut down on our casualties."

Ritchie winced inwardly. He had indeed received via secure Pandora link the e-mail about the use of neutron weapons in the pacification of the eastern seaboard. "Yes, sirs, I received your message," he said.

"So what's your opinion?" Kipper asked, leaning forward into the camera. You had to hand it to James Kipper. He did not fuck around.

Neither would Ritchie. He shook his head. "I am sorry, Mister President. The option is no good. Most of the weapons you're referring to were demobilized and destroyed at the end of the 1990s. I've spoken to my engineers about the matter, and they tell me that it might be possible to build a weapon or two for the purposes you had in mind, but we are probably looking at months, untold millions of new dollars, and questionable effectiveness of the warhead when it's made, anyway. Furthermore, even if it worked as advertised, it's not like the old movies, Mister President. It won't just vaporize the enemy. There is still a significant heat and blast effect that will knock flat a huge part of the city, and even then, even with massively enhanced lethality from increased radiation, many of the enemy will recover from the lethal dose and enter a walking dead phase."

Ritchie paused at that, struck by an odd image running through his mind: pirates with AK-47s lurching through the streets of Manhattan like zombies.

"Walking dead… ase?" Kipper asked as his image and audio faltered a little. "Wha… at?"

"I'm sorry, Mister President. You're breaking up. If you're asking what the walking dead phase is, it's exactly what it sounds like," Ritchie replied. "The enemy so targeted and not killed immediately will recover from an initial bout of illness and survive free of any symptoms for a period that could last anywhere from a few days to a few weeks in any given case. During that time they could cause a great deal of havoc, especially given that they'd know they had nothing left to lose."

Kipper rubbed the bridge of his nose as though he had a bad headache while Culver shifted through his papers.

"What about other weapons?" Culver asked. "Have you had an opportunity to survey our options?"

Ritchie nodded. "I talked to the chemical warfare folks over at Twenty-fifth Infantry before you called. The United States was already in the process of demobilizing and destroying our biological and chemical stockpiles when the Wave struck."

Kipper looked up at the screen, then back at Culver, his face deeply lined with fatigue.

"I understand there are small stockpiles at locations I can disclose via encrypted text transmission. However, there remains the same question as to whether or not those weapons are viable for use," Ritchie said. "Moreover, their tactical value may well be degraded by the specific theater conditions. Despite the mythology, neutron weapons were conceived of as a defense against Soviet armor massed out in the open, not as a way of denuding enemy cities of all life. Plus, of course, it's not an insignificant thing, opening this particular chest of wonders, Mister President. I would like to place on the record my very strong advice that we do not even consider going down this road."

The president stared off to the left somewhere, as though looking out a window, perhaps. When he turned back to the screen, he asked, "Are those weapons secured?"

"The facilities are," Ritchie replied. "We do not have a full inventory of all of the weapons and their status, but that is mainly a human resource issue. The depots themselves are secure."

They were secured, as Ritchie well knew, by a cluster of W62 and/or W78 thermonuclear warheads surrounding the perimeter of each facility. These warheads, with a yield of 170 to 300-plus kilotons, were in turn surrounded by another perimeter of antipersonnel weapons and watched by satellite and hardwire video surveillance. The warheads were arranged in a way that ensured maximum destructive yield over a facility such as the Deseret Chemical Depot in Utah or the Johnston Atoll Strategic Weapons Reserve in the Pacific Ocean. Part of Ritchie's job was to secure all such weapons of mass destruction by any means possible. Since his 1,000-strong Strategic Command Security Force was not nearly enough to even begin to garrison all the sites, it was logical to simply booby-trap them, especially given the fickle nature of loyalty these days within certain elements of the U.S. Army. Blackstone's siren song reached all the way out into Ritchie's command, though he was confident that most naval personnel remained immune to the charms of terrorizing migrants in Texas.

If Mad Jack ever got his hands on a nuclear weapon, however...

"I know ground operations aren't your thing, Admiral," said Kipper, "but do you have any thoughts on the current problem? In New York, I mean."

Drawn away from contemplation of his daily nightmare, Ritchie shook his head.

"I am afraid there will be no easy solution, Mister President. There never is. I will offer this for consideration: How long will the bulk of New York City last without human intervention? We have found significant natural deterioration of the places we've already resettled. Am I correct?"

The president nodded.

"Even if we were to secure the New York City area, and even I agree that it has to be secured somehow, just how long will it be before we need all of the possible living space?" Ritchie asked.

Culver leaned forward. "If current immigration trends continue and our birthrate remains nominal, perhaps a hundred years from now."

Ritchie nodded. "By that point, Mister President, we would need to demolish what is there and build something new. Well, not us, of course, but you know what I mean. Nature will have destroyed the city for us even if we are able to drive the pirates out."

"What do you suggest, Admiral?"

Ritchie backed away from suggesting anything. The idea of mushroom clouds consuming a dead city full of memories and pirates was just too much.

"I have no easy solution, Mister President. That is the best I can tell you."

Kipper did not look happy, and part of Ritchie urged him to leave it at that, but he couldn't. "Do you mind if I speak freely, sir?"

The president seemed surprised he'd asked, but then, he was neither a military man nor a career politician.

"No. Go on," he said.

"Mister President, I understand it is a terrible thing sending men and women into combat. If you are a halfway decent human being, it should weigh on you like no other decision you will ever make in your life. But sir, just because it is emotionally difficult and morally challenging, it is not necessarily wrong. Those men and women were not press-ganged into service. It was not just a choice for them. It was and remains a calling. And sir, no nation on earth can hope to survive long without people who will answer that call. No nation can hope to survive if it does not respect what they have offered and do the hard things that history sometimes asks of us. Sometimes, Mister President, there is no answer but blood."

James Kipper stared out at him from the screen, his hands held together as if praying, pressed against his lips. He seemed to be weighing what Ritchie had said. After a moment he replied.

"Thank you, Admiral. I'll think on that some more."

28

NEW YORK

"CLAYMORE!" Milosz shouted. He squeezed the clacker three times. The intersection before him lit up with a flash and a roar of three claymore anti-personnel mines set up to optimize the body count. When the dust, the smoke, and the ringing in his ears cleared, he could see an intersection full of shredded offal and bone where screaming asswits had been.

"This is like the shooting of monkeys in a barrel, yes?" Milosz shouted as he exchanged an empty magazine for a full one. "Except we are these fucking monkeys. No racial offenses to be intended, Wilson."

Tracer fire punched into the polished stone column behind him, chewing out chunks of powder and sharp, stinging fragments of marble. An armored truck sporting the logo of the Wells Fargo Company lurched into the intersection with a 12.7-mm DShK mounted on top. A rail-thin Somali worked the machine gun around the intersection, spraying the walls with heavy fire. Sergeant Veal laid down return fire with his M240, firing off short bursts of

7.62s while his partner worked her radio. Veal's rounds shattered the armored glass of the truck.

"None taken! I'm more offended that you didn't bring the fifty-cal, Fred!" Wilson roared as he lifted his carbine over the windowsill of the bank at the corner of East 29th Street and Madison to squeeze off a few as Somalis and Yemenis started to pour in around the Wells Fargo truck. Return tracer fire zipped through the air in torrents like deadly horizontal rain, but inaccurately, as if blown everywhere by a squalling wind. Milosz kept his head tucked in so tightly that his neck started to cramp, but straying even an inch too high could mean losing the top of his skull. This was the problem with operating behind enemy lines, he thought: *Always it sounds like such a very glamorous sort of adventure until the fucking enemy turns around and realizes you are there.*

"Throwing white," he yelled over the infernal din before pulling the pin on a smoke grenade and tossing it through the shattered windows and into the street outside, aiming for the center of the intersection.

"White smoke at your three o'clock, over," Tech Sergeant Gardener yelled into her radio headset. There was a brief pause before she yelled again. "Target in platoon strength, one hundred yards south of smoke. Enemy in the open, moving toward us. Over."

Milosz picked up his M4 carbine again and risked a peek over the solid gray stonework behind which they were sheltering. He got a quick picture of two dozen or more men running and darting from doorways to smashed cars, moving from one scrap of cover to the next, firing and yelling as they came. In among them he spotted a lone man who seemed to be directing traffic, his head swathed in what looked like a red scarf. A single round sizzled past Milosz's ear and clanged off something metallic behind him. He heard the speeding projectile as a distinctly separate entity inside the storm of battle, a single shot out of the bullet swarm that raged around them. He leveled the muzzle of his M203 on them and fired a forty-millimeter high-explosive grenade into a car across the street where many of the nig nogs were taking cover. A crunching explosion blew chunks of shrapnel and fresh man meat into the street. A quick check. The scarf was nowhere to be seen.

"Cleared hot!" Gardener yelled, before she grabbed Milosz by the shoulder and pulled him down hard. He heard the thudding roar of a swooping gunship a split second before the deafening buzz-saw howl of its minigun turned the street outside into a mess of flying metal, glass, and spent brass casings. A few seconds later rockets whooshed in, detonating with deadly effect in the concrete valley of Madison Avenue. Milosz risked another look and was horrified to see that one of the attackers—*the asswit in the red scarf, back from the dead!*—had somehow sprinted through the fiery maelstrom and thrown a grenade into Sergeant Veal's position. The air force machine gunner was blown in half as he tried to throw the grenade back. Gardener screamed, and Milosz shook his head, which rang like a giant gong.

The attacker cocked an arm back to throw another grenade into their hiding place. Before Milosz could get his weapon up to snap off a shot, Technical Sergeant Gardener, firing one-handed while still yelling instructions to the gunship pilots, put half a clip from her M4 into his stomach. Milosz would swear that for just a moment he could see right through the man in the scarf to the burning wreckage of the street behind, where secondary explosions were tossing cars around like throw pillows, melting tires and windshields, and blowing out windows high above the street.

"Fucker!" Gardener yelled as she swapped mags.

"Ha! Take that Captain fucking Crunch," Wilson shouted half hysterically. "You like that, huh? Sucks to be you now, don't it, bitch!"

The pirate spun around, ending the weird effect—had it been an illusion?—of being able to see right through the huge, ragged hole in his torso. Milosz and Gardener ducked as the grenade exploded, adding its cracking bass note to the explosive symphony.

"I do not imagine Colonel Kinninmore will be having such a full and frank exchange of views with this motherfucker, eh?" Milosz cried.

"Whoa! Three o'clock!" Wilson yelled, quickly shifting position to one of the big, soaring windows that looked east down 29th Street. "There's more of them."

"Cursed be your mother's anus and your father's testicles!" Milosz roared in demented anger as he scrambled over to cover the new line of attack. "This is not how we do stealth in Polish special forces, I tell you, Wilson. And yet Poles it is who everyone makes joke about. Is this fair, I ask you? *Is this fair?*"

He yelled that last while methodically firing single rounds one after the other into six charging pirate asswits. Most of them wore red keffiyehs like the man Gardener had just killed, and as they charged, Milosz distinctly heard the war cry *"Allahu akbar!"* One came so close that he heard his bullet strike flesh, like the sound of a hand slapping water, and saw a small fizzing cloud of steam puff out from the entry wound. Meanwhile, the thin black ranger was down on one knee, swapping a magazine, while Gardener called in a new close air support mission and covered the burning morass of Madison Avenue lest any more freakishly lucky survivors should emerge from the hot tangle of twisted scaffolding and burning cars.

"Downtown four five, this is Halo two niner, requesting close air. Swing ninety right on last confirmed gun run, white smoke as previous, over," she said into her headset with a shade less urgency and volume than before.

The crackle and wind roar of the blaze triggered by the last Little Bird attack was loud, but not so loud that it drowned out the cries and shouts of the enemy as they pressed forward again.

"Little Birds are pulling out for resupply," Gardener said, checking over Veal's body. The mute sergeant's right arm had disintegrated in the same grenade blast that had split his torso open.

"I'm trying to get some A-10s. They ought to be stacked up between five and eight thousand feet."

"Goddamn! Hope they don't leave us open for too long," spit Wilson. "I'm down to three mags and pistol ammo. What you got, Fred?"

"Two full magazines of carbine ammunition and two rounds for the two-oh-three," Milosz said, banging another two shots down 29th Street, knocking over a crazy black fellow who appeared to be armed with nothing more than a machete. His carbine jammed as he watched the African climb to his feet.

"American piece of shit," Milosz shouted, pulling the charging handle in an attempt to clear the jam.

"Roger that. Cleared hot," said Gardener. "Over. Gentlemen, heads down, please."

Milosz distinctly heard the whine of turbines echoing around the concrete canyons of the city again before a fantastic river of bright yellow tracer fire deluged the street, sweeping over everything in its path like fiendish sorcery. The machete-wielding fool was scythed apart, bursting open in a splatter of blood mulch as though cleaved from shoulder to hip by a giant's invisible sword. It happened in an instant, the lethal radiance unstitching his sprinting form in a malign display of rag doll physics before ribboning up the street to disassemble even more of his comrades. A second later the incendiary hammer fist of Hellfire missiles fell upon 29th Street, atomizing the living and the dead alike in a scorching blast that Milosz could feel in the uncomfortable tightening of all his exposed skin. He shut his watering eyes against the heat, ducking well below the solid stone window box. The turbines howled away, powering the A-10 back into the low clouds over Manhattan.

Gardener's calm voice came from somewhere to the left. "Outstanding work, Downtown four five. Another load of tourists gone to hell."

Wilson was more emphatic as he whooped it up. "Ha! Not so

tough now, are we, motherfuckers? Teach you to disrespect the city ordinances, didn't we? Welcome to explodapalooza, fools."

Milosz squinted into the fierce glare of the small, self-contained apocalypse burning merrily away in Madison Avenue, and there, sure enough, he saw more figures moving, advancing carefully through the fiery debris, some of them in the ubiquitous scarves of the tactical commanders he had learned to look out for.

"Goddamn," Wilson protested. "Don't these ignorant motherfuckers ever get the message? Gardener, is that more of them?"

"I do not know that we should be killing these people, Wilson," Milosz said. "They remind me very much of the bootblack in Horatio Alger story with their sticking-to-it-iveness, yes? Would make excellent citizens now, I am thinking. Perhaps we should discuss possible truce and fast-tracking of naturalization, no? As alternative to being overrun and fast-tracked into early grave?"

"Horatio fucking who? Izzat that fucking nigga in the two-seven always talking about getting out and working salvage in LA?"

"Downtown four five, this is Halo two niner," Gardener said. "Requesting close air again. Over."

"Again with the N-word, which we discussed, Wilson," Milosz said, as he took a pair of binoculars from his battle dress and tried to get a fix on the advancing enemy. "Is this an irregular English noun, perhaps?"

"Downtown four five, please say again, over."

Milosz replaced the spyglasses and tried to find the man he had just seen through them with the scope of his M4, but it proved impossible in the clutter of the burning street.

"You got it." Wilson laughed. Milosz had no idea why anyone would laugh in such a situation. "They are worthless jungle niggas to me. But to you they are the proud and worthy descendants of the Zulu warrior race. Or asswits. Asswits works just as well."

Milosz shook his head in exaggerated dismay.

"Have I mentioned this is crazy fucking country, Wilson?"

"Downtown four five, we have hostiles on the move toward us... how long... goddamn it, no!"

" 'Goddamn no' is not good," said Milosz, suddenly paying more attention to the very pissed off air force controller. "What happened to outstanding work, and excellent shooting of the enemy, and please to killing some more?" he asked.

"They got retasked," she said. "We're on our own."

"On my twelve," Wilson said, without a trace of good humor. He snapped up his carbine and rattled off a brace of single shots. Milosz, too, had switched his weapon to single fire, needing to preserve ammunition. Gardener began fiddling with her radio, adjusting frequencies.

"Air liaison, air liaison, this is Halo two niner, requesting priority patch through to ASOC. Grid reference is..."

"Hey, Alabama," Wilson called over his shoulder. "Don't you let those fucking assholes hang us out to dry here. You get a fucking fifty-two to demolish every fucking block around us if you have to, but you keep those nasty fuckers out of our faces here."

Gardener ignored him and kept at her job.

"Air liaison, air liaison, this is Halo two niner..."

"Wilson, perhaps we need to fall back soon," Milosz suggested as the first rounds of the next attack began zipping and cracking past his head. It was just a few shots to begin with as the pirate asswits pushed forward through the carnage and destruction laid upon their comrades.

At least they could not know that the Americans' air cover had been pulled away, presumably to save somebody more important than they, in even deeper shit.

But who is more important than Milosz? he thought wryly. And surely nobody's shit is deeper than mine right now.

And then, for half a heartbeat, he caught himself out.

For the first time he had thought of himself as American.

"Soon to be dead American," he muttered. What was next? he wondered. A Stetson cowboy hat and a pair of… what did they call them? Shitkickers for my coffin?

"What's that, Fred?" Wilson asked, firing twice at some unknown target.

"…ASOC we are requesting air support at grid reference…"

"Nothing," Milosz shouted. "Just please to keep shooting asswits."

At three minutes to three in the morning, he ran out of ammo for the carbine and the M203.

"I'm out, too," he shouted, joining Gardener in drawing his M9 Beretta and aiming two-handed into Madison Avenue, where at least eight of the enemy were popping up to fire at them with assault rifles, shotguns, pistols, and in one case some sort of hunting crossbow. That had been good for a laugh until one of the wickedly sharp arrowheads had nearly sliced open Wilson's jugular.

"I'm out," the master sergeant declared as the hammer of his M4 clicked on an empty chamber.

"We should really be going now," Milosz said, raising his voice to be heard over the assault, a sonic storm of gunfire and tribal shrieks, ululations, and the occasional *"Allahu akbar"* as the growing horde of attackers drew closer. Gardener swung out from behind her cover, holding two pistols that cracked like whips in the hands of a veteran cowboy. She killed four or five men Milosz could see, adding their bodies to the gruesome pile of the dead that had ramped up in front of their position, and then she stopped, ducked, and checked her load.

"That's it for me, gentlemen. If you don't mind, I'll be saving one bullet for the sake of decorum."

The words were brave, but Milosz could see that the woman speaking them was terrified. The yelling and screaming cycled up outside to something like hysteria, and perhaps it was, an insane mix of fury, terror, bloodlust, and vengefulness all about to burst upon them.

"I'll save this for when they come in," Wilson said, holding up the last grenade.

Milosz nodded grimly while scanning the ruined bank foyer for any possible exit. Unfortunately, there was none. They were cut off as the final charge began with an unholy war cry. He had enough time to wonder where it had originated, what benighted jungle swamp or howling desert these particular nig nog asswits hailed from that they should travel so fucking far and die in such numbers just to have at him.

He had four bullets left for his own Beretta and resolved to put each of them into a different man, standing up from where he'd crouched below the scarred ruins of the bank's high-vaulted windows and assuming a comfortable shooter's stance, taking careful aim with a two-handed grip. His pistol boomed once, and a charging asswit spun and dropped. He fired again, and the throat of another exploded in red ruin. A third shot smacked into the chest of a massively fat man whose momentum carried him forward so far that Milosz wondered if he had been hit at all. He lifted his aim slightly and shot him in the face, which came apart like a rotten melon, spewing its corruption everywhere.

Bullets struck and whizzed all around as he calmly unsheathed his fighting knife and waited to receive the enemy.

At last they drew close enough for him to marvel at the whiteness of teeth bared like canine fangs, as though they might leap the last ten feet and tear him apart like jackals. And then... a murderous wind blew over them, scything them down, carving through them, raking huge chunks of meat and chips of bone from their dancing bodies. So shocked was he that it took another second before he recognized the dense, ripping sound of a high-capacity machine gun coming from somewhere to the north. And then his knee collapsed under him as Gardener kicked it out from behind and dragged him down below the line of the window.

"What the fuck! Is that the cavalry? The real cavalry?"

The ferocious industrial hammering continued without faltering, and Milosz risked a pop up to see what had become of the assault wave.

It was broken.

A few asswits were fleeing back through the flames and the shattered landscape through which they came, some of them tumbling as short staccato roars from the automatic weapons cut them down.

Milosz looked around, desperate to see who had saved them, incredulous that they had survived. There had to be an explanation.

But all he heard was one loud, mocking American voice.

"No, siree. You do not get these from pettin' kitty cats. Hooaahh!"

29

LONDON

"The armorer will see you now, ma'am."

The young gray-suited man pronounced it "marm."

"Thanks," she said. The occasional vestiges of Ye Olde England still amused her greatly. Caitlin swallowed the last of her thin, lukewarm instant coffee with a grimace. That didn't amuse her at all. It was nothing like the potent brew Bret made back on the farm, but it would have been churlish to refuse it. Such offers were not made lightly, even within the confines of the London Cage, where many of the privations suffered by the wider city were ameliorated by black budgets and secondary funding sources.

"I have a few of the usual suspects to see. I'll join you in the briefing room," said Dalby, excusing himself from the scarred Formica table and the trifling remains of a plate of fries—hereabouts known as chips—lying in a puddle of dark brown gravy. Dalby ate his chips with a knife and fork, which Caitlin also filed under Q, for quirk.

They shook hands, the Englishman being a stickler for the formalities. Indeed, the word "stickler" could have been invented just for him. Caitlin picked up her backpack and followed the younger officer out of the staff canteen and into a long corridor lined with closed doors and blacked-out windows. Somewhere nearby a man, or possibly a woman, was crying. Walking behind her escort, she noted that his hair was slightly longer than normal and his chin more heavily stubbled. She wondered if he had just come in from the field—unlikely, given the lowly nature of his duties today—or whether, like everyone else, he was feeling the hardships of the ration system. She was certainly missing the small luxuries of home life at the farm: the fresh eggs and milk, a loaf of bread baked in the wood-fired oven. And Bret and Monique, of course. She couldn't stop wondering how they were faring and how long it might be before she would see them again. Would the baby even recognize her? On cue, her leaky breasts began aching dully.

"Knock it off, asshole," she muttered to herself before mommy guilt could run away with her.

"Excuse me, marm?" asked the suit, turning his head as he continued to stride down the hallway.

"Don't sweat it." She smiled. "Talking to myself. First sign of madness."

"Very good, marm."

They reached a set of stairs at the end of the hall and descended three flights, which would have put them well below the river. The cinder block walls leaked moisture and in places had sprouted cancerous-looking growths between the bricks. Some of the lightbulbs had burned out, making the staircase something of a darkened well. At the very bottom they pushed through a pair of heavy rubber doors into a workshop, an area much better lit by fluorescent tubes and long-life bulbs. Dehumidifiers labored to suck the dampness out of the space with limited effect. The cement floor still had a moist color to it.

Workers in coveralls bent before workbenches laden with the tools of war. Racks of M16s lined the far wall where a couple of men were working with a larger rifle barrel. Probably something that would increase the punch of the pathetically underpowered round. On other workbenches, innocent-looking civilian devices were being stripped down to their component parts and remodeled with secret compartments, special packages, and, in some cases, explosives. Surrounded by the whine of power tools and the scent of machine grease, Caitlin thought it was the sort of place her father would have loved even though he wasn't a gun nut.

The suit handed her off to a middle-aged woman, a short, squat specimen with an enormous mole on one of her nostrils.

"Hiya, Gerty." Caitlin smiled. "Long time."

" 'Ello, pet." The woman grinned back, displaying an alarming mouthful of decaying teeth. "Sending you out again, are they? A woman in your condition; it's a disgrace is what it is, pet. An absolute disgrace. You should be at 'ome with your young one and that lovely man of yours. Sorry to 'ear about 'im, I was, luv, I hope he's resting well. Typical of the Wallies running this place, I tell you. Still, beggars and choosers, eh? Mister Dalby said you'd be needing all your kit 'n' caboodle, then. A lovely chap that Dalby, a gent of the old school, too. So, whereabouts are we off to this time, you poor girl you?"

Gerty's delivery was uninterrupted by the need to draw breath or apparently to pause while injesting the sodden biscuit she dunked into a cup of tea before pushing it into that mouth full of broken tombstones.

"I'm off to Germany, Gert," said Caitlin. "Probably fly out later today."

"Oh, dear," cooed the armorer. "Nothing good ever comes of intrigues with those sausage-eating bastards. They did for my old granddad, you know, Miss Cait. A Stuka got him at Dunkirk. A terrible shock it was to old nan Dorothy, too. And she with her dicky heart an' all. It's a wonder the family line didn't die out there and then."

The woman put one warm, meaty hand through the crook of Caitlin's arm and drew her deeper into the workshop. A few men and women, mostly men, huddled around machine tools, fiddling and adjusting levers and dials. One manned a lathe from which poured a shower of bright, white sparks and a high screeching sound.

"So will you be giving the bally Hun a stand-up floggin', then, Miss Cait? Or doing him quietly with a bit of shiv work and piano wire?"

Caitlin grinned.

"I'll be going into the shariatowns, Gerty…"

"Oh, Gawd…"

"So discretion will be my friend, but…"

They finished the old routine together, *"A sodding great shooter couldn't hurt, neither."*

"All right, then," Gerty said as they came to her personal office, an isolated workbench in the center of the shop. "I understand that discretion may well be the better part of valor, but there's nothing quite so discreet as forty grains of hollow-point silenced by one of these spankin' new Reflex Suppressors we've just 'ad in. It's the very thing to give one of those mad Turks over there pause to think that perhaps he might have misinterpreted the Prophet's teachings about the relative relations between the sexes, not that they're not always thinking about the sexes' relations of course, because if you ask me, that's what's behind most of this argy bargy and ranting on about bloody jihad and all that rubbish. Not nearly enough of the horizontal hokey-pokey for your beardy nutters, Miss Cait, and rather too much time spent fiddling about with livestock behind the woodshed is all I'm saying, it's not natural, is it, wrapping women up in those bloody great bedsheets."

She handed Caitlin a black rubberized nine-inch-long tube that was obviously meant to fit over the business end of a firearm. "Expansion chamber's sleeved back over the first six inches of the barrel on a long arm," Gerty explained, "and they come in these lovely miniatures for a variety of sidearms work. We're issuing the Kimber ICQB pistols at the moment. Got a very generous shipment of them from your homeland awhile ago on an exchange deal of some sort. Here, look at this. There's such lovely workmanship in this gun, Miss Cait. You won't regret slipping it into your purse with the lippy and a couple of clips of h-tipped."

The armorer paused for just a moment to favor Caitlin with a crooked grin.

"But I can see from your slightly disappointed look," she continued, "that you were hoping for something a little more… daring."

Caitlin picked up the Kimber and tried it for heft. It was a beautifully balanced handgun with a great feeling of density and solidity that spoke of real care in the design and manufacture. She assumed that Gerty's stash had to have come from a stockpile somewhere, as the original manufacturer had Disappeared.

Maybe a good backup, Caitlin thought, *but not a primary.*

"It is a beautiful gun, Gerty. I'll give you that. But if I had to clear a room, I'd be standing there pulling the trigger over and over again. I'd get bored, you know. Or possibly shot. One or the other. Neither good."

Gerty grinned hugely, a distressing sight for the unprepared.

"Oh, you always were a kidder, Miss Cait. But point taken. Point very much taken, dear. If you 'ave to pull a gun on one filthy blagger, you might as well 'ave at the lot o' them. I 'ad a good long think about your special needs when Mister Dalby sent through your resource request, an' it's a tad out of the ordinary, but I'd like you to think about carrying a couple of these little beauties."

Gerty drew back a heavily soiled canvas rag to reveal a pair of black, spidery-looking machine pistols. They reminded Caitlin of the MAC-10 submachine guns that had been the rage in the agency back in the late eighties.

"Russian PP-2000s," Gerty said. "We've 'ad a lot of luck with this model since we took a shipment on trial from the manufacturer a few months ago. They provide a very high fire density at close quarters an' all the way out to about two hundred meters. Come with an extra magazine on the shoulder rest. Ivan's used a lot of high-end plastics in the assembly, which makes it very light an' resistant to corrosion. Fewer moving parts than your P90s or MP7s, so it's easier to maintain in the field. There is a silencer, but we've 'ad the Reflex people do some bespoke work for us so we can fit one of their lovely tubes over the muzzle. The thing I do like about this model, Miss Cait, is the new Russian 7N31 P-class armor-piercing round. It'll make short work of most vests, but without sacrificing any stopping power. Just the sort of thing for a young lady on her own in a bad neighborhood."

Caitlin tried the nearest weapon for balance and weight. It didn't have the same lavish feeling of overengineered luxury as the Kimber, but it did sit nicely in her hands, and like many Russian weapons, stressed function over form. Instinctively, she field stripped the weapon on the workbench and reassembled it while Gerty's broken grin grew even wider. She sighted the weapon on the ceiling, brought it back in, and unfolded the stock before taking aim again. The pistol grip fit the palm of her hand perfectly, something she couldn't quite say for the Kimber .45.

It felt like a weapon she could trust.

"Still got the touch, lass." Gerty beamed.

"Rate of fire?"

"Six 'undred to eight 'undred rounds per minute," Gerty said.

"I'll need a lot of caps for this gun, then, Gerty. You got any harnesses for them?" Caitlin asked. "And maybe a sight?"

"Comes with a sight an' a harness already made up in your size, pet. We'll just need to do some adjusting in case you've put a bit a weight on with the baby, excuse my being so forward and all."

"Oh, don't beat yourself up, Gerty. My boobs are about three times bigger than they used to be. Bret's gonna be pissed if I'm away too long and they shrink again."

"Oh, I know, dear," Gerty said. "I remember by the time I 'ad my fourth I 'ad to design a special sling to keep the bloody things from dragging along the ground between my legs. And then Hubby made me wear it for years after I'd done with the breast-feeding anyway. Said it made him right jumpy down in the pants, it did."

Caitlin kept her face as neutral as possible. It was a big ask, as the Brits liked to say.

She caught up with Dalby again up on second floor, where they stored the prisoners undergoing interrogation after deciding to go with both the 2000 and the Kimber. It never hurt to have a backup weapon, and Gerty assured her that Berlin Control would issue a shotgun and sniper rifle on request.

Richardson was somewhere up here, Caitlin knew, although he remained indisposed due to his injuries.

"I'm afraid he's a little too delicate for the sort of debriefing session we'd like to put him through," said Dalby. "But Mister Forbes here did manage to garner a few more tidbits before the CMO intervened."

Forbes was sitting across the table from them in an otherwise empty conference room, running one corner of a yellow manila folder under his thumbnail. He looked to be about fifty years old, with a shock of white hair thinning considerably on the top of his head. The only other notable things about him were the white lab coat he wore over a brown suit and the stethoscope that hung from his neck.

Caitlin raised an eyebrow by way of inviting him to elaborate on Dalby's introduction.

"Thank you, sir, ma'am," he said. Another of the marm brigade, then.

"Upon receipt of the prisoner we subjected him to a controlled course of *anatinus* venom to obtain a modulated hyperalgesic effect and—"

Caitlin shook her head and held up one hand.

"Whoa, sorry, Doc, I bombed out of premed before switching my major to state-sponsored murder. You did what?"

Forbes looked most put out by the interruption, but Dalby nodded at him to explain.

"Platypus venom, Ms. Monroe," he said. "A new trick. From our Australian colleagues. In the correct dose it causes excruciating pain, but without the associated necrotic effect of the snake and spider venoms. A small dose can last for weeks, sometimes months. A fact of which Mister Richardson has been apprised."

"I see," Caitlin said, not really caring much about Richardson's inconvenience, but similarly not really caring for the clinical manner in which Forbes discussed his work, either.

"And the tidbit haul?"

Forbes opened the folder and consulted a page of handwritten notes.

"Before the neuralgia grew too intense—" He looked up from the notes. "—the subject's wounds did not help in that regard, I might add…"

Caitlin pulled a face at Dalby as though they were naughty schoolchildren caught out on a lark.

Forbes pointedly ignored her and continued. "Before the subject's trauma-related and toxin-enhanced neuralgia rendered him insensible, the debriefers were able to elicit some new intelligence, not all of which concerns you."

"Because?" Caitlin asked, putting an edge on the question.

"Because the information concerned the subject's criminal networks in ways that do not intersect with your case."

"*Our* case, you mean."

"Semantics, Ms. Monroe. At any rate, what would be of interest to you was confirmation of the fact that Richardson believed his contact had arrived in London from Berlin at a time that our checks have confirmed Baumer traveled from Tempelhof using the Tariq Skaafe passport."

Dalby interrupted at that point. "A cover that the Germans have origin traced on our behalf to Neukölln. Mister Baumer's home turf. The biometrics on the passport chip are his."

Caitlin folded her arms and took in a breath to give herself time to think. The air in the room was antiseptic and cold, and the only light came from two bare long-life bulbs hanging from electric wires. She let her chin rest on her chest for a moment. It was a given that Baumer was out, released by the French for whatever reason. Or released by the local authorities in Guadeloupe, at any rate. She had to concede that it didn't necessarily have to involve the Elysée Palace. The world had spun apart at a dizzying rate the last four years, and lines of authority did not run as clearly as they might once have. What was that quote from Yeats? The centre cannot hold. Somebody important had said that to her once. Had it been Wales, perhaps?

Whatever.

If al Banna, or Baumer, or whatever name he was going by now was out and coming for her to work through some kind of ragheaded revenge scenario there was only one thing for it: to get out there and lay her vengeance on him first.

"So when do I go?" she asked.

Dalby leaned over and retrieved his battered briefcase from the floor beside his chair. From it he produced a document wallet.

"You're booked on BA, the 18:35 flight to Tegel tonight. I'm sorry about that. Schönfeld would have been better, but there is a complication. You're not going in as a declared operator, so we'll have to send your equipment beforehand via diplomatic pouch. Gerty is seeing to that right now. You'll be able to get your kit at our layup point in Hermsdorf. There'll be a rental car waiting at the airport, but Berlin Control will swap that over for you when you get to the LUP. You'll have to develop the case yourself after that, I'm afraid. Baumer is a person of interest but not enough interest to justify any more resources at the moment beyond a snatch team when he's identified."

Caitlin waved off his apology.

"Don't sweat it, Dalby. I still have some assets off the book over there. I won't need backup."

He regarded her with very obvious misgivings.

"I didn't expect you would have taken it even if it were offered," he said. "However, do bear in mind, Caitlin, that while Baumer may be indulging himself in a revenge fantasy, we are not. This is in no way an autonomous operation. Undeclared, yes. But freelance, no. You are there on Echelon business, and we would very much like to have a long chat with Mister Baumer. Isn't that right, Forbes?"

"Oh, yes." The interrogator grinned. "Very much." In the unforgiving light he looked vulpine.

"Well, I can't promise anything, Dalby. Especially if things get out of hand. But believe me, if it means Doctor Frankenstein here gets to stick a plunger full of platypus jizz into the Banana's ass, I am totally up for that. You tell me it hurts like a bastard?" she said, looking at the man in the lab coat.

"Even morphine doesn't help, marm. The only relief is to put them into a coma. Or into the ground."

"Well, that works for me, too," she said. "But Dalby, my word to you. If it is at all possible to drag this sorry motherfucker back to the Cage, his worthless ass is already here."

"I suppose that will have to do, Caitlin. I understand that it may not be possible, but please do your best. And I would appreciate regular updates, too. Baumer was a significant recruiter, and although his cells are no longer in play, you shouldn't need telling that our European colleagues remain bedeviled by the consequences of the intifada. The Germans in particular, because of their refugee issues. Getting him back here and developing him properly would go a good long way toward improving our links with the federal intelligence lads. He might not be everyone's top priority at this point in time, but he is mine and yours. And as I said, our continental colleagues will always be interested in him."

Caitlin shook her head. "You know, there was a time when those guys were our targets, Dalby."

"I believe I may have already mentioned, Caitlin, that we live in a post-ironic world."

30

TEXAS ADMINISTRATIVE DIVISION

Miguel pondered the odds. Seven men against twenty-three.

Twenty-one now, he corrected himself as he rubbed at the dried, tacky blood on the backs of his hands.

Or rather five men and two boys against twenty-one road agents.

And their camp whores, too.

You couldn't forget them. A man was just as dead with a bullet in his back fired by a woman protecting her lice-ridden rapist as he was shot down by the rapist himself. Miguel Pieraro shook his head slightly, so his companions would not notice. These were not good odds.

He wondered, too, about the mettle of the men he would be fighting alongside. Mormons were not pacifists. Who the hell was in this new world? But neither were they natural killers, unlike the men they were about to confront.

The small group crept forward as stealthily as they could through the tangle of rusted car bodies, waist-high grass, old bottles, and mystery refuse that cluttered the approaches to their goal. They snuck through overgrown suburban yards for the most part, whenever possible avoiding the open streets where they could be spotted more easily. Not that Miguel expected the road agents to have posted lookouts. Nothing of their operation had impressed him so far. They halted at the back of a shed at least a hundred yards from the Hy Top Club.

He carried the Winchester in one hand, and his fingers drummed nervously on the wooden grip. At his hip hung the reassuring weight of the Lupara. Once that dog barked there would be no disguising their intentions. The Lupara was a break-open, sawed-off shotgun loaded with number two buckshot. It was an old Italian weapon, once used for wolf hunting but later taken up by the Mafia in Sicily, and was ideal for clearing crowded spaces of men whose lives and limbs meant nothing to you. Unfortunately, because of the women and the need for silence, he was going to have to be very careful about how and when he used it. That was why he carried a third weapon.

Miguel glanced warily at the two figures to his left, Aronson and the boy, Orin. They were also carrying what looked like heavy clubs in the dark but had M16s slung across their backs. For all that he was wary of the damage his own firearms might do to the women, he was doubly concerned about those unruly cannons. An overlong squeeze of the trigger or poorly controlled aim and half a dozen people could be cut to ribbons regardless of whether they were friend or foe. At least the Mormons had changed from their normal outfit, a white shirt, black tie, and slacks, to dark jeans, shirts, and jackets. Some of them had black or navy blue hooded sweaters, which helped them to blend into the night. They were not camouflaged by any means, but it was adequate; it gave Miguel a spark of hope about them. He motioned them to take a break while he had one last peek at their target.

They all dropped to one knee. A few of them prayed in silence. Miguel could hear a bit of Aronson's prayer.

"Oh, Lord, we pray of thee, give us your strength as we stride forward into battle. We ask that you give us your strong right arm and guide us in our quest for justice…"

Miguel adjusted the night vision goggles to control the bright glow of the burning oil barrels. He scanned the front deck of the club and the driveway to the left, where the agents had dragged couches and recliner rockers from nearby homes to fashion for themselves a handy outdoor party space. He counted eight men in all and two camp whores. As best he could tell, they were all sleeping. There were no signs of the Mormon women. The agents' horses remained tethered in a well-fenced yard a few streets down.

They were not being guarded.

"All right," Miguel said in a low voice. "It must be as we discussed back in Leona. Is there any one of you who doubts your ability to do this? It will not be like shooting a man, which in itself is a difficult enough thing to do. This will be much worse."

He gave Orin a hard stare as he spoke, and the boy blanched but swallowed hard and nodded.

"I—I don't know," a voice piped up.

"Adam, be still now," D'Age warned.

"No. It is good," Miguel said, taking the measure of the young man to whom Sofia had taken a liking. "Any man who cannot carry this through to the end must speak up now. Once committed, we must not hesitate. To falter in striking is to die. Adam, are you certain you cannot?"

The boy shook his head. He could not have been more than sixteen years old. Miguel had come to know him a little the last two days because Sofia had taken to riding with the boys when she could. Teenagers, he thought. The end of the world and they still cannot bear to be embarrassed by being seen with their parents. Well, at least his daughter was safely hidden away with the women and the horses for now. Adam seemed to struggle to find his voice in the dark.

"It is just that… it's…"

He petered out, sounding ashamed of himself.

Miguel reached over and gave his shoulder a reassuring squeeze. "It is not a bad thing, Adam," he said. "To know your own mind and conscience, and to listen to it, that is the mark of a real man. Here, give me that."

He took the sledgehammer from the boy and laid it against the wall of the shed. He could not carry any more himself, his hands being full with his own massive hammer and the Winchester rifle.

"Give it to me," a deep voice rumbled. It was Benjamin Randall. He stood a good foot higher than Miguel and was twice as wide across the shoulders. He took up young Adam's abandoned hammer and hefted it to test the weight. Then he twirled both cudgels experimentally.

"Won't be a problem," he grunted.

Miguel glanced back at the Hy Top to make sure nothing had changed.

"Good," he said softly.

"Adam, you will come with me to get the women. I am most certain they are being held in a room at the back of the club. I observe bars on the window and a padlocked steel door, but we can deal with that. Do you think you will be able to fire a gun? If you have to?"

Miguel was glad to see the young man question himself before nodding, even if he still seemed uncertain.

"I trust you, Adam. And I will need you to trust me."

He turned back to the wider circle of men.

"The boy and I will cut around the block and approach the club from the rear. Give us fifteen minutes to do that. Then move in and take down the men outside as we discussed. There are two women with them. Not yours. If they try to raise the alarm…"

He left the sentence unfinished.

"We understand," said Willem D'Age.

* * *

Miguel took the precaution of going an extra block when circling around behind the Hy Top, taking Adam up South Cedar Street, an unkerbed boggy stretch of dirt road where most of the small fibrocement cottages appeared to have survived intact. A red pickup had struck a power pole outside number 642, bringing it down on the front porch of the white clapboard house, and fat black power cables lay like giant snakes on the road top.

Maybe that had knocked the electrics out back in '03 and saved the suburb from burning like some others in Crockett, Miguel thought. Two more cars had collided a little farther down the road, and they had burned out, but the flames had not spread at the time. Miguel and his teen shadow skirted them and cut through a scrap of open ground into West Bell Avenue. A few more crashed vehicles and a couple of children's tricycles shrouded with stiff rags were all that remained of the original residents. Signaling to Adam to stay close and keep quiet, the vaquero ghosted another block back toward the center of town before swinging right and heading down a long straight road. South Sycamore, a bent and faded street sign declared it. The glow of the burning oil drums back at the Hy Top silhouetted the tree line between here and there, and he heard the snorting of a horse somewhere in between.

Miguel slowed down and pressed one finger to his lips.

The Mormon boy was wide-eyed but resolute.

The faintly glowing dial of Miguel's watch told him he had three minutes to get into position.

"I need you to carry this for me. Just carry it, okay?" he said, passing his sledgehammer to Adam. It was a model sometimes called a Canadian ax, with a traditional flat hammer on one side of the iron head tapering to a wedge point on the other. As the two intruders picked their way carefully through the small forest that had colonized at least three blocks behind the Hy Top, Miguel held his Winchester, ready to snap it up and fire.

He fervently hoped that would not be necessary. They needed to remain hidden from their quarry until the very last moment. Taking up position behind the trunk of a dead white maple, he nodded encouragement to Adam and ruffled his hair to show the lad he was impressed with his fortitude so far. The boy visibly swelled with confidence. It would have been hard for him, losing his family at such an age. In Miguel's judgment, he was very much a young man in need of a strong father.

They had to wait only another minute before the other members of the raiding party appeared without warning from the dark recesses of the woods that had crept up to the other side of South Cottoonwood. The first to materialize was Big Ben, carrying two hammers, one in each hand as though they were no heavier than children's toys. And then came his brothers, as the Mormons referred to each other, all of them hauling a heavy cudgel of sorts. Sledgehammers, axes, and one crowbar. Miguel grimaced at what was about to take place.

The Mormons did not break into a sprint. They did not announce themselves with a war cry to summon up the spirits. They almost floated across the street until they were in among the loose collection of lounge room furniture over which the drunken, debauched road agents were draped, passed out in the warm glow of the barrel fires.

"Come now, quickly," Miguel whispered to Adam, stepping out from behind the tree and taking long, brisk, but careful strides toward the padlocked steel door that led into a small room attached to the back of the club. The stench of urine and cigarette butts slashed through the otherwise clear air.

When they reached the door, their view of the street in front of the building would be obscured, but Miguel was able to see the first moments of the attack as it unfolded. Big Ben swung his hammers like a gymnast twirling her ribbon at the Olympics and brought them down with a gruesome, sick-making crunch onto the heads of two road agents passed out under a blanket on an old brown couch. Miguel, who had seen many terrible things in his time, both before and after the Disappearance, was forced to blink away the sight, flinching involuntarily just before impact. There was no mistaking the wet organic cracking sound, however, as the men's heads split apart like overripe melons. Not half a second later he saw D'Age and Aronson repeat the awful stroke, each man swinging his weapon, another sledgehammer and an ax, respectively, even as Big Ben recovered his momentum and whirled away from his first victims to bash the life out of another two.

Miguel heard a strangled, gurgling sound and spun around to see Adam vomiting into a clump of grass. The boy waved him away as if to say it was nothing. The vaquero tried to keep track of the number of agents as they went down, counting out each dull, chopping thud he heard, but it was impossible.

And then one of the camp whores woke up and screamed.

Her ululating cry was cut off by another muffled blow, and Miguel had his signal.

"Get up, boy. Our time has arrived."

The whey-faced youngster, still dry heaving, nodded and took up position behind Miguel, covering him with an M16 as he went to work on the padlock securing the heavy security door. The first blow rang out like a discordant cathedral bell over the huge graveyard that was the town of Crockett. Miguel's heart tried to leap out of his chest with the huge, jarring boom, but he ignored his galloping fears and swung again, striking the padlock squarely. It disintegrated with a shower of sparks and a metallic crash. He heard screams inside—women's screams—as he wrenched open the door.

"Get out, get out now," he ordered as the door flew back with a wrenching screech of stiff, tortured steel in an ill-fitting door frame.

Adam moved up just behind his shoulder.

"Come on, it's us. Get out of there, you ladies; we have to go now."

Other voices were shouting: deep male voices, angry and confused.

The first gunshot cracked open the night as a woman appeared from within the gloom of the prison at the back of the club. Miguel recognized her as the woman he had seen humiliated by the camp whores earlier in the evening. Her face was streaked with tears, her eyes dark sunken pits. She was shivering with fear and shock and seemed not to recognize Adam when she saw him.

"Come, Sister Jenny. This way, quickly."

The boy took her by the arm and virtually dragged her from the room as the percussive trip-hammer of automatic weapons fire began around the front of the building. More screams followed and then the boom of a heavy single-shot weapon. Miguel almost stopped in midstride.

That couldn't be the Remington, he thought. He had told her to stay behind.

There was no time for that. Sofia would do as she was told.

"Ladies," he said urgently. "It really is time to go now. Quickly. With young Adam here. My name is Miguel, Miguel Pieraro, and I will be rescuing you tonight. But only if you step this way."

Sofia almost lost her meager dinner when Ben brought the sledge down on his first victim's skull. Choking it down, she brought out her Remington and waited for a target to present itself. In the excitement, she nearly opened fire on the first target that resolved in her scope, bracketed against the fires and torchlight of the camp. That would have meant shooting Orin and giving herself away. Sneakiness was the watchword of the evening, she reminded herself. Sneakiness and not shooting the wrong people. She forced herself to wait.

When the first camp whore screamed, Sofia pivoted toward her, but a sledge silenced the woman before she could fire. The woman's boyfriend struggled to rise off the couch, a bearded, shaggy-haired, potbellied maggot with a red bandanna tied over his head. Ben and the other Mormons were distracted by gunfire from the front of the Hy Top.

Sofia brought the crosshairs of her Remington up to the bandanna boy's unibrow, took a deep breath, and let it out.

As she exhaled, she kept the muzzle of the gun on target until her finger completed the pull of the trigger. Bucking in her arms, the rifle put a single round through the agent's unibrow, disintegrating the top half of his skull in a spectacular shower of bloody gruel, dropping the corpse back onto the couch. She felt a surge of anger and… something else. It was a feeling she did not recognize, but it was powerful. No, it was… power itself. She felt her power over the man whom she had shot, whose life she had taken. It was a good feeling. Sofia forced herself to work the bolt mechanically, spitting out the spent .30-06 casing and sliding a fresh round into the chamber. The Mormon men, having discarded their sledgehammers for their M16s, took cover behind the couch and exchanged fire with those who tried to run back into the Hy Top.

Sofia tracked two more agents sprinting for the door, dispatching one with a clean torso shot that spun him off his feet and into a dry wall façade with a crash that shook the entire front of the club building. The other man she drilled in the ass, slowing him down long enough for the Mormons to pour a stream of tracer fire into his back. So intense was the fire that it disassembled him from the hip to shoulder height.

She had expected this to be hard, yet she felt nothing but a deep sense of satisfaction as she scanned the windows of the Hy Top for more targets.

In fact, Sofia was ashamed to admit as she dispatched another road agent firing from a second floor window, it was kind of fun.

* * *

Miguel kept up the banter as two more women emerged from the dark room. He had seen one of them earlier while scouting the building, but the other was unfamiliar, and he quickly noted that Adam did not recognize her, either. Another captive, then, most likely. She did not have the hardened aspect of the longtime camp whores, appearing every bit as traumatized as the Mormon ladies. Miguel moved into the locked bunkhouse and drew his sawed-off shotgun, keeping the internal door covered while Adam rousted the rest of the women out of there.

Sure enough, within a minute he heard somebody scrabbling at the lock on the other side, and within seconds the door flew inward and a road agent stood there, still groggy and half naked. He registered the presence of Miguel, and his bleary eyes had just enough time to go wide as they took in the huge, yawning muzzle of the Lupara, before the cowboy pulled the trigger and all but cut him in two. In the stark white flash of the muzzle blast Miguel caught a glimpse of a corridor behind the agent, stacked with boxes. The man's body jackknifed around the molten comet of lead shot and flew backward, slamming into a tower of crates that toppled to the floor with the crashing tinkle of broken glass. Immediately Miguel smelled alcohol.

"Out now!" he roared, no longer concerned with stealth. He holstered the Lupara, with one chamber still loaded, and pointed his Winchester down the end of the hallway. "Is that all of them, Adam? Are all of your women out?"

The uproar of the gunfight was now so great, so overwhelming, that he wondered if he had missed the boy's reply, but turning around, he saw he had not. Adam was frantically checking and rechecking his small frightened group of women, shaking his head ever more frantically.

"No! No!" he cried helplessly.

"Adam," Pieraro yelled. "How many are missing?"

"It's Sally, Mister Pieraro. Sally Gray." And the raw anguish in his voice told Miguel that this Sally Gray was not just another captive. She was someone special to the boy.

Sofia would be disappointed.

"Take them out the way we came in," he ordered. "Run and do not stop to look back or wait. We shall meet up again at the clearing. Go. Go! I will find your Sally."

"Sir!" called out the woman he knew as Jenny. "I think she was in the storeroom. One of those men took her there not fifteen minutes ago."

"Thank you, Jenny. Now go!"

He waved them off with a fierce gesture and took a moment to compose himself. Battle raged elsewhere in the building, a savage din of staccato weapons fire. Machine guns. Single shots. Men and women crying in fear and outrage. He checked the load on his Winchester. It was still good. He had not yet fired a shot with it. Crossing himself and imploring the help of the Blessed Virgin, he swallowed his fear, which was considerable, and swung into the hallway, covering its length with his rifle. He stepped over the ruptured body of the man he had slain and hastened down the corridor. It was poorly lit, with only a few shafts of lamplight poking in through gaps in the walls to illuminate his way. A door stood locked halfway up, and he considered how best to approach it for all of half a second before kicking it in and jumping out of the way of any return fire. None came, which was a small disappointment. He had been hoping not to have to push farther into the club. Another check of the room confirmed that it was little more than a closet filled with cleaning implements: brooms, mops, buckets, and so on.

Miguel ducked from the knees as a burst of gunfire suddenly tore through the wooden slats of the wall just ahead of him, allowing more light to spill through.

His legs quivering from the adrenaline rush, he cautiously edged up to the hole and took a peek. He seemed to be looking into what must have been the main bar area. It was chaos in there, with a

small fire burning out of control in one corner where an oil lamp
had been smashed or shot to pieces and had spilled its fuel onto
the wooden floor, where spilled liquor and bedclothes had quickly
caught alight. Bodies lay everywhere, some still, some twitching
or trying to drag themselves away from the carnage, But he also
counted at least five road agents still standing and able to give a
good accounting for themselves. They were all hunkered down at
the front of the building, firing out into the street. The shots that
punched through the wall in front of him must have come from
Aronson's men out there.

Miguel furrowed his brow as he took in the scene.

There was no sign of any woman who might be Sally Gray. Jenny
had said she was in a storeroom, but there was no such area off this
corridor. He could see three camp whores from his vantage point,
easily discerned by their sluttish mode of dress. Two were dead, and
one was firing a carbine out into the street. Indeed, the agents were
putting out such a volume of fire that he had to worry about Aronson
and the others. Had they found cover before coming under fire?

How many were alive?

Was it even worth continuing the search for Miss Gray?

Papa should be out of there by now, Sofia thought. She had given up
any pretense of hiding at the edge of the battle, crossing the street
a block up from the Hy Top. Rifle fire popped around her, but she
did not pay it any mind. The adrenaline was flowing through her,
giving her a rush that was far more intense than the flush of deer
hunting. She worked around to the back of the Hy Top.

"Don't shoot me, please!"

The Mormon girl, about the same age as Sofia, fell down in front
of her. She ran up to the young woman and knelt down. Adam
caught up with them seconds later, his weapon leveled on Sofia
until realization took hold.

"Holy hell, Sofia! Your father is going to be furious with you," he said.

"Where is he?" she asked. "He should be out by now."

"Still in the Hy Top," Adam said, bringing her up to speed.

"Anything left in that rifle?" she asked, pointing at the M16 Adam carried.

"Sure," he said. "I've not even fired it yet."

"Give it to me," she said.

"I think not," he said, trying to summon up all the dignity his few months of added maturity might lend him—without any luck. "Your father—"

Adam didn't complete the sentence. She butt swiped him across the face with the flat of her rifle stock. It made a pretty good club.

"Here." Sofia handed her Remington to the crying woman. "What's your name?"

"Jenny," she said.

"I'm not going to kill you. Do you know how to use this?"

Jenny nodded.

"Fine," Sofia said, collecting Adam's M16. "Stay here. I'm going after my father."

Miguel dismissed the unworthy option of cutting and running without a second thought. He had promised Adam that he would do his best to rescue the girl, and even if he hadn't, that did not change the fact that she was a good woman—he assumed—being held captive by the worst sort of men. Were it his daughter and another man had turned away from a chance to save her, what would he think of such a worthless cur?

Not much, after killing him.

Miguel settled on what he had to do and determined to see it through, no matter what. He took a moment to examine the room again, taking care this time to commit to memory as much detail as he could: the positions of the agents firing into the street and those of the dead and the wounded, the cover he might use, the paths he might take through the chaos. He did not have perfect vision of the room, far from it. But life was not perfect, and God expected his children to be about his business anyway.

He checked the Winchester one last time as he walked on a few paces to a door that would surely have to give on to the barroom.

Seven rounds of 30.30 smokeless in the tube.

He made the sign of the cross.

Kissed the small locket hanging around his neck.

Jacked a round into the chamber and stepped into the room.

Working from left to right, Miguel punched 170 grains of 30.30 deer killer through the back of the first man's neck at 2,227 feet per second. The agent crouched next to him lost the top of his head as he turned slightly to see what had happened to his comrade. Miguel worked the lever action and put his third round into the back of the next man in line, who was taking cover behind a structural beam as he fired out into the street. The woman, the camp whore, who had been firing her carbine blindly over the window ledge reacted with catlike speed and managed to turn toward him, cry out a warning over the clamor and tumult, and even squeeze off a couple of rounds. But they hit the ceiling, bringing down a shower of dust and particleboard before her face exploded when hit by his fourth shot. Blood and gray matter spattered the face of the man next to her.

"Dixie!" he cried out, turning on Miguel. "Fucker, you ki—"

Dixie's boyfriend died of a bullet through the heart, and before Miguel could finish the last of them, the final agent, an older man, threw his weapon down and put his hands up.

"Whoa, pardner, don't shoot me! I fucking surrender!" the graybeard said.

Miguel covered him with the rifle, advancing cautiously through the room, still hunched over slightly and flinching as fire from the

Mormons outside continued to smash into the building. All of his senses were singing; light and sound and the reek of gunpowder and death flooded in as time seemed to stretch out forever—as though he might walk across this room, surrounded by the dead and dying, from this moment until the ending of the world.

Something was behind him. He whipped out his Lupara.

A burst of rifle fire cut the shape down before Miguel could pull the trigger. He caught the briefest hint of the agent's head disintegrating in a shower of blood and bone before blessed silence fell and all that remained was the ringing in his ears and the wailing of a woman somewhere in the dark. The man who had been coming at him from a doorway to his left fell facedown onto the floor.

Sofia stood behind the man, an M16 in her hands.

"Papa," she said sheepishly.

31

BERLIN

As she'd expected, the BMW was an older model, an X5 from 2002. The Bayerische Motoren Werke hadn't gone under like so many other automakers, but it had shrunk enormously and had not released a new line beyond the 2003 models. Still, this X5 from Berlin Control was a pretty good SUV crossover. A little stiff in the handling for her taste, but powerful and kitted out with the balance of her equipment in a sealed diplomatic box in the back. No Landespolizei patrols would be pulling her over and poking around in her unmentionables.

Caitlin blinked away the fatigue of a long day's travel. She had risen before dawn in London, and it was coming up on midnight. Six lanes of the A100 ribboned away in front of her, sweeping past the radio tower on her left, lit from below by golden lights. It would have been an almost cheery sight after the drab gray Orwellian tones of London, but she was too tired to care. She was also lonely, an unusual, almost unknown state for her. She'd tried to phone Bret before flying out, but the guard at the safe house had told her that both he and Monique were asleep, and she hadn't wanted to wake either of them. Her breasts felt heavy and ached from not having fed her baby in so many hours, but there was nothing to be done about it. It wasn't like she could express milk in the field, after all. Soon enough her milk would dry up, anyway. She felt an irrational flicker of resentment at that, as if it was the worst thing Baumer had done. Caitlin flicked the air vents to keep the uncomfortably cold AC blowing into her face, warding off drowsiness.

She regretted not bringing a couple of CDs. German pop and rock music made her brain hurt. After flitting around the dial for half a minute she found a local news radio station halfway through a quarter-hour update. Her German-language comprehension was good, but she was a little rusty with the spoken word and practiced by repeating the bulletin after the newsreader.

"Fighting continues in New York, while the British Security Cabinet holds crisis talks with the U.S. Defense minister. NATO ministers meeting in Brussels are expected to release a statement later tonight condemning state-sponsored piracy but urging the Kipper administration to show restraint…"

Caitlin snorted and rolled her tired eyes.

"Enough of that shit," she said, trying a few more stations until she lucked onto a talk radio host ranting about an upcoming vote in the Bundestag to recognize sharia law, applied by mandated local communities as binding in certain classes of civil action. The five-minute tirade was enormous fun to bluster along with, and the callers provided her with an eclectic mix of accents and vocal styles to parrot. It was also a reasonable backgrounder on the sort of suburb she was headed into. Neukölln wasn't a closed community like some of the shariatowns in the east of Germany or the remaining Enclosures in London, for that matter, but it was enclosed in all but name. She, a blond American woman, would have no freedom of movement there. She'd need an escort, someone she trusted, but not a local stringer for Echelon. As Dalby had made clear, this op was deniable. There was a good chance it was going to get bloody.

She yawned and shivered as the X5 hummed past miles of closely packed, low-rise apartment blocks. Unlike London, Berlin had no curfew or travel restrictions, and traffic was noticeably heavier than she'd experienced in the British capital, especially at this time of night. Gas was much cheaper, probably because it wasn't controlled by anything like the Brits' Ministry of Resources. Even so, the city was noticeably quieter than when she'd last been stationed there, working up the brief on al Banna at the start of the decade. The German economy, like Britain's, was much smaller than it had been, and few people had the means to keep a car on the road.

Another ten minutes took her past Tempelhof Airport, where she could see a few stripped and gutted jetliners in the livery of American Airlines and Delta Airlines parked on the apron to the north of the two runways. Shortly afterward she turned left at Britzer Damm and motored quickly past long rows of shuttered shops. Many of them looked as though they hadn't opened in years. The footpaths and gutters were littered with rubbish and scraps of paper gathered into drifts and whipped up in small eddies by her speeding passage. The streets were darker than she recalled, but then they would be, with every second light turned off by the city authorities. Here and there groups of young men clustered together, some of them watching her with sullen expressions as she drove past. Immediately after crossing the rail line at the Hermannstrasse station, she turned left into Emser Strasse and drove for two blocks past whitewashed four- and five-story apartment buildings. Away from the main strip, with its scattering of mean little bars and greasy spoons around which tribes of young men would gather, Emser Strasse was quiet. Many cars were parked neatly by the curb, but even in the dark Caitlin could tell most of them had not been driven in a long time. They were dusty, and more often than not rotting banks of leaf matter were piled up against deflated tires. The GPS module beeped triumphantly.

She was there.

A new, unusued phone came out of her leather jacket, and she keyed in the number taken from Bret's diary back at the farm. A man answered in a voice fogged with sleep.

"Hello? Sayad al Mirsaad."

"Hey, Sadie. It's Caitlin Monroe. Bret Melton's wife. We met at the wedding. I know he was always threatening to visit you, buddy, but I'm afraid you're shit outta luck. It's just me."

The apartment was small: two bedrooms and a single living area that contained a kitchen, dining nook, and sitting room. Mirsaad, the journalist who had rescued her wounded husband from the epic clusterfuck of Iraq, lived there now with his wife and four children, who were all mercifully asleep. His wife, Laryssa, a German national, was standing in the door, clutching a bright pink dressing gown across her chest when Caitlin stepped out of the third-floor elevator door. She was not giving off happy vibes. Her husband looked exhausted, and peering behind Laryssa into the cramped confines of the flat, Caitlin understood why. All the paraphernalia of a newborn was there to see: changing table, bassinet, baby bottles on the kitchen counter. Caitlin regretted calling them without first checking, but she hadn't wanted to let anyone know where she was headed. When it came to Baumer, she had learned the hard way in France to work on her own.

"I'm sorry, Missus Mirsaad, I really am, but I just flew into Berlin and I needed to get in contact with Sadie."

"You could not have waited until morning?" Laryssa asked. It sounded more like a demand than a question.

"Look, I'm sorry about that. Really. I understand. I have my own little one at home. About the same age by the look of things."

She gestured over the woman's shoulder to indicate all the equipment she'd briefly seen.

"We know about little Monique," Mirsaad said in a more

conciliatory tone. "Bret sent us photos by e-mail. But what are you doing here, Caitlin? You surely cannot be working. Not with the baby so young."

Mirsaad's wife, whose red hair and pale skin spoke of a long local family lineage, glared at him for that, but the reporter extended a hand and drew Caitlin gently by the elbow into their main room. The baby was asleep in a crib, which had been pushed into one corner near the changing table. Caitlin's experienced eye immediately recognized the cloth diapers piled up underneath.

The small room reeked of lanolin, disinfectant, milk, vomit, and baby shit.

"Bret told me about you," the woman said, almost accusingly. "He said you were a soldier, like he was once. But you stayed in longer than him."

Caitlin nodded noncommittally.

"Something like that. Soldier for a while. More of a police officer after that. That's why I'm here, Sadie. Bret and Monique have been hurt. Someone attacked them."

Mirsaad lost the last vestiges of sleepiness as his eyes widened in shock.

"Caitlin, I am sorry. Are they all right? I did not know. We hadn't heard. I work for a community radio station here now. I'm afraid it's all very parochial. Was it criminals? I understand there is a lot of crime in England now."

"It didn't make the news, and they're fine. Bret's a little scratched and dented, but not much more than before. And our baby is safe. It was criminals, but not like you think. They were hired by a man from a place near here. Someone with a grudge. They were after me, but I'm afraid they tried to go through my husband and daughter to get to me."

Laryssa Mirsaad glanced involuntarily at the door through which Caitlin had entered. A glimmer of maternal concern clouded her features, quickly turning to anger.

"And you came here?"

Her tone was accusing now. No doubt about it. Caitlin couldn't blame her.

"Don't worry," the American assured her. "I didn't call you about my coming because I wanted to be sure nobody else knew. I wasn't followed or tracked. Everything's cool. But I could use your help, Sadie. If you're up for it. And if Laryssa agrees, too, of course."

"What did they do to your family?" Laryssa asked.

"Tried to kidnap them, we think. There was... some shooting," Caitlin said.

"Oh, my God. What happened? Did the men who did it get away? Were they captured?"

"They're dead," Caitlin said.

It was Mirsaad's turn to look worried.

"Oh, my. Is Bret okay? Really?"

"A few wounds, but he's fine. He's being looked after. Look, I don't want to intrude on your family here. Sadie, is there somewhere we could talk, where we're not going to wake your kids? If that's okay, Laryssa."

Caitlin had quickly scoped out where resistance was going to come from in this arrangement. The German woman looked like it was a thousand miles from okay, but Mirsaad, who had completely regained his faculties, simply nodded.

"Laryssa," he said in a very serious voice. "These people helped us after the war. I would not have escaped the Middle East were it not for Bret Melton interceding on my behalf." His eyes narrowed slightly. "And you, too, I suspect, Caitlin. You are something more than a police officer, are you not? You are someone with influence inside the British government quite obviously. And with Seattle, too. While Bret, like me, is a mere journalist. I doubt his lobbying alone would have secured my transit out of Kuwait after the Holocaust."

She smiled, tired. "Sadie. You did my husband a big favor once. That means I owed you one as well."

"And so now I am in your debt," Mirsaad said in a tone of voice that signaled he would not be dissuaded. "Laryssa, mind the children. I will not be long. We shall discuss what help I might be to Caitlin. We shall be down in Ahmet's."

His wife's threat detectors were all pinging wildly, but before she could object and turn it into a marital issue, the baby stirred and began to cry.

"Oh, just go and don't be more than fifteen minutes," she said.

"It will take me three minutes to change and five for us to walk there. I shall be back soon," he said.

But Laryssa had turned away and was lifting the child from the crib.

Ahmet's was a small coffeehouse and smoking room on the same block as Mirsaad's apartment. Caitlin left the X5 in the basement garage of Sadie's building, secure in the knowledge that Echelon's unique antitheft technologies were more than a match for any would-be carjackers. Even so, she checked the LED on her key ring before they left Emser Strasse just to be sure she'd be alerted if anyone attempted to interfere with the vehicle. The tiny light was glowing green, powered up and hotlinked.

Ahmet's was a brief walk though an unseasonably chilly night, although the weather was so unpredictable these days that the idea of seasons had little meaning. Caitlin maintained her situational awareness, scoping out the street and the surrounding buildings as they walked. Emser Strasse had been blessed with good tree cover once, but the canopy had apparently not recovered from the pollution storms in '03. The trees, which should have been lush with early summer foliage, were still looking sick and straggly. Not unlike Mirsaad himself.

"I'm sorry to turn up unannounced like this, Sadie. But it's better, believe me."

The reporter frowned and burrowed further into the old brown coat he had donned for the brisk walk.

"There will be a price to pay for this with my wife, but for Bret I am willing to pay. For you, too, if it is true you helped get us all back here. He intimated as much at your wedding. For which invite I must thank you. It is a lovely farm you have there, and we were made very welcome. Laryssa was worried."

"Because of you?"

"Because of the government. This Howard fellow is very hard line, no? Much harder than Blair was."

Caitlin rubbed her hands together against the cold as her breath plumed white in front of her. It was hard to believe the weather was still fucked up so long after the Wave. She had indeed been instrumental in clearing Mirsaad's passage to the EU from Kuwait, back to his wife and two children, as they were then. Even though he was married to a German national, there was no guarantee he'd have been allowed back in during the insane time after the Disappearance. And Bret had been insistent that they help him after the Jordanian had done so much to pluck him to safety from the chaos of the American retreat. But of course, mere philanthropy and favor trading would not have been enough for Caitlin to secure the Jordanian's travel permits. Not in the toxic atmosphere of 2003. She had lobbied on Mirsaad's behalf because she knew there was a chance that one day he might be useful as an asset.

That day was upon them.

None of this did she say aloud, of course.

"The Brits aren't so bad," she said, replying to his complaint about the Tory PM. "You have to remember they could have gone down the tubes like France. Looked like they would for a few weeks there."

"But the forced deportations, Caitlin? The Enclosures? Surely these things are excessive. Certainly now, if not then. The moment of crisis has passed. There cannot be any real chance of that sort of violence breaking out again, can there? Have they not got rid of a hundred thousand of these so-called jihadis and their sympathizers? Pure ethnic cleansing if you ask me."

"Probably more than a hundred large," she admitted. "But I won't argue with you about British policy. I can't vote. I'm still a guest there. How they run their country is up to them."

Mirsaad halted at a corner from where she could see the coffeehouse. It was gaily lit, with crowded tables clustered around charcoal burners. The clientele seemed a mixed bunch: old German and Middle Eastern, men and women, some of the latter wearing scarves and some not.

"Ah, but you are not just a guest, are you, Caitlin?" Mirsaad ventured before they got any closer. "And you are not a police officer. In my experience, in Europe at least, police officers do not flit about on their own in the dark."

She smiled. "No, Sayad. I am not a police officer. But I am looking for the man who came after my family and your friend. And I need your help to find him. Or at least to start looking."

"And what about my family, Caitlin? Will they be safe if I help you? I can make decisions for myself, but I cannot recklessly endanger my wife and children with a clear conscience."

She regarded him dispassionately. He was a very intelligent man and street-smart with it. There would be no bullshitting him.

"There is some danger, Sayad. The man I'm after, he's a bad motherfucker. But so am I."

"I believe you are, Caitlin. But Bret loves you and trusts you as the mother of his child. For this reason, because you are a mother and not just a bad motherfucker, I will trust you, too."

"Let's get a coffee," she said.

"Yes," he agreed. "The coffee is good here. Ahmet the Turk is away much of late, but he sends good coffee back to his relatives."

32

TEXAS ADMINISTRATIVE DIVISION

"You can't do this to us, mister. We ain't done nothin' worth a hangin'."

Miguel paused as he made to slip the noose over the man's head. It was the plaintive, pitiful appeal in his voice that nearly stayed the vaquero's hand.

Then he shook his head angrily. "You are a rapist, a slave trader, a murderer, a cattle thief, a taker of land, and a destroyer of good families... I could go on, but we shall just skip to the hanging, I think, my friend."

The road agent's eyes frosted over like a poison lake on a hard winter's morning as the noose went around his neck. He was not long ago a boy, with fresh acne on his cheeks and the full head of thick and springy blond hair that had been washed an hour ago for his execution. That had been his only request of them. There was none of his youth left in him, however, and precious little of the rest of his life in front of him. There could be no doubt he had walked a vicious and depraved path these last few years, and whatever innocence he might have been born with, poor choices and ill circumstances had pressed it entirely from his existence.

"Vete y chinga a tu madre," he hissed, spitting the words in Miguel's face.

Some of the Mormon women trilled and fluttered in disgust, but the Mexican cowboy smiled thinly and tightened the rope around the man's unshaven neck, adjusting the knot back and forth until it sat correctly behind one ear. The young bandit's Adam's apple bobbed up and down as he tried to swallow, and two bright red spots stood out on his unusually feminine cheekbones. Miguel wiped flecks of the boy's warm saliva from his face with the back of one hand.

Sofia, standing not far away, regarded the scene and Miguel with cold, frosty detachment. No one else had seen or knew of the world-class whipping he had given her after she had saved his life. What had startled Miguel was not so much that she'd disobeyed him but that she didn't react to the punishment at all. No tears, no pleading, nothing at all. He might as well have been whipping a couch or a particularly obdurate mule.

Miguel wasn't sure which had frightened him more, Sofia's lack of reaction or the fact that he'd lost control and beat her so much harder for it. And that after she had saved his life. She had, by all accounts, been murderously effective. The Mormons were not even aware she was behind them until well after most of the shooting stopped. She had killed seven men and one woman, a camp whore who had been advancing on Ben Randall from behind with a knife. The engineer had not known until he was told by young Orin, who saw the woman's throat suddenly explode for no immediately obvious reason. Sofia was changing in ways Miguel could not fathom, changing into something he might not care for, and he seemed to be powerless to do anything about it.

This morning, for instance, she was determined to have whatever additional measure of revenge she could take from the hanging. Miguel was of two minds about that. It was an ugly thing to kill a man in cold blood, even for justice, and he would wish to spare her what she was soon to witness. On the other hand, perhaps it might bring some relief if she could see that sometimes bad men did meet a bad end. Perhaps she could have some faith that the agents who had murdered the rest of their family might one day also swing from a rope or die in a pool of their own blood. At any rate, she was here and he would not deny her in spite of her disobedience last night.

Miguel returned his attention to the task at hand.

"You must be a very brave man to be able to spit like that when you are so close to death," he said. "Me? In your shoes I would have a very dry mouth."

"Cocksucker," the agent muttered.

Miguel nudged his horse away from the younger man and pulled lightly at the reins to reposition himself alongside the next road agent. There were three of them, hands tied behind their backs as they perched on their saddles beneath the spreading arms of an elm tree that sat on a small rise overlooking the town. The other two were older than the boy, one a hulking, bearded menace to humanity, forever scowling at Miguel as if through the pure intensity of his loathing he might somehow effect a change in his situation. Whereas the boy and the other surviving agent, a thin, grim-faced streak of misery and tribulation, sat on their horses with their elbows and wrists bound behind them, this black-bearded monster was chained from wrist to shoulder, so fiercely had he resisted the arrangements for his hanging.

"I am going to put the noose over your head now," Miguel told him. "I can understand that you are thinking of resisting with whatever violence you might yet be capable of, but if you trouble me with this, I shall put your eye out with my thumb. Do you believe me?"

The man's small, porcine eyes, almost lost within the folds of his fat face twinkled with malign intent, but he looked at Miguel and saw the simple truth of the vaquero's threat. He nodded once and bent his head forward for the rope.

The third agent was some sort of gang boss. Not the lead agent—Miguel had blown his head off in the Hy Top Club—but a senior lieutenant of sorts. The other two had deferred to him after their capture, and he had tried to negotiate a settlement with the Mormons by which they might retain their lives. Thankfully, the Mormons weren't having any of it.

"Anything to say?" Miguel asked.

The gang boss responded with a sickly smirk.

"Texas will make my reckoning with you, Mexico. And all your family."

He grinned darkly in the direction of Sofia, and Miguel had to restrain the urge to put a knife into his guts.

"Let us pray," Cooper Aronson said, loudly as he opened his Bible with a bandaged hand. Big Ben, Adam, and Willem D'Age knelt in front of him, their heads bowed.

The youngest of the agents broke then. The pimpled boy cried out, "I can't believe you're gonna to do this to us without even a trial. You people are fuckin' hypocrites."

His eyes darted left and right, looking for a sympathetic face in the small group of witnesses, but mostly what he found was scorn and even now, at this late stage, fear. Miguel saw him lock eyes with Miss Gray, the girl he had stayed behind to rescue after young Adam had taken the others to freedom. She was shivering and attempting to break free of his gaze, but he held her with a sort of dreadful hypnotic power.

"You tell 'em, Sally. You tell I didn't mean no harm. It was all just a little fun, weren't it... I didn't hurt you none. You even told me you liked it; you said you wanted it that way."

The poor girl turned a bright shade of red before blanching nearly white and falling into the woman next to her, all but fainting away. Sofia scowled fiercely at the condemned man and hurried over to Miss Gray to see what assistance she might lend. Miguel suspected that if his daughter still had the Remington at hand, the one he had taken from her after last night's violence, she would have put a round through the man's heart.

We need to get through this, he thought.

He prodded his horse forward again and rode up next to the youngest agent.

He spoke in a low voice but with great power. "If I were you, I would be looking to make this as painless a leave-taking as possible, señor. If I were you, I would shut my mouth now, unless I wanted to die with my neck stretched and my insides hanging out over my belt, swinging in the air for the crows to pick."

He casually drew the knife with which he had killed two men the previous evening, stropped it slowly on his jeans, and gave the road agent his stone face.

Tears were leaking from the young man's eyes, and his lips were quivering with the effort of not crying.

"Why don't you shut up and die like a man?" growled the bearded monster beside him.

"Why don't you show me?" the boy spit, and lashed out with his boot, catching the other agent's horse in the flank.

It leapt forward with a shriek. The rope securing the giant to the tree went taut, his massive legs shot forward as he jerked back, and the animal sprang away. Every branch in the massive old elm seemed to shake as his weight pulled the rope tight. Miguel grimaced at the sound of his neck snapping, and a few of the women screamed and turned away in horror. The substantial corpse twitched and kicked a few times before finding its rhythm, a long, swinging pendulum ride.

"Goddamn you, Billy," said the gang boss before clamming up again.

Miguel shook his head sadly, although not too sadly. "Another murder to account for when you reach the other side, boy."

"A murder?" the young man wailed. "But you were fixing to do the exact same thing to him!"

Aronson, who had stopped in shock, resumed his prayers. A baptism for the dead, he'd told Miguel it was, which seemed to have things quite ass-ended around to the cowboy, but he was not one to interfere in the worship rights of others. Only the sound of the young man's whimpering and his urine dribbling down his pants legs into the dirt could be heard as Aronson spoke.

"Willem D'Age, having been commissioned of Jesus Christ, I baptize you, for and in behalf of this man we shall call John, who is just now dead, in the name of the Father, and of the Son, and of the Holy Ghost, amen."

He sprinkled water from a canteen on the heavily bandaged head of his comrade.

"What are they doing?" the boy asked, sniffling up a runny nose.

"Baptizing you," Miguel explained. "So you might have a chance in the next life, since you are shit out of luck in this one."

"But I been baptized. As a proper Baptist, too," he protested. "Tell them no. I don't want their stupid heathen god interfering with me."

Miguel shrugged. "Let them be, boy. It is the same God. And believe me, you have bigger problems today."

Without further preamble he smacked the lad's horse sharply on the rear, and it whinnied in distress before bolting away.

"Hey!" the lad yelped, but whatever protest he might have wanted to make was cut short by the snapping thud of the rope. His body added its fresh rhythm to the dying swing of his comrades.

Aronson splashed more canteen water, this time on Adam's head, and repeated the prayer. "Adam Coupland, having been commissioned of Jesus Christ, I baptize you, for and in behalf of this man, we know only as Billy, who is just now dead, in the name of the Father, and of the Son, and of the Holy Ghost, amen."

The last of the road agents, the boss of the crew, drew in a deep breath as Miguel rode over, but he seemed composed enough now that his time had come.

"Will you tell them your name so that they might baptize you properly?" Miguel asked of the man.

The agent seemed to ponder the matter for a few moments. He took a deep breath of cold Texas air through his nose and held it for a few seconds before slowly letting it out. Then he looked Miguel straight in the eye.

"No," he replied, allowing his gaze to drift away from Miguel to the peaceful vista they enjoyed from the gentle rise overlooking the forested hills to the southwest. "No, I really do not think I will give you or anyone else the satisfaction."

"Satisfaction be damned," Miguel said, letting his anger show through. "You have your orders from Fort Hood, do you not? You have your orders, your mission, your blood money, everything from Blackstone."

The agent smiled.

"Maybe yes, maybe no, maybe neither. You've got my life, *puta*. You can't have my name. And you can't have my country, neither. But rest assured, I will be sure to give your regards to the devil."

And with that, he spurred his own horse out from beneath him and dropped into eternity.

"I would not advise staying here long," Miguel said as they walked away from the freshly mounded graves.

"You think there will be more road agents?" D'Age asked.

"Possibly not. From what I hear, they have their own territories. But there are TDF patrols about, and if they were in contact with these men, they will soon notice that they have gone."

The morning was cool despite the late hour. It would be time for lunch soon, but Miguel wondered whether the Mormons would have any appetite after the foul passage of the day so far. At first light they had buried the dead from the gunfight with the help of the three survivors, laying them down in soft ground near a small water hole not far from the football field. Then they had buried the other three in the same place after hanging them. Three of the camp whores had survived their wounds, and Miguel understood that an intense debate was under way within the Mormon ranks over what to do with them. The smart thing would be to silence them, too, but he had no stomach for that, and the Mormons would not hear of the suggestion. Taking them or leaving them seemed to be the only options, and both were beset with problems.

He wiped his sweating brow. A few wispy strands of white cloud stretched across otherwise hard blue skies, and the sounds of cattle mustering drifted over the tree line.

They had buried Peter Atchison, their horse wrangler, who had been killed by an agent's bullet, under a chestnut tree some distance away. The tenor of the small party was subdued, and their leaders were of a mind to move both cattle and people to the far side of town for a few days' rest before breaking trail again.

Sofia, who had been walking a few yards ahead with Adam and Orin and a fully recovered Sally Gray, dropped out of the group of youngsters and stood waiting until Miguel, Aronson, and D'Age caught up with her.

"I need a moment with my daughter," Miguel said.

Aronson and D'Age nodded. "Of course."

Sofia still seemed stiff, cold, constantly searching her surroundings. Miguel remembered a better time when his little princess had taken an intense interest in anything new, always curious. He placed a hand on her shoulder and guided her off to the side. She came along willingly enough, something Miguel did not take for granted these days.

"Are you all right, Sofia?" he asked in Spanish. He did not want anyone to overhear this discussion.

After clearing her initial surprise at the change in language, Sofia responded in kind. "Suppose so."

This morning was not the first time she had seen death, of course, but it was the first time she had seen men killed in a detached and calculated fashion, if one could call the messy execution that.

"I am sorry about what I did last night," Miguel said. "I lost control of myself."

"I understand," she said in a tone that lacked any warmth or emotion.

"Do you?" he asked. "Do you really understand? You are all that is left to me. You are the future to me. But also my past. Every one of us who has ever lived lives on in you. All of our family. You are everything. For that reason, in small measure, but mostly, almost entirely, because I love you more than anyone or anything in the world. How could it be otherwise? Do you understand how important it is to me that you reach safety?"

She cocked her head to the left, another new tic she had picked up. "Where is it truly safe, Papa? Can you answer me that?"

"Kansas City, of course," he said.

"Are you sure, Papa?" Sofia asked. "Are you really sure about that?"

"The federales are there…"

"And what of the Wave, Papa?" Sofia asked. "The Americanos, for all of their power, were wiped off the face of God's earth by the Wave. Where is safe?"

"The Wave will not come again," he said.

"Are you sure of that?" Sofia asked. "How can you be sure of anything, Papa? I am certain of only one thing now—that feeling safe is an illusion. Can you tell me otherwise?"

Miguel shook his head. He had never had this sort of trouble with Sofia before. She had never questioned his authority like this. He felt rage flickering at the edge of his temper again and quickly did his best to defuse it.

"Papa." She reached out and grabbed his arm. Her grip was firm, solid around his bicep. "We must protect each other. We are all that we have left. And whether you like it or not, I will do my best to protect you. Your belt does not frighten me anymore, not now."

He looked Sofia in the eye. He saw that in some respects he had lost her as well. The laughing, happy daughter, *la princesa,* had passed away just as surely as the rest of his family. In her place was this changeling, this cold, hard…

Woman, he realized.

"Papa." Her voice sounded much as it had years ago when he used to hold her high over his head. "I love you very much, and I could not bear to lose you."

He took her into his arms and held her close, as if it might be the last time. He remembered bringing her those silly little toys out of a McDonald's Happy Meal, how much she had enjoyed them. More so because her papa had brought them for her. He remembered taking the family down to the beach on one of his rare vacations away from the trail, watching the children play in the surf.

Miguel remembered teaching Sofia not to blink when she pulled the trigger, to squeeze the trigger, not yank it, when the ten-point buck came into view. Headstrong even then, Sofia had taken the buck at nearly three hundred yards, which startled everyone to this very day.

"I love you, too," he said.

Later in the day, Miguel gave her back her Remington.

"You should not feel bad about what we had to do this morning or last night," Aronson said as they resumed their trek back to the rest of the Mormon host. "Those men were killers and rapists and thieves. Both Texas and Seattle law allows for summary execution under those circumstances. God will judge them as he judges us all."

Sofia regarded the Mormon leader with some confusion. "I don't feel bad," she said. "I don't feel anything for them. They got what they deserved. That's all that happened this morning."

"But you do not look very happy," he said.

She waited a moment before answering.

"I thought it would help," she said. "I thought it would make me feel better." She shrugged again and then trailed off.

"The only thing that will make you feel better is the thing you can't have," said Miguel. "Everything the way it was. That is what we all want. And that is impossible. But it is possible to have some justice from the sort of men who killed Mama and your brother and sister and the others. And while it may not make us feel better, I can promise you it does make the world a better place every time one of them leaves it."

Miguel turned to Aronson. "I can understand that you might wish some time to recover from all this, and I will abide by your choice, but if you are caught here by Blackstone's men, by the TDF, so close to the evidence of the agents' destruction, it will go badly for you."

"But we were defending ourselves and our women and reclaiming our stock," Aronson protested. "We cannot be punished for doing that, not justly."

"Out here, justice is a bullet," Miguel replied. "You have the most bullets, you get the most justice."

His daughter, he noticed, nodded in agreement with that. Both of the Mormons looked troubled.

"But Fort Hood condemns the road agents," Aronson said. "They send patrols against them and have made membership in the gangs a hanging offense. We hanged those men on that authority."

"They are the first agents I know of being hanged," said Miguel. "None have been caught or punished by the TDF."

He looked up at the sound of a whip crack to see Adam and Orin mustering the herd toward the field on the far side of the road that ran by the football stadium. Martin Luther King Drive or Boulevard, he thought it was called.

"It is not true to say that the TDF does not suppress the gangs," Aronson said. "You know they hanged a dozen bandits in Fort

Hood just last week according to Texas Public Radio. And I have read reports of summary executions on the range."

"They are said to be quite common," D'Age added.

Miguel stopped at a fence post where they had left their jackets and water bottles. He took a long pull from his flask, which was insulated by a neoprene sleeve. The water inside was deliciously cold on his dry throat. He offered it to Sofia, but she produced a small pink hip flask of her own. Miguel had never seen it before and wondered where she had picked it up. It seemed to have a picture of a cat on it and the words "Hello Kitty."

"Hangings are *said* to be quite common," he said to D'Age. "I wouldn't trust a word that comes from Texas Public Radio. It is a Blackstone... how would you say? Piece of mouth? And nobody ever sees them, because they are *said* to take place beyond the boundaries of the settlement. And yes, twelve banditos were hanged last week. And more the week before that. But banditos are not road agents. They are all from well below the Rio Grande. There was a reason those men would not give you their names this morning. It had nothing to do with matters of faith. Agents give up their names and with them their affiliations to Fort Hood on pain of death, or worse."

Aronson took a drink before bending forward and pouring most of his bottle over his head and neck, grunting with pleasure at the cool thrill. When he stood up, he shook off the beaded droplets like a dog.

"That is speculation, Miguel. They didn't give us their real names because they have their gang names. They're like the old Hells Angels or the gangstas in the cities before the Wave. They take a gang name when they join. It is their new identity, like being born again, except into sin. These men are no different."

Miguel gave him a searching look. "How would you know?"

Aronson smiled. "I was a doctor of sociology before the Wave. Urban subcultures were my specialty."

The cattle were moving en masse now to fresh pasture a short distance away, lowing and trumpeting as Miguel's cattle dogs barked and yapped with great excitement to herd them through the gates on the far side of the field. The beasts' earthy scent mingled with the growing cloud of dust as the herd got on the road. Flankers guided the cattle off the ball field with a rudimentary skill that impressed Miguel. The Mormons were fast learners.

"Get around!" he yelled at Red Dog before she was distracted by a blood patch where he had killed the two guards with his knife.

Miguel faced Aronson and turned his palms up to the sky, a "whatever" gesture as his daughter called it.

"Well, I am no doctor, Mister Aronson. But I know what I know, and you will come to regret it if you take the word of Fort Hood on this matter. The road agents are their men, no matter what they say. And if I were you, I would be clear of this place as soon as I could be."

Aronson did not dismiss him out of hand, for which Miguel was thankful. He had often found with educated people that they thought his advice not worthy of listening to because he had not bothered with books and learning beyond what was necessary for his work. He could read, and he could write English quite well—he would not have made it through settler selection otherwise—but he did not have the luxury of doing so for pleasure.

"We shall confer with the women and see what they say," Cooper Aronson conceded. "But even if we are to leave here as soon as possible, we should gather what supplies we can from this town."

Miguel nodded at that. "Fair enough," he said before smiling at an old memory.

"Fair enough" was what Miss Julianne used to say when she got as much of her way as she was ever going to, just before she started plotting to get the rest of it as well.

* * *

He was right about lunch. Although Miguel had a raging appetite, nobody else seemed to need much beyond hardtack and water. Some of the women had gathered fruit, and the storm cellar of the Hy Top had given up a carton of strawberry jam tins. But only Miguel and, oddly enough, young Adam seemed to have any hunger. Sofia nibbled at the fruit and drank plenty of water, but to her father's eye she appeared tired and worn down. Everyone had gathered in the shade under a tree near the football field on which the herd was now grazing. At some point the camp whores had been accepted into the Mormon host, but from what Miguel could see, the graft was not taking well. They sat apart, sullen and suspicious.

The women they had so recently treated as less than human distinguished themselves by the care and consideration with which they attended to the needs of the whores, who had been cleaned up and dressed in more respectable attire. Perhaps that was behind their surly disposition, Miguel thought, smiling to himself. Once they had been prized out of their leather miniskirts and tight T's and draped in long, shapeless floral frocks, all of their intimidating sexual power had vanished. The livid bruising and splints and bandages for their wounds did not help much in that regard, either. Miguel kept his eye on them for a few minutes, but they were being guarded by Trudi Jessup, the woman he had rescued last night, who was neither camp whore nor captive Mormon. He had not spoken to her at length beyond quietly accepting her thanks after the executions. She had spent all her time with the other women, but something about her marked her as being separate and somehow different.

He supposed it was simply because she was not of their church.

After a short while observing her, it was obvious the whores would be given no opportunity to cause trouble, and he relaxed a little. It was not such a wise thing accepting the enemy into camp like this, he thought. Taking a few apples from a plastic bowl, and supplementing them with a slab of biscuit and a small piece of hard cheese, he walked over to where the leadership group was still discussing what they might do. He had always assumed Mormons to be a little backward in their treatment of women—although no more so than many traditional Catholics, he had to admit—but here the women seemed to be equals with their men.

"Come over, Miguel, please," Aronson said when he saw the vaquero watching them idly.

He had met all the women already, of course, but he was never especially good with names, and despite making an effort to commit them all to memory, he could not be certain who was who. Jenny, the betrothed of Willem D'Age, he remembered without a problem. And Aronson's wife, Maive, he recognized, of course. She had been very good to Sofia and the only one who did not appear to judge his daughter for her behavior on the night of the rescue, although Tori, the betrothed of Ben Randall, had taken Sofia aside to thank her for shooting down the murderous harpy who had intended him murder.

Of the others, besides Sally Gray, who was younger and thus no part of this conference, he had no idea, but he was comfortable enough addressing all as ma'am.

A pall still hung over the small band, with all of them speaking as though they were in church, not quite whispering but not speaking as loudly or gaily as one might expect of people who had just escaped death. Miguel supposed the close nature of that escape would naturally suppress their spirits. The wound of losing one of their own, the violence to which they had been a party, and, most serious of all, the outrages committed upon the women would take some time to heal.

"Miguel," said Aronson, "my wife agrees with you that we should not delay long in our departure from this place." Maive surprised him by placing a cool hand on his forearm and squeezing lightly.

She looked over at the camp whores, and Miguel was certain he detected just a flash of ill feeling directed toward them, but Maive

Aronson immediately softened her gaze and went on.

"It would be best to get the women away from here. We have enough supplies from the stop at Leona. We should be gone from here as quickly as possible."

"That is probably wise," Miguel said. "I do not know that there would be much worth salvaging here, anyway. The center of the city is badly burned out and looted already."

"That was the agents," Jenny said, with much more obvious bitterness than Maive. "One of them told me they had been using this town as a base for six months and had destroyed a good deal of the town center for the fun of it."

She sounded as appalled by the suggestion that anyone would do such a thing as she was by having been captured and mistreated by the same men.

"Then we should move on as soon as we can," said Miguel. "Where do you next plan to make camp?"

"Palestine," Aronson said.

33

NEW YORK

No, thought Milosz, you do not obtain military-specification P90s from stroking pussycats. You steal them or buy them on the black market, or, given the way this country was, you loot them from a deserted gun store. But what the hell. He could not care less where the strange hippopotamus man in the very odd Viking helmet and his English lady friend got the weapons that had saved his ass. All Milosz cared about was that his scrawny ass remained in one piece, while back at Madison and 29th the asses of many nig nogs and crazy ragheaded asswits were scattered about the street in many, many pieces.

"You need to get out of this part of the city," Wilson insisted in the same tone of voice Milosz had heard him use when pushing around lower ranks and junior officers.

The man and woman, however, seemed oddly immune to the master sergeant's imprecations. "Imprecations" was another word Milosz had learned from reading Mr. F. Scott Fitzgerald, along with "orgastic," which admittedly remained something of a mystery and not a word he was confident about throwing into this conversation.

"I'm sorry, Sergeant—" the woman began.

"Master sergeant, United States Army Rangers."

"That's lovely. But I'm sorry, Master Sergeant, no, we cannot leave the city until our work is done."

"Your work was hauling rusted fucking car wrecks out to the salvage barges, according to these papers," Wilson said. "Not spooking around Pirate Island capping motherfuckers and looking for fucking treasure maps. Your work didn't involve any of that crazy shit at all."

"Well," the woman said, smiling in a rather sexy fashion, Milosz thought, "our work didn't involve saving your asses from Captain Fucking Feathersword and his merry band of cutthroats, either. But we did. So perhaps you'd be a darling and let us toddle off before your friends arrive. Honestly, being sent back now would ruin our whole day."

Milosz peered out of the office window down into the streets of midtown Manhattan. From their vantage point on the forty-second floor of the building to which they had fled he had a good view of the OPFOR concentrations around the approaches to Madison Square Park. They were a lot less concentrated. A lot more "attrited," as that American colonel had said. The lower end of the city looked like hell. Frankly, he was glad to be out of it for a little while.

He idly examined the office, wondering what kind of business the occupants of this particular floor had carried on. Whatever the case, they'd been busy on March 14, 2003. The leavings of the Disappeared lay everywhere: at desks, in hallways, mounded in a pile of stiff, blackened suits and dresses encircling a box of petrified Krispy Kremes. He did his best to ignore them and Wilson's argument with the smugglers, for that was surely what these two must be.

"Halo to any element, request close air. Location is…" Gardener said into her headset.

He returned to the drama unfolding below, where dozens of city blocks were aflame. Sunrise was mere moments away. Gunships darted in and out of the shattered canyons, hosing long ropy streams of tracer fire onto unseen targets. Every few minutes a jet fighter would fall out of the sky, loosing rockets or bombs into the cauldron of battle, their detonations causing the window in front of him to vibrate. The scale of destruction was fantastic.

"Troops and vehicles in the open," said Gardener. "Approximately one hundred effectives plus five civilian trucks moving toward…"

She sat in a corner that had not been given over to the office of any single executive. A breakout space, she called it, a small open area decorated with a couple of couches and a small coffee table on which lay old magazines and a vase of brown dried-up flowers. Gardener, comfortable on a musty couch, examined the maelstrom through her binoculars, apparently unaware she was sitting on a red dress left behind by one of the lost souls who had worked there. Her muddy boots were propped up on the coffee table, and her carbine lay across her lap. She had taken her helmet off, leaving the radio headset in place, exposing some of her stray blond locks. She pressed her fingers to the earpiece of her headset and called in a string of air strikes, punishing the foes who had killed her partner, Sergeant Veal, and had very nearly taken her life as well.

"I copy, Talon. What have you got?" she asked. She waited a moment and then replied. "Clusters will be perfect. Do you see them?"

She pressed her headset against her ears and nodded.

"Halo copies."

Behind Milosz, Wilson raised his voice again.

"Listen, I am the world's most grateful motherfucker that you happened along and pulled our nuts outta the fire," he said. "But you can't be tear-assing around the AOR on your private business with all of this shit flying around. Have you looked out the fucking window the last few minutes? Huh? We got us Apocalypse fucking Now out there, people. Top-shelf fucking ordnance getting uncorked today. Star Wars shit. Hell, they gonna be firing up the fucking Deathstar and just zapping this whole fucking island to ashes before we're done, believe it. And you want to go back out into it? You are going to get yourselves killed. And since I owe you for me and my people not getting killed, I have to say no, and furthermore, Hell No. When resupply flies in on the roof, you are flying the fuck outta here."

Wilson had worked himself up into such a state that Milosz was actually drawn away from the spectacular bonfire down in the streets that had exploded behind the master sergeant at the end of his rant, lighting the room up considerably. Gardener was all over that detail, anyway. The man and woman—what did they call themselves, Hippo and June?—seemed relaxed and even amused by Wilson's rant. But then, they were the only ones with loaded weapons in the room, and it was clear they wouldn't be giving them up. Plus, Milosz thought, to wear such a stupid helmet with such large cow horns poking out, the hippo man was very obviously an individual who took his amusement where he could find it. He searched his memory for a literary character he might compare this hippo to—an old trick for passing the time and for fixing in his memory the details of books he wanted to remember. But nothing came. Watching them and their utter imperturbability—another Fitzgerald word—Milosz just knew there would be no getting these two evacuated anytime soon. Or ever. They were happy to stay and watch over the Americans until they were resupplied—the hippo, who looked like a former soldier of sorts, as well as a Disneyland Visigoth, had promised them that. But that was the only promise they had extracted from the pair.

"Hey, Wilson," he said in an easygoing, reasonable tone, "what does it matter what the lady and the hippo do? If they get killed, who will blame us? It is not as if they are supposed to be here. I don't suppose anyone but this Rubin they speak of even knows they are still in the city, no?" He tilted his head at them, looking for confirmation.

"It's Rhino, son. Rhino A. Ross," said the man he had mistaken for a hippo. Advancing on Milosz, the giant engulfed his right hand and pumped it three times. "Chief petty officer, United States Coast Guard, in my glorious youth," he continued. "At your service. And you make a good point, son. You're obviously a worldly and educated man. And Polish, too, if I am not mistaken. I served with a Pole once. Bochenski his name was. A marine engineer but a polymath of the first order. Had a gifted amateur's interest in fifteenth-century Florence, which is by the bye, but of immediate and critical relevance is the very point you just made, sir. Nobody is going to care about us except our employer, and I can assure you his interest in our well-being extends only so far as his self-interest allows. In the event of misfortune, we will be quickly replaced and forgotten. No reason, then, we shouldn't be on our way once you're able to see to your own defense again."

Milosz took his hand back with a rueful grimace. The Rhino probably had not crushed it nearly as much as he could have.

"Wilson," he said, "I think we should not be too hasty with the bum's rushing of these two back to rear echelon, no?"

The master sergeant's face clouded over with suspicion. "And why not, Fred? It's bad enough we're going to have to fess up about how they saved our asses. If we let them wander off after that, we're toast whether they make it back or not."

"Not if they simply disappear and we never report them," Milosz said.

The English woman suddenly tensed. "Nobody's disappearing us," she protested, leveling her weapon in their direction.

"Easy," Wilson said. "Be cool, lady."

Milosz endured a second's confusion before understanding suddenly dawned. "No, no," he said quickly, wondering what he would disappear them with if he were so inclined. The only person with any firepower was Gardener, and calling in an air strike on their position was not logical. "I do not imply that we will make you disappear. Just that we will let you disappear. On one condition."

The Viking rhinoceros subtly shifted his grip on the P90, causing the barrel of the weapon to point a bit more in the general direction of Wilson and Milosz.

"What sort of condition?" he asked.

"I believe the American phrase is 'a piece of the action,'" Milosz said, pleased with himself for remembering that vernacular expression.

"Oh, fuck me, Fred. We don't need this George Clooney bullshit," protested Wilson.

"No. You wait on a moment," Milosz said. "I do not know this Clooney character. Perhaps he is your friend, but just think about this. You were nearly killed by pirate asswits last night, and for what? Not even for a lousy paycheck you can depend on. A hundred and forty new bucks that may not be paid you if we even make it back to battalion. Please to forgive my presumption, Rhino A. Ross and, sorry... English Lady Baldwin?"

"Balwyn."

"My apologies. But I presume you are to be paid much more than one hundred and forty newbies, yes? So if we were to help you toward completion of project, we too might be paid by this oil man Rubin, no?"

"I can't believe this," Wilson said, shaking his head.

The Rhino pursed his lips and shrugged. "I suppose so," he said. "If we had Rubin's papers, it wouldn't be hard to get you a cut... a small cut," he added. "But a hell of a lot better than a hundred forty newbies, yeah."

"I would like equity," Milosz said.

The English woman snorted, but more in amusement than dismissal.

"Listen, if we have Rubin's paper, he would negotiate," she said. "But it would take more than just letting us walk out of here. We could do that right now."

She hefted her gun to remind him. Even disabled by some sort of wound to one arm, she looked more than capable of using it.

"If you want a cut, you need to get us closer to his apartment," she said.

"Jesus Christ," Wilson said, dropping his Kevlar helmet to the ground.

"No. Jesus Christ of no use in this situation. But Fryderyk Milosz and Master Sergeant Wilson of U.S. Army Rangers very useful. Oh, and Technical Sergeant Gardener, too. She most useful of all."

"Just shut up and take the deal, Sarge. I didn't get paid at all last month," Gardener shouted from her couch before pressing her headset. "This is Halo. Talon, give me two more of the same on the original target, do you copy?"

Julianne jumped out of the cabin of the helicopter and fought the rotor wash trying to sweep her off the roof. She stayed bent over as she ran forward, clutching the straps of her backpack lest it be ripped away by the furious downblast. She turned and crouched beside an air-conditioning unit and was almost bowled over by the Rhino, who was right on her heels. The dark green chopper snarled even more ferociously as the pilot fed power into the engines and lifted off again. Her dirty, unwashed fringe whipped stinging strands of hair into her eyes, but she watched and waved them off, anyway. The Polish soldier, Milosz, stood in the doorway, grinning hugely. With one hand holding a grab bar, he laid the tips of two fingers under his eyes and then pointed directly at her.

I'll be watching you.

I'll bet you will, Fred, she thought. *I'll just bet you will.*

The Blackhawk leaned over and dropped away below the roofline. Within a minute it had disappeared completely, flying back toward the enormous column of black smoke rising high into the sky above the southern end of the island. It was nearly a mile across at the base and shot through with great tongues of fire and the flashes of exploding bombs, looking for all the world as though a volcano had erupted in Lower Manhattan.

"Well, I must say, I would not have imagined that helping people could turn out to be so fulfilling," Jules said. "And to think my father warned me off it for life."

The Rhino lit up a cigar and took a few puffs with evident satisfaction.

"Damn, that feels good. You know, I had but a few goals in life, Miss Jules. To own my own boat and run charters out of Acapulco, which I've done. To drive an RV around the country having adventures with my dog, Sidney, and our mentor, a ninja master, which, I'll admit, I'm still working toward. And to work for the covert ops section of the CIA and save an ungrateful world on a regular basis, which I can now cross off my list."

Julianne stood up and walked over to the edge of the skyscraper.

"Almost," she corrected him. "The CIA is now the NIA. And you don't actually work for them. Those crooked fucking spec-ops guys just requisitioned a helicopter by claiming you did. The actual agency is probably hunting you down as we speak. And you're not saving the world; you're chasing a fucking quid."

"Close enough!" he said. "Now let's get inside and have a look at that map."

"In a minute," she shot back.

Julianne simply wanted to savor the moment. They had passed through, or over, the worst of the fighting thanks to the intervention of the rangers, although mostly thanks to the quick-thinking avarice of that sneaky Pole. The flight had been a short hop but a useful one, carrying them over the heads of any number of villainous types who might have otherwise interfered with their passage. It would have been nice to have been dropped right at the doorstep of Rubin's apartment, but the Pole had explained he was already pushing things by getting them the lift on false pretenses. He had done as she had asked and gotten them that much closer. She had no doubt that if he survived the next few days, he would come looking for her, assuming she, too, survived and managed to retrieve the Rubin documents. And he was right. Once she had those papers, there would be no problem renegotiating the package with the businessman. Cutting in the rangers as silent partners was simply a cost of doing business in a market as chaotic and challenging as New York. She would see to it that they got their due reward.

But for now, she simply wanted to take a moment before leaping back into the fray.

The air on top of the skyscraper tasted remarkably clean. She had expected to smell the petrochemical reek of burning buildings and military ordnance, but a northerly wind had pushed the ash clouds and general stink of war down toward the bay and the Statue of Liberty, which was just visible beyond the western edge of the towering smoke column. From here, Jules felt as though she stood atop the whole world. The impossibly fast jet planes shrieking down from the heavens, the dark insectile shapes of the helicopters, they were all so far removed and so tiny as to be nearly abstract. Not real things of steel and fire, flown by men, but almost mythical enchantments, tiny airborne fascinators, toys. Gray warships as small as bathtub toys lobbed shells into the ruins, attempting to root out the hard cases. She shook her head.

"Sound, sound the clarion," she said to herself as deadly orange petals of fire blossomed from the top floors of the Flatiron Building. "Fill the fife! To all the sensual world proclaim…"

"What's that, Miss Julianne?' the Rhino asked as he drew up beside her, removing his helmet and rubbing his scalp.

"One crowded hour of glorious life," she said softly, "is worth an age without a name."

"Huh," grunted the Rhino. "Well, shit, yeah. Can we go now?"

"You really don't have the soul of a poet, do you, Rhino?"

"No, ma'am," he answered. "Just the horn of an irascible, endangered pachyderm. And two spares on this excellent fucking helmet."

34

NEW YORK

Yusuf Mohammed had taken his first woman a few years after joining the Lord's Resistance Army. Before then he had been only a child and incapable of being with a woman in the way some of the older fighters so often were. But one day, not long after the Wave had swept over North America and brought chaos and murder to the rest of the world, Yusuf had taken his first living prize after Captain Kono's men had ambushed a small convoy carrying medical aid workers back from the wastelands of Egypt. He did not remember the experience fondly. The woman, a young French nurse, was not broken in spirit and fought him bitterly. Indeed, he still carried a few faint scars from her fingernails on his left cheek.

This young infidel woman, however, was much more pleasing. She submitted willingly to his advances, and although he suspected her enthusiasm was feigned, he did not much care. After the horrors of Ellis Island and his trip down the river and then through eastern Manhattan, it was a comfort to have a woman give herself to him, even though they both knew she had no choice.

Afterward, he felt sorry for her and even, to his surprise, a little ashamed of himself. He'd had good reason of late to recall his capture by Captain Kono and his unhappiness at being pressed into service by the LRA, and as the girl lay next to him in the hotel suite that formed part of the emir's personal harem, Yusuf could not help but wonder what ill fortune had delivered her to him.

She was a young American woman, almost perfectly fitting every preconception he had of young American women: blond and fair-skinned and sweet-smelling. But though Yusuf was unfamiliar with American women, he had the better part of a lifetime's experience of fear, and this woman, for all her pretense of arousal and excitement, was very obviously afraid.

Yusuf had enjoyed having his way with her, but as he lay in bed watching the gentle rise and fall of her shoulders as she pretended to sleep, he realized he had no great wish to be around her much longer. He was unsure what to do. It was a great honor and privilege the emir had given him, and he was profoundly grateful not just for the rest, the food, and the attentions of the slave girl but also for the forgiveness it signaled. Now, though, he found himself eager to return to battle and prove himself. There would be no flinching from the enemy next time. If he was fated to die, it was Allah's will that he should die and he would give up his life willingly.

It was unworthy and probably sinful, but he envied many of the fedayeen who had brought their families with them. When they were not fighting, they probably enjoyed this sort of ease and pleasure back at the settlements. Yusuf couldn't help but dream about a future in which he lived in a nice house tended by his boys. Maybe his wife would even be a young blond like the one in bed with him. After all, though they were fighting the Americans now, it was only because they resisted the message of peace brought by the Prophet. One day, when this was done, Yusuf hoped all the peoples of the world would live together peacefully. A girl like this, he thought, gazing at the sinuous curve of her spine, might even love him for bringing that message, which, Allah willing, would be almost as good as dying in battle.

They were fighting for more than just revenge, he knew. They were fighting for a new home, a place untouched by the atomic evil of the Jews. They were fighting for the future.

He shook it off. If he was to have a family of his own, then Allah would provide.

The question on his mind now was how to get back to the front. Was he to simply walk out and request transport to the front? Did they intend him to join a new *saif*? Yusuf had no idea.

He rolled out of bed and padded across to a window. The deep, rumbling growl of war reached him even up here, miles from the front. The room overlooked the great park in the center of the city, which appeared to have exploded in a riot of plant growth that spilled out into the surrounding streets. Many of the larger, older trees had died some time ago, probably from the great chemical storms that had drifted over the city when the rest of the continent burned. Their stark skeletal forms stood out like witches' claws against the gray clouds that hovered low over the city, obscuring the upper floors of some of the higher towers. Thousands of saplings had sprung up in the deep grass between them, and a dense understory of vines and bushes had crawled over the wall around the park and appeared to be advancing on the hotel in which he was staying.

The emir, in his benevolence and wisdom, had not merely armed and trained his followers for war. On the long voyage here, besides lessons in the art of city fighting and lectures on the tactics and weapons of the Americans and the bandit gangs of the city, there had been some time set aside for more civilized learning. A teacher, a refugee from the Balkan wars, had told Yusuf how the faithful had first come here many hundreds of years ago, how they had settled near this park and set up gardens, markets, and even a mosque. Why had Allah chosen to let his message wither in this place? Yusuf wondered. Why had so much bloodshed been allowed to come of it?

He could see the ragged edges of human habitation on the western side of the park, on the undeclared border with the areas controlled by the Slavs. They would be swept into the firestorm for certain soon enough. A savage people, all but barbaric from what he had been taught of them. They seemed to revel in cruelty.

The Americans, in contrast, killed with the flip of a switch. If they gave a thought to murder, it was before or after the act, not during. And they flipped that switch as far away from their victims as possible, as if they thought themselves little gods. Too good for the ugliness they brought into the world.

He should be out there now, he thought, with his comrades or even with the janissaries, whom he had to admit were just as deeply invested in this fight as the faithful. Their aims were not righteous by any means, but they served God nonetheless.

He should be there.

A knock at the door drew his attention away from the park. He was surprised and not a little embarrassed to find Ahmet Ozal standing at the entrance to the hotel suite. Yusuf was naked and felt his face grow warm with shame. Ozal just laughed.

"You are recovered from your adventures, then?" said the fedayeen commander before grinning mischievously. "These American women, they do not have the modesty of good Muslim women. But they have their uses, yes."

Yusuf also grinned, unsure of himself. He moved toward the bed to put his pants on.

"Yes, get dressed," Ozal said. "We have much to discuss, and then we must both get back to the fight. There will be time for this later." He waved a hand at the the American girl.

Yusuf could see her eyelids fluttering as she desperately tried to maintain the façade of being asleep. He dressed as quickly as he could. His clothes, a black battle dress uniform, were new and unfamiliar, but his old keffiyeh had been laundered and returned to him. It was torn and a few bloodstains still showed, but he was glad to have it back. His boots took a few moments to lace up, and he worried that Ozal would lose patience with him, but whenever he looked up, he found the giant Turk smiling indulgently.

"Tuck your pants into your boots so you don't trip on them," Ozal said.

Yusuf, flushed with embarrassment, did as he was told. Then he tucked in his T-shirt for good measure, pulled on the black battle dress jacket, and hurried over to the door without a backward glance at the slave girl. He wondered if she would have to clean the room.

He found two more men outside wearing the same type of uniform, fedayeen bodyguards for Ahmet Ozal. The corridor was dark, with no natural light to illuminate it at this point. A few ceiling lamps threw small pools of yellow light down on the green-bordered carpet, presumably powered by a generator somewhere in the building. Patterned wallpaper and the shadows of square columns that jutted into the hallway every few feet lent the area a gloomy, almost spooky atmosphere. Yusuf could very easily imagine himself being pursued down this corridor by the ghosts of those who had lost their lives and souls here. A service cart stood abandoned outside one room, still stocked with hundreds of little plastic bottles of shampoo and shower gel. He recognized them from the bathroom in his own suite. A maid's uniform lay next to the cart, rigid and unclean with whatever dried-up soup remained of its owner. Yusuf grimaced with distaste. So excited had he been when he was first escorted up here, he had not even noticed the relic, and he wondered now why it had been left to clutter up the emir's personal harem.

He wanted to ask Ozal how the struggle was going, but his jaw seemed to have been wired shut and his tongue was thick with shyness. The great Turkish warrior, for his part, seemed perfectly happy to amble along smoking a thin cigar he produced from a breast pocket and humming an unfamiliar tune. They entered a fire escape at the end of the hallway and climbed down three flights of stairs. The floor at which they exited was decorated in the same fashion, with old opulent-looking rugs and long golden drapes that had not been dusted in many years. Yusuf could tell immediately that this level was different. The rooms here did not appear to be for the accommodation of guests. There were only a few of them, and they were very large.

"This way, through here," Ozal said. "I'm afraid the facilities are very spare. The Americans are devils for tracking our movements through the city and sending their warplanes against us whenever we let our guard down."

He waved his cigar around as they entered what looked like a large ballroom with a glass roof. There were no tables in there, just row upon row of stackable chairs facing a small raised dais. Yusuf felt his skin crawl as he realized that most of the chairs were occupied by the remains of the dead. There must have been hundreds of them in there when Allah swept up their souls and cast them down into hell.

"The emir has not long been in this hotel," said Ozal, who seemed not to care. "But within a day we shall be gone again. It is not safe to remain anywhere for very long."

"Not even with the prisoners we hold here?" Yusuf asked when he found his voice again. His found it very difficult not to stare at the dark, contaminated piles of clothing, all so neatly laid out in rows. *And their shoes,* he thought with renewed horror, *look at their shoes.* Aloud, he went on, "Would they bomb us here knowing they would kill their own kind?"

Ahmet Ozal seemed to give the question serious consideration as he drew a few deep puffs from his cigar.

"It is hard to say," he admitted. "Their leader, this Kipper, he is not a man given to making hard choices, which are the only kind available in war. But some of his officers? Yes, they would attack in a second. Or perhaps they might send some of their special forces soldiers in an attempt to rescue their women. They are weak like that, the Americans. You will often draw many of them to their doom by staking out just one or two of their number as bait."

Yusuf felt greatly honored to be privy to the grand strategies of his superiors and again reflected with some disbelief that it was not so long ago he had found himself questioning those strategies as he quaked under the ferocious assault of the American war machine. Now he kept his mouth shut and was glad of it when his eyesight adjusted to the gloom of the darkened ballroom and he realized there were other men in there, sitting clustered in a small semicircle of chairs in an alcove off to the side of the room.

Bandits.

"This is Yusuf Mohammed, one of *my* warriors and the only one to survive the American counterattack on Ellis Island," Ahmet Ozal declared in an almost proprietary tone. Yusuf winced as the Turk's enormous hand smacked into the meat of his shoulder.

"I may be wrong," said one of the bandits, a black man but not an African as best Yusuf could tell, "but weren't your fedayeen ordered to give up their lives rather than be captured by the Americans?"

He was dark-skinned with a wild explosion of black dreadlocked hair and a face marked by what looked like ceremonial scars. He spoke in English. Yusuf did his best to keep his expression neutral when confronted with the unspoken accusation.

Ozal nearly growled in reply. "But the Americans did not capture him. Yusuf evaded them as the Prophet evaded the assassins of Mecca."

The hot flush that seemed to suffuse Yusuf's entire upper body was fueled by a sense of shame that anyone would compare him with the Prophet. He tried to speak up, but Ozal held up one hand in a peremptory warning. The boy soldier fell silent. His Turkish commander plowed on.

"The emir is not foolish or wasteful with the lives of his followers. He does not ask that they give up their lives needlessly. By surviving the attack on the island and coming safely back to us, Yusuf provides us with information that we would otherwise not have."

Another of the bandit leaders spoke up. Yusuf had to assume these men had some leadership role, given that they were here. This man spoke Arabic, but his complexion was sallow. He looked European, perhaps from the south, where there was much fighting between the faithful and the unbelievers. Yusuf's own Arabic was still very basic, and he was not yet confident in conversation with fluent speakers, although he was able to follow what others said in the language if he concentrated.

"Your emir might dole out the lives of his own men with the parsimony of an old Jew," said the man, "but he spends the lives of our men like a drunken fornicator."

Yusuf expected Ozal to flare in anger at the insulting comparison, but he was wrong. The Turk simply grinned and folded his arms, which emphasized his huge physical stature.

"We are all bleeding, Jukic," he said with an undertone of threat. "Very few of the fedayeen I have sent to fight the Americans have come back. And then only to have their injuries treated before returning to the fray, as Yusuf soon will. Is that not so, boy?"

Realizing he had been drawn into the conversation, Yusuf nodded. It was not a lie. He desperately wanted to get back to the front. He had something to prove to himself, to the emir and Ozal, but most importantly to God. Of course that meant nothing to the bandit leaders sitting in a rough semicircle in front of him. They all regarded him suspiciously.

"So what is it you have brought us here to learn, Ozal?" asked the one called Jukic.

Ozal pulled up a chair and gestured at Yusuf to sit in it.

"My lad here has done something none of us have managed," he said. "He has passed through those parts of the city claimed by the Serbs and the Russians and noted several of the most important depots and barracks as he did so. The emir has decided that in gratitude for your continued support in our fight against the common enemy, we will share this knowledge with you and make no claim on any plunder that may arise from it. The treasure houses of the Slavs, as much our common enemy as the Americans, are yours for the taking." Ozal paused significantly. "When the battle is done."

Yusuf felt his testicles crawl up inside his body as the bandit leaders suddenly turned their attention on him like the edge of a sharpened blade.

"Go on, young one," Ozal said. "Tell our comrades here what you told my men when you made it back to our part of the city."

Yusuf swallowed twice before he was able to speak. The first time his throat clicked dry, a most uncomfortable feeling. The light-skinned bandit named Jukic tossed him a small clear plastic bottle of water that had been sitting by his feet. Yusuf caught it awkwardly but nodded his thanks for the drink. After a few sips, when he thought he could speak without coughing or gagging, he repeated the story he had told Ozal's men when they had intercepted him attempting to cross the park he had seen from his window upstairs.

"I escaped the Americans by jumping into the water when their bombardment was at its fiercest," he explained, resisting the urge to buff up his story so that it shined with a false glimmer of heroism and adventure. "I was frightened. I am sorry…"

Yusuf flicked a nervous look over at Ozal, but the giant merely shrugged and made a circular motion in the air with the end of his cigar. *Go on.*

"There are no fearless men in battle," Ahmet Ozal said. "Only fools and angels go to war without fear, and there are neither in this room."

Two of the bandit leaders smirked, the one called Jukic and the dark-skinned man with the big hair and the facial scars. The third of the pirates, an African like Yusuf, showed no emotion at all. He simply stared at Yusuf like a bird of prey watching a mouse.

"I drifted for a long time," Yusuf said. As he spoke, he grew a little less nervous. The men seemed interested in his story. He took another sip of water from the bottle Jukic had tossed him.

He could not help staring at the remains of the Disappeared and wondering whether they had been aware of their own deaths. Had God struck them down all at once, or did he take them one after the other so that the last to go knew the terror of what was to happen to them? That had been a favorite tactic of Captain Kono. Instantly he regretted that line of thought. It must surely be blasphemous to compare an animal like Kono with Allah himself. Yusuf's heart began to beat painfully hard in his chest, and sweat broke out on his forehead.

Ozal seemed to note his discomfort. "Go on, boy," he said.

"The streets were all flooded down there," Yusuf said. "It was like the river had come up a long time ago and wasn't going down again. I had no weapon and I did not know where I was, but I knew the emir was somewhere near the big park in the middle."

"How did you walk up the street if it was flooded?" Jukic asked.

"Sometimes I swam," he answered. "Sometimes I grabbed on to whatever was floating by. But there are many cars and other vehicles blocking the roads down there, many of them unseen under the water, and I often hurt my legs on them."

"Did you see any men down there?" the African pirate leader asked. "Any Russians or Serbs?"

Yusuf shook his head emphatically.

"Not down there, no. There is nothing alive down there. It's too difficult and dangerous to move around. I got caught once or twice, my legs trapped and held by something under the water that I couldn't even see. I was lucky it was not raining and the water was not flowing quickly or rising, because I would have drowned. I moved very slowly, sometimes swimming from one building to another, swimming in through the windows, moving from one hiding spot to another so I would not be seen. Sometimes I was able to cover more ground by climbing over piles of trucks and containers that the water had jammed up against one another. There were many shipping containers down there, some of them floating around. I was almost crushed by one as I tried to swim through an intersection."

The men all nodded, none of them interrupting him.

"Go on," Ozal said. "Tell them how you came across your first Slav."

Yusuf exhaled slowly, still shaken by the memory.

"I was floating between a line of buildings, and then my feet were dragging on the ground. Not just touching something solid every now and then but dragging on the road surface."

"You were just floating," Jukic said with open disbelief.

"I was holding on to a big plastic bottle," Yusuf explained. "A really big one. A water bottle, big and empty."

The European seemed satisfied with the explanation.

"I was tired. It felt like I had been swimming for hours. I saw a parking garage where the infidel used to keep their cars stacked on top of each other. The water was lapping only halfway up the office of this garage. I started kicking for it, thinking I might have a rest on the second floor, which was dry.

"It was late in the day, not yet night but maybe an hour or so from getting dark. I was so tired, and I think that's what saved me. I was not splashing or making much noise. I swam in through the big roll-up door and over to a staircase that led upstairs. When I reached the steps, I just pulled myself out of the water and lay there. It was only after a couple of minutes I realized I could hear someone upstairs, snoring. I did not know what to do. I couldn't swim out of the building in case they saw me. Unlike me, they were almost certain to be armed. After a short time I decided to crawl up as quietly as I could. I had done this many times before back home when I fought with Captain Kono. He would often send us into the villages when everyone was asleep. I just did what I have always done, moved as quietly as a snake upon a bird's egg.

"I found him in the first room at the top of the stairs. Just one man with a rifle leaned up against the window, probably looking for people like me coming from the river. You will probably find guards like him on each of the streets leading up from the water."

Ozal and Jukic both nodded in approval. The other two were silent and unmoved, but their faces no longer wore any trace of skepticism.

"I stood behind him for some time, listening for any others, but he was alone. There was a desk in the room with many papers impaled on a thin metal spike. It was the only weapon available without searching any further. The rifleman was leaning back in his chair with his head tipped toward the ceiling. I picked up the spike and removed the papers as quietly as I could. Then I killed him with it. Stabbed him in the neck. It seemed to take a long time for him to die and there was a lot of blood, but I kept my hand over his mouth and he was off balance in the chair, so he could not fight back."

He looked across at Ozal to see how he was doing. The Turk nodded in encouragement.

"After that I was much more careful," he said. "I left that building and swam across into another, a few doors up. It was an older building, an office. Many of the infidel had been in there when they were taken. But it seemed nobody else had been there since then. I stayed there until nightfall. About an hour after darkness some men came to look for their friend. They raised an alarm, but they didn't leave anyone behind to take his place when they left. I followed them maybe ten minutes later.

"The next two days I moved very carefully, staying off the streets where I could be seen."

The black man with dreadlocks and scars leaned back in his chair. "And you can tell us where the Slavs have their main stores and depots?"

Yusuf nodded and turned toward his commander.

"Sheikh Ozal's men gave us much instruction in drawing maps of the city before we left Morocco."

Ozal dipped his head in acknowledgment and agreement.

"We had many maps of the island to practice with," Yusuf said. "They made us draw some parts of the city again and again. We practiced drawing many blocks around areas where we expected to fight. We practiced drawing maps for members of other *saif* as if we were directing them during a battle. We do not have the Americans' technology, their spy planes without pilots, the helicopters and satellites. But we could make do because of the training we received from Ahmet Ozal."

He bowed formally toward his commander. The giant Turk smiled indulgently.

"You learned well, boy. I could only wish that all of my pupils learned their lessons as well as you." He produced a series of papers from a pocket in his shirt, unfolding them and handing them out to each of the bandit leaders in turn.

"Yusuf Mohammed was very careful not to be seen as he made his way back to us," Ozal said. "As he moved through the Slavs' territory and came to understand what he was seeing, he made maps just as he had been taught. These are copies of those maps my men developed from his field sketches. They reveal the location of at least four warehouses, three of them Russian, one of them Serbian. They are clearinghouses for their salvage operations here in Manhattan and so are always well stocked with the finest loot. They are yours for the taking... after we have driven the Americans from the city. When that is done, you have the promise of my emir that we will help you take this treasure but will claim none of it ourselves."

The bandit leaders exchanged a quiet look. The African spoke for them all.

"This will mean war with the Slavs as well."

Ozal showed him a pair of open palms.

"Yes, it will," he said. "But once we have driven off the Americans together, the Slavs will be easy pickings for us. They may not even put up a fight. We shall see. But whatever shall happen, you have the promise of the emir that for your help in defeating the Americans that part of the city and all its plunder shall be ceded to you in equal measure. What say you? Do you still have the stomach for this fight?"

Yusuf Mohammed sat very still. He had known as he stole up from the river toward the camp of his emir that any information he could gather would go to his credit when it came time to plead for a second chance. Now, sitting here in this room surrounded by the ghosts of hundreds of Americans, in a city haunted by millions of others, he was struck by just how forgiving Allah could be.

He had thought himself borne along on a current carrying him to ignominy and doom, yet it was all part of God's design. He had been meant to survive the American assault. He had been meant to wash up in the part of the city controlled by the Slavs who had refused to join in the holy campaign against the Americans. And he had been meant by God to walk a path that delivered him here into this room to cement an alliance with these men who were obviously vital to the emir's plans.

All he needed to make this day perfect was a gun in his hand and directions back to the front line.

35

KANSAS CITY, MISSOURI

President James Kipper felt a surge of pride at the sight of Kansas City Power and Light's restored Number Five generator pumping sanitized white smoke into a clear blue sky. Standing in the parking lot of the Hawthorne plant, on the banks of the Missouri River northeast of the city's still-deserted urban core, he could indulge himself in the guilty pleasure of forgetting for a moment about Mad Jack Blackstone and the horrors of New York, along with the frustrations of politics and the trouble he was in with his wife. For just a few moments, standing next to his oldest friend, Barney Tench, listening to the hum of the transmission lines and the excited burbling of his entourage, he could wallow in a giddy glee rarely experienced since the Wave.

Creation.

The simple joy of creation had been the engine of his life for as long as he could remember. His earliest memories were of building things. Not just wooden blocks and LEGO towers but giant, messy backyard earthworks and dams and pretend farms and shoebox factories and tree houses and secret dens. As a child he had always gone that one step further, driven by what he now recognized as an innate desire to reach out and shape the world. My poor mother, he thought fondly. Oh, how her garden beds had suffered.

"So, boss," Tench said, gesturing at the massive Hawthorne Unit Five smokestack. "What do you think?"

"Impressive," Kipper replied. "You know how much I love a big honkin' power plant, Barn. What's our status?"

Barney gestured at the drab tan structure of the main plant building with a jelly doughnut swiped earlier from the catering table. "With Unit Five fully manned and operational," he said, "we'll have close to four hundred megawatts of juice. Plenty for now."

"Cool. More than enough," Kipper agreed. "What about the gas turbine facility on the east side?"

Barney looked over his notes. "Ah… from what I understand, I think that's meant for the summer months when everyone is, er… *was* running their AC. It is in pretty good shape and could provide backup power on demand. We're still sorting it out, but the coal generator was easier since she's so much like the ones we got back in Seattle."

"Relatively new, isn't it?" Kipper asked.

"Yeah. Umm, perhaps I shouldn't mention this, boss, but this plant has a history of bad luck: a fire back in the nineties that knocked out the transmission lines and an explosion which destroyed the original Unit Number Five," Barney said.

Kipper nodded. "That explains why everything is new, then. What about Units One through Four? Will you be bringing those back online?"

Tench shook his head. "Naw, there's no need for them. Besides, they'd been idled for decades before the Wave. What I really need are more linemen to restore the grid."

"I thought we had an on-site training program," Kipper said.

Tench nodded. "We do. Hell, there's a community college not more than a mile away with everything you need for a program.

Classes were in session when the Wave hit, so we were literally able to pick up the program and restart it in place with new apprentice linemen. Thing is, those folks won't be ready for at least a year. In the meantime, the work is waiting. Can we get any more warm bodies from Seattle City Light?"

"Doubt it," Kipper said. "In fact, they're screaming to get their people back as soon as possible. Got their own repair issues to deal with, and they're shorthanded, too."

Loud metallic squeals and screeches heralded the approach of a train backing into the power plant. Bumping down the tracks past the reinforced checkpoint, the cars were loaded with coal bound for the generating facility. Coal was still the most plentiful means of energy production within the United States, and early in his term Kipper had rammed a bill through Congress providing a fast track to citizenship for any suitably qualified migrant who would work the mines in Wyoming. Watching the three big ATS diesel locomotives slowly hauling the massive line of hoppers into the plant, he recalled the arm-twisting and distasteful outright pork barreling Jed had used to sideline the Greens' bloc vote on that one. They didn't oppose the immigration program per se, of course, but they wanted those immigrants to focus on restoring large swaths of the country to a prehuman state. Forget about power generation or anything resembling a twentieth-century standard of living.

Kipper shook his head. He loved the wilderness as much as any man. More than most, probably. Hell, the first thing he was going to do when he finally escaped from executive office was take himself off into the mountains for a week on his own. Barbara permitting, of course. But to hear the Greens tell of it, he was doing more damage just bringing this one plant back on line than all the firestorms of the post-Wave period.

He sighed. Couldn't they see what a beautiful fucking thing this was? How much better it was going to make life for the people stuck out here in the boonies? And how KC itself was so important to resettling the interior and reaching out to the East? But of course thinking about the East only led to thinking about New York, and for now Kip was determined not to harsh his own mellow, borrowing a phrase his daughter had brought home from school the other day. *Seattle and its fucking hippies,* he thought.

As Barney burbled on about the logistics of this small corner of his empire—"The maintenance facility down on Front Street is fairly well stocked, and the city's P&L did a pretty good job of archiving their work. Only real problem's been figuring out the quirks of Unit Five. Once we get that hashed out, we can probably move on to restore Iatan in Weston, Missouri"—Kipper gently took him by the elbow and steered his reconstruction tsar back toward the catering table. The presidential entourage, about fifty people in all, including his Secret Service detail, all turned and moved with him like a flock of birds in slow motion.

For a change, the heavier armored fighting vehicles of the Secret Service response teams were absent and his own detail was dressed in jeans and denim shirts. Only their sunglasses and earpieces marked them out as bodyguards. Besides the black Suburbans and half a dozen Reconstruction Department pickups, the car park was full of trucks and support vehicles sporting the logo of Cesky Enterprises, one of the rising stars of the post-Wave economy. Pakistani and Filipino migrants worked the catering line, doling out something that was supposed to be Kansas City barbecue among other local treats. Kipper took one discreet whiff of the beef ribs and decided that though they might have been made in the city this morning, it definitely wasn't KC barbecue as he understood it. It smelled like curry. The dark-skinned, bright-eyed young woman wielding the tongs flashed a mouthful of blindingly white teeth at him.

"The barbecue has some extra spice today, Mister President."

"I'm sure it does, ma'am," Kipper said. "But I haven't even had my breakfast doughnut yet. Do you know if Mister Tench has left any for the rest of us?"

She pointed toward the far end of the trestle table, where Kipper could see Jed guarding a precious stash of leftover crullers, muffins, and glazed twists. His chief of staff fixed the recon boss with a forbidding glare.

"I think my wife's been talking to him," Barney stage-whispered to the young serving girl.

"She needed to," said the president, backhanding Tench in the gut. "So how many hours of power a day does the city get?"

Tench took a guilty bite of his glazed doughnut and sucked down a mouthful of rare and precious coffee before answering. The doughnuts, Kip had discovered, came courtesy of a local franchise owner for LaMar's who had been out of the country when the Wave hit. The coffee, he had no idea, but given how difficult it was to get, he'd resolved to limit himself to just one cup so that the plant workers might enjoy the leftovers. Barney wiped a small dollop of jam from his mouth before continuing.

"Right now we get close to eighteen hours a day. More if the trains are consistent. Sometimes that's not the case, though, because you're dealing with train crews from India who are used to doing things their own way. They're efficient and hardworking, but they're, well…"

"They just have their own way," Kipper finished for Barney. "I know. You take the help you can get. And India's been a godsend for us."

"True enough," Tench said. "There is one problem, though, boss. A big one."

Kipper waited as his good mood threatened to curdle and sour.

"No one's been paid for three weeks. Some folks, I just found out, got over four months of back pay on the books. Granted, many of them are refugees who are happy to have three hots and a cot, but it's not sustainable," Tench said.

Kipper sighed. Money. You had to spend money in order to make money. And to spend it, you had to have it or borrow it. He was the first to admit that finances were not his strong suit, but he didn't need a Nobel Prize in economics to understand that the implosion of the world economy, the total collapse of the banking and financial markets, had real-world effects down on the ground, in this very parking lot.

The United States was broke. Living off the stored capital represented by its empty cities and silent infrastructure, it could not pay its debts, had refused to, indeed, for the last three years, in complete contradiction to Alexander Hamilton's advice to the Founding Fathers. An act of treachery according to some of its creditors that could even have led to armed conflict in one case, had China not fallen into civil war. His fine temper of the morning spoiled, Kipper tried to recapture some of the optimism by turning back to the plant and basking in the view again. He tried to convince himself they would get out of this with the same hard work and native ingenuity that the men and women who were reclaiming this city had shown. This wasn't the first time America had been laid low. The nation had been born virtually bankrupt, yet it had managed to climb to the top of the heap in less than two centuries. If they played their hand right, they could recover from this mess as well.

They had to.

"Barney." Kipper put his hand on his friend's meaty shoulder and looked him in the eye. "Your people will get paid. You have my word on it."

But he had no idea how.

An hour later the convoy of Secret Service black Chevy Suburbans made its way across the Chouteau Bridge over the Missouri River. A dredge was visible to Kipper's left, docked alongside Harrah's Casino. Construction equipment and workers toiled to restore the Muddy Mo's traffic channel to navigable status. Trains rumbled along the rail line on the north side of the casino complex. Laden with salvage, food, and cattle, they were bound for a central processing point in the river bottoms on the eastern side of North Kansas City, which had ample warehouse and light manufacturing space to accommodate them. A makeshift train station for passenger traffic had been established at the casino to augment the main facility at Union Station on the other side of the Missouri River. New workers, most of them participants in the Federal Homestead and Resettlement Program, had brought their families in search of a fresh start.

To Kipper's right, they passed a complex of buildings and a BP gas station surrounded by an earthen berm topped with sandbags. A couple of army Humvees rolled out and headed south toward the Kansas City Southern rail yard.

"Local troops, militia," Culver said, taking note of the small fort.

"None of us are local anymore," Kipper said. "What are they doing here?"

"Securing the railroad, I suspect," Culver replied. "They patrol as far as Fort Leavenworth. From there an army detachment takes over."

Kipper watched the storm clouds building on the horizon, pleased with the progress.

"We're getting there, Jed," he said.

"Are we?" Culver asked. The chief of staff had his old briefcase open and was poring over piles of documents. "If we pay Cesky's men at Hawthorne, then other workers elsewhere will demand the same. Budget's a zero-sum game at the moment, Mister President. We can't borrow money; there is no one who will lend us anything near the amount we need. We can't just print it. Economy's like fucking ground zero, if you'll excuse my French."

"I promised them they'd get paid," Kipper said. "We have to make it happen. Not just here. Everywhere. That bastard down in Fort Hood doesn't seem to have any trouble raising money and spending it. He's even using our currency, the sorry son of a bitch.

And he's getting loans! Goddamn Saudis advanced him that big one just last week."

Jed looked up from his paperwork.

"He's selling off assets to fund consumption, Mister President. Remember how we talked about him overreaching? This is just an example of it."

"They're our assets, Jed."

"Possession is nine-tenths of the game, sir. And we do not have the means to enforce our rightful possession yet. Now, as to Tench's problem, you know there is significant opposition to the appropriations for restoring coal-fired power plants," Culver said. "The Greens are united with the Northwest Democrats on this one. They'll keep the money for Hawthorne tied up for months if they have to."

"Can't we find a way around that?" Kipper asked.

Culver nodded. "Sure. Sandra Harvey wants one of her Borg drones appointed secretary of energy. Greens also want more of their people over at EPA. And they want EPA fully empowered. Give 'em that and you'll get your money. But then either your new crazier EPA or your new crazier energy sec will shut down that shiny new power plant we christened this morning and insist on installing thousands of solar cells in its place. Should only take about eighteen years to replace the lost wattage. And a coupla billion new dollars. But they'll want to sell off another aircraft carrier soon, anyway, so maybe the folding stuff won't be a problem."

Jed's smirk was almost purely evil.

Kipper felt a Godzilla headache coming on, sharpening itself within the dark recesses of his mind. He had a war to fight against men who'd carve up and eat the old bones of his country, which he was trying to rebuild and rehabilitate. Sandra Harvey's Greens and their allies on the far left of the Dems, of which he'd once been a member, should be on his side. Some of Harvey's people in particular had been instrumental in the revolution that had swept

Blackstone out of Seattle without firing a shot. Yet they stood in the way of every effort to repopulate the Wave-affected United States. More than a few of them even argued that those areas should be allowed to go fallow and wild.

Forever wild, their motto went. Forever free.

The fucking wing nut faction of the Republicans, in contrast, wanted everyone above the age of sixteen years drafted, school prayer made mandatory, *Roe v. Wade* overturned, every migrant expelled, the borders closed, wars launched on half a dozen problematic foreign powers, and a settlement with Blackstone that would probably see the crazy fucker in the Western White House before Kip and Barb had finished packing their suitcases.

And Jed wondered why he was reluctant to commit to a second term in 2009.

The convoy passed under the Highway 210 overpass and climbed the ramp back toward North Kansas City. As they moved west toward the town, it was possible to see the mass of humanity disembarking from the salvaged Amtrak passenger cars. Faces looked up at the convoy of black Suburbans, most of them dark, some covered in bandages and scars. Kipper expected Jed to speak up and harass him once again about the numbers of refugees they were taking from the atomic ruins of India, but for a mercy his chief of staff remained silent, allowing Kipper to retreat back into his own thoughts.

Watching the new arrivals spill from the passenger cars, blinking in the unexpectedly fierce light, looking nervous but hopeful too, Kip was assailed by a raft of questions. How do you deal fairly with immigrants from a culture so significantly different from your own? How do you provide jobs for them while ensuring that your own population is also employed? How do you pay the bills? What solutions are fair and equitable as opposed to being merely effective or, worse, in the case of Blackstone, genuinely harmful?

We need these people, Kipper told himself. We need them to buy into America, our America, or we're finished.

36

BERLIN

"You had better put this on," Mirsaad suggested, holding out a blue and gold head scarf as they walked through the car park underneath his apartment building. "No sane woman would go uncovered in Neukölln these days."

"What, not even Angela Merkel?" Caitlin teased.

"It is very unlikely she would set foot there," he said. "Such an action would be considered inflammatory."

Caitlin dutifully tied the scarf around her head, thinking that at the very least, with a pair of dark sunglasses, it would provide a basic measure of camouflage should Baumer have anybody on the lookout for her. Plus, of course, Mirsaad was correct. Going into a shariatown uncovered was just asking for trouble. Begging for it, in fact.

"We should take my car," he insisted, regarding her black BMW with open envy.

"I won't argue with that," Caitlin said. "We don't need to attract attention."

She had what she needed from the vehicle already, having kitted up in the airport hotel back at Tempelhof an hour earlier. She wore a long black leather coat that was loosely belted to conceal the twin Russian machine guns nestled at her flanks in Gerty's bespoke combat harness. Her pistol she wore at the hip, with extra clips for all three guns secreted throughout her coat, adding noticeably to the weight. For good measure she wore a spring-loaded blade on her right wrist, and the packet of cigarettes in her left breast pocket was half of a powerful binary explosive. The other half was sealed inside a plastic disposable lighter in her right breast pocket.

They climbed into Mirsaad's vehicle, a rusted, beaten-down old Lada with the logo of his community radio station stenciled amateurishly on both front doors. The car was full of children's toys and smelled of boiled cabbage. He smiled apologetically.

"I am afraid it is not a luxury vehicle, Caitlin," he said. "But the station pays for it and allows me to take it home for family use."

She waved away his apology.

"From what I've seen since getting in last night, you're lucky to have it, Sadie. Main thing is, it's not going to attract attention." She paused. "So you're cool with this?" she asked as they drove out onto the street. "Taking me out as your assistant?"

She mimed invisible quotation marks around the last two words.

"It is nothing," Mirsaad said. "I have been meaning to do a series of reports out of Neukölln anyway. It is one of the local areas where sharia law will be accepted for the resolution of civil cases, you see. If this goes through the parliament, of course. The reality on the ground, as you Americans say, is that German law already holds no sway within the boundaries of the town."

They pulled out onto Emser Strasse and into a cloudy gray morning.

"And do you have an opinion about that, Sadie?"

"It is rank foolishness," he said without hesitation. "People do not understand the nature of law, Caitlin. They seem to think of it as an expression of good manners. It is not. The law is codified violence, a balance of power struck in the words of a statute. To cede that power to a rival, as the German state is doing, is to invite a contest for true power at some point in the future. It is inevitable."

"So you're agin it, then?" She grinned.

"I have daughters," he said seriously—the full extent of his explanation. He hunkered over the wheel to concentrate on his driving. Caitlin recognized the type. Bret was like that, too. She wondered how he was getting on and wished she could call him and the baby.

Neukölln was the next suburb over, little more than five streets away, but in that distance the assassin felt herself pass from the modern world into something altogether archaic and oppressive. Mirsaad motored through a former green belt—now a gray and squalid wasteland—just before entering the suburb. The strip of rubbish-strewn land, pockmarked with mysterious sunken pits, mounds of gravel, and the leafless specters of dead trees, marked a visible discontinuity. Back in Mirsaad's neighborhood she had felt herself in a depressed environment characterized by empty shops, sullen unemployed youths, and occasional bright spots such as Ahmet's coffeehouse. She had recognized the atmosphere of an economically damaged lower-class area and the low-grade hostility that focused on her as she moved through it, so obviously privileged and wealthy in her luxurious SUV.

As they passed into the streets of the shariatown, however, all that changed. The footpaths were thronged with many more people, and most of the streetfront shops were open, although not in their original guise. A thriving souk had grown up here, with the locals taking over previous businesses and establishing small but vibrant markets of their own. Caitlin examined them closely. A former restaurant had been converted into a clothing store, with racks of jeans and windbreakers standing where diners once had sat at their tables. Next to it a former liquor store now sold electronics, and a onetime video rental outlet two doors down played host to a smokers' *maqhah,* a café offering its patrons a selection of tobaccos and possibly more. Dozens of men sat drinking short cups of coffee and drawing on ornate glass hookahs in the weak morning sun. There were women on the streets, many of them, but they were almost all covered head to toe, some in burkas, some in long shapeless olive drab or gray coats with scarf and veil. And they invariably traveled in groups, always with a male escort. Here and there she did notice a few younger women who wore only a head scarf, like hers. But they, too, had male escorts, and their clothing was still modest, revealing nothing of their bodies' true shapes.

"Sadie," she asked, "what chance if we hopped out and had a look through this lively Persian bazaar that I'd find most of this stuff was sourced from the United States?"

Mirsaad grinned diffidently.

"A very good chance indeed, Caitlin. I shop down here a lot. Usually without Laryssa because she does not approve, but it is very cheap and we do not have much money."

"I'm not judging you, buddy. You got kids to look after, and I'm guessing the local ALDI is looking more like some gruesome old East German people's *Kommisariat* these days. I'm just curious. How much of this stuff has been looted from the United States, do you think?"

"Let us see," he said, taking her by surprise as he suddenly pulled over. In spite of the obvious vitality of the local economy, there were still few cars here and he had no trouble getting a curbside parking spot. Before they hopped out, the Jordanian turned to her and spoke quickly and quietly.

"It would be best if you let me do all the talking. At least here. Your accent…" He shrugged helplessly.

"Don't sweat it. You're the man. I believe that's how it's done here."

"It is." He smiled. "Let us go, then."

They alighted, and immediately her fair complexion and a few loops of blond hair peeking out from under her scarf drew attention. But Caitlin had worked for many years in both the Middle East and the various diasporas within Europe. She withdrew her stage presence, dropped her head a little, and fell in behind Mirsaad as he stepped onto the footpath and walked over to the clothing stalls she had seen. Immediately an aged Turkish shopkeeper swooped down on him, offering the best "morning price" and bragging about the quality of his wares. When he asked about the infidel woman, Mirsaad laughed his query off and explained that she was a refugee on a government work-for-welfare program with his radio station. She had no money. At that point the wizened old Turk grinned hugely, exposing a mouth full of missing teeth, and immediately lost interest in her.

As the two men rattled away in Arabic, Caitlin stuck close but took in as much detail as she could. The racks were heavy with U.S. designer labels. Jeans from DKNY, Calvin Klein, and American Apparel, sweats and shirts by Hilfiger and Kors. There were a few European brands in there, too, but not many, and they looked like cheap knockoffs judging by the stray threads and the way the fabric bunched up around the stitching. While Mirsaad and the shopkeeper chattered at each other, she took her time examining some of the items more closely. On a pair of 501s she found a security tag from Old Navy. And three brightly colored Nautica windbreakers still sported price stickers from a Macy's on Fulton Street in Brooklyn.

Looking bored but submissive, she let her eyes wander over the electrical goods piled up on makeshift display tables next door. She could see a lot of Japanese brand names for sale at insanely low prices but imagined she would find they'd all been sourced from the United States if she ventured over and checked them out, looted from somewhere on the East Coast. It meant nothing to her, but she logged the information away. Somebody back at Echelon would want to make a file note. The Brits were absolute maniacs for file notes.

Mirsaad reappeared, looking sheepish and holding up a plain white shirt.

"I had to buy it," he said.

Caitlin said nothing but smiled at him with her eyes.

"Would you like to look around some more?" he asked.

"Maybe the electronics place," she said quietly, staying in character. "I would like to get a small radio... for my dorm."

A few minutes browsing the stolen TVs and microwaves farther down the footpath confirmed her suspicion. The Neukölln markets were so healthy partly because the vendors were getting their stock for free or at least for the cost of looting and transporting it back to Europe, which until last week had been negligible. It would be interesting to come back here in a month and see whether Kipper's Manhattan offensive had made any difference or whether the sellers would be able to find new suppliers. The fighting in New York was intense, but there remained thousands of miles of unguarded Atlantic coastline and hundreds of towns and cities open to pillage.

When they got back into the car and had safely pulled away from the curb, Caitlin took out her wallet and passed fifty euros to Mirsaad.

"I'm sorry you had to buy his stolen rags," she said. "I can pay for them. You did good."

He looked like he was about to object, but she insisted.

"No, Mirsaad. You have kids to feed, and there will be more expense involved before we're done today. Put it on my tab. I'm working, and I'll be reimbursed. You won't."

"Okay, then," he said, obviously grateful. "I did beat him down on the shirt, though. Not as well as Laryssa would, could she bring herself to come in here, but still..."

"Take the fifty, anyway," Caitlin said. "Like I said. Expenses. Now let's have a look around the manor, as my paymasters would say."

* * *

Neukölln was an Enclosure in all but name, with one crucial distinction: The residents had chosen to shut themselves off from the outside rather than being internally exiled as was the case back in London. That helped explain why the township hummed with an energy that was singularly missing from any of the Enclosures. The locals were exercising their power rather than finding themselves subject to someone else's. But there was more to it. Driving around, marveling at the vigor and intensity of the street life—even if it did seem to her as medieval and bigoted—Caitlin had to conclude that the engine of the local economy was fired by a primitive but effective form of reverse colonialism. They were living off riches looted from another country, in this case, the United States and maybe Canada. Vancouver had been no more successful at securing and resettling its eastern provinces than Seattle had.

Mirsaad drove her around for half an hour to get a feel for the place, transiting the center of the village three times. There she found markets that put to shame the small stallholders they had first encountered. A Kaiser's Supermarket had become a prayer room around which hundreds of people gathered, chatting in the midmorning warmth. Restaurants still wearing the livery of their previous incarnations now served as "Red Sea" grocers, halal butcheries, and in one case a pet store. New proprietors had painted over the signage of a former F.W. Woolworth building on Harmannstrasse, whitewashing the old logo and replacing it with a hand-lettered announcement that it was now operating as the Dahabshiil funds transfer bureau for Berlin. From the brief drive-by it also seemed to be trading as a furniture depot and carpet warehouse. Everywhere they went she saw trestle tables piled high with clothes, electronics, and homewares, all of them surrounded by eager customers dickering furiously with the stall owners. The longer she observed, the more convinced she became that she would have to report back to Echelon in much greater detail than that required for a simple file note. There was real wealth here—stolen to be sure, but it was merely the tip of things. All this bustle and activity—so alien to Europe now—spoke to deeper currents of power. Just organizing the logistics train to deliver all this pillage across the Atlantic and through the German border controls—and who knew, maybe even the French or half a dozen other countries, too—all that implied a vast undertaking. Not necessarily by a single monolithic organization but certainly by an unknown number of networks operating in concert sometimes, perhaps in competition or even conflict at others.

It was not Caitlin's area of expertise and certainly not within her mission brief. There would doubtless be other agencies monitoring all this. But her interest was piqued simply because al Banna's trail did lead here, and she found it hard to believe that Baumer would remain disconnected and aloof from all this activity. If nothing else, the movement of goods and people and the wealth it generated could all be exploited for his own ends, whatever they might be. As they drove past a busy Afro-Net Café on Werbellinstrasse, she decided it was time to find out.

"Okay, Sadie, let's head on over to Rollberg. We can get something to eat, and I want to keep an eye on the little council office over there."

"Can you tell me why?" he asked.

"Better if I don't. I'm looking for somebody. Someone connected to the man I need to find."

"The one who sent the criminals to your farm?"

"Not to the farm. They tried to grab Bret and Monique a few miles away, but yeah, that guy."

The Jordanian shrugged. "It is almost time to eat, and I can write up my notes from our tour this morning. This is a fascinating place, do you agree? So full of life and yet darkness, too."

He swung the Lada left into the cross street that would take them through to Rollbergstrasse. A group of youths were lounging on the corner, one of them was wearing a T-shirt emblazoned with the Kurdish flag. A brave choice, she thought, given the large Turkish majority living here. It was also one of the few gatherings of young men she had seen anywhere that morning. Neukölln was a town of women, children, and older men, some wizened like the Turk from whom Mirsaad had bought his shirt, and many others middle-aged and well fed, all deporting themselves with that peculiarly arrogant gait of males who think themselves in charge of their world.

There were comparatively few young men, though.

You tended to miss that, your gaze drawn by the packs of black crows, as Caitlin thought of the women in burkas.

It was as if the young men of Neukölln had all gone off to war.

She allowed Mirsaad to order her lunch, a falafel roll and a glass of black, unsweetened tea. Not that she would have been allowed to order on her own, anyway. She distinctly heard the gray-haired, one-eyed old coot behind the counter ask Mirsaad whether she was unclean. A younger, less experienced operator than Caitlin might have bristled, but that would have betrayed her language skills and she preferred to move about in seeming ignorance of the conversations around her. Also, there was no point investing emotionally in someone's stupidity and backwardness. It was simply data to her, something to be filed away, possibly for future reference, possibly not.

She sat demurely at the small round table under the shade of an awning, watching the small office building across the street. A large sticker, the emblem of the Berlin city council, stood out on the boarded-up front windows. She assumed they had been smashed so often that the glass had been replaced with plywood. A heavy metal grille protected the front door, which opened every few minutes to let visitors in or out.

Mirsaad returned with the rolls before doubling back to fetch their tea.

"This is good?" he asked.

She nodded as the piped in music increased in volume.

Mirsaad leaned forward and spoke in a soft voice, in English. "We can speak freely here if we are careful. I know the owner. He is married to my cousin."

"That old guy?"

She nodded toward the one-eyed troll behind the counter before taking a bite of the roll. It dripped with chili and yogurt sauce, and she enjoyed the pleasing crunch of the falafels and their warm soft filling. The tabouleh, as always, reminded her of shredded weeds.

Mirsaad's mouth sketched a quick grin. "No. He is just filling in. He speaks no English."

She decided to take that information with a pinch of salt. After all, nobody but Mirsaad knew that she spoke Arabic.

Keeping one eye on the small council office across the street, she took a sip of tea and adjusted her posture to stop one of the machine guns from digging uncomfortably into her breast.

"What sort of story are you going to file?" she asked.

The reporter finished chewing a mouthful of food before answering. "Not one that will make me popular with the good burghers of Neukölln," he said quietly. "The shariatown vote is very big news here. Very divisive. It is being used by the right to whip up anti-immigrant feeling. It is being used in the Muslim neighborhoods to further entrench separatism. Meanwhile, guilt-ridden liberal Germans torture themselves over how much respect they must show other cultures because of 'past mistakes.' "

"The best lack all conviction while the worst are full passionate intensity, eh?"

"Something like that, yes," he answered once he understood what she meant.

"And your story?"

"Well, I must be balanced, of course." His cheeky expression implied that he would be nothing of the sort. He leaned forward and spoke carefully. "But I see nothing good coming of this, Caitlin.

Back in 2001, well before the Disappearance, the Islamic Federation of Berlin, after twenty years of trying, finally succeeded in getting the city to allow purely Islamic schools to take in Muslim children. The city no longer controls those lessons, which are more often in Arabic than German and usually are held behind closed doors, especially for girls. Not long after that, the *hijab* became much more common. Girls began leaving school as early as possible. Groups of male students formed associations that now lobby for their schools to become fully fledged madrassas. It is a disaster for these children, and for Germany…"

He paused and glanced around the small café.

"I see this vote on localized sharia law for civil cases as being the same but worse, infinitely worse. Does that make sense?"

"Yes." She nodded while keeping one eye on the building across the street.

"Let me tell you a story," he said, warming to his theme so much that he forgot his lunch. "When I first arrived in Germany in 1992, I came as a trainee for Deutsche Welle Radio. I was hired partly because of my background, partly because of my language skills. I speak five languages; did you know that?"

"Bret did say something about it once," she said, nodding. Two black crows and their male shadow disappeared behind the iron grilled door.

"The flight I caught from Amman stopped in Turkey, and many migrants got on. Families of guest workers. One of them sat next to me. He looked like a goat farmer, because he *was* a goat farmer from somewhere outside Nevsehir. He had never flown before. Probably never been in powered transport at all. I had to do his seat belt for him. Show him how the tray table worked. Show him to the toilet. I don't know what he did in there, but I heard the crew complaining bitterly about it later. He sat next to me in his old sandals and skullcap, working his prayer beads. He was inches away but unreachable. He lived in another time. Another world, Caitlin.

If he is alive, he lives there still, despite having been in Germany for over fifteen years. His body might dwell here, but his mind and soul remain firmly in the past. A past he considers superior in every way to the reality of modern life."

She sipped at her tea and regarded him anew. The lines in his body were all tense, and his jawline bulged as he ground his teeth. She tracked the old shop clerk with her peripheral vision as well as two tables of men who had just sat down on the other side of the café. But the reporter had kept his voice down, and the music was loud enough to have covered his little monologue.

"You ever thought of moving to the States?" she asked. "They're looking for settlers. Five languages would give you a head start on your hundred points to qualify. Your choice of career could have been better, though. That old goat farmer would probably be thought of as more useful than a reporter."

"That old goat farmer would be the death of America," he replied earnestly before suddenly loosening up.

"But yes, I have thought about it. Laryssa and I have even discussed it. She is a qualified nurse. She would easily find a placement there. But the fighting in New York. And this fascist Blackstone. I fear we would be jumping from the frying pan into the fire."

"Could be," she conceded.

The door across the street opened again, and a woman stepped out. She was instantly notable for two reasons. She was dark-skinned but wore modern clothes, and she was alone. No man escorted her.

She stepped out into the street enveloped by a fierce aura, as though challenging anyone to confront her.

Caitlin doubted that anybody would.

Only a fool would cross Fabia Shah.

The mother of al Banna.

37

KANSAS CITY, MISSOURI

If opening the Hawthorne Power Plant was the highlight of Kipper's day trip, visiting the restored North Kansas City Hospital was undoubtedly the lowest point. An unforeseen late-afternoon shower lashed the windows as Kipper made his way down hallways mopped and polished to a high sheen in his honor. The staff, many of them recent migrants and refugees, dipped their heads, watching him in awe as he proceeded to the intensive care unit with Culver in tow, a clutch of colonels and generals flanking him, and white-coated medical staff hurrying to stay in touch.

A doctor waited outside the ward he was to visit. The thirty-something man in green surgical scrubs looked careworn and tired.

"Welcome to North Kansas City Hospital, Mister President," the doctor said, extending his hand. "I'm Alex Leong, director of the facility. Sorry about my appearance. I've just come out of surgery a few minutes ago."

"I hope it went well," said Kipper.

"We'll see," Leong answered as they shook hands. Kip marveled at the man's thin, long fingers, which returned his grip with a truly surprising amount of strength.

"How are the troops?" he asked somberly.

"We've received two hundred and nineteen wounded from New York over the last forty-eight hours," Leong said. "We're finding that their body armor protects them from most fatal wounds to the center mass. Unfortunately, we have seen a spike in traumatic amputations, in some cases multiple amputations."

Kipper could feel his face twisting with distaste and consciously forced himself to frown, trying to mask his distress at Leong's report. He'd learned it freaked people out if he looked like he was getting upset. "Do you have everything you need?" he asked, knowing that Jed Culver would be grinding his teeth at any more ad hoc resource commitments.

The doctor shook his head. "The army is giving us everything they can spare, but some of the supplies are past their expiration date. Bandages and basic needs are holding out well enough, but we are having trouble with pharmaceuticals and other perishable items."

"Jed?"

"Yes," Culver sighed. "Top of my to-do list, sir. I'll contact Senator Clavell and see what can be done."

"There is one other problem," Leong said, gesturing for the presidential party to follow him onto the ward.

"Tell me, Doctor."

"We're desperately short of blood," Leong said.

"What type?" Kipper asked.

"All types."

Kipper turned to his army liaison. "Colonel Ralls, can you get me a hundred people up to the hospital ASAP? I saw a settler train come in this morning. They'd all have their health checks in order. I'm asking for volunteers, so you tell them why we need them. Tell them *I* need them. Can you handle that?"

Ralls nodded. "I'm on it, Mister President," and retreated down the hallway.

"While we're waiting for the colonel to find some donors," Kipper said, rolling up his sleeves, "perhaps we can help."

Culver checked his PDA. "Ah, Mister President, we do have a tight schedule."

Kipper turned and punched Culver on the shoulder. "Jed, there's all the time in the world for doing the right thing. Come on, what are you frightened of, needles or something?"

"No, sir. I'm just afeared for my reputation. If Congress finds out I give blood instead of drinking it, they'll never take me seriously again."

Kipper turned back to the surgeon. "Is that okay, Doctor Leong? I can assure you I don't have cooties. What about the rest of you ladies and gentlemen? Are we cootie clear?"

The military officers seemed a little taken aback, but Leong pronounced himself more than willing to take blood with a little brass in it.

"My patients will love that." He smiled.

From the tired, twitchy look of the gesture, it had been a long time since the doctor had last cracked a grin.

Much to Jed's obvious annoyance, the donation routine took an unscheduled half hour, which Kipper made up by announcing that they'd eat lunch on the move. He was feeling a little nauseous and dizzy after giving blood and didn't much feel like a sit-down meal, anyway. A cookie and a glass of juice were about all he could handle. While a couple of orderlies were off trying to rustle up sandwiches for everyone else, Jed suddenly appeared at his side, brandishing a cell phone like a time bomb.

"For you, Mister President. It's Colonel Kinninmore. From New York."

"I'm sorry, Doc, I really have to take this call in private," Kipper said, apologizing to Leong. "Is there somewhere...?"

"Of course," the physician replied. "A room along here became vacant just an hour ago, I'm afraid."

"Thank you," he said quietly.

A few moments later he and Jed were secure behind the door of a suite containing a bed that recently had been stripped of its linen and presumably its occupant.

"Put him on speaker," Kip said.

"Mister President, are you sure about…"

"Go on, Jed. I doubt anyone could hear us, and even if they could, this hospital is full of soldiers. They know better than you or I what's happening in New York. Go on."

The chief of staff did as he was told but dropped the volume a few notches.

"Colonel Kinninmore, it's Jed Culver. I have the president with me. On speakerphone. We're not in a secure location, I'm afraid."

"Don't worry about that," Kipper said, raising his voice to be heard over Jed. "Just tell us what you've got, Colonel."

Kinninmore's voice sounded tinny and flat, an artifact of the encrypting system Kipper had made redundant by insisting on using the speakerphone.

"Mister President, we haven't obtained any hard human data yet—"

"You mean you haven't captured any of our mystery guys, is that right, Colonel?" Jed asked.

"No, sir," came the answer, crackling through the airwaves. "We've come close once or twice. There are definitely a group of hostiles active in New York, coordinating a disparate group of independent actors, but whenever we've come close to capturing one of them, they've killed themselves."

"What?" Kip said.

"They killed themselves, Mister President. Sometimes self-detonated a bomb belt–type device, sometimes a grenade. We've taken some significant casualties because of that. Once or twice, when that option wasn't available, they simply put a bullet in their own heads. One guy cut his own throat out. Hard core, sir. These guys do not want to be captured."

Kipper exchanged a look with Jed. A "what-the-fuck" look, his wife would have called it.

"So you haven't caught any alive, Colonel," he continued. "But the fact you've called means you have something more than a bunch of corpses to go on."

"Yes, sir. We have managed to lay hands on quite a few of the pirates now. Mostly low-level muscle. And they're much happier to talk once they get a meal and some drink in them."

Kipper was surprised. He'd expected that modern interrogation techniques would run more to water torture and car batteries. He'd reluctantly authorized such extreme measures in the Declared Zones over a year ago, but if Colonel Kinninmore thought a cup of soup and a bread roll would get better results than a rubber hose, Kipper was not going to second-guess him. He was kind of grateful, actually. He really didn't want to go down in history as the "torture president."

"The enemy combatants we have secured," said Kinninmore, "are all singing from the same sheet. About four months ago this crew arrived in Manhattan from somewhere in North Africa. Maybe Morocco, Algeria. Depends on who you ask. One of the post-Holocaust caliphate states, anyway. They were very well armed, well trained. Real discipline. They cut down a couple of the lesser players without drawing breath, but rather than consolidating and working their way up the food chain, they threw the switch to negotiation. Offered all the remaining gang leaders tribute and territory outside of New York if they combined forces to drive us out of the city. They bought their allies and paid a good price, too, by all reports."

It was Jed Culver who spoke this time. "Did you say outside of New York, Colonel? They were offering to carve up turf *outside* Manhattan?"

"Not just Manhattan, Mister Culver. All up and down the eastern seaboard."

"How?" Kipper asked.

"Don't know that yet, Mister President," came the disembodied reply. "None of our prisoners are what you'd call decision makers. A lot of what they're telling us is circulating as rumor on the other side. But the rumors all lock in together. They all sound the same. There is an operator out here who's managed to get these guys working together, most of them, anyway. Apparently, the Eastern European gangs weren't having any part of it. They're sitting this out."

Kipper leaned in closer, feeling suddenly as if he really should be taking the security of the call more seriously.

"And the jihadi angle, Colonel. Any word there?"

Kinninmore's voice disappeared in a wash of static.

"I'm sorry, Colonel," Jed said. "Could you repeat. It's a bad connection."

When Kinninmore came back, Kipper was certain he could hear gunfire and maybe explosions somewhere in the background.

"Some of the prisoners have confirmed that the newcomers have described themselves as fedayeen. There seems to be about four or five groups of them, identifiable by the different color scarves they wear. Their common language is Arabic, but then, a lot of the North African pirates speak that, too. They're devout. They don't miss prayer, but again, some of our pirate captives are no different. The main thing is, Mister President, all of our captives say that these new guys have been acting as leaders or advisers for the pirate gangs during this recent fighting. They are running the battle from the other side. And they're doing a good job. They're not punching it out; they're drawing us in and hitting us with a lot of ambushes and booby traps."

"Booby traps?" Kipper said.

"Yes, sir. That's the really annoying thing. A lot of our casualties aren't even coming from stand-up firefights. We smash them flat whenever they try that. Most of my KIAs and my wounded are coming from car bombs and improvised mines. The city is a nightmare for them. I think they presighted a lot of these things well before we got here."

"Do we have any idea who's running this show?" Jed asked. "Any indications a foreign power might be involved?"

"Nothing concrete, sir. There is a leadership cadre that my prisoners are aware of, but they don't have names or any kind of actionable information. If we could just grab up one of these scarf-wearing motherfuckers…"

Kipper could hear the intense frustration in Kinninmore's voice despite the flattening effect of the encryption software.

"Excuse me, Mister President, I didn't…"

"Don't sweat it, Colonel," said Kipper. "I feel the same way. Like we've been hit by some bastard from out of nowhere. I'm not going to waste my breath telling you we need to lay hands on one of these characters. I'm sure you're moving heaven and earth to do so."

"Thank you, Mister President. You are correct about that, sir."

Kipper stretched his neck, which cracked uncomfortably. The room swam around him, and he reached for the bed head to steady himself. Jed looked worried and tried to lend a hand, but Kipper shook his head and held up the arm from which the medical staff had taken blood. He was just suffering from the aftereffects of losing a pint.

"Colonel, I have to go now," Kip said. "I'm about to go visit some of your men and women in the hospital here. I broke off from my visit to talk to you."

"Do what you can for them, Mister President," said Kinninmore. "They've done you proud out here."

"I'm sure. You stay on it, Colonel. And call me whenever you've got anything you think I might want to know."

"Yes, sir, Mister President. Mister Culver. Kinninmore out."

The connection died, and the phone began protesting the lost signal before Jed shut it down.

"We'd best get on with the tour," Kip said. "Can't keep people waiting."

Culver helped him stand up, and Kip had to wonder how the man was coping with his own reaction to having donated blood. It didn't seem to bother him nearly as much.

"There'll be a formal intelligence brief coming through on this within an hour or so," Culver said. "I'll get it to you as soon as possible. Get NIA working on it with the Euroweenies. And Echelon Group with the Brits. See if they've picked up anything in the chatter."

"Okay."

They emerged from the room to find their escort group standing off a short distance down the corridor, presumably to give them some privacy. As they returned to the party for the short walk to the recovery ward, the first buses full of blood donors from the settler camp pulled into the car park. Kipper watched through a big picture window as the new Americans spilled out onto the tarmac, chattering and grinning and looking all around. *Probably looking for me,* he thought.

"If you'll follow me, Mister President," Leong said.

The recovery ward was hushed as they entered. Here and there a soldier was propped up on pillows, keenly awaiting his arrival. But many of them were unconscious. Feeling like a child in church who has done something wrong but does not know exactly what, Kipper walked down the long line of beds, stopping to talk to those who were awake and responsive. Colonel Ralls was back, standing by with a box of Purple Hearts. The president personally pinned the medal to the pillow of each wounded soldier, whether they were conscious or not, an act he had already performed far too many times over the last three years. He tried to clear his fuzzy head of the conversation with Kinninmore. He wanted to be able to concentrate on meeting these soldiers.

"Hello, son. I'm James Kipper. What's your name?" he asked of a redheaded boy whose right arm ended at a bandaged stump just above the elbow.

"Specialist Neil Tomlinson, sir," the young man barked back as he attempted to salute, forgetting about his injury. Confusion and embarrassment flooded the boy's face, and Kipper felt his heart cracking open inside his chest.

"Don't you worry about any of that stuff, Tomlinson. You're officially excused from saluting and marching and all of that crap."

"And KP, Mister President?" said the specialist, trying for a light tone and almost, but not quite, making it. "No more peeling taters for me."

Kip forced a smile.

"No. Suffered that indignity a few times, have you?"

Tomlinson rolled his eyes in an exaggerated fashion. "More times than I care to remember, Mister President."

"Do you mind?" Kip asked, motioning toward the edge of Tomlinson's cot.

"No, sir," he answered, his butt shuffling over a few inches before Kip could stop him.

The president of the United States sat down on the rumpled blanket and looked to Colonel Ralls, who leaned forward with his box of tricks and retrieved two medals: a Purple Heart and a Bronze Star.

"Well, son, the colonel here tells me that you've been busy on our account. Not just getting yourself wounded and all but doing extra hero duty with it. According to this citation—"

Ralls passed him a sheet of paper.

"—you were part of a platoon that was ambushed by sniper and rocket and machine gun fire at the intersection of Broadway and 26th Street. Says here one of your squad mates was shot and went down in the middle of that intersection and that you ran into the fire to drag him out. Says that's how you lost your arm, Neil."

Kipper read directly from the citation, struggling to keep his voice from breaking.

"Says here that 'by his courage, dedication, and willingness to sacrifice for his wounded comrade, Specialist Tomlinson reflected great credit upon himself and upheld the highest traditions of the United States Army.'"

The president lowered the piece of paper and looked directly at Tomlinson, whose eyes were clouded with a mix of emotions he would probably never understand. Kipper found himself feeling even more poorly as he confronted the human consequences of decisions he had made in comfort many thousands of miles away from places like the intersection of Broadway and 26th, where young men like Neil Tomlinson got their limbs blown off.

"I'm very proud of you, son," he said with some difficulty. "We all are." He tilted his head to indicate the cluster of high-ranking men and women gathered around him. "And you need to know that we are in your debt forever now. I don't know that we can truly pay you back, but you need to know that as long as an American draws breath somewhere, that debt will be acknowledged and honored."

"Thank you, Mister President," Tomlinson said in a quiet voice. "I was really just helping my buddy."

"And that's what makes it admirable," Kipper said as he leaned forward to pin the medals to Tomlinson's pillow.

He bade farewell to the boy and moved on to decorate a number of unconscious patients. Once or twice he had to stop and take a few breaths to get his balance back.

With one of the injured soldiers, however, he couldn't identify the race or gender. Blood-spotted bandages covered the trooper's entire head. An air tube forced oxygen through a fleshy hole that didn't resemble a mouth in any way that Kip recognized. There were no eyeholes cut through the bandages.

He asked why.

"Shrapnel struck this soldier in the face, Mister President," Leong explained without needing to check the chart. "She has lost her lower jaw. She also received additional shrapnel in her sinuses and eyes.

This soldier will never see again, but we believe once we stabilize her, we can send her on to Sydney for reconstructive surgery."

Kipper stayed focused on the soldier. Her chest rose and fell regularly. He placed his hand on her shoulder and whispered into her ear. After stroking her bandaged forehead, he pinned a Purple Heart to her pillow, stood up, and walked on.

Culver asked what he had said to the woman. The military officers and medical staff couldn't help hanging on his answer, either.

The president rubbed his eyes and took a deep breath. "Jed," he replied, "I asked her to forgive me. For my weakness."

38

TEXAS ADMINISTRATIVE DIVISION

Road agents had been through Palestine. Miguel and the other riders stayed on their mounts as the animals slowly clip-clopped down the wide-open thoroughfare, snorting and neighing in distress, their ears twitching nervously. Miguel leaned forward and patted Flossie on the neck to calm her down, taking the opportunity to check on his daughter. Sofia was tight-lipped and pale-faced with her Remington laid out across her lap. She seemed to be holding up well enough, though, all things considered.

"There now, girl, be still," he said to the horse. It was not easy to keep his voice calm and soothing with such a black oily rage threatening to boil up from deep inside his guts.

He had first thought to climb down and lead the mare in on foot after the long ride from their last camp, but now he wanted to be able to spur away if necessary. Unfortunately, that put him on eye level with the corpses. They swung on ropes that creaked and groaned under their burden. Twenty-three of them he had counted so far, all strung up from the cross stays of the telephone and power poles that ran along the street.

"They were from the south," Miguel said quietly.

"How can you tell?" Aronson asked in a tight voice. "They're… pretty far gone."

He was right. The bodies had turned black and bloated with gases before rupturing and spilling over the refuse-strewn footpath below. Crows and other carrion birds had been at them for some time. Drag marks evidenced the efforts of wild dogs and other ground scavengers to carry off a tasty prize.

"The way they are dressed. And their hair," said Miguel. "All of them had black hair. Like mine."

"And Mama's," Sofia said in a strangled voice.

He considered sending her back to the edge of town with Adam, but there was an evil air about this place, and he wanted his only blood kin right where he could see her.

A mechanical click had him reaching for his Winchester, but it was just Adam with a camera. After Crockett, Miguel had taken the lad under his wing, and he had seen that Sofia seemed to relax in Adam's company, too, even though he very obviously had eyes for poor Sally Gray. Adam seemed somewhat wary of Sofia after her actions in Crockett, but Miguel thought he detected admiration there, too.

The cowboy shook his head. Even running for their lives, it seemed there would be no avoiding the *telenovela* of teenage entanglements. Adam's family had Disappeared, a fate he had avoided by virtue of a school trip to Edmonton, sister city to his hometown of Nashville. Miguel had been impressed with the boy during the rescue of the women, not just with his bravery during the fight but with his even greater bravery for speaking up beforehand about his fears. In Miguel's experience, very few men were able to admit they found the idea of doing violence to another completely unnerving. But it was true. He had once heard an old circus boxer say that for normal men, far greater than the fear of being hit was the fear of hitting. It was a secret, shameful thing for most. Young

Adam, though, had come right out and confessed it. And then he had proved himself every bit as courageous as any grown man Miguel had ever known by shepherding the ladies away from the heart of the road agents' lair in the thick of the very worst fighting.

That was why Miguel was so angry with him now.

"What are you doing, Adam?" he asked in a low voice as the boy snapped photographs of their grisly discovery as though he were on holiday. As soon as Adam dropped the camera from his eye, however, the cowboy understood. The boy's face was nearly white with strain, and the muscles in his jawline bunched and unbunched with such fierceness that he could have been chewing on bitterroot.

"Evidence," was all he would say.

"Okay," Miguel said, a little humbled. It had not occurred to him to bother with such a thing.

They came to the burned-out shell of a coffee shop. A charred sign atop a pile of blackened bricks that might once have been yellow read old... gnolia... and Miguel wondered why it had burned when so much of the town center remained intact. Perhaps on the day of the Wave a gas burner had been on and caught fire. But why had it not spread? Was it raining here, then? He shrugged off the idle speculation. Every town they had passed through was the same. Some areas were destroyed. Some looked as though they had merely been abandoned. Modern ghost towns.

Adam's camera continued to click and beep.

To Miguel the wide, dusty streets of Palestine evoked images of the 1930s, the Depression. The scattered, sun-faded hulks of late-model cars ruined the illusion, but the overall sense of the place was one of weariness and abandonment.

Except for the bodies of the lynched settlers, of course. They lent the scene a dark and immediate energy.

Even in the thirties, though, with the Klan active in the South, one would never have witnessed something as gruesome as this. A single corpse strung up from a lamppost, maybe, but not almost two dozen of them. Miguel, bored during the long transit from Australia to Texas, had often attended the history lectures provided aboard the USS *Wasp*. From what he understood, the purpose of lynching one person was to terrorize the rest into submission. This had nothing to do with submission.

This was about extermination.

Aronson dismounted and tied up his horse outside the café. One hand fingered the pistol at his hip while with the other he rubbed at the rough golden-red beard he had lately grown. His eyes were haunted, and Miguel could swear his face had a distinctly green tinge.

"Adam, over here," Aronson called. "Bring that camera. Sofia, please stay back."

Miguel's daughter favored her father with a questioning glance, but he shook his head. A warning gesture.

"Mister Aronson is right, Sofia. You do not need to see any more. Adam neither. Give the camera to us."

"I may want you both to scout around town," he said quietly. "Keep an eye out for anyone headed our way. Understood?"

Sofia and Adam nodded.

He took both of his weapons as he dismounted and tied Flossie to the roof rack of a red station wagon.

A cold wind whipped up dust devils and small twisters of rubbish along the street, stinging his eyes with grit. A traffic light, one of the kind that hung from thick black cables across an intersection, swayed in the breeze, and somewhere a crow shrieked at the gathering gray clouds. Packs of feral dogs could be heard barking in the distance.

"I was wondering why there were only men hanging from those ropes," said Aronson. "Now I know. Brother Adam, Miguel is correct. You need not see this wickedness. Nor Sofia either."

Adam hesitated, drawn by the power of whatever lay within the tumble of charred bricks and roofing iron, but Miguel stepped in front of him.

"Do as your elder says, boy. He is trying to spare you."

Adam bristled and attempted one look over Miguel's shoulder, but he deflated quickly. Sofia looked as though she wanted to climb down off her horse, but she knew her father well enough to be wary of the furious storm clouds that had gathered behind his eyes. Nodding but saying nothing, Adam took himself across the street to drink from his canteen. Sofia wheeled her mount around and followed him. He deliberately avoided walking under or even looking at the hanging corpses, instead investing his attention in the grimy windows of a bookshop. Miguel watched them move all the way across before turning back to the elder Mormon.

"Women?" he asked in a voice as arid as a salt pan.

"And children," Aronson said. "Here, pass me the camera. I'll document it for the authorities in Kansas City. Perhaps we should look around for some clue as to their identities. Papers or a camp of sorts."

The rising tone of his voice was inflected with the thinnest of hopes. Not that Miguel might find such information but that by busying himself with such details, Aronson might pass through the next few minutes without losing too much of himself. Miguel hazarded a quick look inside the collapsed confines of the building and felt his heart hardening with another layer of scar tissue. He was no policeman, but he could tell from the way the bodies were piled up at the back that they had either cowered there or attempted to force an exit through the rear of the building. They had been alive when the coffee shop was set afire.

He cast his eyes down at the road surface and after a few seconds found what he was looking for: shell casings. A weapon or weapons had been used here to force the women and children into the building. Almost certainly to keep them there. He picked up the brass casings and metal clips that had held the casings together. The rounds were larger than those used in the M16, possibly a machine gun. He could not say. He was no expert in these things.

The vaquero shook his head, a banal gesture in the face of such black-hearted malevolence, but since he had nobody on whom he could vent his fury, it was best not to give it free rein.

A crash and a string of muttered oaths drew his attention outward from his cheerless thoughts. Aronson had tripped on a blackened crossbeam. The Mormons were not given to profanity. Even under extreme duress in Crockett the only real cursing Miguel had heard was his own. But Cooper Aronson emerged from the burned-down coffee shop still swearing under his breath. Distant thunder rolled over the town, and Miguel felt a few spots of cold rain on his neck.

Aronson shook his head at the cowboy as if he, too, had nothing else to offer.

"I suppose we had best see to the burial of these poor people," he said in the tone of a man girding himself for something he would rather put off forever. "I'll send Adam and Sofia back to the others. We'll need help."

Miguel nodded. "You and I can see to cutting some of them down. It is not good work for women or boys."

The Mormon leader flared angrily. "It is not good work for us, either, Miguel." But his loss of control was momentary, and he added a quick apology. "I am sorry, my friend. That was unworthy. You are right. We should do as much as we can between us. I'm going to suggest we put all of the bodies in the coffee shop and collapse those walls on top of it. It's not proper, I know, but it's probably the best we can do short of staying longer to dig individual graves."

The rain was coming down harder now, obscuring the silent rail yards to the south of the town in a dark gray band. Miguel shuddered inwardly. This was going to make an already unpleasant task all but unbearable.

"It is a better end than they have come to already, Cooper," he said. "I agree. Those walls will come down without much effort, and they will form a good... what is the word for the grave of stones?"

"A cairn," Aronson said. "They'll form a cairn. We'll just need to be careful that we don't collapse the walls on top of ourselves." He called Adam over from where he'd been investigating the bookstore. The lad hurried back, followed by Sofia, both of them carrying an armful of paperbacks, looking a touch happier than they had been. Miguel read with curiosity some of the titles Adam had chosen. An orange book called *The Martian Chronicles* topped the stack, and beneath it *Hammer's Slammers*. He couldn't make out the writers of those books, but they were not the sort of thing Miguel had read to improve his English for the settler's test. Sofia, he was happy to see, had picked more appropriate reading for a young lady of some bearing. Some literary novels, by the look of them, by a woman named Helen Fielding. Almost certainly a novelist of high literature with a name such as that.

"Brother Adam, I want you to ride out with Sofia and have Benjamin return to help us with the burial of these people," Aronson said. "Tell Willem we will camp by the lake for the night and resupply from the Walmart depot in the morning. Make sure he knows to be alert for more road agents... or Texas Defense Force patrols." He turned to Miguel. "How long do you think it has been since the agents were through here?"

The vaquero rubbed the back of his neck and scowled as he examined the nearest of the hanging corpses, trying to see it only as a thing, not a person.

"I cannot say for certain, but given the state of those bodies, maybe two weeks. They are still black and wet, but they have ruptured from the gases. In cattle that can take ten days. There are many insects on them that you do not see on dry bodies in the desert. So yes, maybe two weeks."

Adam was now looking decidedly green and quickly excused himself to be about his duties back at the camp.

"I'd better get going," he muttered. "Before it gets too dark."

Sofia looked hollow-eyed as she joined Adam.

"Be careful," Miguel called out after them as he hurried back to his horse. He did not like being separated from Sofia, but he was certain now the agents had not been here for some time. It was a short ride back to the main party. They were both armed. And woe betide any fool who made the mistake of assuming Sofia would not pull a trigger on him to defend herself.

The fat drops of icy rain thickened and fell more quickly, forcing the two men across the street and down some, where they could shelter in the recessed doorway of a sports club. It was a large three-story building, the upper floors faced with simple sheets of corrugated iron adorned with giant sun-faded plastic stars. It somehow added an even greater sense of melancholy to the scene. Aronson shivered and hugged himself against the wind, which was now blowing scraps of paper and plastic and drifts of dead leaves up the road.

"Do you think the gang we took on back in Crockett could have been responsible for this?" he asked. There was hopefulness in his question if you looked past the grim tone.

"I'm afraid not," Miguel said, hating to dash the other man's spirits. "This... this makes no sense. The agents in Crockett would have taken your women as slaves, but they would have let them live. Here they have killed women and children without reason that I can see beyond the pleasure of killing itself."

"Ethnic cleansing," Aronson said darkly.

Miguel was not familiar with the term but thought he understood what it meant.

"We are a good forty miles from Crockett," he said, "which was as far north as that band of agents ever ventured according to their camp whores. No, I think this is another group."

Aronson's face grew even longer.

"That would mean that as we head north, we're moving into the realm of the men who did this."

"Yes," Miguel said. "We are."

The rain intensified, solid and heavy enough to raise a roar as it sheeted down on the iron roof of the sports club. Miguel had a sudden urge for a smoke. He had given up the cheap cigarillos of his youth after boarding the golfer's yacht with Miss Julianne and her people. What was that now, three or four years ago? It was a lifetime. There had been a small supply of very fine Cohibas on board, and he remembered fondly sharing a few with the big friendly gringo who called himself a rhinoceros. But they ran out halfway across the Pacific, and there had been no such indulgences in the refugee camps and on the work farm in Australia. So he had learned to do without and been glad of it, too. He breathed much more freely these days. But now, huddled in the doorway of a darkened tomb festooned with plastic stars, watching the obscene and rotting black fruit strung up by road agents swinging in the wind, he suddenly felt a terrible need to fill his mouth and lungs with fresh, strong smoke, as if it might burn him clean of the corruption he had breathed in Palestine.

"Of course," said Aronson, "if it was ethnic cleansing, it would be the case that things went... different... up here because these people were..."

He trailed off, unable to find a polite way of saying it.

"Because they were beaners," Miguel finished for him. "Wetbacks."

The Mormon grimaced but nodded.

"You are correct," Miguel said. "It may be that they treat their white captives differently. But the men in Crockett would still have killed you, no? And in the end we are all the same color."

He nodded at the gently swinging corpses, ruptured and black and crawling with flies and maggots.

The rain didn't help matters. The first corpse dropped to the ground with a solid thump as Miguel sliced through the rope, only to explode across the asphalt. That necessitated another trip to collect brooms, shovels, heavy-duty trash bags, and masks. The masks didn't help much, but the Vicks VapoRub under the nostrils did.

"I saw it in a movie once," Aronson said. "Don't ask me which one."

Miguel didn't. He really didn't want to know if the movie featured entrails and flesh smeared into the greasy road surface. Each scrape of the shovel against the tarmac to collect another body part caused his stomach to twist and gurgle ominously, pushing the bile to the back of his throat. He choked it back down and continued with the task of dumping the body into the heavy bag Aronson held open for him. It was a task that did not get any easier with each thump of the next corpse against the asphalt. Fortunately, most of them came to the ground in more or less one piece.

More or less.

The three men to whom the task fell all wore long and forbidding expressions by the time Benjamin smacked the horses on their rumps to drag away a charred wooden beam that was propping up the last wall. It came free with a giant crack and the deep thunder of tumbling brickwork. The rain had finally eased off an hour earlier, but the mass grave was so thoroughly soaked that the collapse raised no dust.

"We shall pray for them, if you don't mind, Miguel," said Cooper Aronson.

"I shall add my Hail Marys before sleeping tonight," he answered, "but now I will clean up."

Ben Randall looked up from where he'd been untethering the horses.

"If you head on down Main Street, across from the rail yards, that Trudi Jessup was setting up to boil water in a big white shed down yonder. A sign-writin' business, as I recall. She's got soap, clean clothes, and boots, too. Got 'em from the Walmart. I think your daughter and Sally were helping her, too. Finding dry wood for a boiler."

"Thank you," Miguel said, his mood lifting at the prospect of cleaning the remains of the settlers from his body. That Miss Jessup had attended to the preparations also gave his mood some reason to improve. As the only non-Mormon in the camp—besides the whores, of course, who did not count because they could not be trusted—Miss Jessup had proved to be a relief from the sometimes stern and moralizing company of the Saints.

He picked up his rifle from where it leaned against a wall and bade the other two men good-bye as they prepared for another of their strange baptisms for the dead. At this rate, thought Miguel, Mormon heaven would fill up with their dead converts long before they reached Kansas City.

Leading Flossie by the reins, he set off parallel to Main, walking past the sports center where the blue silhouettes of basketballers leapt across the tinted windows. He shivered as what little warmth was left in the day quickly bled away into the gathering dark, reminding him of how wet and filthy his clothes were. He would have to dump them. They were beyond any laundering. Over the road, the windows of the Silver Lady jewelry shop were smashed, and the counters inside upturned and ransacked. A couple of cars parked outside sat on their rims, their tires having deflated long ago. He crossed at Magnolia and Oak, marveling at how the streets of Palestine were so free of car crashes compared with other towns he'd been through. At the next intersection, however, he was forced to divert south by a tree that had fallen and blocked most of the intersection. He was wondering how long it would take to find the place where the ladies had prepared bathing facilities for them, but after cutting diagonally across an open lot, he saw the golden flicker of an open fire outside a big white shed a few hundred yards away.

It was, or had been, as Benjamin had said, some sort of sign-writing business. Miss Jessup appeared from within as he approached, probably alerted by the clopping sound of Flossie's iron shoes. His heart lifted slightly as Sofia appeared at her shoulder. He had been worried about her. She waved, and he raised his rifle to return the greeting. He felt his age, more than had ever been the case before. Every year lay on his back and weighed down his tired arms and legs. This was a hard land. Always had been by reputation. But there was hard and there was bad, and the deeper Miguel moved into the dominion of the road agents, the worse things seemed to get. He hoped Miss Jessup had found deep tubs somewhere so that they might scrub every inch of their bodies clean, but he also knew there were some stains a man might never be rid of. And Miguel Pieraro, trudging back from the site of a mass grave, felt himself covered in just that sort of insoluble corruption.

39

KANSAS CITY, MISSOURI

"Mister President, I have the latest reports on the situation in New York City," said General Franks.

"Go on," Kipper said as a macabre sense of dread crept over him. The faceless soldier in the recovery ward would not leave his mind. He was tormented by flash visions of what she might look like under those bandages: jaw gone, tongue split and lolling obscenely over sharp jutting nubs of bone, loose teeth falling from her upper jaw like broken bricks from a ruined wall.

Did she have children? Many women in the military did. Although if they'd been in the country when the Wave came... He pushed that thought away, but even worse followed. How would her children react when they saw their mommy? He could see his own daughter screaming in terror if Barbara and he came home missing their faces. Kipper shuddered and pushed the images away.

Jesus how do guys like Franks endure this? Or Bush or Clinton, or any of them?

General Franks floated before him, occupying most of a large-screen TV hanging from the wall of the secure videoconference center on the Cerner Campus. Smaller TVs provided feeds from the remaining global news networks, mainly talking heads hashing out the situation in New York City. Most of the equipment was salvage, cobbled together from scavenger runs to Best Buy and Circuit City, combined with whatever military gear was in the area. Some of it was enhanced with more up-to-date cryptography, but for the most part, right down to the KMBC-9 News camera that had been lifted from their downtown KC Studio, the salvaged tech had one redeeming attribute.

It was free for the taking.

Presumably the chairman of the joint chiefs was watching him on a similar but presumably much better setup somewhere at Fort Lewis. The secretary of defense should have been online too, but she was in London at that very moment talking with the British prime minister about what additional assistance the Royal Navy might render in blockading the Atlantic approaches to New York. Kipper suspected that the Brits, though still their allies, would engage in some ugly horse trading for their assistance. Just as the United States had done in the early days of World War II. What was he saying? There were no friends, only interests. He couldn't remember who said it.

Sitting next to Kipper was Jed Culver, bunkered in behind a great wall of ring binders, three civilian landline phones, and one green and black phone from the army. Kip's military aide, Colonel Mike Ralls, stood out of view in a corner of the room, in case he should be needed. Apart from the three of them, the small room was empty. It probably couldn't have held many more occupants, anyway. Kipper's ever-present shadow, the air force officer with the suitcase, was sitting on a plastic chair just outside in the corridor.

"We've managed to push farther up the island of Manhattan, but the weather has turned against us," Franks said. "We've had heavy rainfall for the past forty-eight hours. Given the city's gravely deteriorated condition, the result has been to fill the streets with water, and I mean that literally. It's making movement nearly impossible in some quarters."

That didn't surprise the president at all. For once he probably had a better appreciation of the so-called battlespace than his military commanders. New York was a little like Venice, simply holding back the tide until the day the waters inevitably won.

Franks pushed on. "The enemy, such as they are, have continued to fight for every block of the island in very loose company-size formations. They are using the urban environment to maximum effect, slowing our efforts down even further. Some of them have been donning militia and army uniforms, which increases the possibility of blue on blue casualties."

"Blue on blue?" Culver asked, saving Kipper the effort.

"Friendly fire," Franks said. "It's a lot like the crossroads fighting during the withdrawal from Iraq, Mister President, except, of course, it's our own real estate we're demolishing."

Culver leaned forward from his perch, accidentally knocking over a pile of blue ring binders. "And what can you tell us about the enemy now, General? We spoke with Colonel Kinninmore earlier, and he was adamant that this isn't just some sort of gang war or bandit uprising. It's coordinated by political actors."

Franks's features didn't change much as he registered the question. Kipper wondered if that was significant.

"I've seen the raw intelligence that Colonel Kinninmore is using to make his assessments, sirs. I concur with his findings so far, but that's not telling us much. Until we can capture and properly interrogate some of their leadership cadre, we're thrashing about in the dark."

"Could you speculate, General," Kipper said. "Please."

Franks's shoulders lifted slightly on the screen. He sighed.

"At a guess, sir, New York is collateral damage from the Paris Intifada or the Isreali nuclear strikes, perhaps the British government's forced resettlement schemes, or some combination of them and other factors. There are nearly a billion and a half people on the move around the world right now, Mister President, fleeing conflict or engaging in it. New York is the main game for us, but it's small beer when you look at the global situation. If I had to lay a few newbies on the barrelhead, I'd say somebody is making a simple play to grab up some real estate and colonize part of the East Coast. It's not like we have the people or resources to occupy that territory."

"But why pick a fight?" Kipper asked. "Why not just sneak in there and, I dunno, take over a fishing village or an empty farming hamlet if they really wanted to just settle? Hell, why not just ask? We're looking for immigrants."

"Maybe we're not looking for these ones, Mister President. But I really do not care to speculate on the motives of an enemy I can't even ID yet."

Kip was forced to concede the logic of his point.

"Are there any assets you need that might help us identify them?" he asked.

"Not really," Franks said. "Their communications discipline is very good. At least at command level. Reminds me of looking for bin Laden back in the day. They just don't use the sat phones. I'd speculate they use runners to get their orders out and push a lot of responsibility down to the small unit level. They move around a lot. But they do so under cover. Whenever we get any sign of big concentrations of enemy personnel, we hit them with what we can, although, with respect, sir, we could hit them harder, much harder, if you authorized the use of strategic air assets."

"The big bombers, you mean, General?" Culver asked.

"Yes, sir. I'm afraid that a city like New York provides lots of protection from helicopter gunships and even from the limited air strikes we're able to carry out under our current rules of engagement. It's also a very dangerous environment for close air support. We've lost four jets to shoulder-fired missiles and—"

He checked a piece of paper on the table in front of him. "—and thirteen helicopters so far."

Kipper felt his head reeling at the numbers. They simply could not bear those losses for very long.

"Were they all taken down by missiles, General? Surely we could find out where those things came from."

"Some of them were ours, sir. And no, most of the choppers were killed by very low-tech means. Rocket-propelled grenades, often fired from skyscrapers. As I said, sir, it is a very challenging battlespace."

Jed leaned across his wall of ring binders. "We have discussed this, Mister President. We can use men or we can use ordnance. But at the moment we're not using enough of either. Is that what you're saying, General Franks?"

"Yes, Mister Culver."

"How many troops do we have on the island right now, General?" Kip asked.

"Close to twenty-four thousand regular army, marines, and New York militia, Mister President. The militia element forms the majority of our combat power, probably close to sixty percent. But their effectiveness is mixed depending upon their local commanders," the chairman said. "If you are amenable, I would like permission to deploy an additional marine expeditionary brigade into New York."

"Where would these marines come from?" Kipper asked. The U.S. Armed Forces were a lot smaller than they had once been. You couldn't just go tossing marine brigades around like confetti.

"I'd probably pull them from California. Los Angeles and San Diego. Stripping them down to MCRD San Diego," Franks said. "Things are secure enough that the corps felt they could move boots back to San Diego. At least secure from outside interference at any rate, and using marines there is probably overkilling the issue of zone runners and scavengers. We're scheduled to transfer more of that mission over to the local militia, anyway. May as well move it up."

Jed Culver riffled quickly through a sheaf of papers until he found what he wanted.

"Couldn't we send forces from Missouri and strip units from the garrisons along the Seattle–Kansas City rail line? They're a lot closer, and they're not busy. It's mostly wilderness out there."

Franks shook his head. "I know it looks as if those troops aren't doing anything, Mister Culver, but they keep the rail line secure from interdiction and sabotage."

"Sabotage?" Kipper asked.

"The incidents have been relatively small in number and not coordinated, but all it takes is one train derailment to cause considerable disruption to reconstruction efforts in the Midwest," Franks said. "The Second MEB is vital, but with a third one in—"

"Who the hell's been sabotaging my railways?" Kip asked. If Franks noticed his sudden surge of interest, he didn't react to it, continuing in the same gruff voice as before.

"The bureau is investigating, Mister President. They're not ruling anything out. There's some indication it could be a Deep Green thing or one of the Earth First splinters. But the strikes were pretty far into the interior, well beyond the reach of a bunch of tree huggers and vegan whack jobs. Latest theory is Fort Hood, possibly using a bogus Green front to mess with our supply lines. They do have the capability and motive," Franks said, notably omitting Blackstone's name. It was known that Franks had been part of the effort to oust Blackstone from uniform. Kip understood that he didn't care for the man in the least.

"That Blackstone asshole again?" Kipper exclaimed with a passion that surprised even himself. "This guy is like Satan's own jack-in-the-box the way he keeps popping up. How bad is it, General? And why wasn't I informed?"

Franks didn't look at all uncomfortable with the question.

"It's not as bad as it could be, Mister President, precisely because we have those garrison forces along the line, constantly patrolling. And that's why you weren't informed. Compared to some of our other problems, this one is small potatoes and easily managed as long as we keep those forces in place and on alert. I'd add, though, that the fact they haven't caught anyone does tend to bolster the case that it's not amateurs operating out there."

Kip got his runaway temper under control again. He'd come forward in his chair, and the knuckles on his clenched fists stood out white against the suntan he'd picked up visiting so many reconstruction sites.

"Okay," he said. "But General, and Jed, too, if this sabotage gets out of hand or even if it starts ramping up, I want to know. That rail line is the single most important transport corridor we have."

"Will do, Mister President," Franks said.

"I think you were about to give us a few options for redeploying troops to New York," Culver suggested, moving the discussion forward again.

On screen, Franks nodded.

"We should also be able to redeploy the marines from Kennedy since the cav has now totally secured the airport. Navy is moving some of their assets up from Puerto Rico to seal off access to the city from the sea. At least as best they can. These 'assets' consist of two destroyers and an oil tender. It will be a big help if Secretary Castellato can secure some assistance from the British, Mister President."

"That's why she's there, General," Kipper said. He was due to call Castellato in two hours for an update but saw no point in wasting time speculating on progress until he'd heard from Alida herself.

Franks leaned toward him on the screen, almost filling it.

"I should warn you, sir, that casualties are certain to increase over the course of the next month."

"I'm sorry," Kipper said, certain he'd misheard. "A month? This battle could last a month?"

Franks nodded. "Easily, Mister President. We could deploy

two to three times as many troops without changing the duration of the engagement."

Oh, man, thought Kipper. This was getting worse by the minute.

"I see," he said aloud. "General, did you receive a copy of Admiral Ritchie's brief concerning the possible use of nuclear and/or chemical weapons in New York?"

"I did, Mister President." Franks replied. "And I concur with Ritchie's opinion. We should be very, very careful about going down that path for all of the reasons he outlined. I can understand the attraction of a technological fix, Mister President. I don't like losing precious lives any more than you do."

"Well, then give me some options, General," Kipper said plaintively.

Franks nodded slowly, as if considering the issue for the first time, which was obviously not the case.

"If you are willing to write off large sections of New York City," he suggested after a moment, "we could send a flight of B-52s over."

"What? Conventional bombing?" Kipper asked.

"A massed conventional bombing run would certainly break the will of the irregular forces we face there. The pirates and whoever has been coaching them. Also, it would place the rest of the world on notice that whether or not we actually stand on a given piece of U.S. territory, it is ours and we will do whatever it takes to keep everyone else out."

"Cost," Culver chimed in. "Just how much will this bombing run cost us? In human and capital terms."

"Well, you do the job properly and you'll kill everyone needs killing, Mister Culver. Thousands of them. As for damage, the areas targeted will look a lot like pictures you may have seen of cities that were bombed during World War Two. If you like, I can have a member of my staff send over a brief."

"Jesus, we'd be better off just throwing a nuke at the place," Culver said to himself mordantly.

"To borrow a line from history, we *will* have to destroy part or all of the city in order to save it," Franks said. "New York is too valuable as a port of entry and a strategic location on the eastern seaboard to let anyone else take over there, even if we cannot take full advantage of it. Mister President, we have to give serious consideration to the reality on the ground. We can retake this city, hold it, restore it, but it won't be the New York we remember."

Kipper leaned back in his chair and stretched his back, which was feeling cramped. He poured himself a glass of water and pondered the options.

He knew as a basic tenet of his profession that occasionally you had to demolish something in order to rebuild. But such demolitions were neat, orderly affairs and never hurt anyone. Not on purpose, at any rate. Over the last four years he had proved, he hoped, that he wasn't squeamish about killing America's enemies when necessary, but the senseless destruction of all that property... New York City had such a long history... museums, galleries, Central Park, buildings that had a story, each and every last one of them. They were going to destroy so much of their heritage if they did this.

"Let me think on it, Tommy," Kipper said. "In the meantime, I authorize you to begin redeployment of the marines you mentioned to New York." A door knock behind them drew Kipper's attention, and he saw a young woman tapping her wristwatch apologetically.

"Mister President, we're about to lose the link."

He mouthed "thanks" at the woman and apologized to Franks for the interruption.

"Thank you, General. We're about to lose the satellite. Please, rest assured, I'm not going to dick around with this decision. You'll have word very soon about..."

But the screen where Franks had been sitting was already full of white noise.

Kipper and Jed sat in silence in the hot, oppressive room. For once his chief of staff seemed to understand that he did not want to be talked at. He most wanted just a few moments of quiet to think things through. The president tried to put himself in the place of all those men and women he had ordered to New York, at first assuming he was sending them on nothing more than a brief policing operation. The pirates, after all, were little better than glorified criminals, looters. They were a problem all over the country, not just in New York, and as well armed as they were, they had never presented as anything other than a rabble, until now.

And now?

He had no idea. There just wasn't enough information. How he envied his predecessor in this job. Bush had enjoyed almost infinite resources, the all-knowing intelligence agencies, the all-seeing spy satellites, vast networks of spies. Kipper often found himself having to put aside an almost childish jealousy when he thought of how much information Bush must've had as he prepared to go to war in Iraq. If only he now had but one-tenth of those resources available to him.

Instead he had imperfection, uncertainty, doubt. And fear. The fear that every decision he made was wrong, disastrously so. Every judgment in error. His reasons ill founded.

"Jed, I don't know what to do," he said hoarsely. "I never seem to get it right."

Culver reached across and squeezed his arm.

"No, Mister President, you do get it right more often than not. But you forget that the world is not an engineering problem, sir. You're not dealing with elegance and balance and discretely measurable artifacts. You're dealing with people. Flawed, imperfect people. You can never set right human affairs the same way you can square off a right angle in a technical drawing. Neither the virtues nor the malevolent rottenness of the human soul can be specified to millimeter tolerances. You can only do the best you can."

Kipper let his head fall forward into his hands. He closed his eyes and rubbed his temples, which were throbbing painfully.

"Jesus, Jed, way to cheer a guy up," he said.

He knew the TV screens in front of them were still running loops from the fighting in New York. He did not need to look at them. He would always be haunted by what he had seen there and, even worse, what he had imagined. Crowding out all those hellish images, however, was the woman he had visited in the hospital, the woman whom he had sent into battle and who had come back a broken and incomplete remnant of everything she once was and might yet have been.

The president of the United States of America let his hands fall slowly away from his face. He turned to his military aide, Colonel Ralls, who was standing quietly off to one side as always.

"Mike, can you get General Franks back for me?" he said. "A phone line will be fine. I've made a decision."

40

BERLIN

Caitlin did not follow the woman immediately. Fabia Shah was on her lunch break and would not venture far. She disappeared around the corner about a hundred yards down the street, marching the whole way, stopping to talk with nobody. Caitlin and Mirsaad finished their meals with a couple of very short, strong Turkish coffees before leaving to spend a few hours working on the reporter's behalf. Having found Baumer's mother where she expected, Caitlin could pick up her tail later in the day. Meanwhile, Mirsaad moved about Neukölln, and Caitlin tagged along with him, dutifully playing the obedient intern as he drove from one appointment to another, interviewing the imam of a small reformist mosque that had taken over a Chinese Christian church on Werbellinstrasse, the local welfare officer for the city's Islamic Federation, and the director of a women's shelter operating about a mile north of the shariatown.

As the light began to fail, they headed back into Neukölln's dense warren of faded identikit apartment blocks, the ranks of grimy whitewashed four- and five-story tenements recalling for her a line she'd read sometime in her college years. Aesthetically worthless rent slabs. Caitlin struggled for a second to recall where she'd seen such an evocative description. She frequently had trouble recalling little things like that after the operation to remove her tumor. She knew the line wasn't written about this section of Berlin but was struck by how apt it was.

"This woman you are looking for…"

"Not looking for, Sadie. We found her already. I just needed to confirm she was still here in Neukölln. Do you think you could head over to Mahlower; it's the next right."

They motored through a big intersection on Hermannstrasse and made the turn she had pointed out. Mahlower was relatively short and home to just six apartment blocks, three on each side. Caitlin had him pull over and park.

"This woman we saw today, she is somehow connected to the attack on you, on Bret?"

Caitlin shook her head. "No. Not directly. But she knows somebody who almost certainly was, and for now she's the best link I have to him. He came back here when he got out of jail awhile ago. I'm willing to take a bet she's either seen him or heard from him. It's a start. That's all."

"She is his girlfriend?" he asked dubiously. "Such arrangements are frowned upon here, you know."

"No," Caitlin said. "His mother."

"Ah, I see."

Mirsaad seemed satisfied with that. After all, it wasn't too far removed from the way he might go about tracking a difficult contact for a story. If you can't find them, find the people around them.

"So should we not we go back to the café and follow her?" he asked.

Caitlin smiled.

"No. I have the last known addresses for her. Residential and work. That office has moved, but she moved with it. She was living in a council flat down the end of this street as of three years ago.

My best information is that she's still there. Makes sense. She hasn't gone anywhere else. She'll walk past in a few minutes if she is there. Fabia is a tough old bird, but even she won't linger long after dark on her own. We can wait. Besides, there's not really enough road traffic to hide in if we had to follow her."

Caitlin dimly registered a call to prayer somewhere outside, muted by the closed windows of the little Lada. Here and there she could see groups of people, some small gatherings and others quite numerous, making their way into local prayer rooms. When she had last stalked Baumer, she'd built up an encyclopedic knowledge of Neukölln's ethnic and religious topography. But she had enjoyed much greater freedom of movement back then, and so many things had changed in the intervening time. Thousands more residents had flooded in, for a start, refugees from both France and the charred wastelands of the Middle East, making the already cramped suburb almost intolerably overcrowded. There was very little chance that Fabia would have given up her small but precious council flat.

"So why not just talk to her now, when she walks past?" Mirsaad asked.

"Now is not the time, Sadie. I just need to confirm she's here. Then we're going back to your place. You have my thanks and your marching orders. I'm afraid when I come back in here tonight, I'll be coming on my own."

"But this is madness," he protested, turning his body toward her in the cramped confines of the car. He had to release the seat belt to do so. "You have seen how it is here. You cannot hope to move around unaccompanied. For you it will end badly. Very badly."

"Not for me, buddy," she assured him as movement in her peripheral vision caught her attention. It was Fabia, walking with a woman who was wrapped up in a dull gray ankle-length coat and escorted by a middle-aged man in a baseball cap. They paid the Lada no heed as they walked past, deep in conversation, and Caitlin held up her hand to forestall a question from Mirsaad.

The presence of the other two might prove an inconvenience if Fabia Shah had taken in lodgers or had family staying. It was very common for extended families to squeeze themselves into the tiny one- and two-bedroom apartments. But they stopped and said their good-byes about fifty yards down the street as the man and woman disappeared into a large white-washed apartment block on the left. Fabia waved them off and resumed the marching stride Caitlin had noted earlier in the day. A forceful gait from a woman emanating a very strong "don't-fuck-with-me" vibe.

Good for you, Mrs. Shah, she thought to herself.

Mirsaad watched her, too. A professional in his own right, he said nothing until the woman had entered her tenement at the far end of the street.

"Okay," Caitlin said. "That'll do us for now. Let's get you safely home."

He started the car and drove toward Fabia's place, looking for a spot to perform a U-turn, but a line of angle-parked cars ran the length of the street, blocking the maneuver. It did give Caitlin a chance to scope out the target address as they drove past. Another blank-faced, grimy tenement looking out on the world through small square windows, about half of them dark.

Mirsaad took them around to the left at the end of the road, and another quick left took them back up to Hermannstrasse, the main road back toward the Jordanian's apartment. Within a minute they were approaching the lines of stalls and makeshift markets through which they had driven that morning. The place still hummed with the same level of energy, but it was now all directed toward breaking down and putting away displays, trestle tables, racks of clothes, and piles of cardboard boxes. Street vendors pushed handcarts through the controlled chaos, calling their wares, pushing for a few last euros before their customers finished packing and took themselves off to worship.

"Caitlin, please," said the reporter. He was almost pleading with her now. "I would ask you to reconsider your plan to come back alone. Bret will never forgive me if anything happens to you. There are bands of young men who rove these streets at night. Dignity Patrols they call themselves. They are looking for women just like you. Women they would teach a lesson to."

The car passed out of the oppressive patchwork quilt of tenements and into the small green belt to the south of Neukölln at last. Caitlin turned in her seat to face Mirsaad.

"Sadie, I'm not going to bullshit you. What I have to do tonight is going to be dangerous. But you have to believe me when I tell you it'd be worse if you came along. I know what I'm doing. This is where my talents shine, buddy. But if they shine too brightly, people get burned. I don't want you to get hurt. You've done me a great favor today. I needed you. But now I need you to back off and trust me, in fact, to forget about me and this day altogether. Like I was never here."

Mirsaad frowned as they passed by an Islamic culture center between Thomasstrasse and Jonasstrasse. From the uncovered heads of the many unaccompanied women gathering on the footpath outside, laughing and talking happily, it was most likely a reformist operation. He shook his head sadly.

"I fear, Caitlin, that you are much more than a police officer."

She said nothing. An eloquent response in itself.

"Well, you have my number. If you need help, please do not give it a thought. Just call me and I will come as quickly as I can, but... you know, with the children and my wife to think of..."

"It's your children and wife I am thinking of," Caitlin said.

By eleven-thirty in the evening the streets were almost empty. Caitlin parked in a deserted multilevel garage a good five miles from Neukölln. She hauled a smart phone out of her kit and spent some time typing up a report for Dalby, which she dispatched via an encrypted link to Berlin Control. The file wiped itself from the phone after transmission. Her own mission brief she covered quickly, noting that she had located Baumer's mother and would question her at the first opportunity. The bulk of her transmission, however, detailed her impressions of how much the economy of the shariatown relied on goods obviously looted from the United States. Given the fighting in New York and the resources Echelon and the other agencies were devoting to anti-piracy operations, she knew it would be of interest.

So much interest, it turned out, that the phone buzzed in her jacket pocket about ten minutes after she'd zapped off the data package. Caitlin keyed in the security code and waited while the device exchanged encryption sets with the retransmission facility at Berlin Control. After a final series of bleeps and bloops she heard Dalby in the earpiece.

"Got your message," he said. "Most interesting, I must say. We knew a lot of the product you saw was available on the continent, but not in the significant concentrations you found. Any chance you might look further into the relevant supply chains for us?" he asked. "At your end, I mean."

Caitlin frowned. "I could do that," she said, taking care to remain aware of her surroundings while she spoke in vague generalities with her handler. The call was encoded with military-grade encryption, but there was no sense taking chances. "I do have other purchases to make while I'm here, though. They remain my top priority."

"Of course. Of course," Dalby said. "It's just that we've been asked to pay particular attention to this market, given what's happened of late, and you are well positioned to do that for us. Management and our offshore partners insist."

"I see," said Caitlin. "I'll do what I can, then."

"Good lass," Dalby replied. "Talk soon."

The connection was severed at his end. Caitlin sat there, fuming and trying to get her anger under control. They had sent her out here, undeclared, a deniable asset, and now they wanted to retask her onto a basic intelligence-gathering job that some desk Johnny from the embassy could handle. She was so pissed off that she had to remind herself not to lose situational awareness. The parking garage was empty and looked like it had not been used in a long time, with a lot of rubbish and dead leaf matter lying in pools of dank water all around her car. But that did not mean she was alone there.

She checked her watch. Coming up on midnight. Time to move. Were she in London, she could have relied on the curfew to keep any innocent bystanders out of harm's way. But in Berlin, even though it was eerily quiet compared to her memories of the city, there were still a few groups of young people here and there, and she couldn't immediately mark them all down as hostile. She took a long, looping approach to Fabia Shah's apartment, driving out to the eastern edge of the airport and creeping into Mahlowerstrasse via a street lined with dead trees that ran past a sports field at the northeastern corner of Tempelhof. Like most open spaces in Berlin, it had been dug up and converted to market gardens, with rows of tomato stakes and cornstalks poking up through a light ground mist, contrasting with the stark, leafless branches of all the trees that had died in the pollution storms back in '03.

She parked the BMW under an elm with at least some scattered surviving foliage and killed the engine. She was dressed as before, mostly in black, but had discarded the head scarf borrowed from Mirsaad. A few lights burned here and there and the flickering blue-green shadow play of television screens illuminated a few more windows, but given the two thousand or more people all living within a minute's walk of Fabia Shah, the place was deathly quiet. Just how the Dignity Patrols liked it, she supposed.

Caitlin waited ten minutes behind the X5's tinted glass, one of the Russian machine pistols within easy reach on the passenger seat. A couple of lights flicked out while she maintained her vigil, and one of the late-night TV addicts finally gave up and went to bed. Just after twelve-thirty she moved, holstering the automatic with its twin in the combat harness under her leather jacket and taking a set of lock picks from the small storage bin between the front seats. She set the car's defenses and stepped out onto the grass footpath, closing the door softly behind her. Less than a minute later she was through the front door of the block where Fabia had been living four years ago, and within another a minute she had picked the lock on the letter box bearing a small handwritten name tag: shah.

A gas bill and a flyer from a shoe shop personally addressed to Baumer's mother lay uncollected inside.

Caitlin took a few seconds to listen to the building, sending her finely honed senses out along hard echoing corridors, up stairwells, past doors secured by metal grilles. She faintly heard two babies crying and a couple deep in argument. A television droned on somewhere. Repeats of *Star Trek* dubbed into German to judge by the faint strains of the famous theme music she was able to hear.

But there appeared to be nobody moving about. Nobody lying in wait.

She glided up a set of stairs to her left, empty-handed but ready to go guns-hot. On the third floor, she ghosted along the hallway until reaching the right door. Heavy steel bars protected the entrance, but the lock was a primitive arrangement, easily neutralized in about a minute and a half. The cheap hollow-core wooden door behind it took less than half that time, but it was still an anxious interlude, kneeling in front of the handle with a tension wrench and half diamond and hook pick, obviously up to no good.

She was glad to get through the locks and, after gently unlatching the front door, into the apartment. A short, darkened entry hall lay in front of her, with a doorway into a laundry and bathroom to her immediate left. She could smell detergent and the warm, almost comforting odor of tumble-dried clothes in there. Caitlin took a good two minutes to let her eyes adjust to the darkness. She had rejected the idea of using goggles for fear of being blinded should Fabia suddenly flick on a light.

It did not take long to begin picking shapes and objects out of the charcoal gray dimness. A pair of windows in a lounge room directly in front of her appeared to open onto an internal courtyard. She unholstered one of the machine pistols and fitted the long rubberized tube of the specially designed Reflex Suppressor. With the stock unfolded and resting against her armpit, she felt confident enough to move into the main area of the flat.

A small kitchen sat to the left, just beyond the laundry and looking out over a tiny open-plan living area. There were no more doors on that side and only one to the right. The bedroom. The assassin moved slowly, not even pushing dust motes in front of her. She controlled her breathing and allowed her senses to flow outward in a meditative technique she had learned while studying aikido in Japan. Rather than focusing attention down to a single point and letting the world fall away, she threw open the doors of all her senses and allowed everything to rush in. She could smell the meal Fabia had cooked for herself hours ago. Taste the spices at the back of her mouth. Hear a clock ticking and a woman breathing. Feel the thin, threadbare carpet beneath the soles of her boots. See all the depressing details of the flat's spartan furnishings and the slight phosphorescent glow of a small TV screen on a sideboard crowded with photo frames. She knew that if she took the time to inspect those photographs, she would almost certainly find in some of them, smiling and innocent, the younger face of the man who had raped her back in Noisy-le-Sec.

She ghosted forward.

One hand reached out for the door, and she carefully pushed it open, ready to shoot if necessary. Instantly she was struck by the scent of Baumer's mother. Cold cream. A harsh perfume. Soap. And perhaps an apple-scented shampoo. The woman's breathing did not falter. She snored slightly and ground her teeth together, but Caitlin could tell that she was truly asleep.

She swept the muzzle of the suppressor across the room, but there was nowhere for anybody to hide. Fabia had no room for walk-in cupboards or closets, and just a few outfits hung from a wooden clothes rack pushed up against one wall.

They were alone.

Caitlin shouldered the machine pistol and took a small one-use syringe from her jacket.

She uncapped the business end, flicked the chamber to force any air bubbles up, and squeezed off a small stream of liquid to clear them completely. She carefully crossed the floor to crouch by the bed and without preamble slid the syringe into the woman's neck, pressing down on the plunger. Fabia snorted and moaned slightly. She rolled away from Caitlin, forcing her to follow while she administered the last of the shot.

When she could depress the plunger no farther, she withdrew the needle and waited, more than a little relieved that Baumer's mother had not woken up. With a few minutes to wait before the drug took hold completely, she withdrew from the room and checked the rest of the apartment again, spending some time with her ear to the front door, listening to the corridor outside.

Nothing.

She approached the bedroom with much less stealth this time, walking in and sitting on the mattress next to her mark.

"Fabia," she said in a conversational tone, not too loud and softened with a hint of kindness. "Fabia, it's time to wake up."

The woman stirred and gulped air. She stopped snoring but didn't rouse herself.

"Fabia," Caitlin repeated. "Wakey wakey…"

Jesus, she thought, *I've been in England too long.*

"Fabia, wake up. We need to talk now. About Bilal. I need to find Bilal."

"Bilal? Is that you?"

"No, Fabia. I am a friend of Bilal's. I need to find him. He needs my help."

The woman appeared to struggle against unconsciousness, lifting her head from the pillow, blinking her eyes slowly. She groaned and spoke in a slurred voice.

"Too tired."

"I know you're tired, Fabia. Just tell me where Bilal is and you can sleep. Is he here? In Neukölln?"

"Bilal…"

Caitlin suppressed her frustration. Questioning a drugged subject was never ideal, but Fabia would not raise an alarm and would remember this encounter only as a dream in the morning.

"Fabia, I need to see Bilal. Where is your son? Where is Bilal? Do you know?"

"Tired…"

"Where is Bilal, Fabia? His friends need him. Where is Bilal?"

"Not here," the woman said, speaking so faintly that Caitlin had to lean forward.

"What did you say, Fabia? Is Bilal here? In Berlin?"

"Bilal is gone," she said as the drug broke down more of her defenses. "He's gone away."

"Where?" Caitlin asked, containing her impatience. "Where has Bilal gone?"

"America."

Caitlin's surprise was so total that she nearly missed the snick of the door latch in the entry hall.

Baumer was in America.

But where?

The question answered itself.

He had to be in New York.

And how many possibilities opened up from that, like a poisonous flower budding in the dark? Fabia Shah mumbled on about Bilal and America and somebody called Abu, possibly Abu Bakr Shah, her brother, as Caitlin recalled from the al Banna case history.

There was no time for contemplation or further questioning, however, because somebody was coming.

Caitlin spun up from the bed, as silent as quicksilver, bringing the fat black silencer of the gun to bear on the bedroom doorway.

Whispered voices, both male. Low and guttural.

She stood with knees bent slightly, breathing in through her nose, out through her mouth. Centered. Waiting for it to happen.

Behind her Fabia began to mumble about Bilal and America again.

The voices stopped, and with them all movement in the apartment.

No footfalls. No elbows brushing against walls. No creaking knee joints or the whisper of one pants leg against another.

"Bilal is back but gone. Gone away," Fabia murmured.

Caitlin resisted the urge to turn toward the only voice in the apartment. She kept the oversized suppressor targeted on the open doorway. She closed one eye as a precaution. Her night vision was dark-adapted so completely that simply flicking on a light would be enough to blind her.

Fabia snored, a long and ratcheting hawking noise that ended with a gulp.

Caitlin heard snickers from just outside the doorway.

She heard a few muttered words in Arabic.

"She is dreaming. There's nobody here. Abu smokes too much hash."

"We need to check, anyway."

The outline of a man appeared. Relatively young, she judged. Dressed in sports training gear. His eyes were drawn to the bed where the woman lay, and for a second he did not notice the assassin's form in the darkened room. Caitlin took in all she needed to know in less than a second. The man was carrying a blade and a pistol.

As his partner moved into frame just behind him, she silently cursed herself. She had left the iron cage open at the front of the apartment and all but invited these two inside.

At the very instant she made that judgment the first of them finally realized she was there. A jolt of surprise ran through his entire body, and he swore, back-pedaling into his partner, knocking them both off balance. Caitlin flared into action, closing the distance between them like a dark swift illusion, a flicker of malice. She pivoted on one foot, performing a nearly perfect spin *en pointe,* generating great centrifugal force as she whipped around in a tight circle, the outer edge of which was drawn with the muzzle of the heavy Reflex Suppressor. She smashed the improvised bludgeon into the temple of the nearer intruder, crushing the side of his skull like a chocolate egg. He grunted and dropped, a dead weight hitting the floor with a dense thud and metallic clang as the handgun struck ceramic tiles. Behind him the other man groaned, a small pathetic cry of abject fear, as he raised both hands in front of him to ward off the evil shadow that had just killed his partner. Caitlin pistoned out a front kick, driving it up into the man's groin and feeling a distinct pop as one of his testicles burst like a rotten grape. The pain was enough to cut off his strangled shriek as his body folded violently in half. Flowing forward with the momentum of her attack, she swung the machine pistol down on the back of his head as his body crumpled. Two vicious knee strikes into his face arrested the fall for just a split second as Caitlin swirled around him like a stream around a stone. Her free arm encircled his bloodied head, guiding his descent along the same circular path as her turn, until she savagely reversed direction and snapped his neck with a wet cracking sound.

His body finally tumbled on top of the other.

In the room next to them, Fabia snored again, deep in a drugged sleep.

Shit.

She needed a cleanup crew, *now,* but could not call on Berlin Control for backup.

She would have to extract herself and sanitize the site, but first she had to find out whether these clowns had been working alone. From the snatch of conversation she had heard, she feared not. It seemed as though they'd been alerted to her presence by an observer.

She tasted copper in her throat, and her heart accelerated noticeably. Was this some sort of trap? Had Baumer left people watching his mother, knowing that Caitlin would come looking for him? If he had, he'd chosen his men poorly. Or perhaps not. Perhaps these guys were the trip wire.

A quick inspection revealed the gun to be none the worse for its brief use as an improvised club. She wiped off some torn patches of scalp and blood on the track suit of one of the men she had just killed before folding the metal stock away but leaving the suppressor in place.

She checked the hallway through the small fish-eye lens in the front door. It appeared to be empty, but she stepped out with the gun raised, ready to fire.

Clear.

Caitlin spent a minute finding another stairwell that could take her down to the ground floor. She stopped at every level and checked for trouble. The building's occupants all seemed to be asleep now. Even the night owls and insomniacs had given up and shut down their televisions.

Reaching the ground floor, she was painfully aware of just how much her combat fitness had been reduced by pregnancy and childbirth. Still stronger and faster than many world-class athletes, she was nonetheless well below her own peak levels of readiness. Her breasts throbbed and leaked abominably, and she felt as though she might have torn something inside. Nothing large or vital, but enough to need eventual treatment. Instead, if she was clear, she was going to have to drag two bodies out of Fabia's apartment and do a rough and ready disposal, all in the next five minutes.

She peeked out onto the street, and the situation deteriorated immediately. Half a dozen youths, all of them dressed in flowing shirts and loose pants, some sporting black bandannas and some with baseball caps, were leaning against a brick fence about a hundred yards down the street.

A Dignity Patrol, she assumed.

But why would they be loitering in a quiet street with no passing traffic?

A quick look reassured her that her car was parked out of their line of sight, but she was certain their appearance had to be related to the two idiots she had just encountered.

Maybe they'd been tracking them, looking to impose a little jihadi-style vigilante justice. Or maybe the intruders were part of this crew. She simply did not have enough information, and there was almost no time.

She hurried back up to the flat, less concerned with stealth than with speed now.

Nothing had changed. The bodies lay where she had taken them down. Fabia still was snoring away like a buzz saw.

She had neither the strength nor the opportunity to drag the men out of the building and into her car for safe disposal somewhere far away, and she could not leave them there for Shah to find when she woke up. Caitlin's intrusion would stay with her as a bad dream at worst, easily dismissed and forgotten in the light of day. Two corpses bleeding out on her cheap brown carpet would be more problematic.

There was a quick and dirty solution, however.

She took the uppermost body by the wrists and dragged it out of the apartment, careful not to let any more blood leak out onto the floor. The sensation of having a bad stitch in her guts was back, but she ignored it, pulling the dead man all the way down the corridor to a utility room at the far end. She was ready to whip out her lock pick tools, but it was unnecessary because the door was unlocked. Once the body was deposited, she returned to the flat and repeated the performance, bundling the remains of the second man on top of the first. A quick search of their pockets turned up no ID, but she did find something more useful: a set of keys. Caitlin latched and closed the door before jamming an ill-fitting house key into the lock and snapping it off. That should secure them for a couple of hours in the morning.

A few blood smears marked the dirty tiled floor, but they weren't the only ones she could see. Just the freshest, and they would discolor quickly.

She returned to the apartment and scanned it quickly for anything she might have dropped and left behind, but her training had taken hold at a cellular level and there was nothing beyond the bloodstains on the carpet, about which she could do little. The syringe she'd used on Baumer's mother was sitting snugly in a jacket pocket, recapped with its small orange plastic lid. She knelt down to see if the carpet was one of those old-style ones, laid down in squares that could be peeled up and moved around for occasions such as this—you know, when you've whacked a couple of dudes and don't want their brain fluids and blood on public display. But no, the carpet had been laid in one piece.

She shrugged it off.

It wasn't important because she would be gone from Berlin early the next morning.

This time, when leaving the flat, she closed and locked the door and the security grille. She would have preferred to have taken Fabia into custody for a full debrief, but she was working dark and had to go with what she had.

Baumer was in America.

The light in the hallway seemed flat and harsh after the gloom of Fabia's apartment, hurting her eyes and even making them water a little with the contrast. She double-timed away from the flat, moving toward the staircase she had taken before, machine pistol at the ready, hoping to navigate her way to the rear of the building and slip out onto a side street where she might get away undetected.

The two youths who emerged from the door at the end of the corridor deep-sixed that plan. They were obviously part of the group downstairs, dressed in white *thobe* shirts and loose-fitting cotton pants. They both carried whips, a little like South African *sjamboks,* but the first who emerged was also armed with a sawed-off shotgun. Caitlin did not falter in her approach as she saw them, but they did, obviously surprised to be confronted by a tall blond woman clad in black jeans and leather, covered in blood and advancing on them with murder in her eyes.

"It is her!" one of them shouted. "She is here."

She saw the shotgun start to rise, but it was too late for the shooter. Her PP-2000 was already at shoulder level, the wide black tube of the Reflex Suppressor unwavering as she squeezed the trigger twice. The weapon stuttered, and spent shell casings tinkled off the cold concrete walls as the men's white shirts were puffed and shredded by a small storm of 9-mm Parabellum. The gunman fell away, cracking his head on the wall and then the floor as he crashed down. The other spun backward into the stairwell again, forcing Caitlin to move a few steps forward, lower the muzzle, and put a finishing burst into his head, which came apart in spectacular fashion, spraying bright red sunbursts of blood and bone chips and gray matter everywhere.

"So much for stealth," she muttered before stepping over the men and hurrying down the stairs, sweeping for more challengers as she went.

They were already charging toward her, and these guys looked a lot more capable, all of them armed with hand cannons of some sort and moving as a fluid group, covering one another.

Two single shots crashed out, echoing and caroming off the steel handrail.

"Allahu akbar!"

"Oh, for fuck's sake," she sighed.

She worked quickly, covering the flight below with the machine gun, squeezing out a few bursts as she used her free hand to haul out the cigarette pack in which Gerty had hidden the small but powerful binary explosive. Caitlin stripped off the lid, pushed in the tab that allowed the two elements to mingle, set the rudimentary timer for seven seconds, and then calmly walked down the steps, firing off fast irregular volleys from the Russian gun, keeping the heads of her targets down until she rounded the last landing and tossed the small package down among them. She ducked back behind the shelter of the thick concrete steps as the bomblet exploded with a titanic crash that shook the entire building.

All need for stealth and care now gone, she took out the second PP-2000 and advanced firing both weapons. The second, unsilenced gun roared with an earsplitting report that completely drowned out the sound of the first. As she swung around on the last flight of steps, she saw that two of the men had been caught by the explosion and killed instantly, one of them split from neck to groin as though gutted by a butcher and the other simply taken apart into four or five large pieces. A third man was crawling away from the shattered glass entry, and she stitched him up along the spine, finishing with a head shot as another bullet cracked past her ear.

The fourth and final target had made it halfway to the footpath and was firing wildly over his shoulder. Two more bullets fizzed close by before she could draw a bead on him with the silenced gun. Before she could pull the trigger, his head disintegrated and his lifeless body tumbled over.

She dived for the nearest cover, a concrete pillar.

She scanned the darkness for the second shooter and heard the unmistakable growl of her BMW as it suddenly appeared in front of Fabia Shah's building with Dalby at the wheel.

"Come on," he called out. "Get a bloody move on."

She hurried down the steps as lights went on all over the street and a fire alarm wailed somewhere.

"What... fuck?" was all she could manage as she dived into the passenger seat through the door he had leaned over to fling open for her.

"Sorry," Dalby said. "Might have been fibbing about sending you out on your own."

* * *

"What the fuck, Dalby!"

She waited until he pulled out of the street before punching him on the shoulder. The Englishman drove at the speed limit and was careful not to draw attention to them with any reckless maneuvers. He had mounted a scanner on the dashboard, and they could hear emergency calls going out to the police.

"I'm sorry, Ms. Monroe... Caitlin. But just as you were an undeclared asset, I'm afraid my presence here is, too. We're not inclined to take risks with our continental colleagues anymore."

The shakes took hold of her as they drove along the street where she and Mirsaad had investigated the market stalls early that morning. No, she corrected herself. That was yesterday morning. She was having trouble keeping it all straight and was annoyed at her jittery unprofessional response to the ambush, or at least to the aftermath, including Dalby's unexpected intervention.

"Seriously, I mean it. What the fuck are you doing here, Dalby? And what was the story with all the Universal Exports doublespeak before? What the hell kind of double-blind bullshit operation is this? Do you want al Banna found? Are they fucking serious about tracing the supply chains through here? What the hell is going on?"

Dalby had the decency to look abashed as he drove them out of the shariatown on a heading for the airport. Caitlin could hear sirens as the first responders sped toward Neukölln.

"I apologize, I really do, Caitlin," Dalby said. "But needs must out when the Devil drives. I was not leading you astray when we spoke earlier, although I am sorry I could not reveal I was also in Berlin. We all have our histories, Caitlin, and I'm afraid I have quite a bit of history with this city. I'm not supposed to be here, ever."

He didn't elaborate, and she didn't expect him to. They drove on as a fire engine and two ambulances sped past with sirens howling and lights flashing. Dalby ignored them and stuck to his route, which she was now certain was taking them in a great loop toward Tempelhof Airport.

"I volunteered as your overwatch officer because I suspected something like this might happen."

Caitlin bristled. "I do know how to do my job, you know, Dalby," she said, but regretted her tone. The man had put himself at great risk to help her and probably remained at risk as long as he was in Berlin. "Sorry," she said. "Can you just bring me up to speed with what's happening?"

"What's happening is a rather amateurish attempt at distraction," he said. "We are now of the opinion that the attack on your family was not really personal. It was meant merely to appear as such, to make us imagine that Baumer had returned to Germany after escaping his confinement in Guadeloupe. Attacking your family, then drawing you to Berlin, where you could be ambushed, would play out as a rather neatly packaged revenge scenario had Baumer been able to call on sufficiently competent help. Fortunately for you, he wasn't. Partly because we suspect that having rebuilt his networks quite quickly from the refugee cohort, which has arrived here in great numbers these last few years, he committed the best of his people to New York."

Caitlin shook her head and blinked away a moment of dizziness and nausea as they traversed the northern boundary of Tempelhof.

"So what, you think he's gone into piracy now? That doesn't make sense. That's not the guy I went after back in 2003. He's a believer, not a crook."

"Indeed he is," Dalby agreed. "And believers are always much more dangerous than your common garden-variety villains. That's why we've never lost interest in him. It's why, when he reached out to you through Richardson and his men, we were able to authorize this operation at such short notice and to resource it when there are so many calls on our resources because of New York. There are no coincidences, Caitlin."

"You knew? All the time?" she asked quietly.

Any other man who knew her would have immediately sensed the danger. But Dalby showed no sign of feeling threatened. Only tired.

"No, we didn't. We had our suspicions. I certainly had mine. But suspicions are so common as to be a worthless currency in our trade, Caitlin. We can only know what we know, and until then anything is possible. Up until a few hours ago it was possible that you would actually be reassigned to the very, very important job of finding out where the street traders of Neukölln are sourcing their plentiful supplies of cheap toasters and Levi's jeans. It was only after you were ambushed that I was able to convince our lords and masters you had more important work to do."

"In New York?" she asked.

"Yes," he said as he turned off the main road and onto a disused concrete laneway that led to an open gate on the airport's northeastern fringe. A short distance beyond that a Gulfstream V stood ready on the tarmac with its engines spooled up and cabin lights dimmed. Dalby pulled up as a man popped his head out of the hatchway just behind the cockpit and waved to them.

"I'm sorry I couldn't give you all of the information to which I was privy, Caitlin," he said. "But I honestly did not have much, and information is one thing, meaning is another. We now have, I think, a much better understanding of the meaning of what has happened in New York and how it connects to what happened to you."

"What is Baumer doing?" Caitlin asked as she struggled to maintain her temper.

"He has taken his people to the New World," Dalby said. "There to build a new world for them."

Caitlin was quiet for a moment as she took it all in: the deceit, the betrayals, the shifting agendas and interests. As much as the lines and details shifted and blurred, however, one thing remained constant. She had but one interest, finding the man who had used her family. That was worse, much worse, than imagining he had come after them as part of some intensely personal vengeance trip. He hadn't cared at all. Killing them meant nothing. It was a tactic to buy time, and not much time at that.

"This plane is one of ours. It will take you to a small airfield in upstate New York, where you'll transition to a military craft for insertion into New York. You'll be jumping in, I'm afraid, hopefully just before dawn over there. You're rated for HAHO operations, as I understand. You'll find all of the equipment you need at the other end," Dalby said.

"I won't need any equipment," she said. "I am going to kill him with the same hands that held my baby after he tried to take her from me."

41

TEXAS ADMINISTRATIVE DIVISION

McDonald Lake was a small, brown, roughly triangular patch of brackish water hidden away in a thicket of dense forest a mile or two southeast of where Texas 155 crossed the Farm to Market Road 321. The woodlands, closely woven with black hickory, cedar, elm, sugarberry, and bunch grasses, enclosed a large fenced clearing where the cattle could graze safely without any danger that they might be observed by road agents. Miguel was also hopeful that the vegetation might smother some of the noise that always attended a herd, even now, late at night, with the animals content to stand around occasionally tearing mouthfuls of feed from the earth but mostly settling down to sleep.

A hard chill had returned with nightfall, and both he and Sofia were well wrapped up inside thick lamb's wool jackets. Both still wore their riding gloves, however, rather than thicker winter mittens, just in case they should suddenly have need of their weapons. Miguel still carried his Winchester and Lupara despite an offer from the Mormons of an assault rifle from their armory.

The cowboy acknowledged the greater firepower and range of the M16s, but he preferred to work with a tool that felt as familiar in his hands as his reins. Sofia still carried her Remington, but now she also carried an M4 carbine she had picked up from one of the agents in Crockett. She had trained with the M16, a similar weapon, when they had first arrived in Texas and had taken to training with the carbine for half an hour at the end of each day.

They crunched across a small patch of gravel, the remnants of an old walking track that wound through the clearing. Miguel could hear the sound of the cattle splashing through the mud and water at the edge of the lake as they took a late-night drink. At the other end of the clearing two dark silhouettes, Adam and Ben Randall, patrolled the far edge of the herd. The cattle dogs, Red and Blue, kept pace with Miguel as he walked.

"Papa," she said quietly as they made their rounds of the herd.

"Yes, Princess," said Miguel in a low voice. Part of him was listening to his daughter, but part of him was constantly alive to the possibility that danger might be nearby.

"The men who killed all those people back in that town…"

"The road agents, in Palestine."

"Yes," said Sofia. "Do you think they are nearby?"

Miguel gave her shoulder a squeeze in the dark. "I hope not," he said. "But I think not, too. I think they would have been on us by now if they were near."

He could tell his daughter was not encouraged by the answer.

"We shall be fine," he added for her benefit. "If we are careful and vigilant, they will not surprise us as they did those settlers. And if they try, we shall give them the same treatment we gave those pirates when they attacked us on Miss Julianne's boat. You do remember that, don't you?"

"Of course, Papa. I was not a baby, you know. I even helped that day with the dressings and the ammunition."

Miguel grunted as he gave her a pat on the back.

"Yes you did, little one," he said. "You were very brave. All of the family was."

They both fell into a mournful silence then. Miguel pressed his lips together and shook his head as if in that gesture of denial he might somehow negate all that had happened. But, of course, there was no magic in the world. They simply trudged around the edge of the forest, occasionally squelching through a cowpat, unseen in the dark. Miguel felt Sofia's fingers reach out for and entwine with his.

"I miss Mama," she said. "And little Manny, and *Abuela* Ana, and…"

"I know, I know. I miss them all, too, every minute of every day, and while I sleep and when I wake. But I still have you, Sofia, and you I will not have taken from me."

He stopped next to a small cluster of longhorns that lowed gently and moved away as soon as they saw the dogs. Miguel turned to his daughter and placed both hands on her shoulders. It was good to see her mourn, show some emotion over the loss of their family. For far too long she had been a stranger to him, cold, forbidding.

"I know that some days it is very hard to go on. Sometimes it seems pointless," he said. "But that is not what they would want, Sofia. Your mother especially; she would want me to get you safe away from here so that you might grow up and continue the family. In the end that is all that matters. Not me; my time is almost past—"

He felt her shoulders tense up under his hands but shushed her before she could protest.

"No, it is true. I am not old, not like some of your uncles were, but the family part of my life is over. It has been taken from me. But your life lies in front of you. We will endure this, Sofia. We will survive, and you will rebuild our family, and you will make sure that all of those Peiraros to come know of those who preceded them. That is what God has planned for you. For me… well, for now there is you to look after. And when I have you safe, then we shall settle our score with Blackstone and his men. That is what God means for me to do, *Princesa*."

Leaves rustled in the evergreen trees, and branches creaked as a cold wind blew up from the south. Miguel resumed their round of the herd, opening his senses to the night again, listening for the telltale sounds of men nearby and not hearing them.

"Adam really likes Sally, doesn't he?" Sofia said without warning.

The vaquero was glad of the dark night that hid his smile.

"That is only natural," he said. "They have traveled together, and they are of the same people. I suspect hitting him with your rifle butt in Crockett did not improve your chances."

Sofia laughed. "Maybe, maybe not."

Miguel searched for and quickly found the distant silhouettes of the Mormon boy and the giant engineer. They were on the far side of the clearing. He kept his voice down.

"It is good you make friends with Adam and the others," said Miguel. "We need each other out here. But our paths will part somewhere in the future. You should remember that, too."

He was unsure what to say next. This was the sort of discussion Sofia would have had with her mother or grandmother not so long ago. Miguel would simply have stood in the background scowling and polishing his rifle to put the fear of God into any potential suitors. Now he found himself having to play a role for which he was entirely unsuited. When he thought of Sofia, the age she was, and all the changes that would come as she grew from a young girl into a young woman, he felt himself even more wretchedly alone than before. Perhaps one of the Mormon ladies could help with such things, at least for now, while they shared the trail.

Any further discomfort was forestalled by the return of Randall and young Adam. They cut across the clearing, a half-moon lighting their way. A few of the cattle protested at their passage, but mostly they moved aside. Ben Randall was a massive shape in the dark. He towered over his smaller companion, cursing softly and muttering as he tripped on an unseen obstacle. Of all the Mormons, he was the most likely in Miguel's experience to cuss like a normal person.

"Hey," said Sofia.

"Hey," Adam replied.

"We all good?" Randall asked.

Miguel scowled into the inky blackness of the forest that surrounded them. "Good? No, I would not say that."

Instantly, Randall seemed more alert, his back straighter, his presence more watchful. "Why? You see something, hear something?"

"No, and that is the problem. I see and hear nothing, which might mean there is nothing to fear. But I do not like feeling my way through the dark like a blind man in a roomful of traps. I will not be happy until we know for sure where the men who killed the settlers have gone."

The big man sighed, and his shoulders dropped a little.

"I'm with you on that," he said. "Ever since we buried those poor people, it's like I've been feeling someone's eyeballs staring at the back of my neck. Not a pleasant sensation, no, sir."

They began a slow, careful walk to the northeast, following the path of one of the remnant trails that led off to the farmhouse a mile or two distant, where the rest of their companions had settled down for the night. It was a solid structure with good clear lines of fire all around. It would be easily defensible.

"We should have scouts," Adam said, glancing meaningfully at Sofia.

Miguel agreed with him, but aloud he said, "There are few of us to spare. Where would we look?"

Adam surprised him by answering, "We don't need to look everywhere. We just need to know that the route we're taking is safe."

Sofia confirmed her father's suspicions that the two teenagers had been discussing this issue by quickly following up on Adam's suggestion.

"That's right," she said as they reached the tree line at the edge of the clearing. The going became much tougher there. They did not have the night vision goggles, and the two men had agreed it would be reckless to use a torch that might be spotted many miles away. As long as the moon was out, they had just enough light to pick their way through the undergrowth, but whenever it disappeared behind a drift of cloud, they were forced to proceed much more carefully and slowly. The dogs, in contrast, bounded ahead, crashing through the long grass and occasionally tripping on a tree root without a care.

"It's worth considering," Randall said. "We probably should send riders ahead just to be sure."

"And who would these riders be?" Miguel wondered aloud.

"I'll go," said Adam.

"Me, too," Sofia added quickly.

The night brightened just perceptibly as a meteor streaked overhead. Miguel resisted the urge to stare at it, not wanting to ruin his night vision.

"I do not think so, *Princesa,*" he said. "But you, Adam, you could ride with me if Cooper Aronson allowed it."

He braced himself for his daughter's protest, and it was not long in coming.

"That's not fair," she said just a little too loudly before continuing in a stage whisper. "I can ride and shoot as well as Adam, probably better. No, much better. Sorry, Adam, but it's true."

It was true, Miguel thought. Her performance in Crockett had confirmed that. With her hunting experience, she had all the natural makings of a scout. He often found her looking at the next horizon with binoculars or her Remington in hand. The trail boss in him saw the merit of her argument.

But there was no way he was going to have his only surviving daughter tracking the sorts of monsters responsible for the atrocity in Palestine. Adam was skilled enough to do that sort of work, and after the gunfight in Crockett, Miguel trusted him to keep his head.

The lad seemed most put out to have had his manly virtues dismissed by Sofia. Miguel could tell, even in the dark, that Adam was considering a wounded protest.

The cowboy smiled to himself.

Miss Sally would look all the more attractive to the Mormon boy now.

Cooper Aronson sipped at the steaming mug of coffee. In the soft, guttering candlelight he looked as though he'd aged ten years in the short time Miguel had known him. His eyes stared out from sunken pits, and the cowboy could swear that deep lines and new crevasses scored his face. The Mormon leader stood at a cork-covered island bench with his hands wrapped around the chipped enamel coffee mug as though he were hugging it for comfort as much as for warmth. Only three candles burned in the kitchen, where Miguel, Ben Randall, Willem D'Age, and Aronson had gathered after a modest evening meal of salt pork and beans. All the rest had bunked down in their sleeping bags throughout the farmhouse after the Mormons had tended to the remains of one of the former residents.

"It seems a reasonable idea," Aronson said. "But are you sure that Adam is the one to take with you?"

"He is a good boy," Miguel said. "Brave and reliable. And he will be under my supervision, of course. I will ensure he does not run off the trail and do something stupid."

Ben Randall topped off his mug from the coffeepot standing on the bench in front of them. Maive Aronson had made up the brew after discovering a stash of vacuum-sealed beans in the larder. They were not exactly fresh, but it was still something of a luxury to have them.

"I'm happy to go with Miguel," Randall offered, but the vaquero could tell from the way the lines in Aronson's face grew even longer and deeper that he did not relish the idea of losing a man who had proved himself so capable in the brutal hand-to-hand fight back at Crockett.

"No, I think we will go with Miguel's idea," Aronson said. "If he's the one out scouting for these characters, I think we should leave it to him who he chooses to ride with."

The engineer shrugged off what could have been taken as a slight, but Miguel felt he needed to explain himself anyway.

"My daughter will be here when I ride away," he said. "I would be happier, much happier, knowing you were here to guard her. I saw you beating down those road agents in Crockett, Randall. Sofia will be safe with you."

Randall tipped his coffee mug slightly toward Miguel. "And you can rest assured no harm will come to her while there is breath in my body, Miguel," he said.

"Then we shall head out before first light," said the cowboy. "Adam is already sleeping. He has packed himself a bedroll and supplies for a five-day ride. I shall do the same. But first we should agree on a route, yes?"

He reached along the bench for one of the battered Rand McNally road maps they were using to navigate through Texas. The thick, laminated foldout map was covered in squiggles and notes. It was fraying at the edges and along the creases where it had been folded and unfolded countless times. Miguel made a mental note to pick up a new one when the opportunity arose. They cleared a space between the candles and refolded the document to center it on their current location.

Miguel placed his finger on their location and traced a rough waving line to the north. "We shall follow this path," he said. "Switching and doubling back as we go, clearing a trail, shall we say twenty miles wide, looking for any sign of the agents."

"And if you do find them?" Aronson said.

"Then we shall make sure they do not find us."

42

TEXAS ADMINISTRATIVE DIVISION

The dogs began growling long before Miguel and Adam approached the ridgeline. The vaquero called them back with a nightingale whistle, as they had been taught, and tossed each a piece of beef jerky as a reward.

"Stay. Be quiet," he ordered them before motioning to the boy to dismount and secure his horse. Adam did as he was told, not saying a word, leading his mare to a cedar tree, where he tied her to a low branch before unslinging an M4 carbine fitted with a heavy-looking silencer. Life on the range was pressing all the youth out of him, leaving just the hardy stripling of a young man behind. He was learning quickly.

Miguel took a moment to look behind him, checking all the possible places where Sofia might lurk. After Crockett he was especially sharp to the notion that she might repeat her performance.

Once satisfied that his daughter had stayed behind, Miguel took his Winchester from the scabbard. They advanced cautiously to the crest through a light forest of fir trees, mountain juniper, and a few scattered conifers and Dutch elms. The forest floor was soft with pine needles, deadening the sound of their approach. Miguel could smell wood smoke and roasting pig meat, and his mouth watered involuntarily. A few feet from the top, they both crouched down and snaked forward the rest of the way on their bellies. Miguel gave Adam a brief nod. The boy was doing fine and seemed unaffected by the anxiety that had nearly unmanned him before the rescue at Crockett.

The voices reached them as they warily raised themselves up on their elbows and peered over the ridgeline. The hillside fell away a good three hundred yards down to a plateau that had been cleared of trees a long time in the past. A hunting lodge, most likely constructed from the felled pines and firs, stood facing the west, bathed in the warm light of the late-afternoon sun. A band of men, over twenty of them, lolled about on the soft grass in front of the lodge and on couches and Adirondack chairs sheltered under a generous front porch. A spitted hog fizzed and crackled over a bed of coals, causing Miguel to wonder at its origin. Pigs were one of the animals that had vanished or been killed in great numbers by the Wave. Was this a feral leftover or perhaps a trophy taken from some poor settler family, perhaps even those poor folk they had found back in Palestine?

"Agents?" his companion asked in a low voice.

Miguel nodded. The men were well armed with military weapons, and their camp looked as though it had been professionally supplied. They were dressed in the same ragtag fashion as the agents back in Crockett, sporting outlandish costumes obviously chosen more for effect than for practicality. As he drew a pair of binoculars to study the camp in closer detail, two women emerged from the hut, both attired in the same slutty fashion as the camp whores they had liberated: miniskirts, boots, low-cut T-shirts. None of it was sensible in cold spring weather, but he had to admit they were outfits well chosen to please the men they were with. Miguel studied the camp for five minutes, searching for evidence of any captives, but there were none. Perhaps this band of outlaws preferred to move more freely than would be possible with reluctant prisoners in tow. Perhaps that was why the women in Palestine had not survived their encounter, if these were the men responsible.

Miguel grunted in frustration.

"Anything seem strange to you, Miguel?" Adam asked, keeping his eye to the scope of his weapon.

"What am I looking for?"

"A lot of them are clean-shaven, lean and trim," Adam said. "Not like the other agents."

"I see," Miguel said. "Blackstone's soldiers, perhaps?"

Adam shrugged. "Suspect so."

It was all idle and pointless speculation. They could not know the minds of the men down in that glade, and short of stealing into the camp to snatch a prisoner for interrogation, they never would. And again, what would be the point? They had been lucky in Crockett. The agents there had been sloppy and ill disciplined. There was nothing about this gang that made him think they would be as fortunate a second time around. The camp was well laid out, with garbage and sewage pits dug well away from the lodge and the little spring that presumably provided their water. If they were soldiers, there would be fighting positions, traps, and perhaps even land mines hidden around the exterior of the camp. A line of clothes hung drying in the weak sunlight, attended by the whores who had just emerged from the lodge, and there was even a small vegetable patch situated to catch the northern sun.

No. These men knew what they were doing, which meant they would have patrols out in the woods.

He had seen enough.

"Let's go," he mouthed to Adam.

* * *

"We must divert farther to the northeast," Miguel insisted.

He warmed his hands over a potbellied stove in a holiday house overlooking Pineywoods Lake, a good twenty miles to the west of the road agent's camp. Most of the Mormon party was there save for Benjamin and Maive, who were out riding patrol. The ranch-style home, all timber and stone, had expansive views over the water, which rippled in the glow of a crescent moon. He was able to see out through the picture windows because a few candles and the glowing coals of the stove provided the only illumination, creating just the ghost reflection of the small group of travelers in the glass. Still rugged up against the cold, routinely armed, thin and tired, they presented an almost medieval image when viewed against the background of the moon-dappled lake.

"Are you sure about this, Miguel?" Cooper Aronson asked. "It could add weeks to our traveling time, and I don't need to tell you that every day we're out in the wilderness is another we're at risk."

"I saw them, too, brother," Adam said, speaking with quiet confidence. "They were road agents for a certainty. And a meaner crew than we saw in Crockett. They looked... I don't know... professional."

"He is right," Miguel said. "They were agents, and I suspect they may have been the ones responsible for Palestine. They were close enough for it to fall within their territory if it is true that Crockett was the northern extent of the other gang's turf."

He cast an inquiring eye over at the camp whore called Marsha. Of the women they had taken in after Crockett, she had adapted best to her new role with the Mormons. That did not make her particularly reliable or pleasant company, but she was better than her two sullen friends who sat apart smoking hand-rolled cigarettes and furtively drinking from a hip flask they passed between each other. The Saints did not prevent their drinking—that would have been unfair given that they raised no objection to Miguel taking a sip at the end of the day—but they did not encourage the women to feel comfortable doing so in their presence. Marsha sat well away from the two women but still maintained her distance from everyone else except Miss Jessup, who formed a bridge of sorts between the two groups of women.

"Well, Marsha, do you think it's true?" Trudi asked, in a gentle voice. "From what you knew. Are the men Miguel and Adam saw today likely to be agents claiming the country north of Crockett?"

Marsha glared momentarily at Miguel, who had, after all, blown the head off her man, but she softened under a supportive shoulder pat from Miss Jessup. Sofia rolled her eyes at her father, but he motioned her to be still. There was no sense holding a grudge against this woman for the company she had kept, not when she might be of some use to them.

"Could be," Marsha offered. "The boys didn't like to talk much about that sorta thing. They'd brag all day on a shootin' or some pillage. But old Tom, he cracked down pretty hard on discussin' things like that. You know, turf and politics."

Miguel nodded. "Old Tom was the last man we hanged, yes?"

Marsha glared at him. "He was. And he was a good guy, too!"

Sofia snorted. "He was a murderer and a rapist who got what he deserved."

"I am sure he has gone to his reward," the vaquero intoned in a flat voice before addressing Aronson again. "You know my feelings about the agents. They are Fort Hood men. Perhaps not the lesser rank of them. They would just be thugs for hire, expendable. But the leaders of these gangs, they must answer to Blackstone, and to run their gangs as effectively as they do, they must have some training. The camp today, it was like the army with its discipline. I believe had we delayed long on that ridge, we would have been caught by them. They are not amateurs, and we will have a hard time staying away from them if we pursue our original route. This is why we must divert to the northeast. We cannot go west and into the lands directly controlled by Fort Hood. To them you are federales. Seattle's people. You will not find an easy passage there."

Willem D'Age leaned forward from his perch next to his fiancée Jenny, on the end of an expensive-looking leather couch. He used a small log to open the grille of the wood stove. Tossing in more fuel, he took up the case with Aronson.

"Miguel might be right. We did have trouble with those Texas customs and excise people a few days after we left Corpus Christi. You said at the time it was almost like they were waiting for us. And to tithe us as they did, I still do not believe that to be legal or just."

Miguel folded his arms and nodded. "It is as I said. Out here justice is a bullet. These customs men, they pretended to tax you?"

Aronson snorted.

"No pretending about it, my friend. They took ten percent of our herd and supplies. Said it was a border fee or some such thing. They had papers and issued us with a receipt. It was all very official. Right down to the platoon of Texas Defense Force soldiers standing watch over the transaction. But they also said we would need to pay more tolls if we used the state roads to offset the cost of our protection. That's how we came to ride through the agents' territory. It seemed to us we would have nothing left if we tarried long in Blackstone country."

Miguel stroked the rough beard on his chin and grunted.

"I have heard similar tales of federal ranches similarly taxed despite the exemption from Seattle, although it did not happen to me. Why take something piece by piece when you can have it in one bite, I suppose."

"So do we do as Miguel suggests and ride around these men?" Adam asked, surprising the cowboy and causing Aronson to raise his eyebrows, too. The lad had developed a very mature sort of confidence. Miguel suppressed a smile as he saw young Sally Gray glancing approvingly at the boy, an interlude that his daughter very studiously chose to ignore. She would just have to accept the situation, he thought. The two Mormon youngsters had been spending a great deal of time together when the boy's duties allowed, and although Miguel could see that Adam was drawn to the exotic in Sofia, there was no doubting the attraction of one's own kind in the end.

He did not imagine they would be zipping their sleeping bags together, however. The Mormons maintained a strict propriety regarding such things. Even D'Age and his fiancée still slept apart. For Miguel, who felt Mariela's absence like a suppurating wound, it was an impressive display of abstinence. What he would not give just to lie down with his wife one last time. Just to tell her of the things there had never been time to discuss in the rush of the everyday.

He rubbed at his eyes as they blurred and watered. Nobody noticed the weakness.

"I do not suppose we can hope to stand down this gang if we encounter them," Aronson mused.

Again, before Miguel could answer, Adam spoke up.

"Not a chance," he insisted. "They looked sharp and mean. The best we can hope for is to never see them again. I suggest we move before first light. They will have outriders, and the cattle do raise a dust cloud."

Sally Gray, sitting next to Jenny, nodded vigorously but remained quiet.

"What say you, Willem?" Aronson asked.

"I'm with Brother Adam and Miguel, Cooper. I fear these men might be the perpetrators of that mass murder. And if they are, we will get no quarter from them. Not out here. I think it best if we take ourselves as far away as we can, as fast as possible."

Aronson sat quietly, weighing his responsibilities as their leader. Miguel could see Adam's impatience in every line of the youth's rigid stance. He had placed himself over near the main entry to the large, open lounge area, and unlike the others he was still cradling his carbine as though ready to use it at a moment's notice. Silence fell save for the crackling of the fire and the tinkling of cutlery on plates and bowls as a few of them finished their evening meals—beans and beef stew. Miguel gave Adam a look as if to say calm down, and the boy did visibly relax somewhat. Sofia meanwhile was as quiet and watchful as a cat.

"All right," the Mormon leader said, at last. "I have to agree. We have not the numbers or, frankly, the ability to tangle with men like this and survive the encounter. I suggest that we bed down early tonight and make a start before sunup in the morning. I'll tell Ben and Maive when they return from their patrol."

Miguel nodded in satisfaction as the official meeting started to break up. He had a watch to stand at two in the morning with Adam and hadn't yet eaten, having not long before come back from tending the horses, a role he had taken over after the death of Atchison. He took a ladle of stew from the big pot on top of the potbelly stove and tipped it carefully into a beautifully delicate china bowl, the sort of thing Mariela would have loved to have back at the ranch, something for good company.

"Fancy a drink, cowboy?"

He looked up from his stew, surprised to find Trudi Jessup holding a bottle of wine and two glasses.

"You found that here?" he asked.

Miss Jessup smiled. "They have a cellar. Had one, I mean. Awesomely stocked, too. This is a fucking 1990 Echezeaux Grand Cru!"

Miguel shook his head in bafflement.

"I have had some Tempranillo now and then, but I am not much of a wine drinker. This is good, then?"

"Actually, it's corked," said Jessup. "But what the hell. It's an imperfect world. Glass?"

He shrugged acceptance, and she poured him a solid slug. It had no cork floating in it that he could see, but perhaps she had strained it out. He would have.

The Mormons were clearing away the leftovers of the meal and drifting off to wherever they had found themselves a bed for the night. The two camp whores were still smoking, but he could see in the window reflection that one of them was grinning wickedly at him. Sofia was staring out into the darkness. Miss Jessup raised the bottle inquiringly, smiling with great warmth. Miguel felt very uncomfortable.

"My wife…" he said awkwardly.

She regarded him with a strange questioning look, her head tilting slightly and a weird smile quirking one side of her mouth. Then her eyebrows shot up and her mouth made a surprised little O.

"Oh! Sorry, Miguel. I didn't mean to give you any ideas or have any ideas about, you know… that. I mean, Jesus. How horrible. I'm not even…"

Sofia was watching them now, her attention drawn by the exchange.

Miss Jessup leaned forward, speaking in a lower voice. "I'm not even that into men, you know. I'm not a complete dyke, more sort of… manbivalent."

Now he was entirely confused.

What on earth did she mean by all of this? He felt his face beginning to flush as Sofia pushed herself up off the couch and walked over to join them, obviously intrigued by whatever was happening.

"Well, that is… excellent," he improvised, gulping a mouthful of the expensive corky wine to cover his embarrassment.

"Oh God," she snorted before descending into a fit of giggles. "Oh, no, I'm sorry. Look, Miguel," she said when she had herself back under control. "I like you. And your kid. She's tough," she said, nodding at Sofia, who was now standing beside him. "And you saved my fucking life, if you'll pardon my language… and you're… different, you know. You'll take a drink, for one thing, and you don't get all pussy-faced when I curse up a storm. I'm just saying I'd like a drink is all, and if we're gonna be on this trail together, I'd like us to be friends. Is that cool?"

Miguel forced a nervous smile. He thought he understood now. Sofia's smile was softer, more natural.

"I miss my friends from the camp and the boat," she said.

"Yes. Okay," Miguel said. "Friends are good. I had two very fine lady friends on the boat that got us out of Mexico," he said. "My wife, Mariela, God rest her soul, she liked them, too. Miss Julianne, a real English lady, and Miss Fifi, who had a neck as red as the merciless peppers of Quetzlzacatenango but a heart as golden as Montezuma's treasure room."

"Is that a joke, Miguel?" Miss Jessup smiled.

"It is," he replied a little sadly. "One of Miss Fifi's favorites. But I joke to make well my sadness. She is dead now, I'm afraid."

"I'm sorry to hear that," Trudi said. "It's a hard world, isn't it?"

"Yes, Miss Jessup. It is."

Adam appeared just then, saving him from further entanglement and awkwardness. Miguel saw his daughter searching the room for Sally Gray, but she had disappeared into the kitchen to help with the cleaning.

"Miss Jessup," said the boy. "Miguel. I'm going to bunk down now. Do you need me to wake you later? I got this new watch today. Found it in the study upstairs. It's one of those that keeps wound up just by the movement of your arms when you walk. It has an alarm, too."

"That would be good. Thank you, Adam," said the cowboy, wishing he could offer the boy a drink as a way of keeping him with them a little while longer. Instead he spooned up a mouthful of stew.

Miss Jessup, who seemed to have recovered her poise entirely, reached across and took Adam's wrist between her long brown fingers.

"That's a beauty, Adam. A TAG Heuer. It'll last you a lifetime if you look after it."

"You think so?" he asked.

"Oh, for sure. Hey, I don't suppose you can take a little drink, can you?" she asked conspiratorially, winking at him.

"Oh, no, ma'am. That would be sinful. For me, that is. You're welcome to, though. And Miguel, of course. He's Catholic. They drink *a lot*."

She rolled her eyes and laughed, a warm full-throated sound.

"Oh, Adam, I was schooled by nuns way back in the last century, so I figured that out a *long* time ago."

"Sofia," said Miguel, "would you like a mouthful of wine? Miss Jessup tells me it is very good."

"Oh, please call me Trudi. You're making me feel like an old schoolmarm with the Miss Jessup thing. And yes, Sofia, it is a very nice wine, if slightly oxidized."

Miguel was not a puritan. For a few years now he had allowed his oldest child a small occasional glass of wine and water with dinner, when appropriate. Both he and Mariela had always thought it best not to surround the taking of strong drink with too much magic and mystery the way the Mormons did.

"I'd like that," Sofia said. "We had wine at home sometimes. But I don't know how good it was."

Miguel allowed her to sip from his glass before Miss Jessup— sorry, Trudi—topped it off. The Mormons were all gone now, although he could hear the sounds of cleanup coming through from the kitchen. Marsha had stretched herself out on the couch under a colorful Navajo blanket and turned away from them. The other two whores were still smoking and muttering together, but they had lost interest in Miguel and Trudi. Adam, who was looking a little excluded, glanced about cautiously before reaching out for Trudi's glass.

"Perhaps just a sip," he said. "To see what all the fuss is about."

She beamed and let him take a mouthful, giggling again at the face he pulled.

"Tastes like cordial syrup or something," he said, apparently unimpressed.

"Well, officially, it smells like vanilla, orange peel, and cigars and tastes of sweet fruit, smoke, and a balancing acidity with spicy notes in the finish."

Both Miguel and Adam stared at her as though she were crazy. Sofia seemed fascinated, however.

"I used to be a food writer," she explained.

"You wrote recipes?" Miguel asked.

"Like cookbooks?" the boy added.

Sofia shook her head and sighed as though on stage. "No," she explained on Trudi's behalf. "I'll bet you used to write for magazines and stuff, didn't you? Like *Vogue* or something."

Trudi smiled, but she looked disheartened to Miguel.

"Yes, Sofia. I wrote restaurant reviews. For magazines and newspapers. Not much call for that sort of skill these days, though."

"Ah," Miguel said, suddenly understanding. "I knew a man once who worked for McDonald's. I used to manage their herds in Mexico. So you would write stories about eating in such places?"

"Oh my God, Papa," his daughter said as though he'd fatally embarrassed her.

Trudi Jessup, however, seemed to give the question a good deal of thought, and whatever she thought, it apparently amused her.

"Yes," she said after a moment. "That's what I would do. I'd eat in places... *like* McDonald's... and write a story about it. That's how I came to miss the Disappearance. I was in Sardinia, researching a story for *Gourmet Traveller*."

"I know that magazine," Sofia said. "There were copies on Miss Julianne's boat, after the Wave."

It wasn't exactly like a silence fell over them. The Wave had long ago receded, after all. But their good humor was subdued a little.

"I was in Edmonton," Adam said. "On a school trip."

"Oh," Trudi gasped unexpectedly. "You poor boy."

Miguel wondered what she meant, and she registered his puzzlement immediately.

"Don't you understand, Miguel?" she asked. "Edmonton was

cut in half by the Wave. The city was madness, they say. Pure killing madness."

Adam nodded, and the candlelight gave him a haunted look.

"It was," he said. "It was like a curtain of bright sparkles high in the sky. I saw a pair of police cars and an ambulance cross the Wave and crash into buildings on the other side. Another cop ran past me, shouting for people to get back while she was talking on her radio. The Wave reached out and snatched her."

Adam shook his head.

"I saw her eyes… She didn't even get a chance to scream."

Adam shivered.

"This is why we drink," said Miguel, taking his refilled glass from Trudi Jessup.

"Amen to that," she said.

43

NEW YORK

Yusuf Mohammed could think of no prouder moment than this as he stood in the shell of a ransacked department store to meet the warriors of his very first *saif*. The store, housed in a grand old building, had been thoroughly looted. Every window on the ground floor was broken, letting in the wind and rain and an acrid smell of burning chemicals from the battle that rumbled a few miles to the south. For the most part his men, all Africans like him, all of them converts to the religion of peace, were recent arrivals. Only Tony Katumu, a former Serengeti National Park ranger, had been in America for more than a month. The others—two Ugandans, one Kenyan, and a lighter-skinned Algerian—had all arrived via the Canadian wastes in the last two weeks. They were all seasoned fighters, but they could not keep the look of wonder from their eyes whenever they moved through the city streets. Even as a tomb, New York had the power to overwhelm a newcomer. Yusuf remembered his own sense of insignificance the first time he had glimpsed Manhattan's skyline from a distance. He'd felt as though he was trespassing in a burial ground for ancient gods. A blasphemous thought, of course, that he flinched away from the very moment he'd had it.

His men—he was still getting used to that characterization, *his* men—checked their kits one final time before heading out. Around them, in the cavernous ruins of the department store's ground floor, the warriors of the other *saif,* all of them newly arrived via the overland route from the north as well, were busy with final checks and preparations. They did not look much like an army. No two men were dressed alike, and although most were armed with AK-47s, the rest of their equipment was a grab bag of scavenged body armor, webbing, helmets, packs, and a jumbled bazaar of civilian clothing, bits and pieces of military camouflage, and whatever trinkets each man thought useful or necessary to have. Some carried extra water; some had pockets bulging with energy bars. The men of Yusuf's *saif* traveled light, at his insistence: their personal weapons and extra ammunition, a fighting knife, two canteens of water and a dozen water purification pills, a map, a small first-aid kit. As the commander of a *saif,* Yusuf was supposed to have the option of night vision goggles, but there were not nearly enough to go around, and he was comfortable fighting in the dark at any rate. Most of the raids he had carried out as a member of the Lord's Resistance Army had taken place after dark. He also worried about being blinded by bright flashes while he was wearing them.

"Tony," he said, "I am told you are familiar with the part of the city where we are to fight."

The former park ranger nodded as he adjusted the sling of his assault rifle.

"When I first arrived in New York, I was sent down there with four men from Dar es Salaam," he said. "They were bandits, but their clan had negotiated passage and salvage rights in our part of the city in return for providing fighters. I watched over them while they picked over a couple of blocks. But I made my own notes and maps as we had been taught. I know it well."

"Then you shall lead us down there," said Yusuf, "once we find out exactly where they need us most."

The Algerian, a wiry brown-skinned fisherman by the name of Selim whose livelihood had been ruined by the Israelis' nuclear contamination of the Mediterranean, grinned wickedly. "They want us to go to hell," he said. "It's just down that way."

He jerked his thumb as if to point somewhere off to the south.

The other men all chuckled or grinned. It was nervous laughter. The sounds of battle reached them as a dull volcanic roar rolling up out of the gray distance. Even when the rain fell heavily enough to make conversation difficult, it was still not so loud as to drown out the thunder of the Americans' big bombing raids and the constant crash of their artillery. Yusuf had learned since becoming the commander of his own *saif* that the island he had been able to see from his dugout on Ellis was the location from which most of the American shelling originated. Governors Island it was called, and the governor of New York, an infidel known as Schimmel, was actually based there, as was the regiment of militia he controlled. They were fighting alongside the army in Manhattan now, and Yusuf had been told that they were not nearly as formidable an opponent as the regular American soldiers he would meet. Indeed, Sheikh Ozal's lieutenants, who had sat him down and all but overwhelmed him with information and details about the battle as soon as he was elevated to the level of commander, had insisted that whenever he found himself faced by a militia unit, he should press forward at all costs, for if the American line was to break anywhere, it would be there. To that end Yusuf had driven his small band of men to distraction, making them memorize the differences in uniforms and equipment between regular U.S. Army units and Governor Schimmel's militia, who were very helpfully dressed in gray camouflage, not green and brown.

"While we wait, we should look at those photographs of the American soldiers again," Yusuf said, drawing a chorus of groans and pleas from his men.

"Not again," said Selim. "Please, not again."

As they burned off nervous energy waiting for their orders to head out to the front line, a strange quiet descended. Yusuf turned around and found that Ahmet Ozal and, even more surprisingly, the emir himself had appeared at the rear of the store. All discipline evaporated as fifty or sixty fighters pressed forward to get closer to their leaders. As sworn members of the Fedayeen Ozal, their first loyalty was to their Turkish lord, but the emir was a legendary figure, almost mythical, and his very rare appearances were always eagerly discussed and fondly remembered by the men afterward. The emir never spoke harshly to anyone. He had a knack of remembering a man's name and the smallest, least important details of his life, if he had met him once before. He was also generous to a fault, often sending out small gifts and tokens of appreciation to the men for their efforts even when his duties precluded him from walking among them. It was rumored that he took no plunder from the city, spending any and all tribute, which was rightfully his, to support the families of his fighters instead. The story of how he had not punished Yusuf for his self-confessed failure of spirit on Ellis Island but had instead rewarded him lavishly for returning to the fold with useful information had spread rapidly through the ranks of the fedayeen. Yusuf, who had expected to be shunned as a coward and detailed into some demeaning or even suicidal role, found himself the object of envy and much good-natured ribbing at having shared the delights of the emir's personal harem, even if only for a day. The man did not simply inspire loyalty. Looking upon him for the second time in a week, Yusuf understood something his enemies never would: The emir inspired love.

He did not look happy today, however. The dark and somber cast of his features matched almost perfectly the bleak weather and deteriorating news from the front. As the emir weaved his way through and around the trashed store displays, hopping over a mannequin and crunching the broken glass of an empty jewelry cabinet under his boots, Yusuf could not help worrying that something had gone terribly wrong. His worst fears were confirmed as the emir held up both hands and gestured for the fighters to gather around him and be quiet.

"My friends, I bring ill tidings," he announced. A troubled murmur ran through the small gathering of armed men. "I have had word from the front. The Americans have cut through our allies…"

The grumbling turned much darker and uglier, but the emir hushed the angry crowd with a gentle gesture of his hand. "It is only to be expected," he said. "They are pouring everything they have into this battle, and our… allies… are not as well equipped or trained as you. Nor do they fight for a higher purpose. We cannot expect them to bend themselves to God's will and do his hard work when they do not have faith. All they have is their greed. Do not blame them for this. Pity them and forgive them as Allah would."

Yusuf was surprised to find a tear welling up as his throat tightened. As he listened to the emir, his anger at the failure of the bandits turned to pity and even a little shame.

"Even so, there is now more hard work for us to do. We are preparing a fearsome defense upon which the Americans will perish like sailors dashed against the rocks by a great storm."

The mood in the room changed again at that. The fighters became more attentive. Yusuf noted his own men clustering around him and lifting their faces expectantly to the emir, who had climbed atop what looked like an old cabinet in a perfume display.

"We need time to ready that defense, and I'm afraid I must ask you men to give me that time. It almost certainly means asking you to give me your lives."

A single voice cried out. "Our lives! Our souls! For you, anything, my sheikh."

The crowd erupted in a single roar of agreement. Yusuf found himself shouting along with everyone else.

"There is more," said the emir, raising his voice to be heard above the clamor but not actually shouting. He seemed to have a way of projecting his words so that they reached right to the back of the assembly. "I'm afraid it is not so simple a matter as laying down your lives in battle. There are women and children in the path of the American onslaught."

Yusuf was stunned. He'd had no idea any of the families were even on the main island of the city. Although he had no woman of his own yet, he understood that all the families of the warrior-settlers were maintained safe and far away from the fighting. When he thought of them caught up in Kipper's infernal war, his reaction was identical to that of his comrades—outrage. The emir gestured for calm again before the men's anger could run away with them.

"A small party ventured downtown a few days ago after we received reports of a sizable food store that remained untouched. They set out before the current fighting began, gathering supplies for the main family camp, when they came under fire from the Americans' artillery. Soldiers soon followed, and they took shelter, hiding nearby in the public library. They are still there now with just a handful of guards. The American numbers are small, just a platoon of militia, but more will surely follow. We need to get them out, along with whatever supplies they have salvaged, and then we need to hold that position as long as possible. *You* need to hold that position as long as possible. If you can do that, if you can give me the time, I will prepare a trap for the infidel that will break him at last. I ask you now, as men of the the Fedayeen Ozal, my very finest warriors, who is willing to give up his life that our women and children might live and our enemies fail?"

The answering roar drowned out the sound of the rain and the rumble of battle for the first time Yusuf could recall.

* * *

They ran, heedless of the rain that lashed at them, sometimes making
it impossible to see more than half a block ahead. They ran, heedless
of the many pitfalls and traps that lay in their way. Half-submerged
wreckage and debris on which a man might trip and shatter his
leg. Lethal depths, open manholes, yawning concrete mouths where
rusted steel grates had given way and now lay like the jaws of the
city, waiting to consume anyone foolish enough to fall headlong into
them. They ran, bounding over barricades of crashed cars, darting
inside the husks of looted shops whenever the dull chopping thud
of rotor blades echoed through the empty canyons above them,
warning of the approach of American helicopter gunships. They
ran carrying the burden of their weapons and the extra ammunition
they had been given, weight they bore by dropping food they would
not need. They ran even when their legs grew hot and their muscles
trembled and terrible barbed knots of pain spread through their
bodies, starting as stitches in their guts and flaring into white-hot
incandescent flames that burned their lungs. They ran without
checking for snipers. Or mines. Or the cruder man traps left by
the pirates and bandits who had passed through here before them.
They ran counting the blocks they passed, but only at first. They ran
when they lost count, and they ran all the harder when they had no
idea how much farther they had to run.

A couple of blocks from their destination Yusuf heard the crack
and bark of small arms fire. The rain that had served to cover
their passage down the long avenue that ran down to the library
building had eased off, allowing him to spot the muzzle flashes of
the American militia well before he blundered into them. Tony
Katumu proved his worth immediately, pulling Yusuf and the
other men of the *saif* off the main boulevard and nearly half a block

to the east, where they threaded their way through a shambles of collapsed scaffolding, overturned buses, and crushed taxicabs in front of some sort of school or university.

"If we cut through here, we can get into the library through a park just behind it," Tony said. "Without the Americans seeing us."

Fighters from maybe half a dozen more *saif* had followed Yusuf and his men for no reason other than they looked like they knew where they were going. As they waded through filthy knee-deep water, the spasmodic gunfire increased in intensity. The other fighters were presumably engaging the enemy on the street. Yusuf wished he had some way of coordinating with his fellow *saif* commanders, but none of them had radios, and indeed they had never been trained to use them, even if they'd been able to salvage some. Instead, he was forced to do as commanders had done for millennia.

"Quickly, gather on me," he cried out. The small war band, maybe twenty or thirty men strong, all of them heaving and gulping for air after their long run down through the city, followed him under a tower of iron scaffolding from which torn and ragged sheets of plastic flapped in the wind and rain. He hoped it would be enough to hide them should any Americans fly over. With everyone undercover, he explained the simple plan.

"We are going to follow Tony through this block and across the road into a park behind the library where our people are trapped. We cannot get in through the front doors without being seen, but I hope… I am certain that God willing there will be another way in from the rear. If there is, we will take it. We will rescue our women and children, and the men of one *saif* will escort them back."

He could tell from the way the men looked at one another that nobody was likely to volunteer for a task that involved running away from the infidel.

"There is no shame in doing this," he insisted loudly. "Not only will those men bring honor to the Fedayeen Ozal, but they can aid the fight of those who stay here by returning with reinforcements and ammunition. We are going to need both *because many Americans will die by our hands here today.*"

He finished his speech with a rousing war shout, or as rousing as a boy of his age could manage when addressing a band of hardened fighters, many of whom were older than he. It worked, however. The men answered fiercely with their own shouts and cries.

"Let us go, then," he said loudly over the drumming of the rain on the discolored plastic sheeting above them. "Tony, you lead."

Tony Katumo seemed to stand a few inches taller with pride as he called out, "Follow me," and led the combined fedayeen of half a dozen *saif* into the fight.

44

On what level of hell do we find these people? thought Kipper.

The satellite link was not the best, and at times the woman on the screen disappeared behind a blizzard of electronic snow. When the reception was good, however, there could be no mistaking the murderous look in her eyes. It was, thought the president, something akin to true madness, but a cold and watchful madness.

"I'm sorry, Mister President," the woman shouted over the noise of the big military aircraft, "but my mission parameters are slightly different from that. I am not equipped for the sort of task you want me to undertake, nor do I have any of the overwatch or support I would need. I am on my own, sir, and hostile rendition is not my mission specialty."

She's an assassin, Kip thought. *She's going into New York to kill this guy, and she has no interest in anything else.* He did his best to keep his reactions under control so that Ms. Monroe could not see him shaking his head in dismay. She bounced and shook on screen as the laptop into which she was talking was affected by turbulence. He wondered why they bothered with the encrypted video link. It seemed to make things just that much harder. He knew that Jed could feel him tensing up as the exchange went on and tried to wave off his chief of staff without the gesture being picked up by the little camera at his end of the exchange. The woman—the agent, he reminded himself—seemed to have little trouble maintaining her self-possession. But then, he thought, she probably wouldn't be very good at her job if she lost her cool at the first provocation or frustration.

"Agent Monroe," he said trying to find the reasonable tone of voice he used when he was looking to avoid a fight with Barb. "I can understand this is difficult for you. They told me what happened to your family and that this Baumer guy, this emir or whatever he's calling himself now, was behind it…"

Although that does raise the question of what the hell you're even doing working this case, he thought but did not say.

"And we are indebted to you for tracing him so quickly to New York. But we need him alive if at all possible. I know it won't be easy. But they tell me you are very good at what you do…"

"What I do, Mister President, is kill people. On orders from a duly constituted authority. I am the people's executioner, sir, not their fucking dogcatcher."

The madness, or maybe it was just the anger, in her eyes finally flared, and Kipper was able at last to see the human being to whom he was speaking to rather than a flat, affectless functionary who seemed more than happy to hide behind the bursts of static that frequently interfered with their connection.

"…orry, Mr. President," she said as she emerged from a cloud of white noise. "I apologize for my outburst. But my point remains. New York is a combat zone, and Bilal Baumer is deeply entrenched there. He will be surrounded by his people, all of whom are tooled up for major combat operations. I cannot just walk in and put a bag on him. I can, however, decapitate his command and control network."

"You mean kill him," Jed Culver said, taking the opportunity to speak at last. The secure communications room was small, not much more than an annex to the main area where the military had set up all its electronic gear and from which they were able to monitor the battle in New York in real time. Jed was forced to lean across as he spoke.

"I mean kill him and everyone around him, including his first rank of commanders," the Echelon agent replied. Again, Kip had to stop himself from shaking his head. She was an unremarkable-looking woman, quite pretty but not at all as physically imposing as he would have expected. From what he could see of her on the little screen, she did not look much bigger through the shoulders than his wife, and once when she brushed a few strands of hair out of her eyes, he could see that her hands, although strong-looking and possibly a little scarred across the knuckles, were not as big as his own. He could not help but wonder what life paths had led her to be in a C-130, flying through the night toward the slaughterhouse of Manhattan. She seemed no more concerned by what she was heading into than Barb did when heading off to Pike Place Market. Less so, probably.

Kipper was about to speak when Jed cut in over the top of him again.

"Of course, the president could order you to secure Mister Baumer," he said.

The woman appeared to smile behind the wash of static that briefly obscured her. "Yes, Mister Culver, he could. And I would die trying. But then you would have nothing. At least my way you have a chance to disrupt their command of the battle, and that can only mean fewer American casualties." She appeared to be looking directly at Kip as she said that.

"How long before you go in?" the president asked in a resigned tone.

She didn't need to check. "I have forty-three minutes until I jump," she said.

"And how can you possibly locate him?" Kipper asked.

"It won't be easy, sir, but the army and air force have sent through their latest intelligence, which will be a big help. And they have some good scans of midtown. Thermal imaging. There's a pretty little heat bloom coming out of the old Plaza Hotel and some foot traffic in the area that seems to indicate it's some sort of staging post. I'll start there. It's right in the middle of their turf and very close to my insertion point."

"But how are you going to—" Kipper started to ask before Jed laid a hand on his forearm and squeezed gently, shaking his head. "Sorry, natural curiosity. I don't need to know."

Kipper was sweating under the armpits and wondering what sort of leadership model he must be presenting to this strange homicidal female. He knew that many in the military were uncomfortable serving under a president who'd never served a day in uniform and was famously reluctant to commit to military action. But at least they took their uniforms off at the end of the day. This woman, this killer... he knew from his briefing notes that she had a family and that they were largely the reason for her involvement in all this. But nothing about her demeanor suggested a nurturing or loving side. She didn't have a uniform to take off. She was a killer down to her core.

"Okay, look," he said. "I've made it something of a virtue in this job not to question the judgment of people in the field. I didn't like it when politicians used to do it to me, and I don't intend to start doing it to anybody else. Agent Monroe, you know best how to do your job, so I will leave you to do it. It will be difficult enough as it is. I acknowledge your point that taking out Baumer's leadership group should go a long way toward reducing our casualties. But do bear in mind that it would be of *enormous* value to us if we could talk to this character, whether he's their emir or sheikh or whatever he's calling himself or whether he's just middle management. Because if he is, snuffing him out might well end this fight, but there will be another one in the future. You mark my words."

The woman disappeared again inside a brief wash of static and white noise. When she reemerged, she was nodding. "...do what I can, sir."

"We are all doing what we can, Agent Monroe," Kip said. "I thank you for your efforts. I know they have taken you away from your family at a difficult time, and I know what you're doing is very dangerous."

She looked as though she was about to say something, but the screen went black and a single electronic tone replaced the audio feed.

"Looks like we lost her," Jed said.

Kipper leaned back from the screen over which he'd been hunched without realizing it. He let go a long, ragged breath.

"Jesus, Jed, where the fuck did she come from? And what the hell is she doing chasing after this guy when she has a personal involvement?"

The White House chief of staff pushed his chair back from the table. He seemed entirely nonplussed by the exchange with Agent Monroe. "She's here *because* she has a personal investment, Mister President. Agent Monroe is not supposed to be out in the field anymore."

Kip stood just as Colonel Ralls opened the door to their small, enclosed hot box and relayed the apologies of the tech guys for losing the link. He waved away any concerns. Broken communications links were an unfortunate reality nowadays.

"You have an update from Governors Island on the supply situation, sir," Ralls said.

"Thanks, Mike. Just give us a moment, would you?"

His military aide backed out of the room, closing the door behind him. Kip wished he'd left it open. Even the brief draft of slightly less stale air from the big combat information center outside had been refreshing.

"You were impressed with Agent Monroe, Jed," Kipper said. "I suppose she appeals to your Machiavellian side. And before you answer, just know that I am deeply unhappy to find out we ever had assassins on our payroll, let alone that we are still employing them."

Culver broke the seal on a new bottle of water and sipped before he replied, "Well, technically, she works for the Brits now. Her file has her on attachment to them as a consultant since 2003. She transferred from U.S. line management after her mission in Paris went south."

Kip deployed one of his darkest, most skeptical glares to let his chief of staff know he was not impressed with the rhetorical footwork. It only seemed to inspire Culver to come right back at him.

"Okay. Am I impressed with her? Yes, dammit. I am. I didn't have a lot of time to read the deep background on the woman. London only told us about her mission, which was effectively freelance, about two hours ago. But yes, what little I've been able to find out about her does impress me. For one thing, she came *this* close to nailing the rat bastard who's been giving us so much grief on Manhattan and who, I might point out, came very close to taking your life and mine, before going on to cause us thousands of casualties. Frankly, Kip, if I knew we had the option of turning someone like her on this fucking tinpot mad mullah and saving ourselves all of the blood and sadness we've had to suck up the last few days, I would not have hesitated to recommend doing so."

Kip knew that Culver was getting deadly serious whenever he dropped the honorifics. He was tempted to launch into a little speech about how his administration could not sanction murder, but it felt hollow with so many lives already lost in New York. Unlike Jed, he could not find it within himself to admire somebody who made her living from killing in the shadows. He had to acknowledge that Monroe had done them a great service in confirming the theory that the recently arrived jihadi fighters were playing an entirely different game from that of the pirate gangs scavenging the eastern seaboard.

But he just could not see himself allowing any government of which he was the leader to remain in the business of state-sponsored murder. And that was what Monroe was. Not a soldier. Not like Mike Ralls or Colonel Kinninmore or that poor, poor woman he had visited in the hospital. She was a publicly funded serial killer.

"For now, I am willing to let her out on a long leash," said Kip. "But don't get any ideas about coming back to me in the future with plans to bring Agent Monroe home so you can call on her services for any other outstanding issues. And you know what I'm talking about, *who* I'm talking about."

Culver shook his head. "Caitlin Monroe was very happily settled down on her farm in Wiltshire before Bilal Baumer tried to reach out and fuck with her. She could have come home, but she didn't. I think she understood she wouldn't be welcome."

Kipper began moving toward the door, steering his chief of staff toward the exit with him. He couldn't fail to recognize the tone of disapproval in Culver's voice, just as he noted that Jed had not answered him directly, deftly sidestepping the issue of Agent Monroe's future.

"I am sorry, Mister President," General Franks said on the screen back in the main room of the improvised combat center. "We do have stockpiles of weapons, but they're dispersed all over the country, often in places we haven't even surveyed yet. Funding for those survey teams is tight at the best of times, which draws out our lead time to exploit and recover ordnance, weapons, parts, and the like from any given site."

Kipper rubbed the palms of his hands deep into his eye sockets. Painkillers had no effect on his headache, which had started well before he spoke to Caitlin Monroe and now gripped his head like an iron glove. His stomach quivered as the room threatened to begin spinning around him.

"Everyone assured me that we had more than enough firepower," he said. "Not enough men but plenty of firepower."

"On paper we do, Mister President," Franks said.

"On paper doesn't count, General. On paper. In our dreams. Somewhere in never-never land. It's all bullshit," Kip said, raising his voice as his anger got away from him.

"What's done is done," Culver said off to his side. "What's your read of the situation in New York, General Franks? What do we need to do now?"

"The blocking force is in place in Upper Manhattan," Franks explained. "Even if the assault force in Lower Manhattan is unable to reach all of their final objectives, we should still see appreciable results from the second phase."

"What's the problem with your assault force, General?" Kipper asked. "Is it that they don't have enough ammo or support or whatever?"

Franks shook his head. "No, sir, or not entirely, no. We have significant elements of the First Cavalry and Schimmel's militia held up with resistance in the New York Public Library. Found a real nest of vipers in there, Mister President. Hundreds of them. So our advance there is behind schedule. First Infantry's two brigade combat teams are continuing to push up the West Side, with lead elements entering the Javits Convention Center an hour ago. The expected resistance along that axis has melted away. The Serbs and Russians are smarter than the average pirate, I guess. They saw us coming and just bugged out. Advance teams from Marine Regimental Combat Team One are securing the west end of Manhattan from the convention center to the Metropolitan Opera House. Lastly, we did manage to effect a resupply of the firebases on Governors Island," said Franks. "If the Marines continue to move east toward Broadway, I think we can relieve pressure on 1/7 Cavalry and make up for lost time."

It sort of made sense to Kipper if he thought about it in the same way as cleaning his basement. The units were like his push broom, shoving dirty water, or in this case the enemy's fighters, toward the drain. They would sweep the pirates and their jihadi allies toward the heaviest concentration of his forces, the Seventh Cavalry Regiment.

"Okay. Keep pushing, Tommy," Kipper said. "Keep pushing. And my apologies for losing my temper. I shouldn't have."

"That's perfectly understandable, sir," Franks said, before signing off.

Kipper wondered whether he could take another couple of Advils for his head. He was already feeling nauseous from them. At least another dozen officers from all the branches of the military were standing behind him, all waiting for a moment of his attention. He decided to skip the painkillers, instead seeking out his aide, Colonel Ralls, who was standing behind Jed.

"Mike, can you get me somebody from the air force to talk me through their plans for this bombing run? How much longer do we have before they're ready to go?"

Ralls consulted with a USAF general who was standing nearby clutching a manila folder full of documents.

"Mister President," the air force man answered. "General Wisnewski, sir. The units you're asking about will be over the city in twelve hours on present projections."

Kipper nodded, quietly admonishing himself. They'd already told him that not half an hour ago. He was having serious trouble holding it all in his head.

Something else was bugging him. Something he had forgotten…

"Jed," he asked when the memory came to him. "Agent Monroe. She does understand that she's working to this timetable, doesn't she?"

"Yes, Mister President. She knows she is on the clock. If she is still in the AOR when times runs out, there's very little we can do for her."

Jed paused, favoring him with a worried look.

"It's why she was reluctant to commit to rendition, sir. She simply does not have time."

"No," Kip sighed. "I guess she doesn't."

45

NEW YORK

The loadmaster leaned over and checked Caitlin's rig, pronouncing himself happy with a brusque nod. The roar of the MC-130H in flight, the military free-fall helmet she wore, and the oxygen masks they both needed at thirty thousand feet in an unpressurized cabin rendered any kind of verbal communication impossible. She ran through a final check of her loadout and tried to center her thoughts. She had not expected the call from James Kipper, and it had thrown her completely, especially the last-minute attempt to redefine her mission. What the fuck did he think he was doing? There was no way she had the resources to grab al Banna and throw him over her shoulder. Especially not with the countdown she was now working to. The more she thought about it, the more pissed off she became. She made a conscious effort to let go of her frustration and annoyance, to focus instead on what lay immediately ahead of her: a high-altitude high-opening parachute drop into the middle of a city being fought over by multiple factions, warlords, nut jobs, and the remnants of what had been the most powerful military force in the world.

She had settled on a relatively light weapons and ammo package. A sawed-off Mossberg 500 shotgun. An M4 carbine. The Kimber CQB pistol she had picked up at the London Cage. And two Gerber fighting knives, one at her hip and one tucked into a scabbard on her reinforced jump boots. The rest of her equipment she wore or carried in some of the many pouches sewn into her black, insulated jumpsuit and combat assault vest. A GPS unit with locator beacon and IFF transponder, a small but rugged PDA, altimeter, goggles, gloves, spare oxygen tanks, a full-face mask, and the FF2, a pressure-activated device that would pop her chute if she happened to pass out from hypoxia on the drop.

The engines whined in protest as the pilot brought them around on the correct heading for an HAHO insertion over the city. She could not see New York yet. She could see nothing in the darkness outside the cabin windows, which were streaked with freezing rain. The plane banked as the pilot made one final adjustment, and then she was just able to make out some of the city skyline far below and to the south, silhouetted by angry flashes of light.

At two minutes out the jumpmaster lowered the rear ramp and raised his arm, telling Caitlin it was time to stand up. He extended the same arm with the palm up at shoulder height before bending it to touch his helmet. She took a deep breath and exhaled slowly and powerfully as she pushed up out of her seat and moved to the rear of the MC-130. Her equipment was secured and the ram-air steerable chute hugged her like a child. Even with every inch of her body covered, she could feel the drop in temperature as the damp, subzero air swirled in.

As she stood in the dim red light looking out into the darkness, Caitlin imagined that her own child was out there, sleeping safely in Bret's arms. Red lamps clunked over to pale green, and the jumpmaster gave her a pat on the shoulder. She stepped on the ramp, flexing her knees slightly against the buffeting of the plane. She didn't look back or wave. She strode forward and stepped into the infinite dark.

The drone of aircraft engines, muted by her helmet, fell away completely as she dropped toward the earth. The weather was poor—foul, really—and she had only intermittent visibility before she popped the chute after a few seconds of free fall. It deployed with a fierce tug, and she allowed herself a minute's glide through the inky gloom before checking her altitude and position via the GPS unit.

She was thirty miles north of the insertion point, the Great Lawn of Central Park in the middle of Manhattan. The PDA attached to her right forearm fed a continous stream of updated weather data, helping Caitlin adjust her glide path toward the landing spot. For the first few minutes she descended through a black void, enveloped in clouds and rain. Droplets beaded her goggles and the readout of her instruments, necessitating a continual juggle between steering the chute, checking her position, and cleaning off the small green-lit screens.

At twenty-one thousand feet, however, she emerged from the cloud cover to find herself where she should have been, gliding south-southeast over the lower reaches of the Hudson, with the New Jersey Palisades passing by far beneath her boots. The U.S. Air Force was maintaining a clear corridor for her to drop through, but she saw that far away in the gloom the skies over southern Manhattan were alive with military aircraft. The great battle caused a curious inversion in the scene, with a terrible storm appearing to rage on the ground within the canyons of the city, lighting the gray featureless clouds that formed a ceiling over the tempest. Caitlin noted with professional detachment that very little antiaircraft fire chased the fighters through the bleak diorama, but she knew it would be different for helicopters dawdling close to any of the enemy hidden high above street level on the upper floors of office buildings or apartment houses. A lot of choppers had been raked out of the sky by low-tech countermeasures such as RPGs. That wasn't the reason she was parachuting rather than riding in, but she was still grateful not to have to contend with that sort of bullshit.

Another check revealed that she had drifted off course by a mile, pushed off her line of approach by a freshening westerly. The slightest gap between the glove on her left hand and the cuff of her jumpsuit let in a knifing wind to cold burn her skin and remind her of just how hostile was the environment through which she was passing. As Caitlin steered herself back on course, a small rain squall blew through, making the correction that much more difficult. She fought the chute, the elements, and her momentum as she angled across the dark void of the river just north of the George Washington Bridge. Here and there below her, she could make out single points and occasional small clusters of light, far distant from the fighting in the city. Were they small pirate bands, perhaps? Or possibly even the camps of Baumer's people? The latest intel digests she had read on the flight from Berlin to upstate New York to change planes had spoken of small camps of civilians, previously thought to be wildcat settlements, now possibly tied in with Baumer's crazed colonization scheme.

She checked her position again as she lost more altitude but gained on her landing spot. The singular points of light were so tiny and isolated, they did not look as though they could have any connection to the vast conflagration tearing at the heart of the metropolis. But Caitlin knew better than that. Even the smallest, most insignificant things could be connected to the great engines that drove human affairs at the level of states and peoples. The eastern bank of the Hudson passed beneath her, all but invisible in the gloom. GPS and altimeter readings had her back on track, and she put out of her mind any speculation or idle thoughts about anything but her mission. She was coming up the most dangerous part of the insertion, navigating over the city itself, a city unlit save for the fires of combat at the other end of the island. High-altitude jump specialists in the army had calculated her approach, and she couldn't fault it on paper, but even so, it was a hellishly difficult business falling through the night in bad weather over a blacked-out, war-torn city to land in a small field without being detected by hostiles or simply crippled by a bad landing. As she floated down over City College—or what the GPS told her was City College—she checked her watch and peered south into the murk and the fires of battle. The guns would begin firing soon.

She thought she detected the flash of artillery as she sailed in over the northern corner of Central Park. The hard, angular lines of the built environment, visible in the flash of exploding ordnance, gave way to the much softer, undefined shapes of the natural landscape. She reached above her head and pulled her night vision lens into place over her goggles, being careful not to stare off to the south. Within a few seconds she heard the first of the shells come shrieking in from the firebase at Governors Island, dropping on the southern reaches of the park, where they detonated with extravagant malevolence, uprooting ancient trees, utterly destroying the carousel, and, she hoped, drawing the attention of any onlookers away from the black figure silently dropping through space toward the waist-high swards of grass that covered the Great Lawn.

Caitlin focused on her landing site. With the ground so overgrown, there was no guarantee she wasn't about to break her legs crashing into a hidden concrete bench, but that was a risk she mitigated by aiming for the center of the large open area. Through the NVGs, the earth rushed at her with unpleasant speed. She flared at the last moment, then touched down at a run, her feet finding hard ground and good purchase.

She was down.

The artillery barrage was short-lived but effective. Caitlin disposed of her chute and free-fall helmet, allowing her to fit the night vision goggles more comfortably before she moved out for the first objective, the Plaza Hotel. She wasn't challenged as she pushed through the park. Her briefing notes had predicted she would find the area unoccupied. The open space was simply too dangerous for insurgents or pirates to move through without being interdicted from the air or by an artillery bombardment such as the one the army had used to cover her landing. Central Park was very much a no-man's-land.

She stuck to the paths as she ran, moving forward in small increments to avoid running headlong into trouble, should there be any. If she had been confident of her footing, it would have been better to avoid the pathways, but so much of the park was overgrown and pitted with shell holes that she could not risk it. It took her nearly half an hour to make her way to the tumbledown ruins of a little stone bridge near the pond at the corner of Fifth Avenue and Central Park South. She could smell the freshly churned earth and the metallic burning tang of high explosives from the diversionary attack. A few flames licked at the ruins of the old carousel off in the distance, but the persistent drizzle had put out most of the fires.

Caitlin could see that the Plaza was occupied. It wasn't ablaze with light or crawling with activity, but here and there a few rooms appeared to be lit with the dim flickering of candles, and once or twice she saw figures outlined in those windows. In the fifteen minutes she lay concealed in the rubble of the old bridge, she saw three men leave the building and head downtown; two arrived at a trot, jogging through the Pulitzer Fountain. Her briefing documents had speculated that the Plaza was being used as some sort of rest and recreation facility. It had not been targeted partly because of the White House policy of preserving as much of the city's infrastructure as possible but also because there were some indications of Americans and possibly other nationals being held captive there.

To Caitlin that felt a lot more like Baumer than this whole bullshit

Jolly Roger routine. It would amuse that rapist motherfucker no end to fill his camp brothel with prisoners taken locally. It would probably also help establish his credibility as a player with some of the cruder gang lords he had recruited as muscle. It seemed as good a place as any to begin the search for him. She checked her watch. The sky was lightening just perceptibly in the east. She had maybe half an hour until dawn and then seven hours until the U.S. Air Force came through and pounded this place flat. Well, maybe not the Plaza, but definitely any other concentrations of enemy personnel in the midtown area. She had to move quickly.

Some tree cover had survived on the far side of the Pond, and Caitlin used it to safeguard her approach to the hotel. The hammering of weapons fire, the dull crump of air-dropped munitions, and the continual drumming of artillery all drifted up from the lower end of the island, helping to mask her approach as she double-timed it from one scrap of cover to the next, looping around from her hiding place to the southern edge of the Park. Central Park South was jammed with the wreckage of hundreds of vehicles that had piled into one another when they lost their occupants. She perched behind a yellow cab that had been knocked on its side by a truck, taking a few minutes to scope out her final approach.

She didn't intend to effect an entry directly into the Plaza. Without knowing the disposition of the enemy inside, that was asking for trouble. A much smaller building abutted the hotel on Central Park South, however, and after observing it for a few minutes through the night vision goggles, Caitlin felt confident enough that it was empty to use as her way in. It appeared as though the roof of the building, housing apartments, perhaps, ought to give her access to the fifth or sixth floor of the hotel via a window. She unholstered her pistol and took a moment to fix the suppressor that Gerty had given her back at the London Cage. With the merest hint of gray, dismal dawn pushing back the shroud of night, Caitlin closed in on her quarry.

46

"Go ahead. Try again. See what happens."

The man glared at Caitlin over the fat black tube of the silencer-suppressor. A girl was huddled on the bed with her knees drawn up under her chin and a white cotton sheet pulled tightly around her. Her eyes were large with fear, flicking from Caitlin to the dead man bleeding out on the carpet just inside the door of the hotel room.

"No, please," Caitlin said to the man. "I mean it. Try and call for help again. It's been all of two minutes since I killed a man. I could use the practice."

He looked European, possibly from the south. Caitlin gestured with the silenced pistol, and he raised his hands above his head.

"Hands behind your head," she said. "Weave your fingers together and get down on your knees."

"Who… who are you?" the girl asked in a quivering voice.

Caitlin did not take her eyes or her aim off the man kneeling in front of her. "Well, I'm not the hotel dick, sweetheart. Why don't you get yourself dressed. You'll need warm clothes and decent walking shoes if you can find a pair."

"Are you here to rescue me?" The hope in her voice teetered on the verge of being both pathetic and heartbreaking.

"No," Caitlin answered. "Rescues are totally not my thing. But if you want to slip out the window when I'm done and try to get away, be my guest. You're a prisoner here, right?"

She could hear the girl moving off the bed. Her voice still sounded shaky and upset, which was only to be expected given that she had just witnessed Caitlin blow a man's brains out.

"We're all prisoners here," she said. "There's a bunch of us. But they keep us apart, don't like us talking, I guess. Are you going to help the other girls?"

Covering her prisoner, she moved a few feet to the left, where she could keep the young woman in sight. "No," she said. "I'm not going to help the other girls. I won't be here that long. And if you want to live, you'll get going, too."

"Are you going to kill him or something?" the young woman asked as she climbed into a pair of jeans she took from a dresser drawer.

"That depends on how helpful he is," Caitlin lied.

Her captive bristled at that. "You will get nothing from me, you whore."

"Dude, as the guy who was raping this young lady not five minutes ago, I think it's a little fucking disingenuous of you to be casting aspersions on my moral standing."

He frowned, apparently having trouble following her.

"Disingenuous. It means do as I fucking say or I'll shoot you in the face."

He opened his mouth to retort, and Caitlin did indeed shoot him, but in the hip, striding over quickly to launch one booted foot into his solar plexus as he spun to the floor. The snap kick drove all the air from his body, cutting off the scream that had begun to form in his throat. The woman cut off her own shriek of horror by jamming a couple of knuckles into her mouth. Caitlin quickly glanced at the door through which the bodyguard she'd killed just before had come, but she heard nothing in the hallway outside.

"Do you mind if I ask your name?" she asked in as soothing a voice as possible.

"Donna," replied the woman. "Donna Gambaro."

"Okay, Donna. Do you know if there are other guards on this floor? I haven't had a chance to check it out. Lucky you, yours was the first room I tried. That's why you need to close your windows. Even in a nice hotel like this one."

The Gambaro woman visibly attempted to compose herself. A train of emotions ran over her face. Fear. Shock. Rage. All them morphing together. She took a deep breath and let it out slowly, pointing at the man who'd been using her for his pleasure.

"If you're worried about him hollerin', don't," she said. "You hear screaming like that all the time around here."

Caitlin took a second to examine the woman properly. She was half dressed now, buckling up her jeans and adding a gray T-shirt. This chick was not going to wait around for a second chance.

"So this was your room, Donna? This is where you stayed the whole time? Did they let you out at all? I'm trying to get a sense of what's waiting beyond that door, is all."

Donna pulled on an old jacket. It didn't fit and looked as though it might have belonged to a man.

"They caught me a month ago," she said, her voice faltering. "I was working salvage with my brother in Toronto. We were… freelancers."

Caitlin shrugged. What did she care about somebody looting a dead Canadian city?

"Your brother?" she asked.

"He's gone. They killed him when they took me."

Donna Gambaro looked like she was thinking about giving her captor a couple of kicks in the head to settle some of that debt.

"I'm sorry about your loss," said Caitlin, "but I have to ask for your help. I need you to focus, Donna. Have you been out of your room at all? Can you tell me about the setup here? How many men? What sort of security?"

Caitlin could see tears welling in the woman's eyes and knew she had very little time before she fell apart. She decided to try a different line of approach.

"I don't suppose you know the name of our friend here, do you?"

"I've heard his bodyguard call him Mister 'You Chick' or something," she said. "Something kinda foreign like that."

Keeping her gun trained on the man, who was moaning and snaking about in great pain, Caitlin powered up the PDA Velcroed to her gun arm.

"Sounds like 'You Chick,' you say? All right, let's see, then. That is ringing a bell for me."

She tried a few spelling combinations until the database threw up a possible match.

"Jukic? Does that sound right? Danton Jukic?"

He groaned as though she had struck him again, and Donna nodded enthusiastically as she wiped away a few tears.

"That's him. Rat bastard ass fucker. Not so fucking tough now, are you? Huh?"

Caitlin shifted position slightly to put herself between the two of them. Jukic was sweating profusely, and deep body tremors had taken hold of him. He was having trouble keeping his moans quiet.

"Are you like a cop or something?" Donna asked. She pointed at the PDA. "That looks like one of those computers they used to have in cop cars."

"No, I'm not a cop. They don't get to shoot people on general principles. Or torture them. You hear that, Jukic? We'll be moving along with the torture in a minute. Just so you know."

His groan was noticeably louder, and he kicked out with one leg as though trying to push himself toward the door. Donna Gambaro fetched a pair of running shoes from the same dresser drawer in which she had stored her jeans. She sat on the end of the bed to pull them on. Caitlin could see that her hands were shaking, but she was doing her best. She kept the gun on Jukic as she spoke to Gambaro.

"Do they have guards in the hallways, Donna, do you know?"

Donna paused in the job of trying to untangle a knotted shoelace.

"Not always, no," she said. "Only the big guys get bodyguards. Sometimes some of the guys who came through here were just fighters or soldiers, you know. They got sent here as a reward. I talked with some of them. They weren't all bad. Some were pigs, of course. You never knew what you were getting. But that's men all over, isn't it? Anyway, no. There's not always guards in the halls."

Caitlin fetched a couple of photographs of Bilal Baumer from one of her pockets.

"You ever see this guy come in?" she asked.

"No," Donna said, after a brief look. She began searching the drawers, as if looking for something lost in the clothing. Jukic levered himself up on one elbow and gave the impression of a man who was about to start protesting again, leading Caitlin to drive another kick into his guts to quiet him down.

"That's good to know," she said. "Now, Donna Gambaro, you look to me like someone who can handle herself. That's good, too. The thing is I have to ask old Jukic a few questions, and... well, things are probably going to get ugly. Very ugly. I'm afraid I can't let you go until I have the answers I need. When I get them, we can both leave together, out the same window I came in. I'll be on my way then. But if I were you, I'd probably get my ass hunkered down somewhere nearby as quickly as possible. Do you understand?"

"Miss," Donna Gambaro said as she located a locket that obviously meant something to her, "I don't know who you are, but I used to wait tables at Hooters. I know when things are about to get ugly and when it's time to go. You won't need to tell me twice. Are you going to torture him?" she asked, pointing at Jukic.

Caitlin took the fighting knife from the scabbard in her boot. "A little bit," she said.

In fact, she hardly needed to hurt him at all. Jukic, an Albanian, who was listed in her files as running a medium-size pirate crew of mostly Balkan origins, gave up the information she needed a few seconds after she cut off the tip of his little finger. She had thought she was going to have to harvest at least half of his digits, but perhaps kneeling on his hip wound as she made the cut helped.

She got an address no more than a few blocks away that the Albanian gang leader insisted was the last command post he knew of for the jihadi fighters who had brought so much grief to New York. It didn't show up on her PDA, so chances were that it hadn't been known to the military. There was no guarantee Baumer would be there, but if it was manned by his own people rather than pirates, she might have a shot at getting to someone with better information than Jukic.

He was now balled into a fetal position on the floor, shaking and sweating and keening in a high-pitched, almost childlike fashion as he bled all over the carpet. "Fucking Germans. Fucking Turks," he repeated over and over again until Caitlin put two bullets in his brain and shut him up forever.

She killed him without warning or obvious provocation, causing Donna to jump with fright again.

"Sorry," Caitlin said. "You don't mind, do you?" The former Hooters waitress looked at her the same way one might regard a dangerous dog one had stumbled across in a dark alley.

"No," Gambaro said, but none too certainly. "No, fuck him, I guess. Can we go now?"

The window in the bathroom was still open, giving them access to the roof of the apartment house across which Caitlin had come.

She hadn't intended to enter the hotel through that particular window until she noticed the flickering light of a candle inside as she approached. The sash was already raised a few inches, and Caitlin was able to lift it without too much effort, although she did have to take her time with it lest the sound of the wooden window frame rumbling upward alerted the occupants. Luckily, Donna had had Jukic well and truly distracted as Caitlin came calling. It was her scream, however, upon seeing the assassin silhouetted in the doorway to the bathroom that had brought Jukic's bodyguard into the room. Caitlin had shot him twice in the head before pistol-whipping his boss into submission.

Amazing what can happen in a New York minute, she thought as the two women dropped a couple of feet onto the roof of the neighboring building. Despite being loaded down with all her equipment and wearing heavy jump boots, Caitlin landed almost without a sound, whereas Donna struggled and grunted and heaved herself through the aperture before touching down with a loud bang.

"Ma'am, do you think I could come…"

"No," Caitlin said before she could finish. "I'm sorry, Donna, but you can't come with me. It's gonna get a lot worse before I'm done. You'd be way better off just hiding out in one of these buildings. It won't be more than a few days before things shake themselves out here. Whatever you do, though, Donna, do *not* go back to the hotel. Even if you have friends there, leave them. Do not try to rescue them. You'll fail and you'll die."

The rumble of distant explosions grew louder as if to emphasize her point. They had reached the tiny cabin at the top of the stairwell providing access to the roof of the apartment house. The sun had not yet fully arisen, but there was more than enough light to make them out. Caitlin hurried the woman along out of sight.

"You don't need to go much farther," she said. "But you do need to get out of this building. They'll look for you here. But if you take yourself along the street a ways, get yourself bedded down, and then keep your fucking head down, you will get through this, I promise."

Donna Gambaro looked anything but certain as Caitlin entered the stairwell, but throwing a glance back over her shoulder at the Plaza seemed to strengthen her resolve.

"All right, then," she said. "Whatever you say."

"Remember," Caitlin said. "Do not go back to the hotel. Move quickly and get out of sight. You've got maybe half an hour till Jukic is missed."

She gave Gambaro a reassuring pat on the shoulder before turning and hurrying down the darkened stairs.

If she was following the playbook, Donna Gambaro would have been dead, too, or at least trussed up and stashed away somewhere so that she couldn't interfere with the run of events. But as somebody who'd once been held captive and abused in a very similar fashion to the former waitress, Caitlin was well past giving a shit about the playbook.

Good luck, kid, she thought.

47

NEW YORK

The shopping was a terrible disappointment. Jules had been hoping there might be one or two choice items somewhere along Fifth Avenue that she could take home as a souvenir of their visit to New York, but everyplace she looked had been comprehensively looted. Takashimaya was a burned-out shell in front of which a headless body swung by its heels. And Lord knew she'd never had any luck at Saks, anyway, so why bother trying now, especially when that particular block appeared to be swarming with jihadi whack jobs and pirate asswits—she really did like that cheeky Polish character—all heading into Rockefeller Center.

Jules used her binoculars to scope out that stretch of the avenue from their hiding place within the rubble of St. Patrick's. There was a lot of movement down there, which meant it couldn't be long before there was a response from the U.S. Air Force. Every time the pirates massed in any numbers, they got pounded flat.

"Looks like they're gonna make a stand there," the Rhino said around the stub of an unlit stogie. He was growing impatient, grunting and shaking his enormous and ugly head, which still was magnificently ornamented with the stupid Viking helmet.

"Do you think we might be done with the retail therapy soon, Miss Jules," he asked. "We really shoulda stayed over on Madison. Fifth seems to be lousy with tourists."

Jules ignored him. He was grouchy from having to drag his oversized ass through the tumbledown ruins of the cathedral to reach a safe vantage point where they could observe the activity on Fifth. There appeared to be a real concentration of ragheaded crazies in the shell of Saks. Every window in the department store was broken, and half the stock seemed to have been piled into a sodden heap out on the road. As she watched, dozens of fighters emerged from the building, but rather than scattering and heading into Rockefeller Center like their comrades, they took off at a sprint downtown.

"What do you think that means?" she mused out loud.

"It means the U.S. Air Force is going to be along very shortly to bomb the living bejeezus out of anyone foolish enough to be loitering in the vicinity of fucking Fifth Avenue," the Rhino said. "Come on, we've ticked all the boxes, reconnoitered like champions. We can see the place is crawling with vermin. But it's not our concern unless they make us. We should get going back over to Park Avenue. Quieter there. Wide-open spaces. It's a more amenable environment for your average pachyderm. And it's not like you're going to find anything you like here. I think you've probably left your shopping till a bit late."

"You're right," she admitted as she adjusted her sling, which was slipping off her injured shoulder, and crawled backward down the mound of rubble on which she'd been lying. St. Pat's was a gutted ruin, burned out and open to the sky where the roof had caved in. She wondered if it had been reduced to this state on purpose. Small jagged jewels of stained glass lay everywhere, and anything of value had been looted long ago. The vestibule in which they hid reeked of human excrement. "There's nothing worth having here now," she said. "Best we push on, I suppose."

"Yes, best we do," he muttered.

Just two blocks away, on Park Avenue, the city was surprisingly quiet again, indeed all but abandoned, allowing them to move with more freedom as long as they exercised some caution. The large number of enemy fighters in the blocks around the Rockefeller Center buildings had caused them a few hours' delay as they picked their way around the obstacles, with Jules insisting that they move slowly and take note of where the gangs had gathered their forces. It never hurt to know where your competition was setting up shop, although from what Milosz and the others had told them, perhaps it was time to stop thinking of the pirates as competitors. They seemed to want to actually take over the joint now rather than just clean it out.

The overnight downpour had abated, and the worst of the flooding was over, although great oily pools of water lay everywhere and small rivulets and streams ran out of some buildings with damaged roofs. The dull background roar of battle to the south probably explained the abandoned streets, Jules thought, as thousands of gang members rushed to join the battle. It couldn't be long before somebody else pushed in to fill the vacuum created by their departure from this part of midtown, however.

"It's all just fucked," she muttered to herself.

"What's that?" he asked as they paused at the corner of 52nd Street and Park, sheltering behind an overturned meat truck while they scoped the next block of real estate.

"Oh, it's just so fucking disappointing, isn't it," she grumbled. "I used to love this town, Rhino. And especially this part of it. I was just sort of hoping that... you know."

He paused in his scan of the terrain ahead of them.

"That it might not be completely fucked. That there might be some little trinket you could put in your pocket and carry home with you? A keepsake from the past, Miss Jules?"

"God, you put it like that and it sounds so naive."

"That's because it is naive. This is the reality now." He gestured with his gun at a bloated corpse lying half in and half out of a Citibank across the street.

"September 11 was the end of the fucking golden age here. The Wave just came in and washed the debris away. There wouldn't have been anything more after that. Come on," he said, dashing from the wreckage of the van to the cover of another pileup a hundred yards farther north. Half a dozen cars had collided with a big blue bus, forcing them to weave around the twisted wreckage. Gray water had gathered in a small depression, deep enough to reach the top of her boots, and Jules was slowed down considerably by nursing her shoulder injury. "Sorry," she gasped, a little winded.

He shrugged and took up his surveillance of the next hundred yards of ground.

"I'm not even a local, you know, and I have more faith in the city than you," Julianne said, continuing her thoughts from before.

"Miss Jules, your ironic detachment is almost Buffy-like in its awesomeness. But how about we get our game faces on? According to that Polish guy, it's gonna start getting dicey once we're nearer the park. Milosz reckons it's still crawling with bad guys, even with most of them heading downtown, and it's six to five the gangs from the West Side are going to push through there anyway once they figure out there's nobody to really push back."

Jules conceded the point with a nod and took a grip on the P90 with her good hand. She wore it slung around her neck and clipped to a combat harness, but taking hold of the weapon did help focus her mind again.

"I'm sorry," she said. "Game face on. It was just that apart from Sydney, this is the first time since the Wave I've really been in a big city I knew and loved. And, of course, Sydney was full of people. This is…"

She gestured helplessly, a sweep of her gun muzzle taking in the ruined metropolis stretching away to the north. From their new vantage point she could see how a suddenly driverless yellow cab had punted a street vendor's cart through one of the huge plate glass windows of an office building, and a solid river of mangled steel appeared to have frozen at the intersection of Park Avenue and 54th. Heavy traffic flowing east on the morning of the Wave was now piled up in a giant, crumpled concertina of metal and broken glass. It wasn't impassable, but they might have to climb over it if they wanted to keep heading north. The Rhino scanned the block ahead, checking for stay-behinds, ambushes, lone operators, whatever. But Jules was becoming very attuned to the subtle changes in the city's mood as they passed across the invisible boundaries between one piece of turf and the next. And this felt... abandoned.

"Yeah," the Rhino grunted. "I know. I might have lived the last twenty years in the court of King Bubba, but my folks were Pennsylvania Yankees going all the way back to the thirteen colonies. I came here every year with my mom and dad. We had family in New Jersey."

He spit a wad of dark, viscous tobacco juice out the side of his mouth. It landed with a plop in a small puddle of filthy rainwater.

"Sorry," Jules said. "My selfishness can be staggering at times. Legacy of that landed gentry lineage."

"Well, you're earning your keep now, missy. So let's get to work."

A sniper opened up on them just short of 59th and Park Avenue, although "sniper" was probably too grand a word to describe the crazy man dressed in a florid yellow shirt leaning out the fourth-floor window of a tall brownstone building and unloading on them with an AK 47. At least the Rhino insisted that was what it was. Jules didn't much care. All that mattered to her was that somebody was firing lots and lots of bloody big bullets at her, and were it not for the shooter's obvious incompetence and the riot of jungle that had grown up over the median strip along which they had been progressing, she would probably have been ventilated at six hundred rounds a minute. As it was, she found herself huddled up against a concrete planter, leaking blood from somewhere and all but vomiting and fainting from the small white supernova of pain that had exploded in her damaged shoulder.

"Stay down," roared the Rhino, entirely redundantly. She wasn't moving anywhere. Park Avenue was gridlocked for at least a mile in either direction with a massive pileup of smashed, burned-out auto bodies—the reason they had been creeping toward their objective along the relatively unobstructed center strip. Unobstructed, that is, save for three or four years of unrestrained plant growth along the strip that formerly divided north- and southbound traffic. At times the Rhino had been forced to hack a path through with a machete, but they had chosen the slow path along the thin overgrown corridor because it provided good cover from anyone enjoying the high ground on either side of them. Anyone like the drug-addled pirate asswit currently trying to kill her, for instance.

He had to be fucked on kif or something, she was certain, because he was playing "Who Let The Dogs Out?" on a giant portable stereo and singing along, laughing hysterically, as he unleashed a whole clip of 7.62-mm on them. The gun roared sporadically with impossibly long strings of rapid-fire pops and booms, reminding her, insanely, of a woodpecker on speed and all but drowning out the most annoying song in the world and the fairy rain tinkle of shell casings tumbling four floors to the sidewalk. Jules huddled in close to the small concrete revetment as dozens of rounds zipped and zooped and cracked around her, chewing up the foliage and showering her with hot, sharp splinters of wood, metal, and cement.

No. She would not be moving anywhere soon.

She didn't even dare turn her head to see where the Rhino had gone. She had a brief impression that he'd dived to the right, somehow arcing over the crumpled hood of a flame-scorched yellow cab, but how he'd managed to get such an enormous mass of Rhino flesh airborne at speed, she had no idea. The firing stopped for a few seconds, but not the music or laughter. Reloading presumably, although she wasn't quite ready to test the theory by hopping up and exposing herself to another fusillade. Perhaps if she'd been close enough to hear the hollow clunk of a mag swap...

The frantic drumming of the Kalashnikov started up again, disintegrating leaf and branch all around her, caroming off car bodies, and shattering the odd unbroken window. Jules's shoulder was in agony. Black spots bloomed and spread across her vision. And then the terrible din abruptly ceased, cut off by two short bursts of fire from a P90. The glassy tinkle of falling shell cases terminated with a giant crash, causing her to jump.

"Nothing to worry about, Miss Jules," the Rhino announced, as he suddenly appeared from behind the body of the trashed yellow cab. "That was just his boom box hitting the curb."

"Thank Christ for that," she said, finding her feet somewhat shakily and brushing off the worst of the mud and foliage with her good arm. "What do you think his story was?" she asked.

The Rhino slitted his eyes and peered at the building from which they had been sniped after a fashion.

"Dunno. Mighta slept in and missed all the fun downtown," he suggested. "Doesn't seem likely from what those rangers told us, though. They reckon the pirate clans have been working almost professionally together. Fighting in big units."

"The enemy of my enemy..." Jules said.

"Something like that," he answered, scanning the block ahead of them. "Whatever the case, we'll want to be on the stick from now on. This part of the city was never going to be completely deserted one way or another. Let's get under cover and check the map again."

The Rhino helped her up and over the hood of the nearest car wreck, and they hurried into the foyer of an office block on the corner, jumping straight through the hole where a plate glass window had been smashed. Given the lack of water and rubbish in the foyer and the neatly presevered remains of the Disappeared, perhaps a dozen of them in all, it appeared the window had been intact until very recently. There was a chance the shooter with the boom box had taken it out, for there seemed to be no evidence that the foul weather of the previous twenty-four hours had encroached in there. The smugglers retreated from the street front, where they might be seen and targeted, and laid out the map of midtown that the soldiers had helpfully updated for them.

Central Park was still listed as no-man's-land, but the Serbs and Chechens were present in much greater concentrations on the far side of that wilderness than the Rhino's last update had indicated. They faced off against each other across West 64th, and the Chechens were thought to have pushed into the park, taking over the Tavern on the Green as they attempted to flank their Serbian rivals. That was as far into the park as any raider clan was known to have pushed. According to the female soldier they'd met, the air force had armed drones constantly over the area and standing orders to fire on any movement within the confines of the park.

"Wouldn't surprise me to see 'em drop an air assault force in there real soon," said the Rhino, circling a couple of open greenswards with one huge, filthy finger.

"In helicopters, you mean?" asked Jules.

He shrugged.

"I suppose they could paradrop the Eighty-second, but I'd lay money on the cav or the One hundred first going in. They're faster. They hit harder. And they can keep their shit together a lot easier. If you are in a parachute and strike a bad wind, you and your buddies end up all over midtown getting picked off in detail. We learned that lesson on D-day."

"Did we indeed." Jules smirked. "How about we stick with our current little war, General Patton."

"Ah, recovering our wits, are we, after the excitement of being rescued by a rampaging American Rhino?"

"Lets just get on with it," Jules countered. "If you're right and the army does try to take the park, this whole part of town is going to become a free fire zone. I'd prefer to be well away from here by then. How much farther to Rubin's apartment?"

"Two blocks north and one west," the Rhino said without bothering to consult the map.

"So do we try our luck on Park Avenue again?" she asked. "Or do we—"

Jules didn't finish her question. Instead she cried out in surprise as a bomb of some sort exploded outside, shattering the foyer windows. The angle of the blast and the mass of the concierge's desk on which they were examining the map protected them from the worst of the blast, but even so, as she dropped and rolled, awkwardly trying to bring up her machine gun, she noticed that the Rhino's Viking helmet was gone and a sizable flap of skin was hanging down over one eye, pouring blood in bright red torrents over his face and chest.

That wasn't the most disturbing aspect of this unpleasant development, however.

Much more upsetting was the heavily accented voice crying to them from the street.

To her.

"Helloooooo… Miss Choolia. And Meester Rhino. Welcome to New York. Meester Cesky sends his regards."

Mister who? thought Jules as the foyer erupted under the impact of hundreds of rounds of automatic weapons fire.

48

NEW YORK

She came at her target from the north, looking for an older office building at the corner of 59th Street and Park. Her last update from G2 had the Plaza as the northern outpost of Baumer's forces, almost all of which now appeared to have been drawn south toward Rockefeller Center. After leaving the hotel and Donna Gambaro, she had faded back into the cover of Central Park, trusting in her IFF transponder to protect her from air strikes by any orbiting drones. With the clock running down, she hurried through the park, exiting just opposite the remains of the Temple Emanu-El on 65th and diving into the network of streets on the other side. They were not entirely deserted, and once or twice she was forced to take shelter from small numbers of men who appeared to be roaming around aimlessly. Avoiding such encounters slowed her considerably, delaying her arrival at the address she'd tortured from Jukic. The gunfire started up when she was two blocks away.

It wasn't a large-scale engagement like some of the battalion-size encounters shaking themselves out downtown, and it seemed to come in two waves: a brief, shattering eruption of fire that lasted a few minutes but involved only a few shooters, followed by a larger engagement that sounded willing enough to make extra caution on approach advisable. She could make out a few of the weapons types from their reports: at least one AK-47, the street fighter standby; a curious, almost paramilitary mix of M16s and M4s like her own; a shotgun of some sort; and a couple of chunky, large-caliber pistols. All of them were punctuated by two noticeably different discharges of high-capacity automatic fire from something nasty and brutish. She wondered whether she was too late and some freelancing Lord Jim spec-ops type had beaten her to Baumer.

Sheltering in the lobby of a brownstone, Caitlin listened intently as the small gunfight played out. At one point, early on, she was certain she could hear amplified music, tinny but distinct: that dumbass song with a bunch of barking dogs that had been huge about a year or two before the Wave. The snarling bark of an automatic weapon—a P90, she was certain—seemed to cut off both the music and the hammering of a lone AK at about the same time. She scanned the street outside in case anybody else was being drawn into the confrontation, and occasionally she checked the darkened lobby of the building in which she was standing. It had suffered some desultory looting but did not seem to have attracted the attention of any systematic scavenging efforts. The foyer had flooded recently, however, and the place reeked of decay and contamination.

When she heard nothing for a few minutes after the music died, Caitlin resolved to push on. She needed to give herself time to examine the building she had to infiltrate. It was unlikely that Baumer would have an obvious security presence out on the street; that would do nothing but attract the attention of the air force drones constantly buzzing over the city, looking for signs of enemy concentrations. And she had no idea what part of the building his people were using. Jukic had merely given her the street address and said it was a large building. There could be forty or fifty floors on which they had set up camp, if they were even still there. To do the job properly would take days of careful observation, but she had only hours left before extraction. Her mission brief had been adamant about that. This afternoon midtown Manhattan was going to become a "nonsurvivable environment."

The Echelon agent performed another equipment check by rote before easing herself out onto Park Avenue to continue her quiet approach to the enemy camp. She was just turning her mind to how she might handle the last couple of hundred yards when another gun battle erupted not far from the location of the last one. Caitlin quickly took cover behind the body of a rusted Town Car that had had a prime parking spot in front of the apartment block on the morning of the Disappearance. Focusing on the intersection a few blocks down with a pair of compact binoculars, she caught a small band of men, maybe seven or eight of them, hurriedly picking their way through the snarl of auto wreckage that was always so much thicker wherever the traffic streams had met back in 2003.

"Motherfucker," she said quietly.

There could be no doubt about it. They were attacking the very same building she was headed for. Cursing quietly, she returned to the lobby of the brownstone. She wasn't sure why, but the feeling of an unnatural presence was particularly strong here. Perhaps it was the remains of the Disappeared that lay in great profusion in the mud and muck that had flooded in with the recent bad weather. She hurried through the lobby regardless of the flesh-crawling sense of being watched and judged from beyond the grave.

Caitlin shuddered.

She was someone who dealt with death as a matter of routine. It was odd that she should suddenly find herself unsettled and affected by it now. She put it down to exhaustion and hurried on, her jump boots splashing through the filthy brown watery ooze. The fire escape was over near the elevator shafts, and she racked a round into the chamber of her shotgun before entering.

The stairwell was empty and pitch-black. So little ambient light made it in there that her night vision goggles struggled to illuminate the space. She hurried up three flights of stairs and exited after carefully sweeping the hallway for potential adversaries. There were none, just that same creepy feeling that recalled to her mind a line from her Shakespeare studies at the academy in Colorado Springs.

Now entertain conjecture of a time, when creeping murmur and the pouring dark fill the wide vessel of the universe.

"Or I could just shut the fuck up," she muttered to herself in the dank, musty confines of the unlit third-floor hallway. Caitlin tried the door of the nearest apartment that she judged likely to have a view down Park Avenue. It was locked. She flipped up her night vision goggles and drove one powerful side kick into the wooden door just up and back from the handle. The latch and part of the frame shattered inward as the door flew open, flooding the hallway with a weak gray light.

A few strides carried her over to a pair of double-hung sash windows looking out across the overgrown median strip of Park Avenue. From there she could see the small band of men she'd observed two minutes earlier down on the street. Using the binoculars, she was able to count eight of them. They had two down already, one dead with half his head missing. The other was thrashing about screeching and clutching at the stump of one arm. A burst of fire had severed it just below the elbow, and he was bleeding out in great extravagant fountains. None of his comrades had moved to help him. They were all too focused on putting fire into the lobby of the building she was supposed to infiltrate. From the volume of return fire, which was accurate but by no means overwhelming, Caitlin judged there to be only two or three targets inside. Their bursts were much more discriminating, indicating a greater level of professionalism but also a more modest supply of ammunition. She scanned the face of the building with the binoculars, looking for the telltale signs of shooters preparing to drop plunging fire down on the attackers.

There was no sign of any such activity, meaning that either Jukic had lied under the duress of torture or his information was wrong or out of date. Caitlin favored the latter as the most likely explanation. The air force had been pounding any command and control cells it located, necessitating frequent movement by the jihadi leadership cadre.

"Well, that's just great," she said aloud. "Another excellent plan down the crapper."

Her plan, such as it was, was predicated entirely on a swift but stealthy assault up the chain of command to put her within striking distance of her man. It was always going to be subject to the risk of critical failure at any number of points, but it was way galling to have it fail before she'd even really begun.

Caitlin dropped her attention back to street level. Another of the attackers was down, leaving five. She took her time to scope them out. None looked like the African or Caribbean pirates allied with Baumer's fedayeen warriors. These guys looked more like they might even have belonged here once upon a time. They appeared to be Latino, possibly Mexican, or maybe a crew from farther south. It was impossible to say, of course. But none of them were sporting keffiyehs or dreadlocks or any of the other giveaway headgear that might mark them as being linked to Baumer. Looking at these guys, Caitlin had the impression she was watching a small gang of dope smugglers on a day trip away from one of the struggling *narcotraficante* settlements down in the vast graveyard of Mexico City.

She ate an energy bar from one of her pockets and washed it down with a canteen of warm water.

This was going to take some figuring out.

49

NEW YORK

"We gotta get out of here, Miss Jules," the Rhino shouted over the tearing snarl of his P90. "This particular pachyderm is feeling very much like an endangered species right now."

Jules poked her weapon above the rim of the concierge desk and squeezed off a short burst.

"Totally with you. My ass is way too pert after all the exercise I've had recently to have it shot off by Henry fucking Cesky's goons."

That was what really hurt. Not her busted shoulder or the flesh wound she'd picked up just over her left hip that was leaking blood at an alarming rate. It was the fact that their entire trip to New York—a hazardous, grotesquely expensive, and diabolically difficult exercise in subterfuge, risk taking, and really, really hard work on that fucking road clearance gang—*it was all a fucking crock*. There were no Rubin documents, no maps of the Sonoma oil field, no title deeds, no contracts for exploration and extraction, nothing. There was nothing but a fucking trap, which they had walked into like a pair of numpty fucking nuff-nuffs. There probably wasn't even a Rubin. After all, they'd never met the guy face-to-face, just his supposed fucking lawyer. And he had sent them on a fucking cross-country snipe hunt for the sole purpose of delivering them to an address in New York, the most dangerous city in the world, where they could be ambushed by a bunch of hired guns and their bodies added to the mass graves of thousands of pirates and soldiers and ragheaded lunatics who were all going to be plowed under by the time this was finished.

And all because she kicked him off the boat back in Acapulco.

Jesus fucking Christ, but some people knew how to hold a grudge.

The Rhino crab-walked sideways a couple of feet from his last firing position to retrieve his battered-looking Viking helmet. It was badly dented and one of the horns was broken, but he put it back on after pushing the flap of skin hanging down from his forehead back under the rim. With so much blood coursing from that wound down his face and over his chest, he looked like a true barbarian as he popped up and loosed another short burst over the top of the concierge desk. She wasn't quite sure, but Jules thought that maybe there was slightly less fire coming their way than before. The taunting had certainly dropped off as their would-be murderers concentrated on the job at hand. The Rhino was pretty sure he'd taken out one of them with a head shot, and she knew for a laydown certainty that she'd pretty much scythed off the arm of another attacker who foolishly had jumped up to taunt them some more about how stupid they were for believing in fairy tales and how much Mr. Cesky was going to reward him for killing and raping her, possibly in that order.

"How's your ammo?" the Rhino shouted.

"Three and a half clips. How about yours?"

"I'm afraid I'm down to my last, Miss Jules."

"Jesus Christ, Rhino. This isn't a fucking video game, you know."

The deep bass boom of a shotgun thundered three times in rapid succession just before Jules heard the dry click of a hammer striking an empty chamber. She launched herself upward, bringing the

P90 around with her good hand and sighting on a figure who was charging toward them through the shattered remains of the lobby windows. As he leapt a good three feet into the air to clear a jagged fang of broken glass, she fired, punching a hypersonic lead fist into his center mass while he was still airborne. He screamed briefly, but the concentrated swarm of lethal projectiles disassembled his lungs, air passages, and throat, instantly reducing his protest to a wet, strangled gargle.

Jules saw her chance as he dropped like a sack of old shit to the floor.

"Go," she cried out, pointing at the fire escape door a few feet away. "Go now."

The Rhino got moving with surprising speed, accelerating from a lumbering start to a full-throated charge in less than a second. He hit the door with all his mass, and it crashed inward while Jules crouched and fired short discrete bursts whenever she saw color or movement outside. No sooner had the Rhino entered the stairwell than he swung his weapon around the corner and began to provide covering fire for her. Jules ran, heedless of the pain in her shoulder and hip, firing her weapon blindly as she held it across her body. A few shots chased her into the fire escape, but they were poorly aimed and she made it without a mishap.

"So what do we do now?" the Rhino asked.

"We go up, quickly. Come on. Move it."

They hit the stairs at a sprint from a standing start, or as close to a sprint as they could manage in the extremes of exhaustion and stress. Jules could feel her thighs burning with lactose buildup after three flights. That was enough for her. Dizzy from blood loss, she shouldered open the door and tumbled into a hallway. It was an unremarkable space: elevator doors, dead potted plants, an empty water dispenser, and the remains of the Disappeared everywhere. Something about them caught her eye, but she was too busy to stop and think about it.

"Come on, we got to get ourselves barricaded in," she puffed.

The Rhino was laboring and wheezing a little bit, too, which was only to be expected given how much more weight he had to haul up the stairs with a bunch of murderous thugs on their heels. It didn't slow him down much, however. He continued at high speed through the doors of an office directly in front of the elevators and the fire escape they had just emerged from. Jules followed him, dodging out of the way as he began to throw desks and filing cabinets up against the entrance. There was no chance of hiding now, no pretense of stealth. He was trying to build a barrier from which they might fight. She tried to help as best she could with her wounds, tossing a couple of office chairs out into the hallway, where they might trip anybody who came out of the stairwell at speed. She kept her gun trained on the entrance, using her injured arm.

After a few minutes, she judged the impromptu defenses good enough and called out to the Rhino, who was about to turn over a heavy, old-fashioned manager's desk as a second line of defense. Julianne took up position covering the fire escape and waited for the next phase of the attack to begin. She expected the Rhino to join her and had one of her spare mags ready for him. After a tense minute, however, she realized he wasn't coming.

"Rhino! Excuse me, Rhino. I thought this would appeal to you. Glorious fucking death in a hopeless last stand and all that. Remember the Alamo? We've even got the fucking Mexicans for it. So do you think I could get a little bit of help out here, you know, with me being a mere lady and having one gammy wing and all?"

"Sorry, Miss Jules," he said, finally appearing at her side clutching a sheaf of papers. "I found something."

"It would want to be something really special to distract you from seeing off this bunch of villains who are... hmm... let's see, oh, that's right, trying to fucking kill us!"

The Rhino accepted the spare magazine from Julianne and

took up a firing position behind a couple of filing cabinets and an overturned desk.

"Have a look at these," he said. "I'll cover the door."

"You've got to be kidding me."

"Rhinos do not kid, Miss Jules. We charge and we gore. And that's about it. Go on, have a look; it won't take long."

Jules glanced down for the briefest moment at the papers he handed her. One of them seemed to be a hand-drawn map of the midtown area covered in circles and arrows and Arabic writing. She tossed it on the floor.

"Oh, for fuck's sake, Rhino. What do we care about any of this? And where are Cesky's men? They should be blundering in here by now."

The Rhino maintained his steady aim at the door through which they expected the contract killers to come, but he wasn't letting the issue of the documents go.

"Miss Jules, this place is full of this stuff. And none of it's old. There's ration packs, empty drink bottles, muddy boot prints everywhere, and lots and lots of paperwork like this. Jules, I think this used to be some kind of jihadi pirate command post."

Julianne's heart had only just begun to slow down after the the shock of the ambush downstairs, but it began hammering away again as she took in the import of what the Rhino had just said. Cesky's crew could not be very far away now. They had to be sneaking up the stairs as quietly as possible, which gave her all the more reason to be anxious. She had been hoping they'd come running through the door like macho fools, pants down around their ankles as they tripped over in front of her so she could put a bullet into each of their skulls with as little fuss and bother as possible.

Not to be, apparently.

A quick reconnaissance of the office confirmed what the Rhino had just said. It looked like it had been occupied until quite recently and abandoned with some haste.

"Rhino, I think we might have made—"

"Put the guns down. Lace your fingers behind your heads. Get down on your knees and shut the fuck up."

The voice was soft but menacing. Jules almost jumped out of her skin as she spun around.

"Whoa, lady, back off," the Rhino protested as he turned and saw the figure in black combat fatigues who somehow had materialized behind them, glaring at him with an expression as serious as heart disease. She traversed the muzzle of her weapon, some sort of assault rifle with an underslung grenade launcher, from the Rhino to Jules and back again with a minimum of fuss. Julianne had no doubt that she could and would drill them both in the space of a heartbeat. The only thing that gave her any hope was the woman's American accent and her military fatigues.

"I don't know who you are, GI Jane," she said, "but some very unpleasant characters are going to come spilling through that door behind us any moment now, and they *will* be shooting at everything on this side of the room."

"Not gonna happen," said the woman. "And I said get down on the floor. I will shoot you in the knee if I have to."

"But…"

The muzzle of the assault rifle dropped until it was pointing at the Rhino's kneecap.

"You look like a fucking Minnesota fan in that dumbass helmet," the woman said. "I lost money on those useless fucking Vikings once. Just so you know."

He didn't need telling twice, laying down his weapon as he quickly knelt and placed his hands behind his head. "Just get down, Jules," he said. "At least that way you'll be behind cover when they get here."

The woman shifted her aim to Julianne, who decided the Rhino was right. She quickly followed his lead and dropped to her knees, laying down her P90 and trying to raise both arms above her head.

She winced as her injured arm and flank flared with pain.

"It's okay," the woman said. "The arm in the sling you can leave."

"Lady, really," said the Rhino. "You're making a big mistake. What are you, some kind of forward air controller? We're not the bad guys here. *They're* coming up the stairs after us."

The woman adjusted her position slightly to put more of the impromptu barricade between herself and the fire exit. But she didn't seem particularly concerned.

"If you're talking about the comedy relief downstairs, you can relax. They're all dead. Eight hostiles. Two of them neutralized in your first exchange of fire. One more as he tried to enter the building—"

"Hey, I got him," Jules said.

"Congratulations," the woman replied. "You killed a moron at close range with an extremely powerful submachine gun. I'd give you a gold star, but I'm fresh out. And... there's five more dumbass *mantones* deader than disco down in the lobby. Was that all of them?"

Jules felt the muscles in her back relax just fractionally as the threat of being shot down from behind by Cesky's men seemed to recede a little. An even greater threat appeared to have materialized in front of them, however, in the form of this crazy ninja bitch with the boiler suit fetish.

"We don't know how many of them there were," Jules said. "They ambushed us. There wasn't time for taking roll call. I'm sorry."

The woman appeared to be processing the same details that the Rhino had tried to draw to her attention. The abandoned supplies and refuse. The tactical documents. Even a couple of cheap, soiled foam mattresses. It was then that Jules had a moment of clarity about what she had seen as they emerged from the fire exit at a rush. The remains of the Disappeared had all been pushed up against the walls as though they'd been swept there.

The Rhino was right. This place had been used recently.

"Ma'am, I hope you don't think me too forward," he said,

smiling but being very careful to keep his hands in place behind his oversized noggin. "But the name is Rhino A. Ross. Formerly of the United States Coast Guard. Now more of a freelance operator in the way of legitimate salvage and—"

"Shut up, tubby, or I'll demonstrate the radical weight-loss benefits to be had from a close-up discharge of a Mossberg 500 shotgun. You look to me like you could do with some trimming down."

"Goddamn but you've got some spunk there, woman," he shot back, practically beaming and apparently not at all put out at having his ample frame so cruelly traduced. "Really, where you from? You AFSOC? CIA—"

"It's the NIA now, you fucking wanker," Jules corrected him. "I already told you that."

The black-clad commando kept her gun on them while she gathered a couple of pieces of paper from a nearby desk, giving them a cursory once-over.

"No," the woman said. "None of those. I'm the person who took out the five hitters from the Guerrero cartel while you were up here building your little kiddy fort. So let's proceed on the assumption that you owe me, since I have the gun and I saved you both from a life-changing episode of humiliating ass fuckage by a bunch of sombrero-wearing gaucho dipshits. So, introductions. Who the fuck are you? What the fuck are you doing here? And what do you know about the people who were using this place before you?"

"Goddamn," the Rhino marveled. "You have to be CIA. Old-school, too. What were you, like, hunting bin Laden up in the Tora Bora when the Wave hit? Did I mention, ma'am, that I served my full hitch in the U.S. Coast Guard? Makes us almost colleagues, don't you think? So perhaps I could get up off my knees now, which trouble me more than they used to, what with me being an aging Rhino these days and—"

"No," she said. "You can stay right where you are for the moment. And you, lady, what's your name and backstory? Judging by your accent, I'm guessing some kind of desperado from *Tatler* magazine."

"Oh, please," said Jules. "Don't make me roll my eyes. My family were murdering Frenchies at Agincourt under their own heraldic banners when most of those arriviste try-hards were still gathering dog turds at tuppence a ton for the local fucking tannery."

The woman grinned at that, just the ghost of a smile.

"So you'd be smugglers, zone runners, something like that?" she said.

"Something like that," Jules admitted. "But not so that we'd have any reason for bragging about it. I'm afraid, well, it's a little embarrassing…"

The Rhino spoke up again, relieving Jules of the need.

"We were hired, or so we thought, by a man called Rubin, a businessman back in Seattle, who told us he had papers here in New York that would prove a claim he had to an oil field off California. He hired us to retrieve the papers."

"Go on," said the woman.

"Well, of course it was all bullshit, wasn't it?" said Jules, picking up the story. "There was no Rubin, probably no papers. For all I know there may be no bloody oil field. The whole thing was a setup by a man called Cesky. I did him a bad turn in Acapulco just after the Wave, and I suppose this was his way of repaying the favor. So thanks very much for the helping hand. Very glad not to be murdered right now. But my colleague and I should probably be on our way."

"Okay," their captor said. "You can get up and move out of the line of fire from that stairwell if you want. Don't bother with the P90s. And you still haven't told me what you know about the men who were here before you."

Jules climbed slowly and painfully up off her knees. They creaked and ached terribly, and her shoulder was throbbing something awful. She was dizzy from blood loss and needed to patch up that flesh wound. She really just wanted to sink into a hot bath with a stiff gin and forget about this entire fucking disaster.

"The reason we haven't told you anything is that we don't know anything," she said. "We took shelter in here, in this building, after we were fired on outside. End of story. If the men you're looking for—I assume you're looking for them—had still been here, I imagine we'd already be dead."

The woman continued to cover them with her carbine, but she was losing interest. The documents the Rhino had discovered were beginning to take more of her attention. Not that Jules had any ideas about trying to make a grab for her gun or escape. Everything about this woman suggested practiced lethality: her minimal movements, her conservation of energy, the impression she gave of being aware of everything around her whether it was the focus of her attention or not. Jules had known any number of ruthless people long before family misfortune had tipped her into the smuggling game. And then afterward, of course. But no one she had ever encountered had emanated such a chilling aura of clear and present danger. She had no doubt that were she foolish enough to try anything, her brains would be running down the wall before her body hit the floor.

"If you want my opinion, ma'am," said the Rhino, "what you have here is an intelligence bonanza."

"No," she said. "What I have here is a cold trail and two fucking chancers I couldn't trust as far as I could throw them, which in your case, buddy, is a fucking vanishingly small distance indeed."

"So you're looking for these guys?" Jules asked.

"No, I'm looking for one guy in particular. The one in charge."

"Ha!" said the Rhino. "I knew it."

"Well, look, I don't know if it helps," Jules said, "but we saw a bunch of those guys come charging out of Saks on Fifth Avenue and tearing off downtown like a greyhound with chili pepper stuck in its arse."

For the first time since she'd snuck up on them, the woman regarded Jules as something other than a potential target. "You," she said, pointing at the Rhino. "You can make yourself useful gathering up every bit of paper and documentation in this place."

"Yes, ma'am," he said. "As you say."

Jules noted that the woman shifted her stance slightly to be able to track the Rhino with a small movement of her automatic rifle. *Who was this chick?* She knew the Americans were so pressed for manpower these days that they'd opened up a lot of their combat roles to women. But this woman was no grunt.

"Go on," she said. "What did you see at Saks?"

Jules tried to recall the memory with as much detail as possible.

"We were tucked away in the rubble of St. Patrick's, I think it was. Dozens of these characters suddenly emerged from the department store and took off downtown in groups of five and six. It was noticeable because there were a lot of other fighters heading into Rockefeller Center in even greater numbers. They're holing up there, I think."

"I know. Were many of them wearing headscarves? Keffiyehs? You know, like you used to see on the Palestinians on television?"

"I have been to Palestine, you know."

"Why am I not surprised?" said the woman. "Did you see anyone near Saks who looked like they might have been part of the leadership group, somebody who could have been in charge?"

"Of the beardy nutters, you mean?" Jules asked. "No, I'm sorry. We didn't. We were just checking out the ground. Making sure we didn't get caught up in somebody's turf war."

The Rhino confirmed her story with a shake of the head that nearly tipped off his helmet. "Sorry, ma'am. But no, we didn't see anyone like that." He approached her carefully, holding out a massive paw full of papers. She gestured for him to put them down on a nearby table.

"Okay, then. I'm gonna go. And so are you. You need to get yourself uptown and bunkered down, and you need to go now. There's nothing here for you anymore."

"You don't need to tell me that," said Jules.

"What about those documents?" the Rhino said. "You're not going to have time to deliver them to anyone. And they're important. They need analyzing."

"I can't believe I'm being lectured by a busted-ass smuggler without the fucking sense to do some basic research before he takes on a job. So what, Coast Guard, are you offering to come on board for the big win now? You going to carry these precious documents back through Injun country, are you? Because that would mean I'd have to give them to you first, which would make me a bigger fucking idiot than you."

"Such spunk!" The Rhino grinned. "I *like* her, Miss Jules. I like her a lot. This is the reason America is still chewin' gum and kickin' ass."

Julianne sighed. "What's your name?" she asked.

"Irrelevant."

"Okay. Fine. Look, mystery girl, you've got all sorts of whiz-bang-looking comms gear hanging off your spanky little outfit. If you can talk to the military, get hold of some special forces bods we ran into; they'll vouch for us. We did save them from their own unpleasant incident of ass fuckage, as you put it so very well. We can carry your papers back if they okay us. As you said, there's nothing here for us now, and frankly, I'd like to get the hell out of New York. It's all been a very bloody fear-and-loathing trip, to tell the truth."

"Hell yes!" said the Rhino. "We were somewhere around the edge of the city when the drugs began to take hold and the giant bats swooped down. Remember that, Julesy? The giant bats?" He grinned maniacally.

Jules couldn't help but giggle at the incongruous fucking madness of it all.

The woman with the gun shook her head. "I hate this fucking city."

50

NEW YORK

"Down, down, down!" Wilson shouted, taking cover behind the splintered, pockmarked doors leading to the public reading room of the library.

"I am down, Wilson," Milosz yelled back. "And I am staying down now until stupid asswits and ragheads get bored and go home. This is not so much fun anymore."

Tracers spewed out of the vast reading room into the smaller catalogue area where the rangers and militia troops were holed up. They poured through in a lethal torrent of tracers, cutting down anyone foolish enough to stick his head in the way. Milosz kept himself well out of the line of fire, which was coming from a makeshift stockade constructed of dozens of upturned wooden desks and the wreckage of a large, dark wooden booth that appeared to divide the vast cavern of the room on the other side of the doorway. The uproar of gunfire and screaming from inside was so loud that you had to shout into someone's ears to make yourself heard.

"Worthy's had it," Gardener hollered, dragging the militiaman back toward them, using the cover from the old catalogue files. Worthy had lost his melon and most of his gray matter trying to throw a frag into the main room. The same grenade had gone off a few yards away and clipped two exposed members of the New York militia, who were screaming as a medic did his best to shut them up.

"Got one critical here," he yelled.

"Get some of those militia pukes to drag his ass out of here," Wilson shouted. "Fred, we need to gather up some claymores. And a bucket. A big fucking bucket. Gardener, can you handle that?"

"Holy shit," she protested. "Sex discrimination case? Would you like me to come back barefoot and pregnant, too?"

"No, just fetch me a fucking bucket, zoomie."

The Polish NCO snaked forward, his ass puckered and his head down. Hundreds of rounds zipped and cracked through the air just above him. "You have a cunning plan, Wilson?"

"I always have a plan, Fred."

Milosz stuck his carbine up over the ruined cabinet behind which he was sheltering and popped off three rounds. Elements of their ad hoc team were trying to break into the reading room from multiple points of entry, but where those other points were, Milosz had no idea. He tossed another precious frag into the reading room, where it went off with a cracking roar that seemed to interrupt the volume of fire coming at them for a second or two. Charred and burning pages of God only knew how many good books came drifting back into the anteroom.

Milosz shook his head.

This was not right. Destroying a library like this. Libraries were sacred places—his father had taught him that. Hallowed halls where silence and stillness and modest learning was the order. Not screams and gunfire and crazy fucking schemes involving explosive mines and big fucking buckets that Master Sergeant Wilson would not even bother to explain to him.

More hammering automatic fire started up somewhere behind and above them, but he had no idea where.

"Motherfuck—"

"Man down!" someone shouted.

"Worthless fucking militia," Wilson muttered, using his 203 launcher to plunk another 40-mm HE grenade into the reading room. The boom sent another dirty snowstorm of shredded, smoking paper into the air but this time it did very little to turn down the volume of fire coming their way.

Gardener's feet squealed and skittered across the marble floor as she returned with two steel buckets and a mop.

"Damn, we didn't need the mop," Wilson shouted over the din.

"Sorry," Gardener cried out. "Couldn't hear you. Fred, give me your claymore, buddy."

Milosz unlimbered the olive drab bandolier holding two M18A1 claymore antipersonnel mines. He fired a burst of suppressing fire through the door and tossed it underhanded to Gardener across the deadly gap between them.

Tech Sergeant Gardener spilled the contents of the bandolier onto the floor.

"You're supposed to leave the mine in the bag," Milosz said, regretting it instantly. He simply couldn't help himself.

"I didn't know this was a common task test, motherfucker!" Gardener shouted back.

"It is just that I have investments now," he called back. "A reason to live. I plan to die as wealthy oil tycoon, not stinky-ass soldier with head blown off."

She ignored him and unrolled a copious amount of slack from the spool of firing wire. "How much do you think we need?"

"Thirty feet," Wilson said.

"Right." She unspooled thirty feet of slack and set the wire at her feet before jamming the mine into the bucket. Milosz smiled as he read the words front toward enemy. That always made him smile.

Perhaps they should have had a tag at the end of their rifle: bullet comes out here. very fast.

Using "hundred mile an hour" tape, the air force lady fixed the mine firmly in place and opened the detonator well.

The tracer fire abated just a little, and Milosz could hear voices through the ringing in his ears. The sound of a muffled footfall reached him. A lieutenant from the 82nd Airborne dived and slid across the floor to fetch up beside him.

"You Sergeant Milosz?" he asked at full volume.

"Not if you are from Immigration."

"What?"

"Sorry. Bad joke. Relieves tension of waiting for pointless death. Yes, yes, I am Milosz. You bring good news for me, yes? Otherwise, you will please to be fucking off backward out door through which you slid. Nice work, by the way."

"Thanks. I'm looking for you and a Master Sergeant Wilson and—"

"Present!" cried out Wilson.

"And T.S. Gardener."

"That's me," she yelled without stopping her work on the improvised mine. Milosz was beginning to worry about the punch she was trying to pack into those two buckets. Wilson had collected another three claymores from the militia troops scattered about the room.

"I'm Lieutenant Cleaves," the airborne man explained. "I got sent here by battalion. They need to confirm you met a couple of civilian contractors, a—" He checked a small piece of folded paper and frowned. "—a Mister Rhino A. Ross and a Ms. Julianne Balwyn."

"That's Lady Julianne," Milosz corrected as Wilson looked up and gave him a warning look. "Her family once had castle and everything. Not so much now, though. Why you ask?"

"We've had flash traffic from a classified source. Says they have some documents and need airlift immediately."

Milosz leaned around the corner of the cabinet and squeezed off a round. The tracer fire resumed, impacting against the marble wall above his head, steadily chewing through the masonry and showering him with stinging chips of hot rock. The small clutch of militiamen hiding over there scurried away to find better cover.

"Is this hippo man and lady saying they have documents or classified source?" asked Milosz.

Cleaves could only shake his head in confusion. "Sorry?"

"Does not matter? What for you need to speak to us?"

"Command needs to verify these people before it'll task airlift to get them out. The source says you can do that."

Milosz, Wilson, and Gardener had a whole conversation without saying a word. Milosz had no idea what was going on but had to assume that the smugglers had found whatever they needed and had somehow lucked into a way of getting out of the free-fire zone. It was infuriating that he didn't know for sure, but what was he to do? He just had to assume that if they could talk their way into an airlift, they could talk their way out at the other end, especially if they convinced this "source" to help out. He hoped that didn't mean a further dilution of his cut. And if it did mean he got his ass kicked, so what? Soon enough Fryderyck Milosz would be a wealthy former soldier whose only care was how to get the wealthy former Technical Sergeant Gardener to show him a good time.

"Yes," he said at last. "Tell battalion they should pick them up. These are good guys, this hippo and Jules lady. They saved my Polish ass from angry pirate asswits."

"Good to know," Cleaves said. "Do you, er, think I could get a little covering fire?"

Milosz and Wilson obliged, with a couple of the militia pukes throwing in for good measure as Cleaves exited the anteroom as quickly as he'd arrived.

"What the fuck was that about?" Wilson shouted.

"Ours is not to know, Master Sergeant. Ours is but to protect our investment in offshore oil field and not get fucking heads shot off like dopey militia unit inappropriately named Worthy."

Another surge in fire from the reading room had them fucking the marble floor and Gardener demanding to know how much ammunition the towelheads had, anyway. As Milosz watched, she gave herself a meter of slack; taking the plug from the detonator well of one of the claymores, she slid the blasting cap through and with great care screwed the plug back into place, arming the mine.

"Got 'em both," she said. "Would have been quicker with a satchel charge."

"This is the army, my friend," Wilson said. "We go with what we got; now give me one bucket. And give Fred the other one. You keep the firing devices."

She handed them over and allowed Wilson to connect the device, the "clacker," to the firing wire.

"You motherfuckers had better knock that shit off," Wilson shouted at the reading room.

The fire slackened momentarily. "Fuck you, George Bush!"

The Americans looked at each other in astonishment.

"Man," said Gardener. "Some people just cannot get their heads out of the past."

Milosz popped around the corner, sighted in on the loudmouth, and punched a single round through his forehead.

"Ha! Stupid nig nog!" Milosz shouted. "Second Amendment trumps First every time."

Wilson stared at him like he was insane.

Milosz shrugged. "For what purpose is that look, Wilson? I am forced to learn civics classes for citizenship but not to use knowledge learned for taunting pirate asswits?"

Wilson shook his head. "Let's just ram the corncob in the hole."

He turned to address all the shooters he had at his command.

"Sergeant Milosz and I are going to save your worthless asses in just a second with a display of ranger awesomeness that will make you pee in your fucking pants every time you remember it for the rest of your lives. But first you got to give us covering fire when I say go. That means hauling your sorry asses up off the ground and actually sending some joy downrange on the fucking enemy. It also means fixing bayonets right now and following us into there when I tell you. Are we clear?"

The ragged response forced him to yell.

"ARE WE CLEAR?"

That drew a louder roar, and Wilson raised his eyebrows at Milosz.

"Good enough, you think, Fred?"

"Soon to be finding out, Wilson. Shall we go?"

Wilson tossed him the heavy bucket loaded with high explosives and shrapnel as the other men in the anteroom clicked their fighting knives into place at the ends of their rifles. When Milosz caught the can and set himself to take off, Wilson yelled.

"GO!"

The unexpected savagery of the Americans' coordinated fire slammed a lid down on the jihadi defenses, giving the two rangers time to leap up and sprint for the door to the reading room.

"Fire in the hole!" Wilson shouted as he heaved his bucket through the door a fraction of a second before Milosz. The heavy improvised bombs arced up high into the air over the improvised palisade from which the jihadis were fighting. In the surreal silence that seemed to hum inside Milosz's head he distinctly heard Gardener give both clackers three squeezes.

Detonated by a small electric spark, the tightly packed C-4 of half a dozen claymores detonated over the heads of their enemy, unleashing a steel rain of more than four thousand ball bearings all traveling at 3,995 feet per second. The explosion was far louder than any other noise in the confined space of the library building, and the concussion was enough to knock Milosz to the floor, even shielded as he was by the thick walls of the reading room.

"Go, go, go!" Wilson shouted. "Off your asses now!"

Milosz was dimly aware of glinting steel closing on him from behind as he spun around the corner of the great double doors and opened fire.

"Fuck you, George Bush!"

Selim the Algerian was the last man of his *saif* to die, shot through the forehead, his brains and half his skull spraying out behind him, blinding Yusuf with a foul, hot organic gruel that stung his eyes as he wiped it away.

He could not believe anyone would be so foolish as to martyr himself for the momentary satisfaction of taunting the enemy. Yusuf Mohammed shook his head and burrowed farther into the small foxhole he had built for himself inside the massive chaotic fort fashioned from dozens of desks and chairs and heavy wooden cabinets. Thousands of pieces of paper and cardboard notes and handbooks spilled out, strangely reminding him of his days in the mission school back at the village where he had lived simply and, he supposed, happily until Captain Kono had come and taken everything from him.

It was odd the way that memory worked. All his life he had never been able to recall anything but the merest fragments of dreams from that time. But just in the last hour or two, as he had come to realize he would probably die in this room, he had found himself able to recall what he had to believe were intensely remembered images and moments from a life he had never really known before. A woman with huge soft arms and a big belly on which he bounced and giggled as she sang to him and tickled him until he was nearly sick with laughter. An old man, gray around the temples and thin, led him down to a river, carrying two poles strung with fishing line. He ran across a bare dirt field, squealing with happiness as he kicked a ball, and other children chased after him, calling out his name. He knew they were calling out his name, but no matter how hard he concentrated, he could not quite make it out.

"Fuck you, George Bush!"

And then Selim died so foolishly and wastefully as he sprayed the memories of whatever childhood he had known in Algeria all over Yusuf's face. The former child soldier, all grown up now, screamed in rage and hoisted the familiar weight of his AK-47 up above the rim of the overturned table behind which he was hiding, firing off the remainder of his clip until the hammer clicked and clicked and nothing happened.

His head swam and his ears felt as though somebody had jabbed a sharp stick in them, so loud was the noise of the battle reverberating around the huge empty space of this room. It must have been beautiful once, he supposed, before war came to it. The mural on the ceiling was smoke-damaged and pitted and gouged with bullet holes and long dark scorch marks that all but obliterated the original artwork. It was a shame. He knew some members of the faithful looked disapprovingly on all forms of art, taking the Prophet's admonitions against such images much more generally that Yusuf imagined the Prophet intended.

He ducked as he saw the small, dark shape of a hand grenade come flying through the door. It detonated with a great crash and showered his barricade with deadly shrapnel. How much had changed in such a short time. Not so long ago he would not have dared to advance his own opinions or interpretation of the Prophet's works, especially not when they did not agree with those who were his elders in the faith. But as he wiped a sharp white fleck of bone from his cheeks and contemplated his own demise, he thought he understood much more of what the Prophet wanted from his followers and even the leaders of his people than some of those leaders did.

Honesty, courage, modesty, righteousness, even kindness and mercy—they all had their place in life. Yusuf shook his head again in bitter despair as he saw the bodies of the women and children they had come to protect. There were only three of them left alive. The fedayeen had done what they could to construct a bunker inside where the innocents might shelter, but the Americans had thrown so many explosives in there with such abandon, and some of the children had panicked and broken away from their mothers, and…

His stomach contracted mightily, and he dry wretched for half a minute.

What were they even doing in the city?

What fool had sent them here into a battlefield?

The Americans' fire tapered off for a moment, giving him hope that they might be withdrawing, but it soon returned with increased intensity.

Surely the emir could not have done so, knowing how dangerous it was? Not when there was so much preserved food and even wild roots and vegetables that could be harvested away from the fighting.

He swapped the clip on his Kalashnikov, the last of his ammunition. There had to be some explanation, some mistake, he told himself. Unfortunately, mistakes were as common in war as death and sorrow. Perhaps the emir had been misinformed. After all, he was only a man.

Yusuf lifted the gun above the line of the barricade and fired two single shots in the general direction of the little room where the Americans were trapped. He scolded himself for his lack of faith. Not in God, of course, but in the messengers he had sent to earth. The emir, Ahmet Ozal, all the other fedayeen commanders—they were but men and so subject to the failings of all men. He himself had more than enough experience to understand that. After all, his failure on the island at the start of this great battle had not been a failure of judgment but one of heart, of courage. He had failed his god and his comrades because he was a coward. And now here he was, having been given a chance to redeem himself, and he was blaming others for yet another failure of his own.

Yusuf Mohammed resolved to do better in what little, little time he had left, to stop questioning and doubting and forever finding fault elsewhere when the fault lay within. So many had died for the dream of this new home, where the light and grace of Allah might shine on all who opened their hearts to his love. And yet Yusuf still lived. To what end?

None.

He felt the sickness steal over him again. The nausea of an existence without meaning.

He tightened the grip on his weapon, drew in a deep breath, and prepared to die with God's name on his lips. He pushed himself up from his hiding place and, standing tall, aimed his rifle into the darkened room from which a river of deadly fire was now pouring.

"Allahu akbar!" he cried out as he fired again and again at the enemy.

Flashing lines of tracer zipped past his head while unseen rounds cracked and fizzed all around him. Allah smiled on him, however, protecting him from harm. At least for a brief while. The Americans' fire was a terrible wind that swept over his comrades, cutting down more of them even as he stood in the storm, untouched.

"Allahu ak—"

The cry died in his throat as he saw the strangest and most unexpected of things in all his time in this city of wonders: two large metal buckets covered in tape slowly arcing through the air, turning end over end, trailing a pair of wires as they flew.

Yusuf Mohammed eased off on the trigger of his weapon and stood staring at the flight of those most unusual objects. He had another moment of intense dislocation, a feeling that he had somehow lost his tether to this world and slipped back into another he had lost many years ago. He was a small boy again, standing at the edge of a stream that ran near the little village. The tall thin man with the patches of gray at his temples stood by him, teaching him how to cast a fishing pole. He was not very good, this being his very first time, but the man was not just patient with him, he seemed to take joy in the little boy's squeals and giggles of delight as his brightly colored lure flew everywhere but where it was intended. The sky wrapped itself around them, an endless blue, soft and resplendent with a warm sun.

The old man told him not to look into the sun, but Yusuf Mohammed did not listen. He smiled and smiled, and the sun smiled back on him, filling the whole world with bright, white light.

"Cease fire!" Milosz shouted. "Cease with the fucking fire already!"

The clatter of weapons fire died down in much the same way his tractor at home wound down after he shut it off. A few bursts stitched the walls, followed by sporadic single pops, finally punctuated by a single hollow thump.

An ear-piercing wail reverberated off the marble interior of the reading room. Milosz could just barely make out, through the smoke and mist, a woman cradling a child in her arms. She rocked back and forth, adding her own screams to the baby's protests.

The fighting had shattered the cathedral-like windows, letting the driving rain pour inside. As the rain dispersed the smoke, Milosz could see them.

Bodies. They lay strewn amid the tables and chairs of the reading room. They held children close, curled up with their backs to the door he and Gardener had just fought their way through. Along the walls were stacks of canned goods, jars of sauces, meats, and other food that was still edible, if a bit questionable.

A can of pineapple rolled to a stop against Milosz's boot. Through a hole it leaked a thick yellow syrup onto the floor, which mixed with the dark blood of a little girl who was missing the back of her head.

Two of the surviving militia men who had covered the assault from the upper level looked at each other.

"How many frags did we throw in here?" one of them asked.

The other shook his head. "I have no idea."

"Too many," Gardener said, wiping her brow. She was sweating profusely despite the cold rain, preversely reminding the Pole of a wheel of cheese. "Or not enough. It doesn't really matter now, does it?"

"Are we going to get in trouble for this?" the one who had asked about the frags wondered.

"I doubt it," Milosz said. "They will probably give you medals. And one hundred and forty new bucks this month. Probably."

51

KANSAS CITY, MISSOURI

The city never slept. The demands of reconstruction meant there was always something going on somewhere, and Kip took solace from that as he sat at his desk in the early morning, eyes burning with fatigue, struggling to write something original in each letter of condolence. Handwriting each letter, each comma, and restoring his rusty cursive script after decades of disuse helped provide a sort of penance for the men and women dying on his command. "Dear Mrs. Kohler," he wrote, ignoring the cramp in his fingers, "I am terribly sorry to have to write you this letter…"

He had begun writing after a long night of briefings and video meetings with his military chiefs, and the brief, frustrating talk with Agent Monroe. It was nearly four-thirty before he finished the last of the letters, and his head swam with fatigue. He was sick of it and desperately wanted nothing more than to climb into bed next to Barbara back at home and fall asleep for twenty years, waking only when all this was history. Instead he spent the next hour inhaling coffee and reviewing reports from Manhattan. When the first silver bands of dawn softened the eastern horizon, he asked his security detail chief—Agent Shinoda was asleep—if she could organize a morning run for him with some troops.

Forty minutes later he was pounding down Highway 210, surrounded by a platoon of U.S. Army rangers, who seemed flattered to have been called on in such a fashion by their commander in chief even though he had signed orders yesterday sending them all to the slaughterhouse of New York.

Kipper would never understand the military mind.

The rangers took the president past a QuikTrip and a recreation center that were both open despite the early hour. The QuikTrip's red façade had faded to pink after four years of weathering, but the doors opened frequently as men and women from the night shifts grabbed a meal or perhaps a nightcap and some early birds came around looking for an easy breakfast. As he jogged along, he watched others make their way into the rec center for a shower, a swim, or perhaps, strangest of all in an era of renewed physical labor, a workout. Through the windows of the center he could even see militia troops playing basketball as part of their physical training. He felt guilty at the sight of them. The militia was suffering by far the worst of the fighting in Manhattan.

The runners took a turn down past the Northtown's city hall, where the FBI had set up shop along with the restored Metropolitan Kansas City Police Force. A couple of officers in green fatigues on the front steps noticed their commander in chief and snapped out salutes as he headed north toward the high school where newly arrived immigrants were processed and given rudimentary medical treatment and a meal in the cafeteria. To them he was nobody, and they ignored him. KC was crawling with small groups of military men and women pounding the bitumen. That was a strangely satisfying experience. The rangers continued past the red brick three-story building and the football stadium. A glance over the rock walls revealed the olive drab tops of army tents, where many of the refugees would spend their first night. The Missouri militia watched over the football stadium from plywood guard towers.

Kipper made an effort to keep up with the rangers, who were singing a song, or a cadence as they called it. There was a rhythm to it that was supposed to help one endure the double time, but Kipper kept tuning it out, lost in his own thoughts, mostly haunted by images of his trip to the hospital.

Her face!

Moving farther north, they passed a high school campus and turned east by a large park dominated by cracked tennis courts and weed-choked baseball diamonds. A few abandoned cars filled the parking lot, probably belonging to runners who'd been getting in a morning jog when the Wave took them. The rising sun silhouetted the bulk of North Kansas City Hospital from here, reminding him of yesterday's visit. Running alongside the men who would be going into New York City on his say-so, he was haunted by visions of them reduced like that poor woman yesterday. Faceless, limbless, hobbled and broken for the rest of their lives.

Why risk their lives for a dead city or country?

He couldn't help wondering. If you took away the uniforms, they were just regular people, young and fit, for sure, but not supermen. Not giants or comic book heroes. They were average guys with the same problems as any other average guys: overdue bills, relationships, family problems. The usual.

Why do this when he couldn't even guarantee they'd be paid this week? Why not hire themselves out to private contractors who valued their skills and would pay well for them? Why did they do it? Because, as Barbara kept telling him, somebody had to.

Kipper increased his pace a fraction until he was running alongside the rangers' squad leader, or platoon leader, or whatever. That made him a... lieutenant... he was pretty sure. There was no way of telling from the man's running gear.

"Son," he puffed, "I reckon I've had enough of this sweaty bullshit. How about we head back and win us a war."

"Hooah, Mister President!"

"Yeah," said Kip. "Plenty of that today."

Having made the call to throw everything into the maw, Kipper found himself strangely calm as he examined the results a few hours later from almost exactly one thousand miles away. It was possible, if the satellites and the stars were aligned at the precise moment, to watch the unfolding battle for New York City on the screens in the ad hoc command center the army had quickly established once he'd decided to stay in the Midwest hub settlement. Kip wasn't sure where all the extra personnel had come from, whether they'd been here when he arrived or had flown in over the week, but the Cerner Campus was suddenly overrun with uniforms, and the rather quiet building in which he had his local office was swarming like a busted ants' nest.

It reminded him of the first week after the Wave, when Seattle's city council tower had been all but invaded by Mad Jack Blackstone's people from Fort Lewis. Dozens, perhaps hundreds of phones rang constantly. The corridors were crowded, sometimes getting on for impassable, as hundreds of men and women scurried about, carrying sheets of paper, folders, ring binders, phones, files, maps... all the mountains of paper generated when the United States committed itself to battle. The small conference room where he and Jed had often met to run the country was now crowded with communications gear, computers, and dozens of wide screens. He had relocated to a boardroom up on the top floor, similarly overrun and stocked with electronics but at least not as hopelessly crowded as downstairs, with only a handful of military officers able to cram themselves in around him.

Kipper sat between Jed and Colonel Mike Ralls, who had

changed out of his dress greens and into the standard fatigues of the U.S. Army. He looked a lot more comfortable than Kipper felt as the aide used a smartboard to provide a running commentary on the engagement.

"The Second Marine Expeditionary Brigade has established their blocking positions to east of Rockefeller," Ralls said. "The One hundred first is inbound."

Kipper rubbed his forehead, which was aching a little. He was dreading what the day would bring. There was no ignoring the fact that he'd ordered the destruction of a huge part of the city, something he'd once promised himself he would not do. Homes, businesses, streets, churches, memories. All would be gone. He built such things, helped provide water, power, and other service to homes just like that. New York City wasn't his town by any means, but the destruction still offended him.

The shattered, faceless female soldier in the hospital offended him more, however.

"Mister President?" Another aide stepped through the door. Their numbers had suddenly metastasized like the dancing brooms in that old Mickey Mouse film.

"Yes?"

"Colonel Kinninmore reports that the last of the resistance at the old library has been neutralized and he's transferred the bulk of his forces there to reinforce the cordon around Rockefeller Center. G2 is estimating the bulk of the enemy have dug themselves in there now."

"Good," Kip said.

"Copy that," Lieutenant Colonel Alois Kinninmore replied, handing the phone back to an aide. It had been a long time since anything had surprised the cavalry commander, but his new orders did. *Finally,* he thought. *The end is coming.*

He walked over to the map of Manhattan that covered half a

wall inside 1/7 Cav's latest tactical operations center in the small, ravaged wasteland of the park behind the New York Public Library. Thick columns of smoke poured from the upper floor of the building, and the last time he'd stepped outside his command Bradley, he could even see flames through one or two windows. A small and miserable-looking band of prisoners from that fight were still sitting on the muddy ground in the rain at the rear of the library, being guarded by a squad of resentful militia.

Kinninmore was flanked right and left by liaison officers from the 101st and the Marine RCTs who were tasked with backstopping his push toward the enemy.

"Gentlemen," he said. "That was General Murphy at Fort Lewis. The president has authorized us to proceed."

"About goddamn time," the marine growled.

Major Holt, Kinninmore's XO, pulled a printout from the fax. "Do you want me to execute this fire mission Colonel?"

"Affirmative," Kinninmore said. "Forward that to fire support for immediate action."

"*All* the bridges, sir?" Major Holt asked. "Won't we need them to press into Brooklyn and Queens?"

"Rules have changed, Major. We're fighting to win now. That's the extent of our new rules of engagement."

Realization dawned on Holt's face. "Sergeant Cathey, send this fire mission ASAP."

Kinninmore picked up his helmet and retrieved his personal weapon. He turned to his colleagues from the U.S. Marine Corps and U.S. Airborne Division. "Gentlemen, I'm going forward. Care to join me?"

Governors Island had reverted to a natural prehuman state in the four years since the Wave had swept over it. After the pollution storms, only the hardiest trees had flourished, their roots and trunks shrouded by the rapid growth of underbrush and weeds—until the U.S. Army arrived and began returning the island to its earlier role: a fort. The gun bunnies of 1/5 Field Artillery and the Sixth Field Artillery dug themselves into the fields around Fort Jay, establishing Firebase Euler, home to the long guns, heavy mortars, and rocket batteries that had chopped down wave after wave of pirates, insurgents, and freebooters inside the city. The island also housed the core of the local civilian administration, run by the appointed governor, Elliott Schimmel, and protected by a battalion of troops from Schimmel's irregulars—now reduced to a mere company by the need to reinforce the army on the main island.

Governor Schimmel was a New York native, an historian who had been guest lecturing in Japan back in March 2003. From the battlements of Fort Jay he watched the skyline of his city shrouded in dark oily smoke, an ungovernable rage churning in his innards.

"Governor Schimmel?" one of his officers called over to him. "I just got word from the firebase commander."

"Any news of resupply?"

"Yes, sir," the officer replied. "It is coming now. ETA twenty minutes. But what I wanted to tell you, sir, is that they're going to blow the bridges."

"What?" Schimmel roared, turning on his underling.

Before he could say another word, the 155-mm howitzers barked into the dawn. The metal-on-metal crash of the guns spit their ordnance out toward Long Island. Metal boxes on tank tracks swiveled until they, too, were facing Brooklyn and Queens. Stacks of fresh ammunition for the multiple rocket launch system sat a safe distance away, ready for use.

No, Schimmel thought. *Not the bridges.* The president had promised him they would not do this. Not to his city.

He jumped a few inches when the first missile shrieked into the sky, ripping at the very fabric of the morning. Others followed immediately, filling the firebase with white acrid smoke.

In the distance he heard the first rumble of thunder as the high-explosive shells began to pound his precious bridges into scrap.

Manhattan was being cut off, and all who stood on it without the say-so of the American people would soon have no choice but to surrender their liberty or their lives.

Having gathered another thirty troops along the way, Colonel Alois Kinninmore arrived at Fifth Avenue and West 48th Street, where the sharp end of the U.S. Army's Seventh Cavalry Regimental Combat Team was located. To say the cavalry was assembled at the intersection would be to gloss over the reality. The wounded streamed south down Fifth Avenue toward aid stations set up in the shells of once-fashionable shops. A murderous stream of tracers poured into the cross streets from the 1930s Depression era concrete skyscrapers that made up Rockefeller Center. Kinninmore and his scratch team of marines, militia, and soldiers kept their heads down and their weapons up and edged along the walls, mindful that there was no safe place to be found.

"Colonel!" someone shouted from a cluster of troops right at the edge of the fighting. "Have you lost your fucking mind?"

Kinninmore grinned. "No, but I lost my sense of humor around Forty-second Street."

The soldier ran over to Kinninmore, mindful of the tracer fire hosing down the intersection. Captain Frankowski didn't bother to salute his commanding officer. No one needed a sniper to know that he was around.

"Pretty fucking sporty up here, sir," Frankowski said. "If you don't mind my saying."

"I don't," Kinninmore replied. "Status?"

Frankowski turned and gestured toward Rockefeller Center. "We're hung up on these fucking scrapers. Depression-era shit built with old-fashioned concrete, rebar, and probably more than a few bodies courtesy of the mob. No good estimate on effective combatants, but they've set it up as a strongpoint with good intersecting fields of fire. I think we're gonna find almost all of them in there, Colonel. It's a great defensive position."

"I can see that," Kinninmore said. "Don't fret, son. We have them exactly where we want them. Who's the on-scene commander?"

"I was until you got here. Colonel Callahan took a shot to the chest. While the medics were working him, he got another one to the melon. Game over. You're it, sir."

"Any contact with higher up?"

"Sporadic," Frankowski said, ducking against a roar of gunship turbines. Kinninmore saw the black burst of explosives against one of the larger skyscrapers, which had been defaced by so many such strikes that it looked like an ancient ruin.

"Who have we got on our flanks?"

"Fourth Cav combat team on the Avenue of the Americas; they've worked their way up to Fiftieth Street," Frankowski said. "Fifth Cav is to the east over on… looks like Park Avenue. They're chopped up pretty bad, and I've not had any word from them in the last hour."

Kinninmore pulled a map from his cargo pocket and unfolded it. "Any support fire available?"

"Fifth Field Artillery is up. They're at Firebase Euler, but the support has been somewhat spotty. These skyscrapers are really fucking with our comms, especially since we lost the retrans unit up in the Chrysler Building," Frankowski said. "You need to know our ammo situation is critical as well. I've had our troops strip the wounded and the dead, our guys and the enemy, but we're still hurtin' for certain."

Kinninmore got the map out and started making notes, placing units where Frankowski described them. He pointed at Madison Avenue. "Fifth Cav got anyone on this?"

Frankowski shook his head. "Not near as I can tell."

"Get me a commo dog over here who knows his shit. Anyone. I don't care who they are or what branch."

"I'm on it," Frankowski said.

Kinninmore tossed his map onto the ground and pointed to his scratch collection of trigger pullers. "All of you with me. We're moving fast, and we're killing anyone who gets in our way."

"Where are we going, Colonel?" one of the marines shouted.

"Over to Madison," he shouted back. "It ain't Iwo, but it'll have to do. Let's move out!"

Kinninmore ducked behind an overturned trash truck, and gathered a few of his team members around him. The rest of the scratch team engaged the vehicles, not waiting for a dramatic command or any heroics from their commander. Looking back the way they had come, the colonel could see a thin, scrawny figure running down the sidewalk toward him, a radio antenna prominent on his back. Two other men flanked him, watching for fire from above. There were snipers everywhere.

"Over here!" Kinninmore shouted. He tapped the female military police trooper next to him. "Hold this position, Sergeant. No matter what."

"I've got it!"

Kinninmore ran toward the commo dog and shoved him through a doorway. One of the two rangers escorting him actually bulled Kinninmore out of the way.

"Watch where you going, ignorant shithead," he shouted in a thick Polish accent. "We have had enough of being pushed around today."

"Anybody teach you to use cover, son?" Kinninmore shouted back. "What's your name? Do I know you?"

A tuft of blond hair poked out from under the first soldier's Kevlar helmet. "It ain't son, sir. It's Sergeant Bonnie Gardener. USAF TAC. Someone said you needed a rainmaker. Well, I'm it."

52

NEW YORK

Motherhood was making her soft. There was no way, in her salad days, she would have bothered helping out a couple of losers like these two. She didn't need them to get the documents back to G2. She could've dialed up a chopper to swoop in and grab them any time she wanted. But as the three of them hunkered down against the blast of the rotor wash from the descending Blackhawk, Caitlin told herself she was just acting rationally. Their lives might not mean much to her, but they weren't hers to throw away, either. Not nowadays.

These two might be a pair of idiots, but they weren't bad people, just inept smugglers. And they hadn't been lying about rescuing a special forces team a day earlier. There were a couple of rangers and a forward air controller who were drawing breath today because Balwyn and Ross had put themselves in harm's way on their behalf. They hadn't had to do that, the same way she didn't have to do this.

The chopper came down quickly, much more quickly than she was used to when working with the military, but the chances of getting an RPG up the ass increased exponentially the longer a pilot hovered around squeezing his johnson and taking in the view. The smugglers had taken themselves off a few yards away and were clutching all the documents they'd gathered up downstairs in a couple of packages like they were carrying newborn babies and feared they'd be snatched away and blown over the edge of the roof. It was a long way down to the street. Caitlin couldn't fault them for that. Those documents were probably going to keep them out of a federal prison if they could find themselves a good lawyer and cut a plea bargain for running the zone. Assuming, of course, they didn't just disappear in the old-fashioned way inconvenient people used to disappear. This guy Cesky they were talking about, he was a big name back west. A heavy hitter plugged deep into the administration. Nothing they had to say about him was going to make anybody very happy. In fact, the more Caitlin thought about it, the better off they would be jumping out of this chopper at the other end and running as hard as they could for the horizon.

Oh, well, not her fucking problem.

She turned her head and squeezed her eyes shut as the Blackhawk landed and blew a stinging cloud of dust and grit up from the roof. When she looked up again, the chick was there—Jules, she called herself, even though she was entitled, as in genuinely entitled, to be known as Lady Julianne.

"Look," Jules yelled out. "We got off to a bad start, but I just wanted to say thanks for everything. If you hadn't taken out Cesky's guys... well, you know. Thanks. And for this, too," she shouted, jerking a thumb back over her shoulder at the helicopter.

Caitlin nodded and waved her on board, but she wasn't really paying attention. She had been working out how she was going to get herself into the ruins of the Saks department store on Fifth Avenue, where she was almost certain Baumer was holed up. But she stopped worrying about that when she saw the man who hopped out of the chopper and hurried across to her, bent over and squinting against the storm of dust.

It was Wales. Her old controller. Wales Larrison, a deputy director now, coordinating all the Echelon branches from the new headquarters in Vancouver. Her heart swelled at the sight of him, the closest thing she had to a father in what was left of the world, but she winced, too. Wales wouldn't fly into New York just to wish her good luck. Like her, he was smiling, but sadly, as he wrapped his arms around her and gave her a fierce, protective hug.

"I'm sorry, Caitlin," he said. "Not this time."

"No, Wales. No. You can't!"

Her cry was so pitiful, so heartfelt, and so loud that the Balwyn woman hesitated with one foot raised to hop into the cabin of the chopper. A cavalry trooper brandishing a shotgun pulled her up, anyway.

"I'm this close, Wales. Just give me an hour and I'll put my fucking hand inside his chest and squeeze off his heart. An hour, Wales, that's all I'm asking."

He shook his head unhappily.

"Not this time, I'm afraid. They sent me to make sure you got on the chopper. President Kipper sent me. Rang me himself and told me to get my ass over here to make sure you got out. I barely made it."

"But Wales," she cried in anguish. "My family. You know what he tried to do to my family. I have to finish this. I'm the only one who can do this and be sure."

Wales took her by the arm and began to lead her across the roof to the helicopter. They both knew she was more than capable of resisting him.

"You don't have time, Caitlin. There's a storm front coming in from the west. They've moved everything forward ahead of it. Air cav is assaulting into Central Park right now. As soon as they're down, air force is going to hammer the city flat. Or at least that part you want to head into. You don't have an hour, Caitlin. They are in the air now. Bombed up and inbound."

He was right. She could see the leading edge of the air assault coming in over his shoulder. Small black dots for now but growing larger every second, resolving themselves into an airborne armada of UH-60s and their gunship flankers. There looked to be about a dozen in the first wave and another two waves stacked up behind them, probably formed up in one of the new, stripped-down regimental combat teams the army was testing. Say, four hundred men on the ground within a quarter of an hour.

Wales almost had her into the cabin when she finally dug her heels in. She could see the smugglers and the cavalry troopers in the helicopter staring at her as though she were mad. But she didn't care.

"Wales, if we let him get away this time, he will be back in our faces worse than ever. You know that. He will come back at me. I know it's not personal, but it is. If that makes any fucking sense. You have to let me go. You have to let me get him."

"I can't, Caitlin," he said, looking older and more worn down than she had ever seen him before. "I'm not just following orders. I'm here because I don't want you to die. My daughter died four years ago. And my wife. And my brother and his wife and their kids. Everybody I cared for in the world is gone. Everybody but you. You have your own family now, Caitlin. I understand what that means. I understand the madness and the fear of it, because you are my family. You are all I have left. You are my daughter now, and I can't let you go."

She felt her throat closing up tight and her eyes beginning to water. She turned away so that nobody in the helicopter could see her. Wales Larrison stepped up around in front of her and raised her chin with his forefinger.

"He won't win, Caitlin," he said, projecting his voice through the thudding of the rotor blades. "He won't even get close. And I can give you my personal guarantee that he will never get within a thousand miles of Bret or Monique again. Ever."

"Why? How? Are we going to surround them with traps and razor wire?"

"No, Caitlin," he answered, gently steering her back toward the cabin. "Because he's going to die sometime today, or he's going to die in the very near future when you put your hand inside him and squeeze the life out of his heart. But not today."

She was numb. Numb and exhausted and somewhere out over the edge of things where she might be free-falling or floating or possibly even drifting away from the world.

Caitlin climbed into the chopper and sat in the front of the cabin, refusing to make eye contact with anyone. Wales strapped himself into the seat beside her and placed one arm around her shoulders. That was all it took. She fell apart and started crying, covering her face with her hands as the chopper lifted off from the roof.

"I believe 'I told you so' would be appropriate at this point, Miss Jules."

The roar of the helicopter's takeoff was loud enough that Julianne could have pretended not to have heard the Rhino, but she was past caring anymore.

"About Cesky and Rubin, you mean?" she said. "You never told me anything about that other than your plans for spending the money."

"No," he insisted as they left the roof of the office building on East 60th Street behind. "I meant that." He pointed out of the cabin behind her, over toward Central Park. Jules had to lean forward to see past the door gunner who was covering their ignominious exit from New York. She had no idea what was going on with Wonder Woman and the old guy up front. She looked like she'd dropped her entire bundle in the last two minutes.

The sky over Central Park was swarming with helicopters just like theirs, Blackhawks full of troops. Sleeker, deadlier-looking gunships weaved through the congested air traffic, protecting the airborne assault, just as the Rhino had predicted. Unlike him, she was not a military enthusiast, and she had no idea how many men were involved or what it meant beyond a dramatic escalation of the war that was tearing the city apart block by block.

"What is that?" the Rhino bellowed over the racket. "One hundred first Airborne?"

One of the soldiers riding shotgun in the cabin—literally riding shotgun, Jules thought as she took in his armament—nodded. "The Screaming fucking Eagles, man," he shouted back. "Playtime is over."

As the helicopters stacked up one behind the other in a sort of layered effect to begin landing their troops, two of the waspish-looking gunships peeled off and began to pour a storm of machine gun and rocket fire down onto an unseen target over on that side of the city. And then Jules's chopper banked around and swung out toward the East River, taking them away from the action, the worst of the danger, and off toward the unknown. She had a package of papers tucked away inside a ballistic vest the flight crew had given her. She hoped they would go some way toward securing her immediate future, even though she had no idea what was in them, just that they had guaranteed her passage out of the trap Henry Cesky had set for her.

Jules ground her teeth and bit back on a throat full of bile when she thought of him. Her father had long ago advised her against investing in any scheme that had vengeance at its heart. But Cesky had invested heavily in his plan to settle up with her for leaving him and his family behind in Acapulco. What side of the equation did that leave her on now? Was she the vengeance seeker or the one upon whom vengeance was to be visited?

She had no idea.

53

TEXAS ADMINISTRATIVE DIVISION

Miguel could not shake the creeping fear that wanted to run wild as they mustered the cattle out of the little valley. But at least it was a sensible fear, not like the preternatural dread that had stolen over him back in Leona. This was merely a rational fear of being caught by the road agents he had observed the previous day. The vaquero had no illusions about how such an encounter would go. Oh, they would give a good accounting of themselves for sure, possibly taking down one or two agents for each of their own who fell. But in the end, they would be overwhelmed. Of that there could be no doubt. And then Sofia, if she lived, would be their prey.

And so, in the hours before dawn, they snuck away from Pineywoods Lake. With the agents so far to the west, there was no need for any elaborate displays of subterfuge. Still, he could not help keeping his voice down as he spoke to the other riders and called out to the dogs as they orbited the edge of the herd. Protesting cows, the muffled crunch of thousands of hooves on soft ground, a few whip cracks and whistles, his daughter riding high in the saddle next to him—it was all so familiar yet so alien in this empty landscape.

The coming sunrise had not yet burned off the early-morning fog as they began to move north, heading for the Johnson National Grasslands up near the border with Oklahoma. Miguel's head felt thick and fuzzy with the lack of sleep and the four or five glasses of red wine he had shared with Miss Jessup last night. After finishing the first "corked" bottle, she had produced another and pronounced it perfect. A chilled cerveza would have been perfect for Miguel, but he had to admit that the red wine did go down without too many protests.

"Hungover, cowboy?"

He turned to find that the very woman had ridden up behind him, catching him woolgathering and unaware. She was not a natural in the saddle. Indeed, the gelding struggled a little with its inexperienced passenger. But the strange "manbivalent" woman with the cheeky sense of humor and the warm laugh rode easily enough at this sedate pace. Most folks did nowadays, at least in the countryside.

"Good morning, Miss Jessup. And no, I am not so used to drinking as I once was," he admitted, tipping his hat to her.

"None of us are, Miguel," she replied.

"Oh, Papa was never much of a drinker," said his daughter, teasing, as he she rode over. "Not much of a drinker or a rider or shooter, really."

He showed her the back of his hand, but he was only playing, of course, and glad that Sofia's mood had lifted enough for her to be able to joke at his expense. Miss Jessup's face he could not see in the gloom, but he sensed that she was smiling, too, if a little sadly.

"It used to be nothing for me to finish a couple of bottles on my own," she said. "Occupational hazard. You know, I've dropped five sizes since the Wave came. Only put one back on last year, and I like to think that was muscle mass as opposed to table muscle."

"Table muscle?"

"Fat," Trudi said flatly. "Lard."

"Ah," he replied, turning his attention back to the cattle.

The herd was a heaving, dusty river, flowing north now, away from danger. He took in the scent of morning glories and honeydews that mingled with the stink of the beasts. A hint of rain in the air, perhaps. He wasn't sure of the weather, and there was no way to check. Most of the AM band Texas radio stations had fallen behind them, and the stations outside Texas concentrated on the weather in Seattle or Kansas City, which didn't help their situation one bit. Batteries to power the one radio they had were precious in any case, and no one was in the mood to listen to the gibberish coming out of Fort Hood or Governor Blackstone.

Miguel relaxed in the saddle and released a pent-up breath he hadn't even noticed he was holding. The morning sun started to peek through the chilly fog, ready to burn the thin sheath of frost off the land. With every minute that passed he felt better about leaving, about adding so many miles and weeks to their trip.

"Penny for your thoughts?" Miss Jessup asked.

"I am sorry to be so quiet," Miguel said. "Tell me, what did you do, Miss Jessup? This last year, I mean, that you should find yourself in Texas, captured by road agents?"

As soon as he asked the question, he regretted it, thinking himself too forward and rude for inquiring about another's personal business. But Trudi Jessup seemed not at all put out.

He saw her shoulders lift in silhouette.

"First up, my name is Trudi. Remember. Second, I was working for Seattle, like everyone else," she said. "Or so I thought. Before I wrote for magazines, I used to work in restaurants and catering. A lot of it is just logistics. Knowing how much food to have in store, predicting demand spikes and troughs, organizing transport. But you'd know some of that if you worked for the Golden Arches."

In fact, he had merely bossed their herds in one particular part of Mexico and knew very little about the hamburger clown's wider business. Once the cattle were out of his care, they were no longer his concern. And where all the potatoes for fries and apples for pies came from and went to he had no idea. Although he had heard dark rumors that the globby, glutinous filling of Ronald McDonald's apple pies were not apple at all but some sort of reconstituted root vegetable in sugar syrup. A rumor he dismissed as foolishness but one that never seemed to go away. Even down in Australia, they still talked about the apple pies as though they were made of mystery vegetables and secret chemistry tricks. When the family—again, a knife twisted in his chest as he thought of them—had passed through Sydney on their way back to America to join the resettlement program, he had taken them to spend the last of their local currency at a McDonald's down near the port from which they were to leave. Miguel Pieraro would swear on his life that the apple pie contained only apples and maybe some sugar.

"Well," Miss Jessup continued, unaware of his private musing, "I put all that down on my forms when I got back from Sardinia. I would have stayed; it is absolutely gorgeous there with so much history and culture. And the food…"

Miss Jessup… *Trudi*… sighed.

"But with the Arab-Israeli thing and my funds turning into so much pixelated static, it just wasn't tenable to hang out in that part of the world. So the feds paid for my passage, and I signed away five years of my life, figuring I wouldn't be doing much more than digging ditches or clearing roads. God or the cosmic dice must love me because I got sent down here to organize the logistics train from settler farms like yours back to Seattle and up to KC. That's how I got caught by the agents. I was out inspecting homesteads not far from where Aronson's congregation got themselves bushwhacked."

Miguel whistled at Red Dog and sent her forward to chivvy a couple of head that looked like they might have been splitting off from the herd. The little cattle dog, a streak of fur in the dark, flashed off at his command, barking and leaping. Without being asked, Sofia urged her mount forward to support her.

"So, before you were captured, did you have other problems with Fort Hood, in your work, I mean?" Miguel asked. He was forever searching for information about Blackstone that might help when he arrived in Kansas City.

Trudi laughed. "Oh, you have no idea.

"I learned pretty quickly not to route any requests through there," she said. "Blackstone's all but replicated the federal bureaucracy back in the Northwest, you know, and at first I thought that was a good thing. It can take a long time to hear back from Seattle, and I figured, naively, I suppose, that we were all in this together. So early on I tried cutting a few corners, sent out a few feelers to Fort Hood, to see if maybe we could get a few back-channel contacts going, you know, help each other out with stuff. All the usual informal give-and-take you get when people are making do in pretty rough circumstances."

"And they were no help?"

She laughed again, but not happily.

"They tried to shitcan me! Said I lacked the requisite 'credentials.' Said I'd have to sit a course and exam in Fort Hood before they could even deal with me. Do you believe that shit? Academic credentials in this environment?"

She waved her hand around.

"That's when I knew they were just dicking me around. I've been doing this sort of work for longer than most of those assholes had been in uniform. But that wasn't enough, of course. When I pushed back, they complained all the way back to my head office about me trying to subvert their duly constituted authorities and systems and structures and all sorts of petty Weberian bullshit?"

Miguel did not understand exactly what she meant by "Vayberian," but he had a pretty good idea.

"It is as I thought," he said. "It is even possible, Miss Jessup—"

"Goddamn, Miguel. I'm Trudi! My name is Trudi."

"Sorry, I forget. The nuns beat me for bad manners when I was a boy. It is even possible… Trudi, that you were targeted by the agents *because* you were sent by Seattle."

She was silent at that, riding along for nearly half a minute under the cold fire of the stars.

"Possible," she conceded at last. "It wasn't but a few hours before meeting them that I had a nasty brush with the TDF. Some bald clown with a goatee and a really filthy chaw tobacco habit."

Miguel could see that the riders ahead of them had turned the herd to the northeast, as agreed. They had traced out the next week's trek on a new road map taken from the study of the holiday home. For much of the journey they would follow the road network, avoiding some difficult geography between here and the grasslands, although the final approach to the first reserve would see them traverse a long forested valley north of the town of Commerce. Of that part of the state they had no knowledge, although it was so far from the cluster of federal settlements in the south that Miguel did not expect to encounter any problems there. In his experience, one was more likely to rub up hard against the Texas Defense Force and the agents near areas resettled by the federales.

He looked east and found the skyline there discernible at last, just a faint difference in shading between earth and heaven at that point but enough to let him know that dawn was not far off. He found himself wishing that Miss Julianne and Miss Fifi and all his friends from the dead golfer's boat were with him. By the Sacred Mother, they would make short work of any agents who attempted to interfere with them. Those mountain men from Nepal, if he remembered, the soldiers she had hired… Gurkhas! He could never remember their unusual names, but he well remembered how fiercely they had fought to protect the boat and his family from pirates down at the bottom of the world.

Miguel shook his head.

Pirates. At the bottom of the world.

What strange paths his life had taken.

* * *

Midafternoon and storm clouds building up in the west confirmed what Miguel's nose had told him earlier. The road agents were unlikely to get them now even if they had helicopters or planes to help them. The purple thunderheads, livid and bruised at the heart and tinged with green at the edge, already were flashing with a malicious promise of violence. Thunder, distant but ominous, rolled over gentle hills toward them. The weather front advanced rapidly, blotting out the clear sky as it came. At its current speed, Miguel could see it would overtake them long before they left the valley.

The herd stirred with agitation, calling to one another. Flossie snorted, shaking out her mane, struggling against the reins. She started to back-step and fight the bridle.

"Easy," Miguel said, giving the reins a short, sharp tug. He leaned forward to stroke Flossie's neck and whisper a few reassuring words in her twitching ears.

"Don't see many of them at this time of year."

Cooper Aronson had ridden up and was examining the wall of cloud as though it meant to give him personal offense.

Miguel pointed at the storm with his Stetson. In the few minutes he had been watching, the storm front had cut the distance between itself and the herd appreciably. Anxiety sat heavily just beneath his heart, and he cast around for his daughter. She was riding on the far side of the herd, chatting with Trudi Jessup. He had to suppress the urge to cut across and tell her to be wary. They might have a half hour, perhaps even less. "No," he said. "That looks like a summer storm, one of the worst kind, but the weather, it has been *loco* for years now."

"I had thought it was calming down some," Aronson ventured. "At least these last twelve months."

"Maybe the last twelve months, but not in the next two hours," Miguel said. "I do not like this, Aronson. Look at the land around here. We are driving through a wide valley, and as I recall from your map this morning, there are at least four streams within a few miles of us."

"A risk of flash flood, you think?" the Mormon asked.

"There is a lot of rain in that storm," Miguel said.

The protests of the cattle grew more insistent as lightning strobed through the huge, evil-looking bank of cloud and the trailing thunder grew noticeably louder than before. Miguel could see all the riders turning in their saddles to examine the spectacle as the shadow of the front fell over the tail end of the herd. His dogs began barking, and he called out harshly to them to be quiet. He did not need them spooking the herd any worse than it was already. Sofia, he was glad to see, gave him a querying glance before edging her horse onto slightly higher ground. She appeared to call to Miss Jessup to follow her, and the former restaurant woman did just that.

The rapid clip-clop of thudding hooves preceded Willem D'Age's approach at speed. He and Aronson acknowledged each other with brief nods before D'Age spoke up.

"I think it might be best if we moved the herd and ourselves to the nearest high ground," he said.

"Miguel feels the same," Aronson replied, "but of course on high ground we'll be exposed to the danger of lightning strikes."

Miguel waved off that point.

"That is a concern, Aronson, but a very small one. There is a chance of being hit by lightning but a certainty that many of these animals will drown, and us with them, if this valley floods."

The storm seemed to emphasize his point by unleashing a cannonade of thunder and lightning at that moment.

"How far is the nearest town or settlement; do we know?" Miguel asked. A cold breeze started up, bending long stalks of grass and a few scattered saplings to the west as the giant cell began to draw air into itself, as if to fill its lungs. The cattle, he noticed, had picked up their pace, trotting now, to match the increased urgency of their protesting calls.

"There is nothing close, nothing on high ground for a good twelve or thirteen miles," Aronson said, without consulting a map. "There's a small crossroads village there. I don't know whether it's on the floodplain, but the land does appear to rise in that direction."

He dipped his head to the north.

"Then we should hurry," Miguel said, looking to D'Age for support. He often found the younger Mormon to be the more cautious and reasonable of the two, perhaps as a result of the encounter at Crockett. Miguel snapped his reins and sent Flossie forward at a canter to match pace with the herd and the other riders.

The storm front passed over the sun then, snuffing it out and causing an almost startling drop in temperature. The first real crack of thunder split the sky, and the cattle started moving at speed, the drumming of their hooves becoming a frenzied tattoo. Another quick glance across the vast, seething river of mottled brown cowhide and bobbing longhorns found Sofia and Trudi turned around in their saddles, watching the storm race toward them. His daughter caught him staring at her and gave him a thumbs-up. Whips cracked and outriders yelled, attempting to keep the mob together. Adam and Orin galloped past him, doing their bit. It was no small thing herding thousands of cattle that were already spooked and this close to stampeding in panic. He wished he was over with Sofia. And Trudi, too. She was unusual. Not at all right, yet he could not help but warm to her. The Mormons were good men and women, but by the Blessed Virgin they were a tightly stitched bunch, and Miguel, for all his own hard exterior, did enjoy the company of people who knew how to enjoy themselves.

CRACK!

The flash of lightning and the hard-edged peal of thunder were nearly simultaneous. He felt rain on his face, a few droplets at first but quickening to a downpour that slapped down on them with real force. He was drenched through within seconds by the cold, stinging rain. And then it stopped abruptly, and a sickly green light lay over the valley floor, flattening the scene, as though he were riding into a photograph in a book.

Uh-oh, he thought.

The first hailstone fell as a single white rock, bouncing off Flossie's sweat-streaked shoulders. He just had time to hunker down and cinch the drawstring on his Stetson so that it sat tightly before a huge white fist smashed down on them all, a sudden roaring storm of ice that slammed into the earth, raising a shrieking, braying protest from the cattle, and nearly unseating the rider in front of Miguel with shock.

The vaquero spurred forward at a gallop, ignoring the stinging, burning pain of an Old Testament stoning from above. He recognized D'Age ahead of him, about to tumble from the saddle. Flossie was streaking forward at her top speed now, and Miguel was drawing on decades of horsemanship to maintain his balance. He drew up beside the Mormon and saw the fear in his face, the terror of having lost control of a big beast, compounded by the pounding riot of the stampede a few feet away.

Yes, the cattle had gone over now. No longer a controlled herd but a fear-shot panicking mob, barreling forward, plowing under any of their own number that fell, their cries like the horns of a thousand ghost trains. Miguel leaned across the gap between his horse and D'Age's, precariously teetering on the edge of his balance. He grabbed at the other man's reins and took a firm grip on the first attempt, applying hard but steady pressure, letting the animal know that it was under the control of a higher power. Calming it. Steadying it.

The horse never slowed. It was caught in the flow of the great mass of flesh up the valley floor, but after a few moments Miguel felt its wild terror and abandon subside noticeably.

"Take the reins," he yelled at D'Age, and for a wonder, the

man did so, getting his own fear under control, too.

He tried to find Sofia in the storm, but there was simply no chance. He could see no more than a few yards in any direction. He prayed as he had not prayed since the murder of his family that she would be all right. Truthfully, he had no faith in prayer anymore, but the Hail Marys and the pleas to look after his only surviving child arose unbidden, anyway.

Without warning, the hailstorm transitioned to a ferocious downpour, and visibility contracted to just a few feet. A howling banshee wind bit down on them, blowing the gray sheets of water horizontal. Miguel could feel himself being pushed forward by the strength of the wind and water. It shrieked in his ears and lashed at every exposed inch of skin, burning like acid.

Even the uproar of the stampede faded beneath the monstrous assault of the storm.

He looked about for his dogs but could see them nowhere. He could see very little indeed.

He hoped they had just fallen behind, unable to keep up. They were well trained and would not have let themselves get close enough to be trampled, but he could not still the anxious rodent of fear he felt gnawing at his guts.

CRACK!

A fat white bolt of pure electric energy speared into the ground not fifty yards away. He was certain he heard the wet air fizzle and split apart a microsecond before the blinding light seemed to turn the whole world into an X-ray display. The crash of thunder was enormous, enough to swallow whole planets, let alone the tiny creatures running back and forth across the land. He felt the reverberation of the sonic boom deep inside his chest, like a cathedral bell tolling, making his nuts contract in fright.

A single longhorn peeled away from the mass and took off at a right angle to it. Flossie all but reared up and dismounted him, but at the last moment she veered and threaded herself around the moving obstacle. He flowed with the horse, gripping with his thighs. So closely bonded was he with the animal that he felt the ground change under her hooves. Her grip on the soil became less sure, and he looked down and saw that Flossie was throwing up great geysers of water as she hammered up the valley.

At the same instant Miguel heard the sound he had been dreading since the storm clouds first had piled up in the western sky.

The rumble of something huge chasing them. Something bigger and more deadly than a mere stampede.

A wall of water.

The flood.

54

NEW YORK

The flight of the Second Bomb Wing of the much reduced U.S. Air Force was largely uneventful. Ten of the B-52H Stratofortresses left Whiteman Air Force Base in Missouri just before sunrise, lumbering up into a low gray mass of rain clouds that turned reduced visibility in the predawn gloom to near zero. The bombers climbed high over the storm system, heading east into the sun. The mission commander, Lieutenant Colonel Andrew "Havoc" Porter, was glad of the cloud cover not for any tactical reason but simply because he found it depressing to fly over hundreds of miles of empty countryside and burned-out cities, knowing that down there the remains of millions of his countrymen still lay unburied, unsanctified.

Porter was not one for dwelling on the old horror. He'd met his fair share of cranks and obsessives in the years since the Disappearance, all with their own patented explanations of the cataclysm. The bomber pilot preferred not to think about it. That way lay madness, in his opinion, because if you could not explain why it came and went away—and *nobody* could—you could never be certain it would not return. Best to just get on with the task in front of you and the work of living in a changed world. Christ knew, there was plenty to be getting on with. Behind him and in the other planes, flight crews passed their time, prepping for the mission with computer simulations while nine other pilots like him kept their bombers on course at thirty thousand feet.

This would be different from their previous sorties over Manhattan, where they often loitered in the battlespace for hours, depending on the availability of a tanker, occasionally releasing precision-guided ordnance on high-value targets, usually at the behest of an individual forward air controller somewhere down in the meat grinder. Porter clicked his tongue—an old unconscious habit—as he thought of the FACs who went out into that fucking madhouse. You had to respect those guys. And girls, he reminded himself. Sometimes they deployed with small spec-ops teams, sometimes with half-trained, ill-equipped militia units. Often enough they were they only thing standing between a ground unit and total annihilation. It was why their life spans were measured in hours once they hit the streets of Manhattan. As Porter brought the wing around on a new heading, taking them farther to the north, he wondered, not for the first time, who the hell joined the air force to go get themselves fed into the shredders with a bunch of dumbass grunts.

Exceptional motherfuckers, without a doubt, that was who.

For him, the job for the moment meant little more than a numb ass and a sore back after flying around for a day or so. He didn't even need to worry about triple A or enemy air response. But he wasn't foolish enough to downplay the importance of what he and his comrades were about up here. Because of them, thousands of dumbass grunts lived when they might have died, and thousands of pirates and raiders got handed the shit end of the stick.

He grinned darkly behind his flight mask. If this mission went ahead as planned, there might very well be no more pirates left by the time he set foot back on terra firma. And how fucking sweet would that be? Those ragged-ass jumped-up motherfuckers had been given a free pass for too long now in the considered opinion of Lieutenant Colonel Andrew "Havoc" Porter. It was high time they learned New York was an expensive place to visit. And he was just the man to learn 'em.

There had been some vintage scuttlebutt around the refurbished officers' mess back at Whiteman before they'd suited up for this run. Lots of fevered talk about uncapping a nuke on the Big Apple, after all leaves were canceled and every crew hauled back. Granted, there had been some AWOLs who were probably making their way down to Texas at this very minute, but they could go fuck themselves and the horses they rode off on. They wouldn't be getting their back pay updated. Only when the entire wing had been sequestered, paid—glory be!—and fed a rare meal of steak and potatoes had the pilots learned the nature of their mission. Nothing like it had been tried since World War II, and no one was quite sure if the weather conditions were optimal for the mission parameters.

Havoc thought it was probably going to be a bust. The rain in the Manhattan area of operations was moving into a third day of downpour thanks to a front stalled over the eastern seaboard. But what the hell? They were finally gonna be bringing some real pain for a change. And even if the primary mission parameters didn't play out, the bomb bay of Colonel Porter's venerable old BUFF was loaded with an altogether different but equally unpleasant surprise.

"Time to target?" he asked his navigator.

"Ten minutes," said Major Chaplin.

Porter nodded and checked his panel. A small pocket of turbulence connived to buck the old bomber around as they approached the city from the southwest.

"Think this will work?" Porter asked.

His copilot, Captain Hernandez, put her thermos of coffee away and smiled at him. "What do you care? You got a hot date to get back to?"

"Seems like a waste of ordnance to me," Chaplin said. "You know, in this sort of weather. I have to admit I'm not comfortable with our mission."

"Havoc, this is Eightball," the radio crackled. "We're coming up on the target now."

"Copy, Eightball," Porter said. He waited a few seconds to see if any last-minute countermands came in from the National Command Authority. Porter didn't much care if they flattened all of Manhattan with nukes or with conventional munitions. It was their job to kill the enemy, and he was fully prepared to drop every last bomb in his plane, return to base, load her up, and do it all over again. He did know, however, that the civilians who gave him his orders could be fickle and that there was every chance that having flown all the way here, they might just turn around without shooting their wad. Like that time he'd been sent out to scare off a convoy of illegal refugee ships bound from India to California. At the last minute, the mission was scrubbed and the refugees were instead met by officials from the Immigration Service.

"Eightball, this is Havoc," Porter said. "Stand by."

"Strike Force One is over the target, Mister President," Colonel Ralls reported. "Orders?"

Kipper could see the satellite track on the main screen in the operation center, a series of green symbols with attached alphanumerics over a wireframe map of Manhattan. Cloud cover obscured keyhole imaging from orbit, but several Predators and one of the Global Hawks were down below the cover with their eyes on midtown. Bursts of pale green and gray light flared on the screen, and flickers of tracer fire zipped back and forth at odd angles between clusters of individuals all over that part of Manhattan. He wondered how the military sorted any of this chaos out.

In his mind he had drawn a line around the lower end of the island, from the remains of the Flatiron Building down to Castle Clinton, and decided that was the part of old New York that he needed. Pretty much the same amount of land the Dutch originally bargained for when New Amsterdam was born. From Central Park North, a huge wedge of land to which only display was devoted, there was silence and stillness. But from about Times Square south, block after block was alight with fire and thunder. Dozens of screens displayed the inferno, but on the main window wall dominating the center of the room, eight linked displays were all focused on a few blocks around Rockefeller Center.

"Shouldn't the bombing already be in progress?" Culver asked.

"Very soon," Ralls said uncertainly. "Unless there's a last-minute change in orders."

Kipper shook his head. "Not this time. Can you patch me through to the commander of that wing, or flight, or whatever you call it?"

Ralls nodded. "We can, sir. If you'll wait one second."

"Strike Force One, stand by for a message from the National Command Authority," the radio crackled.

"Ah, shit," said Porter. "Here we go." He requested authentication and got it. "Havoc copies. All Strike Force One elements, hold for instructions."

"They're calling it off," Chaplin said. "Waste of bombs, anyway."

"Least we got a steak dinner out of the flight," Hernandez said.

"Havoc, this is Architect. Do you copy?"

"Architect?" Chaplin asked. "Who the fuck would that be?"

Porter shook his head and keyed his mike. "Architect, this is Havoc. I read you five by five, Mister President. Go with your traffic."

He swapped a what-the-fuck look with his navigator.

"I won't take long, Colonel. I simply wanted to wish you good luck and good hunting. I also want you to understand… I want everyone in your flight to understand that today's orders are for you to carry out, but the responsibility for what you're about to do is mine and mine alone… Uh, over. Is that what I say. Over?"

"Yes, Mister President." Havoc grinned. "And thank you, sir. I will forward your message to the rest of the wing. Over."

"Thank you, Colonel. Go do it. Kipper over and out."

Porter shook his head as KC severed the comm link.

"What kind of a call sign is Architect, anyway?" Chaplin asked.

"Secret Service," Porter said. "That was the president of the United States, and the mission is on. Havoc to Eightball, do you copy? Over."

"Eightball copies. Over."

"Execute when ready, Eightball. Follow us in. Over."

"Eightball acknowledges. Out."

The sky around New York was dense with air power, almost half the remaining air force and a quarter of the U.S. Navy's once-proud naval air arm. Flashes of lightning and rain lashed the veteran bombers as they felt their way through the storm front by radar and GPS. If bombing a sizable chunk of American real estate bothered any of the men or women in Porter's crew, they showed no sign of it as they began to descend toward the target area.

"We have uplink and hard target data confirmed," said Major Chaplin.

"Open her up, let in the fresh air," Porter said a second before a thick merchanical chunking sound preceded a moment's whirring as the giant bomb bay doors swung open.

"All boards are green. All packages hot."

The Second Bomb Wing emerged from the wall of thunderheads banked up to the southwest of the city. The way ahead was clear, and for the first time Lieutenant Colonel Porter felt some regret at what he was about to do. The city in front of them was the cradle of civilization in modern America, the place where all its creation myths began. Under the cloud cover and the slowly wandering smudges of rainfall it looked little different from his memories of the place from the world before the Disappearance. A cloudburst over the southern reaches of Manhattan obscured any view of the fighting in midtown. At this height, in the thick of the weather, the only evidence of the battle ahead was the murky bursts of gray-blue light that throbbed beyond the misty shroud.

"Pull 'em back. Pull 'em back," Kinninmore yelled into his headset. The order went out across the battalion's comms net, pushed down to company commanders, who sent it on to platoon commanders, who barked the directive in person at their senior NCOs, and before a minute had passed the U.S. forces laying siege to the main enemy concentrations holed up in Rockefeller Center began to withdraw along prepared axes. The shattered buildings and piled-up traffic provided good cover from the plunging fire, but dozens of smoke grenades soon bathed the scene in a thick, white fog of war.

Kinninmore waited with a small squad for personal protection, listening intently to his company COs reporting in as they made for the layup point two blocks back to the south. The volume of fire from the dark, hulking labyrinth of the center increased viciously, and he ducked as rounds began to whip past his head, pinging off metal car bodies, shattering nearby windows, and occasionally striking flesh with a dull, terrible thud.

Within six minutes the tactical withdrawal was complete, and the colonel signaled to his own detail that they could bug out, which they did with considerable speed and profanity. Kinninmore felt one bullet snag a fold in his pants leg as he sprinted away from the buildings, but he didn't dive for cover, knowing that he was in much greater danger remaining in close proximity to them. At one point, just as he ducked out of the main line of fire, he was tempted to look up to see if he could spot any of the laser designators painting the landmark, but he plowed on, calling himself an idiot for even entertaining such a foolish notion.

"FAC confirms all friendlies have exited. We are cleared to release."

"Weapons," said Havoc, "you have a go. Bring down the sky, Michelle."

He heard the acknowledgment and a brief burst of chatter down the link before two heavy clunks signaled a sudden loss of weight beneath the wings of the Stratofortress, causing it to jump nearly a hundred feet higher into the air. He tried to watch the pair of hardened penetrators as they began their fatal dive toward the target, but the GBU-28s quickly disappeared into the cloud cover and there was no chance he would have seen them anyway. He just couldn't help himself. He knew they would fire their little rocket motors in a second, accelerating the pair of five-thousand-pound bunker busters down toward the city. The kinetic impact alone would be enough to destroy vast swaths of any normal target, but the 630 pounds of high explosive that would detonate deep inside the target building, collapsing it from within, would seal the deal.

"Adios, Captain Hook," he quipped over the intercom before turning the huge, lumbering plane around to the west and climbing another five thousand feet to prepare for the secondary attack.

Simultaneous with Havoc's release of the two laser-guided bombs, nicknamed Deep Throats, four other B-52s released identical packages. Ten of the twenty-five-foot-long, superhardened lances speared down toward the famous cluster of buildings. They dropped silently, tiny servomotors adjusting the stubby fins on their tails as the intelligent seeker heads at the nose of the bomb maintained an obsessive lock on ten separate points, all of them illuminated by infrared dots sourced from small laser devices operated by special forces high up in skyscrapers a few blocks back from the target.

"Oh, man, this is gonna be so fucking sweet," Wilson said.

Milosz forced himself to stay fixed on the complex of four buildings within the greater Rockefeller Center that had been indentified as harboring the greatest concentration of enemy forces. He was acutely aware of Technical Sergeant Gardener crouched next to him, keeping the laser designator pointed at the window where he could see at least two men firing wildly into the thick banks of drifting smoke down on the streets below. Her blond hair and the sweet scent of chewing gum were driving him to distraction, but he did not wish to miss this moment. It would be, as Wilson had said, so fucking sweet.

And then it happened. A blur. A thin black flicker that shot down at a steep angle and punched right into the window he had been watching. The two men standing there disintegrated in a spray of bright pink mist and colorful clothing. The very walls on either side of them seem to shudder, and then there was a brief eerie moment when nothing happened.

He knew intellectually exactly what was going on over there. The long iron spike was spearing itself into the guts of the building, waiting until the small chip in its warhead decided it had embedded itself deeply enough to do the maximum amount of damage.

And then the bomb detonated.

All ten of them did at the same time.

The four buildings flew apart as though constructed of honeycomb and icing sugar. The blast atomized massive slabs of thick gray concrete, blowing them outward, removing a significant supporting structure from the overall building, which began to collapse in on itself with a volcanic roar. The three special operators were four blocks away, high in a residential tower, but Milosz could feel the destructive power of the strike in his very guts, under layers of Kevlar and ballistic plate.

"Goddamn," Wilson hooted. "Didn't I say that'd be sweet?"

Gardener placed a pair of binoculars to her eyes and smiled.

"When you want the job done, send a grunt. When you want it done properly, call the United States Air Force. The best is yet to come, gentlemen. Observe. This is a little trick we learned from our jihadi brethren."

Milosz watched where she pointed at half a dozen undamaged buildings out of which hundreds, maybe a thousand or more enemy fighters were now fleeing.

Lieutenant Colonel Porter frowned as he banked his plane around and lined up for the incendiary run.

It didn't seem fair that the first time they'd been allowed to get medieval on these cheeky little fuckers, the weather had shut down any chance of him enjoying the spectacle. Indeed, he had to wonder whether this next phase of the mission was even worth bothering with, given the wet conditions on the ground. He waited, expecting orders to scrub, but the radio link to Fort Lewis remained silent.

"We have good uplink data for the second package," his weapons officer reported.

"Release on my mark," said Havoc. "Aaand… mark!"

Hundreds of incendiary bombs fell away from the cavernous interior of the fuselage, whistling down toward the streets of Manhattan, where the survivors of the bunker buster attack had flooded into the open to escape what they thought must be an inevitable second strike.

* * *

As Milosz watched, a strange and unexpected sick feeling churning his stomach, the swarm of antlike creatures pouring into the streets around Rockefeller Center were suddenly consumed in a volcanic eruption. Hundreds of firebombs rained down on them, ringing the pocket of the city into which they had been carefully penned by the fighting of the previous days. Vast, apocalyptic rivers of flame, hundreds of feet high, poured through the canyons, washing over the tiny creatures below, wiping them from the face of the earth.

Even at this distance from the carnage it sounded like the end of the world. An epic rip in the fabric of things as the world tore itself asunder and the flames of hell came gushing out.

"Is very much like Dante's *Inferno*. Or perhaps *Towering Inferno*. Except down on the ground," said Milosz.

Technical Sergeant Gardener put an arm around him and gave the Polish commando an unexpected squeeze.

"You're quite the poet, aren't you, Freddy?"

55

TEXAS ADMINISTRATIVE DIVISION

Just a minute or two before Miguel had been riding over flat, dry ground, but his horse was now splashing through a wide racing stream, a filthy torrent befouled with the churned-up mud and manure left in the wake of the herd. To his right, only dimly visible in the ferocity of the storm, two thousand head of cattle plunged wildly through the rising water, bellowing their distress and unbridled terror. Riders added their cries to the caterwauling din, Sofia among them.

He was wild with fear for her, which was made worse by his utter powerlessness. The flood had come up so quickly and the storm was so intense, he was completely cut off from her on the other side of of the panicked, stampeding herd.

"Come left, come left," he yelled to D'Age, who had surged just a little ahead of him.

There was slightly higher ground out there. But the Mormon was too far ahead, lost in the savagery of the tempest. The valley channeled the worst of the storm's power right over them, and in its folds strange, contrary twisters and sudden shifts of wind direction did their worst to disorient him. How would Sofia be coping? Was she even still alive, or had she been swept from the saddle and trampled already? The one thin hope to which he could cling was the memory of her and Trudi Jessup spurring on for slightly higher ground before the worst of the storm hit them. Trudi was a good woman, he knew. She would not let any harm come to Sofia if she could help it at all.

Dark shapes peeled off the herd as cattle bolted in all directions, driven mad by their panic. Miguel could feel Flossie's terror in every twitching sinew and muscle. He began to ease her away from the black, heaving mass of the stampede, leaning her toward the slightly higher ridgeline he knew was somewhere to their left.

But the water piled up beneath them with shocking speed. The flood had started as a stream down at her fetlock and risen quickly. As they attempted to escape the churning rapids, they plunged into a trough, the roiling gray ice water suddenly splashing the horse's flanks, soaking in through Miguel's boots and pants. He felt the powerful mare lose her footing once or twice as the water threatened to sweep her away. A lesser rider might have dug in the spurs or whipped her with a crop, but Miguel leaned forward through the howling squall and laid his head down by hers, patting her straining neck, squeezing with his knees, reassuring the animal that he was still there and still in charge. He was the master of her destiny. Not the storm.

The roar of the torrent was huge now, a crescendo overwhelming all else. The rumbling thunder of the stampede was gone, washed away by the white-water rapids. Miguel thought he might have heard human screams once or twice, but so cut off was he from his fellow riders, so perfectly isolated within the fury of this instant hurricane, that he could not tell whether he alone survived at that moment.

Flossie struggled and wrestled against the flood, gaining purchase with her hooves, then losing it, then finding a foothold again. Just as it seemed she might tire and succumb, Miguel felt her connect with solid earth again, somewhere down below the rushing water, and with a titanic heave she launched herself up out of the death grip of the flood and onto the slight rise.

"Go, girl, go, go," the cowboy cried, urging her on.

The great beast, the finest of his mounts, repaid his faith in her, pushing onward and upward, finding a small, gentle ridgeline submerged beneath just a foot of water.

He reined her in then lest they plunge into greater depths again.

A longhorn appeared out of the white squall, bawling with fear, charging for them. Before Miguel could turn Flossie around, she saw the danger and veered, increasing her speed. He could see that a collision was inevitable, though. The steer was going to broadside them in just a few seconds.

Miguel acted without thought, whipping out his saddle gun and blasting the animal in the head. It roared with agony and outrage, half its face torn away by the Lupara, but just as it seemed as though momentum might carry it into them anyway, the beast's front legs buckled and it tumbled end over end, a thousand pounds of muscle, meat, and bone crunching into the ground, throwing up a massive fantail of floodwater.

Miguel felt his bowels tighten and shudder with the shock of near death. The horse whinnied her alarm but had sense enough to thread herself quickly around the airborne steer. She found good purchase on the small rise and galloped on. Miguel thought to rein her in, then decided to trust the animal's instincts. She was probably better suited than he to surviving this.

On they raced for a few minutes more, Flossie following the natural rise of the land and only once or twice plunging into unexpected depths, drenching them both again. Miguel kept his head down and his attention focused on the remains of the herd to his right. He strained with all his might to make out some sign of his daughter through the violence and chaos, but there was nothing. As the wind and rain finally began to abate, it became clear that few of the cattle remained. The hellish squall faded back to a hard downpour, and finally he was able to see more than a few feet in any direction. A river now ran off to his right, a violent, roiling dark brown flow in which floated the carcasses of dozens of dead animals, most of them cattle but also a few horses, some still saddled, and one sheep, bloated with gas, its four legs pointed skyward.

Pulling on his reins, at last he brought Flossie to a halt on a small mound of waterlogged earth that seemed high enough to have avoided inundation. Three longhorns already stood there, but they moved aside silently for the newcomers. Miguel turned in the saddle and peered back up the valley, into the rain. Even with visibility still reduced, it was possible to see that a hugely destructive force had scoured the wide shallow gorge of animals and plants in a short time. He spied an uprooted tree heading toward him from the south, along with what looked like an old car body. The Lord only knew where that had come from. He had seen no sign of human habitation, new or old, for miles.

"Hello!" he cried out. *"Can anyone hear me?"*

Of D'Age, who had been so close at one point that he'd been able to reach out and steady his ride, there was no sign. He heard a plaintive barking somewhere behind him and craned around to see Red Dog a few hundred yards away, standing atop a truck-sized boulder, wagging her tail and spinning in circles. She was safe from the flood there, but he saw nothing of the other dog, Blue.

"Hey. Over here!"

A female voice, coming from the north and a little to the east, on the far side of the still-roaring river that had sprang into life.

Miguel found her waving from a tree.

Miss Jessup, and with her Sofia.

His heart felt as though it might burst from his chest.

One of the camp whores appeared from behind them, too, but he could not tell which, so thoroughly bedraggled and mud-covered was she.

"Stay there," he cried back. "Do not move until the water falls or someone comes to help."

Sofia yelled something in reply, but he could not make it out.

Miguel waved in what he could only hope was a reassuring fashion as he spurred on, looking for other survivors. He saw hundreds of dead cattle, some of them jammed up in massive natural dams formed when one or two had caught on a tree trunk, providing a temporary obstacle against which even more had piled up. A few minutes on he found D'Age's body, smashed against a rocky outcrop, the head staved in and resting at a horribly unnatural angle. The young man's eyes were open, staring up into the storm that had killed him. Miguel did not dismount. There was nothing to be done for the dead at this time, whereas the living might be in need of his help.

Another body just a short way farther on turned out to be Jenny, Willem D'Age's fiancée. Miguel recognized her fine red leather riding boots sticking out from the crushing weight of a dead longhorn.

He crossed himself and offered a quick prayer for the souls of the departed. It was a mechanical gesture, something programmed into him by the nuns of his childhood. In his heart he no longer felt as if he was talking to God. There was only a void and a world full of pain and wickedness.

"Miguel… over here…"

He almost didn't hear the faint voice crying out over the raging waters and the still hammering rain, but the crack of a rifle shot drew his attention back across the flood stream to where Adam stood atop another large boulder with a woman. His spirits lifted as he recognized Maive Aronson, but then his mood palled again. He just knew that her husband must be dead. Cooper Aronson, the leader of this small band who had taken him and Sofia in, who had adopted them, really, after Crockett, had been riding on the far side of the herd with his wife. Miguel knew the man well enough to understand that he would not have let himself be separated from her even in the worst of the storm. That he was nowhere to be seen was an ill omen indeed.

Miguel waved and gestured for them to stay put, nodding when Adam signaled that he understood. Shivering in his sodden clothes, the vaquero rode on to survey the extent of the damage.

"All gone," Aronson's wife whimpered. "All of them?"

"I am afraid so," Miguel said, the words like ashes in his throat. It was he who had suggested—insisted—that they head to the northeast to avoid entanglements with the road agents, but in doing so he had doomed the small party to utter destruction.

Four more hours he had ridden that day, up and down the length of the flood, until it receded, leaving a hellish landscape. Dead and broken cattle. Shattered trees. The bodies of the missing, save for Adam's sweetheart, young Miss Gray, who remained unaccounted for. Wrack and ruin.

The herd was scattered to hell and beyond.

His own horses and Blue the cattle dog had perished.

The few surviving souls clustered around a sputtering, rusted iron stove in an old corrugated iron shed on high ground, a good five miles from where they had lost everything. Himself. Sofia. Maive Aronson. Adam and Trudi Jessup. And the camp whore named Marsha, rescued, cleaned up, and dressed in a very damp pair of Adam's jeans and a grossly oversized flannelette shirt and lamb's wool jacket from Miguel's pack.

Just another hour would have seen them clear of the worst effects of the flash flood. Had the storm held off just that brief while longer, they could have laagered up here on this hill, easily high enough to have sheltered all the cattle and the humans who watched over them.

A steady downpour fell outside, and occasional gusts of wind blew miserable drifts of cold rain and even sleet into the shelter, which looked to Miguel to be an outstation for a large ranch. A workbench ran along the back wall, and rusted bridles, and one stiff cracked ancient saddle hung neatly from the rafters. He stoked the oven fire from a supply of hardwood stored neatly under a tarpaulin, well back from the entrance to the shed. As the others warmed themselves and absorbed their shock, he did his best to hang the tarp over the gaping entrance, providing them with a barrier against the weather.

Somebody had once cared well for this small outpost, he could tell, probably camping there overnight after a long trek from the main homestead of this ranch, wherever that might be. He had even discovered a few logs of pitch wood under the canvas sheet, sticky with resin and easy to light even in the damp conditions. Miguel had no idea where they had come from. Such fuel was not common in Texas.

Upon finishing the makeshift canvas wall, he returned to the stove, where the others now sat silently and Red Dog lay curled up in his daughter's lap, as close as possible to the heat. Sofia stroked her with shaking hands and appeared to be staring at something a long, long way off in the distance.

A small burst of orange sparks floated out of the open grille as he tossed in two more logs, old gray hardwood this time. They would burn slowly for hours. Night had fallen outside, and with it came a killing chill. Adam and the women huddled around the warmth, wrapped in old horsehair blankets they had found hanging in the shed. Their own sodden blankets and sleeping rolls were draped from the same drying racks.

Miguel busied himself with food, a few hunks of good meat he had cut from the rump of a longhorn he had found suffering from two broken legs. After putting the animal out of its misery, he'd dressed the kill and returned to the shed in the last failing moments of daylight.

Miss Jessup had been a great help, taking the bloody steaks from him without a qualm and tending to them on the stove. Poor Maive Aronson was beyond talking to anybody and merely sat, shivering and staring into the coals. Sometimes her chest would hitch with sobs, and she would whimper a few words. But mostly she just sat and gazed.

Miguel had tried to apologize, to tell her how dreadfully sorry he was, how this was all his fault, but she had waved him off.

Adam had spoken for her.

"This is nobody's fault, Miguel. Not yours. Not Brother Aronson, who chose this particular path. Not God's. It is not even the fault of those agents we came through here to avoid. These things are... God's design... but not his fault," the young man said, although he did not seem at all convinced.

"You must eat. We all have to eat," Miss Jessup said quietly as she pulled the seared rump steaks off the griddle built into the top of the stove.

They smelled fine, but Miguel felt awful when his stomach growled and spit flooded into his mouth. It seemed unworthy and wrong.

But she was right, of course. They were still on the trail and could not indulge themselves in the luxury of not eating because they did not feel like it. Tomorrow might well bring even more severe tests than they had faced today, and only the lucky and the strong would survive.

He nodded to Trudi, who passed over a piece of rump steak on a long, thin metal skewer. Miguel had no idea where she had found it, but all their camp utensils had been lost, so he took the crude implement gratefully. Adam followed him, taking an extra piece, which he handed to Marsha. Miguel had determined that it would probably be best if he stopped thinking of her as a whore. In her pathetic, bedraggled state she could not have been less alluring. Miss Jessup passed a chunk of meat to Sofia, who took it without comment. Another piece went to the dog, who scarfed it up without ceremony, her tail beating a fast tattoo on Sofia's thigh. Miguel was relieved to see that even Maive shared in the meal, although she did so mechanically, consuming the food as fuel and nothing else. Certainly not as a comfort.

The remnants of the storm still lashed at them, but the shed had been well placed in the lee of the hill, probably for that reason. Weather tended to come from a particular direction in Miguel's experience, and the ranch owners had obviously prepared well for it with this humble shack. With the tarp hung over the entrance, trapping more of the warm air inside and blocking the occasional gusts of wind and rain that curled around to seek them out, they might even have been cozy. But Miguel could not help seeing the remains of the dead, now hastily buried a mile away. It felt as though he had abandoned them out there, and he imagined that Adam and Maive felt the same way, only much more intensely. Adam, indeed, nearly had to be restrained at the end of the day, when he'd insisted on continuing the search for Miss Gray.

It was only the discovery of one of her boots still containing a foot, and a bloodstained shred of her dress that had convinced him she was gone and there would be no finding her.

Even so, Miguel resolved to venture out later while the others slept and see if he might locate her body or some sign of her.

Without torches or lamps it would be hazardous going, but there was nothing for it. He would not be able to sleep while she remained lost, even though he knew in his heart that she, too, was gone.

"Have to round up the cattle in the morning."

The flat, emotionless voice surprised him. He had not thought Maive would speak at all tonight, certainly not that she would discuss such banalities. But then, he thought, people often did that in moments of great shock and sadness.

Miss Jessup laid a worried look on Aronson's wife and went immediately to her side, sitting down and putting an arm around her shoulder. The simple human contact seemed to collapse some final, fragile defense, and Maive let loose a terrible howl, a searing, animalistic wail of impacted grief and loss and rage. It turned to long racking sobs and then weeping as the two women embraced, bathed in the flickering golden light of the camp stove. Sofia's face crumpled, too, and she pushed the dog from her lap to hurry over and comfort the woman who had been of such comfort and support to her these past weeks.

"All gone. All gone," Maive whimpered. "All gone."

"I know, honey. I know," Trudi Jessup said as she rocked and stroked the woman like a child. "I know."

Sofia placed her arms around the Mormon lady and hugged her fiercely, repeating over and over again, "I'm sorry."

Miguel thought for a second that he might lose his humble dinner, but the wave of nausea and self-loathing that washed over him passed with surprising speed.

He could not bring this woman's husband and friends back.

But he could do what he had promised to do in the first place.

Get them safely to their destination and his. To Kansas City.

"In the morning," he said softly, "we shall start again."

ACKNOWLEDGMENTS

Halfway through writing *After America* I broke my arm. My writin' arm. That's why you're holding this weighty tome about twelve months after I expected to get it to you. The busted wing threw a lot of schedules and deadlines out of alignment. Mega thanks are due to all my editing and publishing friends who helped out as I slowly got back to work. Cate Paterson and Joel Naoum in Sydney; Betsy Mitchell in New York; and a whole heap of magazine and newspaper eds along with them. And in the realm of a thousand thank-yous, I dips me propeller beanie to my faithful researcher and occasional co-conspirator S. F. Murphy, of the great state of Missouri.

As I was punching through the deadlines on *After America,* I received invaluable help from an unexpected source. The Cloud. Specifically from my followers on Twitter who were an amazing fount of obscure factoids and information such as the color of the carpet in the Plaza Hotel in 2003. Hundreds of them contributed in one way or another to this book; thousands of them if you count the people who stood on the electronic sidelines each day cheering me on. Extra special mention must go to my regulars and lurkers over at cheeseburgergothic.com, my personal blog. They know who they are and what they contribute. Nuff said.

And as always, my poor, poor family. Goddamn they put up with some shit.

ABOUT THE AUTHOR

John Birmingham is the author of *Without Warning, Final Impact, Designated Targets, Weapons of Choice, He Died With a Felafel in His Hand, The Tasmanian Babes Fiasco, How to Be a Man, The Search for Savage Henry,* and *Leviathan,* which won the National Award for Nonfiction at Australia's Adelaide Festival of the Arts. He has written for *The Sydney Morning Herald, Rolling Stone, Penthouse, Playboy,* and numerous other magazines. He lives at the beach with his wife, daughter, son, and two cats.

ALSO AVAILABLE FROM TITAN BOOKS

JOHN BIRMINGHAM'S BLOCKBUSTER

WITHOUT WARNING
TRILOGY CONTINUES!

Angels of Vengeance
With a conflicted US president struggling to make momentous
decisions in Seattle, and a madman fomenting rebellion in Texas,
three women are fighting their own battles—for survival, justice,
and revenge.

"A seamless fusion of alternate history, post-apocalyptic fiction, and
espionage-fueled thriller… Birmingham's story is tightly woven and
deeply considered." *Publishers Weekly*

TITANBOOKS.COM

ALSO AVAILABLE FROM TITAN BOOKS

THE COMPANY OF THE DEAD
BY DAVID KOWALSKI

Can one man save the *Titanic*?

March 1912. A mysterious man appears aboard the *Titanic* on its doomed voyage. His mission? To save the ship. The result? A world where the United States never entered World War I, thus launching the secret history of the 20th century.

April 2012. Joseph Kennedy—grand-nephew of John F. Kennedy—lives in an America occupied in the East by Greater Germany and on the West Coast by Imperial Japan. He is one of six people who can restore history to its rightful order—even though it would mean his own death.

"Exciting action, twisty and ingenious characterization, and complicated time-travel plotting deftly handled." S.M. Stirling, *New York Times* bestselling author of *The Tears of the Sun*

"A magnificent alternate history, set against the backdrop of one of the greatest maritime disasters." *Library Journal*

"Time travel, airships, the *Titanic*, Roswell: from these well-worn bones, Kowalski builds a decidedly original creature that blends military science fiction, conspiracy theory, alternate history, and even a dash of romance." *Publishers Weekly*

TITANBOOKS.COM

ALSO AVAILABLE FROM TITAN BOOKS

THE LOST FLEET
BY JACK CAMPBELL

Dauntless
Fearless
Courageous
Valiant
Relentless
Victorious
Beyond the Frontier: Dreadnaught
Beyond the Frontier: Invincible

After a hundred years of brutal war against the
Syndics, the Alliance fleet is marooned deep in enemy territory,
weakened and demoralized and desperate to make it home.

Their fate rests in the hands of Captain "Black Jack" Geary, a man
who had been presumed dead but then emerged from a century of
survival hibernation to find his name had become legend. Forced by
a cruel twist of fate into taking command of the fleet, Geary must
find a way to inspire the battle-hardened and exhausted men and
women of the fleet or face certain annihilation by their enemies.

Brand-new editions of the bestselling novels containing unique
bonus material from the author.

"Fascinating stuff... this is military SF where the military
and SF parts are both done right." *SFX Magazine*

TITANBOOKS.COM